# of love & life

Three novels selected and condensed
by Reader's Digest

Reader's
Digest

The Reader's Digest Association Limited, London, Montreal

CONTENTS

DEBBY HOLT

Love Affairs for Grown-Ups

My initial idea for Love Affairs for Grown-Ups *was to write about two very different sisters. I was also keen to see if I could create a convincing leading man who at first glance was not leading man material at all. A family holiday in France gave me my setting and in fact I began to write the story while I was out there. What I did not foresee was that I would fall completely in love with my unconventional leading man. I do hope you do too!*

Debby

CHAPTER ONE

A Difficult Introduction

CORNELIUS STOOD on the deck and watched the white cliffs of Dover slowly recede into insignificant dots. He was not in a good mood. In fact, he was in a very bad mood and it was all Douglas's fault.

Douglas had been working for Cornelius for three years now and possessed many sterling qualities. He was an excellent office manager. He was bright, ambitious and quick to learn. He liked people; he liked to *help* people. He was friendly and sociable and full of enthusiasm. On the minus side, because Douglas was sociable and liked people, he didn't understand anyone who wasn't sociable and who didn't like people.

Consequently, Douglas was impregnably convinced that Cornelius would *love* to meet Douglas's wife's solicitor friend on the ferry out to Boulogne. He was convinced that Cornelius would *love* to give a lift to the unknown woman all the way down to Montélimar. Douglas thought it was a harmonious coincidence that Cornelius and the solicitor woman were both travelling to the same destination. And, even better, they could travel home together again as well.

Cornelius had tried to make his feelings clear. He had raised a variety of genuine objections. He wasn't sure which part of August he would be spending in France; he was an erratic driver; he might decide to stop off for a night in Troyes. And furthermore, he would *not* be able to bring the woman home since he was only going to be in France for a week.

Most people would have understood what Cornelius was *trying* to say. Not Douglas. Douglas assumed that everyone was as friendly and as eager to perform charitable acts as Douglas. In the face of such *niceness*, Cornelius found it difficult to explain that he *wasn't* very nice.

He was reduced to throwing up objections which Douglas swatted with the same lethal success that he applied to errant wasps. The solicitor woman was happy to travel in whichever part of August suited Cornelius. The solicitor woman was apparently no stranger to erratic driving since she was teaching her son to drive. The solicitor woman would be very happy to spend the night in Troyes since she had always wanted to see its famous medieval architecture. And finally, Cornelius *would* be able to give the solicitor woman a lift back because she only wanted to stay a week in France anyway.

What Cornelius wanted to say was that he didn't like to share his car with people he *did* know, much less with some stranger who would probably talk like a hyperactive monkey. What he *did* say, faced with Douglas's implacable good nature, was that while he would be able to give the woman a lift, she should be warned that he would no longer be staying overnight in Troyes itself but would instead book a simple bed and breakfast in a primitive hamlet some twenty kilometres away.

Douglas reported back that the solicitor woman thought the hamlet sounded fascinating. Cornelius hated her already.

When he drove his car onto the boat, he contemplated the tempting idea of failing to find her. His conscience, always unpredictable, would not let him pursue this train of thought. More to the point, the ferry was far too small and intimate to guarantee the success of such a possibility. The woman had sent him an email in which she told him that she would have a blue and white striped canvas bag and she would wear a red rose fixed to her jacket lapel. The red rose carried with it a terrifying connotation of romantic assignations. For a terrible moment, Cornelius wondered if Douglas had been trying to play Cupid.

Glumly, Cornelius left the deck and wandered past the duty-free shop and up the stairs. His eyes scanned the bar where passengers were already scoffing croissants and Danish pastries. Did they not *know* that they would soon be landing in a country that overflowed with the freshest of baguettes? He checked the tables down the left side of the boat and began to feel hopeful. Then he turned to the right side.

A woman was sitting at the back, a book in her hands, gazing out of the window. It had to be her. On the table in front of her was a large blue and white canvas bag. Attached to the top buttonhole of her denim jacket was a generous red rose. He saw her take a mobile from her bag, and as she checked it, he studied her surreptitiously.

From what he could see, she was short and reasonably slim. He guessed she was in her early forties. She had soft brown shoulder-length hair and a wispy fringe that was far too long. She put down the mobile, looked up and caught his eye. Escape was impossible. He squared his shoulders and moved forward towards her.

Katrina hadn't even wanted to go to France. When she thought about it, her relationship with her sibling was punctuated by the numerous occasions on which she had agreed to do something which almost immediately she had regretted. These moments would be followed by long periods of self-loathing in which she would promise herself that she would never again be talked into doing something she had not wanted to do. And the phone would ring and ten minutes later she would be hitting her head with a cushion, furious with her lemming-like behaviour in the face of her sister's assurance that Katty would always think everything she suggested was brilliant.

There was the occasion twelve years earlier when her sister had decided to have a party to celebrate the fact that she was changing her name from Margaret to Rose. ('I've met this wonderful man,' she told Katrina. 'He's amazingly perceptive. He says Margaret has had a hold over me for far too long. He says I am definitely a Rose.') She insisted that the party could not go ahead without Katrina, and though Katrina knew very well that it could, she still found herself travelling down to Salisbury with her children. Once there, she was given a lukewarm cup of coffee before being dispatched to Longleat with her sister's children as well as her own, so that Margaret, or rather Rose, could concentrate on getting her nails and her hair done. Katrina drove her charges round the safari park, and it was while they were in the lion and tiger enclosure that twelve-year-old Cam vomited over her companions in the back of the car. Katrina was unable to turn round and drive back; nor could she open the windows, let alone the doors, since there were countless posters telling her to keep them firmly shut. By the time they got to the exit gate, there wasn't a child in the car who wasn't threatening to throw up.

The most infuriating point about that entire weekend had been the fact that Katrina had *known* she would have a terrible time. And yet she never learnt.

Just a few months ago, Rose, in mourning for her husband who had died quite unexpectedly last summer, made one of her more exacting requests. She rang Katrina and came to the point immediately. 'I want you to have our cat,' she said. 'You know how Roger adored him. Every time I see that little furry face, it reminds me of Roger and I start crying all over again. Omo has to go. You will have him, won't you, Katty?'

Katrina did, even though she didn't like cats, even though Omo was possibly the nastiest and smelliest feline that had ever stalked the planet. Omo had immediately taken possession of Katrina's favourite armchair. Katrina had retaliated by making a list of all the things she had done for her sister that she had not wanted to do, to make sure she had a tangible warning she could whip out whenever the need arose. The list was long and infinitely depressing.

So when Rose rang, in April, to invite Katrina to spend some of her precious six weeks' annual leave in France, Katrina reached for the list. Unfortunately, Rose was, as she reminded Katrina, at her most vulnerable. 'I still can't believe Roger has died,' she said. 'I'm trying so hard to make a new start and it isn't easy after twenty-seven years of marriage. Anyway, I've bought a house in France—'

'You've bought a house in France!' Katrina exclaimed. 'I thought you were moving up to London next month? You've only just bought the flat in Kensington! You're not planning to move abroad, are you?'

'Of course I'm not,' Rose said. 'I've bought it as an investment. I shall let it out for holidays. And it will also be a bolt hole for me and the kids. Katty, you'll love it; it's in the Drôme region—all lovely mountains and vast plains. We're going out for the month of August. I'd love to invite your two but Sam and Cam are both bringing their partners of the moment and there isn't the room. You will come, won't you?'

Katrina gripped her list and swallowed. 'That's very sweet of you but there's no way I can take a month off work and—'

Rose interrupted her. 'Surely you can manage two weeks at least?'

'Not really,' said Katrina, staring at her list. 'I mean, there are the children to think of and—'

'They're hardly children any more,' Rose said. 'Susie's in her last year at university, for heaven's sake! Were you planning to go on holiday with them? What are you doing?'

'Nothing *as such*,' Katrina conceded. 'Ollie's starting work with a car-hiring company as soon as his A levels are over and Susie's spending most of August in Edinburgh with her boyfriend. But I thought I'd take one or two weeks off and catch up on the garden. It looks like a jungle.'

'That sounds very dull! And what will you do if it rains? Come to France! Come and swim in our pool! Get a suntan! Oh, Katty, do come.

It's virtually my first holiday without Roger and I shall be the sole adult there in the presence of two pairs of very horny young lovers . . . Please come!' There was a pause and Katrina heard Rose give a forlorn sniff. 'I really do need some support at the moment.'

It was the sniff that did it. Katrina said that it *would* be fun to see the new house. She agreed that Ollie was quite capable of looking after himself for a fortnight. She agreed it would be lovely to spend some quality time with her niece and nephew. It was only after she rang off that Katrina remembered that Rose had, in fact, had three holidays since Roger's death.

Katrina went through to the sitting room, picked up a cushion from the sofa and hit herself on the head with it.

The next day, at work, Katrina snapped at the blameless trainee solicitor with whom she currently shared her office. This was unfair. Carol, an energetic young woman with a puppy-like enthusiasm, had been quite in order to ask her about the seminar on communication skills that afternoon and Katrina apologised at once, explaining that she had just agreed to go on holiday to France in August.

'Oh, I see,' said Carol, who clearly didn't see at all.

'I know,' Katrina admitted ruefully. 'I'm very lucky and I sound horribly ungrateful, don't I? It's only that, to be perfectly frank, I'd far rather stay at home for a fortnight. And there's the journey. It's right down in the south of France in Montélimar and my sister's expecting me to drive there and French roads terrify me.'

'Montélimar isn't nearly as far as you think,' said Carol, trying to be helpful. 'It's more in the middle of France than the south.'

'It's still far too far away,' Katrina said. 'France is a very big country.'

Carol laughed and went out, which surprised Katrina because, in the short time she had known her, she had discovered that Carol never abandoned a problem without finding a solution to it.

Three days later Carol came into the office with a smug smile on her face. 'I've sorted it,' she said.

Katrina eyed her warily. 'You've sorted what?'

'Your holiday! As soon as you said Montélimar, it rang a bell and then when I got home and told my husband about it, he reminded me. Douglas's boss is going to Montélimar in August and Douglas has asked him if he could give you a lift down there and he said he'd be delighted! He'll give you a lift back as well.'

Katrina directed an appalled glance at her trainee. 'That's very nice of your husband but I certainly can't ask someone I don't know to give me a lift all the way to—'

'He wants to help you!' Carol crowed. 'End of story!'

Katrina stared at her trainee solicitor. She wanted to say that she would rather risk the dangers of driving on the wrong side than have to make polite conversation with Douglas's boss all the way down to Montélimar. 'Look,' she said, 'it's very kind of you and your husband and his boss but—'

'There's only one problem,' Carol conceded. 'He's only going for a week and I know you were planning to go for a fortnight.'

Katrina hesitated. Could she really turn down such a perfect excuse to halve her holiday with her sister? She smiled at Carol. 'A week would suit me very well.'

'I'm sure you'll get on,' Carol said. 'Douglas thinks he's very nice, though he also says he's rather odd. And he has a very peculiar name . . .'

So now, thanks to Carol, she was sitting on the ferry waiting for a rather odd man. If she failed to find him, she could get a train down to Montélimar and get Rose to meet her at the station. Her mobile made a noise and Katrina reached into her bag. She pulled it out and was intent on reading the message when she suddenly felt conscious of being watched. She glanced up and caught the eye of an extraordinary-looking man. She saw him glance at her bag and wondered if he were Douglas's boss. He wore green corduroy trousers, a grey shirt and a battered-looking black velvet jacket. He was very tall and very thin and his limbs looked as if they had been stuck to his frame at the last moment. He had a tousled mass of rust-coloured curls and an aquiline nose on which perched a pair of large, dark-framed spectacles. She reckoned he was older than her: probably in his late forties or early fifties. His appearance was strangely familiar, yet she was sure she'd never seen him before. Flustered and unsure whether to hail him or not, she turned back to her phone.

Cornelius saw her look down at her mobile again and wondered if she really was the solicitor woman. He approached her uncertainly. He could see she possessed a superb complexion. Her skin was almost translucent. He gave a small cough and said diffidently, 'Excuse me, my name is Cornelius Hedge and I think I'm supposed . . .'

The woman looked up at him and promptly burst into tears.

Cornelius stared at her in horror and suppressed a craven urge to turn on his heels and run. The woman was *really* crying: heaving shoulders, tears coursing down her cheeks. He reached into his jacket pocket, pulled out a handkerchief and held it out. 'I'm so sorry,' he stammered. 'I . . . I didn't mean to startle you . . . I'll go . . .'

The woman shook her head violently. She had covered her mouth with one hand and accepted the handkerchief with the other.

Cornelius could sense a swell of interest from passengers across the aisle. 'Would you like some coffee?' he asked desperately. 'Shall I get you some strong black coffee, or tea? Would you prefer tea?'

The woman nodded gratefully but continued to keep her hand clamped to her mouth. Despite the hand clamp, a strangulated sob managed to escape. The woman was like a pressure cooker, primed to explode, and Cornelius made a hasty escape to the refreshment bar. He had no idea whether she wanted tea or coffee, so he decided he would order both. He kept his eyes fixed on the pastries, which now seemed rather enticing— funny how stress always made him hungry. Silently, he cursed Douglas.

When he returned to the woman, she was holding her book in front of her. She sat, rigid and stiff. Her eyes were red and puffy but at least she'd stopped crying.

He put the tray he was carrying on the table. 'I thought you might be hungry,' he said, 'so I bought a couple of pastries.'

'That's very kind but I had a sandwich when I got on the boat.' She put down her book and, fixing him with anxious eyes, waited until he had sat down opposite her. 'I must apologise,' she said. 'You must be wondering who on earth you've been landed with.'

'Yes,' said Cornelius, 'I did rather . . . I mean, I don't know that I—'

'Can we start again, please?' The woman extended a hand. 'I'm Katrina Latham.'

Cornelius shook her hand. 'And I'm Cornelius Hedge. I've got you a choice of drinks. This is tea and that's coffee.'

Katrina helped herself to the tea. 'Thank you. This is perfect.'

Cornelius tried to think of something to say, something that would divert her from attempting to explain why she'd been crying, because if she *did* try to explain why she'd been crying, she would inevitably start crying all over again. 'Is your book interesting?' he asked.

'It's a biography of Mary Shelley,' she said. 'She's one of my heroines.'

'Really? How fascinating.' He would have liked to ask her why but she blinked furiously and he surmised that for some reason Mary Shelley was not a safe topic of conversation.

The woman swallowed once more. 'Are *you* reading anything at the moment?' she asked with a pretty impressive assumption of interest.

'I am indeed,' Cornelius said. He pulled from his jacket pocket a dogeared paperback. '*Hegemony or Survival* by Noam Chomsky. It is the most brilliant book. It is a *total* book, if you know what I mean.'

Katrina moved her cup to one side and rested her arms on the table. 'No, I don't.' She gave a small sigh. 'What *do* you mean?'

'It's a particular sort of book.' Cornelius spoke with a nervous enthusiasm, propelled by a desire to convince the woman that he had already forgotten her extraordinary behaviour. 'It makes one see everything in a totally different way. Basically, Chomsky's thesis is that given the choice of hegemony over the world or survival of the species, American governments have always gone for hegemony. It's very interesting. He makes a distinction between American *people*, whose energy and enthusiasm he admires, and American presidents, whose collective arrogance appals him. He doesn't have a good word to say about any of the presidents.'

'Does he have any gossip about them?' Katrina asked.

'*Gossip?*' Cornelius repeated. 'No, he's not that sort of man.'

'What a pity,' Katrina said. 'You can learn so much from all the little personal stories.'

Cornelius raised his eyebrows. 'Can you? I'm not sure I agree.'

'I've always felt this about history textbooks,' Katrina said. 'They tell you all about political trends and movements and wars and forget that the people who start them are just like us: influenced by headaches and love affairs and misunderstandings. Shall I give you an example?'

'Please do.' Despite himself, Cornelius was interested.

'For the first few years of his reign,' Katrina said, 'Louis the Sixteenth had a minor sexual abnormality that made his erections painful. Consequently, he got rid of his frustrations on the hunting ground. As a result, he spent too little time finding out how discontented his people were, and bingo! The French Revolution happened.'

'That is very intriguing,' Cornelius allowed. 'But I can't help thinking the causes of the French Revolution might be a little more complex.'

'Of course they are. I'm simply saying that one man's sexual malfunction played a part in it. The personal is always important.' Katrina picked up her cup and drank her tea. 'I think I'll go and freshen up. And then I might get a little fresh air. I'll make sure I'm back here before the boat docks. It gets in at midday, doesn't it?' She stood up. 'Thank you for the tea. I will see you in a little while.'

'Yes, indeed,' Cornelius said. He waited until she had left and then he rearranged his limbs, stretching his long legs out under the table. He looked out of the window and wondered what had upset the solicitor woman so much. He sincerely hoped she wouldn't cry again. He sighed, picked up one of the Danish pastries and began to eat it.

Katrina fled to the ladies' and locked herself in a cubicle where she could weep in peace. It was clear that the poor man with the funny name thought she was completely crazy. Why had she had to burble about the failings of a man's penis, for heaven's sake? Even if it was a French king's penis. She was hopeless. How could a name on a text message reduce her to this shrivelling body of incontinent emotion? How, after so many years, could Lewis still have the power to hurt her? It was so *sad* and *pathetic* and *feeble* and *wet*.

Katrina met Lewis Maltraver the day after her twenty-fifth birthday. She was acting for a television company that wanted to buy the warehouse it had been renting for the last few years. She had arranged to meet the client at the warehouse itself, and when she arrived he gave her a tour of the place. She had glimpses of television cameras, colourful costumes, gesticulating people. The best part of the tour was the last room she was taken to. She couldn't believe it. There in the flesh in front of her were her favourite soap-opera stars from the *Medical Alert* series: sexy Dr Rubin, terrifying Mr Garside, capable Sister Green and, currently crying her eyes out, Dr Rubin's on/off girl-friend, Angelica.

Angelica put out a faltering hand. 'But I love you!' she cried.

'You have sucked me dry!' Dr Rubin shouted. 'You have . . .' He stopped suddenly and grinned broadly. 'I am sorry,' he said, 'but there is no way I can broadcast to the nation that Angelica has sucked me dry.'

The client coughed nervously by the door and said that perhaps they should move on. Reluctantly, Katrina followed him out but not before she had taken one last look at gorgeous Dr Rubin and not before, mira-cle of miracles, he had glanced across the room and smiled at *her*.

After her meeting, the client invited her to have lunch with him in the canteen. They were standing in the queue when Dr Rubin himself came up. 'Tom,' he said to the client, 'Gary wants to see you.'

'I can't,' said the client. 'I'm having lunch with my solicitor.'

'I'll have lunch with her if you like,' said Dr Rubin. 'Gary needs to see you now.'

The client looked anxiously at Katrina. 'I'm so sorry,' he said. 'Do you mind if Lewis here looks after you instead of me?'

Katrina smiled. 'I'm sure I can manage.'

Lewis was a little smaller than he looked on television but his eyes were just as warm and rich and sympathetic. He kept those eyes on her all the time and he made her, for the first time in her life, feel she was beautiful and beguiling.

When he asked if he could take her to dinner on Friday, she didn't hesitate.

He picked her up and drove her to a pub overlooking the Thames. She drank too much ('I'm driving,' he insisted. 'You have to drink for both of us.') and listened to the stories of backstage gossip with rapt attention. Over coffee he took her hand and put his face close to her own. 'Do you want to know what I want to do? I want to take you home,' he said. 'I want to take your clothes off. I want to put my tongue in your mouth, taste you and feel you and love you. Shall we go?'

Katrina was a solicitor who specialised in commercial property law. She had successfully seen off office Lotharios and she prided herself on being able to distinguish between genuine feeling and phoney seduction lines. And yet she responded to Lewis's outrageous proposition with a shameless and indeed breathless affirmative.

When she woke the next morning, she felt his hand stroke her thigh and knew she had to make love to him again. Which was a pity since her daughter came in at that precise moment and demanded to know who was in bed with her.

'I'm a friend of your mother,' Lewis said, removing his hand from Katrina's thigh. 'How do you do?'

Susie giggled and asked him if he'd like her to show him her polar bear. Lewis said he would love to see it and the little girl ran out.

Lewis cast a quizzical glance at Katrina. 'You didn't tell me you had offspring,' he said.

'Does it matter?' she asked.

'Of course it does,' Lewis said. 'A few minutes ago, I was hoping to make love to you again and now'—he paused as Susie rushed back in with her bear—'I am going to be introduced to a bear.'

He left after breakfast, assuring Katrina that he would ring the next day. He didn't. By Wednesday, Katrina had stopped jumping every time the phone rang. She didn't tell anyone about him. She was ashamed that she had behaved like the worst sort of star-struck fan.

Then, late on Saturday evening, he came to see her. He told her he had tried to stay away but he couldn't. He told her the publicity people had said that the main reason for the popularity of *Medical Alert* was the sexual chemistry between Dr Rubin and Angelica. In order to foster this, they liked the public to think that Lewis Maltraver and Penny Darlington were romantically involved in real life. He and Penny had promised not to flaunt any private relationships with other people. 'If we had a relationship,' Lewis said, 'we'd have to keep it secret. You don't deserve that.'

'In that case,' Katrina said, 'why are you here now?'

Lewis thrust his fingers through his luxuriant brown locks. 'I've tried to keep away,' he said, 'I really have tried.' He smiled suddenly. 'My teachers always said I had no self-discipline.' He had a lovely smile. 'Look at you,' he said. 'You have not the first idea how sexy you are.'

There was no doubt about it. Sex with Lewis was incredible. Sex with her husband had been regular and efficient. His attitude to lovemaking had been like his attitude to food. He appreciated it but he didn't want to spend too long on it. Lewis was a true gourmet. He liked to take his time; he liked to try different things. Katrina was utterly in thrall to him.

Six weeks later, he came to supper and told her it was over. Katrina had prepared a special meal: cream of Stilton soup, trout with caper sauce and lashings of spinach, and a fresh fruit salad. He told her he cared for her deeply but his career had to come first and he couldn't combine his job and a relationship. After he had gone, she played Patsy Cline's 'Crazy'. It was how she felt. She *was* crazy for crying and she *was* crazy for loving him.

Then one evening, while sitting in bed with the *Evening Standard*, she saw a photograph of a smiling bride, with the caption: *Angelica Marries Her Very Own Doctor.* Underneath, a few lines stated that Penny Darlington from *Medical Alert* had married her boyfriend, Dr Peter Woodstock. Lewis Maltraver, the journalist had added a little coyly, arrived at the wedding hand in hand with another member of the *Medical Alert* cast, prompting speculation that Dr Rubin and Sister Green clearly enjoyed playing doctors and nurses.

Katrina never heard from Lewis again.

As they drove off the ferry, Cornelius suggested a quick lunch in Boulogne. They parked and settled at a pavement café. Cornelius left Katrina to choose a table while he plunged into the café to order lunch. When he came back, he set a glass and a small stoneware jug in front of her and sat down. 'I've got you a small *pichet* of house red,' he said.

'Aren't you having any?' she asked.

'I'll stick with water,' Cornelius said. 'I have a long drive.'

Katrina poured herself a drink. 'Well, then,' she said, 'cheers!'

'That rose on your jacket,' Cornelius said, 'looks remarkably fresh.'

'That's because it's not real. Carol—the wife of your friend Douglas—gave it to me. The red rose in the lapel idea was hers. She said I needed something to mark myself out. I thought it was all rather tacky . . . like one of those ghastly blind dates when you both hold copies of the *Communist Manifesto* and wear flowers in your buttonhole.'

'Have you ever been on a blind date?' Cornelius asked.

'Only once,' Katrina said. 'Once was enough.'

'Was it so terrible?'

'Depending on one's point of view, it was either a brilliant success or an absolute disaster. I ended up marrying the man.' For a moment her eyes met those of Cornelius and then she looked away.

'Well,' said Cornelius, 'well . . .'

Now she was looking at him again. 'Cornelius,' she said, 'I want to say something . . .'

Oh God, he thought, she's going to tell me why she was crying and then she's going to start crying *all over again*! He had to do something. He leapt to his feet. 'I'm terribly sorry,' he said, 'I've just remembered something. I would like to buy some local cheese for my friends while I'm in Boulogne. I won't be long. Will you be all right on your own?'

'Of course,' Katrina said. 'It's a beautiful day and I'm sitting on a pavement in France with a glass of wine in my hand!'

He strode off. He felt irritated with her for making him feel guilty and for making him dream up some spurious excuse. He didn't even know if there *were* any cheeses peculiar to this area.

He found an excellent delicatessen in the rue Thiers and purchased a quite superb local cheese called Cremet du Cap Blanc-Nez. This acquisition put him in such good humour that he felt he could cope with anything Katrina had to tell him. Food shops in France always put him in a good mood.

Their lunch was on the table when he returned and he felt another twinge of guilt. 'You shouldn't have waited for me,' he reproached her.

'The waiter brought it only a few moments ago,' Katrina assured him. 'Cornelius, before you went, I wanted to tell you something.'

'You did?' asked Cornelius feebly.

'Yes,' said Katrina. 'I wanted to say that I insist on paying for this meal and for our dinner tonight. We'll also go halves on petrol. It's very kind of you to give me a lift but I insist on paying my way.'

She was not going to reveal her inner turmoil. He was almost beginning to like her. 'You can pay for lunch,' he conceded handsomely, 'but you certainly won't pay for supper.' He was aware that he had lost her attention and followed, enquiringly, her line of vision.

'You see that girl walking towards us?' Katrina whispered fiercely.

The young woman was slight and blonde and very well dressed. Cornelius waited until she had walked past them. 'She's very attractive,' he said politely.

'Shush!' Katrina commanded. 'Watch her.'

The young woman reached the end of the pavement. She stopped, turned, stamped one foot twice and then the other. Then she proceeded to walk back towards them. She looked neither to the right nor to the left. She walked past them and when she got to the edge of the Grande-Rue she stopped, stamped her feet twice, one after the other, and turned again.

'I've been watching her,' Katrina said, 'ever since you went off. I thought she might be waiting for some friends but all she does is walk backwards and forwards, backwards and forwards, and every time she gets to either end of the pavement she stamps her feet with such precision. She's young, she's beautiful, but I think . . . I really, really think . . . she must be mad.'

Cornelius blinked. 'Isn't that a rather premature judgment? There could be all sorts of reasons for her behaviour. She might have gum on her shoes. You think she's mad because she's doing something for which you have no obvious explanation. It seems to me that people are far too ready to dismiss as mad those individuals who choose to be different. Peculiar people are only peculiar until you know them.'

'Sometimes,' Katrina retorted, 'you only realise people are peculiar once you *do* know them.'

'Well,' said Cornelius, 'all I can say is that I know many people who are often described as crazy and they are not at all.'

'Really?' asked Katrina. 'Give me an example.'

'Well,' said Cornelius, frowning thoughtfully, 'I have a friend who's always wanted to be a robin. Whenever he's stressed, he goes into his garden and he spends half an hour being a robin.'

Katrina's chip remained suspended in her hand. 'I'm sorry?'

'He goes into the garden and he imagines himself into the state of mind of a robin and then he stays in that state of mind for half an hour. It does him no end of good.'

'Right,' said Katrina.

Her eyes were very expressive. Her eyes were laughing even before her mouth turned up at the corners. It was good to see her smiling. 'I have another friend,' he said. 'He spends his free time trying to be picked up by aliens.'

'How does he do that?'

'Oh, you know,' said Cornelius airily, 'he goes to the sorts of places that aliens might be interested in and walks around looking hopeful.'

'You have some very odd friends,' said Katrina.

'You might think James is the oddest of all. I'm spending the next week with him and his wife. He used to be an extremely successful merchant banker. When he was thirty-seven, he fell in love with a French schoolteacher called Odile. He followed her out to France, gave up his job and took up painting.'

'Is he a good artist?'

'He is an appalling artist. He has never sold a painting in his life. Some people think Odile is mad because she thinks he's a genius. They live on Odile's income. He brings up their children and paints terrible paintings. A lot of people think he's mad.'

'I don't think that's mad,' Katrina said. 'I'd love to give up being a solicitor. I'd much rather spend my time painting bad pictures.'

'Why don't you?'

Katrina laughed. 'My daughter has just finished her degree and wants to be an actress which means I will probably have to support her indefinitely. My son is going to university next year. I shall have to carry on working for a long time yet.'

'Doesn't their father help with money? I would have thought—' Cornelius stopped, momentarily paralysed by the terrifying thought that Katrina's weeping fit might have been caused by the very man he was now referring to. 'I'm sorry,' he said. 'It is none of my business.'

Fortunately, Katrina remained quite composed. 'I promise I'm not offended! My ex-husband can't afford to help. He has far too many other children. My sister always calls him the Serial Propagator. He left me before Ollie was born. He married again and had two more children. Then he abandoned them and took up with someone else. He left her when their child was four. Now he's on his fourth partner. She's pregnant with their second child so he'll probably leave *her* soon.'

'Oh, dear,' Cornelius said. 'He sounds a little careless.'

'Try irresponsible,' Katrina said. She took a sip of her wine. 'Tell me about the friends you're going to stay with. Do they live in Montélimar?'

'It's their nearest big town. They live in a little village called Cléon d'Andran. Are you staying in Montélimar?'

'No, it's near a place called Pont-de-Barret. If you drop me anywhere near Montélimar my sister will pick me up.'

'There's no need for that. Pont-de-Barret is only a little further on from Cléon d'Andran. I'll be happy to drop you at—'

'Jul . . . *eee!*' The frantic, anguished shout stopped him in his tracks. Both Cornelius and Katrina turned and saw a lanky, unshaven man running down the street towards them. He was flaying the air with his arms as if he was besieged by locusts.

Cornelius saw that the blonde girl had halted her march and come to rest a few feet from their table. She stood absolutely still.

The young man cried once again, '*Jul . . . eee!*'

It was as if that second shout destroyed some terrible enchantment. Quite suddenly the girl smiled and cried, '*Armand!*' before running into his arms like a little lost girl who's found her mother.

Cornelius looked at Katrina. 'You see?' he told her. 'I told you she wasn't mad.'

When Katrina awoke, they were no longer on the motorway but travelling along a tree-lined avenue between vast, flat fields. 'I'm *so* sorry,' she said. 'How long have I been asleep?'

'A couple of hours.' Cornelius sounded unconcerned. 'We should be there soon.'

'I am *so* sorry,' Katrina repeated. 'I'm not used to drinking at lunch.'

'Don't apologise.' Cornelius swung right. 'It's only now that I need some help. There's a map in the glove compartment. I've circled the village we're looking for. We came off the motorway at exit number thirty . . .'

Katrina had never been very successful with maps. She opened out Cornelius's map and said in what she hoped was a confident voice, 'What road are we on now?'

'It should be the D8. Can you see it?'

Katrina frowned. She turned the map upside down. After due consideration, she said judiciously, 'I think it *might* be a good idea if we stop for a moment.'

Cornelius braked and put on his hazard lights. 'Let's have a look.'

A moment later, a knock on his window made them both jump. Cornelius wound it down. A short, balding gentleman with small black eyes and a bulbous nose nodded politely. 'You are English,' he said. He was stating a fact, not asking a question.

'Yes,' said Cornelius, 'I'm afraid we are.'

'You are lost,' said the man. He was clearly a man of some prescience.

'I'm afraid we are,' agreed Cornelius. He reached over for the map and showed it to the Good Samaritan. 'We're trying to get *there* and I know we're somewhere *here*.'

The man nodded again. 'I see you and I stop,' he said. 'I am the mayor! You follow my car and I indicate the road you must take.'

'Thank you,' said Cornelius. 'You are very kind.'

The man gave a magnificently Gallic shrug. 'I am the mayor,' he said.

Cornelius followed the mayor's car as it turned left at the T-junction. Their subsequent progress was slow since the mayor responded to every salutation from passers-by with a cheery wave. Finally, he stuck out his hand and pointed to the right with a dramatic flourish. Cornelius hooted his thanks and turned right into a narrow country lane.

'What a lovely man!' cried Katrina. 'And everyone knows him! *That's* why I'd love to live in France! Name me one provincial town in England where the mayor is recognised by anybody! I *wish* I lived in France.'

'Really?' asked Cornelius. 'Would that be your only reason?'

'Why not? It's a jolly good reason. But I'd also move because the French appreciate beauty. No one in Britain ever plants trees along the roads. I like tree-lined avenues.'

'You'd get on very well with my friend James,' said Cornelius.

'Why?' asked Katrina suspiciously, sensing an insult.

'He loves tree-lined avenues too. He goes on and on about tree-lined avenues. He can talk about tree-lined avenues for hours. He's very odd.'

Katrina folded her arms. 'Your idea of "odd",' she told him, 'is very different from my idea of odd.'

Cornelius laughed. 'That is the precise point I was trying to make during lunch.'

Cornelius had a lovely smile. His severe face looked completely different. Katrina felt absurdly pleased that she had made him smile.

'Aha!' said Cornelius. 'Here we are!' He turned into a large square and parked in front of a big house with white shutters. The door was opened by an attractive woman who greeted them effusively. Cornelius surprised both women by breaking into fluent French and engaging madame in polite interrogation. Finally, he turned to Katrina. 'Apparently, there's only one restaurant here and it closes early. Do you mind if we set out in twenty minutes?'

'Fine,' Katrina said. 'Knock on my door when you're ready.'

Katrina's room was clean and cheerfully decorated. She threw off her shoes, went to her bed and lay down. Within thirty seconds she was on her feet again. She was *not* going to think about Lewis tonight. She was not going to inflict any more scenes on poor Cornelius. She was going to try very hard to be an entertaining companion.

She went through to the bathroom. She stared at her reflection in the mirror and her mouth dropped. She looked horrific. The ravages of her epic weeping on the boat and her big sleep in the afternoon had conspired to make her resemble a squashed tomato, while her hair appeared to have received some electric-shock treatment. Katrina swallowed and prepared to execute a hasty damage-limitation exercise.

Cornelius came to collect her and they walked across the square, past the bar and down a narrow street to the restaurant.

Katrina followed him in and glanced round the small, spartan room. The orange-painted walls were bare but for an old, curling poster advertising some long-gone festival. The whole place smelt of defeat. Or perhaps of cabbage.

To the right was a bar behind which stood a bald-headed man with bags under his eyes and a dark, drooping moustache.

'*Bonsoir, monsieur,*' Cornelius said. '*Je voudrais dîner . . .*'

The landlord sighed, turned away and called, 'Brigitte!'

Brigitte emerged. Katrina wondered if she'd been called after Brigitte Bardot. She didn't look like Brigitte Bardot. She wore a grubby white apron and had protruding eyes which, together with the fact that she had lost teeth on either side of her mouth, gave her the appearance of a frightened rabbit. As she listened to Cornelius, her brow furrowed and then she launched into a long explanation that was accompanied by a variety of hand movements, all of which seemed to indicate that a delicious supper was not on the way.

'Right,' Cornelius said, once they were outside on the pavement again. 'This is the situation. Brigitte and her husband don't usually cook beyond eight in the evening. She suggests we go to the bar in the square for half an hour while she sees what she can put together for us. I have to warn you . . . the main course will be tongue.'

Katrina blinked but refused to be downhearted. 'Well,' she said bravely, 'that will be a new experience at any rate.'

The bar had an altogether jollier atmosphere. A young couple sat at a table with their small son. At the bar itself sat a handsome woman who was holding forth to the young barman and two elderly gentlemen.

'Remember,' Katrina said, 'I'm paying for this evening.'

'We can discuss that later,' Cornelius said. 'Let me get the drinks.'

She watched him go to the bar and hail the barman. The woman immediately engaged him in animated conversation. At one point she turned and smiled at Katrina, who smiled back and wished she'd paid more attention to her language lessons at school.

Her attention was diverted by the small boy from the end table. He came up and pointed a silver pistol at her heart. '*Pan!*' he said.

Katrina duly pretended to be dead and the little boy crowed with pleasure before running back to his parents and shooting them too.

Cornelius came over with two champagne flutes and a slightly reddened complexion. 'They all insist that we try the local champagne,' he said. 'I hope you don't mind.'

Katrina laughed. 'Do I mind drinking champagne? That's like asking if I'd mind winning the lottery!'

'Well, I'm not sure I would like to win the lottery,' Cornelius retorted. 'Either I'd have to turn to philanthropy, which would involve lots of meetings with people I don't know, or I'd have to justify my good fortune by transforming my life and that would cause a whole host of problems.'

'I'd be happy to have problems like that,' Katrina said. She was aware that her companion was giving her a rather strained smile. 'Is something wrong?' she asked.

'Katrina,' Cornelius whispered urgently, 'would you mind very much if I held your hand?'

Katrina stared at him impassively before putting her right hand on the table. Cornelius patted it for a few moments and gave another ghastly smile. Katrina's mouth twitched.

'I hope you don't mind,' Cornelius murmured, 'but I told that lady you were my wife.'

'I'm flattered,' Katrina said, 'but she probably assumed that anyway.'

Cornelius shook his head. 'No, no. She told me she *hoped* you were my sister. I think'—Cornelius paused to give an unhappy sigh—'she has taken a liking to me. It seemed *safer* to tell her we were married. I think we should just keep talking as if nothing is happening.'

'Right,' said Katrina. She couldn't think of anything to say.

'Well, now,' Cornelius said, in the desperate tones of one who has never mastered the art of polite conversation, 'you must be looking forward to your holiday. You said you're staying with your sister?'

'That's right,' Katrina said. 'She's older than me but she looks much younger. She looks like Catherine Zeta-Jones.'

'Ah!' For a moment Cornelius looked mystified and then his face cleared. 'Yes. I've heard of her.'

'I should think you have!' Katrina retorted. 'Really, you are a very peculiar man. Tell me, have you ever looked at *Heat* magazine?'

Cornelius shook his head.

'When was the last time you went to the cinema?'

Cornelius stroked his chin thoughtfully. 'I like going to the cinema,' he said, 'but I haven't been for some time. I don't know why.'

'Do you have a DVD player?'

'I'm afraid I don't.'

Katrina grinned. 'It's just as well we're not really married,' she said, 'because we have nothing in common at all. Whenever my daughter's at home, I read every page of her *Heat* magazine. I regularly go to the cinema and one of the highlights of my life is when I treat myself to a new DVD.' She paused. 'Actually, that makes me sound very sad, doesn't it?' She took another sip of champagne and hoped Cornelius would contradict her. He didn't. He was shading his eyes with his hand.

'Oh dear,' he said.

Katrina, initially disconcerted by his response, soon realised that his remark was occasioned by the sudden arrival of the French woman at their side. The lady was holding a bottle of champagne. '*Bonsoir, madame*,' she said. '*Vous aimez la champagne?*'

Katrina smiled enthusiastically. '*C'est magnifique!*' she said.

The lady replenished their glasses. '*Votre mari est très beau*,' she declared. '*Il est beau comme un dieu.*'

'*Oui*,' Katrina responded with just as much conviction and a lot less comprehension. '*Vraiment magnifique!*'

The lady gave a raucous laugh, clapped Katrina on the back and returned to the bar. Katrina noticed that Cornelius had gone very red. Behind her she could hear the people at the bar laughing loudly. She looked at him suspiciously. 'What did she say to me?'

'She said that . . .' He paused and shrugged his shoulders. 'I think she was just making a joke. She's a little drunk.'

Behind them there was more raucous laughter. 'Well, it was obviously very funny,' Katrina said. 'What was it she said?'

'She said,' Cornelius said in a voice that was devoid of any expression, 'that I was as handsome as a god.'

'Oh,' Katrina said. 'I see.'

'And you agreed,' Cornelius continued in the same flat tone, 'that I was truly magnificent.' He nodded politely. 'Very kind of you.'

Katrina looked at Cornelius and, for the second time that day, a smile broke across his countenance. It really was a very nice smile.

After bidding self-conscious farewells to the barman and his customers, Katrina and Cornelius made their way to Brigitte's restaurant. They were ushered in by the landlord, who waited for them to sit down before muttering a query in which Katrina happily recognised the word 'vin'.

There was no one else in the room. 'This is terrible,' Katrina murmured. 'Poor Brigitte was probably looking forward to putting her feet up and now we've wrecked her evening.'

Cornelius glanced at the sea of empty tables surrounding them. 'Well,' he said, 'we can't leave now so the best we can do is appreciate what she gives us and look grateful.'

The landlord reappeared with bottles of water and wine. He opened the wine, poured a little out for Cornelius to try and, as soon as Cornelius nodded his satisfaction, filled both their glasses. Cornelius said something and monsieur waved his left hand, became suddenly animated and, after a quick waterfall of words, left them with a smile.

Katrina took a sip. 'It's good,' she said. 'What were you talking about?'

'I said I thought the wines in this area were excellent. He agreed.'

'I wish I could speak French like you,' Katrina said. 'Of course, you sell wine. Carol says you're based in Dulwich. I suppose you come to France all the time. Carol says her husband loves working for you. She says you have these lovely mornings when you get everyone in your office to sample your wines and as a result Douglas won't let her buy cheap plonk any more.'

'I'm sure that's not true. There are many excellent wines on the market that are quite inexpensive.'

'Are you here on business now? Are you going to go round Montélimar, sniffing all the vines?'

'I don't go in for a lot of vine-sniffing and I don't sell wines from that region anyway. I'm simply visiting friends.'

From the kitchen came a sound of a saucepan lid crashing to the floor. Cornelius ignored it, so Katrina did too, asking, 'Where *do* you buy your wines from?'

Cornelius moved his long legs from under the table and let them stretch out to the side. 'I buy them from all over the world,' he said. 'There's a chardonnay in Uruguay I particularly like. In France, I suppose I tend to concentrate on Bordeaux, Burgundy, the Rhône . . .'

The kitchen doors swung open and Brigitte appeared, looking frazzled, bearing their first course on two big white plates. She launched into a long speech which appeared to be a passionate apology for the food she was serving them. Cornelius responded soothingly.

'Actually,' Katrina said to Cornelius as soon as Brigitte had departed, 'this looks great. I love couscous salad. Did you tell her how pleased we were to be here?'

'I did,' Cornelius said, 'and I thought she was going to burst into tears.' His eyes met hers involuntarily and Katrina bit her lip.

Both she and Cornelius turned their attention to their couscous salad. Finally, Cornelius coughed and made what Katrina recognised was a brave attempt to retrieve the situation. 'Do you often go on holiday with your sister?' he asked.

Katrina responded with a polite shake of her head. 'No,' she said, 'I hardly ever do. But her husband died a year ago and her children are coming out with their current partners and she said she'd be feeling rather lonely. So here I am.'

'That's very nice of you.'

'Not really. My children are doing their own things this summer and Rose is giving me a rent-free stay in a lovely house with a swimming pool. It's no great sacrifice.'

The kitchen doors opened again and Brigitte came through to collect their plates. '*Merci, madame,*' Katrina said enthusiastically. She was rewarded with a wan smile before Brigitte disappeared again.

Her exit only emphasised the silence. Cornelius stared thoughtfully at the bottle of water. Katrina stared at the empty table on their right. She squared her shoulders and looked steadily at Cornelius. 'This isn't working. I want to tell you why I was crying this morning.'

'Really,' said Cornelius, 'there is no need.'

'Really,' countered Katrina, 'there is. Neither of us can relax while you're thinking I'm some crazy, hysterical woman who's going to start making another scene any moment.'

'I assure you I don't think you're some crazy, hysterical woman.'

Katrina smiled. 'Thank you,' she said, 'but you *are* worried I might start crying again. I promise you, I'm not in the habit of weeping copiously when I meet someone for the first time. Actually, I'm not in the habit of weeping copiously, full stop.'

'Right,' said Cornelius. 'I'm sure you're *not* and even if you *are*, I promise I don't need you to tell me anything—'

'I understand *that*,' Katrina said impatiently, 'but *I* need to tell *you*.' She finished her glass of wine and then waited while Cornelius refilled it. 'After my husband left me, I fell in love with an actor. Actually, you might remember him. He was Dr Rubin in *Medical Alert*. Did you ever see it?'

'No,' said Cornelius, 'I'm afraid I didn't.'

'Of course you didn't,' said Katrina. 'Anyway, I fell in love with him and I thought that he fell in love with me. And then I discovered that he hadn't at all and we stopped seeing each other. I felt pretty foolish. I never told anyone about it.' Katrina swallowed hard and gripped her wineglass with both her hands. 'On the boat, just before you introduced yourself to me, I found out that he is currently staying at my sister's house in France and the reason he is staying there is because he's my sister's new boyfriend. She sent me a text. She thinks I'll be thrilled. She knew I used to watch *Medical Alert*. Everyone used to watch *Medical Alert*. Everyone except you.'

The kitchen doors banged open again and Brigitte reappeared. 'Ah!' said Cornelius with an attempt at enthusiasm. 'This will be the tongue!'

The tongue exceeded Katrina's expectations. It sat on the plate surrounded by a mountain of pale cabbage, like an old, flaccid phallus. When Katrina took her first bite, she was pretty sure it tasted like an old, flaccid phallus. She swallowed hard and reached for the wine.

'You don't like it,' Cornelius said.

Katrina tried to think of a polite way to describe it. 'It's different.'

'Eat some cabbage,' Cornelius suggested. 'You can leave the tongue.'

'If I leave the tongue,' Katrina said, 'Brigitte will be upset.'

'I'll eat your tongue.'

'You hate it too,' she said. 'I can manage it. If I keep drinking wine with it, I'll be fine.' She took another mouthful.

By the time she finally finished her ordeal she had downed three full glasses. She and Cornelius put their empty plates to one side and regarded each other with the respect of two mountaineers who have finally conquered Everest.

Cornelius poured out yet another glass for them both.

'I think I can say,' he declared, 'that that was, without doubt, the most disgusting thing I have ever eaten and that'—he frowned thoughtfully—'you are an exceptional woman for eating it.'

Katrina flushed with pride. 'Thank you,' she said, adding graciously, 'and you are an exceptional man.'

'Thank you.' Cornelius cleared his throat. 'Before we leave the subject, I would like to tell you that the doctor man doesn't deserve you.'

'Well, he doesn't want me,' Katrina pointed out, 'so whether he deserves me or not is immaterial. And he isn't a doctor. He's an actor.'

'My wife,' Cornelius said, 'is an actress.'

'Is she?' Katrina was surprised. Fleetingly, she tried to picture Cornelius surrounded by over-expansive thespians. 'What's her name?'

'She's called Lucy Lambert. She's not as successful as she should be. She is an excellent actress but Lucy says it's all about looks for women. She is very attractive but most writers and directors seem to lose interest in women over twenty-five, however attractive they are.'

Katrina sighed. 'Lewis was very attractive.'

Brigitte arrived with two cups of black coffee and offered her guests cheese or fruit, which was politely declined by both of them. Katrina waited until she had left and then said she felt as if she would never be able to eat anything again. Cornelius agreed that he felt unpleasantly full.

Another crash came from the kitchen. 'We ought to leave,' Katrina said. 'Poor Brigitte looks so tired and we're stopping her from going to bed.' She saw Cornelius reach for his wallet and added, 'I'm doing this. I absolutely insist.' She pushed back her seat, walked towards the kitchen and called out, '*Madame? Nous finishons! L'addition, s'il vous plaît.*'

Madame reappeared, wiping her hands on her apron and pulling a notebook from its pocket. Katrina returned to the table, picked up her handbag, opened her wallet and produced a wad of euros, saying brightly, '*J'ai includé un tip. C'est tout pour vous et mucho merci!*' Then Cornelius reached into his pocket and pressed some more notes into Brigitte's hand.

Cornelius and Katrina saw with dismay that Brigitte's eyes were shiny with tears. She uttered a low '*Merci*', went over to Katrina, kissed her on both cheeks and then did the same with Cornelius. After another heartfelt '*Merci*', she called her husband and showed him the money and suddenly he was gripping their hands and murmuring, '*C'est trop! Oh, merci, merci beaucoup! Je vous souhaite tout le bonheur possible!*'

By the time they got outside, Katrina felt quite overwhelmed. She took one last look through the window. Monsieur and Brigitte were embracing each other.

'Cornelius,' Katrina said, 'you are a very nice man. You must have given them one hell of a tip.'

Cornelius looked a little sheepish. 'I enjoyed the evening,' he said. 'I enjoyed it very much.'

Katrina laughed. 'You're just relieved that I didn't start crying again.'

'I *was* relieved,' Cornelius admitted. For a few moments they walked on in amicable silence and then Cornelius spoke again. 'I am not very good at polite conversation. I have never known how to talk to strangers. But I didn't feel you were strange.'

As they reached their temporary home, Cornelius took out the key he had been given by madame and let them both in. Katrina stopped outside her room and thanked Cornelius for the evening. 'I have to tell you,' she said, 'that I wasn't looking forward to this evening either. But I also enjoyed myself.'

'I'm very glad,' Cornelius said. 'I told madame we'd have breakfast at eight. Is that too early for you?'

'Not at all.' Katrina took out her room key. As Cornelius turned towards his own room she called his name softly. 'I just wanted to say,' she said, 'that I didn't find you strange either.'

CHAPTER TWO

A Plan is Made

WHEN CORNELIUS CAME DOWN for breakfast the next morning, he found a table for two laden with fresh croissants. Madame bustled in and asked if she should bring in the coffee. Cornelius told her that was an excellent idea and assured her with more optimism than conviction that Katrina would be here at any moment.

In fact, Katrina appeared shortly after the coffee. Her complexion was wan and she held herself in a manner that suggested her body was made of the finest bone china. She sat down carefully.

Cornelius offered her a croissant and she shook her head. 'They look lovely, but I think I'll just have coffee.'

'Are you all right?' Cornelius asked. 'You look rather white.'

Katrina swallowed. 'It's entirely my own fault,' she said. 'I drank too much last night.'

'I don't think you can blame yourself,' Cornelius said judiciously. 'It was the only way you could eat the tongue. It really was quite—'

'Do you mind if we don't talk about the tongue?'

'Of course. I'm sorry.' Cornelius poured her out some coffee. 'You can sleep in the car. You'll feel much better once you've had a good sleep.'

'I'm sure you're right.' Katrina took a sip of her coffee. 'When do you think we'll get down to Montélimar?'

'If we don't stop for lunch,' Cornelius said, 'we should be there by midafternoon. It's a beautiful day.'

Katrina glanced at the sunlight pouring through the window and winced slightly. 'When do you want to leave here?'

'Well.' Cornelius looked at her doubtfully. 'I thought about leaving in twenty minutes but we can leave later if you like. There's no hurry.'

'Twenty minutes will be fine.' Katrina swallowed. 'I think if you don't mind I'll go back to my room for a little while.'

Cornelius watched her leave the room. He helped himself to another croissant and resigned himself to a late departure.

He had underestimated Katrina. Looking even paler than she had done earlier, she appeared at the precise time she had said she would. Having ascertained that Cornelius had settled the bill with madame, she insisted on paying her share at once. Then, as if exhausted by such a sudden flurry of activity, she got into the car.

Cornelius turned on the ignition. 'Don't talk,' he told Katrina. 'Shut your eyes. Go to sleep.'

'Thank you,' Katrina murmured and duly closed her eyes. Cornelius shot her a swift glance. There was no doubt about it. She was an impressive woman. Anyone who could force a plate of tongue and cabbage down her throat without complaint was not the sort of person to habitually indulge in emotional excess. Her stoicism over breakfast was further proof. She must have been very much in love with the doctor man and Cornelius hoped she wouldn't discover she was still in love when she saw him again. He was not impressed by the sister's behaviour. If she'd asked Katrina to come and keep her company, it was not very thoughtful to tell her at the last minute that there would be a boyfriend there as well. The more Cornelius thought about it, the more it seemed to him that the sister and the doctor man were made for each other. He would have liked to pass on this thought to Katrina once she woke up but was not sure that she would appreciate it.

Cornelius shot another look at her. It was extraordinary that even though she was a relative stranger, he did not find her company either jarring or uncomfortable. This was a rare experience.

She did not stir until some hours later when Cornelius brought the car to a stop. She opened first one eye, then the other and said, 'Are we here?'

'No,' said Cornelius. 'I left the motorway. I thought we'd stop for lunch. I could do with a break and it might do you good to get some food inside you. This is Bellevue. I've spotted a brasserie at the end of the road. I think we should try it.'

Katrina nodded. 'Fine. I'm sorry I've been such a useless companion. I *do* feel better.'

Surprisingly, when the waitress brought them their meal, Katrina found that she was able to eat at least half her pizza. Her headache no longer felt as if it would tear her skull apart. She even felt able to talk again.

'Cornelius,' she said, 'how did you get your name? It's very unusual.'

'It was my mother's choice,' he said. 'I think perhaps she didn't like me. I was an unprepossessing baby.'

'That doesn't sound very likely. There's no such thing as an unprepossessing baby. Have you ever asked her?'

'There's not much point. She has always had a rather selective memory. I'm pretty sure it isn't a family name. It could have been worse. I knew a boy at school called Endymion.'

Katrina blinked. 'You're right,' she said. 'It could have been worse. Poor Endymion.'

'Katrina's a good name,' Cornelius mused. 'Very strong.'

'Thank you,' Katrina said. 'I like it. My sister *will* call me Katty.' She bit her lip and wished she hadn't brought up her sister. She wished a miracle could happen, she wished Cornelius's car would break down, she wished Cornelius would trip and break his leg in such a way that he would need her to drive him back to an English hospital. She wished that *she* would break her leg.

Cornelius did not trip over anything, and neither did she, and the car did not break down either.

Cornelius had noticed that his companion's mood had darkened and he had guessed that she was contemplating the unwelcome reunion with her former lover. He did think of reminding her that after so many years the actor/doctor man might have lost his appeal, but the fact that he had secured the affections of the Catherine Zeta-Jones woman did suggest that he hadn't. He checked his watch. They were now on the other side of Lyon. Another forty minutes and they'd be there.

They had left the motorway for the last time when Katrina spoke again. 'Cornelius,' she said, 'I want to ask a favour of you. It is a very big favour but it doesn't involve you having to *do* anything. It does involve you not mentioning your wife to my sister.'

'I had no intention of mentioning anything at all to your sister.'

'No,' Katrina agreed. 'The thing is my sister always found it difficult to understand how a woman can be happy without a man. Certainly, she finds it impossible to understand that *I* can be happy without a man. I gave up trying to enlighten her a long time ago and I don't care at all any more that she feels sorry for me. But—and I know it's silly—I find that I *do* mind the idea of Rose . . . *and Lewis* . . . feeling sorry for me, both at the same time. I'm not sure I can bear to spend a week with both of them being kind to me. So, what I was wondering was whether you would mind if I let them think that you and I are possibly more than just acquaintances. I know it's presumptuous . . .'

Cornelius shifted uncomfortably in his seat. 'No, no, not at all. But I don't think I quite understand.' He rubbed his forehead nervously. 'You want us to pretend we're having an affair?'

'No, no, I want them to think you're not married, I want them to think we're having a perfectly legitimate relationship. You wouldn't have to do *anything*. I've worked it all out. Rose would probably want to invite you to dinner at some time but I shall say that you want to concentrate on your friends.'

'I'm not sure I *do*,' said Cornelius. 'I'm quite sure my friends don't want to spend every minute of the holiday with me . . .'

'That doesn't matter. The point is I shall only say that in order to spare you the need to come round and be polite to Rose and Lewis.'

'I see. I would certainly like to avoid that.'

'I know, I know. All I want is that you let me introduce you when we get to the house and you avoid mentioning your wife if possible.'

Cornelius gave a sigh. 'The thing is,' he said, 'I don't like telling lies.'

'Oh.' Katrina reddened. 'I see. Of course you don't. I'm sorry, it was a crazy idea. It only occurred to me because . . .' She stopped and turned her head away.

Cornelius looked at her enquiringly and then, as understanding dawned, returned his gaze to the windscreen. '. . . because I pretended you were my wife in the bar last night. I did indeed tell a lie. I panicked. I shouldn't have done that.'

'No, I don't mean that. It doesn't matter. It was a silly idea.'

Cornelius glanced at Katrina. She sat stiffly, her face closed and tense. He said, 'If your sister were to ask me about my marital status—and I see no reason why she should do so—I could say that my wife is planning to divorce me.'

Katrina shook her head. 'That's very kind of you but you're right. There's no reason why you should have to tell lies for me.'

'That wouldn't be lying. My wife *is* planning to divorce me.'

'Oh.' Katrina looked confused. 'I'm so sorry.'

'I don't see why you should be,' Cornelius said. 'It isn't your fault. The only reason I mentioned it is that it does at least mean that you can legitimately be in a legitimate relationship with me.'

'Are you sure you don't mind?'

'No, I don't mind. We don't have to hold hands or anything, do we?'

'No. In fact, you probably won't have to do anything at all. I might not even say anything. It's just nice to know that I can if I want to.'

'As a matter of interest,' Cornelius said, 'how long have we been seeing each other?'

'I'm not sure. I know I told Rose I was getting a lift down with you but I can't remember what else I said. I think it might be safer if we met for the first time on the boat and discovered we had a mutual affinity for . . .' Katrina tried to think of a mutual affinity and could come up with none. 'Never mind,' she said again. 'We can say we just got on together. That'll do. Cornelius, I am very grateful.'

'Not at all,' said Cornelius. 'Ah. We're coming into Cléon d'Andran.'

Katrina's eyes widened. 'This is your village. So we're nearly there?'

'Do you have directions?'

'Yes, yes, I have.' Katrina pulled two photocopied sheets out of her bag. 'I've got one for you as well. It has the phone number in case you need to ring me.' Her mouth felt horribly dry all of a sudden. 'The house is not actually in Pont-de-Barret, it's a couple of kilometres before and it's a little way off the road. We have to look out for a stone farmhouse and a pair of big sky-blue gates.'

'Fine,' said Cornelius. 'We'll be there in no time.'

Katrina stared despairingly out of the window. On one side were fields with dying sunflowers that stood to attention like tired old soldiers. On the other were rows of short, bushy trees with small, pretty leaves. In the distance, Katrina could see banks of mountains undulating gently along the horizon. Rose was right: the place was beautiful.

They drove on in silence until Cornelius turned left towards Pont-de-Barret. 'You know,' he said carefully, 'you might take one look at this man and wonder why you were ever worried. It's been a long time.'

'I might,' Katrina said. She craned her head forward. 'Cornelius, I can see a stone house on the right.' She gulped. 'I can see the blue gates. Cornelius, you will come in with me, won't you?'

'I will.' Cornelius turned into the drive and parked the car outside the gates. 'We're here,' he said. 'Shall we go in?'

The gates opened onto a large, enclosed courtyard. On the left, an azure-coloured pool could be glimpsed through a series of tile-topped stone arches, and on the right was the farmhouse, its shutters the same colour as the gates. A delighted 'Katty?' from the pool area could be heard; Rose ran towards them, resplendent in a flame-coloured swimming costume, split to the navel, that clashed gloriously with her voluminous Titian tresses. It was hard to believe Rose would be fifty next year. It was even harder to believe she was a grieving widow. 'Katty!' she cried again and ran up to her sister, enveloping her in a lavish embrace. 'You are here!'

Katrina was horribly aware of her crumpled linen trousers and her paste-like flesh. 'Gosh,' she said feebly, 'you're so brown!'

'So will you be soon,' Rose assured her. She turned to Cornelius and bestowed a brilliant smile on him. 'And you are the kind man who brought my sister to me! Hello. I'm Rose.'

Cornelius put down Katrina's suitcase and shook Rose's hand. 'I'm Cornelius Hedge. How do you do?'

'Cornelius Hedge?' Rose clapped her hands. 'I'd die for a name like that! That is an amazing name! May I call you Corny?'

'No,' said Cornelius, 'you may not.'

'Well, *Cornelius*!' Rose laughed. 'I'm sure I don't blame you!'

And now, through the archway, like a long-awaited star taking his place on the stage, came Lewis.

His hair was shorter than she remembered. He was not bald. He was not fat. Years of probable decadence had neither coarsened his features nor dulled his eyes. Like Rose, his skin was the colour of burnished bronze. He wore black bathing shorts that revealed a taut and muscular and undeniably desirable body. He came towards them with the heart-stopping smile that Katrina remembered so well. She heard herself saying with admirable coolness, 'Hello, Lewis, how are you?'

She thought his smile faltered momentarily but it was difficult to be sure. She heard Rose say, 'I don't believe it! Do you know my gorgeous man, Katty?'

Katrina had practised what to say. 'We met very briefly a long time ago. I doubt if Lewis remembers. I was doing some legal work for the television company that was responsible for the *Medical Alert* programme and I seem to remember we had lunch together in the canteen.'

'Of course I remember you,' Lewis said warmly, grasping her hands. 'You haven't changed a bit. How lovely to see you, Katrina.'

'How extraordinary that you've met each other,' said Rose. 'I'm so glad, my darling, that you didn't try to snap my sister up. You might have been my brother-in-law and that would never have done!' She put her arms round Lewis's waist and smiled lovingly up at him.

For the first time in her life, Katrina was glad to hear the words 'Aunty Katty!' Until four years ago, Cam and Sam had been happy to call their aunt 'Katrina'. Four years ago, they discovered irony and rechristened her 'Aunty Katty', which Katrina loathed. She had long ago given up trying to stop Rose from calling her Katty but to have the ghastly sobriquet used by Cam and Sam was excessively irritating. Worse still was the 'Aunty' that preceded it. It made her feel middle-aged, which, of course, to her constant surprise, she was.

Cam and Sam had obviously been swimming. They came towards their aunt with their partners trailing behind them. All of them were beautiful. Cam was a nubile blonde with a bow-shaped mouth and extravagantly long eyelashes. Her boyfriend had equally blond hair and his grey floral bathing shorts were a perfect complement to Cam's pink bikini. Sam had short spiky hair enlivened by what looked like expensive highlights. His girlfriend wore a green bikini that strained to contain her generous breasts. All four of them held themselves with the careless confidence of people who are used to being admired.

'Thank God you're here, Aunty Katty.' Sam spoke in the exotic south London cadence peculiar to those who wish to conceal a privileged education. 'Mum and Lewis won't play any card games with us.'

'They're hopeless,' Cam agreed. 'They go to bed straight after supper.'

'Cam, you're such a liar,' Rose said with an indulgent smile. 'Now, children, come and meet Katty's friend. Cornelius, this is my daughter, Cam, her boyfriend, Francis, my son, Sam, and his girlfriend, Sassy.'

Katrina watched Cornelius murmur something unintelligible and knew it was time to rescue him. 'We mustn't keep you,' she told him. 'Your friends will be wondering where you are.'

'Do you have far to go?' Lewis asked.

'Cléon d'Andran,' Cornelius said. 'Katrina's right. I really should go.'

'But you're only down the road!' Rose said. 'You must come to dinner!' She rubbed Lewis's chest with her hand. 'Wouldn't that be fun, darling?'

'Terrific fun,' said Lewis.

Katrina was aware that Cornelius had planted a rigid hand on the small of her back. 'I'm afraid that isn't possible,' she said. 'Cornelius is on a working holiday, really. He's a wine merchant and when he's not with his friends, he'll be out every day visiting vineyards.'

'I'm sure he can get out for at least one evening,' said Rose.

'No,' said Katrina, 'he can't. He doesn't see his friends very often. And besides, their marriage is going through an extremely rocky patch at the moment and they're both looking to Cornelius to help them.' She took Cornelius's spare hand. 'I'll see you to the car,' she said.

As soon as the gates were closed, Katrina released him. 'I'm sorry I made up that stuff about your friends,' she whispered, 'but if I hadn't said something Rose'd have been knocking on their door.'

'I quite understand,' said Cornelius. 'I hope I looked . . . I wasn't sure what to do . . . The hand on your back . . .'

'Very good,' Katrina assured him, 'very convincing. Thank you so much. I am so sorry to have dragged you into all this.'

'That's quite all right.' Cornelius climbed into his car. He shut his door and wound down the window. 'I hope the holiday goes well for you. Phone me if you have any problems. If you need anything . . .' He scribbled down a number and gave it to Katrina.

'Thank you, I'm sure I'll be fine. You've been so kind. Whatever else happens, I've had a lovely holiday so far.'

Cornelius watched Katrina grow smaller and smaller in his driving mirror. She looked so forlorn. He didn't like the idea of leaving her to the four personifications of arrogant Youth, the Lewis man who had clearly forgotten all about her and the Rose woman who did not in fact look anything like Catherine Zeta-Jones. He was aware he had not acquitted himself well in front of them. The only confident and glamorous people he had ever really known were his mother and his wife. He still didn't understand his mother, and as for Lucy . . . The first time he had met her he had been struck by incoherent love. Lucy told him later she had found his silence mysterious and intriguing, and by some miracle she had ended up loving him too. He had never understood why.

He remembered the last time he had seen her. Her beautiful eyes had been full of tears so that they had shone like pools in the sun. He gripped his steering wheel. He was not going to think about his wife while he was in France.

There were several reasons why Katrina accepted a glass of chardonnay at half past six that evening, thus breaking a newly minted resolution to avoid alcohol for the rest of the holiday.

On returning to the bosom of her family after waving goodbye to Cornelius—and feeling oddly bereft in so doing—she had had to endure a litany of teasing questions and innuendoes from Cam *and* Sam *and* Rose about the nature of her relationship with him, none of which were amusing or interesting or based on any semblance of reality.

She had taken an instant liking to Sam's girlfriend, Sassy, who asked Katrina if she always had to put up with such Gestapo-like interrogation about her private life. Francis was a different matter. While he was undeniably easy on the eye, his facial repertoire seemed to be limited to knowing smiles and lustful leers.

Having finally wearied of the subject of Cornelius, Rose had decided to take Katrina on a tour of the house. Katrina was invited to admire the large sitting room, the grand wooden staircase, and Rose's bedroom and en suite bathroom. She found that her own bedroom, a small, monastic cell, was sandwiched between those of the two pairs of young lovers. 'I hope they're not too noisy,' Rose said with a grin. 'We had to put you in here; it's the only single bedroom in the place.'

The final straw was when Rose announced that the four 'Young' were in charge of supper. 'You and I and Lewis will sit by the pool and have a drink and we'll tell you how we met. Isn't this *fun*?'

In answer, Katrina said yes, it certainly was, and in answer to Lewis's query, agreed that she would love a glass of wine. Then she sat back on her sun-lounger and tried to appreciate her surroundings, which were indeed delightful. Beyond the pool and the small stone wall, there was a long field with a stream at the bottom. Beyond that, gentle hills, decorated with elegant poplars and bushy almond trees, formed a gracious counterpoint to the cloudless blue sky.

Concentrating on the cloudless blue sky was infinitely preferable to concentrating on Lewis, who lay stretched out between the two sisters like a gorgeous piece of steak. Rose, for reasons that Katrina found perfectly comprehensible, could not stop touching him, stroking first his chest, then sitting forward and grasping his thigh. Lewis, for reasons that Katrina also found perfectly comprehensible, did not touch Rose. It was a sort of consolation that he did seem to feel a little uncomfortable about lying between a past and present lover.

'Tell me, Katty,' said Rose, 'how do you think I look? Everyone tells me I am positively glowing these days!'

'You look wonderful,' Katrina agreed.

Rose laughed and swung back her hair. 'It's love! I tell you, it's better than any beauty treatment! Do you want to hear how Lewis and I met?'

'I'm sure,' Lewis murmured, 'that Katrina isn't interested.'

With anyone else, Katrina would have whole-heartedly agreed. As it was, she said she would *love* to hear every last detail.

'Well,' said Rose, 'do you remember when I moved up to London?'

Katrina did indeed remember. She and Ollie had spent a whole weekend moving furniture.

'Well,' said Rose again, 'a few days after I finally settled in, I met the couple on the floor below. They made me feel I'd known them for ever. Martha and her husband, Anthony—he's a QC, absolutely brilliant—insisted on throwing a party for me, which was ever so kind because there I was, a poor little widow, who didn't know a soul . . .'

'Rose, you know hordes of people in London,' Katrina said, 'not least your children, who live within a fifteen-minute radius of your flat.'

'I know, but I've never been the sort of mother to foist myself on my young. So I went to the drinks party and I met some wonderful people, and then Lewis walked in and—it was extraordinary. Martha said later she could almost *see* an electric current pass between us. We just looked at each other and he came over and we talked and he made the most outrageously naughty proposition to me. You won't believe what he said.'

'Oh,' said Katrina, 'I think I can imagine exactly what he said.'

'If that's true,' said Rose with a smirk, 'you will be horrified to hear that I agreed straight away! We made our excuses and went back to my flat and . . . I will leave the rest to your imagination! Lewis and I have been inseparable ever since.'

'It all sounds very romantic,' Katrina said briskly. 'So tell me, Lewis, are you still acting?'

'Oh, yes,' Lewis said. 'I was in *The Bill* a few weeks ago and I had a part in *Casualty* in February.'

'Really?' Katrina brushed away a wasp from her trousers. 'What were you? A corpse?'

'I had quite a meaty role. I played a man whose wife leaves because she's in love with a younger man. My character is left alone in the house and he's utterly distraught and he sits down with a bottle of whisky and gets drunk and falls asleep with a lighted cigarette in his hand . . .'

'And he goes up in flames? So you *did* play a corpse!'

'It was actually very moving,' Lewis assured her. 'You had to see it to appreciate it.'

'The funny thing is,' Rose said, 'I *did* see that episode and I remember thinking how wonderful Lewis was!' She laughed. 'I'd better go and check on the kitchen and make sure the children are cooking something that is actually edible.'

'Let me go,' said Katrina. 'I've done nothing since I arrived.'

'Absolutely not!' said Rose. 'Not on your first day here! You can cook tomorrow if you like. Lewis will keep you company, I won't be a minute.' She stood up. 'Now, Katty, I know how you disapprove of public displays of affection so look away while I give Lewis a kiss!'

'I shall go and admire the view,' Katrina said. She walked over to the wall, looked out on the wooded slopes and wondered how she was going to endure the next few days. A buzzard rose from the undergrowth and hovered soundlessly in the sky before plummeting dramatically back to earth. She wished her children were here.

She jumped when a voice beside her said, 'Katrina.' Lewis had joined her by the wall. 'Are you all right? This is an odd situation, isn't it? I want you to know I had no idea that you were Rose's sister.'

Katrina gave a light smile. 'I'm sure you didn't,' she said. 'And even if Rose had told you she had a sister called Katrina Latham who lived in Greenwich, you still wouldn't have known who I was because I'm pretty sure you'd forgotten all about me.'

'Of course I didn't forget you. I recognised you at once. You forget I'm an actor. I didn't know how you wanted to play it. I didn't know if you'd even told Rose about us . . .'

'It's pretty obvious I hadn't,' Katrina said acidly. 'I think she'd have remembered something like that.'

'You know what I mean. I was following your lead. If I'd known you were her sister, I'd have refused Rose's invitation to come out here.'

'That makes two of us,' said Katrina. 'Anyway, I'm sure I'm very happy for you. It must be so nice for you not having to hide your love affairs from your adoring public any longer.'

'Katrina,' said Lewis, 'I was young and irresponsible when I met you. I look back and wonder how I could have behaved with such jaw-dropping callousness. There aren't many things I'm ashamed of and you'd be surprised if you knew how often I have thought about you.'

Katrina gave a little nod of agreement. 'I'd be very surprised.'

'I can offer no defence. I can only tell you I was terrified of responsibility. The idea of getting involved with someone who was a mother was . . . I couldn't cope. My earnest hope is that you can understand how very sorry I am.' He took her hand in his and squeezed it lightly. 'Did I make you *very* unhappy?'

Katrina removed her hand. 'No,' she said. 'You made me very angry.'

'I'm sure I did,' Lewis said. 'I was a scumbag.' He gave a deep sigh. 'I can't bear to have you hate me.'

'I don't hate you. I don't like you very much, that's all.'

'I understand.' Lewis took off his sunglasses and put them on the wall. 'I'm getting in that pool,' he said, 'and I shan't rise to the surface until you tell me you forgive me.' He turned and jumped into the water.

Katrina watched him form a tight ball on the floor of the pool. The man was an idiot. No doubt he expected her to jump in after him and confess her undying love for him. She glanced across at the courtyard. She wished Rose would come out again. She looked back at Lewis. He was still crouched, foetus-like, at the bottom of the pool. Katrina gnawed at her bottom lip. Suppose he *didn't* come up? She glanced again at the courtyard. This was ridiculous. Finally, she couldn't bear it any longer. She slashed the water with her hands. 'Lewis,' she yelled. 'Come up at once!'

His face, alarmingly puce, appeared in a second. 'Tell me,' he gasped, 'tell me you forgive me. I shall go back down unless you forgive me.'

Despite herself, Katrina laughed. 'You're mad,' she said.

Supper was lively, if rather late. Conversational topics ranged easily from the weather, to Rose's plans to set up as a garden consultant, to the latest make-up freebies that Cam had acquired through her job in the beauty department of *Simply Fashion* and, finally, over coffee, to

Lewis's forthcoming rehearsals for a new television serial.

'I think it could be good,' Lewis said. 'I have a great part. I'm an MP, very charming and charismatic. I seem to be an all-round Mr Nice Guy. And then, with each passing episode, we learn more and more terrible things about me and my family . . . incest, adultery, stuff like that.'

'Just like real life, then,' Sam said. 'Do you have the main part?'

'In theory,' Lewis said. 'Unfortunately, I die in the first episode.'

Rose gave a loud yawn. 'I think I'm rather tired! Lewis, darling, shall we go to bed?'

'I do feel a little sleepy,' Lewis said, rising from his chair with a swiftness that suggested otherwise.

No sooner had the happy couple left than their absence was filled by the arrival of two enormous May bugs which, after circling the light, started making kamikaze assaults on the table. Sam eventually caught them and hurled them out into the night.

'Yuck!' said Sassy. 'Horrible things! What shall we do now?'

'Have some more wine,' said Sam, reaching for the bottle. 'Tell me, Aunty Katty, what do you think of Mother's new boyfriend?'

'Very charming,' Katrina said.

'Now, that,' Sam said, 'is the sort of remark you make when you can't think of anything nice to say.'

Francis gave one of his silly laughs. Katrina tried hard not to give him a sour look. Her first impression of him had been right.

'I think he's lovely,' Cam said. 'I think Mother's very lucky.'

Katrina refused Sam's offer of the wine bottle and stood up. 'It's been a long day,' she said. 'I think I'll go up.'

When she got into bed, she reached out for her biography of Mary Shelley. She was *not* going to think of Lewis and Rose. She read two pages before she realised she had not taken in a single word. She turned out the light and started counting sheep. After she'd watched the hundred and twenty-seventh jump over a wall, she gave up. She had no idea how she was going to get through the holiday. All sorts of mean, ugly, petty thoughts were sticking to her like molluscs on a rock. If she was absolutely honest, her extreme irritation with the four specimens of youthful beauty was inspired by jealousy. They were young and gorgeous and confident and she was not. And then there was her sister. It was pathetic, it was nasty, it was grotesque for a middle-aged woman to be jealous of her older, recently widowed sister. Yes, said a hateful voice inside her head, particularly since she's a wealthy widow who has never had to worry about work or bills or mortgages. For twenty-seven years, Rose had been cosseted and adored by a sweet man with oodles of money. And now, having been on her own for hardly any time at all, she was being cosseted and adored by Lewis.

Katrina turned to the left and then to the right. She hated this. Rose hadn't stolen Lewis from her because Lewis had never belonged to her. He would never have wanted to stay with a not wildly attractive solicitor who lived in a terribly untidy terraced house in Greenwich.

Eventually she heard the voices of Sam and Sassy on the stairs. Katrina tried to imagine herself lying on a velvet blanket and falling, falling, falling into it. It was an infallible yoga trick she'd been told about years ago and it had never worked yet but there was always a first time.

She stiffened as she heard the bed springs from Sam's room start a rhythmic squeak. Great. Katrina tried to concentrate on the velvet blanket but the more she tried to concentrate, the louder Sassy's cries were: 'Oh, Sam! Oh, Sam! Oh, Sam!'

Katrina started counting sheep again. Then she heard Cam's voice: 'Oh, Francis, Francis, Francis, don't stop!'

Francis didn't stop. Francis went on and on and on. And on.

Katrina got out of bed and went out to the pool. She swam ten lengths before returning to bed. All was quiet. She fell asleep at last.

Katrina came down the next morning, dressed in her swimming costume and clutching her towel. As she had hoped and expected, the house was silent. She went out to the pool, took a deep breath and slipped into the water. She lowered her head and swam slowly but purposefully up and down the pool, letting the nocturnal cacophony of childlike, nasty thoughts and resentments fall away. I am a mature and intelligent woman who is happy in her own skin, she told herself. I am cool, I am calm, I am content.

Raising her face for a gasp of air, she noticed a pair of feet by the side of the pool. The feet belonged to Lewis. She felt oddly affronted as if she had been caught in an act of intimacy. 'Hello,' she said.

'This must be the first time since I've been here that anyone's been in the pool before eleven,' Lewis said. 'I'm off to Cléon to get the croissants. Why don't you come too?'

'Thanks,' Katrina said. 'I think I'll swim for a little longer.'

'I'll see you later, then.' Lewis put on his sunglasses and walked away. In his cream linen shorts and crisp white T-shirt he looked like someone who'd stepped out of a washing-powder advert.

Katrina could swear she had detected a note of surprise, perhaps even of pique, in his voice when she declined his offer to tag along. *Yah boo sucks, Mr Beautiful Buttocks, that'll show you!* What it was she had shown she was not sure. She was beginning to get tired but she could not get out of the pool until she was certain Lewis had gone. She turned and did yet another length. *I am a mature and intelligent woman who cannot get out of the pool in case my sister's boyfriend is still around.*

She heard the sound of a car engine and gratefully heaved herself out of the water. If she got pneumonia she would jolly well blame Lewis.

A hot shower improved her spirits, as did the sight of her reflection when she put on her new wraparound sundress. She might be immature and impossibly uncool but she still had a decent figure.

Unlike her sister—who had an outstanding one. When Katrina came downstairs, she found Rose making coffee in a diaphanous lilac skirt and a tiny pink vest.

'Katty!' Rose said. 'Did you sleep well?'

'Very,' lied Katrina. 'I've had a lovely swim.'

'Isn't this place just too beautiful? Really, I feel quite blessed!'

'I should think you do,' Katrina said. 'I was a little surprised to get your text on the boat. I thought I was coming out here to console a grieving widow. I suspect I'm quite surplus to requirements.'

'If I didn't know you better, I'd think you were quite put out to find I *wasn't* a grieving widow! You *are* happy for me, aren't you?'

'Yes, of course I am, it's just that—'

'Good, because I am quite *deliriously* in love! I've made the coffee, so we can eat as soon as Lewis comes back. Would you like some orange juice? Get us a couple of glasses from the tray and we'll sit outside. I don't want to miss a moment of the sun.'

They sat at a table in the courtyard, sipping their juice. Rose adopted a concerned, even sorrowful expression that made Katrina instantly apprehensive. 'I'm glad we're on our own at last,' she said. 'I want to talk to you. I know you're hiding something. Lewis and I were talking about you last night.'

Katrina swallowed. 'Were you?'

'We were. I told him I'd hate to be you.'

'Really? Thank you for sharing that with me.'

'Don't take offence, Katty. I meant it in the best possible way. I admire you so much. You've had to work so hard to bring up Ollie and Susie without any help from that awful ex-husband of yours. And you live this nunlike life. I told Lewis it makes me weep sometimes.'

'What did Lewis say?'

'He said it was a terrible waste.'

'How very nice of him.'

'I'd love to see you as happy as I am. Which is why I want to talk about your friend Cornelius. I could see you didn't want to talk about him in front of the Young but you can tell *me*! Is there romance in the air?'

'Would you be happy if there was?' Katrina asked, playing for time.

'I'm sure he's very nice,' Rose said, 'if a little peculiar.'

'I don't see how you can think he's peculiar,' Katrina said hotly. 'You only met him for a few minutes.'

'You have to admit he was a little brusque when I asked if I could call him Corny.'

'How would you like to be called Corny?'

'I wouldn't mind. He didn't have to be so short with me.'

'He's not very good at small talk, that's all. He doesn't like it.'

'I'm sorry,' said Rose, 'but that is so self-indulgent! Have you ever met anyone who *does* admit to liking it? When you meet someone for the first time, you *have* to start with small talk and it helps if you can do so with at least a modicum of common courtesy.'

'I don't think Cornelius meant to be rude. He was simply telling you he didn't like to be called Corny. He has very strong opinions about speaking the truth.'

'Very laudable, I'm sure,' said Rose without any conviction. 'I have to say that he's not my type but if *you* find it fun to be with him then I adore him already. Of course'—Rose paused to kick off her sandals—'he is a little odd-looking. He looks like a scarecrow.'

'He does not!'

'He does, you know he does! I'm not being rude. He looks like a very nice scarecrow. I'll tell you something else. He looks exactly like that ugly pop star you always liked: Jarvis Cocker!'

'Of course!' Katrina clapped her hands. 'I *knew* he reminded me of someone. Apart from his hair, he looks just like him!'

'Well, that explains everything,' Rose said. 'Now I understand why you like Cornelius! Can I take it you're an item?'

Katrina shifted uncomfortably in her seat. 'We might be,' she said. 'We only met for the first time on the boat. My trainee at work is married to his office manager. When she told him I was coming out here, he got Cornelius to offer me a lift. It was very kind of him.'

'So,' said Rose, putting her hands together like an inquisitorial judge, 'you met on the boat. And then what? Was it like me and Lewis? Was it love at first sight? Did you know at once that something was going to happen? Did Cornelius look surprised or shaken the first time he met you?'

'Yes,' said Katrina truthfully. 'He was definitely shaken.'

'So then you got to France and you stayed the night en route. My next question is simple: one bed or two?'

Katrina was about to hotly deny that there had been any bed-hopping but the thought that Rose and Lewis had been solemnly bemoaning her celibacy goaded her into a more ambiguous answer. 'I am not going to discuss my sex life with you. And—'

'You slept together! Oh, Katty, I'm so happy for you! It is so frustrating that you won't let me ask him over. If his friends are arguing all the time, he might be very glad to spend a bit of time with us.'

'No, he won't,' Katrina said firmly.

'Well, it's very annoying . . .' The gate clanged open behind them and Rose turned and held out her arms. 'Lewis, you're back!'

Katrina stood up. 'I'll go and get the coffee.'

After breakfast the three of them went on an expedition to the hypermarket. Katrina, sitting in the back like an awkward child, tried not to notice the way Rose kept stroking Lewis's thigh.

'We need to get some more booze,' said Rose, 'and olive oil and water and tomatoes and something for supper.'

'I'll cook tonight,' Katrina said. 'How about ratatouille and sautéed potatoes?'

'Let's have some chops as well,' said Lewis. 'I can cook them on the barbecue.'

'Don't you agree, Katty,' said Rose, 'that there's something terribly sexy about men doing a barbecue?'

Katrina folded her arms. 'I wouldn't know,' she said. 'I've never had much experience of barbecues.'

For some reason Lewis and Rose found this terribly funny. Katrina sat sourly in the back and consoled herself with the thought that she had only six days left before she went home.

She had to remind herself of that again later in the day. She had emerged after a swim to find Sam and Lewis playing backgammon. It was funny to think that she had introduced this game to both of them.

She had taught Sam when he was only ten and he had proved a quick pupil. Lewis had been less adept and had never managed to beat her. One of Katrina's most besetting sins was her intense competitiveness where card and board games were concerned. She was probably the only mother who had never let her children win at anything. So now she could not see the backgammon game without saying casually to Sam, 'I'll play the winner.'

A few minutes later Sam called her. 'He beat me! Come and tear him apart, Aunty Katty!'

'No problem,' she said. She took Sam's place by the table.

'You haven't a chance of beating Aunty Katty,' Sam said.

'Really?' Lewis picked up the dice. 'Would you like to go first?'

'That's all right, you throw.' Katrina pulled her chair closer to the table. For the first time this holiday she felt on superior ground.

Lewis had improved. In the old days he would move his counters with little thought, interested only in bouncing his competitor. He was different now, ready to sacrifice instant gain in order to pursue eventual success. When she threw a double six and sent two of his counters back to his corner, she couldn't resist glancing up at him with a triumphant curl of her lip.

'Katrina,' he said, 'you have a very nasty streak.'

'First rule of backgammon,' Katrina said crisply, 'never underestimate your competitor's desire to win.'

'I can assure you,' Lewis said, 'I would *never* underestimate you.'

Perhaps it was the way he looked at her that led her to carelessly expose one of her counters. Six goes later, Lewis had won.

Katrina was mortified. 'I can't believe you beat me!'

Lewis gave a modest little shrug. 'I play a lot these days. I'm better than I used to be.'

'That's for sure,' Katrina said. 'And of course you were terribly lucky. That was a one-off. You do realise that, don't you?'

Lewis smiled sweetly. 'Far be it from me to suggest you are a sore loser,' he said. 'I can see it's quite hard for you to accept I can play this game rather well.'

'To hear you two talk,' Rose said, 'you'd think you've played together loads of times!' She laughed and walked towards the house. This time Katrina was more careful, only allowing herself to be momentarily distracted when Cam and Sam and their partners jumped into the pool and splashed her legs.

This time she won. She looked up and beamed at Lewis. 'That's better,' she said.

Lewis smiled at her. 'It's just like old times,' he murmured.

Katrina glanced fleetingly at the occupants of the swimming pool. 'I am trying very hard,' she said in a low, urgent voice, 'to forget about old times.' She shut the backgammon case. 'I think,' she said, 'it's time you went to see Rose.'

It's just like old times.

Katrina did not sleep well that night. She kept replaying that comment of Lewis's. Why had he said that? Did he mean anything at all by it? Given that he had behaved so disgracefully in old times, he had considerable nerve in referring to them in tones of such wistful nostalgia.

There was something else that kept Katrina awake. Her relationship with Cornelius had developed at an alarming rate in the last twenty-four hours, progressing from a gently burgeoning friendship into a full-blown passionate love affair. It was only fair that Katrina should inform Cornelius of this development. She should never have told any lies in the first place: they were constantly threatening to spiral out of control.

She slept late the next morning and came down to find a funereal atmosphere round the breakfast table. This was because the sky was the colour of tarmac and the rain was falling with such ferocity that it looked like a divine hosepipe was aiming itself directly at the house.

After a long and agonised discussion about the possible causes of the transformation (global warming, Katrina's arrival), and the likely duration (one hour, one week, for ever), Rose decided that there was only one possible solution. 'We shall go out to lunch,' she said. 'We shall go to the restaurant near Cléon and have a nice, long, lazy meal.'

So once again Katrina found herself watching her sister stroke her ex-lover's leg as they drove through the rain. Katrina would have almost preferred to go in the other car with Cam and Sam and Sassy and Francis.

Les Voyageurs was a jolly, sprawling place with a main concourse and a few anterooms; it was to one of these that their party was shown. Katrina sat at one end of the table while the others sat on either side of her. Katrina imagined them all playing footsie with their partners and tucked her own feet primly behind her chair legs.

She felt better when the first course arrived—a salmon mousse which was quite delicious—and she enjoyed hearing Sassy talk about her travails as a script editor.

It was during the main course that things went wrong. It began quite innocently with Cam asking after Ollie and Susie.

'They're very well,' Katrina said. 'Ollie's working in an office at the moment. He's hoping to earn enough to go travelling with a friend next January. And then he'll be off to university.'

'Ollie,' Rose told Lewis, 'is three years younger than Susie but he looks older. He's tall, dark and drop-dead gorgeous and he has not got the first idea that he is an utter babe magnet!'

Sam gave a wince. 'There should be a rule,' he said, 'that no one over twenty should describe anyone as a babe magnet.'

'I don't think *anyone* should describe *anyone else* as a babe magnet,' Cam said. She rested her elbows on the table and nodded encouragingly at Katrina. 'So tell me about Susie. She's done her finals. What's my lovely little cousin doing now?'

'She and her drama group are up in Edinburgh. They put on *Hamlet* in the spring and it did so well they decided to take it to the Festival. I was very impressed when I saw it. Susie was a great Ophelia.'

'We must introduce her to Lewis,' Rose said. 'He'll be able to give her all sorts of advice, won't you, darling?'

'I'd be delighted to be of any help I can,' Lewis said. 'Is she going to drama school?'

'She got through the first three auditions for RADA,' Katrina said, 'and then they turned her down. She's determined to try again. Susie is absolutely passionate about acting. The plan is for her to get a job and earn as much money as she can in the meantime.'

'Is she still going out with her stand-up comedian?' Cam asked.

'You'd like him,' Katrina assured her. 'He's very charming. He's just finished university, like Susie, but he's been earning money from his comedy all through his student years.'

'Susie,' Rose told Lewis, 'is a brown-haired beauty.'

'How funny,' Lewis said. 'I imagined her blonde.'

'I can't think why,' Rose said, 'unless you think all pretty girls are blonde.'

'You know very well,' Lewis countered, stroking Rose's hair, 'that I do not think that at all. I suppose I just assumed she'd have the same colour hair as her cousins.'

'Well, she was blonde when she was young,' Rose said. 'She was a funny little girl; she went everywhere with this horrible old moth-eaten polar bear. Do you remember, Katty?'

Katrina did remember and, after a fleeting glance at Lewis, was pretty sure he did too. 'I'm sorry.' She gave an apologetic smile. 'I wasn't listening. I thought for a moment I could hear Cornelius in the other room. There's someone out there who sounds just like him.'

'There's no hope for you, Katty,' Rose said. 'It must be love!'

The diversionary tactic had worked. Lewis's unwise comment had been forgotten and instead, for the next few minutes, Katrina had to endure yet another family inquisition.

Things got worse as the meal progressed. Rose went off to the lavatory and came back, bursting with news. 'Katty, you'll never guess! You *did* hear Cornelius! He's in there with his friends and they all look very happy. They have two children with them who are absolutely adorable.'

'You didn't speak to them, did you?' Katrina asked.

'Well, of course I did. Did you expect me to ignore them? I said we ought to invite them for a meal or a drink. I told Cornelius we were very keen to get to know him better!'

'I think,' Katrina said hastily, 'I'll just go and say hello.'

She went through to the main concourse. She spotted Cornelius at once. He was sitting between two little boys. He had made a hat out of his napkin and was offering it to the smaller child. Their parents—a bearded man with shoulder-length hair and a fine-boned woman with a loose chignon and a big smile—looked like people that Katrina would like to know. She took a deep breath and walked up to them.

Cornelius stood up immediately. 'Katrina! This is James and this is Odile and these two are Luc and Pierre.'

'Hello . . . Hello,' Katrina said quickly. 'I'm so sorry to interrupt your meal . . . Cornelius, it's blatantly obvious that your friends are very happy together and so Rose is determined to have you all over and that would be disastrous because . . .' She paused and turned to James and Odile. 'I'm so sorry, this must all seem very confusing to you . . .' She turned back to Cornelius. 'The thing is, you and I are now very much in love and I'm really sorry but it just kept escalating and they all want to look at you and you would definitely loathe it and so of course you mustn't come over and I am so sorry but short of you getting your friends to stage a fight in the restaurant I can't think what you can do.'

'I see,' said Cornelius, who clearly didn't. 'I see.' He glanced across at James who was, not surprisingly, regarding Katrina with a mixture of curiosity and bewilderment.

'Look,' said Katrina desperately, 'you're going to have to come over to us at some point and refuse Rose's invitation. If I tell Rose you're coming over to say hello, then she won't come over to invite you but . . . Anyway, see what you think . . . I'm so sorry . . . This love affair has got so out of control and I don't really know why . . .' She gave a hopeless shrug, said an anxious goodbye to Cornelius's companions and returned to the table from hell.

'Well?' Rose demanded. 'What did they say?'

Katrina sat down and reached for her wineglass. 'Oh,' she said airily, 'they were very nice. Cornelius introduced me to his friends.'

'Don't you think they looked jolly? Did you invite them over to see us?'

'Yes,' said Katrina, 'but Cornelius didn't think it was a good idea.'

'Well, for goodness' sake, I'm only suggesting a drink—'

'But Cornelius is going to come and say hello to you all before they leave and so,' Katrina said, mentally apologising to Cornelius, 'you can ask him yourself.'

'I shall do,' said Rose, raising her chin.

Katrina could see Cam and Sam exchanging glances and she knew exactly what they were thinking. Poor Aunty Katty was in love with a man who was so far from interested that he couldn't even bother to drive the three kilometres from Cléon to call on her. Katrina contemplated the idea of refilling her glass and getting mindlessly drunk. She drank some of her water and made herself concentrate on the present conversation, which had switched from the subject of Cornelius to plans for the next day. Sam was saying that he and Cam and Sassy and Francis were planning to drive down to the famous gorges of the Ardèche and go white-water rafting. 'Of course we won't go if the weather's like this, but as long as it's not raining—' Sam stopped and Katrina, following his gaze, saw that a rather nervous Cornelius and a considerably more relaxed James had come to their table.

Rose turned and beamed at them both. 'How lovely of you to come over!' she said. 'You must be Cornelius's friend from Cléon.'

'James Armitage,' said James, taking Rose's outstretched hand.

Rose batted her eyelashes at him. 'I was saying to Katrina that I would love you all to come over and see us.'

Katrina, inwardly cringing, stared intensely at Cornelius, trying desperately to convey her remorse in her eyes. Cornelius looked every bit as unhappy as she was. He said feebly, 'I don't know what to say.'

'I'm afraid,' James said firmly, 'that you've caught us at a bad time.

I'm sure you'll understand if I don't go into details. Cornelius is being a tower of strength but I know you'll appreciate why we're turning your kind invitation down.' He smiled directly at Katrina. 'I'm sure we'll be seeing *you* again . . . hopefully in happier circumstances.'

The man was brilliant! Katrina stood up and quite spontaneously kissed him on the cheek. 'Thank you,' she said with heartfelt gratitude. 'Thank you so much!'

'Well,' said Cornelius, 'we'd better get back.' He looked down at his shoes for a moment and then sidestepped James to give Katrina a peck on the cheek. 'I'll see you soon,' he said. He cleared his throat. 'You look very nice in that . . . That dress is very . . . I'll see you soon.'

The next day the weather was still grey but at least it wasn't raining. Katrina came down at nine and was impressed by the fact that the white-water rafters were already up. She waved them off while wondering how she could avoid playing gooseberry for the day ahead. Before they had gone to bed last night, Rose had suggested that the three of them go to Montélimar. Apparently, there was a wonderfully romantic restaurant there that Katty would just adore.

The thought of being in a romantic restaurant with Lewis and Rose made Katrina's skin crawl. What she needed was a guardian angel or, even better, a white knight, to come along and whisk her away on his white charger.

And then the telephone rang.

CHAPTER THREE

A Temporary Liberation

CORNELIUS REGARDED James and Odile as two of his closest friends and thought he knew them well, but that afternoon they displayed reservoirs of brilliance he had never seen before. He had told them nothing about Katrina other than the fact that she had proved to be far less irritating than he had expected. She had burst in upon them at the restaurant, her darting eyes apparently contained only by the dark shadows that sat beneath them. In their place, he would have assumed she was, at the very least, demented.

When she left them with the same suddenness with which she had arrived, Odile had immediately responded with the practicality that never failed to impress him. 'Cornelius,' she had said, 'your friend is in trouble. We must help. I do not understand. Please explain.'

So Cornelius had explained. He told them that Katrina had only found out on the ferry that the love of her life was now the love of her sister. He told them that she was anxious to demonstrate that she was free of past affections by inventing an attraction for Cornelius. As far as he could gather, he said carefully, Katrina had somehow been compelled to embroider the initial fabrication and pretend that she and Cornelius were very much in love. He told them that in order to save him any embarrassment arising from the deception, she had manufactured a scenario whereby his warring friends were in dire emotional turmoil thus excusing him from having to accept any awkward invitations. Unfortunately, since her sister had seen that there was no evidence of any such turmoil, she was intent on inviting them all over. He told them that it was all very confusing but . . .

'I understand perfectly,' Odile said. 'You and James must go over to their table now. Cornelius, you must try to look passionate. James, you must try to look unhappy. So, go!'

And they had gone. And James had been superb. Later, Cornelius was the first to admit that *he* had been hopeless. He had seen Katrina sitting at the end of the table like an unwanted bottle of cheap wine, and he had been so angry he had found it difficult to even look at the three couples in front of her. But James had been magnificent. He had said everything that needed to be said and he had nudged Cornelius with a whispered, 'Passion!' Cornelius had no idea how he was supposed to show this but he had at least sort of kissed Katrina and had also managed to pat her arm. His final memory of that lunch would be of Katrina, sitting there, bestowing on him a smile of true sweetness, while her awful sister wittered on about nothing.

When he woke the next morning, he found that Katrina was lodged in his brain like an M25 traffic jam, blotting out all other matters of interest. It was clear she was having a ghastly time. It was during his second cup of coffee over breakfast that he said abruptly, 'I think I might ring Katrina, suggest I take her out for the day. She'll probably say no but it would be nice to ask. Will that be all right with you?'

James shook his head gravely. 'I don't know,' he said. 'I thought we were supposed to need you here in order to prevent domestic discord breaking out.'

'*Que tu es bête*,' Odile said calmly. 'Go to the telephone, Cornelius. Talk to Katrina.'

Which was fine except that Cornelius had no idea what he was going to talk *about*. He did not want her to think his call was inspired by compassion. Cornelius had never liked being an object of pity and he was fairly sure that Katrina would feel the same. There was also the possibility that he had misinterpreted her situation. He realised he had almost talked himself out of ringing, and when he did press the numbers he decided he would put the phone down if no one answered quickly.

He heard Katrina's voice, slightly breathless and with an appalling accent, enunciate, '*Bonjour?*'

He got as far as saying hello when she interrupted him with an enthusiastic, 'Oh, Cornelius, how lovely to hear you! How *are* you?'

'I'm very well. I wondered if . . . I thought I'd do some sightseeing today and I wondered if you'd care to accompany me?'

'Oh, I would! Cornelius, you are so kind, I would love to come out with you, I would really, *really* love to. Thank you.'

He was both relieved and disconcerted to be the focus of such untrammelled enthusiasm. 'Shall I pick you up in half an hour?'

'I'll be ready and waiting!'

She was indeed waiting for him by the side of the road, clasping her bag in front of her, like a schoolgirl at the bus-stop with her satchel.

'Cornelius, this is so kind of you,' Katrina breathed, putting her bag down by her feet and fastening her seat belt. 'All the Young have gone off to the Ardèche and you have saved me from having to accompany Rose and Lewis to a restaurant in Montélimar that Rose says is incredibly romantic. So thank you. I feel like I've been liberated. Are you sure your friends don't mind losing you?'

'I felt almost aggrieved,' Cornelius said. 'They didn't mind at all.'

'I did like them! And the way James referred to his disastrous marriage was masterful. Will you tell him how grateful I was?'

'I will. I must say that I had no idea he was such a consummate liar. He and Odile thought you were very nice, by the way.'

'I'm not nice,' Katrina said solemnly. 'I'm not nice at all. Ever since I came here, my head has been full of the most horrible thoughts. I am jealous and bitter and twisted and nasty. And the worst of it is that I know I should be so happy for Rose. She lost her husband of twenty-seven years and I should be so pleased that she's found someone else, and I'm not pleased at all. I'm cross that she didn't tell me before, and I can't stand Cam's boyfriend, and . . .' Katrina sighed deeply. 'If I'm absolutely honest, the person I'm really cross with is *me*. I knew the holiday would be a disaster as soon as Rose mentioned it. I should never have agreed to come.'

'I don't see why,' Cornelius said. 'No one could have predicted all this.'

'That's just it! *I* could have. If it hadn't been Lewis it would have been something else. There's *always* something else where Rose is concerned. Like once, she rang and said she was worried about me, I sounded so tired. She said she and her family were going to Florence at half-term and would I like to bring Ollie and Susie down for a restful break in the country? She and Roger had a fabulous house in a village near Salisbury and I thought: why not? So off we go, and find Cam there. She hadn't wanted to go to Florence, apparently. Which was fine except that Cam was just sixteen and made Lolita look like Little Bo Peep. Then I find a note from Rose asking me to make fifty fairy cakes that evening, for the church festival bring and buy. Then, the next evening, Cam goes out to a party and ends up in casualty after drinking too much cider. And then the day after that, some builders come to install Rose's new kitchen. Rose told me later she'd booked the holiday to Florence because she knew she wouldn't be able to abide the mess. I think it was the worst half-term I've ever had.' She put her palms together and shook her head. 'Actually, I think it's better if we don't talk about Rose. You have no idea how wonderful it is to get away. Where are we going?'

'Quite a long way,' said Cornelius. 'I thought I'd take you up to the Vercors: limestone mountains thirty miles long and twenty miles wide with a huge plateau in the middle. French Resistance camps hid out there during the war. We're driving to a little village called Vassieux. There's rather a sad story attached to it.'

'Tell me,' said Katrina.

So Cornelius did. 'A week after D-Day,' he said, 'all the members of the underground for miles around were summoned by the Allies and General de Gaulle to join the resident Resistance groups on the plateau. The plan was that they would all rise up against the enemy. Nearly three thousand men turned up. The Allies promised four thousand paratroops, proper weapons and supplies. The idea was that the Allied troops would land on the south coast of France and the Resistance groups in the Vercors would attack the Germans from the rear.'

'And something went wrong?'

'Something went very wrong. The Allies never did land on the south coast and the promised troops and supplies never arrived. Once the Germans realised there was to be no invasion, they invaded the Vercors. Twenty thousand German soldiers devastated the area. One of the villages they destroyed was Vassieux.'

Katrina grimaced. 'How terrible. Was everyone killed?'

'Some of the Resistance people escaped but not many. One man who got out sent a signal to London. It's a masterpiece of understatement: "Arrested. Tortured. Shot. In good health." People were very brave.'

'It's funny,' Katrina said. 'Here we are driving through all these little towns with people like us who are worrying about mortgages and marriages and what to eat for supper. And sixty-odd years ago, their grandparents were facing death and betrayal on a daily basis.'

'Nothing's changed,' said Cornelius. 'Do you remember all the journalists and historians telling us that the end of the Cold War would bring an end to all conflict? And then think of Rwanda and the Balkans and Palestine and . . .' He shrugged. 'People haven't stopped doing unspeakable things to each other. In that context, I don't think your irritation with your sister can be described as evil and twisted.'

'On the contrary,' Katrina said, 'everyone knows that in a war people will do things they'd never dream of doing in peacetime. I *am* living in peacetime so I have no excuse.'

Cornelius glanced fleetingly at Katrina. 'I'm of the opinion,' he said, 'that in time of war, you would be one of the nice people.'

They had lunch at a roadside café and ate baguette sandwiches under the watchful eye of an enormous sheepdog. For the first time since she had come to France, Katrina felt in a holiday mood: relaxed, stimulated by her surroundings, conscious that she was enjoying herself and pretty certain that she was going to go on enjoying herself. 'I wish Ollie was here,' she said. 'He's fascinated by the Second World War. If he were with us now, he'd be bombarding you with questions about the Resistance.'

'He sounds impressive,' Cornelius said.

'The thing about Ollie is . . . Well, you know how some people'—Katrina hesitated but restrained herself from naming any of the occupants of her holiday residence—'some young people can make one feel inherently absurd simply because one has wrinkles? Well, Ollie isn't like that. Neither is Susie, actually. They are both enthusiasts. I think enthusiasm is very attractive, don't you?'

Cornelius was slow to answer and Katrina thought perhaps he hadn't heard her. She was about to repeat herself when he said with great finality, 'It is the very best of qualities.'

Katrina looked at him uncertainly. He looked so *desolate*. She sipped her drink and waited for him to speak again.

He glanced at her suddenly. 'I'm sorry,' he said. 'I was thinking of an Australian girlfriend I once had. She was very enthusiastic.'

Cornelius might not like telling lies but Katrina had a strong suspicion that he had just told one. She was quite certain that it was not some Australian girlfriend who had caused him to look so unhappy. Nevertheless, she gave an encouraging smile. 'Were you fond of her?'

'I suppose I must have been, until one day I realised she laughed like an elephant.'

'You can't possibly know how elephants laugh,' Katrina said. 'I don't think elephants *can* laugh.'

Cornelius rubbed his chin thoughtfully. 'You may be right,' he said. 'But if they *could*, they would sound like my Australian girlfriend.'

The road up the mountain was steep and it curved like a helter-skelter. They pulled into a lay-by near the top and got out and looked down at the tiny little cars at the bottom. 'I feel I'm on the top of the world,' Katrina said. She looked up at Cornelius. 'I am having such a good time today. Thank you for bringing me here.'

'It's a pleasure,' he said. He felt a twinge of disquiet and said abruptly, 'Shall we go on?'

They arrived at Vassieux soon after. Inside the museum there were tattered uniforms, old tobacco tins, flags and last letters from young men to their mothers and their girlfriends. The last time Cornelius had been here he had found the place fascinating. This time he found it less easy to look at the photos of young boys and the letters that tried so hard to conceal their fear and their homesickness.

They walked back to the car. Katrina said, 'Thank you for taking me to that place. It certainly puts into perspective all my silly preoccupations with Lewis and Rose.'

'We all have silly preoccupations,' said Cornelius, 'and most of them aren't silly, they're just normal. It's war that's not normal.'

'I bet you don't have any silly preoccupations.'

Cornelius gave a short laugh. 'In the last few days,' he said, 'I have wasted huge amounts of time wondering whether to send my wife a postcard or not. I spent a whole day worrying that I had a terminal illness after a game with Luc in which I dropped the ball too often. I only stopped worrying after I finally beat him. And then after James told me that I was the least convincing lover he'd ever seen, I started worrying about that.'

'That doesn't count. You were simply contaminated by my own preoccupations; and anyway, I thought you were a jolly good lover.'

'Thank you,' Cornelius said. 'I shall be sure to tell James what you said. I was wondering . . . Do you have to go straight home? Why don't you come back and say hello properly to James and Odile?'

'After yesterday's pantomime? I'm far too embarrassed.'

'I know they'd like to see you.'

'Well . . .' Katrina hesitated. 'I would like to apologise to them. Perhaps we could just stop off for a few minutes.'

It was soon clear that there was to be no quick getaway. Cornelius had bought the boys a croquet set and James had just finished setting it up when they arrived. Cornelius and Katrina were quickly press-ganged into playing. Cornelius discovered that Katrina was every bit as competitive as Luc, and Luc's delight over his final narrow victory was all the sweeter for Katrina's furious attempts to beat him. Katrina would almost certainly have taken up Luc's challenge to another game had not Odile appeared with bread and juice for the children. She told James and Cornelius to fetch more suitable refreshment for the adults. When they returned to the garden they found the women in intense conversation about the difficulties of growing hibiscus bushes in Britain. It was only when James offered Katrina a second glass of wine that she looked guiltily at her watch and said she should get back to Rose.

By mutual agreement, Cornelius dropped Katrina by the side of the road. When Katrina tried to thank him again, he felt another sharp twinge of discomfort. 'Katrina,' he said, 'please stop being so grateful. I did not take you out as an act of charity. I enjoy your company. I have enjoyed today and if you wish to come out again, you only have to ring.' He gave her a mock salute. 'C. C. Hedge at your service.'

'Thank you,' Katrina said. 'What does the second C stand for?'

'I'd rather not talk about it,' said Cornelius. 'My second name is even worse than my first.'

'Actually,' Katrina smiled, 'Cornelius is definitely growing on me.' She hoisted her bag onto her shoulder. 'It has been a fabulous day. You are a good man and I promise I won't take up your kind offer to ring you. You've done more than enough. I'll see you on Saturday with my suitcase packed and I'll be ready as early as you like.' She turned and walked quickly towards the blue gates.

In the kitchen, Rose was slicing tomatoes and Lewis was chopping mushrooms. Rose looked up and raised her eyebrows. 'So the wanderer returns. I suppose we should be honoured that you're good enough to come back and eat the meal we are cooking for you.'

Katrina put her bag on the table and glanced a little apprehensively at her sister. 'Rose,' Katrina said, 'are you angry with me? I left a note.'

'Why should I be angry? I invite you for a holiday and you waltz off with your new boyfriend for a whole day. Why should I be angry?'

'I can't imagine,' Katrina said crisply. 'Cornelius rang and invited me to go out sightseeing with him. Given the choice between playing gooseberry with you two and going out on an expedition with Cornelius, it seemed far more sensible to go for the latter. I did not think my company would be required in a romantic restaurant in Montélimar. I'm sorry you're upset but I assumed you'd be pleased.'

'Well, I think I know better than you what I want. And I think it's rude of Cornelius not to come in and say hello. Anyone would think he didn't want to talk to us. Am I really so disagreeable?'

'That is the sort of question,' Lewis said, 'that only a beautiful woman would dare to ask. There's no point in putting the risotto together until the Young get back. Why don't we open a bottle of wine?'

'All right,' said Rose. 'I'll go and put a cardigan on.' She went across to Katrina and gave her a light hug. 'I forgive you, darling. It's impossible to be cross when Lewis says such nice things! I won't be a moment.'

Katrina felt very strongly that she had nothing to be forgiven *for*. She watched mutinously as her sister disappeared through the sitting room, and then went over to the cupboard to get some glasses.

Lewis took a bottle of rosé from the fridge. 'Katrina,' he murmured, 'it wasn't you Rose was cross with. Sam had told her they'd be back by five and she was worried. Cam rang just before you got in to say they'd be here soon and Rose was cross they hadn't rung earlier.'

'There was no need for her to take it out on me.'

'You're right. Have a glass of wine. What shall we drink to?' Lewis mused. 'Friendships renewed?'

Katrina gave him a withering look. 'I shall drink to you and Rose. I can't think of any two people who deserve each other more.'

Lewis grinned and took a sip. 'Where did you go today?'

'We went to the Vercors mountains. We had a great time.'

'I'm glad to hear it.' Lewis pulled out a chair from the table and sat down. 'Your friend Cornelius seems a nice man. You seem to have got to know him remarkably quickly.'

'Yes,' Katrina said, 'I suppose I have.'

'I almost feel jealous.'

Katrina looked at him sharply. 'That's a very stupid thing to say.'

'It was,' Lewis agreed. 'Let's forget I ever said it.'

'That won't be difficult,' Katrina said. 'I make a practice of discounting everything you say.'

'Darlings!' Rose wafted in. 'I'm quite good-humoured again! I need a big glass of wine and then I want to hear about your day, Katty.'

That night Katrina lay in bed, her mind a kaleidoscope of thoughts and pictures. She had promised herself she was not going to think about Lewis and instead she thought back to her conversation with Odile that afternoon. 'Cornelius is happy in your company,' Odile had said. 'He has been sad for so long.'

Katrina felt warmed by Odile's observation and hoped it was true. It was obvious that Cornelius still loved his wife. What was her name? Lucy Lambert? Katrina couldn't imagine why any woman would want to leave Cornelius. She wished she knew him well enough to tell him that.

Cornelius arrived promptly at nine on Saturday morning. Katrina was opening the blue gates before he had even got out of the car. 'Hi!' she said brightly. 'My suitcase is in the kitchen!' It was clear from her constricted smile and resolute cheerfulness that something was wrong.

He followed her into the house.

'Good morning, Cornelius,' Rose said. 'Would you like some coffee?'

It was at that moment that Cornelius realised Rose was wearing a flimsy nightdress that left *absolutely* nothing to the imagination. He swallowed and glanced at Katrina, who responded immediately.

'We must go,' she said. She went over to kiss her sister. 'Goodbye, Rose, thank you for everything. This is a beautiful place.'

'I suppose,' Rose said, 'I should be grateful you've deigned to visit us at all. Heaven knows when we'll see you again.'

'Look,' Katrina said, 'I never meant to upset you. If it really means so much to you, then of course I'll come to your party.'

'And you'll bring Susie and Ollie?'

Katrina looked as if she were trying to digest a particularly hard piece of gristle. 'I'll bring Susie and Ollie.'

'Thank you, Katty!' Rose stood up to embrace her sister.

'We really *must* go,' Katrina said. 'Goodbye, Lewis.'

'Katrina,' Lewis said, 'am I allowed a kiss?'

Cornelius hoped she'd say no but she offered her cheek for the briefest of moments before saying gaily, 'Say goodbye to the Young for me. Please don't come out.'

Lewis, however, insisted on taking Katrina's case to the car. Cornelius and Katrina got in and Lewis went over to Katrina's window which Katrina, after a moment's hesitation, opened. Lewis bared his teeth at Cornelius. 'Drive safely,' he said. 'You have someone very important in the car with you.'

Cornelius, having turned on the ignition, gave in to an irresistible urge to put his foot on the accelerator. He didn't say anything to Katrina until he had turned onto the main road, and then murmured a muted apology for the suddenness of their departure. 'We have a long journey,' he said stiffly. 'I thought we'd better get on.'

'Please,' Katrina said, 'don't apologise! I am *so* glad to get away!' Her face was tense and her arms were folded tightly in front of her.

Cornelius grunted sympathetically but said nothing. He found it difficult to understand why someone as intelligent as Katrina should be in love with someone so supremely pleased with himself.

'Rose and I had a stupid row last night,' Katrina said. 'She's having a party in a few weeks. She wants to *introduce* Lewis to everyone. I said the children and I couldn't come but I didn't have any time to think of a good excuse so I said we were having Amy and her husband to dinner—Amy is one of my partners—and of course Rose got mad and said I see Amy at work every day and why couldn't I change the date and then I said . . . Well, it doesn't matter what I said because now I've agreed to go and the whole thing is a disaster.' She shook her head and then smiled suddenly. 'You've been invited too, by the way.'

'Oh,' said Cornelius. 'Do you want me to . . . ?'

'No, no, I wouldn't dream of making you endure one of Rose's parties. The whole thing is stupid. Let's not talk about it any more. It's so nice to be going home. I can't wait to see Ollie. And Susie will be back next week.'

'How old is she?' Cornelius asked.

'She's twenty-one. She's just graduated from York University. At the moment she's in Edinburgh with her boyfriend. They're both perform-ing in the festival.'

'Is the boyfriend nice?'

'Liam? He's lovely. Great fun and never stops talking. I wouldn't care if he wasn't great fun. I'm just glad Susie has a boyfriend.'

'Why?' Cornelius asked sympathetically. 'Is she ugly?'

'Of course she's not ugly! Actually, she's very pretty. She hasn't had a boyfriend in years, that's all. She was very badly hurt when she was six-teen. She met a boy called Ash. He was three years older than her, a friend of Cam and Sam. She met him at one of their birthday parties. She thought he was wonderful and then at a party they kissed and it was all incredibly romantic, and then some friends came up and they got separated and when she finally found him again, he was locked in a passionate embrace with someone else! What do you think of that?'

'Well,' Cornelius said, 'speaking as the devil's advocate, they weren't involved in a relationship at the time and indiscriminate kissing does seem to be something that teenagers do these days.'

'Yes, but they'd been flirting for months. For Susie, that kiss was the culmination of a courtship. And after that he totally *blanked* her. Actually, I never trusted him. He was one of those good-looking boys who think they can get anyone. What do girls see in boys like that?'

A vision of Lewis flashed before Cornelius. 'I can't imagine.'

'Anyway, as far as Susie was concerned, that was the end of romance. I seriously thought she'd spend the rest of her life stuck in some sterile time warp, mourning the end of her teenage love affair. The first time she brought Liam home I felt like hugging him.'

They had arrived at the motorway. Katrina didn't speak again until Cornelius had successfully negotiated his way into the fast lane and past two enormous lorries. 'I've noticed something about us,' she said sternly. 'Whenever we're together, I always end up talking about me. We never talk about you. You know about my pathetic little affair with Lewis, you know about my family. All I know about you is that you're a wine merchant and you are divorcing your wife.'

'*She* is divorcing *me*,' Cornelius corrected.

'I can't think why,' Katrina said loyally. 'Are you so difficult?'

'I suppose I must be.' Cornelius hoped Katrina would change the subject but she remained with her head cocked to one side, her eyes expectant and sympathetic. 'When we married,' he said, 'she used to call me her strong, silent husband. By the time she left me, I think she just thought I was silent.'

A fly appeared from nowhere. Cornelius opened his window and the insect flew out towards the sky. Cornelius closed the window and glanced at Katrina. He suspected she hadn't finished with the subject of his marriage. 'Tell me,' he said, 'why are you so interested in Mary Shelley?'

'It started at school. We had to study Shelley's poetry and I didn't like it very much so of course I felt sorry for his wife and then I discovered she'd had to cope with so much right from the start. Her mother died soon after giving birth to her, and then there were the children.'

'What children?'

'Mary's children. Shelley and his friends were always complaining about Mary's bad moods. It occurred to none of them that the deaths of three of her four children might have had something to do with the fact that she wasn't always a little sunbeam. What that poor woman had to go through . . .'

They stopped at Dijon for lunch. By then, Cornelius had learnt so much about Mary Shelley that he felt he could confidently deliver a lecture on her. They sat by the canal, eating baguettes. 'What I don't understand,' said Cornelius, 'is why Mary is a heroine for you? I mean, I know she wrote *Frankenstein* and was married to a romantic poet who treated her badly but—'

'It's what happened *after* the marriage that's interesting,' Katrina said. 'Shelley kept falling in love with stupid women and yet she never stopped loving him. I think that's rather noble. She was only twenty-five when Shelley died yet she never married again.'

'Of course,' Cornelius mused. '*There's* the connection.'

'Where? What are you talking about?'

This happened to Cornelius sometimes, usually when he was particularly interested in something. He would come to a conclusion and then surprise himself, and often his companions, by articulating it. The last time he had done this was at a dinner party given by one of Lucy's acting friends. Cornelius had become increasingly intrigued by his host's hair, which sprang from his forehead with quite extraordinary exuberance. Cornelius had been wondering if he used curlers to achieve such an effect. Finally, understanding dawned: the man was wearing a toupee! He did not even realise he had voiced this discovery until he saw everyone looking at him. Lucy had been furious and had lectured him all the way home.

'What is?' Katrina asked. 'What is the connection?'

'Nothing,' Cornelius said, sensing danger. 'I was talking randomly.'

'No wonder you hate lying,' Katrina said. 'You're rotten at it. Now tell me what you meant.'

Cornelius fixed his bottle of water with an intense stare. 'Well,' he said, 'Mary went on loving Shelley for the rest of her life even though he'd treated her badly and, in the same way, Lewis still has the power to seriously upset you even though he treated you badly. Just like Shelley.'

'That,' Katrina said hotly, 'is entirely different.'

She didn't, he noticed, say *why* it was different. 'I'm sorry,' he said. 'I was thinking aloud. My wife always says I need to learn about tact.'

Now she smiled. 'That's all right,' she said. 'Let's change the subject. Tell me about that book you were reading on the boat.'

'The Noam Chomsky?' Cornelius brightened. He felt as if she had pulled him out of quicksand. 'I'll tell you about it in the car. Are you ready to go?'

The rest of the journey passed surprisingly quickly. Cornelius enjoyed talking to Katrina: conversations with her rarely seemed to reach a rational conclusion; they diverged into unexpected areas, picking up unusual nuggets of information along the way. Harmonious relations were only endangered one more time when they were halfway across the Channel and Katrina discovered that Cornelius intended to drive her back to her house. 'I live in Clapham,' he said. 'You're hardly any distance from me. If you think I'm going to abandon you in the middle of the night, you're wrong.' Katrina protested vigorously and only stopped when Cornelius told her that if she persisted in being so tedious he would start talking about Noam Chomsky again.

They arrived outside her house at a little before midnight. Cornelius carried her case to the door and refused her offer of coffee.

'You will at least come to Sunday lunch with us soon?' she asked. 'I'll email you next week. Will you come?'

'Thank you,' Cornelius said. 'I shall enjoy that.'

'Good,' Katrina said. 'And thank you so much. The best bits of my holiday . . . they were all with you. You've been so kind.'

'Not at all.' Cornelius cleared his throat. 'I was thinking . . . Are you sure you wouldn't like me to come to Rose's party with you?'

'Of course not.' Katrina laughed. 'It was bad enough making you go through that silly pretence in France. I have no intention of prolonging your agony. I shall wait a few weeks and then inform Rose that you have definitely dumped me.' She reached up to kiss him on the cheek, said, 'See you soon,' and disappeared into the house.

Cornelius returned to the car. He felt oddly bereft, which was ridiculous. Why should he be upset by the news that he was about to terminate a non-existent relationship? He turned the ignition and drove off, furiously castigating himself. If he'd been Lewis, he'd have told her that meeting her was the best thing that had happened to him in a very long time. If he'd been Lewis, he'd have told her that he would very much enjoy taking her to Rose's party. Not for the first time in his life, Cornelius wished he wasn't stuck with being Cornelius.

CHAPTER FOUR

Respite

HOLIDAYS, KATRINA DECIDED, were brilliant. Was there any mechanism better suited to developing an appreciation of one's domestic environment? She had been away for only a week and yet here she was, sitting in front of her favourite pub, waiting for her son to bring out the drinks and feeling that of all the places in the world, Greenwich was the very best in which to live. The sun was shining, the sky was blue and the geraniums in the window box across the road provided a vibrant splash of crimson colour.

Ollie emerged from the bar and set down the drinks and put the nuts in the middle of the table. 'I've ordered food,' he said. 'Tim says he'll bring it out when it's ready.'

Ollie, of course, was the icing on the cake. There could be *nothing* better than to sit in the sunshine and see his cheerful face, a face that was utterly foreign to smirking or leering or thinking he was beautiful. Unlike Francis, who obviously thought he was God's gift to everyone, Ollie had never been satisfied with his appearance. He thought he had a nose like an aardvark. He didn't. It could almost be described as Roman; almost, since God had taken His eye off the ball for a moment, leaving a slight indentation in the middle. In recompense, he had been supplied with dark, arching eyebrows, eyes set wide apart, great cheekbones and a determined chin. The last two years had seen a transformation. He had lost all his puppy fat, his shoulders had broadened and he had grown at least a foot. Katrina thought he was beautiful.

He sat down opposite her, took a sip of his beer and gave a contented sigh. Ollie was as transparent as a mountain stream. His moods and thoughts rippled across his features like a gentle breeze. It was arguable, of course, that Katrina's view of him was not wholly impartial; nevertheless, she felt particularly blessed that her son just happened to be the nicest young man she had ever met.

'I'm sorry I wasn't in when you got back,' he said. 'I was playing poker with George and Dan. I thought you weren't getting home until the early hours.'

'I was lucky. The ferry came in on time and Cornelius insisted on giving me a lift all the way home.'

'The man who drove you down? What was he like?'

'Very nice. At first I thought he was going to be rather scary. He's quite imposing to look at, he's very tall and very thin with lots of hair. But he couldn't have been kinder. I'm going to invite him to Sunday lunch soon and then you'll meet him.'

'And how was Rose? Is she missing Roger a lot?'

Katrina took a sip of her wine. 'No,' she said, 'I don't think she is. She has a boyfriend. He was there.'

Ollie's eyes widened. 'She has a *boyfriend*? That is so *weird*! Roger was so cool. Do you like the new man? Is he like Roger?'

Katrina reached in her bag for her sunglasses. 'No. He's not like Roger at all. He's urbane, confident, dresses well. He's an actor, extremely good-looking. He and Rose seem to be very happy.' She looked at her son expectantly. 'Now, tell me about you. How's the job?'

'It's mind-numbing. It's a terrible job.'

'But?'

'But what?'

Katrina laughed. 'For someone who went to bed at three and got up only an hour ago, you are extraordinarily wide awake and . . . and bouncy. Something has happened!'

Ollie folded his arms and looked earnestly at Katrina. 'There's this girl,' he said. 'I don't want to talk about her, really. I mean, I don't think anything's going to happen, you see, so . . .'

'That's fine,' said Katrina. 'I quite understand.'

'She's called Sophie. She's a friend of Hannah who was in that school play with me—about dead people, remember? She's very small but she has a fantastic figure and she has these blue eyes that look straight at you when she talks and she's really into the environment and she's a supporter of the Green Party but she also does a brilliant karaoke of KT Tunstall. She's pretty amazing, actually . . .'

'But you don't want to talk about her.'

Ollie gave a sheepish grin. 'I know. I can't help it. I really like her but I don't want to mess it up so I'm going to play it really cool and be just friendly at first—you know, talk about ice caps and things . . .'

'Very sensible.' Katrina stopped to smile at the fresh-faced young man who was approaching their table with two plates of chicken and chips. No question, holidays were brilliant.

After lunch, Ollie went off to see friends in the park. Katrina went home with the laudable intention of unpacking her suitcase and cleaning the kitchen floor, which had developed an unpleasantly sticky sheen under Ollie's supervision. But the weather was beautiful and she had another week before she had to go back to work. The unpacking and the floor could wait.

She took a deck chair and the phone and went out into the small garden at the back of the house. She sat down, and for a few moments closed her eyes, enjoying the sensation of the sun on her face and the sweet sound of a chatty bird in the garden next door. Then, with a sigh of pleasure, she settled down to ring her daughter.

'Mum! It's *you*! *Hello*! How *are* you?'

Katrina could always tell in the first two seconds how her daughter was. A tired, downward-inflecting, 'Hi, Mum, how are *you*?' presaged clouds and rainfall. There was no middle way with Susie: she was either happy or she was sad, and today she was very, very happy.

'I'm very well,' Katrina said. 'It's good to be home again.'

'Did you have a good time in France? What is Rose's house like? Is Rose still missing Roger terribly? Tell me everything!'

'The house was lovely; huge swimming pool, gorgeous courtyard. Rose was fine. She has a boyfriend. He was there with us.'

There was a brief hiatus while Susie processed the information. 'I thought you said the only reason you were going out there was to stop Rose from feeling lonely?'

'That's what I thought. It turned out I wasn't necessary at all.'

'I'm sorry, Mum! You didn't want to go out there in the first place. I can't believe she has a new man already. What's he like?'

'He's an actor,' Katrina said. 'He's called Lewis Maltraver. He used to be a well-known soap-opera star. I met him once when I was arranging a purchase for a TV company. He's . . . he's charming.'

'What's wrong with him?'

'Nothing's wrong with him! He's an attractive man and he and Rose are very happy. I can't say I enjoyed myself hugely, though. He and Rose were all over each other, and Cam and Sam were all over their partners too. Oh, dear . . .' Katrina paused. 'I'm sounding terribly ungrateful.'

'Course you're not. Rose got you there under false pretences. What about the man who was giving you a lift? Was he all right?'

'He was lovely. Rose thinks he looks just like Jarvis Cocker.'

'What do *you* think?'

'I think she's right. He has different hair but otherwise he's very similar. He's tall and thin and he has the same sort of glasses and he often has an expression on his face that makes it difficult to see what he's thinking. He was nice. I enjoyed his company.'

'Is he married?'

'I said I enjoyed his company, Susie, nothing else! He is married but he's getting divorced and I get the feeling he doesn't want to be. His wife's an actress: Lucy Lambert.'

'Never heard of her.'

'Well, that's not surprising given that only one in ten thousand actors are successful.'

'Mum, there is no point in giving me your Acting is a Ruinous Profession lecture because I don't care! Oh, Mum, I am having the best time of my life, I am so happy!'

Katrina smiled and leaned back in her chair. 'Tell me,' she said.

So Susie did. She was living in a flat with what sounded like the entire cast of *Hamlet*. For their first performance, only three people came, but the night before, thirty-four people had come and everyone said Susie's mad scene was incredible.

'And what about Liam? Is he getting good audiences?'

'Better than us and he's had some fantastic reviews. And, Mum, we've met this really nice girl called Honey. That's not her real name, she won't tell us her real name, she says it's terrible. She was born in Knutsford like Liam, isn't that funny? She's going to come and see me when we get home. You'll like her. And, Mum, can Liam stay the first two weeks in September? He told me to send his love to you. It's all so exciting up here. Life is so good!'

Yes, Katrina thought, when she finally rang off, life was very good. She had two wonderful children, she loved her home and she could look forward to a week of gardening and reading and meeting friends. For the next week, at least, she was going to relax and be happy and she was not going to allow herself to think about Lewis Maltraver at all.

She almost managed it. She tidied the garden. She vacuumed every room in the house. She drove down to Sussex and spent a pleasant day with her friend, Alicia, who made exquisite silver jewellery in an old shed in the garden of her equally exquisite Tudor house. Only the nights were bad. She would fall asleep quite easily but would wake quite suddenly at five and find the same question going round and round in her head: What am I going to do about Lewis?

For once, she was happy to go back to work.

Carol was there before her, eager to fill her in with the events of the last two weeks (one resignation, one birthday, one new client, one very angry old client and a fascinating new training scheme on people skills), and anxious to know if Douglas's boss had been a satisfactory driving companion. Katrina assured her that Cornelius had.

'I'm so glad,' Carol said. 'Douglas says he can be a little odd.'

'He isn't odd at all,' Katrina said irritably. 'I thought he was courteous and considerate. Anyway'—she gave a dismissive smile—'I must get on.' She turned to her computer and frowned at the long list of emails.

Amy dropped by twenty minutes later. 'Are you free for lunch? I'd love to hear about your holiday.'

'Great. I'll see you at twelve thirty.'

Katrina worked steadily throughout the morning. She answered her emails, spent thirty precious minutes soothing the very angry old client, cold-called one potentially amazing future client and went through two hideously complicated documents. At half past twelve, she pushed back her chair and went off to find Amy.

No one could look less like a probate lawyer than Amy. At a cursory glance she might be mistaken for a little old lady with her small spectacles, her cheerful round face, her white hair parted in the middle and held back in a small bun, her long linen skirt and her broderie anglaise blouse. A closer inspection would take in the lively blue eyes, the merest smattering of wrinkles, the ever-present dimples and the silver elephant earrings.

Amy was indeed an expert on probate but she was certainly not a little old lady. She was one year off fifty. For most of her twenties she had been unhappily in love with a man who promised her everything but the babies she yearned for. On her thirtieth birthday, he left her. At the age of thirty-five she fell in love with a client, a fifty-three-year-old widower. He asked her to marry him and promised her a football team of children. They went back to his home and were making passionate love when he made an odd little sound, fell on top of her and died. After that, Amy packed away her dreams of babies and of love. Her career flourished.

Four years ago, she met an accountant called Eddy who had an Errol Flynn moustache and a wicked smile to match. Three months later, with a speed that had startled all her colleagues, he and Amy were married.

Amy was one of the reasons why Katrina enjoyed her job. At least once a week they had lunch together at the small café five doors from their office. Today, as they sat eating linguini salad Katrina regarded her friend with warm affection and said, 'It's good to be back.'

Amy twinkled sympathetically. 'Was your holiday *that* bad?'

'Worse,' said Katrina. 'My bedroom was sandwiched between two pairs of young lovers, which meant that I had to listen to their sexual marathons in stereo. Don't laugh, Amy, it wasn't funny. And on top of that, my poor, grieving sister turned out not to be grieving at all and was there with a brand-new man who just happened to be an old boyfriend of mine from years ago.'

'How fascinating. Since your sister is enamoured of him, I assume he is still attractive.' Amy put her fingertips together. She reminded Katrina of a schoolteacher considering some arcane academic problem. 'Was he pleased to see you?'

Katrina shrugged. 'I don't know. He's an actor. He's good at concealing his feelings.'

'So what did you do?'

'I counted the days till I could come home.'

'I'm not surprised,' Amy said. 'What did Rose think about it?'

'I didn't tell her. I just said I'd met him once, long ago. Lewis was obviously quite happy to keep her in the dark.'

'How horribly difficult for you.' Amy adjusted her spectacles and took a sip of her water. 'What's he like? Have I heard of him?'

'Do you remember *Medical Alert*? He was Dr Rubin.'

'I do remember! It was my mother's favourite programme. Dr Rubin was the handsome one, wasn't he? Is he still just as handsome?'

'Yes, and he knows it. He must spend half his life in the gym because his body is so well toned and his arms are really muscular—'

'I take it you weren't paying him much attention . . .'

'You couldn't help but pay attention. He spent most of the holiday wandering round the place in little black bathing shorts. He and Rose kept going off to make love. Everyone was making love. You have no idea how lovely it was to get home and see Ollie again.'

'I can imagine,' Amy said. 'Poor old you. How is the gorgeous Ollie?'

'He got his A level results a few days ago: two As and a B, so that's all right. And he's fallen in love.'

'I adore your son. He always makes me feel he's pleased to see me.'

'That's because he *is* pleased to see you.' Katrina had noted the wistful tone in Amy's voice. 'How are you getting on with your stepson? How long has he been with you now?'

'Three weeks.' Amy twirled the linguini onto her fork with careful precision. 'He's very nice. He doesn't say very much to me; he grunts politely, if you know what I mean. He watches a lot of television.'

'He's only staying with you for a couple of months, isn't he?'

'That was the original plan. Now his mother's boyfriend has managed to get him a job in this record company near Covent Garden and they've offered to keep him on until he goes travelling in February.'

'Oh,' Katrina said. 'That's quite a long time.'

'I'm sure I'll get used to him,' Amy said doubtfully. 'It's silly. I mean, I always wanted children and now I have one living with me. If you can call an eighteen-year-old a child. The thing is, I realise I don't know anything about eighteen-year-old boys. Is it just Stephen or do they all have a particularly distinctive aroma about them?'

'Stephen is not alone,' Katrina said. 'I know the smell well.'

'It's certainly very strong. He doesn't seem to shower very often.'

'Do Stephen and Eddy get on?' asked Katrina.

'They do. It's lovely to see them together. They go off to horror films and football matches and now Eddy's bought this motorbike—'

'Eddy's bought a *motorbike*?'

'It's a monster, a great big black monster. I'm terrified he'll kill himself with it.' Amy folded her arms. 'I don't know. It all feels so easy when you fall in love with someone. You never think of all the people and history that trail along behind. Eddy's so happy to have Stephen around, which is marvellous, but sometimes now I almost feel like I'm the one who's the visitor. Occasionally, very occasionally, I do marvel at the fact that I married Eddy without a thought. I jumped off the cliff without even wondering if I had a parachute.'

Cornelius climbed out of his car and reached in the back for the wine and the flowers. The door was flung open by a tall, dark-haired teenager with an engaging smile. 'Hi,' the boy said, 'you must be Cornelius. I'm Ollie. Come on in.' He ushered Cornelius into the hall. 'Go on down. I don't know where Mum is. I'll go and find her.'

'Thank you.' Cornelius watched Ollie leap up the stairs, two at a time. Surveying his surroundings, he admired the blue and yellow striped wallpaper and the ancient mirror to the right of the front door. To the left of Cornelius there were some stone steps going down to the floor below. Following Ollie's instructions, Cornelius proceeded down them and found himself in a large, airy kitchen that encompassed the entire lower-ground floor. It was clear what Katrina's favourite colours were. The walls were sky blue and at intervals along the central length of the room hung three canary-coloured metallic lamps.

Beyond the circular pine table (on which stood two very promising bottles of Merlot), French windows looked out onto a pleasantly scruffy small garden. Cornelius thought of his own cramped and windowless kitchen. This room was clearly the heart of the house. Drawn by tanta-lising smells, Cornelius wandered over to the stove. The roast beef sat on top of it like the crown jewels. Its pink-coloured flesh and its crisp coating of fat made him remember he was hungry. He allowed himself one last respectful glance and then turned his attention to the notice board on the wall by the fridge.

There was a council leaflet on recycling, a flier advertising a production of *Hamlet*, two passport-sized photos of Ollie making a funny face and a *Far Side* calendar which almost obliterated a cut-out article on *How to Tone Your Bottom*.

He was reading about the importance of clenching one's pelvic muscles when Ollie came back, followed by Katrina who looked flus-tered and sounded breathless. 'Cornelius, I am so sorry. I got some fat on my shirt and went to change. It is *lovely* to see you!'

Cornelius was unsure as to whether he should kiss her cheek or not. Instead, he held out the wine and the flowers.

'How very generous,' Katrina said. 'Do you see the cream jug by the sink? Could you put them in there for now and I'll have a lovely time arranging them later.' She tore a piece of foil from the roll and covered the meat. 'I'll leave it to stand for fifteen minutes and then we can eat. Susie will be down in a minute. Ollie, get Cornelius a drink.'

There was a difference about her: she had a confidence that had been absent in France. In her green linen trousers and cream-coloured shirt, she looked, Cornelius thought, like spring. He unwrapped the roses, filled the jug with water and stuck the flowers in it.

Ollie went to the fridge and took out a bottle. 'If you don't like this,' he said, 'then it's my fault. Mum told me to go and get some good white wine and the man at the off-licence said this was his favourite. Mind you, the man at the off-licence has a poster of Dannii Minogue on his wall so I'm not sure I can trust him.'

'It looks very good,' Cornelius assured him.

Katrina took out four glasses from one of the kitchen cupboards as a stunning girl, dressed in jeans and a pink vest, came through the doorway. 'This is Susie!' she said proudly.

Katrina's daughter had slate-coloured eyes and long brown hair that shone like burnished copper. She was blessed with her mother's flawless complexion. 'Hello,' Cornelius said. 'How very nice to meet you.'

The girl took one look at him and burst into tears.

Before Cornelius could say anything—not that he could think of anything *to* say—the girl turned on her heels and fled upstairs.

Katrina put down the glasses. 'Ollie,' she said, 'if I'm not back in five minutes, stir the gravy. If I'm not back in ten, baste the potatoes.' She turned to Cornelius. 'I'm so sorry. Make sure Ollie gives you a drink.'

After she had gone, Ollie poured some wine into a glass which he gave to Cornelius. 'I hope it's all right,' he said.

Cornelius took a sip and gave an encouraging nod. 'It's very good.'

'That's a relief.' Ollie poured himself a glass. 'Well, we might as well sit down. I'm sure Mum will be back in a minute.' He pulled out a chair.

Cornelius followed him and sat down.

'I'm sorry about Susie.' Ollie scratched his head, directed an anxious glance at the ceiling and sighed. 'She was fine before you came.'

'Oh, dear,' said Cornelius. 'I'm so sorry.'

'I don't mean that you had anything to do with it, I just mean that . . . you know . . . She *was* all right. She got back from Edinburgh two days ago. She was in the festival there.'

'I see,' said Cornelius.

'Have you ever been to Edinburgh?' he asked.

'No,' said Cornelius.

'Neither have I,' Ollie said.

It was clear that Ollie, like Cornelius, was struggling. In the ensuing silence, they could both hear the sounds of Susie's desperate sobs upstairs. Cornelius racked his brains for something to say. 'I went to a concert last week,' he ventured.

'Did you?' Ollie asked with an impressive simulation of interest.

Cornelius nodded. 'Yes. I saw the Zutons. They were very good.'

Ollie's face lit up with genuine enthusiasm. 'I *love* the Zutons.'

'So do I. And they are excellent live performers. I felt very *positive* for at least three days afterwards. I tried to recreate their sounds on my guitar but—'

'Do you play the guitar? I want to get a guitar. Are you good?'

'I'm afraid I'm rather bad. I bought one six months ago and I've been teaching myself with the help of a book.'

'I'm just the same. I have a friend who's brilliant and he's taught me a bit. I'm hoping Mum will give me a guitar for Christmas. I'd buy one myself but all my earnings are going towards travel. I'm off to Thailand as soon as I've earned enough money.'

'It's a beautiful country,' said Cornelius. 'I went there last year. And I visited Vietnam. And Laos . . .'

But Ollie had leapt from his chair and was pulling out the huge atlas from under the pile of photo albums. He put it in front of Cornelius. 'Can you show me where you went?'

Cornelius took another sip of his wine and opened the atlas. He felt the familiar surge of excitement he always experienced when he looked at the strange territorial shapes and the wide expanses of blue.

When Katrina returned, they both jumped guiltily. Katrina made straight for the neglected gravy. 'Luckily for you two,' she said severely, 'it is just about all right. Susie will be down in a second. Ollie, lay the table. Cornelius, would you be able to carve the meat?'

The meal was perfect: soggy Yorkshire pudding, buttered cabbage, thick, aromatic gravy, crisp and crunchy roast potatoes with deceptively fluffy insides. Susie came down when Cornelius was standing over the stove, attacking the joint for the second time. She went straight to him. Her eyes were red-rimmed and puffy.

'I want to apologise,' she said. 'I didn't mean . . . I'm so sorry.'

Cornelius, flustered, said, 'Not at all, not at all, it happens all the time.' He caught Katrina's eye and hastily corrected himself. 'I mean, it does happen sometimes . . . Can I give you some beef?'

He noted approvingly that she was as impressive as her mother. She responded politely and when she took her seat at the table she listened gravely to his rather stilted enquiry about her career plans. She told him that she had always wanted to be an actress and was already selecting her pieces for auditions to RADA and LAMDA and Guildhall.

'My wife is an actress,' Cornelius said.

'Mum told me. Does she get a lot of work?'

'She hasn't done as well as she'd hoped. The last play she was in was three years ago. She does the odd voice-over. At the moment she does the voice in the Terrible Tots advert.'

Katrina's mouth twitched. 'I think you mean Trimble Tots.'

'I know that advert,' Susie said. '*Trimble Tot nappies for discerning tots!* Your wife has a lovely voice.'

Cornelius nodded. 'She does. She's a very good actress. Everyone says so. She should have been more successful. It seems very unfair.'

'I'm afraid,' said Katrina, 'that unfairness is the major characteristic of the acting profession. For most people, rejection and humiliation and poverty are the order of the day . . .'

'You've said all this a thousand times,' Susie said. 'And I don't know why, because you know I don't care. I want to act.'

'You are beautiful,' Cornelius said thoughtfully, 'so you might just make it.' He looked enquiringly at Katrina. 'Do you mind if I have another Yorkshire pudding?'

You do realise,' said Katrina, as she walked Cornelius to his car, 'that you achieved the impossible? I am *so* glad you came today!'

'I'm sorry,' Cornelius said, 'I don't follow you.'

'Susie wasn't eating a thing. Then you told her she was beautiful and she ate her food. Thank you!'

'I wasn't trying to cheer her up or compliment her . . .'

'I know. You said it as if it was a simple, obvious fact and that made it all the more gratifying. Cornelius, I . . .' Katrina paused and, for the first time that day, looked uncomfortable. 'I don't want you to think that our family makes a habit of bursting into tears in front of strangers. It isn't something we usually do.'

'I'm sure it isn't,' Cornelius said.

'It was unfortunate timing, that's all. When you arrived, Susie was on the phone to her boyfriend. They'd both made friends with a girl in Edinburgh. Now he's told Susie that he and the girl are rather more than friends. The girl's name,' Katrina added with venom, 'is Honey. She was supposed to be coming to stay.'

'If I were her,' Cornelius said, taking in Katrina's glittering eyes, 'I'd give that a miss.'

'If I were Honey,' Katrina said, 'so would I.' She waited while Cornelius got into his car and wound down his window. 'Thank you for coming today,' she said.

'I had a good time,' Cornelius said, 'and I like your children.' He put his key in the ignition and glanced up abruptly. 'I wonder if you would be able to help me out next Saturday? I'm sure you're busy but—'

'I'm not,' said Katrina. 'What can I do?'

'Elizabeth, my mother, is having her eightieth birthday party. She lives in Kent. She is very fond of my wife and refuses to believe our marriage is over. She keeps ringing Lucy in an effort to get her to come back to me. It occurred to me that if I were to take a female companion with me to her party she might realise that her campaign is futile.'

'Well,' said Katrina, 'since I made you become my lover for a week, the least I can do is become your companion for an evening. Of course I'll come. I'd be delighted to help.'

'Thank you. Can I pick you up at seven? Good. Good. Goodbye, then.' Cornelius drove off quickly. What had he *done*? He had told a *lie*! He had no idea whether his mother was still in regular contact with Lucy or not. That he had spoken out of panic was hardly an excuse. He had had the feeling that Katrina was saying goodbye to him and that he would never see her again and out of his mouth, without any thought, had come this fully formed story. For a man who valued honesty beyond all else, he had proved to be remarkably adept at telling a falsehood. But at least he would see Katrina again.

When Katrina came back to the kitchen, she found Ollie consuming another helping of fruit salad. 'Where's Susie?' she asked.

'She's taken the phone up to her room,' Ollie said. 'Your friend was nice. He looks very like—'

'Jarvis Cocker, I know.'

'Except for the hair. Susie reckons he's still in love with his wife.'

'I think Susie's right,' said Katrina. 'It's very sad.'

'I wonder why she left him.' Ollie reached for the cream. 'He told me he went to see the Zutons last week.'

'What are the Zutons?'

'Only one of the best groups in England today. I can't believe you haven't heard of them. I play their music all the time. How can you not have heard of them?'

'I can't imagine.' Katrina studied the remains of the meal.

'Cornelius went to Thailand last year *and* he went to Vietnam. I'd like to go there. Shall I show you the route he took?'

'Yes,' said Katrina, transferring the remains of the beef from the carving dish to a plate, 'after we've done the washing-up.'

On Saturday evening, Katrina gave herself an hour to get ready. What did one wear to an elderly lady's birthday party? In the end, she wore the same black dress that she wore to everything.

Cornelius arrived punctually at seven. He had obviously made an effort but he still resembled a scarecrow. He wore navy pinstriped trousers that made his legs look even longer than usual. He wore a crumpled but clean white shirt and a navy tie. His curly, springy hair looked as if he had at least tried to brush it.

'I'm all ready,' Katrina assured him. 'Now, have I got . . . No, wait a minute.' She dashed back into the hall and collected her gift. 'I didn't know what to get. I hope your mother likes orchids. Right! Let's go!'

Cornelius opened the car door for her and then went round to his own side. 'You look very pretty,' he said and switched on the ignition.

Katrina smiled at him. 'You never fail to surprise me,' she said.

'Really? Why is that?'

'You're not the sort of person to give charming compliments. And I don't mean that in a bad way.'

'The thing is,' Cornelius said, 'it is factually correct that you look pretty, so I thought it was worth saying in case you hadn't noticed.'

'I hadn't,' Katrina said. 'And it's very kind of you to tell me but I think it's an indisputable fact that not everyone would agree with you and that therefore it is a subjective judgment on your part.'

'I wasn't being subjective. I spoke as a disinterested observer.'

Katrina laughed. 'You see, now you've spoilt it by telling me that.'

'Should I tell you that I'm interested?'

Katrina's eyes met his and for a moment Katrina felt nonplussed since Cornelius both looked and sounded as if he genuinely wanted an answer. Almost immediately, she berated herself. What a sad person she was that she could allow one kind sentence to lead her into such an absurd deduction. 'Just remember,' she told him, 'that this evening, that is exactly what you are supposed to be!'

'I will do my best. How are Ollie and Susie?'

'Ollie is *very* well. After talking to you about Thailand and Vietnam, he's full of plans for next year. Susie, on the other hand, is still very subdued. It's horrible, she's lost all her bounce. She cries a lot and keeps trying to work out where she went wrong with Liam. Yesterday she even asked me if I thought she had an irritating voice. I tried to explain that the fact that Liam has fallen for Honey doesn't necessarily mean that Honey is more attractive than she is, but she just said that I haven't seen Honey. I must say, the more I hear of her the more I dislike her. She is obviously a vile, conceited liar.'

Cornelius smiled. 'Another disinterested observation?'

'Not at all. I am happy to tell you I subjectively hate the girl. What really gets me is that Susie is just like she was when that horrid boy, Ash, treated her so badly five years ago. What if it takes her another five years to get over Liam? She's starting her job next week so I hope that will distract her a little.'

'What is she going to do?'

'It's just a waitressing job in a fairly seedy hotel. At least she has a friend who is starting at the hotel at the same time and I suppose it will keep her busy.'

'Yes,' said Cornelius. 'And that's the best thing she can do. She should be busy. She should be very busy. She should be so busy that when she goes to bed she falls asleep at once. Keep her on the move.'

'I'm sure you're right.' Katrina cast a sideways glance at Cornelius. She presumed he was talking from experience and wondered if he was thinking of his looming divorce. She wished she knew him well enough to offer sympathy. Instead, she said briskly, 'Anyway, tell me about tonight. Do you know who will be there?'

'Yes,' said Cornelius. 'You'll see my sister, Juliet, and her husband, Alec. They live in Sussex. They've organised the party for Elizabeth.'

'What are they like? Does Juliet look like you?'

'Fortunately for her, she does not. She has my mother's looks. I think you'll like her. Alec is nice too. He's a typical Scot: he's lived in England for thirty years but retains a thick Scottish accent and gets sentimental on New Year's Eve.'

'Are you and Juliet the only children?'

'Yes. Mother married twice more after my father died and we collected various stepbrothers and stepsisters along the way but none of them stuck.'

'So who else will be there?'

'I hope my nephew and niece are coming but when I spoke to Juliet yesterday she thought it was doubtful. Michael's wife is pregnant and is being sick all the time and apparently Jenny has flu. Henry and Amanda are coming. They're neighbours. They're both expats and used to live in Kenya. Henry's very fat and looks like a walrus. Amanda has a very racy past. And then there'll be Dennis, who is very dull but loves my mother so she likes to have him around.'

'What happened to your mother's husbands?'

'Husband number two got the sack very quickly. He drank too much. Husband number three died in mysterious circumstances a few years ago. Juliet and I are almost certain he got fatally overheated in a massage parlour. He was the dirtiest of dirty old men.'

'It must have been very difficult for your mother.'

'I don't think,' Cornelius said dismissively, 'that she ever noticed.'

Cornelius's mother lived in a small village that looked just like one of those locations beloved by Hollywood when shooting films set in England. Cornelius parked outside a cottage at the end of the immaculate high street and said without much enthusiasm, 'Here we are.'

The door was opened by an elderly man with a green bow tie, green and brown checked shirt and a pale brown cardigan. 'Cornelius, dear boy,' he said, 'how very nice to see you.' Katrina instantly decided that this must be the dull would-be lover.

She was right. 'Hello, Dennis,' Cornelius said. 'This is Katrina.'

'Delighted to meet you,' Dennis said, with unabashed curiosity. 'Come in.'

The door opened into a large, flagstoned sitting room. The windows both had window seats, on one of which sat an elderly lady in a long, shimmering kaftan of the palest pink silk. Standing on either side of her stood a generously proportioned matron in a green and yellow striped dress and a red-faced gentleman who did indeed look exactly like a walrus. In the middle of the room, a short, stocky man was opening a bottle of champagne while an attractive lady in a grey linen skirt and matching top hovered by his side.

As the newcomers stepped into the room, there were cries of 'Cornelius!' but the eyes of everyone were fixed on Katrina.

A moment later all was action. Introductions were made and champagne was poured. Katrina gave her orchid to Elizabeth, who declared that she *adored* orchids. 'Katrina, come and sit by me here. It is so sweet of you to buy me a present.'

Katrina joined Elizabeth on the window seat. 'It's very kind of you to invite me,' she said. She felt increasingly uncomfortable. Unwittingly or not, Cornelius had given her the impression that his mother was cold and possibly remote. This woman with her cheerful eyes, round face and expansive gestures was charming, eminently likable and clearly intrigued by Katrina's presence.

'I was saying only a little while ago to Amanda that I was delighted when Cornelius asked if he could bring you.'

Amanda nodded. 'Elizabeth has been *very* excited. In fact, we've all been dying to know what you look like, and I know I shouldn't tell you that but one of the very best things about getting older is that you no longer worry about anything you say!'

The walrus snorted vigorously. 'I have to say, Amanda, that as long as I have known you, you have *never* given a damn about anything at all. You're about as tactful as a fox in a chicken run.'

'Nonsense, Henry,' Elizabeth said. 'Amanda just tells the truth, that's all. Of course we've been dying to see Katrina but our motives are pure, I assure you. We have been so concerned about poor Cornelius. Now *do* tell us: how did you meet?'

Katrina glanced desperately at Cornelius, who was standing at the other end of the room talking to his sister. She saw him smile at her and felt a surge of irritation. Did he not know that she needed him? 'Well,' she began, 'I suppose—'

Cornelius did know. Cornelius was wonderful, for Cornelius had left his sister to come and join her, and with exquisite timing said, 'Do you mind if I interrupt?'

Katrina looked up into his face and smiled gratefully.

'I'm sorry to break up the conversation,' Cornelius said, 'but my sister is very keen to talk to Katrina.'

Katrina rose with an alacrity that she hoped was not too obvious and joined Juliet, her husband and Dennis, who were all standing by the fireplace. Alec gave her an amiable grin. 'Cornelius said you needed rescuing. Being grilled by Amanda and Elizabeth is an unnerving experience at the best of times.'

'You are a very wicked man, Alec,' said Dennis. He smiled reassuringly at Katrina. 'Elizabeth and Amanda are both delightful women. And I think you should know, Katrina, and I know Alec will confirm this, that Elizabeth,' he paused to fix Katrina with an intense scrutiny, 'is a wonderful *mother-in-law*.'

'Really?' said Katrina faintly.

'Dennis'—Juliet put a hand on his arm—'there's a plate of baby sausages on the Aga in the kitchen. Would you be very kind and go and get them? And Alec, I think a few glasses need refilling.'

'We have our marching orders, Dennis,' Alec said. He gave a mischievous wink to Katrina and walked off with Dennis.

Juliet's eyes twinkled sympathetically. 'I hope you're not regretting you came,' she said.

'Not at all,' said Katrina.

'Cornelius tells me,' Juliet said, 'that your son wants a guitar for Christmas.'

'Well, yes, he does.'

'I might be able to help. My son used to be a guitarist in a Goth band.'

'What does he do now?'

'He's an accountant. The guitar is in very good condition; he got another one a year after we bought it for him and so it's not been used too much.'

'It sounds perfect,' Katrina said. 'You must let me pay you for it . . .'

'We can sort something out. You and Cornelius should come and stay for a weekend with us and you can take a look at it.'

'Yes,' said Katrina a little doubtfully.

'We live in Sussex, in a village called Alfriston; it's not far from Lewes—'

'I love Lewes! I know it well! I have a friend who lives in Chailey. Whenever I stay with her, we always go to Lewes and I spend far too much money. My children used to adore the castle there.'

'Ah, the castle,' Juliet sighed. 'Cornelius has always loved the castle. I remember we used to . . .' She stopped and glanced in the direction of her brother. Cornelius was standing, listening gravely to the walrus. Amanda had joined Elizabeth on the window seat.

'My brother can be very clever occasionally,' Juliet said. 'He has found the perfect way to deflect our mother's curiosity.'

'Why? What has he done?'

'Henry joined a wine-tasting club a year ago. He is convinced he is now the world's greatest expert on wine. So Cornelius asks a wine-related question, the answer to which he knows better than anyone, Henry starts pontificating and Amanda and Elizabeth can't get away quickly enough. All Cornelius has to do is stay awake.'

'Very clever!' agreed Katrina. She wondered why Juliet had changed the subject. She was pretty sure it was deliberate.

At dinner, Katrina sat between Dennis and Alec. Alec was interested to hear that she was a solicitor, having retired from the law himself a few years earlier, and he regaled her with numerous and probably apocryphal stories about judges he had known. Katrina darted occasional glances at Cornelius, who sat between Amanda and Elizabeth. She could see that Elizabeth constantly deferred to her son, touching his arm with her hand. With each solicitation, Cornelius responded with a slight nod and an expressionless face.

At the end of the meal—Juliet had produced a splendid feast of salmon, couscous, new potatoes, spinach salad and tiny crab cakes, followed by an enormous strawberry pavlova—Dennis tapped the table with his hand.

'If I may be so bold,' he said, standing and surveying the table, 'and speaking as Elizabeth's most fervent admirer, I would like to say a few words about our *birthday girl*! I know I can speak on behalf of Henry and Amanda when I say that the three of us are honoured to be representing your friends tonight—'

'All the others have died,' Henry said.

For a moment, Dennis looked slightly flummoxed by this observation. 'I'm sure that's not true,' he said.

'Oh, it is,' said Elizabeth without any visible sign of distress.

'Well, be that as it may,' Dennis persisted, 'we three *veterans* are proud to be here!' He took a sip of his wine and cleared his throat. 'There are many things I could say about Elizabeth—'

'Keep it clean, Dennis,' Henry chortled.

'Henry,' Amanda said calmly, 'you have a mind like a sewer. Carry on, Dennis.'

'Thank you, Amanda,' Dennis said, pausing only to look slightly reprovingly at Henry. 'There are many things I could say about Elizabeth. I *could* tell you that she is an example to us all. I *could* tell you that she has a lightness of spirit and a generosity of soul that gladdens the heart of all those who know her. I *could* tell you these things—'

'You bloody well have done!' Henry pointed out.

'*However*,' Dennis said, ignoring Henry with visible difficulty, 'I felt that my best course would be to tell you what she means to *me*. I have known Elizabeth for twenty-four years, and I think I can safely say that she has enhanced my life. We have spent many an intimate evening—'

'Keep it clean, Dennis!' Henry chortled.

'Shut up, Henry,' said Amanda calmly.

'We have spent many an intimate evening playing Scrabble or Racing Demon, and if ever I have been brought down by the state of the world, she is always ready with a merry quip! I well remember once when I voiced my fears about global warming and Elizabeth said, "Never mind the environment, Dennis, where's my gin and tonic?"' Dennis chuckled at the recollection. 'She is a very special lady. Now, without further ado, I will pass on the baton to Cornelius who I am quite sure has his own thoughts about this happy occasion!'

There was a burst of enthusiastic applause after which everyone looked expectantly at Cornelius.

Cornelius cleared his throat. 'I don't believe,' he said, 'I can add anything to Dennis's speech.'

There was a momentary hiatus in the proceedings, a collective air of bewildered disappointment, and then Juliet rose from her seat with her glass in her hand. 'Quite right,' she said. 'Dennis said everything we could want to say. Will everyone raise their glasses to my beautiful mother? To Elizabeth!'

Katrina wondered if anyone else noticed that Cornelius raised and lowered his glass without actually drinking from it.

'I have to tell you,' Katrina said, as she and Cornelius drove back along the Kentish lanes, 'that I felt extremely uncomfortable. Everyone seems so excited about our great new romance. I bet you the moment we left they all started talking about it.'

'Of course they did. They like nothing better than a good gossip.'

'I feel like an impostor. Don't you feel bad about deceiving your family?'

'I haven't. I told them I wanted to bring a friend of mine to the party. That was true. Can I help it if they leapt to the wrong conclusions?'

Katrina cast a shrewd eye at him. 'You knew very well they'd jump to the wrong conclusions. I had Dennis assuring me that Elizabeth was a wonderful mother-in-law. I had your sister saying that you and I must go and stay with them.'

'That would be nice,' said Cornelius, adjusting his driving mirror.

'No, Cornelius, it would not be nice. Well, at least I now know what I put you through in France. The thing is, I didn't expect your family to be so *interested*. They obviously worry about you a great deal. I thought everyone was very nice.'

'You must have your sister's party coming up soon. When is it?'

'I'm dreading it. It's next Saturday. It will be appalling. I'm strongly inclined to insist you come to it.'

'I've told you I'd be happy to do so.'

'It's kind of you to offer to come but it's not necessary. I've worked out everything. You and I are going to break up in the next few days.'

'Are we? May I know the reason?'

'You are not ready to start a new relationship yet, and so I go to the party, supported by my children, looking sad but resigned.'

'Why don't you let me drive you all to the party and then we can go in and you can look happy and romantic?'

'That's all very well but you'd have to look happy and romantic too.'

'I can be romantic,' Cornelius said confidently.

'Right.' Katrina glanced at him doubtfully.

It was later, while she was taking off her make-up, that she became aware that the evening had left an unpleasant residue of unease in her mind. She liked Cornelius's family and she had enjoyed the drive back. She was grateful that Cornelius was coming to Rose's party next week but . . . and there was no question about it, there was now a very big 'but' about Cornelius. She remembered what he had said after Dennis's speech. In effect, he had quite deliberately thrown a bucket of cold water on the festivities. His sister had acted quickly and avoided any possible awkwardness but the fact remained that Cornelius had made an extraordinarily mean-spirited response to Dennis's invitation to speak. In fact, throughout the evening, Cornelius had not displayed the slightest warmth to his mother.

Katrina was aware that, owing to the unusual circumstances of their first meeting, Cornelius had progressed within a few hours from being a stranger to being a friend. Now, for the first time, she realised how little she knew the man and, for the first time, she felt a small, chilly stirring of doubt.

CHAPTER FIVE

The House of Broken Hearts

THERE WERE TIMES when work provided a positive haven of peace. On Monday, Katrina took a possible new client out to lunch and explained why she could handle his work better than anyone else. On Tuesday, she spent two hours sorting out a land dispute between two companies, had lunch with Amy and sympathised with her anxiety about her husband's infatuation with his motorbike. In the afternoon, she finally finished sorting out the very angry client who, for the first time in months, sounded almost civilised as a result.

So long as Katrina concentrated on work, she needn't dwell on her unsettling thoughts about Cornelius—and why *should* they unsettle her? Cornelius was just a friend, after all, and possibly not even that. At least thinking about Cornelius was less unsettling than thinking about Lewis . . .

On Wednesday evening, Rose rang to announce that she was back from France, she looked fantastic, so did Lewis, and they were both looking forward to seeing her and the children on Saturday.

'Can I bring Cornelius?' Katrina asked.

'Of course you can. So . . .' Rose paused. 'You two are still together? I shall tell Lewis he was wrong.'

Katrina bridled. 'Why? What did he say?'

'He reckoned you two wouldn't last beyond the holiday.'

'Actually, he couldn't be more wrong. Cornelius and I are very happy.'

'I'm so glad,' Rose said. 'We will look forward to seeing all of you on Saturday, then. And Lewis is *most* insistent that I send you his love!'

That night Katrina did not sleep well.

On Saturday morning, Katrina came home from the supermarket to find the house still quiet. She put her bags on the kitchen floor and glanced at the clock: half past eleven. Ollie had been out last night but Susie had stayed in, and when Katrina went to bed she had left Susie watching an old black and white horror film, her eyes fixed blankly on the flickering screen. She sighed and began to unpack the groceries.

Twenty minutes later, Susie drifted in. Her hair was pushed behind her ears, exposing the pallor of her complexion.

'Hello, there,' Katrina said with determined cheerfulness. 'Do you fancy some coffee? I've just put the kettle on.'

'Thanks.' Susie went to the fridge and took out the orange juice.

Katrina spooned coffee into the cafetière. 'What are you going to wear to Rose's party tonight? I thought I'd wear my black dress.'

'Mum, you've worn that to every party Rose has ever had. Last time, she asked you if you *had* anything else in your wardrobe.'

'There's nothing else that's suitable. I thought about wearing my linen trousers but I haven't anything smart enough to wear with them.'

Susie sat down at the table and pulled the paper towards her. 'You can borrow my red top if you like—the one we bought at Topshop.'

'I can't wear that, I'd look ridiculous. It's far too low and it's far too clingy. There's nothing worse than a middle-aged woman trying to look like her daughter . . .'

'It's better than a middle-aged woman trying to look like her mother. At least *try* the red top.'

'All right.' Katrina brought the coffee over to the table. 'But you have to promise to be brutally honest if . . .' She stopped as her son shuffled into the room in pyjama bottoms and a once-white T-shirt. 'What time did *you* get to bed this morning?'

Ollie sat down opposite his sister and emptied the contents of the cereal packet into his bowl. 'I don't know,' he sighed.

'Did you have a good time last night?'

'No,' said Ollie. 'I had the worst evening of my life.' He gave another deep sigh. 'Susie, I now know exactly what you're going through. Last night,' Ollie went on in a doom-laden voice, 'was *hell*. Nick asked Sophie out and Sophie said yes. I mean Nick is the biggest sleazeball you've ever met. I really do feel,' he added, pouring a vast amount of milk onto his Coco Pops, 'as if my heart has been broken.' He stared sadly at his bowl and absently put a very full spoonful of cereal into his mouth.

Susie cast a look of smouldering disgust at her brother. 'I cannot *believe* that you are comparing your stupid crush with my relationship with Liam. I went out with him for five months. You haven't even been on a date with this Sophie girl, you just fancy her—'

Ollie protested indignantly but it was difficult to understand him since his mouth was congested with Coco Pops.

'You have *no* idea what I'm going through,' Susie continued, her voice rising a couple of octaves. 'You have no idea at all, and if you did, you wouldn't be able to stuff your face like that.' She pushed back her chair and stormed out of the kitchen.

Ollie was outraged. 'I don't see why Susie thinks she's the only one in the house who has a right to be miserable. I *seriously* like Sophie. I can't believe she likes Nick. He is *horrible*.' He bit his lip, picked up the cereal packet and shook it. 'Do we have any more?' he asked.

Given her newly ambivalent attitude to Cornelius, Katrina had not expected to be so pleased to see him when he arrived outside her front door. Perhaps it was not so surprising since her children were both sunk in gloom. She had tried to brighten Susie's mood by promising she'd wear her red top. It was only when she saw Cornelius's face that she remembered her earlier reservations.

'You think I'm mutton dressed as lamb, I can tell,' she said without bothering to say hello. 'Susie told me to wear this. Should I change?'

'Definitely not,' said Cornelius. 'You look magnificent.'

'Anyway,' said Katrina, 'there isn't time. If we arrive on time we can leave early. Ollie! Susie! Cornelius is here. We're going.'

Another reason to be grateful to Cornelius: she knew her children would behave in his presence. On the journey, she spoke earnestly to the two of them. 'Now listen, Cornelius is doing me a great favour by coming tonight. In return, you must both help me to look after him. If any of Rose's more difficult friends try to monopolise him, go to his rescue.' Katrina swung her head to look at Cornelius. 'I promise you we will get away as soon as we can.'

'Katrina,' Cornelius said, 'you really do not have to worry. I am happy to stay as long as you want to.'

'You don't understand,' Katrina said. 'Not one of us wants to stay a minute longer than we have to.'

In the back, Ollie's phone let out an enormous belch. He answered immediately. 'Hello, George . . . Cool. Cool.'

Katrina turned round again and watched Ollie slip his phone back into his pocket. 'That was a very quick phone call,' she said.

'George and Rob are in town. I agreed to meet them at ten. Do you want to come along, Susie?'

'No,' said Susie baldly and then added more softly, 'But thanks for asking me.'

Katrina felt her spirits lift. Susie and Ollie were very close and she always hated the rare occasions on which they fell out.

The party was in full swing when they arrived. Rose opened the door to them; behind her the large sitting room was already more than half full. 'Darlings, how lovely to see you!' she said. 'Katty, you look very . . . *dramatic*! Cornelius, doesn't she look dramatic?'

'I think,' said Cornelius, letting his eyes wander round the room before resting on Rose, 'she's the best-looking woman in the room.'

'Really?' said Rose, who was wearing a diaphanous, pale blue dress over a navy slip. 'What a *very* sweet thing to say! Now, circulate!'

Katrina had meant to stay with Cornelius throughout the evening and she was not sure how they came to be separated. Instead, she found herself talking to various people such as Rose's neighbours from downstairs (very nice) and Cam's boyfriend, Francis (just as irritating in England as he had been in France). At one point she saw Lewis chatting to Ollie and Susie. The sight of the three of them together made her muscles clench. She tried to make her way towards her children but was hailed by Rose who insisted on introducing her to two of her female friends; they were just as glamorous as Rose and looked less than excited at the prospect of meeting her sister.

At various times she looked around for Cornelius. Once she saw him standing on the balcony with Ollie. The two of them seemed to be eating their way through a plate of smoked-salmon sandwiches. Another time she saw him talking to Susie and Cam. A third time she saw him standing with his back to the wall looking down at a short, orange-haired lady in a black and white dress who gesticulated energetically at him. The lady looked like a bumble bee attacking a flagpole.

She was about to go and rescue him when she heard a soft 'Katrina?' and turned to face Lewis. His tanned complexion made his blue eyes appear even more striking than usual. 'Katrina,' he said again, 'you ought to wear red more often. It suits you.'

Katrina finished her glass of wine. 'I am very aware that it's far too young for me. It belongs to my daughter; she insisted I wear it.'

'Allow me.' Lewis held a half-full bottle of wine in his hand and he took her glass and filled it. 'You never did know how to accept praise. Are you well?'

'Never better.'

He stared at her intently. 'I'd like you to have a meal with me soon.'

'A candlelit dinner for two, perhaps?'

'If that's what you want. I *was* thinking of lunch. This situation is so extraordinary. I think we should talk about it.'

Katrina took a sip of her wine. 'Some time in the future, it might be a good idea. Now, if you'll excuse me, I must go and rescue Cornelius.'

She turned and left him, only to be stopped by Cam who was anxious to know if she could stay in Greenwich for a couple of nights in November. 'We're doing a photo-shoot there. It's going to be at somewhere called the Queen's House. Have you heard of it?'

'Of course. It's a beautiful building, built by James the First for his wife. It has a beautiful spiral staircase that—'

'That's why we're doing it there. My boss wants to drape models over the staircase, and apparently there are some fab colonnades as well. She has this idea of putting ordinary people behind the columns, peeping out at the models. You could be one if you like.'

'An ordinary person? Thank you, Cam. It sounds very tempting. Anyway, it will be lovely to have your company.'

'Good.' Cam looked across at Susie. 'I'm trying to persuade Susie to come out with us after the party. She can stay the night with me and Sam. Sam says he'll drop her back tomorrow.'

'Well, that's very sweet of Sam . . .' Katrina paused, her attention diverted by the sight of Lewis in intense conversation with Cornelius.

'Susie!' Cam called and waited while Susie wove her way through the guests. 'Susie, you *will* come out with us tonight, won't you? It's so long since we've been out together!'

'Well . . .' said Susie, her eyes flickering fleetingly at her mother.

It would have been easy for Katrina to come to the rescue, she could have used any number of excuses. Instead, she simply murmured, 'I must go and rescue Cornelius,' and wandered off. She knew Susie was sometimes irritated by her cousins but going out on the town with them had to be better than sitting morosely in front of late-night television.

Katrina made her way across the room towards Cornelius and Lewis. 'I think,' she said to Cornelius, 'it's time we were going.'

As soon as they got into the car, Katrina kicked off her shoes. 'Oh,' she breathed, 'I'm so glad that's over! I shall sleep and sleep tonight. Thank you for coming with me. It was far more bearable with you there.'

'Did you find the party difficult?' Cornelius asked.

'Not once I got enough wine down me. In a way, it was even nice to get out. My children are testing my patience at the moment. Susie is still stricken over the end of her relationship with Liam and now Ollie is grieving over a relationship he's never even had. I am discovering that my sympathy is definitely finite. Anyway, enough of that! What did you think of the party? Did you hate it?'

'No,' Cornelius said. 'I enjoyed talking to your children.'

'I saw Lewis bear down on you. What did *he* want?'

'He wanted to know about you and me. In the politest manner, of course.'

'What did you tell him?'

'I told him I was far more interested in his relationship with Rose.' One side of Cornelius's mouth twisted slightly. 'I was always a very truthful person before I met you.'

'I'm sure you were. I'm sorry. I ought to be given a *degree* in telling lies. Oh dear! Everything is in such a mess at the moment!'

'Is it?' Cornelius asked. 'Why?'

'Oh . . .' Katrina waved her hands in the air. 'Don't pay any attention to me. I've drunk far too much and I always talk rubbish when I drink too much.' She sat back in her seat and stretched her arms. 'Ollie didn't say goodbye to me. Did you see him go?'

'Yes. He said you were talking to a lady with a very dark tan and long blue fingernails. He thought he might get sucked into your conversation if he came to tell you he was off.'

'I wish he *had* got sucked into it. Oh, I'm so glad it's over! I drank far too much. Have I said that already?'

'I think you might have mentioned it,' Cornelius said politely.

'Well, I'm sorry but it's true. I shall have to drink loads of water before I go to bed. Have you heard of an American writer called Robert Benchley? He drank too much. Someone once asked him if he realised that drinking was a slow death.'

'What did he say?'

'He said, "So who's in a hurry?"'

Cornelius laughed and Katrina, encouraged by his response, launched into a long and very convoluted anecdote about the first time she drank too much. She only reached the end of it as they drew up outside her house. 'Cornelius, thank you so much for this evening!' She leaned forward to kiss his cheek, somehow caught his mouth instead, saw him recoil instantly and as quickly withdrew herself. 'Sorry,' she said, 'I am so sorry. Thank you for the lift. Good night.'

She fled from the car without waiting for a reply.

From: katrinalatham@parter.co.uk
To: cornhedge@winemart.co.uk
Sent: September 18, 23:30

Dear Cornelius,
First, I want to thank you for your company on Saturday evening. Secondly, I would like to apologise to you for abusing our acquaintance by drinking too much and therefore forcing you to drive back with a rambling, incoherent, deeply pathetic individual. I feel embarrassed and ashamed by my improper behaviour. I can only assure you that I shall neither expect nor ask you to take any further part in this ridiculous masquerade in which I forced you, against your better judgment, to participate.
Best wishes, Katrina

From: cornhedge@winemart.co.uk
To: katrinalatham@parter.co.uk
Sent: September 19, 08:45

Dear Katrina,
I had presumed we were friends rather than acquaintances and, as far as I am concerned, friends are those with whom one can feel free to behave properly or improperly according to circumstance. I very much enjoyed Rose's party. I had a long and delightful conversation with your son and a shorter but no less pleasant one with your daughter. I feel I should remind you that you did not ask me to come to the party; I asked you if I could come, because I enjoy your company. On our journey back from the party, I did not find you rambling or incoherent or deeply pathetic and if the continuation of the masquerade means that I have more opportunities to spend time in your company, I am only too happy to remain a participant. Finally: how are the broken hearts? A little less broken, I hope. Do let me know.
Cornelius

From: katrinalatham@parter.co.uk
To: cornhedge@winemart.co.uk
Sent: September 20, 23:00

Dear Cornelius,
You are so good! You are indeed a friend and I only used the word

'acquaintance' because I was not at all sure you would want to be my friend after seeing how foolish I could be. As far as the masquerade is concerned, I am determined to end it. Despite my undoubted capacity for telling lies, I am not happy with deceit and I felt very uncomfortable at fooling your extremely welcoming family. (Incidentally, I still want to buy your sister's guitar for Ollie. If you give me Juliet's email address I can contact her and arrange a time to see her when I visit my friend who lives near her.) Finally, an update on the broken hearts: Ollie is still very sad. As for Susie, it is all a DISASTER and it is ALL MY FAULT. At Rose's house, Cam invited her to go out with them after the party. I knew Susie did not want to go but I thought it would be good for her to get out. STUPID, STUPID ME! Susie DID go out with Cam and Sam and met a few of their friends, one of whom was ASH! The HORRIBLE young man who behaved APPALLINGLY to her and who broke her heart when she was sixteen. I should have known this would happen since Susie originally met him while out with her cousins. He's one of their oldest friends. So Susie comes back on Sunday afternoon in the company of Ash who has apparently been KIND and SYMPATHETIC and UNDERSTANDING. Susie's heart is healing with a speed that I can only describe as alarming. According to Susie, Ash has no designs on her but is proving to be a WONDERFUL friend. Since I am so pleased to see that Susie is no longer drifting round the house like a lonely ghost, I am unable to remind her that her new saviour is a RAT of the first order. The worst of it is that if I hadn't made her go out with Cam and Sam, she would never have met him—Ash, that is—again. Otherwise, everything is fine.

Very best wishes, Katrina

From: cornhedge@winemart.co.uk
To: katrinalatham@parter.co.uk
Sent: September 21, 11:00

Dear Katrina,

I understand that mothers have an unrivalled capacity to blame themselves for anything that goes wrong in the lives of their daughters but I don't see how you can take responsibility for the re-emergence of Ash in Susie's life. She could, after all, have told her cousins that she did not want to go out with them on Saturday night and she could also have chosen to reject Ash's overtures. Furthermore, if she told you he was only being a friend, then might it not be possible that he is indeed nothing more? Perhaps he is genuinely moved by Susie's grief and wants to make up for his past behaviour. I don't see that you can interfere since Susie is of an age when she needs to make her own decisions. Since you can do nothing, you might as well stop worrying. As far as I can remember, misery is an entirely natural state for most people between the ages of seventeen and twenty-five. At that age, misery can almost be enjoyable. As far as Ollie is concerned, one can only hope that a more perspicacious girl crosses his path very soon.

Cornelius

PS What were you like when you were twenty-one?

From: katrinalatham@parter.co.uk
To: cornhedge@winemart.co.uk
Sent: September 22, 22:30

Thank you for your kind words and you are right, of course. There is no way I can influence the life of my daughter and I have been trying very hard not to say anything at all. Having said that, it is very difficult to watch her teetering on the edge of making a mistake the size of the universe. In the circumstances I think I've been quite tactful and, personally, I think Susie was unfair last night to tell me that I should try to stop living my life through her. All I did was to warn her to be a little wary of Ash and to remind her of his behaviour five years earlier. Anyway, I have now decided to be a hundred per cent silent. Meanwhile, Ollie continues to be sad about Sophie. He saw her last night with some friends and he says it was very frustrating because he and she get on so well and they have so much in common. Sophie's mad about music like he is and, even more spookily, wants a guitar for Christmas. (Which reminds me, remember to send me your sister's address.) Hope I haven't bored you with all this; don't bother to answer.

Love, Katrina

PS At twenty-one, I was completely unacquainted with misery (unlike you: why were you so miserable?). I had met Paul and was madly in love and preparing to get married and live happily ever after.

PPS I should have listened to your advice about Susie.

From: cornhedge@winemart.co.uk
To: katrinalatham@parter.co.uk
Sent: September 23, 18:10

Actually, Katrina, I feel guilty about attempting to give you advice about Susie. Having never had a daughter I am totally unqualified to pontificate. I only suggest that you cannot be certain that Ash is indeed a mistake. I enclose an attachment containing my sister's email address and website. I can imagine you at twenty-one and rather wish I had met you then, except that I think you would have found me unbearable. You ask me why I used to be miserable and I suppose that it was easier to be miserable than to be cheerful. I am glad to say that these days misery no longer holds any charms for me.
Cornelius

Katrina was alone in the house when the phone rang. Susie was out with friends and Ollie had gone over to see Rob to discuss their plans for transglobal exploration. Ollie and Rob had had at least three 'discussion' evenings already and, as far as Katrina knew, the only conclusions reached thus far were a joint agreement to exclude Chechnya, Iraq and Siberia from their route.

'Katty, darling!' Rose's voice was breathy and urgent. 'I haven't spoken to you since my party. Thanks for your card! How *are* you?' Rose sounded buoyant and enthusiastic. Something had put her in a very good mood.

'I'm very well.' Katrina kicked off her shoes and settled herself on the sofa. Rose's phone calls were usually very long.

'And how is Cornelius?'

'Actually,' Katrina said, deciding now was a good time to put an end to the ridiculous charade she had inflicted on him, 'I wanted to talk to you about me and Cornelius.'

'How extraordinary,' exclaimed Rose, 'because that is exactly the reason why I rang you! And before I start, I don't want you to think I've been interfering or trying to mess things up for you because I haven't. My sole concern has been a strong desire to look out for my little sister. So I'm going to be perfectly frank and put my cards on the table—'

Katrina had been glancing idly out of the window, enjoying the tranquil scene of a robin pecking at the lawn. At the sight of Omo streaking across the grass and narrowly failing to slaughter the poor bird, she felt compelled to interrupt Rose. 'Your horrible cat,' she said, 'has just carried out an unprovoked attack on a sweet little robin.'

'He *is* a horrid cat, isn't he?' agreed Rose. 'I never liked him.'

'Neither do I,' said Katrina, settling back onto the sofa.

'I'm sure that's not true,' said Rose comfortably. 'I wish you wouldn't interrupt me . . . What was I saying?'

'You said you wanted to put your cards on the table.'

'That's exactly what I'm going to do. Ever since you mentioned the name, it's been running through my head like one of those songs you can't stand but you can't stop singing—you know what I mean?'

'No, I have no idea what you mean. If you're referring to Cornelius—'

'No, of course I'm not. A name like Cornelius doesn't run through your head, it bursts straight into it like a question mark. I am talking about Lucy Lambert, of course. A few evenings ago I was showing Lewis some of my old photo albums and suddenly there she was, staring at me from the end of the row in front of Miss Drommett!'

'Who is Miss Drommett?'

'Miss Drommett was our maths teacher—she'd gone by the time you came. Anyway, then I knew. Lucy Lambert was at school with me! She was in my class!'

'Are you talking about Cornelius's wife?'

'Unless there are two Lucy Lamberts,' Rose said impatiently, 'of course I am. Really, Katty, you're very slow tonight. I have to say I'm not surprised I didn't remember her. We were never close friends. She was rather a drama queen even then. Anyway, as soon as I saw the photo I said to Lewis that I just had to get in touch with her.'

'I don't see why. If you never liked her.'

'I didn't say I didn't like her. It's simply that we had very little in common. But somehow I felt fate was telling me to seek her out.'

'It wasn't that you were dying of curiosity . . .'

'Well, I admit I was a little interested, who wouldn't be? So, I set to work and I got in touch with Emily Sharp—do you remember Emily? The year you arrived, she was head girl. I knew that if anyone knew where Lucy was, it would be Emily, and of course I was right. So then I rang Lucy and of course she was *thrilled* to hear me and I suggested we have lunch and so we did!' .

'You had lunch with Cornelius's wife?'

'Yes, I did. Today. She's very nice. I liked her. She's very pretty in a washed-out, Mia Farrow sort of way; wonderful voice, very soft and low. We had a lovely chat about the good old days and then I said I thought it might be possible that she was married to my sister's boyfriend—'

'Rose,' Katrina said sternly, 'do you realise you've been completely out of order? Cornelius is a very private person. I'm not at all sure he would be happy with you ferreting about like this.'

'I don't care. What I do care about is your happiness and if I can stop you making a huge mistake it's worth incurring his anger. I always thought there was something funny about Cornelius.'

'Rose, I do not want to hear a long list of grievances from an estranged wife, and this whole conversation is making me feel very uncomfortable.'

'Katty, this is important. I am going to tell you why Lucy walked out on Cornelius. And once you've heard, I doubt very much if you'll want to see him any more.'

For many years now, Katrina's brain had harboured two angels, a red one and a white one. Both were ever ready to offer advice and, generally, the latter proved far wiser than the former. When Paul had asked Katrina to marry him, the white angel suggested that a man who had already been engaged three times in the last four years might not be the steadiest of husbands. When Katrina had fallen in love with Lewis, the white angel queried the credibility of a man who refused to be seen outside her house with her. Now, right on cue, the white angel was on hand to help. 'Tell Rose you don't want to hear any more. Tell Rose you are happy to wait for Cornelius to tell you about his life in his own time.'

'Rose,' Katrina said, 'how do you know this woman is reliable? She left her husband so she's hardly likely to speak with any sort of impartiality. For all you know, she might have told you a pack of lies.'

'She's not bright enough to tell lies,' Rose said. 'She never was. And besides, she was genuinely upset. You should have seen her cry when she showed me the photo of their son.'

'Cornelius doesn't have any children.'

'I *thought* he told you that!' Rose crowed. 'I told Lucy I thought he told you that! Of course, that just set her off crying again.'

'I can't remember if he *did* tell me that. I just assumed . . .'

'Katty, what sort of relationship do you have with this man? How can you not know whether or not your boyfriend has children?'

'Cornelius doesn't like talking about himself.'

'Well, I can see why! He doesn't like talking about himself because he knew you'd be horrified if you knew what he's really like. The man had a son. I saw the photo. He was called Leo and he looked just like his father. He would be twenty-three now.'

'Two years older than Susie.' Katrina frowned. 'What do you mean, he *would* be twenty-three?'

'He died,' Rose said. 'He died about fifteen months ago. Cornelius was with him when it happened. They'd all been out to dinner to celebrate Leo's degree results. He'd just heard he'd got a first. The next morning Cornelius and Leo walked down to the florist's to get some flowers for Lucy; it was her birthday or something. They were outside the shop when Leo collapsed and fell. I gather Cornelius tried mouth-to-mouth but it was no good. He just died.'

'*Why?* What happened? Was it a heart attack?'

'Lucy said it was something called Sudden Adult Death Syndrome—it's the grown-up equivalent of cot death, apparently, a sort of instantaneous heart failure. It's pretty rare and it was just jolly rotten luck.'

'Yes.' Katrina swallowed. 'I can't imagine how they could bear it.'

'Well, Lucy couldn't,' Rose said flatly. 'She told me that all she could remember of the first few weeks was lying on Leo's bed all day and crying into his pillow. But your dear boyfriend was completely useless. He refused to talk about Leo, he didn't even try to comfort poor Lucy. And then, to cap it all, he came home one day and told her he was taking two months off work so they could go and visit the Far East.'

'He probably thought it would do them good to get away.'

'It was a *crass* idea. Cornelius knew very well that Leo was planning to go to Vietnam and places. It was the most incredibly tactless thing to suggest, and Lucy was in no state to go anywhere anyway. She says she told him all this and all he said was that he'd go on his own. And he did! He left his wife, who was having a complete nervous breakdown, and he buggered off to Thailand or wherever without her!'

'He obviously needed to go.'

'We all *need* lots of things; it doesn't mean we can have them! In a proper marriage, each partner will respect the *needs* of the other.'

Rose never failed to amaze Katrina. For a woman who had raised selfishness to an art form, such outrageous self-righteousness, such blatant hypocrisy could only be responded to with speechlessness.

'So, anyway,' Rose said, 'he goes away and leaves Lucy entirely on her own, even though he knows very well she might do something dreadful to herself. Her friends, of course, were appalled by his behaviour and Lucy says they saved her. One of them persuaded her to come and join her in some interior-design business and Lucy says it kept her sane. And now she's doing voice-overs and is making good money for the first time in her life. Anyway, Cornelius finally came home after a couple of months and Lucy told him it was over. Can you blame her?'

'I don't know. I'm sure she thought she was completely in the right but even you must realise she's not going to have an objective opinion. Can you imagine anything worse than watching your child die? Cornelius must have been in the most terrible state.'

'I'm sure he was. That doesn't excuse the fact that he failed to take any notice of the fact that his *wife* was in a terrible state.'

'Rose,' Katrina said, 'I really don't feel happy talking about this. I feel disloyal. And, anyway, I have to go. I'm cooking supper.'

'But you said you had something to tell me about you and Cornelius?'

'Oh,' said Katrina, 'I can't remember now. It can't have been very important.'

'Well,' said Rose darkly, 'don't say I didn't warn you.'

Katrina switched off the phone, leaned back against the cushions and shut her eyes. She could *see* Cornelius and his son walking purposefully down the road, intent on their mission . . . And then, when it happened, she could imagine all too clearly the bewilderment, the panic and, finally, the terror Cornelius must have felt as he watched his son dying in front of him . . . Oh, it was horrible, horrible!

Rose's revelation was like a persistent tummyache. At the most unlikely moments Katrina would be attacked by a twinge of discomfort. She was at a very boring meeting on Tuesday morning when her eyes suddenly filled up, and on Wednesday Carol was telling her about the flat that she and Douglas just *had* to have, when a crystal-clear image of Cornelius in front of a florist's came into her mind.

All in all, it was a relief to meet Amy for lunch on Thursday. They had a pleasant time dreaming up subversive responses to Andrew Tennyson's latest email. Andrew Tennyson was in the conveyancing department and this year he was organising the forthcoming bonding weekend in Essex. He had sent out an email asking each partner to prepare an individual party piece with which to entertain their colleagues at the end of the three-course dinner.

'I think the whole "party piece" idea stinks,' Katrina said. 'It's all right for people like Andrew who love standing up and showing off. I shall have nightmares for weeks about it.'

'I had a nightmare last night,' Amy said. 'I dreamt I blew up Eddy's motorbike.'

Katrina laughed. 'That sounds more like a wish-fulfilment dream. On the positive side, it's nice that he's found a new passion.'

'Not if it's going to kill him. The thing terrifies me. I'm sure they both think I'm utterly pathetic. I suspect Stephen can't understand why his father married such a sad old woman.'

'Forty-nine is not old.'

'It is to Stephen. Do you realise his mother is ten years younger than me? I catch him looking at me sometimes and I know what he's thinking. He's wondering what on earth his father ever saw in me.'

'That is rubbish and, what's worse, it is paranoid rubbish.'

Amy gave a bleak smile. 'I feel so *old* at the moment. I feel old beside Stephen and Eddy. I wish I didn't, that's all.' She moved her plate and put her elbows on the table. 'Right. We've talked quite enough about me. What about *you*? What is happening in your life?'

'Susie was on the phone to Ash last night. Only twenty minutes.'

'But they're still just friends?'

'So Susie says. She hardly ever mentions the late, unlamented Liam any more so I should be grateful. I just have this awful feeling of doom whenever she mentions Ash's name. And poor Ollie is still sad about Sophie. He is definitely smitten. I've been dreading him going off on his travels but now I'm counting the days. At least when he's in Thailand or India or Africa or wherever he decides to go, he'll have lots of new experiences to distract him. I wish I was going away somewhere.'

'You are going somewhere,' Amy pointed out. 'Have you forgotten our exciting night at the Green Ring Hotel in three weeks' time? You and me and our sexy colleagues bonding like mad over all the hilarious party pieces?'

In bed that night, Katrina's mind was far too active for sleep. She had had another email from Cornelius, telling her about an upcoming radio programme on the Vercors. Katrina had planned to fire off a reply but found that she could write nothing. As long as she didn't acknowledge her awareness of his tragedy, she knew she could not recapture the ease that characterised her dealings with him. After supper, she had sat down at her desk and, having struggled with numerous, ever more convoluted efforts, she had written one final version.

Dear Cornelius,
It appears that your wife and Rose were at school together.
They met for lunch recently and Lucy told her about your son, and Rose
told me. I just wanted to say how sorry I was.
Love, Katrina

She didn't hear from him for nearly a week. His email was short.

Thank you for your condolences.
Cornelius

Condolences: such a cold and formal word. The more Katrina read
that sentence, the more it seemed to her that Cornelius had in effect
terminated their friendship. Intensely private as he was, he must have
judged that she had transgressed the boundary. It was absurd to use a
word like betrayal in this context—after all, she had simply listened to
her sister's account of a conversation with Lucy—but a part of her felt
that she deserved to forfeit his confidence. Perhaps it was that sense of
guilt that had stopped her from telling Rose that her relationship with
Cornelius was over. How ironic that this was now almost certainly true.
She had exiled herself from the small circle of his trusted friends. She
was not sure why this upset her so much. All she knew was the bloody
red angel had won again.

CHAPTER SIX

A Disgruntled Ex-Husband and an Angry Sister

KATRINA HAD BEEN PLANNING to ring her ex-husband for a fortnight now.
She didn't ring him very often. Usually, it was to remind him of important dates like the children's birthdays. Invariably, Paul's partner,
Clarrie, would answer the phone and would regale Katrina with the
latest list of Paul's inadequacies as a father, all of which Katrina would
hear with sympathy. Tonight, she got Paul.

'That's weird,' he said. 'It must be telepathy. I was about to ring you.'
'Very weird,' Katrina said. 'Paul, I want to talk to you about—'
'Clarrie's left me. Three days ago, she left me.'

'Oh.' Katrina pulled out the chair by her desk and sat down.

'She's broken my heart. You can't imagine how I feel.'

'Well, actually,' Katrina said, 'I can. You probably feel how I felt when *you* left *me*.'

'You don't understand,' Paul said. 'She's taken the children.'

'The *children*?'

'My daughter and my unborn son. I mean, I left Rachel to be with her.'

'I seem to remember,' Katrina said, 'that you left Rachel and your son, Caspar, to be with Clarrie. Before that you left Ruth and your sons, Crispin and Bertie, to be with Rachel. Before that you left me and—'

'The point is,' Paul said, 'no one's ever left *me* before. You wouldn't believe the things Clarrie said to me. She's been so cruel and vindictive. I've never been cruel. Do you remember when I told you I was leaving you? Do you remember I bought you a lovely bunch of flowers?'

'You did. You also told me I was like a comfortable pair of old slippers. You said Ruth was like a pair of high heels and at your particular stage in life what you needed was high heels.'

'Well,' said Paul, 'there you are. At least that's not cruel.'

'Paul,' Katrina said, 'as a matter of urgent information, I must tell you that no woman wants to be compared to a pair of old slippers.'

'I don't know how the stupid hob works,' Paul said plaintively. 'I keep burning my food. I'm a wreck, Kat. I look terrible.'

'I'm sorry. Perhaps Clarrie will come home soon.'

'She won't. She said such terrible things.' He gave an incredulous laugh. 'She even told me I was hopeless in bed.'

'Really?'

'I know. Can you believe it?' He paused. 'I'm not hopeless. Am I?'

'No . . . Well . . . No.'

There was another pause. 'That's not exactly the ringing endorsement I was looking for.'

'Paul, I don't think Clarrie left you because of your sexual technique. I think she probably left you because she felt you weren't giving her much support. Perhaps you should ring her, go and see her . . .'

'No way,' said Paul. 'She left me, remember? I'm not going to crawl to her. I've been thinking a lot lately. I really miss you and Susie and Ollie. You know it's my birthday in three weeks? I'd really like my family about me then.'

'Which one?' Katrina asked. 'You have so many.'

'Don't pretend to be obtuse, Kat, it doesn't suit you. Rachel and

Caspar are in Madrid. Ruth won't let Crispin and Bertie near me. As far as I'm concerned, you and Susie and Ollie are my proper family now. Will you come and stay for my birthday?'

'I can't. I'm going off to a conference in Essex. I'm not sure about the children. I know Cam will be staying here—'

'Who's Cam?'

'Oh, for goodness' sake, Paul, you know who Cam is. She's my sister's daughter and she's helping to organise a fashion shoot in Greenwich that week. I don't suppose she'll mind being on her own for a bit. I'm sure Ollie and Susie will try and get over to you if they can.'

'Will you tell them to ring me? And tell them I really need them right now, tell them I'm right at the edge. By the way, why did you ring me?'

'I can't remember. It can't have been that important.'

'Kat, was I really hopeless in bed?'

Katrina sighed. 'No. You were a tiger.'

Over supper that night, Katrina told Susie and Ollie about their father's misfortune. She was not entirely surprised to find they were less than sympathetic. Susie said they had always wondered how Clarrie could put up with him. Katrina said that was all very well but it didn't alter the fact that Paul was very unhappy and needed their support. 'He wants us to go and stay with him on his birthday. I've got this beastly conference weekend in Essex so *I* can't go. I know it's a pain but if you don't go, he'll have his wretched birthday all on his own.'

'If we do go,' Susie pointed out, 'all three of us will have a wretched weekend. The house will be a tip and he'll want me to do all the cooking. And I'll have done a full day's work at the hotel.'

'But he's so looking forward to seeing you. It's only for a weekend.'

Susie gave a theatrical groan. 'My weekends are very precious. If we do go, I'm not getting him a birthday present. I can't afford one.'

'Your father won't mind about presents. He'll be happy that you've made the effort to go and see him.' Noting the stony silence that followed this assurance, she thought it best to change the subject. 'Anyway,' she said brightly, 'what are you both doing this weekend?'

'I'm going to Nick's party,' Ollie said gloomily.

'Won't that be fun?'

'Mum!' Susie admonished. 'How could you forget? Nick is going out with the love of Ollie's life!'

'You may mock,' Ollie said with dignity, 'but actually she is.'

'If you ask me,' Susie said, rising from her chair and collecting the plates, 'if Sophie prefers Nick to you, she doesn't deserve to be the love of your life. Nick is so pleased with himself. He always has been. I remember him at school. Yuck! Just promise me, Ollie, you won't spend the whole night staring wistfully at Sophie.'

'I'm not quite that sad,' he said. He got up and went to the fridge. 'Anyone for a yoghurt?'

'Yes, please,' said Susie. 'I'll get the spoons.'

Katrina looked hopefully towards her daughter. 'I thought I'd get a film out on Saturday. I want to see *Little Miss Sunshine*. What about it, Susie?'

Susie returned to her seat and yawned. 'I'd love to but I'm going to meet Ash in the afternoon. He wants me to help him buy a birthday present for his sister.'

'Oh,' said Katrina, 'that's a pity.'

'A pity I can't watch a film with you or a pity I'm going out with Ash?'

'That's very unfair. I didn't say a thing.'

'You don't have to, Mum, you're *so* transparent! Ash and I are friends. If I can forgive him for upsetting me, isn't it time you did?'

'I just . . .' Katrina paused. 'I just don't want you to get hurt, that's all.'

'I have no intention of getting hurt! Ollie, are you bringing those yoghurts over or not?'

Ollie brought them over and sat down. 'I rang Cornelius today,' he said.

His intervention had the desired effect. Katrina lost all interest in Ash and stared at her son. 'Why?' she asked.

'There was nothing to do at work and I was plotting my travel itinerary. I've lost the piece of paper with Cornelius's suggestions on it so I gave him a ring. I asked him to lunch on Sunday.'

'You did what? Really, Ollie, you might have asked me first. I'm sure he has much better things to do with his time. What did he say?'

'He said he was sure *you* had better things to do with your time than cook for him. So I said you wanted him to come round.'

'Well, really, Ollie, why did you say that?'

'Because otherwise he wouldn't have agreed to come and I need to talk to him.'

'Do you mean he said he *would* come?'

'Yes. Why wouldn't he? That's all right, isn't it?'

When the doorbell rang on Sunday, Katrina could feel her face go crimson. She was glad that Ollie was on hand to let Cornelius in. As he came down the stairs, she busied herself by checking the roast chicken.

At least, she reassured herself, Cornelius could assume that her heightened colour was due to the heat from the oven.

Once again, he had brought flowers and wine and dismissed her embarrassed thanks with an easy, 'Please, Katrina, I am happy to bring them. It is so kind of you to feed me.'

'Mum loves feeding people,' Ollie said.

'Well, I enjoy being fed,' Cornelius responded. He gave Katrina a warm smile. 'It is very good to see you again.'

'Cornelius,' Ollie said, 'I've got the atlas out. Can I show you my latest ideas?'

Cornelius followed Ollie over to the table while Katrina stirred the gravy and steamed the spinach. She was happy, quite ridiculously so. Cornelius had smiled at her and she saw they were still friends. He was not cross with her, he was not cross at all.

Relief made her talkative. Over lunch she flitted from subject to subject. She talked about her love of Greenwich and the Argentinian delicatessen round the corner. She talked about Carol at work. She was about to give her views on the condition of the welfare state when Cornelius suddenly raised a hand.

'I have something to say,' he said. 'I can't believe I forgot about it.' He turned to Susie. 'The other day I was talking to my wife,' he said, pronouncing the last two words a little self-consciously. 'I told her about you. She rang me yesterday. She has a friend who's involved in a new production. I gather it's a horror film . . . aliens taking over humans. Lucy says there's one scene where the hero visits his dentist and, as he goes in, he smiles at the sweet young dental nurse and she says, "Please come this way." She only has the one line; it's important because she says it in a very unusual manner—you know, a menacing but distant sort of manner so the hero knows that she has been taken over. Anyway, the point is, Lucy has arranged for you to go along to an audition for the part. The audition's next Thursday afternoon in Soho. I don't know if you can get time off work but—'

'Of course I can!' Susie breathed. 'Oh, Cornelius, this is so exciting. Thank you so much! You are so *good*!'

Cornelius looked a little taken aback by such effusiveness. 'Well, it's only one line and Lucy organised it. I simply told her about you.' He reached into his jacket pocket and pulled out a folded piece of paper. 'I've written down the details and also the line you have to say—'

'"Please come this way." I know, I shall practise and practise it!' Susie leapt up. 'Mum, do you mind if I get down? I must make some phone calls. Cornelius, please thank your wife!' And she was gone.

'Well,' Katrina said. 'Susie will think of nothing else until next Thursday.' She smiled at Cornelius. 'You've made her very happy.'

'She might not get the part,' Cornelius warned.

'I think she'll get it,' said Ollie. He gave a significant nod. 'I have a feeling this week that the Latham luck is changing.'

Katrina, knowing what was required of her, said, 'Why do you think that, Ollie?'

'Last night,' Ollie said, 'Sophie and Nick split up. I don't know why.' He caught sight of the clock and pushed back his chair. 'Mum, I said I'd meet George in town. I've got to go. Cornelius, thanks for all your help. Come and have lunch with us next Sunday!'

There was a slightly awkward silence after Ollie's departure and then Katrina and Cornelius both spoke at once.

Katrina said, 'Do come to lunch next week!'

Cornelius said, 'You must be very irritated by your son's kind habit of asking me to lunch with you. I assure you I don't take it seriously. It's been a lovely afternoon, however. I was *going* to ask if I might take you out to dinner next week.'

Katrina laughed. She could see now that he had been worried she had been bounced into inviting him today. 'Dear Cornelius, you do not have to take me out to dinner. I love having you to lunch and it's perfectly clear the children do too. I do it every week, and one more is no bother at all. Of course you must come next Sunday!'

'Well,' said Cornelius, 'thank you very much. Let me clear the table.' He stood up and began to collect the pudding bowls. 'Have you seen Rose and Lewis lately?'

'No,' said Katrina, 'and I don't want to either.' She was glad he had brought up Lewis. It reminded her of his kindness to her, his support-iveness. Since he had brought up the subject of Lewis she felt it was all right to bring up Lucy. 'I gather you're on speaking terms with your wife, then?'

'Oh, yes,' said Cornelius. 'It's all much better now. We're going for the two-year separation and consent route.'

'I'm so glad.' Katrina spooned coffee into the cafetière. 'Did you know that Rose told her you and I were—were an item?'

'Yes,' said Cornelius. 'Yes, Lucy told me that.' He carried the bowls over to the island unit and cleared his throat. 'I meant to tell you, the other day I was in the National Portrait Gallery with my niece, Juliet's daughter, Jenny—she's an art historian and is doing her best to educate me—and we saw a portrait of Mary Shelley.'

'I'd like to see it,' Katrina said. She was sure that Cornelius had indeed meant to tell her this. She was also sure he had brought it up *now*, because he had wanted to change the subject. She and Cornelius might be friends but it was clear that he was still not prepared to discuss his private life with her.

At work the next day, three new jobs landed on Katrina's desk. They were all potentially lucrative, which was good, and they all needed to be done as soon as possible, which was bad.

Amy dropped by at twelve and said, 'Any chance of lunch today?'

'Sorry.' Katrina shook her head. 'I've ordered a sandwich. I'm up to my eyes at the moment. Let's have lunch on Wednesday.'

'You're on!' Amy waved and left.

Twenty minutes later, her phone went. 'Ms Latham?' It was Rebecca from reception. 'I have your sister here and she wonders if you'd like to meet her for lunch.'

Katrina sighed. 'Will you tell her I'd love to but I have far too much work at the moment. Tell her I'll ring her this evening.'

She heard Rebecca's prim voice relaying the fact that, unfortunately, Ms Latham was too busy for lunch, and then she heard Rose's voice, loud and furious: 'You tell Ms Latham that I won't MOVE from here until she comes down and tells me if she was EVER planning to let me know that MY boyfriend is the father of HER SON?'

There was an appalled silence. At last, Katrina heard Rebecca's voice again. 'Ms Latham, your sister says—'

Katrina stood up. 'I heard,' she said. 'I'm coming down.'

Will you stop frog-marching me out of the building?' Rose demanded. 'And you're hurting my arm!'

'I don't care,' Katrina hissed. She tightened her hold on her sister's arm and marched her purposefully down the street. 'I have spent *years* building up a solid reputation at work and you have just blown it to pieces in two seconds. It will be all round the office in five minutes that I've been involved in God knows what.'

'You *have* been involved in God knows what and . . . Where exactly are we going? We've just passed a perfectly adequate wine bar.'

'We are going to the Embankment Gardens.'

'I don't want to go to the gardens; I want to have some lunch.'

'Well, tough. If you think I'm going to sit in an enclosed space while you're in this mood, you are very much mistaken. We will go to the gardens, we will have a conversation and then I will go back to work. How *dare* you make a scene like that in front of Rebecca of all people, flinging ludicrous accusations about—'

'Are you saying none of it's true? Are you saying my boyfriend is *not* the father of your son?'

'No, I am saying that he was *not* your boyfriend when he *became* the father of my son and . . . How did you find out, anyway?'

'If you'd just slow down a bit, I'll tell you. And you can let go of my arm now. I expect there'll be a huge bruise tomorrow.'

Katrina let go of Rose's arm.

'Thank you.' Rose straightened the sleeve of her jacket. 'If you must know, on Sunday afternoon, Lewis and I visited his mother and—Katty, will you please *slow down*?—in her sitting room there was a large framed photograph of her grandmother. She wore her hair up and the photo was in profile and she was wearing a high-necked dress like Victorians do, or did, or do I mean the Edwardians? Anyway, the point is, I was drawn to it like a moth to—what *is* it that moths are drawn to?'

'Flames.'

'Yes, well, I was drawn to it like a moth to a flame. I mean, it was bizarre. There was this lady from some bygone era, sitting in profile, and she was the spitting image of Ollie! She had his nose with the funny little dip in the middle, his eyebrows, his chin . . . It was like looking at Ollie in drag. I thought it was too funny for words and I pointed out the likeness to Lewis and he could see it right away. And Lewis just stopped talking. I had to make all the conversation, which was not easy, and Lewis kept staring at the photograph. And then we drove back and Lewis asked me when Ollie was born and I said it was a few months after your horrible husband left you, and he looked . . . he looked so odd. I knew something was wrong and I kept insisting he tell me, and finally he confessed he had once had a fling with you and . . . Why didn't you *tell* me, Katty? How could you *abuse* my hospitality like that? You were out in France, at my invitation and—'

'I went out to France because you told me your children would be frolicking with their partners and you wanted some company. So I get on the ferry and you text me to tell me you are madly in love and frolicking yourself! What am I supposed to do? Should I arrive at your house and tell you the new love of your life is an ex-lover of mine who happens to be the father of my son? Would *you* do that?'

'Yes,' said Rose.

Katrina sighed. 'Yes,' she agreed. 'You probably would.'

'And another thing,' Rose said. 'Why didn't you tell me ages ago? I'm not a prude, I would have understood. If I'd been married to Paul, who is a complete bastard, I'd have been as unfaithful as I could be.'

'I was *not* unfaithful to Paul. I met Lewis two weeks after Paul left me. And then Lewis left me a few weeks after that. In fact, he left me the day after I found I was pregnant. I didn't tell *you* about it for the same reason I didn't tell any of my friends. I had been a fool, I had been humiliated and I didn't feel like broadcasting my humiliation.'

'So you let poor Paul believe he was the father?'

'"Poor Paul"? I thought you said he was a complete bastard?'

'Even bastards,' Rose said piously, 'deserve to be told the truth.'

'I *did* tell him the truth. I told him what happened. He was very kind. He said he'd take responsibility—'

'Excuse me,' said Rose, 'but when has your ex-husband ever taken responsibility for anything? Did he ever contribute a penny?'

'You know he didn't, but it was still kind of him to pretend to be Ollie's father. Sometimes I think he's forgotten he *isn't* Ollie's father.'

'Well, that doesn't surprise me. Most of the time Paul seems to forget he's anyone's father. Have you told him about all of this?'

'No. I was going to. I even got as far as ringing him but . . . he's going through a difficult time right now.'

'Paul is the sort of man who spends his life going through difficult times. Oh, thank heavens, there's a bench by that tree. I have to sit down, Katty, my shoes are killing me.'

Katrina glanced at her watch. 'Ten minutes,' she said.

Rose fell onto the bench, and began rubbing her feet. 'Come and sit down!' She waited until her sister joined her and then looked at her enquiringly. 'Were you in love with him?'

'Who?'

'Lewis, of course. Were you in love with him?'

'Yes, I suppose I was.'

'Do you want to talk about it?'

'Not really.'

'Why didn't you tell him you were pregnant?'

'I was going to. I'd made a special supper. Then he told me it was over and it didn't seem . . . appropriate.'

'He's stunned, Katty. You can imagine it: one moment he has no children and the next he finds he's the father of his girlfriend's handsome teenage nephew. You can see why he's stunned.'

'Yes,' said Katrina, 'I can see that.'

'He's going to ring you. And he wants to see Ollie.'

'He can't. Not yet. Tell him he can't.'

'Katty, he's his *father*. You're going to have to let him see his son.'

'Not yet. I'll have to speak to Paul first and I'll have to speak to Ollie. Tell him he'll have to wait a bit.'

'All right. I still can't believe you never said anything. You are such a secretive person. I'll tell you something that will make you feel better.'

Katrina blinked. 'What's that?'

'I've forgiven Lewis for everything.' She gave her sister a benevolent smile. 'And I forgive you too.'

'Thank you,' Katrina said. 'That *does* make me feel better.'

Katrina set a fast and furious pace back to the office. When she arrived at her destination, she went straight upstairs without even a cursory nod at Rebecca. She was going to concentrate on her work, she was going to complete all the tasks she had set herself and she was not going to think about Lewis or Rose or Ollie until she went home.

Her reward, when she finally walked out onto the street at a quarter past seven, was a crushing headache.

For once she was glad the house was empty when she got home. Susie was doing a late shift at the hotel and, judging by the empty pizza carton on the table, Ollie had eaten and gone out. Katrina took herself to bed. She would have to ring Paul, she would have to talk to Lewis and at some point she would have to talk to Ollie. But not yet. Not yet. She needed advice, she needed . . . and it suddenly became quite clear . . . she needed to talk to Cornelius.

She rang him before she could have second thoughts. 'Cornelius,' she said. 'I'm sorry to bother you. Are you watching television?'

'No,' Cornelius said, 'and you're not bothering me at all.'

'You're not eating your dinner?'

'No, I was practising my guitar. I am very pleased to be interrupted.'

'Thank you.' Katrina took a deep breath. 'I want to ask your advice about something. I've had some news which might—which *will* be upsetting to members of my family. If I . . . if I sit on it for a while I might be able to think of a way of . . . of making it sound more palatable, but the danger is that then someone else might break the news. You must think this all sounds very mysterious and I'm sorry I can't tell you anything more at the moment . . .'

'You don't need to,' Cornelius said. 'I think the answer is quite clear. If this news is going to come out in the end, you might as well be the one to announce it and you should do it as soon as possible. If you don't, you'll only get more and more upset about the prospect.'

Katrina gave a little sigh and twisted a lock of her hair round her index finger. 'Thank you,' she said at last. 'I knew you would help.'

As she walked into Parters, Sorenson and Company, Katrina was careful to establish eye contact with Rebecca and give her a serenely smiling, 'Good morning, Rebecca.' Katrina worked hard throughout the day, responding to anyone who approached her with a steely smile and a significant glance at her watch. She left the office at seven and rang Susie to tell her she would be late home.

'I'll make supper,' Susie said. 'I'll do some pasta.'

'You're wonderful,' Katrina said. 'Is Ollie in tonight?'

'Yes. Why?'

'No reason,' Katrina said. 'I'll see you later.' Perhaps Susie would go out later. Perhaps she would have a chance to talk to Ollie, to pave the way. How *would* she pave the way for the revelation that she, his mother, had lied about his parentage from day one?

At home, the reason for Susie's readiness to cook was soon apparent. Over the tagliatelle and mushrooms, she announced to her mother and brother that she needed their help. 'I've been working on my audition,' she said, 'and I realise I have to convey two messages. I mean, I know I should appear to look like a sweet, attractive young dental nurse but at the same time I have to invest "Please come this way" with an undercurrent of menace and a lack of humanity so that the hero is almost certain, but not totally certain, that I am now an alien. I wish I had time to go and do some research—'

'Into aliens?' enquired Ollie. 'Do you know any?'

'Into dental nurses, stupid! But I haven't got time so it doesn't matter. I reckon there are three possible ways of doing it and I want you to give your opinion on each of them. This is Number One.' She stood up, cleared her throat and fixed Ollie with a seductive smoulder.

'Please'—she flicked her hair back—'come this . . . way.'

Ollie took his plate over to the stove. 'I think that's probably the worst impersonation of a dental nurse I've ever seen,' he said. 'You look like that girl in the advert who keeps flicking her hair back and jumping in puddles because she's so happy to have her own hairspray.'

'OK,' said Susie, 'this is Number Two.' She fixed her eyes on the French windows. 'Please—come—this—way.'

Ollie gave a decisive shake of the head. 'No,' he said. 'You sound like a robot. It's far too obvious.'

'All right,' said Susie. 'This is Number Three.' This time she favoured Ollie with an enchanting smile and said sweetly, 'Please come this way.'

'Better,' Katrina said. 'But I don't think you should smile. I think you should look straight at the patient and speak very seriously. What do you think, Ollie?'

'Well,' said Ollie, 'there's a James Bond film on ITV4 in a few minutes and I'm pretty sure there's a dental nurse in the plot . . .'

Katrina could, of course, confide in Amy but she knew she would not. They had been friends for years, during which time Katrina had had three unhappy and humiliating love affairs. She had told Amy about none of these relationships for the same reason that she would not talk about her current crisis concerning Ollie. Katrina had a reputation at work—at least, she thought bitterly, she *had* a reputation until Rose's appalling outburst—for being a woman who managed her life as successfully as she managed her career. Since Katrina believed that her personal life, apart from her children, comprised a series of spectacularly wrong decisions, it was important to her that in the office she could count on the respect of her peers. Cornelius was an exception in that he had witnessed her in meltdown, and she assumed that that was why she had contemplated seeking his advice. Amy was different. Katrina had no wish to reveal the extent of the mess she had brought upon herself.

Consequently, at lunch on Wednesday, when Amy told her with a quizzical eye that rumours were flying round the office, she merely laughed and said, 'I knew they would be. Rebecca's eyes were practically gleaming on Monday. My sister discovered I'd once had a fling with Lewis and started acting like I was still having an affair with him.'

'Has she calmed down now? How did she find out?'

'From Lewis. I should have told her before but it's the sort of thing that gets more difficult to reveal the longer you leave it . . . The whole thing is so annoying, I don't even like to talk about it.'

'Well, in that case,' Amy said briskly, 'let's change the subject. Eddy has come up with a brilliant idea for our cabaret piece at the bonding weekend—'

'*Our* cabaret piece? Are we doing it together?'

'Yes, we are! I was ranting to Eddy about the cabaret turns and he ran out of the room and came back with his book of favourite film dialogues. You and I are going to perform the final scene from *Some Like It Hot*—you know, the one where Jack Lemmon in drag tries to tell his millionaire admirer that he cannot marry him, and finally whips off his wig and tells him he's a man, and the millionaire shrugs that nobody's perfect.'

'Brilliant!' said Katrina. 'And you can introduce it by delivering a little lecture about the dangers of chasing impossible targets!'

'I thought you could do that. Why don't we go up together?'

'Great,' said Katrina. 'I'll drive. We can practise on the journey.'

At home that evening, Susie was out, doing an extra shift to make up for her absence the following afternoon. Having ascertained that Ollie was staying in, Katrina decided that tonight she would try to broach the subject of Lewis.

Over dinner, Ollie chatted about the tedium of his job, Katrina told him about Amy's suggestion for their cabaret piece, and all the time she felt her heart beating faster and faster. Finally, she sat back and said, 'Ollie, it's so interesting, watching you and Susie growing up. It makes me remember my own youth and all the mistakes I made . . .'

'Actually, Mum,' Ollie said earnestly, 'I want to talk to you about that.'

Katrina blinked. 'You want to talk to me about my youth?'

'Yes. When you were young, did you ever go out with a boy who'd been like . . . like, you know, like a *friend*?'

Katrina sighed and realised they were talking about Sophie. 'I did,' she said, 'when I was seventeen. He was a good friend too, but I think I always secretly fancied him. He was called Paul.'

'Paul?' Ollie sounded disappointed. 'It was Dad?'

He's not your dad, actually. Actually, Ollie, your dad is . . . 'No, it was another Paul. We went out for two weeks and then he said he didn't want to risk losing our friendship by being romantically involved.'

The phone rang and they both jumped. 'I'll get it,' Ollie said.

Katrina poured herself another glass of wine and heard her son say, 'Really? Great! Great! Thanks, George, I'll be there in five minutes.' He put down the phone and smiled at Katrina. 'I've got to go, Mum. George has sighted Sophie in the Rat and Fiddle. I'll see you later!'

Katrina heard the front door slam and felt her heartbeat return to normal. She wasn't sure whether she was glad or sorry that Ollie had been called away.

The phone rang again and Katrina heard a voice say, 'Hello, Katrina,' and felt her heart start up its crazy dance again.

'Hello, Lewis,' she said.

From: katrinalatham@parter.co.uk
To: cornhedge@winemart.co.uk
Sent: October 19, 21:15

Dear Cornelius,
I am very sorry but something has come up and I won't be able to give you lunch on Sunday. I have to go out. I am consequently in the doghouse with my children who are not only annoyed that their mother will not be cooking the only good meal of the week but are also sad to be missing you. I suspect Ollie wanted to bore you with yet more location possibilities for his big adventure and Susie wanted to tell you about her audition. She's pretty sure she didn't get the part; she says there was a girl there who was a combination of Gwyneth Paltrow, Julia Roberts and Katie Holmes, none of whom I suspect you have heard of. The audition was held in some fusty old building in Soho and Susie loved every minute of it. She was told she would hear next week and I'll let you know what happens. Sorry again about Sunday.
Love, K

From: cornhedge@winemart.co.uk
To: katrinalatham@parter.co.uk
Sent: 20 October, 09:06

Dear Katrina,
I am sorry I won't be seeing you on Sunday. Do tell Ollie I am happy to give him advice without the lure of an invitation to Sunday lunch. He can ring me at any time. I am glad Susie enjoyed her audition and I shall keep my fingers crossed for her. I have heard of Julia Roberts and Gwyneth Paltrow but not Katie Holmes. Should I have done?
Yours, Cornelius

Katrina woke early on Saturday morning and tried, without success, to return to unconsciousness. Eventually, she gave up trying. Damn Lewis, she thought, damn Rose, damn everyone.

After she got up, she put on an old Pulp CD—Jarvis Cocker's 'Common People' had to be the best record of all time—and got to work, cleaning the kitchen. She only stopped when Susie came in, complaining that she *really* didn't feel like working today.

After Susie had gone, Katrina went out into the garden and ruthlessly pruned the buddleia in the back flowerbed. When she'd finished, it resembled a Bruce Willis haircut. After that, she lost the urge to attack anything else and she returned to the house. She stood in the middle of her kitchen, unable to summon much enthusiasm for anything and unsure what to do. She wished she could be like Ollie, who possessed an enviable ability to sleep until midday.

This was unbearable! Cornelius was right. She had to speak out as soon as possible. She would go and buy a nice lunch for the two of them and then she would come home, wake Ollie and sit by his bed and tell him the circumstances of his birth in a calm manner.

She splashed out on half a dozen slices of prosciutto and a large tub of ricotta cheese and returned home, practising her forthcoming exposition. She would take his hand and everything would be all right.

Except it wasn't. When she got home, she could hear Ollie in the shower upstairs and when he finally came down, he told her he had to rush as he was taking Sophie out to London Zoo for the day as part of his being-a-good-friend-who-will-become-more campaign. It was obvious that now was not the time to deliver traumatic news.

At lunch, Katrina ate her prosciutto and ricotta in solitude, with only Radio 4's *Any Questions* for company. The last question put to the panel was a query about the most valuable quality in today's society. One of the panel chose honesty.

It was at that point that Katrina lost her appetite. She cleared away her meal, pocketed her house keys, walked out of the house and set off for the park.

Greenwich Park, in Katrina's biased opinion, was the best of London's parks. Not only did it possess undulating slopes and majestic trees, it also boasted the best view in the capital, and it was to this that Katrina made her way. She walked fast and furiously and finally arrived at the top of the hill near the famous Observatory. She sank onto the grass and looked down at the elegant old buildings that flanked the dazzling white Queen's House. Cam's beauty people were right: it would form a perfect backdrop for a fashion shoot.

Katrina lay back on the grass and let herself go over Lewis's phone call on Wednesday. He had been composed and dignified but very determined. He *had* to see her as soon as possible. He suggested a small Italian restaurant in Denmark Street. She had been on the point of asking if Rose was coming when he told her that Rose had decided not to join them since she felt it was a private matter between the two of them. 'Also,' Lewis admitted, 'an old friend has invited her to lunch at the Ivy, and Rose would miss her grandma's funeral for an offer to eat out at the Ivy.' Katrina nobly refrained from informing him that Rose had indeed missed her grandma's funeral two years ago, in order to go to a friend's party in Paris.

Katrina had not wanted to go out on a Sunday—it was the only day she could be sure of seeing both her children, and she didn't like letting Cornelius down—but Lewis had been insistent. He was rehearsing all week and he had promised to attend some function with Rose on Saturday. There was another reason why Katrina was less than happy about waiting till Sunday to see him. She knew that until she met Lewis, every waking moment would be spent obsessing about what he was going to say to her and what she was going to say to him.

Cornelius was right. Life was far simpler if one always told the truth. She wished Cornelius were here now. She would tell him everything about Lewis and Ollie, and he would say something sensible in his dry, succinct manner and somehow she would feel better. On the other hand, of course, he might look at her with distaste and ask her how she could have saddled Ollie with an incompetent fake father when he could have known his real one. At the moment, she could think of no rational justification or even explanation for her conduct. And if *she* couldn't, how the hell would Ollie or Lewis?

Later, back at home, prompted by her conscience, she rang Paul. When Katrina told him, hesitantly, about Lewis, he exploded. What right did a man like that have to swan into Katrina's life and demand his paternal rights when it had been Paul who had shouldered those responsibilities for the last sixteen years and it had been Paul who had cherished the boy as if he were his own? Katrina felt it prudent not to remind him that Ollie was, in fact, eighteen, nor did she suggest that 'cherishing' was perhaps an odd word to apply to occasional phone calls. Instead, she assured him that Ollie's view of Paul would not be affected by the arrival of Lewis. (She was pretty sure *this* was true.) Mollified, Paul proceeded to promulgate his latest theory about his life, which was that he and Katrina would have been far happier if he had never left home. He suggested he came up and spent the evening with her, at which point she forgot her recent decision to tell the truth at all times and invented a pressing engagement.

She woke late the next morning and glanced at her radio clock. Three hours to go. She got out of bed, put on her dressing gown and went downstairs. In the kitchen there was a smell of stale beer and tobacco but the place was tidy. She opened the bin, fished out a collection of beer cans and two bottles of what had been extremely cheap white wine and transferred them to the recycling bin.

She made some coffee and, yawning, wondered who the children had been entertaining late last night. Had Ollie spent the evening as well as the day with Sophie? And what about Susie? I am not going to worry about Susie, she thought. Not today. She took the paper and her mug of coffee to the table and was soon absorbed in an extremely interesting article. The writer suggested that all prime ministers who stayed in office for more than five years went mad. It cited Margaret Thatcher and Tony Blair as evidence and made a pretty persuasive case.

At last, Katrina went upstairs. She emerged from the bathroom forty-five minutes later with the feeling that she had taken her hair, skin and teeth to the dry-cleaner's. Going to her wardrobe, she pulled out the item that had made her conscience act like a diva deprived of her orchestra. On Friday lunchtime, despite an appalling workload, she had gone shopping. The result was a pinkish-grey dress of deceptive simplicity that gave her hips that even Kate Moss (all right, not Kate Moss, but certainly Meryl Streep) would be envious of.

Katrina justified the expense by telling herself that she needed to be confident while confronting Lewis. Her conscience remained unimpressed by this excuse and continued to throw a tantrum.

At twenty to twelve, she went downstairs. Susie was sitting at the table and did not look up from her perusal of the film reviews. 'Did you have a good time yesterday evening?' Katrina asked.

'Great, thanks.'

'I thought I heard you with some friends last night,' Katrina continued carelessly. 'Was there anyone I know?'

'Just friends.' Perhaps Susie was aware of her mother's disappointment with this limited response because she glanced up and immediately whistled. 'Mum, you look wonderful! That's a new dress, isn't it?'

'This?' Katrina said, looking at the garment as if she'd only just noticed she was wearing it. 'Yes, it is quite.'

'Well, it's fabulous! *Who* did you say you were having lunch with?'

'Just an old friend,' Katrina said, feeling herself blush. 'I must go or I'll be late. Help yourselves to anything in the fridge for lunch.'

She arrived at the restaurant to find that Lewis was waiting for her and had already acquired wine and olives.

She walked over to their table and Lewis looked up and fixed her with his blue eyes. 'Wow,' he said, 'you look amazing.'

'Really?' Katrina raised her eyebrows. 'I must say—'

'Just for once,' Lewis said, 'allow me to pay you a compliment without throwing it back in my face.' He poured her a glass of wine. 'I think we should make a toast,' he said. 'To our son.'

Katrina paused and raised her glass. 'To Ollie,' she said.

'Do you know something?' Lewis said. 'I wish I could have a word with my thirty-something self. If I could, I would warn him that he would be crazy to leave you.'

Katrina gave an involuntary laugh. 'That wouldn't work,' she said, 'because *I'd* be telling my twenty-five-year-old self that she should take one look at you and turn on her heel.'

'I would hope,' Lewis said, 'that my thirty-something self might be able to prove that he did possess some redeeming features.'

Katrina wrenched her eyes from his with difficulty and took a supportive gulp of wine. 'That would be difficult,' she said. 'As soon as you realised I had a child you couldn't get out of my house fast enough.'

'I came back, though.'

'Yes, after you'd made up a story that anyone else would have seen through at once. I still can't believe I swallowed it . . . *I'm afraid I can't be seen in public with any women other than my co-star . . .*'

'I was a bastard,' Lewis said. 'But you should still have told me you were pregnant.'

Katrina raised her chin. 'I *was* going to tell you. You probably don't remember the last dinner I cooked for you. I spent a fortune on it. I was about to tell you I was pregnant when you told me you didn't want to see me any more. It didn't seem a good idea to say anything after that.'

'Were you *ever* going to tell me?'

'As a matter of fact, I was. Within minutes of Ollie's birth, I decided that you had a right to know. He was such a beautiful baby! Then Paul came to visit me; he brought grapes and a paper. After he'd gone I picked up the paper and saw a photo of you and Sister Green holding hands at the wedding of your co-star. Whatever happened to Sister Green, by the way?'

'I married her.'

'How nice for you.'

'Not very. She left me five years later. I wasn't a very good husband.' He smiled. 'Shall we study the menu?'

As soon as the waiter had left with their order, Lewis leaned forward. 'What kills me,' he said, 'is that all these years I've had a son growing up just a few miles away from my home. I've missed *so much*! You should have told me.'

Katrina took a hefty slug of wine. 'Lewis,' she said, 'tell me honestly: if, after you told me that your career left you no time to take on any responsibilities, I'd told you I had just discovered I was pregnant by you, would you *truly* have said you were thrilled by the news?'

Lewis opened his mouth and shut it again and shook his head. 'Truly,' he agreed, 'I wouldn't. But it doesn't alter the fact that I'm finding it very difficult to accept that you kept my son's existence secret.'

There was a large lump in Katrina's throat which she removed with a further swig of wine. 'In our very brief relationship,' she said, 'you made it painfully clear that anything to do with children terrified you. It was therefore pretty obvious that if you knew you were a father you would be devastated. Nevertheless, every time I saw you on television, I agonised about my decision not to tell you. I have *never* felt comfortable about the decision I took. So you may have spent the last eighteen years not knowing your son existed but I have spent the last eighteen years worrying about what I had done and what I should do. When I was on that boat to France and Rose texted me that you were going to be there, I felt like . . .' She stopped.

'Tell me. You felt what?'

'I felt as if Nemesis had finally tracked me down. I didn't know what to do. I was in a terrible state. So don't lecture me about keeping silent all these years, because everything you said and did indicated that you were the last person in the world to want to be the father of my baby, and I've had to live with the consequences for a hell of a lot longer than you have.' Her eyes were brimming with tears and she took another slug of wine. Thank God she hadn't driven here.

'Katrina,' Lewis said, 'please don't cry.' He leaned forward and kissed her very gently on the mouth.

'For God's sake!' Katrina exploded. 'What was that for?'

Lewis gave an apologetic smile. 'I can't bear to see women cry.'

Perhaps it was just as well that the waiter arrived at that moment with their first course: bruschetta and artichokes, liberally sprinkled with Parmesan and mint and oozing olive oil. Lewis ordered a bottle of Chianti and Katrina concentrated on the plate in front of her.

'Katrina,' Lewis said, 'I can't say I'm not sad about missing Ollie's childhood but I am absolutely not trying to suggest you were wrong in any way to keep his existence from me. In any case, I'm not interested in recriminations. I am anxious to see my son, that's all.'

'You've seen him already,' Katrina said, wilfully misunderstanding.

'I have. I keep thinking back to Rose's party. I remember telling her what a good-looking nephew she had. Don't you find it *extraordinary* that we should all meet up like this?'

'No, I always had the feeling that you'd turn up again.'

'Did you?' Lewis asked softly.

'Yes. And I don't mean it like you think I do. You imagine me spending my life wistfully clinging to the hope that one day I'd see your bronzed and muscular body once more.'

'Do you really think I have a bronzed and muscular body?'

'Shut up, Lewis. For your information, what I *meant* was that I always felt that one day you'd turn up and find out the truth, so stop looking as if you know you're irresistible, because you're jolly well not.'

'I hate to think I ruined your life,' Lewis said.

'You didn't. I can't imagine my life without Ollie.'

'That's very generous of you.' Lewis leaned forward. 'Look here—'

'Tell me,' Katrina said, 'what are you working on at the moment?'

'Katrina . . .' Lewis paused, gave a light shrug and began to talk about his success in extending his part to a second episode. It was only after he finished that Lewis returned to his major preoccupation.

'Look,' he said, 'I know this is difficult for you but I want to see Ollie. I want to see him soon. I want to see him this week.'

Katrina bit her lip. 'You have to let me tell him about it all first. I'll do it soon.'

'I don't want to put pressure on you but—I'm going mad here. I can't sleep, I can't think. Ollie is my son. *I have a son!* Let me come round one evening this week—'

'No!' Katrina exclaimed. 'Don't do that. I'll tell him. I'll tell him tomorrow and I'll get him to ring you.'

Lewis pulled out a notebook. He tore out a piece of paper, scribbled a number and passed it to Katrina. 'That's my mobile number. If I haven't heard from either of you by the end of the week, I'll ring you.'

'But there's no pressure.'

Lewis grinned. 'None at all.'

Katrina gave a reluctant smile. It was impossible to resist his charm. It might have been easier if she hadn't drunk so much of the very good Chianti.

'I wish,' Lewis said, 'you hadn't aged so well.'

Katrina frowned. 'I *beg* your pardon?'

'I look at you,' Lewis said. 'I want to have a rational conversation about Ollie and creating a relationship with him, and there you sit, looking like a Christmas present that is just waiting to be unwrapped . . .'

At that moment Katrina knew she would like nothing more on earth than to be unwrapped by Lewis. She swallowed and took another sip of her Chianti. 'Tell me,' she said, 'how is Rose?'

CHAPTER SEVEN

Reverberations

CHARM, KATRINA THOUGHT as she sat in the train the next day, was an overrated quality. It was true that Lewis knew better than anyone just what to do to make a woman feel desirable; it was true that he himself remained outstandingly desirable. It was also true that as the boyfriend of Katrina's sister, he should not have flirted so outrageously with Katrina, particularly since he was trying to persuade her that he was unable to think about anyone else except his newly discovered son.

Nevertheless, she thought, as she stepped from the train, she must talk to Ollie as soon as possible. She was quite convinced that the dull headache currently afflicting her was caused by her anxiety about this. It certainly had nothing to do with the fact that she had drunk a little too much at lunch yesterday.

At one, Katrina was chewing thoughtfully on a mozzarella baguette when Susie rang to say she would not be back for supper. The coast was clear. But how could she ensure that Ollie would not go out? Illumination dawned and she rang Ollie at once. 'Hi,' she said, 'I thought we might have a takeaway this evening.'

Ollie sat with a glass of beer in front of him. Katrina had an equally large glass of water. Her tension headache had disappeared in the early afternoon despite the fact that the tension hadn't. Between them there was a plethora of cartons.

Katrina waited until they were well into the meal before finally clearing her throat. 'Ollie,' she said, 'I want to talk to you about Lewis.'

'Lewis?' Ollie said. 'Rose's boyfriend, Lewis?'

'Yes,' said Katrina. 'I don't think I've told you this but I met him many years ago, long before Rose did. In fact, I met him . . . nine months before you were born.'

'Did you?' Ollie took a poppadom and dipped it into his vegetable korma. 'That is weird. Mind you, it's not as weird as Hannah's parents. They were at nursery school together and Hannah's dad can remember hating Hannah's mum—'

'Yes, that's very weird,' Katrina said. 'I can remember exactly the day I met Lewis. Paul had just left me. I was organising the purchase of a building by a TV company and while I was being shown round the place, I met Lewis. He was busy rehearsing. In those days, he was quite famous. He was a star of a soap opera. We started seeing each other.'

'Did you?' Ollie actually took his eyes off his food. 'So Lewis is your ex-boyfriend?'

'Yes,' said Katrina, 'I suppose he is.'

'Why didn't you tell me before? When you went to France did you recognise each other? What did you say to Rose? Did she mind?'

'I didn't tell her. I found it all a little embarrassing.'

'Poor you. No wonder you didn't like your holiday. Can you pass the chicken tikka?'

Katrina passed the chicken tikka. 'Yes,' she continued doggedly, 'it wasn't an easy time. You see, when I was . . . seeing Lewis, I was very smitten by him and then . . . *nine months later* . . . you were born.'

'Cool,' said Ollie. 'Were you and Lewis still seeing each other then?'

'No, we only went out for a few weeks. Lewis felt he couldn't sustain both a career and a relationship, so he decided to end our relationship.'

'Poor old Mum. So are you going to tell Rose?'

'Am I going to tell Rose what?'

'That you used to see Lewis.'

'I *have* told Rose. I've told her something else too. The thing is . . . as I've just said . . . I was with Lewis for just a few weeks and then . . . *nine months later* . . . you were born.'

'Poor old Mum,' Ollie said again. 'You must have been very miserable when I was born.'

'Well, yes . . . no. No, of course I wasn't, you were the most beautiful baby, but that's not the point . . . The thing I'm trying to tell you . . . is that you are not actually Paul's son.' Katrina braced herself. 'In fact, your real father . . . your biological father . . . is Lewis.'

Ollie gawped at her. 'Lewis is my *father*?'

'I should have told you before. Ollie, I am so sorry . . . I never told Lewis about you because I didn't think he'd want to know. But he does know now and he is very upset that I didn't tell him.'

'I don't understand. Why couldn't you tell me before?'

Katrina's throat felt raspingly dry. She raised her glass to her lips and drank deeply. 'I didn't want people to know that I'd had a short and obviously failed relationship so soon after Paul had left me. Paul was happy to claim you as his son and it seemed the easy thing to do. I know it all sounds ridiculously prim and self-indulgent and—'

'So Dad isn't my dad?'

'Well, no . . .'

'Phew,' said Ollie. 'Well, that's a relief.'

'A relief?' Katrina burst into near hysterical laughter. 'Of all the reactions I imagined, I have to tell you this one didn't come close!'

'Be honest, Mum, would you want Dad . . . I mean, Paul . . . as a father? Is he still Susie's father?'

'Well, of course he is.'

'Poor old Susie!' Ollie's eyes narrowed in thought. 'Hey! Does this mean I don't have to go to Croydon on Dad's birthday?'

'Of course it doesn't. Paul loves you. He regards you as his son.'

'Damn.' Ollie went over to the fridge and collected a second beer. 'So when did you tell Rose and Lewis all this? That must have been crazy!'

'It was,' Katrina said with a heartfelt sigh, 'but I didn't actually tell them. They found out. Rose went with Lewis to see his mother and on the wall there was a framed photo of his grandmother or his great-grandmother. Rose says you are the spitting image of her.'

Ollie frowned. 'I look like his *grandmother*? Yuck!'

'Anyway, then, of course, I had to tell them everything. Lewis is desperate to see you.'

'Is he?' Ollie looked less than excited by the prospect. 'But I hardly know him! I wouldn't know what to say.'

The phone rang. Katrina went to answer it.

'Katrina, it's Lewis. I had to ring . . .'

'I've just told Ollie,' Katrina said.

'Oh God. Can I speak to him?'

'Hang on.' Katrina went over to Ollie. 'It's your father,' she said.

'Which one?' Ollie hissed.

'Lewis,' Katrina murmured. 'It's Lewis.' She took the cartons of food to the stove to keep them warm, trying not to look as if she was straining to follow her son's conversation.

'Yes,' Ollie said. 'Yes, it is . . . Yes, I am . . . Yes . . . I don't know, really . . . Yes, it's in Fulham . . . Yes, all right . . . Yes . . . Bye, then.' Ollie passed the phone back to Katrina and made straight for the stove.

'Hello, Lewis,' Katrina said.

'Katrina, I love you! You are a wonderful woman. Thank you for giving me your son!'

'Well, I haven't *given* him to you—'

'He's meeting me after he finishes work tomorrow. I'll take him out for an early supper. I'll speak to you soon. Thank you!'

Katrina put the phone back on its base and looked at Ollie. 'I hear you're meeting him for a meal tomorrow. He sounds very happy.'

Ollie—back at the table, tucking into second helpings—said glumly, 'I hope he doesn't want to hug me.'

In the circumstances, perhaps, the row was inevitable. Susie came back from work the next day in a foul mood. The film people had said they'd let her know by Monday and they hadn't even bothered to ring her. Also, she'd had a miserable day at the hotel.

Katrina came back from work in a foul mood because she was on tenterhooks about Ollie's meeting with Lewis. Also, she'd had a miserable day at the office. Had Katrina not been so tired and preoccupied, she would have noticed that Susie's conversational tone was unusually clipped and humourless. As it was, she commiserated with her daughter about the appalling bad manners of people who forgot to make phone calls when they had said they'd make phone calls. And then she served up the sausage casserole and tried to suggest in as tactful a way as possible that now might be the time for Susie to reconsider her future. Later, of course, she realised that there was *nothing* tactful about choosing this particular evening to deliver such a lecture.

'The trouble with these casting people,' she said, 'is that they can choose from thousands of people. Everyone wants to be famous these days, everyone wants to act. You are a very good actress. You're extremely talented—'

She should have stopped there. Perhaps she would have if Susie hadn't rolled her eyes and said, 'You so don't believe that! You've never had any faith in me. You have always been waiting for me to fail!'

'That is not true. If you'd got into drama school first time round—'

'Oh, right, so I didn't get into drama school so therefore I should give up straight away and get a proper job, a really boring job like you. You may be happy to have a boring life but I'm not. Ash says that—'

'Oh, Ash says . . . What on earth does Ash know about anything?'

'A lot more than you do, as it happens. I can't believe you are so vile about Ash. You haven't seen him for years—'

'If I don't know anything about Ash, it's not my fault. You're so secretive about him. I have no idea whether he's a friend or a boyfriend—'

'I cannot *believe*,' Susie exploded, 'that you are accusing *me* of being secretive. That just makes me want to *laugh*.' Susie let out a sound that was not even an approximation of a laugh. 'Ollie rang me tonight when he was on his way to meet Lewis. Did you *really* think he wouldn't tell me what you told him? Were you ever going to tell me?'

'Susie, I'm so sorry, I didn't think—'

'I have as much right as Ollie to know whether we share the same father or not! I suppose if Rose hadn't started seeing Lewis you'd never have told us anything! You are such a *hypocrite* and if there's one thing I know it's that I don't want ever to be like *you*. I'm going out!'

Katrina heard the front door slam. This isn't fair, she told herself, none of this is fair. She began to cry helplessly.

A good bath with a liberal dose of bath oil helped assuage the damage wrought by her weeping fit. She went to bed with Susie's latest magazine and was disturbed from an in-depth analysis of celebrity cellulite by a knock at the door.

Katrina said, 'Come in,' and braced herself for whichever of her children came through the door.

'Mum,' Ollie said, 'sorry to bother you . . . I ate supper *hours* ago and there's some sausage stuff in the fridge. Are you keeping it or . . . ?'

'Go ahead. Finish it up. But Ollie, tell me, how did it go with Lewis?'

'Oh,' said Ollie, in a tone that suggested he'd already forgotten his momentous meeting, 'it was all right. We went to Pizza Express and I had a Margherita with extra salami and—'

'Ollie, I don't care what you ate. Did you get on? Was it difficult?'

'A little bit at first but he was nice. I liked him. He didn't try to hug me or anything. He wants me to meet his mother some time and I said I would.' Ollie stood up. 'Rob's downstairs. If you're sure we can eat it all, I'll let him have some sausage stuff too. Good night, Mum.'

Her son was amazing. He genuinely didn't seem to mind that his mother had lied to him. Katrina wished she could say the same about her daughter.

Susie rang Katrina the following afternoon. 'Mum, can't stop, my tea break is over, but had to tell you. I've got the part! Bet you can't believe it!'

'Oh, Susie,' Katrina breathed, 'I am so pleased! Darling, I am so—'

'I know, me too! Gotta go! Bye now!'

Katrina left work early that day. She stopped off at the supermarket. She bought champagne, salmon fillets and a chocolate gâteau. Her mobile rang just as she'd struggled home with her bulging bags.

'Mum? Don't worry about supper for Ollie and me. We're staying in town, we're going to celebrate with friends. See you tomorrow!'

Katrina switched off her phone and tried to swallow the aching disappointment she felt. She reached for the notepad.

Darling Susie,

Hope you had a great evening. If you're not working tomorrow night, can we celebrate here? Please feel free to invite Ash. I am very proud of you.

All love, Mum

She attached it to the fridge with some Blu-Tack. She began to empty the supermarket bags. It was only when she took out the champagne that she started to cry.

From: katrinalatham@parter.co.uk
To: cornhedge@winemart.co.uk
Sent: October 26, 21:30

Dear Cornelius,
Susie WILL be a dental nurse! She got the part! She and Ollie are out

celebrating this evening. Susie is a little distant with me at present. That's my fault: I have failed to hide my antipathy towards her choice of career and her choice of boyfriend. I am determined to be more positive now and have suggested that the terrible Ash comes to dinner tomorrow night. Will you please thank your wife for providing Susie with such an exciting opportunity? Tell her that Susie is over the moon.
Love, Katrina

From: katrinalatham@parter.co.uk
To: jul@homefind.co.uk
Sent: October 26, 21:45

Dear Juliet,
I am coming to Sussex the weekend after next to stay with a good friend in Chailey. Are you still interested in selling your son's guitar? If so, might it be convenient for me to pop in and look at it on the Saturday or Sunday? Let me know.
All best, Katrina

From: cornhedge@winemart.co.uk
To: katrinalatham@parter.co.uk
Sent: October 27, 10:55

I have passed on your message to Lucy and she is delighted Susie has got the part. Please pass on our congratulations. Do you remember me telling you about my friend who had an affinity with robins? He is also a folk singer in his spare time and is performing at a pub in Greenwich in two weeks' time: November 11. Would you care to accompany me? I hope your meal with Ash is satisfactory,
Cornelius

From: katrinalatham@parter.co.uk
To: cornhedge@winemart.co.uk
Sent: October 27, 21:30

I would love to have met your robin friend but I have a tedious work do I have to attend. Can you come to lunch this Sunday? I know Susie and Ollie would love to see you and I'm busy the next two weekends. The evening with Ash was not satisfactory since Ash couldn't come. I

do hope you can come on Sunday. I feel unaccountably gloomy at the moment and your company would lift my spirits.
Love, Katrina

In fact, Katrina knew exactly why she felt gloomy. She was gloomy because Susie was barely speaking to her and because she was meeting Rose for a drink after work on Friday.

Katrina arrived to find Rose sitting at a table with two glasses and a bottle of Chablis. 'Katty, you look so tired,' she cried. 'Let me pour you a nice big drink and you can relax. How *are* you?'

'I've been better,' Katrina admitted. 'I've had a frustrating day—'

'Don't talk to me about frustration!' Rose exclaimed. 'I went to the hairdresser this afternoon and Jon cut at least an inch too much off my hair. See? What do you think?'

Katrina studied Rose's glossy auburn locks and said, quite truthfully, that Rose looked wonderful, adding a little sourly that she wished *she* had time to spend an afternoon at the hairdresser's.

'You should make time,' Rose said. 'Your hair does look a little *limp* at the moment.' She smiled and raised her glass. 'Here's to you, Katty! I want to tell you I feel no bitterness or resentment towards you. I admitted to Lewis last night that I felt a little sad because I wished *I* could be the mother of his child, and do you know what he said?'

'No,' said Katrina, feeling pretty sure that whatever it was she wouldn't like it much.

'He said if it hadn't been for me, he would never have known he *had* a child and then he said that Ollie was my nephew and therefore was more or less my child anyway. He said we have the same smile!'

Katrina did not trust herself to speak.

'He's so happy, Katty. He says he and Ollie have the most extraordinary rapport. Lewis is so good with young people. We saw Susie and Ash last week . . . Did Susie tell you?'

'No,' Katrina said, 'I don't think she did.'

'I've known him since he was tiny. He's such a nice boy. He and Sam are terrific mates and his parents are my dearest friends. And I have to tell you, Ash and Susie make a lovely couple. Which reminds me: I've invited Susie and Ollie, and Ash of course, to lunch on Sunday.'

'But I've invited Cornelius!' Katrina protested.

'Have you?' Rose narrowed her eyes thoughtfully. 'Do you know, I think that's rather serendipitous! Lewis said I must invite you too, but given the circumstances, your presence might be a little tricky. It is such a bizarre situation. Cam and Sam find it absolutely fascinating.'

'Do they?' Katrina poured herself some more wine.

'Of course they do. I was talking to my friend Dinah, and she said—'

'I don't want to know what she said. I suppose I should be grateful you haven't made an announcement about it in *The Times*. As far as Sunday is concerned, I'm not sure that Susie and Ollie can come. Cornelius was looking forward to seeing them.'

'Well, they've already accepted, and anyway, Katty, I hate to say this, but I think you need to guard against being a tiny bit *proprietorial* about Ollie. I can see why you're jealous—you've had Ollie to yourself all his life; you have to learn to share him. And of course that shouldn't be too difficult for you *now*.'

'Why now, particularly?'

'Well, after all,' said Rose, 'it's not as if you're on your own any more. You have Cornelius!'

On Sunday morning, Ollie kissed his mother goodbye, sent Cornelius his regards and set off for the bus-stop. Perhaps it was just as well that Susie had stayed the night with Sam and Cam. Susie would have noticed at once that the fridge did not seem well prepared for a Sunday lunch with Cornelius.

Cornelius was not coming to lunch. Katrina had looked at her emails before going to bed on Friday night and had found a disappointingly brief message from him to say that he was otherwise engaged on that day.

So now here she was on her own, with a perfect opportunity to work out how to repair her relationship with her daughter. In the past she had fantasised about a time when she would be able to tell her children about Lewis. She had imagined how wonderful it would be to unburden herself of the secret she had carried for so long. Well, now she had revealed her secret and the effect had been like a stone thrown into a muddy pool, stirring up great dollops of guilt and recriminations and darkening her relationship with Susie. Both her children were drawing ever closer to Rose and Lewis and would probably end up adopting them both as preferred parental figures, leaving Katrina to moulder away in Greenwich on her own.

Ollie rang at five to tell his mother not to worry about supper for him or Susie since they had only just sat down to lunch. Katrina could hear lots of noise and laughter in the background.

In the evening Katrina looked at her emails and found one from Juliet inviting her to lunch next Saturday and giving her some details about the guitar. It was the last sentence that transfixed Katrina. 'Cornelius came down for lunch today and told us you two were no longer seeing each other. Alec and I are so very sorry . . .' Katrina sat and looked at the screen without moving. Finally, she sent a reply accepting the invitation. She wondered why she felt so desolate at being dumped by a non-existent boyfriend.

At midday on Wednesday, Katrina received a call from an unusually coy-sounding Rebecca in reception to say that a Lewis Maltraver was downstairs and would like to take her out to lunch.

'I'll come down,' Katrina said. She was pleased she was wearing her blue skirt and long-sleeved white T-shirt today, and immediately she was cross with herself for wanting to look good for him.

In the lobby, Rebecca was twirling her necklace round her fingers and laughing. Katrina had never heard her laugh before.

'I have loads of work,' Katrina said uncertainly.

'Forget that,' said Lewis. 'I'm taking you out. I have no rehearsals today so I thought—'

'Oh,' Rebecca breathed, 'are you an actor? I thought I recognised you! Are you rehearsing something interesting?'

'I think it might be,' Lewis said modestly. 'It's a serial for BBC2.'

'Oh!' Rebecca leaned forward. 'How terribly exciting!'

'I do hope you'll watch it. I would be fascinated to know what you think of it.'

'I'm sure you would be,' Katrina said. 'Perhaps you can come back some time next year and ask Rebecca for her opinion. Now, I think we should be going—' She gave a brisk nod to Rebecca, put her arm through Lewis's and propelled him from the building. 'Honestly,' she muttered, 'you are the most shameless flirt . . . "I would be *fascinated* to know what you think of it" . . . You are so *blatant*. Where are we going? I can't be too long.'

'I thought,' said Lewis, 'I'd take you to Gordon's Wine Bar.'

'Oh,' said Katrina. It was stupid to be so impressed by Lewis's choice of venue for their meal. It was, after all, only a few minutes' walk from her office. It was purportedly the oldest wine bar in London, and it happened to be Katrina's most favourite place in the world; the fact that Lewis had chosen it meant, she told herself sternly, nothing at all.

'So,' she said, 'why have you no rehearsals today?'

'Until a few days ago,' Lewis said, 'I thought my part was finished. I died last Thursday. However'—he paused and smiled broadly—'the powers that be have decided to resurrect me. They're doing a couple of episodes in flashback. They want to show me engaging in various sinful incidents—'

'Which no doubt involve intimate scenes with sundry nubile young actresses?'

'It's hard work,' sighed Lewis, 'but someone has to do it.'

A stunning woman with long hair and a short skirt walked past them. Katrina noticed that the woman's eyes settled on Lewis for a moment. She also noticed that Lewis's eyes had settled on the woman. 'So what have you been doing this morning?' Katrina asked. 'Have you been getting into character, making yourself think lecherous thoughts about any young girl who comes your way?'

'Actually,' said Lewis, 'I've been to the Velázquez exhibition at the National Gallery.' He glanced at Katrina and grinned. 'Don't look so surprised. I'm not quite the philistine you obviously think I am.'

'Really? I stand corrected. What did you think of the exhibition?'

'Superb. His paintings are so real, they instantly connect you with the past; you can imagine *meeting* these people, and his technique is incredible. There's a portrait of Philip the Fourth of Spain. His wife and his son had recently died and the eyes show such weariness and loneliness that . . . Well, it's strangely affecting.'

Katrina stared at Lewis. First, he had chosen her favourite wine bar and now he was displaying a sensitivity that she had never seen before.

They had arrived at the wine bar. They went through to the cellar and sat at a table with the candlelight flickering on Lewis's face, revealing the fact that his eyes were directed solely at her.

Katrina took a sip of her wine and tried to take command of the situation. 'So,' she said, 'why are you taking me out to lunch?'

'That,' Lewis said, 'is a very silly question. Any man would want to take you out to lunch. I wanted to see you and I thought I'd surprise you.'

'I don't like surprises.' She glanced at him suspiciously. 'Why are you grinning like that? It's very annoying.'

'You look so funny when you're cross. I know exactly what you must have looked like when you were a little girl. I am so glad you are back in my life. You enrich it. And as a result I've found our son. Isn't that extraordinary? We have a son! You should be so proud of him. He has such energy and enthusiasm and honesty. I think I'd love him even if he weren't my son. It's funny: those two words, *my son*, they make me feel so . . .' He bit his lip and blinked furiously.

Startled, Katrina hesitated before replying. She had been so preoccupied with her own feelings, she had never considered how traumatic this whole business must be for him. 'In my defence,' she said slowly, 'all those years ago, I knew that you lost interest in me the moment Susie came into my bedroom.'

'That's not true. I admit I was taken aback—'

'Just supposing I'd come and sought you out when you were in the throes of your romance with Nurse whatever-her-name—supposing I'd told you I'd just had your baby—can you honestly say you'd have welcomed me with open arms?'

'I don't know. I suppose I wouldn't. I was such an idiot then.' He reached for her hand. 'I wish you had come to lunch on Sunday with your children. We missed you.'

Katrina knew she should remove her hand but it seemed churlish to, and it had been a long time since her hand had been held by anyone. 'I'm sure you didn't,' she said. 'I'd have been the spectre at the feast.'

'You have to face them all some time.' He released her hand and reached out to touch her face. 'I must have been mad to walk out on you.'

'Lewis—'

'It's still there, isn't it? That chemistry between us? And don't tell me you're in love with Cornelius. I know a little about chemistry and there is not a drop of it between you. But you and me—'

'Lewis, stop this. You're supposed to be in love with my sister.'

'I am,' he said. 'I'm in love with both of you.'

Fortunately for Katrina, she was spared the need to make a response by the arrival of their meal. She used the interruption to collect herself and to decide that the best policy was to ignore his last remark. She tucked in, and asked Lewis if he knew that both Pepys and Kipling had lived in the house above the cellar. Katrina told him she had once learnt by heart Kipling's poem 'If' simply because she had loved it so much.

'It's always been a favourite of mine,' Lewis said. He put down his knife and fork, put his hands in his lap and proceeded to recite it.

Lewis was an actor so it was no surprise that he could bring such an air of depth and understanding to the famous words of advice from a father to his son. For once, however, Katrina did not doubt his sincerity. They were both silent for a while when he finished.

'Well?' he said.

'Well what?'

'Aren't you going to tell me more of the history of this place?'

Katrina bridled. 'Are you telling me you aren't interested?'

'On the contrary. I must confess, however, that I'm rather more curious as to what you think about my problem.'

Katrina swallowed. 'What problem is that?'

'You and Rose. I'm in love with both of you.'

Katrina gripped her glass. 'I'm afraid,' she said lightly, 'I have no solution for you.'

'I have,' Lewis said. 'Do you remember that couple from downstairs? They've been very kind to Rose. They're moving. They are putting their flat on the market.'

'Rose will miss them.'

'Katrina, do you not understand? It came to me this morning: why don't you buy the place? Sell up, leave Greenwich and move into their flat? It has three bedrooms, plenty of room for you and Ollie and Susie.'

'I'm sorry,' Katrina said, 'I'm being very dense but . . . are you suggesting Rose and I *share* you?'

'Don't say anything now. Just promise me you'll think about it.' He glanced at her plate. 'Aren't you going to eat the rest of your meal? I thought you liked it.'

'I do,' Katrina said, 'but I seem to have lost my appetite.'

On Saturday morning, Katrina packed her overnight bag and drove away from Greenwich. It was a perfect autumn day.

As she sped towards Sussex, she reflected that she had never in her life been so glad to leave her children behind. Ollie, of course, was being wonderfully relaxed about everything but if she were absolutely honest— and heaven knew, it was high time she *was* a little more honest—it was extremely irritating to find that Ollie was far more concerned about the lack of progress in his pursuit of Sophie than about the duplicity of his mother. If Katrina had known he would be so unconcerned, she would have told him a long time ago and saved herself years of guilt and angst. And meanwhile Susie had discovered that her mother was a liar, and could barely speak to her without revealing her hurt and sense of betrayal. It was, very definitely, a good time to get away.

Alfriston was a picture-book perfect village on the edge of the South Downs. Katrina drove slowly through the main street, noticing with delight the big beamed pub, the tiny shops and the thatched cottages. Following Juliet's directions, she drove on towards Seaford and turned off up a long, narrow track. She reached the end of the track and stopped in front of an old gate beyond which was a field and open country. The house on her right made her gasp with pleasure. The salmon-painted mill sat on the top of the hill like an inverted ice-cream cone. A discreet L-shaped extension had been attached to its rear and in the front a sprawling lawn rolled down the hill. It was the most gorgeous place Katrina had ever seen.

'Katrina, how nice to see you!'

Alec, wearing baggy brown cords and a pale yellow polo shirt, was flanked on either side by two golden labradors with waving tails.

Katrina walked towards him. 'This place is amazing,' she told him. 'And you're so lucky to have the Downs right on your doorstep. I'd love to explore them. They look so inviting!'

'If you're up to it,' Alec said, 'we could go for a quick walk now. Juliet prepared lunch this morning but she's had to visit a friend in hospital in Lewes and won't be back for another half-hour.'

'I would *love* a walk!'

'Good! Do you hear, boys? Walkies!'

Both dogs responded with feverish excitement and yelps of delight. As soon as Alec opened the gate, they careered across the field like drunken missiles, following first one smell then another.

Alec was an agreeable companion, amiable and relaxed, with an obvious love of the countryside in which he lived. Katrina felt a million miles away from the traumas and the turmoil of the last few weeks.

'I must tell you that we were all so sorry to hear that you and Cornelius have fallen out,' Alec said.

'So am I,' Katrina said, and even as she said it, she wondered why it was that she felt she was telling the truth.

'Elizabeth is heartbroken! She thought you were perfect for her son!'

'I thought she was great fun,' Katrina said. She hesitated. 'When we went to his mother's birthday party, I couldn't help noticing that Cornelius was a little distant towards her. It seemed rather sad.'

One of the labradors bounded up towards Alec and he bent down to throw a stick for him. 'One of Juliet's most treasured possessions,' he said, 'is a letter Cornelius wrote to her two weeks after she'd started university. He must have been about eleven then. It was very short: *Dear Juliet, I hope you are enjoying university. I wish you were still at home.*

Yours sincerely, C. C. Hedge.' He laughed. 'Cornelius is not an easy man to get to know.'

'That,' Katrina said, 'is the understatement of the year.'

'I first met him when he was twelve and I still don't understand him. He was thirteen when his father killed himself.'

'Killed himself?' Katrina repeated. 'His father killed himself?'

Alec nodded. 'I liked his father. Peter was an interesting man, passionate about poetry and wine. He always said he'd have liked to have been a wine merchant. It's a pity he never lived to see his son go into that world. He was a stockbroker, a very good one, I imagine, since he made a lot of money. He adored his children and they adored him. When we were at university, Juliet was always talking about him.'

'Why did he kill himself?'

'He was a manic depressive. He had a difficult relationship with Elizabeth. She was very pretty, used to flattery and attention, neither of which Peter was particularly adept at providing. When it happened, we were far away. Juliet and I were students at Keele University. Juliet always says that Elizabeth felt left out of the closeness that existed between her husband and her son. Cornelius has never talked about any of this. To her credit, Elizabeth told us what happened and, despite what you might think, it would be wrong to paint her as the villain of the piece.'

'I don't understand.'

'Elizabeth has always had a rather *flexible* attitude towards reality. Sometimes, she says things for effect; sometimes, she says things she would like to be true. It's not so much that she means to tell lies, it's simply that she gets carried away by the moment. I gather that on this particular occasion she had a violent row with Peter in front of Cornelius and told him that Cornelius was not his son.'

Katrina swallowed. 'What a terrible thing to do! Was it a lie?'

'Of course it was. It was a stupid lie. Cornelius was the spitting image of his father. Had Peter been even halfway rational he would have known it was ridiculous. But Peter was not a rational man at the time. That night he took himself off to the garage and hanged himself. Cornelius found him in the morning.'

'Oh my God,' Katrina whispered. 'Poor Cornelius.'

'Yes,' said Alec, 'and poor Elizabeth. She fell apart, begged Cornelius to forgive her, told him of course it wasn't true, and then she had hysterics. It must have been ghastly. And Cornelius didn't say anything. He never said anything. It was impossible to know what he thought. I'm telling you this because it explains why he doesn't display the . . . kindness . . . you might expect him to show towards his mother.' He sighed again. 'I'm sorry. This is not a good subject for a beautiful autumn morning. Let's go home and have some lunch.'

Inside, the mill was every bit as impressive as it was outside. The hall was dominated by a huge brass gong; on the right, Katrina had a glimpse of an elegant, circular sitting room. She followed Alec through the doorway on the left into the more recent extension, a large open-plan area. Finally, there was the kitchen, and it was there they found Juliet, cutting up chives. She kissed Katrina's cheek, apologising for being late, explaining about her sick friend and announcing that lunch was ready.

It proved to be a cornucopia of mouth-watering tastes and glowing colours. The chives had been prepared for the main dish, a combination of smoked trout, horseradish, potatoes, onions and soured cream. There was also a carrot and coriander salad, a dish of French beans and a plate of gorgeous, crumbling ciabatta.

Katrina, initially disconcerted by the trouble that her hostess had taken, soon relaxed. It was a long and leisurely meal and only after coffee did Katrina realise how late it was. Juliet caught her anxious glance at the clock and suggested they go upstairs to look at the guitar.

The spare room, pleasingly circular, was part of the original mill. Its windows opened out onto the garden below and the walls were painted a dusky pink. However, it was the framed photo on top of the chest of drawers that interested Katrina most. She went over and picked it up. Cornelius beamed out at her. On his left was a smart young man with short dark hair; on his right was another young man, with a shy smile, an aquiline nose and hair that looked every bit as undisciplined as that of the man beside him.

Katrina looked enquiringly at Juliet. 'Is that Cornelius's son?'

'You know about Leo?' Juliet looked surprised.

'Yes. It must have been terrible.'

Juliet came over and nodded. 'It was a nightmare. It was so sudden, and Leo had never been ill in his life. My two adored him, especially Jenny. We used to visit the castle at Lewes when he was small and he loved it and would run around shrieking with delight. Jenny was five years older than him and she would run along behind him, terrified he'd fall down the hill! That photo was taken at Michael's wedding.'

'They all look so happy.'

'They were. It's hard to believe that less than two years later, Leo was dead.' Juliet smiled. 'He was a lovely boy. He had all sorts of plans. He was determined to go to the Far East before he was twenty-five, South America before he was thirty . . .'

'Did he and Cornelius get on well?'

'Oh, yes. They had what I'd call a healthily combative relationship. Leo thought Cornelius was appallingly apathetic about politics and the environment. Cornelius thought Leo was a philistine about classical music and kept trying to interest him in Mahler and Bach. They enjoyed arguing with each other. There are still times now when I can't believe Leo isn't alive.'

'When I heard about it,' Katrina confessed, 'my first reaction was one of utter selfishness. I thought of my own children, I thought how I would feel if either of them went, and I felt so grateful I had them.'

'I know. I think that's quite natural. What can be worse than losing one's child? That's why Cornelius and Lucy split up. They were happy for a long time. Lucy was a tower of strength in the early days when Cornelius was building up his wine business, and Cornelius was so proud of Lucy's acting talent. We were all surprised by their separation. The trouble was, they both mourned their son in different ways. Lucy thought Cornelius was cold and uncaring, Cornelius thought she was wallowing in her grief and it embarrassed him. Even today, Cornelius can't bear to talk about Leo. It's a terrible business. They've both been so unhappy.' She looked directly at Katrina. 'I'm sorry things didn't work out between you and my brother. I really thought you might make him happy again.'

Katrina flushed. 'Well,' she began, 'I don't think . . .'

'I'm sorry,' Juliet said quickly, 'I really didn't mean to bring this up. Now, let me show you our guitar!'

It was clear that Juliet was as eager as Katrina to change the subject. For the next fifteen minutes, the two women threw themselves into a bout of hard bargaining with Katrina demanding she pay more and Juliet insisting she wanted far less. Eventually, a settlement was reached.

When Katrina finally said goodbye, she left with the knowledge that in different circumstances she would have wanted to keep in touch with them. As she drove towards Chailey, she kept thinking of that photo. She had never seen Cornelius smile like that. Perhaps he would never do so again.

It was good to arrive at Alicia's beautiful home and find that her friend's only pressing preoccupation was the litter of six puppies that had been born to her dog three days earlier.

The revelation came to Katrina as she drove back to Greenwich the following afternoon. Something Juliet had said kept bothering her, hooking itself in her mind like a jumper snagged by a bramble. Leo and Cornelius used to argue about music and the father tried to interest the son in Mahler and Bach. It didn't make sense. Cornelius liked the Zutons and the Arctic Monkeys. Juliet had said Cornelius wasn't interested in politics. That couldn't be right either. Cornelius, after all, had been gripped by that book by Noam Chomsky. None of this added up.

It was only when Katrina joined the M25 and narrowly missed being crushed by a vast black lorry that she suddenly understood. It was Leo, not Cornelius, who had been interested in contemporary music, history, politics and the Far East. But when Leo died, Cornelius had picked up his baton and embraced the concerns of his son. He had behaved in the same way with his father. Hadn't Alec said that Cornelius's father would have liked to become a wine merchant? Surely it was no coincidence that Cornelius had chosen to go into that very same profession?

Those who said he was a cold fish who didn't know how to mourn the deaths of his loved ones could not be more mistaken. What Cornelius had done with both his father and his son was to live their lives within his own. Every day that Cornelius lived, he made choices that ensured that the legacies of Leo and his father continued. Cornelius wasn't peculiar or eccentric, Katrina thought: Cornelius was amazing.

CHAPTER EIGHT

Some Like It Hot

From: katrinalatham@parter.co.uk
To: cornhedge@winemart.co.uk
Sent: November 6, 22:10

Dear Cornelius,

I had lunch with your sister and her husband yesterday. (Do you remember I wanted to buy your nephew's guitar for Ollie's Christmas present?) I like Alec and Juliet so much and do hope we shall meet again some time. They both expressed regret at your news about our 'break-up'. I know it is absurd to be upset about the end of a fictitious relationship but I confess I feel a little bereft! Time to get back to the real world, Katrina! Hope you are well.

Love, Katrina

The following week was horrendously busy and the tranquil landscape of the Sussex Downs soon seemed a million miles away. The bonding weekend was starting on Friday, which meant that five days' work had to be fitted into four, and at home, the mood in the house remained sombre. Ollie was preoccupied by the fact that his campaign to win Sophie's friendship had worked only too well, rendering it impossible for him to change gear and become Mr Sex on Legs. Susie was sullen about going to Croydon at the weekend, particularly since this was also the week of Cam's photo-shoot in Greenwich and Cam had suggested Susie join her and her colleagues on the Friday evening. Ollie had tried to lighten Susie's mood by pointing out that he had far more reason to be cross about going to Croydon, since he was not even related to Paul. Susie responded by shouting that it wouldn't surprise her if Paul wasn't *her* real father either. Katrina then lost her temper with Susie, Susie lost her temper with Katrina, and Ollie—very sensibly—retired to his bedroom. Full civil war was only prevented by a timely call from Cam to confirm that she was arriving on Thursday evening and to ask if Susie would come out with her and the photographer that night so he could use her as a stand-in model while he tried different shots of the Queen's House. Susie was more than happy to do this and for a few glorious minutes almost forgot she was angry with her mother.

Katrina stayed at the office until eight on Thursday evening. At home, she poured herself a large glass of wine and joined Ollie in front of a TV drama about a psychopathic misogynist on the loose in Berkshire. After the fourth murder she decided to check her emails (still no word from Cornelius), and then went upstairs to pack her bag.

Susie and Cam came in just as Katrina was going to bed. Cam told her the photographer had fallen for Susie. Susie told Cam she was talking complete rubbish, but she had the glow of a woman who knows she is admired. She said good night to her mother, which was good, but failed to make eye contact with her, which was depressing.

It was good to be in the car with Amy the next morning, driving up the A12, conferring good-humouredly about their forthcoming cabaret spot, rehearsing the last lines of *Some Like It Hot*. At the climactic moment, Katrina, playing the Jack Lemmon part, would confess not that she was a man but that she was a solicitor, at which point, Amy, playing the millionaire, would conclude with the final famous line, 'Nobody's perfect'. By the time they had turned off the A12, both women were convinced they would be the stars of the evening.

Four hours later they were on the road back to London.

'We're going against the traffic,' Katrina said. 'That's good.' She glanced across at Amy and noted the tense rigidity of her face and body. Katrina bit her lip and concentrated on overtaking the van in front of her. 'We'll soon be there,' she said. 'I promise you, we'll soon be there.'

'Stupid, stupid, stupid!' Amy muttered. 'That stupid motorbike! I *knew* something would happen! He's going to die! So *stupid*!'

'Amy, stop it! You don't know that. You don't know that at all. You said yourself you could hardly understand what Stephen was saying. The poor boy is hysterical and almost certainly doesn't have a clue what is really going on.'

'Stephen was crying. He thinks his father is going to die, I could tell. He said Eddy was trying to avoid a cat. Can you believe it? I can't believe it.' Amy gave a strangulated sob.

'Breathe deeply,' Katrina said. 'Concentrate on breathing deeply.'

Amy took a couple of breaths. 'I should never have married him,' she said. 'This is all my fault. He's younger than me. He married an older woman and he yearned for excitement. It's my fault.'

'You're right,' Katrina said. 'And while you're about it, I think it's time you took responsibility for all that's happened in Darfur and Iraq and Palestine and Chechnya and New Orleans . . .'

'I'm serious.'

'I know you are and it's really scary. I always thought you were an intelligent woman. I've never heard anything so ridiculous. If you want to blame someone, blame the cat. I can't believe you're so stupid!'

Amy sniffed. 'I *am* stupid. I wish I was like you. I wish I had a calm, ordered, dignified life—'

'Really? Now that *is* stupid. You have no idea. If you only knew.'

Amy stared out of her window for a few moments and sniffed before turning back to Katrina. 'If I only knew what?'

Katrina shook her head. 'It doesn't matter.'

'Yes, it does. Tell me. I need to be distracted. Please distract me. Make me feel good about myself. Tell me you make mistakes, like me.'

'Oh,' Katrina sighed, 'I make mistakes. I make planet-sized mistakes. My daughter is currently not talking to me because she has just found out that I have been lying to her for most of her life.'

'What do you mean?'

'Ollie and Susie have different fathers. Do you remember me telling you that Rose was going out with an old boyfriend of mine?'

'The actor in *Medical Alert*? Don't tell me he's Ollie's father?'

'I met him just after Paul left me. I fell in love, Lewis did not, and the result was Ollie.'

'Katrina! You never said a thing!'

'Of course I didn't. I was thoroughly ashamed. It wasn't calm, it wasn't ordered and it certainly wasn't dignified. And by the way, since then, I've had three very undignified and completely disordered and totally disastrous affairs . . .'

A merry tune had risen from the depths of Amy's bag. 'Stephen! Yes! . . . What? . . . Stephen, please slow down, I don't understand . . . Right . . . Oh God! . . . No, it's all right, I'm fine . . . I know, I wish I were too . . . Good . . . I'll see you soon. Bye for now.'

Katrina swallowed.

'The doctor's spoken to him,' Amy said. 'He thinks Eddy's going to be all right. He's not unconscious any more.'

'Oh, Amy!'

'Stephen said he wished I was with him. I said I wished I were too.'

Amy's phone began to chirp again. 'Stephen? . . . What? . . . Thanks for telling me . . . All right . . . I'll see you soon. Bye now.'

Amy put the phone back in her bag. 'He wanted me to know,' she said in a shaky voice, 'that Eddy wanted *me* to know that he doesn't want to ride motorbikes any more.'

Katrina would never forget the sight of Amy dashing into the hospital, her white hair flying in all directions. Katrina had spent about twenty minutes trying to find a place to park, then she had rushed to the hospital to be met by a tall, gangly boy, deathly white, with an arm in a sling. Amy was with Eddy, he told her. Eddy was conscious and he was going to be all right. He had surprised Katrina by hugging her and they had both had tears in their eyes when she left.

As she drove through Deptford, it began to rain. She yawned. The frantic drive to the hospital had exhausted her. She gripped the steering wheel and drove cautiously the rest of the way.

Taking her bags from the car, she walked up to her door and unlocked it. The hall light was on, and Katrina's eyes were drawn to a large bouquet of flowers on the table below the mirror; she picked up the card and began to read it.

A giggle from the sitting room made her stiffen. Susie! Susie was in there with Ash; Susie had not gone to Croydon. Furious, Katrina marched through the open door into the sitting room and then stopped, dumbstruck. She had forgotten that Cam was staying, but it wasn't the sight of Cam that made her freeze.

Katrina cleared her throat and Cam instantly disentangled herself from her companion, pulling an errant shoulder strap back into place.

'Good evening, Cam,' Katrina said in a voice as cold as ice. 'Would you mind leaving Lewis and me alone for a little while?'

Cam looked at her aunt and walked silently out of the room.

'Katrina,' Lewis said, rising with some difficulty from the sofa, 'you are jumping to conclusions—'

'Conclusions are staring me in the face. I come home late in the evening and there on the sofa I see my twenty-four-year-old niece up close and personal with her mother's boyfriend . . .'

The sound of the doorbell made them both jump. 'I won't be a minute,' Katrina said. 'You stay right there.'

She went to the hall, pushed her hair back, straightened her shoulders and opened the front door.

Cornelius stood in the doorway, a tartan scarf round his neck, the faded black jacket with the too-short sleeves making him look more than ever like a scarecrow.

'Cornelius!' she stammered. 'What are *you* doing here?'

'I know it's very late,' he said, 'but I was driving past and I saw you had lights on. I hope you don't mind . . .'

'No,' said Katrina faintly, 'it's just that at this precise moment—'

Behind her, she heard Lewis say, 'Hello, Cornelius.'

Katrina turned and hissed, 'Will you *please* go back to the sitting room?' She tried desperately to recover her composure. 'I'm afraid, Cornelius, this isn't a very suitable time.'

'No,' said Cornelius, 'I can see that it isn't. I think, no, I *know*, that I would rather not see you any more. Goodbye, Katrina.'

The words were all the worse for being spoken in a tone of polite and measured consideration. Katrina watched Cornelius stride down the path, climb into his car and drive out of her life.

Behind her, Lewis said, 'What a very peculiar man!'

Katrina turned on him. 'Don't you *dare* say anything about Cornelius! You know *nothing* about him!'

'Perhaps,' Lewis suggested, 'I should go.'

'Yes, I'm sure you'd love to, but before you do, I want an explanation.' She pulled him back into the sitting room. 'Do sit down,' she said. 'You might want to do up the buttons on your shirt.'

Lewis sat down on the sofa, rubbed his face with his hands and took a deep breath. 'Right. This is the truth. Cam rang me on Wednesday. She told me she was going to be here on Friday evening and needed to talk. She refused to say what was worrying her over the phone and she didn't want Rose to know. She sounded upset. I was curious and I suppose I was a little pleased that she felt she could confide in me. So I came here, we had supper and she told me she was tired of Francis and depressed because she could never meet a man she could really like. After supper, suddenly Cam is telling me how attractive she finds me and she's stroking my thigh . . . I mean, it's a terrible situation—'

'It sounds like absolute hell for you.'

'You can mock all you like but I am the victim in this. *Cam* was trying to seduce *me*. I swear I did not come here in order to seduce Rose's daughter. The whole situation is extremely awkward.'

'You didn't look very awkward when I came in, Lewis. You looked very comfortable. I don't know. Perhaps if I'd come in three seconds later, I'd have found you giving Cam a moving talk about the depth of your love for her mother. Perhaps you'd better go home, Lewis, because right now you're making me feel very sick.'

'If you don't believe what I say, ask Cam.'

'I will talk to Cam. Now, I really do think you should go. It's been a long day and I'm very tired. Just go home. Don't worry. I won't say anything to Rose.' Katrina walked past him into the hall and opened the front door. 'Good night, Lewis.'

He came up to her and hesitated for a moment. 'I know I'm bad, Katrina. But I'm not that bad, I promise you.'

Katrina shut the door and murmured 'Liar!' under her breath. She heard the clatter of pans coming from the kitchen and went down to find Cam washing up.

'Leave that,' Katrina said. 'I'm making tea. Do you want some?'

Cam sat on one of the high stools. 'I'm sorry about this,' she said. 'I thought you weren't coming back till tomorrow. What did Lewis tell you?'

'He said you were trying to seduce him.'

'I didn't have to try very hard. Why did you come back early?'

'A colleague's husband was hurt in a motorcycle crash. I drove her back to London.'

'Is her husband going to be all right?'

'I think so.'

Cam kept her eyes fixed steadily on Katrina. 'I'm not in love with Lewis. I quite fancy him, though. Don't you?'

Katrina's mouth twitched. 'I don't find him as attractive as I used to.'

Cam raised a defiant chin. 'When I realised I'd have the house to myself, I rang Lewis. It seemed too good an opportunity to miss. I couldn't ask him round to my flat. Sam's always around. I've been planning it for ages. What's funny is that it seems pretty silly now, really. I only wanted revenge.'

'Revenge? Revenge against whom?'

'Against my mother, of course.'

'I often think,' Katrina said, 'that you and Sam are the only people your mother has ever loved. What on earth could she have done to warrant your behaviour tonight?'

'Quite a lot, actually. When I was seventeen, I started seeing someone. I liked him. I liked him very much. He was our gardener and Mum didn't approve. Then I told her I didn't want to go to university. She thought it was because of Sean but it wasn't. She decided the relationship had to stop and so she stopped it.'

'What did she do? Did she sack him?'

'No,' Cam said. 'She slept with him.'

Katrina, in the process of pouring boiling water into two mugs, looked up at her niece in surprise and then swore as she realised one mug was now overflowing. 'How do you *know* Rose slept with him?'

'I came back from school, heard some sounds, walked into Mum's room and found them. Poor Sean leapt out of bed like he'd been electrocuted. Mum was lying back, looking like she'd just swallowed heaven knows what.' Cam raised her eyebrows. 'She probably *had* just swallowed—'

'Cam!'

Cam smiled. 'I'm sorry, Aunty Katty.'

'I wish you wouldn't call me that. You have no idea how much I hate it. Katrina will be fine.'

For the first time that evening, Cam looked taken aback. 'I'm sorry,' she said. 'I didn't realise.'

'Well, you do now.' Katrina handed Cam her tea. 'What happened to you and Sean after you found him with Rose?'

'Nothing happened to me and Sean. I took great care to make sure I never saw him again. So Mother was very successful.'

'Cam, I'm not trying to defend Rose here, but in her own peculiar way, she probably thought she was doing the right thing for you.'

'Oh, I know. She told me. I also know she fancied Sean like mad.' She smiled. 'Poor Aunty Katty—sorry, Katrina—you're trying so hard not to look shocked.'

'I *am* shocked, you're right. But I also know that Rose loves you very much. Do you really want to spoil her relationship with Lewis? She loves him.'

'Yeah, but it doesn't stop her bonking Uncle Teddy, though.'

Katrina blinked. 'Who's Uncle Teddy?'

'He's an old family friend. He's an old, *rich* family friend. They get together every few months for a weekend of sex and sin and shopping. They've been at it for years.'

'Cam, how do you *know* all this?'

'After the Sean business, I snooped around a bit. I nearly told Dad. I'm glad I didn't.'

'So am I.'

'It's funny,' Cam said. 'I feel a lot better now. I don't want to have sex with Lewis any more. The thing is, I'm pretty sure he *would* have succumbed to my wicked wiles.'

'So am I,' said Katrina grimly.

'So now,' Cam said brightly, 'I don't need to do it.' She smiled at Katrina. 'You won't say anything to Mum, will you? I suppose I don't actually want to muck things up between her and Lewis.'

'I won't say a thing,' Katrina said. 'I've thought for a long time that she and Lewis are made for each other. By the way, when did those flowers in the hall arrive?'

Cam yawned. 'Your neighbour brought them round. She said a florist arrived with them in the morning and she took them in for you.' She kissed her aunt on the cheek. 'Good night, Aunty—Good night, Katrina.' She picked up her tea. 'Did I hear Cornelius come round earlier? He's a wine merchant, isn't he? Where is he based?'

'I believe he's in Dulwich. Good night, Cam.'

Katrina waited until Cam had left the room and then she gave a long sigh. She remembered the cold contempt in Cornelius's eyes. In the hall, she picked up the card and read it again. *I want my slippers back. xxx* It was typical of Paul to send the most irritating romantic message of all time. She dropped the card in the bin and went upstairs to bed.

From: katrinalatham@parter.co.uk
To: cornhedge@winemart.co.uk
Sent: November 13, 09:28

Dear Cornelius, I am sorry you left so abruptly on Friday and while I, of course, respect your wish to terminate our acquaintance, I would just like to clarify what must have seemed like a compromising situation in which I was betraying my sister with Lewis Maltraver. I assume you concluded I was behaving badly. I confess I am a little hurt that you think I could behave so shabbily, but nevertheless . . .

Katrina felt almost relieved when the phone interrupted her. It was Ollie, wanting to check that Katrina would be at home in the afternoon. Both he and Susie had left their house keys behind. Katrina assured him she would indeed be at home.

She put down the phone and looked at her half-finished email. Then she sighed and pressed the Cancel button. There was no point in humiliating herself by writing a pleading message to Cornelius. The fact that he was so quick to see the worst showed what he really thought of her. Her relationship with him—such as it was—was over. It was time to turn her attention towards her children.

Thus it was that when her children returned, they were ushered into the kitchen to find homemade scones—and Susie's favourite, carrot cake *with* icing—waiting for them on the table. 'Sit down and tuck in,' Katrina said, filling the teapot with boiling water. 'How was Paul?'

Susie threw her bag on the floor. 'It was just as I said it would be. The house was a tip. I spent most of Saturday cleaning it. And Dad is *so* sorry for himself. He kept telling us he's a man who can't live without a woman. He said he sent you some flowers.'

'He did,' Katrina said. 'They arrived with a rather cryptic message.'

Susie nodded. 'I think he's planning to come and live here.'

'You're joking.'

Ollie nodded sagely. 'I'm sure he is. He mentioned the Irish stew you used to make, three times. He hates living on his own.'

'Oh dear,' Katrina said. 'Poor Paul.'

Susie gave a theatrical shudder. 'That's what Dad kept saying: "Poor Paul!" He makes it very difficult to feel sorry for him because he feels so very sorry for himself. And he's mean. He ordered a takeaway last night and I swear he only ordered enough for two people.'

'Yeah, Mum,' Ollie said without rancour, 'and meanwhile you were eating a three-course meal at a posh hotel.'

'Actually,' Katrina said, 'I wasn't. We were getting ready for our wonderful three-course meal when Amy's stepson rang to say that Eddy had crashed his motorbike and was about to die.'

'Oh my God!' Susie exclaimed. 'Poor Amy! What did she do?'

'I drove her back to London and we went straight to the hospital. Basically, Stephen had panicked. Eddy's going to be fine. He has a broken collarbone and lots of bruises. I spoke to Amy this morning. She says the funny thing is that she and Eddy were planning to attend a special screening of *Easy Rider* tomorrow evening.'

'That reminds me,' Ollie said. 'Don't make me supper tomorrow. I'm going to the cinema with Sophie.'

'Really?' Katrina smiled. 'Do I take it the campaign is working at last?'

'Not yet,' Ollie said. 'I keep waiting for the right moment.'

'A nice romantic film will do the trick,' Katrina said. 'What are you going to see?'

'The Al Gore documentary,' Ollie said gloomily.

'Oh,' said Katrina. She passed the carrot cake to Susie. 'Will you be in tomorrow? I could get us some nice steak, if you like.'

'Don't bother,' Susie said coolly. 'I'll be out.'

'Fine,' said Katrina. She might have known it would take more than a carrot cake, even if it did have icing, to make Susie forgive her.

The phone was ringing when Katrina came back from work on Monday. She flew into the study, picked up the receiver and uttered a breathless, 'Hello?'

'Katrina, it's Paul. How are you?'

'Well, I'm very well.'

'Good. Did you get my flowers?'

Katrina sat down. 'Yes, I did. They are lovely, very colourful . . .'

'Good. Katrina, there is no easy way to say this—'

'In that case,' said Katrina with desperate energy, 'I wouldn't say anything. It was sweet of you to be so generous. Now—'

'Katrina, Clarrie's decided to come home!'

'Oh!' Katrina kicked off her shoes. 'Oh, Paul, I'm so glad!'

'That's very generous of you. You might have been thinking that . . . But, of course, I owe it to the children. You must see that I'm doing the right thing here, don't you?'

'Of course I do,' Katrina said warmly. 'And I hope you'll be very happy. Thanks for ringing. Goodbye now.' Katrina put down the phone and rolled her eyes. Trust Paul to assume she was gagging to have him back. Absolutely typical. She stared at the computer but resisted the temptation to turn it on. She had checked her emails before leaving the office and there was nothing from Cornelius. There *would* be nothing from Cornelius.

The telephone rang. 'Darling, it's your big sister! Listen, I want you and Cornelius to come to supper on Saturday. What do you say?'

Katrina pushed her hair back. 'I'm afraid,' she said carefully, 'that we can't. Cornelius and I have decided to stop seeing each other.'

'No! Why? When did you decide this?'

'This weekend, as it happens.'

'How frightfully annoying! We've got Roger's cousin and his wife coming and they're deadly dull and they'll want to talk about poor Roger, which won't be much fun for poor Lewis. I can't think of anyone else I could inflict them on. Why have you broken up?'

'Well, Cornelius is a very private person, very reserved. It's not easy to have a relationship with someone like that . . .'

'Well, really, Katty, talk about the pot calling the kettle black!'

Katrina frowned. 'What do you mean?'

'You must be about the most buttoned-up person I know, for goodness' sake! You never tell anyone anything! If you want to tell me you've split up with Cornelius because he's so odd-looking or because he has no charm or manners or because he has no dress sense or because he's boring, I'd agree with you one hundred per cent. But don't tell me you've split up with him because he's *reserved* because I bet you know more about him than he knows about you!'

'That's not true,' said Katrina, 'and this conversation is very silly. I was merely trying to explain why we can't come to dinner on Saturday.'

'Damn! I suppose you could come on your own.'

'I'm afraid I'm busy that night. I'm going on a speed-dating evening.'

'Oh, very funny. Well, if you can't come I'll have to try someone else.'

Katrina put the receiver down and put a hand to her flushed cheeks. Then she went to the fridge and took out a bottle of wine.

It was an hour later, when she was sitting in bed reading a new book—a biography of Mrs Jordan, mistress of the future William IV and mother of his thirteen children, who was cruelly dumped by him just before he became king—that Katrina started to cry.

It was horrible. She couldn't stop. Great rending sobs that seemed to uproot her insides kept issuing from her, one after the other and when she remembered that the last time she had cried like this had been on the ferry with Cornelius, she cried even more. She only stopped when she was surprised by a knock at her door.

It was Susie, who took one look at her mother and rushed to her side, embracing her fiercely. 'Mum!' she said. 'Mum, don't cry!'

In the presence of such sympathy from a daughter who had been so cruelly wronged, Katrina started crying all over again, finally managing to gasp, 'I'm sorry I'm such a bad mother!'

Now Susie started crying too and in no time tissues were littering the duvet like snowflakes. Mother and daughter hugged each other and then Katrina blew her nose and said, 'I'm sorry . . . I'm fine now.'

'Oh, Mum,' said Susie, 'I've been so unhappy!'

'I know.' Katrina nodded her head violently. 'So have I!'

'It's just . . .' Susie paused and bit her lip. 'I've always told you everything and then I find out that Ollie and I have different fathers and it made me feel like our whole relationship was based on a *lie* and you weren't the person I thought you were at all. It was like . . . like you didn't care about me.'

'Listen, Susie.' Katrina took her daughter's hand and stared at her earnestly. 'The reason why I didn't say anything is because I felt so ashamed. Your father walks out on me and within weeks I've fallen for a smooth-talking actor who's only interested in a bit of fun. And then, all these years later, he turns up again and this time he's properly in love with my glamorous sister who's never had any trouble getting people to love her. I know I should have told you, but I didn't want you to see me as this poor, plain woman who can never live up to her sister. I can't bear you thinking our relationship isn't important to me when it's one of the few things in my life I've been really proud of and . . .' Katrina stopped and groped for yet another tissue.

'Oh, Mum!' Susie pressed her mother's hand. 'And you're not poor and plain! And you *can* keep a man! Ollie and I know about Cornelius. Cam told us ages ago. And we really like him.'

Katrina bit her lip. 'Susie,' she said, 'I have one last confession to make. Cornelius and I do not . . . We aren't . . . There is no romance between us. There never has been.'

'But Cam says—'

'When I met Cornelius on the ferry, I had just received a text from Rose. It told me that she had a new lover who was in France with her and his name was Lewis Maltraver. I was upset. I couldn't bear the thought of Rose and Lewis being deliriously soppy together and feeling sorry for me. So . . . so I asked Cornelius if we could pretend we had fallen for each other. There was . . . There is no relationship.'

'But . . .' Susie frowned. 'You seem so good together and he came to Rose's party and he's been over to lunch . . . He does like you!'

'He likes you and Ollie,' Katrina said, 'and he felt sorry for me. So'— she raised a watery smile—'there you are! And meanwhile I've been so involved with all my problems I didn't even notice what was happening to you. I know I've been prejudiced about Ash. Please tell him he is welcome in this house. I take it you are in love with him?'

'I'm not sure,' said Susie. 'After what happened with Liam, I've decided it's best to be a little more . . .'

'Circumspect? Cautious? Careful?'

'All those!' Susie gave Katrina a quick hug and stood up. 'I must go to bed. I have an audition with RADA in the afternoon.'

'Oh, Susie, you never told me!'

'I know. I'm sorry. They're letting me jump the first audition stage as I got so far last time. I'm really nervous.'

'Will you ring and let me know how it goes?'

'Of course. But it's going to be weeks before they let me know if I've got through to the next round.' Susie went to the door and paused. 'I'm glad we're friends again. I hate that I made you cry.'

'I love you, Susie.'

'I love you too. No more crying. Good night.'

Susie went out and shut the bedroom door softly behind her. Katrina shut her eyes. It was a relief to have told Susie everything. She had pulled herself out of the sticky mire of deceit into which she had fallen.

Five seconds later, she opened them again. She had *not* pulled herself out of the mire. She had *not* told Susie everything. Worse, she had let Susie think she was crying about Susie when in fact she had been crying about . . . She was not even going to think about the person she had been crying about.

CHAPTER NINE

Improved Relations

AN UNEXPECTED CONSEQUENCE of Cornelius's entanglement with Katrina had been a renewal of communications with his wife. She had rung him in September and he was rather taken aback when he heard her voice. He hadn't spoken to her for at least six months.

'Cornelius,' she said. 'How are you?'

Cornelius was so surprised, he had to sit down. 'I'm well,' he said and then, when she didn't speak, he added, 'How are *you*?'

'I'm well. I'm very well.' There was a pause and then a hurried, 'I'm feeling a little *guilty*, actually. An old friend rang me out of the blue and suggested lunch and she told me you were going out with her sister . . . which I'm very happy about.'

Cornelius had no idea what she was talking about and was about to tell her so when he remembered Katrina. He should, of course, tell Lucy that he was *not* 'going out' with Katrina but he had a strong sense that such a denial would be disloyal to Katrina. On the other hand, he also felt that he was being disloyal to Lucy by not telling her the truth. He compromised by saying nothing at all.

'The thing is,' Lucy said, 'I was always a bit in awe of Margaret—'

'I'm sorry,' said Cornelius, 'but who is Margaret?'

'She's changed her name now. I don't know why. She's called Rose these days. At school she was always so popular and confident. I suppose I was flattered that she'd got in touch with me. And she's great fun. You met her, of course, in France.'

'I did,' said Cornelius. 'And I agree with you. She is certainly confident.'

'Anyway, she took me to a very expensive restaurant and we had some lovely wine and I probably drank too much, and we got talking about you, and I think . . . I think it's possible I might have sounded rather cross and resentful when speaking about you and I felt bad afterwards, but Margaret—I mean, Rose—was so understanding and sympathetic, and you know how it is when . . . Well, you probably don't know, Cornelius, but most normal people find sympathy is a little like chocolate or tobacco: once you get a taste of it, you want some more, and it was very nice talking to someone who wanted to *listen* to how I felt . . .'

Lucy's voice, initially crestfallen, had risen to a pugnacious crescendo and Cornelius said quickly, 'Lucy, I quite understand. I don't mind what you said. I'm sure I deserved everything you said about me.'

'Well, I must say,' said Lucy, her voice reverting to its previous softness, 'I think you *do* but I don't want you to think I was trying to . . . to sabotage your new relationship by speaking out of turn.'

'Of course I don't.'

'It's just . . . Well, it was nice to talk to someone about . . . about Leo.'

She waited for him to respond and Cornelius wanted to respond, he really did, and he could tell by the careful manner in which she had voiced that last word that she wanted him to say something and that, if he did, everything that had gone wrong between them might begin to go right. But he couldn't. He couldn't say anything, and so he was silent.

Lucy gave a little sigh and then she said brightly, 'So! Are you going to tell me anything about her?'

'Who?' asked Cornelius.

'Your new lady, of course! Really, Cornelius, you are so obtuse!'

'Oh. Well,' Cornelius said cautiously, 'it's early days, you know.'

'You're hopeless,' Lucy said, but she sounded quite good-humoured. 'You always were. I wish you'd come back to the house some time and let me cook you a meal. You won't, though, will you?'

'Ah, well, I don't know . . .'

'I do. I wish I could do *something* for you. It doesn't seem right that I'm living in our lovely house in Wimbledon while you're holed up in a grotty little hovel in Clapham.'

'Clapham is a perfectly decent place and it is not a hovel, it is a flat—'

'It's a *hovel*. Michael told me.'

'Michael?'

'Your nephew Michael, who helped you move in? I still do talk to your family, you know. Michael says your place is hideous.'

Cornelius looked round at his sitting room/dining room and tried to see it through the eyes of Michael. He would not approve of the grey linoleum or the threadbare orange rug. 'I'm happy here,' he said firmly.

'I wish I could help you in some way. I'm feeling guilty again.'

'Well,' Cornelius said slowly, 'perhaps you *could* do something. Katrina has a daughter, a lovely girl who is dead set on being an actress.

She's waitressing while trying to get into drama school. It occurs to me that you might have some contacts . . .'

'My contacts aren't what they were,' Lucy said, 'but I'll certainly see what I can do. I'll ring you if anything comes up.'

'Thank you,' Cornelius said.

'Are we friends, Cornelius? We are friends, aren't we?'

'We are very good friends,' Cornelius assured her.

'Goodbye, then,' Lucy said and rang off.

He stared at the rug for a few minutes. He was trying to work out why he felt no shame in deceiving her about Katrina. It dawned on him that he didn't actually feel he *had* deceived her. He did feel—he very strongly felt—that he was indeed 'going out' with Katrina, the only slight area of difficulty being that Katrina was unaware of this state of affairs. He sighed, picked up his guitar, arranged his fingers with care and began practising the first few bars of Del Shannon's 'Runaway'.

Two weeks later, Lucy had rung again. 'Cornelius! You owe me big time! I've got an audition for your girlfriend's daughter! It's for a tiny part in a new sci-fi film. They want a nice young girl to play a dental nurse who gets taken over by aliens. If you're interested, I can email you the details.'

'I am *very* interested,' Cornelius said. 'You are a very kind woman.'

'I'm glad to be of help. Tell her not to get too excited. There will be dozens of other would-be dental nurses. How are things going with Katrina?'

'Oh, well, you know.' Cornelius shifted uneasily in his chair. 'It's—'

'It's early days, I know! Cornelius, let's meet for lunch. I'll treat you. What are you doing on the twenty-first?'

'Nothing, but I assure you, you don't have to treat me.'

'I want to. I've just received a very nice cheque for my loo advert. We can go to the Japanese restaurant in Wimbledon. And I promise I won't interrogate you about Katrina.'

Cornelius smiled. 'Can I have that in writing?'

When he finally came off the phone, Cornelius felt an unaccustomed lightness of spirit. For months he had been haunted by his last meeting with Lucy and the recurring image of her face crumpling while he had stood there, unable to say anything to comfort her. Who would have thought that they had just had a protracted, cheerful and affectionate conversation together? It was a minor miracle.

When he arrived at the restaurant later in the month, Lucy was waiting for him. She was looking particularly lovely.

'You look marvellous,' he said.

'So do you,' Lucy said, 'though I wish you'd get rid of that old jacket.
It's falling apart.'

'I like my old jacket; it's comfortable.'

'It looks like you slept in it. Would you like some wine?'

Cornelius studied the label. 'Lucy, this is expensive.'

'It's on me. You wouldn't believe how much money I'm making from
one little advert *and* I've now been offered another one for disinfectant.'

'Disinfectant,' he murmured. 'Well done.'

'I've never earned so much for doing so little. That's one of the things
I want to talk to you about. Money. I've done a lot of thinking and I
feel—I do really feel—I'm ready to sell the house now.'

'Lucy,' Cornelius said, 'there's no need. I told you—as far as I'm concerned, you can stay there for ever if that's what you want.'

'I know. I think it's healthier if I move on. I don't need that big house
and I . . . I feel . . .' She pushed back her hair. 'I know you don't like
talking about the past but . . .'

Cornelius felt the old panic forcing its way up to his throat. He
managed to say, 'No . . . I would rather we didn't.'

'I was only going to say that I realise now I don't need to be surrounded
by . . . by what we used to have. So I have arranged for estate agents to
come round on Monday. And when we've sold the house, we'll share
the proceeds. I won't argue about this so let's not say any more about it.'
She smiled. 'I saw Margaret yesterday.'

'Who's Margaret?'

'Oh, really, Cornelius, do you listen to anything I say? Margaret is
Rose! Anyway, she was in a terrible state.'

'Was she?' Cornelius took a sip of his wine. It was very good. 'I imagine Rose gets into a terrible state quite often.'

Lucy laughed. 'That's not entirely fair. If I found out that my
boyfriend was the father of my sister's son, I think I'd be upset too.'

Cornelius had been checking out the meal on the next-door table.
Now, he directed his entire concentration on his wife. 'I'm sorry,' he
said, 'but can you repeat what you just said? I don't understand.'

'Oh Lord!' Lucy bit her lip. 'I assumed you would . . .'

'Are you telling me Lewis is Ollie's father?'

'Cornelius, I'm so sorry. It didn't occur to me that Katrina wouldn't have told you. I promise I'd never have . . . Are you very upset?'

Cornelius nodded. 'Yes. I'm pretty sure I am. If you could meet Ollie . . . I can't understand how he can be the son of Lewis.'

'It doesn't worry you that Katrina has said nothing to you about this?'

'I think she did try to,' Cornelius said, 'in a rather oblique sort of way. But, no, it doesn't worry me. Why on earth *should* she tell me?'

'Well, if you're not worried, I suppose it doesn't matter, but . . .' Lucy began and then stopped as the waiter arrived. 'Here's our food!'

Cornelius said nothing as the food was served. He stared at his shoe.

Lucy waited until the waiter had left them and then asked, 'What are you thinking about?'

Cornelius sighed. 'I was trying to imagine myself as a woman,' he said. 'And I was wondering what I would feel if Lewis made advances to me, and I honestly think he would leave me cold.'

Lucy smiled. 'Oh, Cornelius,' she said, 'I do miss you sometimes!'

'Did *you* ever come across Lewis?'

'Years ago I met him at a party. He was mildly flirtatious.'

'Did you find him attractive?'

'I suppose so, but I wasn't interested. I was madly in love with someone else.'

'Really? Who was that?'

'Funnily enough, it was you.'

'Oh,' said Cornelius, trying not to look pleased.

'I do remember he had a wonderful way of making me feel as if I were the only woman in the world he wanted to talk to.'

'I have to say,' Cornelius said, 'speaking as someone who is totally unprejudiced, I find him a rather loathsome creep. The funny thing is, Ollie doesn't look anything like him.'

'That's what Margaret—I mean, Rose—said. Apparently, Lewis took her to meet his mother and there was a picture of his great-grandmother, and Rose said she took one look at her and guessed the truth. Then it all came out that Lewis and Katrina had once had a short-lived liaison. And so Rose marched round to confront Katrina . . .'

'Poor Katrina.'

'Well, yes, but I think you should have some sympathy for Rose. Why didn't Katrina tell her what had happened?'

'Why should she? It was nothing to do with Rose.'

'It's nothing to do with Rose that her nephew turns out to be the son of her boyfriend? I know your aversion to gossip, Cornelius, but there is a difference between gossip and profound truths.'

'There is nothing profound about Lewis,' Cornelius said grimly.

'Well, we're not going to agree about this so let's change the subject. How's your sushi?'

'It's very good.' He scrutinised her carefully. 'You really are looking very well.'

'I'm feeling well.' She eyed him intently. 'I have a boyfriend.'

Cornelius strove for an appropriate response. 'Well!' he said and then, sensing disappointment, elaborated a little. 'Well, well!'

'He's younger than me. He's seven years younger. And he's not really a boyfriend yet. He asked me out a month ago and I said no, and then I thought about him a little more and I thought: why not? So I rang him and we went out to dinner. He's nice. Of course it's . . .'

'Early days? I hope it works out for you.'

'Do you?' Lucy asked. 'You don't mind at all?'

Cornelius put his head to one side and considered. 'I don't mind.'

Lucy gave a rather tight smile. 'Good.'

'Perhaps,' Cornelius corrected himself, 'I mind a little.'

'Cornelius,' Lucy said, 'you're a rotten liar.'

A few days later, Cornelius had got the email from Katrina saying that Susie had won the part of the dental nurse. This was good news but the tone of the email was flat and low-key and he wondered if she was still pining for Lewis. He wished he had the confidence to drive round and see her. Yet again, Cornelius wished he possessed even a little of Lewis's expertise. He needed advice from someone who knew about women.

Of all his friends, Edward was the most suited for this role. Edward was a folk singer of deeply romantic love songs. His voice could melt even the hardest heart. So when Edward rang to tell him he had a forthcoming engagement in a pub in Greenwich, Cornelius decided to confide in him.

'Edward,' he said, 'I've made friends with a lady called Katrina.'

'Katrina? That's a good, strong name.'

'That's what I think,' Cornelius said, encouraged by his friend's perspicacity. 'The thing is, we've become good friends. I've met her children. They're both exceptional.'

'Have you met her husband?'

'She's divorced. I've been to Sunday lunch with her twice.'

'Is she a good cook?'

'She is a fantastic cook but that's irrelevant.'

'You only say that,' Edward said sadly, 'because you have never been married to a woman who can't cook.'

'The point is,' Cornelius said, 'I need to know how I can move from the good-friend level to the . . . to the more-than-good-friend level.'

'Oh,' said Edward, 'that's easy. Invite her to my folk evening. Every time I sing, "You Are the Key to My Door" people fall in love.'

Edward spoke with such conviction that, despite himself, Cornelius was impressed. As soon as he put the phone down, he fired off an email to Katrina.

Katrina replied that she had to go to a work do that night. Instead she invited him to yet another Sunday lunch. It was painfully clear that Katrina had no interest in exploring any other levels. In time, he thought, he would learn to be happy with just her friendship. For the time being he was relieved that he could genuinely turn down her invitation since his sister had already invited him down to her house in Sussex. To be exact, she had invited him and Katrina, but Cornelius, aware of her discomfort at his mother's party, had not even thought of passing on the invitation.

Cornelius had only been in his sister's house for one hour when Juliet said for the third time that she was so sorry Katrina couldn't come with him. Cornelius decided to bring to an end any further speculation about his mythical love life. He told Juliet and Alec that he and Katrina were no longer seeing each other and that he would rather not talk about it. Not for the first time he was grateful to his brother-in-law, who interrupted Juliet's immediate request for more information with a long and very funny story about their neighbour's attempts to sabotage their son's latest relationship with a soft-porn actress.

For the next week or so, he was moderately successful in putting her out of his mind. His big mistake was to go to Edward's folk evening. When Edward sang 'You Are the Key to My Door' Cornelius felt such a longing for Katrina that he could concentrate on nothing else. The fact that he was just a few minutes away from Katrina's house was too tempting.

Surely she'd be back from her work meeting by now. He had to see her, he had to at least try to explain what he felt.

He walked up the path, took a deep breath and rang the doorbell. What exactly *was* he going to say? Then, suddenly, the door was opened and there stood Katrina.

'Cornelius,' she said. 'What are you doing here?'

She didn't look particularly pleased to see him. Cornelius swallowed and squared his shoulders. 'I know it's very late,' he said, 'but I was driving past and I saw you had lights on. I hope you don't mind . . .'

Katrina looked as if she *did* mind. She said, 'No, it's just that at this precise moment—'

And then Lewis sauntered into the hall from the sitting room, looking as if he owned the place. 'Hello, Cornelius,' he said. Most of the buttons on his shirt were undone and he had a smirk on his face that made Cornelius itch to hit him.

Katrina turned back to Cornelius. Her face had gone pink and she sounded acutely embarrassed as she said, 'I'm afraid, Cornelius, this isn't a very suitable time.'

'No,' said Cornelius, 'I can see that it isn't. I think, no, I *know* that I would rather not see you any more. Goodbye, Katrina.'

He turned on his heels, walked away from her as fast as he could and climbed into his car. As he drove away, he put on the windscreen wipers and it was a few seconds before he realised it was his eyes, not his screen, that needed wiping.

It was not the end of the world. A few months earlier he had not even known of Katrina's existence. He had been fine. He would be fine. All right, at the moment he felt as if Katrina had shone a torch on his world, revealing for the first time the dank and empty cave in which he lived. Once the memory of that light faded—and fade it would—he would readjust, learn to see again in the dark. He would be fine.

It was not easy. He had agreed to meet his niece at the Tate Modern on Saturday. Every picture he looked at seemed to connect him to Katrina. The Bonnard painting with its jolly pink-chequered tablecloth reminded him of Katrina's own warm and welcoming kitchen. A Picasso painting of flowers recalled the roses on her sideboard. One particular painting, a dark-red rectangle, was a perfect representation of his jealousy of Lewis. Cornelius gritted his teeth and forced the image of Lewis's unbuttoned shirt from his mind, only for it to be instantly replaced by a memory of the drive back from Rose's party and his barely controlled urge to take Katrina in his arms and kiss her.

It was all right. It would be all right.

On Tuesday he was working in his office when his secretary came in and said his niece wished to see him.

When the door opened again, Cornelius looked up and frowned.

Instead of Jenny, there was a blonde young woman in a short black skirt. He tried to remember where he had seen her before.

'I *am* a niece,' the girl assured him, 'it's just that I'm Katrina's niece. I wasn't sure you'd let me in if I told you who I was. And then as soon as I said it, I thought that you might not even *have* a niece. I take it you do have one?'

'Yes,' said Cornelius. He remembered her now. Rose's daughter.

Cam pulled up a chair. 'It took ages to find you. No one in Dulwich seems to have heard of you. I can't imagine how you sell any wine. I'll come straight to the point. I've come to see you about Katrina.'

Cornelius stiffened. 'I'm afraid I'm a little busy at the moment. In fact, I'm extremely busy. So I really don't have time to—'

'I won't be very long. My mother rang her last night and Katrina said you and she had stopped seeing each other. I wanted to tell you, you're making a big mistake.'

Cornelius straightened his back. 'I don't wish to be rude but—'

'Yes, you do,' Cam said. 'You think it's nothing to do with me, but you're wrong. I'm the reason why you walked out on my aunt.'

'I assure you that—'

'I was there,' Cam said baldly. 'I was in the kitchen on Friday evening. I heard everything. You thought Aunty Katty—Katrina was about to embark on a night of passion with Lewis Maltraver.'

Cornelius couldn't speak. He nodded at the girl.

'Actually, Katrina had only come in a couple of minutes before you. I was the one who was about to set sail with Lewis.'

Cornelius stared at her blankly. Nothing she said made any sense.

'It's not something I'm proud of,' Cam said. She tossed her hair back from her face. Her tone was calm and conversational. 'My mother had behaved badly to me and I wanted to get my own back. It was silly, but there you are. I was staying at Katrina's for a couple of nights. Katrina was staying the night in Essex on some work jaunt and my cousins had gone to see their father in Croydon. It seemed a good opportunity . . .'

Cornelius was still bewildered. 'A good opportunity for what?'

'A good opportunity for seduction. I wanted to seduce Lewis, and I would have done too if Katrina hadn't come back.'

'I don't doubt that for a moment.'

Cam gave a faint smile. 'That's what Katrina said! The trouble is she *did* come back.'

Cornelius cleared his throat. 'Would you mind telling me why?'

'One of her work friends had a husband who was rushed to hospital, and so she and Katrina left the hotel and Katrina drove her back to London to the hospital and then she came on to Greenwich and found Lewis and me in the sitting room. Katrina was furious with both of us.'

'Was she?' Cornelius smiled faintly and gripped the edge of the table with his hands, fearing that, if he didn't hold on to it, he would jump up and embrace this charming young girl who, with a few words, had shot down the dark cloud of despair that had so recently engulfed him.

'Knowing my aunt, she's unlikely to come over here herself and explain to you what really happened and I don't want to be responsible for wrecking her love life. Katrina is different from my mother and me. We're not very nice people. Katrina is.' She stood up. 'If I were you, I'd get over there quick and start grovelling.'

Cornelius pushed back his chair. He walked over to Cam and held out his hand. 'Thank you *very* much for coming to see me. It was good of you to take the trouble. I think you *are* a very nice person.'

Cam's face went a little pink and she suddenly looked a lot younger. 'Thank you,' she said. 'I hope you sort everything out.' She shook his hand and walked out of the room.

Cornelius stood for a few moments and then pushed his hands through his hair. 'Oh my God,' he said aloud. 'What have I done?'

At half past six, Cornelius strode up the path to Katrina's house. He carried a very good bottle of wine with him. As he pressed the bell, he cursed himself for his ineptitude. He should have brought flowers.

Ollie answered the door and gave him a welcoming grin. 'Hi, Cornelius, I didn't know you were coming round. Come on in. I'm making a cup of tea. Do you want one?'

'No. Thank you.' Cornelius followed Ollie down to the kitchen and watched him fish a tea bag from his mug. 'How are *you?*' he asked.

Ollie gave a despondent shrug. 'I'm all right.'

'You don't sound all right.'

Ollie poured a little milk into his mug. 'I'm really keen on this girl. Did I tell you about her? She's called Sophie. And we're very good friends but it's impossible to tell her that I really like her, and we keep seeing each other and *nothing happens*. I think I'm just going to stop seeing her. It's a bit depressing.'

'May I offer you some advice?'

'Feel free.'

'Tell her what you feel. Nothing will happen unless you tell her. Ring her. Tell her you want to take her out to dinner. Be direct. Be honest. Be brave. *That* is what you should do.'

Ollie looked slightly taken aback by Cornelius's enthusiasm. 'Do you think so?' he asked uncertainly. 'It could be really embarrassing.'

'Sometimes,' Cornelius said, as much to himself as to Ollie, 'you have to risk embarrassment. Look at Galileo or Darwin or Copernicus. Do you think they'd have ever changed the world if they'd worried about looking stupid?'

'I wonder if Galileo had problems with women,' Ollie said gloomily.

'I rather think . . .' began Cornelius and promptly forgot what it was he did think because he heard the front door.

'Mum!' Ollie called. 'We're in the kitchen!'

A few seconds later, there she was, and when she saw Cornelius she went bright red and just said, 'Oh!'

His face felt like it was on fire. He stood up and said, 'Hello.'

Ollie took a package from his mother's hand. 'You've bought a new book. Noam Chomsky! Sophie likes Noam Chomsky!'

For a moment, Katrina's eyes met those of Cornelius.

Ollie put the book down. 'I'll be back in a moment,' he said. 'I want to make a phone call.' He went to the door and smiled at Cornelius. 'Wish me luck!'

'I'm sure you don't need it.'

'What's that all about?' Katrina asked. 'Why does Ollie need luck?'

'He's going to ring Sophie, I think.'

'He's always ringing Sophie.' Katrina went to the fridge. She pulled out a bottle of white wine and said, 'There are glasses over there.'

Cornelius got the glasses and watched her pour the wine.

'I must say that I'm a little surprised to see you,' she said. 'I seem to remember you said you never wanted to see me again.'

'I wish I could tell you,' Cornelius said carefully, 'that I worked out on my own how stupid . . . and . . . offensive I have been. In fact, I've had help. Your niece visited me this afternoon.'

'Cam?' Katrina gave him a startled glance. 'Cam came to see you?'

'Yes. She wanted me to know about her plan to—er—seduce Lewis. She thought I might have got the wrong idea.'

'And did you?'

'Katrina, I know better than most people how strong your feelings are for Lewis. On the boat—'

'Cornelius, I did not weep copiously on the boat because I was madly in love with Lewis. The reason I was crying was—'

'About Ollie being Lewis's son. I know all that.'

'What? *How* do you know that? Did Ollie tell you?'

'No. Rose told Lucy. Lucy told me.'

'I see. You never said anything.'

'Of course I didn't. It was none of my business.'

'Oh.' Katrina was silent for a moment. 'I wish you *had* said something. I so wanted to talk to you about it. When I got that text on the boat, I felt like everything was falling apart. I wasn't jealous about Rose being with Lewis . . . No, that's not quite true. I *was* jealous. I was jealous that she'd found an attractive man to love her.' She gave a short laugh. 'I don't know why I'm telling you all this. As you so rightly said, none of this is any of your business.'

Cornelius cleared his throat. Take a risk, Cornelius; remember what you said to Ollie. Remember Darwin and all those others. 'Katrina,' he said, 'I've been jealous as hell of Lewis.'

'*Jealous?*' The word shot out of her mouth and before Cornelius could work out if she was shocked or disgusted or just surprised or even sympathetic, Ollie rushed in and seized Cornelius's hands in his.

'It worked! You were right! You are brilliant! I said to her, "Look, Sophie, I'm fed up with being a friend to you and I can't do this any longer. I want to be more than friends and it's driving me crazy," and then . . . Do you know what she said?'

Cornelius dragged his eyes away from Katrina. 'I have no idea.'

'She said, "You took your time!" Can you imagine? So then I said, "Wait there. I'm coming over and I'm taking you out to dinner!" and she said, "Good," and then she rang off! Can you believe it? I'm going to put on a clean shirt. I'll be back in a minute!'

'*Please* take as long as you like,' Cornelius said.

Ollie waved and disappeared up the stairs, singing.

'Well,' Cornelius said, 'that's nice.'

'That's very nice,' Katrina said. 'What was it you said just now?'

Cornelius felt sick. 'I'm not sure I have the nerve to say it again.'

Katrina glanced up at him. 'I wish you would.'

'I said I've been jealous as hell of Lewis.'

Katrina gave a small sigh. 'You *did* say that! When your sister emailed me and told me you'd announced the end of our "relationship", I thought you didn't want to be friends with me any more.'

'I didn't,' Cornelius said. 'At the risk of imitating your son, I was fed up with being your friend. I think I've loved you ever since I watched you struggling with that terrible tongue we ate in France.'

Katrina's eyes were shiny with tears. She bit her lip. 'I've been so unhappy since Friday. I thought you despised me.'

Cornelius went over to her. 'Katrina,' he said, 'I'm mad about you.'

He lowered his head, raised her chin with his hand and kissed her. And then, because it was so wonderful, he kissed her again. He would have happily gone on doing so for ever if Katrina hadn't broken away and exclaimed, 'Oh, dear, this is terrible!'

'I'm sorry,' Cornelius said. 'I thought—'

'You don't understand! Susie was so hurt when she discovered I'd not told the truth about Ollie and Lewis. I've virtually promised I will always tell her the truth from now on. I told her there was no romance between you and me and now . . . here we are . . . and she'll think I've been telling whoppers all over again!'

'No problem,' said Cornelius. 'You can tell her I came over here and proclaimed my love for you and that I persuaded you to give me a chance.'

'That's no good,' Katrina said vehemently. 'I have to . . .' She stopped as Ollie flew into the kitchen again, with his unbuttoned shirt flapping round him. 'I need some advice,' he said, doing up his shirt buttons and apparently oblivious to the fact that Cornelius had his arms round his mother. 'I'm going round to Sophie's now. I have twenty-two pounds. Where can I take her out for a romantic dinner for not more than twenty-two pounds?'

Cornelius reached into his pocket and pulled out his wallet. He extracted eight ten-pound notes and gave them to Ollie. 'Be my guest,' he said. 'Go anywhere. I'm trying to tell your mother I love her.'

'Oh,' said Ollie. He gave them both a broad grin. 'I thought you'd done that ages ago. Are you *sure* I can have all this?'

'Ollie,' said Cornelius, 'if you don't go now, I might take it back.'

Katrina waited until she heard the front door slam and then looked at Cornelius severely. 'You gave him far too much money.'

'It was worth it. Why can't you tell Susie what I said? It's the truth.'

'No, it isn't. That's the trouble.' Katrina reached up to stroke his face with her hand. 'You didn't have to persuade me to give you a chance. I love you, Cornelius. I absolutely love you.'

Cornelius was glad that the telephone rang at that precise moment. To be the recipient of such life-transforming information was almost too much to bear.

Katrina murmured, 'Damn,' and picked up the handset.

'Susie!' she said. 'How funny—I was just talking about you! . . . Oh, wow, that's amazing! Will you tell Ash I am truly grateful? . . . Darling, that's the most wonderful early Christmas present. Thank you! . . . Yes, that's a good idea. I will ask him. He's here now, as it happens. In fact, I wanted to tell you . . . Oh, all right, I'll speak to you later.'

She put the phone down and looked at Cornelius with shining eyes. 'That was Susie,' she said. 'And you'll never guess! Ash has got hold of two tickets to a Jarvis Cocker concert at the Roundhouse in Camden on December the sixteenth!'

'Jarvis Cocker?' Cornelius queried.

Katrina laughed. 'Don't tell me that a man who knows all about the Zutons has never heard of Jarvis Cocker! He is the greatest songwriter in the world! And Ash has got two tickets and he and Susie are giving them to me! She said I ought to ask you to come with me. Will you?'

Cornelius took her hand. It seemed to him she had never looked so beautiful. 'I'd go to anything with you,' he said, 'anything at all.'

'You'll like Jarvis Cocker,' Katrina said. 'Jarvis Cocker is gorgeous.'

'I *have* heard of him,' Cornelius said. 'I've seen photos of him. I wouldn't say he's gorgeous.' He felt a twinge of jealousy. 'I would say he looks rather peculiar.'

Katrina laughed. 'You do realise,' she said, 'that you look just like him?'

'No, I don't!' Cornelius said. 'Do I?'

'You're better-looking.' Katrina said. She put her arms round his waist and looked up into his eyes, and as Cornelius bent to kiss her again he knew that for the first time in what seemed like for ever, he was quite happy, in fact he was *very* happy, in fact he was *completely* happy to be Cornelius Coriolanus Hedge.

Debby Holt

Did you always want to be a novelist?

Oh definitely, yes. But I never thought I would be. When I was little, I had fantasies about being a writer. On car journeys I used to bore my five siblings with very, *very* long stories. Then I grew up, became a bad history teacher, took time out to have five children, and then returned to being a truly rotten supply teacher. I moved from long verbal stories to writing short stories that were published in women's magazines, and was then persuaded by my writing group to tell longer tales again—and I did. When I took the call from my agent to say that my first novel, *The Ex-Wife's Survival Guide*, had been taken by a publisher I was so delighted that I danced round the car park in Portmeirion, frightening a coach full of elderly tourists!

What is the best thing about being an author?

You are never bored. If ever I am on my own anywhere, in a queue or taking a walk, I've always got something to think about. Writing is like pushing a rock uphill—hard slog but so gratifying when you get to the summit.

How did you get the idea for *Love Affairs for Grown-Ups*?

It all started with the idea of two sisters—one incredibly selfish, Rose, and the other loving and giving, Katrina. I also wanted to create a male character, a male hero if you like, who most people would think was a bit odd. I wanted to show that, actually, there are individuals who you might think are eccentric but are really worth knowing. My father was regarded as a great eccentric by many but I thought that he was wonderful. So I created lovely Cornelius Hedge, who isn't conventionally charming or romantic, but I hope readers will come to love him as much as I did.

The novel is set partly in France, is it a country you know well?

While the novel was taking shape in my head we had a joint family holiday with my sister's family in France. It was really lovely and while I was there I wrote notes about the place and what we had done on the drive down and that became the focus for the beginning of the novel. I then added two strangers, Katrina and Cornelius, forced to take the long journey together.

Do you think that falling in love after forty is more complicated than falling in love at twenty?

I love the fact that we are *never* too old to fall in love. I have quite a few friends in their late forties, early fifties, who have found themselves single again. At that age you are more set in your ways than you were in your twenties, perhaps less keen to change. Some at that stage in life have possessive teenagers; all have a past. When I was at university I worked in an old people's home where a couple fell in love in their nineties and got married. I strongly believe that love is not the monopoly of the young—but mature love can have its complications!

Did you ever have such a disastrous meal as Cornelius and Katrina when they are forced to eat tongue and cabbage?

Yes, that happened to us almost exactly as it appears in the book. Tongue and cabbage—*the* most disgusting meal ever. Quite revolting. I ate as much as I could and then hid what was left of the tongue under the cabbage.

What do you like to do to relax?

Every morning before I start writing I go to the gym or the swimming pool. I find that I just can't get going unless I've done some exercise. It sets me up for the day. I also love to watch soppy films, lunch with friends and have a good gossip . . . and read, of course. Also, when I'm writing I love to go for walks to help me think—*but* it has to be exactly the same walk so that I won't be distracted by new sights, smells or sounds.

I read that you are a huge Cary Grant fan. If you had to choose between Cary and your hero, Cornelius Hedge, who would it be?

In my business I am forced to spend a lot of time thinking about gorgeous men—it's a tough job but someone's got to do it! But that's an unfair question as I adore Cary Grant—he was one of the most genuinely sexy men—and I had a real crush on Cornelius. I would have to say . . . No, sorry. I just can't choose.

The Help
Kathryn Stockett

I'm pretty sure I can say that no one in my family ever asked our maid Demetrie what it felt like to be black in Mississippi, working for our white family. It never occurred to us to ask. It was everyday life. It wasn't something people felt compelled to examine.

I have wished, for many years, that I'd been old enough and thoughtful enough to ask Demetrie that question. She died when I was sixteen. I've spent years imagining what her answer would be. And that is why I wrote this book.

Kathryn

AIBILEEN

MAE MOBLEY WAS BORN on a early Sunday morning in August, 1960. A church baby we like to call it. Taking care a white babies, that's what I do, along with all the cooking and the cleaning. I done raised seventeen kids in my lifetime. But I ain't never seen a baby yell like Mae Mobley Leefolt. First day I walk in the door, there she be, red-hot and hollering with the colic. Miss Leefolt, she look terrified a her own child. 'What am I doing wrong? Why can't I stop it?'

It? That was my first hint: something is wrong with this situation.

So I took that pink, screaming baby in my arms. Bounced her on my hip to get the gas moving and it didn't take two minutes fore Baby Girl stopped her crying, got to smiling up at me like she do. But Miss Leefolt, she don't pick up her own baby for the rest a the day. I seen plenty a women get the baby blues. I reckon I thought that's what it was.

Here's something about Miss Leefolt: she not just frowning all the time, she skinny. Her legs is so spindly, she look like she done growed em last week. Twenty-three years old and she lanky as a fourteen-year-old boy. Even her hair is thin, brown, see-through. She try to tease it up, but it only make it look thinner. Her face have a pointy chin. Fact, her whole body be so full a sharp knobs and corners, it's no wonder she can't soothe that baby. Babies like fat. Like to bury they face up in you armpit and go to sleep.

Mae Mobley two years old now. She got big brown eyes and honey-colour curls. But the bald spot in the back of her hair kind a throw things off. She get the same wrinkle between her eyebrows when she worried, like her mama. She ain't gone be no beauty queen. I think it bother Miss Leefolt, but Mae Mobley my special baby.

I lost my own boy, Treelore, right before I started waiting on Miss Leefolt. He was twenty-four years old. He had him a little apartment over on Foley Street. Seeing a real nice girl name Frances and I spec they was gone get married, but he was slow bout things like that. Not cause he looking for something better, just cause he the thinking kind. He even start writing his own book, bout being a coloured man living and working in Mississippi. But one night he working late at the mill, lugging two-by-fours to the truck. He too small for that kind a work, too skinny, but he needed the job. He was tired. It was raining. He slip off the loading dock, fell down on the drive. Tractor trailer didn't see him and crushed his lungs fore he could move. By the time I found out, he was dead.

That was the day my whole world went black. Air look black, sun look black. I laid up in bed and stared at the black walls a my house. Minny came ever day to make sure I was still breathing, feed me food to keep me living.

Five months after the funeral, I lifted myself up out a bed. I put on my white uniform and put my little gold cross back round my neck and I went to wait on Miss Leefolt cause she just have her baby girl. But something in me had changed. A bitter seed was planted inside a me. And I just didn't feel so accepting anymore.

'Get the house straightened up and then go on and fix some of that chicken salad,' say Miss Leefolt.

It's bridge club day. Every fourth Wednesday a the month. A course I already got everthing ready to go—made the salad this morning, ironed the tablecloths yesterday. Miss Leefolt seen me at it too. She ain't but twenty-three years old and she like hearing herself tell me what to do.

I arrange the-this and the-that for her lady friends. Set out the good crystal, put the silver service out. We set at the dining room table. Put a cloth on top to cover the big L-shaped crack, move that red flower centrepiece to the sideboard to hide where the wood all scratched. Miss Leefolt, she like it fancy when she do a luncheon.

I'm used to working for young couples, but I spec this is the smallest house I ever worked in. It's just the one storey. Her and Mister Leefolt's room in the back be a fair size, but Baby Girl's room be tiny. The dining room and the regular living room kind a join up. Only two bathrooms, which is a relief cause I worked in houses where they was five or six. Miss Leefolt don't pay but ninety-five cents an hour, less than I been paid in years. But after Treelore died, I took what I could. Landlord wasn't gone wait much longer. And even though it's small, Miss Leefolt done the house up nice as she can. She pretty good with the sewing machine. Anything she can't buy new, she just get her some material and sew it a cover.

The doorbell ring and I open it up.

'Hey, Aibileen,' Miss Skeeter say, cause she the kind that speak to the help. 'How you?'

'Hey, Miss Skeeter. I'm all right. Law, it's hot out there.'

Miss Skeeter real tall and skinny. Her hair be yellow and cut short above her shoulders cause she get the frizz year round. She twenty-three or so, same as Miss Leefolt and the rest of em. She wearing a white lace blouse buttoned up like a nun, flat shoes so I reckon she don't look any taller. Her blue skirt gaps open in the waist. Miss Skeeter always look like somebody else told her what to wear.

I hear Miss Hilly and her mama, Miss Walter, pull up the driveway and toot the horn. Miss Hilly don't live but ten feet away, but she always drive over. I let her in and she go right past me and I figure it's a good time to get Mae Mobley up from her nap.

Soon as I walk in her nursery, Mae Mobley smile at me, reach out her fat little arms.

'You already up, Baby Girl? Why you didn't holler for me?'

She laugh, dance a little happy jig waiting on me to get her out. I give her a good hug. I reckon she don't get too many good hugs like this after I go home. I say, 'Aibileen.'

She say, 'Aib-ee.'

I say, 'Love.'

She say, 'Love.'

I say, 'Mae Mobley.'

She say, 'Aib-ee.' And then she laugh and laugh. She so tickled she talking and I got to say, it's about time. I tote Mae Mobley into the kitchen and put her in her high chair, thinking about two chores I need to finish today fore Miss Leefolt have a fit: separate the napkins that started to fray and straighten up the silver service in the cabinet.

I take the tray a devil eggs out to the dining room. Miss Leefolt setting at the head and to her left be Miss Hilly Holbrook and Miss Hilly's mama, Miss Walter, who Miss Hilly don't treat with no respect. And then on Miss Leefolt's right be Miss Skeeter.

I make the egg rounds, starting with ole Miss Walter first cause she the elder. She scoop a egg up and near bout drop it cause she getting the palsy. Then I move over to Miss Hilly and she smile and take two. Miss Hilly got a round face and dark brown hair in the beehive. Her skin be olive colour, with freckles and moles. She wear a lot a red plaid. And she getting heavy in the bottom. She ain't my favourite.

I move over to Miss Skeeter, but she wrinkle her nose up at me and say, 'No, thanks,' cause she don't eat no eggs. I tell Miss Leefolt ever time she have the bridge club and she make me do them eggs anyways. She scared Miss Hilly be disappointed.

Finally, I do Miss Leefolt. She the hostess so she got to pick up her eggs last. And soon as I'm done, Miss Hilly say, 'Don't mind if I do,' and snatch herself two more eggs, which don't surprise me.

'Guess who I ran into at the beauty parlour?' Miss Hilly say. 'Celia Foote. And do you know what she asked me? If she could help with the Benefit this year.'

'Good,' Miss Skeeter say. 'We need it.'

'Not that bad, we don't. I told her, I said, "Celia, you have to be a Junior League member to participate."'

'Aren't we taking non-members this year? Since the Benefit's gotten so big?' Miss Skeeter ask.

'Well, yes,' Miss Hilly say. 'But I wasn't about to tell *her* that.'

'I can't believe Johnny married a girl so tacky like she is,' Miss Leefolt say and Miss Hilly nod. She start dealing out the bridge cards.

I spoon out the salad and take round ham sandwiches. When I get round to Miss Walter, she don't take but one little old half a sandwich for herself.

'Mama,' Miss Hilly yell at Miss Walter, 'take another sandwich. You are skinny as a telephone pole.' Miss Hilly look over at the rest a the table. 'I keep telling her, if that Minny can't cook she needs to just go on and fire her.'

My ears prick up at this. They talking bout the help. I'm best friends with Minny.

'Minny cooks fine,' say ole Miss Walter. 'I'm just not so hungry like I used to be.'

Minny near bout the best cook in Hinds County, maybe even all a Mississippi. The Junior League Benefit come round ever fall and they be wanting her to make ten caramel cakes to auction off. She ought a be the most sought-after help in the state. Problem is, Minny got a mouth on her. She always talking back. The only reason she waiting on Miss Walter so long is Miss Walter be deaf as a doe-knob.

'I think you're malnutritioned, Mama,' holler Miss Hilly. 'That Minny isn't feeding you so that she can steal every last heirloom I have left.' Miss Hilly huff out a her chair. 'I'm going to the powder room.'

In the kitchen, Baby Girl's up in her high chair, got purple juice all over her face. Soon as I walk in, she smile. She don't make no fuss being in here by herself, but I hate to leave her too long. I know she stare at that door real quiet till I come back. I pat her little soft head and go back out to straighten the silver. Miss Hilly's back in her chair.

'Oh, Hilly, I wish you'd use the guest bathroom,' say Miss Leefolt. 'Aibileen doesn't clean in the back until after lunch.'

Hilly raise her chin up. Then she give one a her 'ah-hems'. She got this way a clearing her throat real delicate-like that get everybody's attention without they even knowing she made em do it.

'But the guest bathroom's where the help goes,' Miss Hilly say.

Nobody says anything for a second. Then Miss Walter nod, like she explaining it all. 'She's upset cause the Nigra uses the inside bathroom and so do we.'

Law, not this mess again. They all look over at me straightening the silver drawer in the sideboard and I know it's time for me to leave. I stand around the kitchen a minute but I ain't got nothing to do in there. I need to be in the dining room so I can finish my silver straightening. And I still got the napkin cabinet to sort through today but it's in the hall, right outside where they setting.

I wait a few minutes, wipe a counter. Give Baby Girl some ham and she gobble it up. Finally, I slip out to the hall, pray nobody see me.

All four of em got a cigarette in one hand, they cards in the other. 'Elizabeth, if you had the choice,' I hear Miss Hilly say, 'wouldn't you rather them take their business outside?'

Real quiet, I open the napkin drawer, more concerned about Miss Leefolt seeing me than what they saying. This talk ain't news to me. Everwhere in town they got a coloured bathroom, and most the houses do too. But I look over and Miss Skeeter's watching me and I freeze, thinking I'm about to get in trouble.

'I bid one heart,' Miss Walter say.

'I don't know,' Miss Leefolt say, frowning at her cards, 'With Raleigh starting his own business . . . things are real tight for us right now.'

Miss Hilly talk slow, like she spreading icing on a cake. 'You just tell Raleigh every penny he spends on that bathroom he'll get back when y'all sell this house. All these houses they're building without maid's quarters? It's just plain dangerous. Everybody knows they carry different kinds of diseases than we do. I double.'

I pick up a stack a napkins. I don't know why, but all a sudden I want a hear what Miss Leefolt gone say to this.

'It would be nice,' Miss Leefolt say, taking a little puff a her cigarette, 'not having her use the one in the house. I bid three spades.'

'That's exactly why I've designed the Home Help Sanitation Initiative,' Miss Hilly say. 'As a disease-preventative measure.'

I'm surprised by how tight my throat get. It's a feeling a shame I learned to keep down a long time ago.

Miss Skeeter look real confused. 'The Home . . . the what?'

'A bill that requires every white home to have a separate bathroom for the coloured help. I've even notified the surgeon general of Mississippi to see if he'll endorse the idea. I pass.'

Miss Skeeter, she frowning at Miss Hilly. She set her cards down face-up and say real matter-a-fact, 'Maybe we ought to just build you a bath-room outside, Hilly.'

And Law, do that room get quiet.

Miss Hilly say, 'I don't think you ought to be joking around about the coloured situation. Not if you want to stay on as editor of the League, Skeeter Phelan.'

Miss Skeeter kind a laugh, but I can tell she don't think it's funny. 'What, you'd . . . kick me out? For disagreeing with you?'

Miss Hilly raise a eyebrow. 'I will do whatever I have to do to protect our town. Your lead, Mama.'

When Miss Hilly gone, I put Mae Mobley in her playpen, drag the garbage bin out to the street cause the truck's coming by today. When I go in the kitchen, Miss Skeeter's in there. She leaning against the counter, got a serious look on her face, even more serious than usual. 'Hey, Miss Skeeter. I get you something?'

She glance out at the drive where Miss Leefolt's talking to Miss Hilly through her car window. 'No, I'm just . . . waiting.'

I dry a tray with a towel. When I sneak a look over, she's still got her worried eyes on that window. She don't look like other ladies, being she so tall. She got real high cheekbones. Blue eyes that turn down, giving her a shy way about her. It's quiet, except for the little radio on the counter, playing the gospel station.

'Is that Preacher Green you're playing on the radio?' she ask.

'Yes, ma'am, it is.'

Miss Skeeter kind a smile. 'That reminds me so much of my maid growing up.'

'Oh, I knew Constantine,' I say.

Miss Skeeter move her eyes from the window to me. 'She raised me, did you know that?'

I nod, wishing I'd said nothing. I know too much about that situation.

'I've been trying to get an address for her family in Chicago,' she say, 'but nobody can tell me anything.'

'I don't have it either, ma'am.'

Miss Skeeter move her eyes back to the window, on Miss Hilly's Oldsmobile. She shake her head, just a little. 'Aibileen, that talk in there . . . Hilly's talk, I mean . . . do you ever wish you could . . . change things?'

And I can't help myself. I look at her head on. Cause that's one a the stupidest questions I ever heard. I turn back to my washing, so she don't see me rolling my eyes. 'Oh, no, ma'am, everthing's fine.'

'But that talk in there, about the *bathroom*—' and smack on that word, Miss Leefolt walk in the kitchen.

'Oh, there you are, Skeeter.' She look at us both kind a funny. 'I'm sorry, did I . . . interrupt something?' We both stand there, wondering what she might a heard.

'I have to run,' Miss Skeeter says. 'See you tomorrow, Elizabeth.' She open the back door, say, 'Thanks, Aibileen, for lunch,' and she gone.

Baby Girl hold her arms out for her mama to pick her up, but Miss Leefolt act like she don't see.

'You and Miss Skeeter looked like you were talking awful serious about something.'

'No, ma'am, she just . . . asking do I want some old clothes,' I say.

Miss Leefolt huff and go out to the garage. I figure she looking at where she gone build me my new coloured bathroom.

Six days a week, I take the bus across the Woodrow Wilson Bridge to where Miss Leefolt and all her white friends live, in a neighbourhood call Belhaven. Down the road from Belhaven is white Woodland Hills, then Sherwood Forest, which is miles a big live oaks with the moss hanging down. Nobody living in it yet, but it's there for when the white folks is ready to move somewhere else new. Then it's the country, out where Miss Skeeter live on the Longleaf cotton plantation. She don't know it, but I picked cotton out there in 1931, during the Depression.

So Jackson's just one white neighbourhood after the next and more springing up down the road. But the coloured part a town, we one big anthill, surrounded by state land that ain't for sale. As our numbers get bigger, we can't spread out. Our part a town just gets thicker.

I get on the number six bus that afternoon, which goes from Belhaven to Farish Street. The bus full of maids heading home in our white uniforms. I spot Minny in the back seat. Minny short and big, got shiny black curls. She setting with her legs splayed, her thick arms crossed. She seventeen years younger than I am. Old lady like me's lucky to have her as a friend.

The bus cross the bridge and make the first stop in the coloured neighbourhood. A dozen or so maids get off. I go set in the seat next to Minny. She smile, bump me hello with her elbow.

'What you feed Miss Walter at bridge club today? I worked all morning making that fool a caramel cake and she wouldn't eat a crumb.'

That makes me remember what Miss Hilly say at the table today. 'I think I heard Miss Hilly say something about that, bout her mama getting skinny.' I say this careful. 'Say maybe she getting mal-nutritious.'

Minny look at me. 'She did, did she?' Just the name make her eyes narrow. 'What else Miss Hilly say?'

I better just go on and say it. 'I think she got her eye on you, Minny. Just . . . be extra careful around her.'

'Miss Hilly ought to be extra careful round *me*. What she say, I can't cook? She say that old bag a bones ain't eating cause I can't feed her?' Minny stand up, throw her bag up on her arm.

I watch her through the window, stomping off towards her house. Miss Hilly ain't somebody to mess with. Law, maybe I should a just kept it to myself.

A couple mornings later, I get off the bus, walk the block to Miss Leefolt's house. Parked in front is a old green lumber truck, with two coloured mens inside.

Mister Raleigh Leefolt still at home this morning, which is rare. Whenever he here, he look like he just counting the minutes till he get to go back to his accounting job. Even on Saturday. But today he carrying on bout something. I hide out in the washroom.

'This is my damn house and I pay for what goddamn goes in it!' Mister Leefolt yell. 'I put up with the new clothes, all the damn trips to New Orleans, but this takes the goddamn cake!'

'But it'll increase the value of the house. Hilly said so!'

'We can't afford it! And we do not take orders from the Holbrooks!'

Everthing get real quiet for a minute. Then I hear the *pap-pap* a little feetum pyjamas.

'Da-dee?'

I come out the washroom and into the kitchen then cause Mae Mobley's my business.

Mister Leefolt already kneeling down to her. He's wearing a smile look like it's made out a rubber. 'Guess what, honey?'

She smile back. She waiting for a good surprise.

'You're not going to college so your mama's friends don't have to use the same bathroom as the maid.'

He stomp off and slam the door so hard it make Baby Girl blink.

Miss Leefolt look down at her, start shaking her finger. 'Mae Mobley, you know you're not supposed to climb up out of your crib!'

Baby Girl, she looking at the door her daddy slammed, she looking at her mama frowning down at her. My baby, she swallowing it back, like she trying real hard not to cry.

'She keeps getting up,' say Miss Leefolt. 'I put her back in bed three times this morning.'

I rush past Miss Leefolt, pick Baby Girl up. 'Cause somebody needs changing. Whooooweeee.'

Miss Leefolt tisk, say, 'Well I didn't realise . . .' but she already staring out the window at the lumber truck.

I go on to the back, so mad I'm stomping. Baby Girl been in that bed since eight o'clock last night, a course she need changing! Miss Leefolt try to sit in twelve hours' worth a bathroom mess without getting up!

Baby Girl stare up at me while I take off her diaper. Then she reach out her little hand. She touch my mouth real soft.

'Mae Mo been bad,' she say.

'No, baby, you ain't been bad,' I say, smoothing her hair back. 'You been good. Real good.'

I live on Gessum Avenue, where I been renting since 1942. The houses all be small, but every front yard's different. I got a few red camellia bushes out front a the house. My grass be kind a spotty and I ain't got no trees. But the backyard, now it looks like the Garden of Eden. That's where my next-door neighbour, Ida Peek, got her vegetable patch.

Ida ain't got no backyard to speak of what with all her husband's junk—car engines and old refrigerators and tyres. So I tell Ida she come plant on my side. That way I don't have no mowing to tend to and she let me pick whatever I need, save me two or three dollars ever week.

I pick me a poke salad and a tomato out a Ida's garden. I fry up some ham. I set at my table to eat, turn on the kitchen radio. I skip over Pastor Green playing his sermon and stop on WBLA. Memphis Minny get to singing how lean meat won't fry, which is about how the love don't last. Time to time, I think I might find myself another man, one from my church. Problem is, much as I love the Lord, church-going man never do all that much for me. Kind a man I like ain't the kind that stays around when he done spending all you money. I made that mistake twenty years ago. When my husband Clyde left me for that no-count hussy up on Farish Street, one they call Cocoa, I figured I better shut the door for good on that kind a business.

A cat get to screeching outside and bring me back to my cold kitchen. I turn the radio off and the light back on, fish my prayer book out my bag. My prayer book is just a blue notepad I pick up at the store. I been writing my prayers since I was in junior high. When I tell my seventh-grade teacher I ain't coming back to school cause I got to help out my mama, Miss Ross just about cried.

'You're the smartest one in the class, Aibileen,' she say. 'And the only way you're going to keep sharp is to read *and write* every day.'

So I started writing my prayers down instead a saying em. But nobody's called me smart since.

I turn the pages a my prayer book to see who I got tonight. A few times this week, I thought about maybe putting Miss Skeeter on my list. I'm not real sure why. She always nice when she come over. It makes me nervous, but I can't help but wonder what she was gone ask me in Miss Leefolt's kitchen, about do I want to change things. I scan down my prayer list. My Mae Mobley got the number one rung, then they's Fanny Lou at church, ailing from the rheumatism. My sisters Inez and Mable in Port Gibson that got eighteen kids between em and six with the flu.

My tea kettle start fussing on the stove, bringing me back to real life. Law, I reckon I just go ahead and put Miss Skeeter on the list, but how come, I don't know. Which reminds me a what I don't want a think about, that Miss Leefolt's building me a bathroom cause she think I'm diseased. And Miss Skeeter asking don't I want to change things, like changing Jackson, Mississippi, gone be like changing a lightbulb.

My phone ring, making me jump. Before I can even say hello, I hear Minny. She working late tonight.

'Miss Hilly sending Miss Walter to the old lady home. I got to find myself a new job. And you know when she going? Next *week*.'

'Oh *no*, Minny.'

'I been looking, call ten ladies today. Not even a speck a interest.'

I am sorry to say I ain't surprised. 'Don't you worry, Minny. We gone find you somebody deaf as a doe-knob, just like Miss Walter.'

'Thank you, Aibileen. Miss Hilly been hinting round for me to come work for her. But you know I never take Yule May's job away . . . Now come on, Miss Walter, eat up a little green bean for me.' Minny say goodbye and hang up the phone.

For the next two days, that old green lumber truck is there again. They's hammering and digging going on in the front yard. I don't ask Miss Leefolt no questions about it and Miss Leefolt don't offer no explanation. She just peer out the door ever hour to see what's going on.

Three o'clock the racket stops and the mens get in they truck and leave. Miss Leefolt, she watch em drive off, let out a big sigh. Then she get in her car and go do whatever it is she do when she ain't nervous bout a couple a coloured mens hanging round her house.

After while, the phone ring.

'Miss Leef—'

'She telling everbody in town I'm stealing! That's why I can't get no work! That witch done turned me into the Smart-Mouthed Criminal Maid a Hinds County!'

'Hold on, Minny, get your breath—'

'Before work this morning, I go to the Renfroes' over on Sycamore and Miss Renfroe near bout chase me off the property. Say Miss Hilly told her about me, everbody know I stole a candelabra from Miss Walter!'

'Minny, I know you honest. God know you honest.'

Her voice dip down, like bees on a comb. 'When I walk into Miss Walter's, Miss Hilly be there and she try to give me twenty dollars. She say, "Take it. I know you need it." And I bout spit in her face. But I didn't. No sir.' She start making this panting noise, she say, 'I did *worse*.'

'What you did?'

'I ain't telling. I ain't telling nobody about that pie. But I give her what she deserve!' She wailing now and I feel a real cold fear. Ain't no game crossing Miss Hilly. 'I ain't never gone get no work again, Leroy gone kill me . . .' Minny hang up without even saying goodbye.

I don't know what she talking about a pie. But Law, knowing Minny, it could not have been good.

I'm stringing beans in Miss Leefolt's kitchen and the phone rings. I'm hoping it's Minny to say she found something. I done called everbody I ever waited on and they all told me the same thing: 'We ain't hiring.' But what they really mean is: 'We ain't hiring *Minny*.'

Even though Minny already had her last day a work three days ago, Miss Walter call Minny in secret last night, ask her to come in today cause the house feel too empty, what with most the furniture already taken away by Miss Hilly.

'Leefolt residence.'

'Um, hi. This is . . .' The lady stop, clear her throat. 'Hello. May I . . . may I please speak to Elizabeth Leer-folt?'

'Miss Leefolt ain't home right now. May I take a message?'

'This is . . . Celia Foote. My husband gave me this number here and I don't know Elizabeth, but . . . well, he said she knows all about the Children's Benefit and the Ladies League.' I know this name, but I can't quite place it. This woman talk like she from so deep in the country she got corn growing in her shoes.

'I give her your message,' I say. 'What's your number?'

'I'm kind of new here and, well, that's not true, I've been here a pretty good stretch, gosh, over a year now. I just don't really know anybody. I don't . . . get out too much.'

I remember then who she is. She the one Miss Hilly and Miss Leefolt always talking trash on cause she marry Miss Hilly's old boyfriend.

'I give her the message. What you say your number is again?'

'Oh, but I'm fixing to scoot off to the grocery store.'

'She don't reach you, she leave a message with your help,' I tell her.

'I don't have any help. In fact, I was planning on asking her about that too, if she could pass along the name of somebody good.'

'You looking for help?'

'I'm in a stitch trying to find somebody to come all the way out to Madison County.'

Well, what do you know. 'I know somebody real good. She known for her cooking and she look after you kids too. She even got her own car to drive out to you house. Her name is Minny Jackson, she at Lakewood eight-four-four-three-two.'

Baby Girl tug on my dress, say, 'Tum-my hurt.'

I get an idea. I pretend to cover the mouthpiece and say, 'Hold on, what's that Miss Leefolt? Uh-huh, I tell her.' I put the phone back to my mouth and say, 'Miss Celia, Miss Leefolt just walk in and she say she ain't feeling good but for you to go on and call Minny. She say she call you if she be needing help with the Benefit.'

'Oh! Tell her I said thank you. And I sure do hope she gets to feeling better. And to call me up anytime.'

'That's Minny Jackson at Lakewood eight-four-four-three-two. Hang on, what's that?' I get a cookie and give it to Mae Mobley, feel nothing but delight at the devil in me. I am lying and I don't even care.

I tell Miss Celia Foote, 'She say don't tell nobody bout her tip on Minny, cause all her friends want a hire her and they be real upset if they find out she give her to somebody else.'

Soon as we hang up, I dial Minny quick as I can. But just as I do, Miss Leefolt walk in the door. I quickly hang up again. This a real predicament. I gave this Miss Celia woman Minny's number at home, but Minny working today cause Miss Walter lonely. So when she call, Leroy gone give her Miss Walter number cause he a fool. If Miss Walter answer the phone when Miss Celia call, then the whole jig is up. Miss Walter gone tell this woman everthing Miss Hilly been spreading around.

Miss Leefolt head to her bedroom and, just like I figured, the first thing she do is tie up the phone. First she call Miss Hilly, then the hairdresser. Soon as she hang up, she come out and ask what they having for supper this week. I pull out the list.

Mae Mobley's dancing a hot-foot jig trying to get her mama to notice her. And just when Miss Leefolt about to bend down to pay her some attention, whoops! Miss Leefolt run out the door cause she forgot she got a errand to run.

I can't make my fingers go round that dial fast enough. 'Minny! I got a job lined up. But you got to get to the phone—'

'She already call.' Minny's voice is flat. 'Leroy give her the number.'

'So Miss Walter answer it,' I say.

'Deaf as doo-doo and all a sudden it's like a miracle from God, she hear the phone ringing. I'm going in and out a the kitchen, not paying attention, but at the end I hear my name.'

'Well. Maybe Miss Walter didn't tell her them lies Miss Hilly started. You never know.' But even I ain't fool enough to believe this.

'Even if she didn't, Miss Walter know all about how I got back at Miss Hilly. You don't know about the Terrible Awful Thing I did. I'm sure Miss Walter tell this woman I'm nothing short a the devil hisself.' Her voice sound eerie. Like she a record player going too slow.

'I be praying for you.'

We hang up and I go to mopping. Mae Mobley come up holding her tummy, say, 'Make it not hurt.'

She lay her face on my leg. I smooth her hair down over and over till she practically purring, feeling the love in my hand. And I think about all my friends, what they done for me. What they do ever day for the white women they waiting on. That pain in Minny's voice. Treelore dead in the ground. I look down at Baby Girl, who I know, deep down, I can't keep from turning out like her mama. I close my eyes, say the Lord's prayer to myself. But it don't make me feel any better.

Law help me, but something's gone have to be done.

Baby Girl hug on my legs all afternoon to where I bout fall over a few times. I don't mind. After while me and Mae Mobley go in the regular living room. I got a load a Mister Leefolt's shirts to iron. Miss Leefolt come in and watch me ironing. She do that sometimes. Frown and look. Then she smile real quick when I glance up.

'Aibileen, I have a surprise for you.'

She smiling big now. 'Mister Leefolt and I have decided to build you your very own bathroom.' She clap her hands together, drop her chin at me. 'It's right out there in the garage.'

'Yes ma'am.' Where she think I been all this time?

'So, from now on, instead of using the guest bathroom, you can use your own right out there. Won't that be nice?'

'Yes ma'am.' I keep ironing.

'So you'll use that one out in the garage now, you understand?'

I don't look at her. I'm not trying to make no trouble, but she done made her point.

'Don't you want to get some tissue and go on out there and use it?'

'Miss Leefolt, I don't really have to go right this second.'

'Oh.' Miss Leefolt lick her lips a few times. 'But when you do, you'll go on back there and use that one now, I mean . . . only that one, right?'

I say what I know she want to hear: 'I use my coloured bathroom from now on. Then I go on and Clorox the white bathroom again real good.'

'Well, there's no hurry. Anytime today would be fine.'

But by the way she standing there fiddling with her wedding ring, she really mean for me to do it right now.

I put the iron down real slow, feel that bitter seed grow in my chest, the one planted after Treelore died. My face goes hot, my tongue twitchy. I don't know what to say to her. All I know is, I ain't saying it.

MINNY

STANDING ON that white lady's back porch, I tell myself, *Tuck it in, Minny.* Tuck in whatever might fly out my mouth and tuck in my behind too. Look like a maid who does what she's told. I rehearse what to say, what to keep to myself. I go ahead and punch the bell.

The doorbell rings a long *bing-bong*, fine and fancy for this big mansion out in the country. It looks like a castle, grey brick rising high in the sky and left and right too. Trees surround the lawn on every side.

The back door opens and there stands Miss Marilyn Monroe. Or something kin to her.

'Hey there, you're right on time. I'm Celia. Celia Rae Foote.'

The white lady sticks her hand out to me and I study her. She might be built like Marilyn, but she ain't ready for no screen test. She's got flour in her yellow hairdo. And flour all over that tacky pink pantsuit.

'Yes, ma'am. I'm Minny Jackson.' I smooth down my white uniform instead of shaking her hand. I don't want that mess on me. 'You cooking something?'

'One of those upside-down cakes from the magazine?' She sighs. 'It ain't working out too good.'

I follow her inside and that's when I see Miss Celia Rae Foote's suffered only a minor injury in the flour fiasco. The rest of the kitchen took the real hit. The counter tops, the double-door refrigerator, the Kitchen-Aid mixer are all sitting in about a quarter-inch of flour snow.

Miss Celia says, 'I guess I have some learning to do.'

'You sure do,' I say. But I bite down hard on my tongue.

Miss Celia, she just smiles, washes the muck off her hands in a sink full of dishes. I wonder if maybe I've found myself another deaf one, like Miss Walter was. Let's hope so.

'I just can't seem to get the hang of kitchen work,' she says and even with Marilyn's whispery Hollywood voice, I can tell right off, she's from *way* out in the country. I look down and see the fool doesn't have any shoes on, like some kind of white trash.

She's probably ten or fifteen years younger than me, twenty-two, twenty-three, and she's real pretty, but why's she wearing all that goo on her face? I'll bet she's got on double the make-up the other white ladies wear. She's got a lot more bosom to her, too. In fact, she's almost as big as me except she's skinny in all those places I ain't.

'Can I get you a cold drink?' she asks. 'Set down and I'll bring you something.'

I look at Miss Celia Rae Foote hard. I've never in my life had a white woman tell me to sit down so she can serve me a cold drink.

'Maybe we better go on and see the house first, ma'am.'

'Oh, of course. Come on in yonder, Maxie. I'll show you the fancy dining room first.'

'The name,' I say, 'is Minny.'

Maybe she's not deaf or crazy. Maybe she's just stupid.

All over that big ole doodied-up house she walks and talks and I follow. There are ten rooms downstairs and one with a stuffed grizzly bear that looks like it ate up the last maid and is biding for the next one. We move on and it starts to look like any nice white house. Except this one's the biggest I've ever been in and full of dirty floors and dusty rugs, the kind folks who don't know any better would say is worn out, but I know an antique when I see one.

'Johnny's mama wouldn't let me decorate a thing. I had my way, there'd be wall-to-wall white carpet and gold trim and none of this old stuff.'

'Where your people from?' I ask her.

'I'm from . . . Sugar Ditch.' Her voice drops down a little. Sugar Ditch is as low as you can go in Mississippi, maybe the whole United States. I saw pictures in the paper one time, showing those shacks. Even the white kids looked like they hadn't had a meal for a week.

Miss Celia tries to smile, says, 'This is my first time hiring a maid.'

'Well, you sure need one.' *Now, Minny—*

'I was real glad to get the recommendation from Missus Walter. She told me all about you. Said your cooking is the best in town.'

That makes zero sense. 'She say . . . anything else about me?'

But Miss Celia's already walking up a big curving staircase. I follow her upstairs, to a long hall with sun coming through the windows. Even though there are two yellow bedrooms for girls and a blue one and a green one for boys, it's clear there aren't any children living here.

'We've got five bedrooms and five bathrooms over here in the main house.' She points out the window and I see a big blue swimming pool, and behind that, *another* house. 'And then there's the pool house out yonder,' she sighs.

I'd take any job I can get at this point, but a big house like this should pay plenty. And I don't mind being busy. I ain't afraid to work. 'When you gone have you some chilluns, start filling up all these beds?' I try to smile, look friendly.

'Oh, we're gonna have some kids.' She clears her throat, fidgets. 'I mean, kids is the only thing worth living for.' She looks down at her feet. A second passes before she heads back to the stairs.

It's back in the dining room that Miss Celia starts shaking her head. 'It's an awful lot to do,' she says. 'All the bedrooms and the floors . . .'

'Yes, ma'am, it's big,' I say, thinking if she saw my house with one toilet for six behinds, she'd probably run. 'But I got lots a energy.'

'. . . and then there's all this silver to clean.'

She opens up a silver closet the size of my living room and I can see why she's looking so doubtful.

After the town got word of Miss Hilly's lies, three ladies in a row hung up on me the minute I said my name. I ready myself for the blow. *Say it, lady. Say what you thinking about me and your silver.*

'You got a big, pretty house,' I say. 'All the way out here in the country. Lot a work to be done.'

She starts fiddling with her rings. 'I guess Missus Walter's was a lot easier than this would be. I mean, it's just us now, but when we get to having kids . . .'

'You, uh, got some other maids you considering?'

She sighs. 'A bunch have come out here. I just haven't found . . . the right one yet.' She bites on her fingernails, shifts her eyes away. 'I knew it was gonna be a chore finding someone, and if I were you I wouldn't want to clean this big house either.'

'When you hear me say I don't want a clean this house?'

'It's all right, five maids have already told me it's too much work.'

I look down at my hundred-and-sixty-five-pound, five-foot-zero self practically busting out of my uniform. 'Too much for me?'

She blinks at me a second. 'You . . . you'll do it?'

'Why you think I drove all the way out here to kingdom come, just to burn gas?' I clamp my mouth shut. *Don't go ruining this now, she offering you a jay-o-bee.* 'Miss Celia, I be happy to work for you.'

She laughs and the crazy woman goes to hug me, but I step back a little, let her know that's not the kind of thing I do.

'Hang on now, we got to talk about some things first. You got to tell me what days you want me here and . . . and that kind a thing.' *Like how much you paying.*

'I thought . . . Monday through Friday? Eight to four with some time for lunch or what-have-you.'

'That's just fine.'

Miss Celia looks down. 'Missus Walter said you were a real good cook and I'm hoping you'll teach me. How much was she paying you?'

'Dollar an hour,' I say, feeling kind of ashamed. Five years and not even minimum wage.

'Then I'll pay you two.'

And I feel all the breath slip out of me.

I sit in the sagging seat of the Ford Leroy's still paying his boss twelve dollars every week for. Relief hits me. I have finally gotten myself a job.

'**S**it down on your behind, Minny, because I'm about to tell you the rules for working in a white lady's house.'

I was fourteen years old to the day, bout to quit school and start my first real job. I sat at the little wooden table in my mama's kitchen eyeing that caramel cake on the cooling rack, waiting to be iced. Birthdays were the only day of the year I was allowed to eat as much as I wanted.

'Rule number one for working for a white lady, Minny: it is nobody's business. You keep your nose out of your white lady's problems, you don't go crying to her with yours. Remember one thing: white people are not your friends. They don't want to hear about it.

'Rule number two: don't you *ever* let that white lady find you sitting on her toilet. If there's not one out back for the help, you find yourself a time when she's not there, in a bathroom she doesn't use.

'Rule number three: when you're cooking white people's food, you taste it with a different spoon. You put that spoon to your mouth, think nobody's looking, put it back in the pot, might as well throw it out.

'Rule number four: you use the same cup, same fork, same plate every day. Keep it in a separate cupboard and tell that white woman that's the one you'll use from here on out.

'Rule number five: you eat in the kitchen.

'Rule number six: you don't hit on her children. White people like to do their own spanking.

'Rule number seven: this is the last one, Minny. Are you listening to me? No sass-mouthing. You sass a white woman in the morning, you'll be sassing out on the street in the afternoon.'

First day at my white lady's house, I ate my ham sandwich in the kitchen, put my plate up in my spot in the cupboard. When her little brat hid my pocketbook in the oven, I didn't whop her on the behind.

But then the white lady said: 'Now be sure and handwash all the clothes first, then put them in the electric machine to finish up,' and I said: 'Why I got to handwash when the power washer gone do the job? That's the biggest waste a time I ever heard of.'

White lady smiled at me, and five minutes later, I was out on the street.

Working for Miss Celia, I'll get to see my kids off to Spann Elementary in the morning but since no bus goes all the way out to Miss Celia's, I have to take Leroy's car.

'You ain't taking my car every day, woman, what if I get the day shift and need to—'

'She paying me seventy dollars cash every Friday, Leroy.'

'Maybe I take the bike.'

'I'm here, Miss Celia.' I stick my head in her bedroom that first morning after the interview and there she is, propped up on the covers with her make-up perfect and her tight Friday-night clothes on even though it's Tuesday, reading the trash in the *Hollywood Digest* like it's the Holy B.

'Good morning, Minny! It's real good to see you,' she says, and I bristle, hearing a white lady being so friendly.

'When can we get to our first cooking lesson?' she asks.

'In a few days, after you go to the store and pick up what we need.'

She thinks about this a second, says, 'Maybe you ought to go, Minny, since you know what to buy and all.'

I look at her. Most white women like to do their own shopping. 'All right, I go in the morning, then.'

Then I tell her she needs to go on in the living room, let me do my work in here. When she's gone, I eyeball the room, at how neat it all looks. Real slow, I open her closet and just like I thought, forty-five things fall down on my head. Then I look under the bed and find enough dirty clothes to where I bet she hasn't washed in months.

That afternoon, Miss Celia and I make a list of what to cook that week, and the next morning I do the grocery shopping. But it takes me twice as long because I have to drive all the way to the white Jitney

Jungle since I figure she won't eat food from a coloured grocery store. When I get to work, I'm ready to fight with her over all the reasons I'm late, but there Miss Celia is on the bed like before, smiling like it doesn't matter. All dressed up and going nowhere. For five hours she sits there, reading the magazines. But I don't ask. I'm just the maid.

At one o'clock, Miss Celia comes in the kitchen and says she's ready for her first cooking lesson. She settles on a stool.

'What you know how to cook already?' I ask.

'I can boil potatoes. And I can do grits. We didn't have electric current out where I lived. But you'll teach me to cook right, won't you?'

Lord. I've never met a white person worse off than me except for crazy Mister Wally, lives behind the Canton feed store and eats cat food.

'I'll try,' I say, even though I've never told a white woman what to do and I don't really know how to start.

I turn on the flame and we watch some fat melt in the pan. 'Chicken's been soaking in the buttermilk,' I say. 'Now mix up the dry.' I pour flour, salt, pepper, paprika and a pinch of cayenne into a paper sack.

'Now. Put the chicken parts in the bag and shake it.'

Miss Celia puts a raw chicken thigh in, bumps the bag around. 'Like this? Just like the Shake 'n Bake commercials on the tee-vee?'

'Yeah,' I say and run my tongue up over my teeth because if that's not an insult, I don't know what is. Real careful, I lay the dark meat in the pan. It bubbles up like a song and we watch the thighs and legs turn brown. I look over and Miss Celia's smiling at me.

'What? Something on my face?'

'No,' she says, tears coming up in her eyes. She touches my arm. 'I'm just real grateful you're here.'

I move my arm back from under her hand. 'Miss Celia, you got a lot more to be grateful for than me.'

'I know.' She looks at her fancy kitchen like it's something that tastes bad. 'I never dreamed I'd have this much. I've never been happier in my whole life.'

Underneath all that happy, she sure doesn't look happy.

That night, I call Aibileen.

'Miss Hilly was at Miss Leefolt's yesterday,' Aibileen says. 'She ask if anybody knew where you was working.'

'Lordy, she find me out there, she ruin it for sure.' It's been two weeks since the Terrible Awful Thing I did to that woman. I know she'd just love to see me fired on the spot.

'What Leroy say when you told him you got the job?' Aibileen asks.

'Shoot. He strut around the kitchen like a plumed rooster cause he in front a the kids,' I say. 'Later on though, we in bed and I thought my big old bull for a husband gone cry.'

Aibileen laughs. 'Leroy got a lot a pride.'

My first week at Miss Celia's, I scrub the house until there isn't a dust rag or a stripped sheet left to wipe with. Second week, I scrub the house again because it's like the dirt grew back. Third week, I am satisfied and settle in my ways.

My housekeeping tasks fall on the same day for every job I take: on Monday, I oil up the furniture. Tuesday, I wash and iron the damn sheets, the day I hate. Wednesday is for scrubbing the bathtub real good even though I wipe it down every morning. Thursday is for polishing floors and sucking rugs, minding the antique ones with a hand broom. Friday is heavy cooking for the weekend and what-have-you. And every day is mopping, washing clothes and ironing shirts so they don't go getting out of hand, and generally keeping things clean. Silver and windows, they're as needed. Since there aren't any kids to look after, there's ample time left for Miss Celia's so-called cooking lessons.

Miss Celia never does any entertaining, so we just fix whatever she and Mister Johnny are having for supper: pork chops, fried chicken, baked ham, fried tomatoes, mashed potatoes, plus the vegetables. Or at least I cook and Miss Celia fidgets. When the lesson's over, she rushes back to laying down. In fact, the only time Miss Celia leaves the *house* is to get her hair frosted and her ends trimmed. So far, that's only happened once in the three weeks I've been working.

'Do you think I'm getting any better at cooking?' she says, and I look at her. She's got a pretty smile, white straight teeth, but she is the worst cook I have ever seen.

'Get the ham hock out, make sure you got enough water in there, that's right. Now turn up the flame. See that little bubble there, that means the water's happy.'

And when Miss Celia burns the beans, I try and use some of that self-control my mama swore I was born without. 'All right,' I say through my teeth, 'we'll do another batch fore Mister Johnny get home.'

Miss Celia stares out the back window at the coloured man raking up the leaves. She's got so many azalea bushes, her yard's going to look like *Gone With the Wind* come spring. I don't like azaleas and I sure didn't like the way they made slavery look like a big happy tea party. If I'd played Mammy, I'd of told Scarlett to stick those green draperies up her white little pooper. Make her own damn man-catching dress.

'I know I could make that rose bush bloom if I pruned it back,' Miss Celia says. 'But the first thing I'd do is cut down that mimosa tree.'

'What's wrong with that tree?' I don't even have a shrub, much less a tree, in my entire yard.

'I don't like those hairy flowers.' She gazes off like she's gone soft in the head. 'They look like little baby hairs.'

I get the creepers with her talking that way. 'You know about flowers?'

She sighs. 'I used to love to tend to my flowers back in Sugar Ditch. I learned to grow things, hoping I could pretty up all that ugliness.'

'Go head outside then,' I say, trying not to sound too excited. 'Take some exercise. Get some fresh air.' *Get out a here.*

'No,' Miss Celia sighs. 'I shouldn't be running round out there. I need to be still.'

It's starting to irritate me how she never leaves the house, how the maid walking in every morning is the best part of her day. 'Maybe you ought to go make some friends,' I say. 'Lot a ladies your age in town.'

She frowns at me. 'I've been trying. I can't tell you the umpteen times I've called those ladies to see if I can help with the Children's Benefit. But they won't call me back. None of them.'

I don't say anything to this because ain't that a surprise. With her bosoms hanging out and her hair coloured Gold Nugget.

'Go shopping, then. Go get you some new clothes. Go do whatever white women do when the maid's home.'

'No, I think I'll go rest awhile,' she says and two minutes later I hear her creeping round upstairs in the empty bedrooms.

MISS SKEETER

I DRIVE MY MAMA'S Cadillac fast on the gravel road, headed home. Patsy Cline can't even be heard on the radio anymore, for all the rocks banging the side of the car. Mother would be furious, but I just drive faster. I can't stop thinking about what Hilly said today at bridge club.

Hilly and Elizabeth and I have been best friends since Power Elementary. At college, at Ole Miss, Hilly and I roomed together for two years before she left to get married and I stayed on to graduate. But today, she threatened to throw me out of the League.

I turn up the lane that leads to Longleaf, my family's cotton plantation. The gravel quiets to smooth yellow dust and I slow down before Mother sees how fast I'm driving. I pull up to the house and get out. Mother is rocking on the front porch.

'Come sit, darling,' she says, waving me towards a rocking chair beside her. 'Pascagoula's just waxed the floors. Let them dry awhile.'

'All right, Mama.' I kiss her powdery cheek. But I don't sit. I lean on the porch railing, look out on the three mossy oak trees in the front yard. Surrounding our yard lie 10,000 acres of Daddy's cotton fields, the plants green and strong, tall as my waist.

'Did I tell you?' Mother says. 'Fanny Peatrow got engaged.'

'Good for Fanny.'

'Not even a month after she got that teller job at the Farmers Bank.'

'That's great, Mother.'

'I know,' she says, and I turn to see one of those lightbulb-popping looks of hers. 'Why don't you go down to the bank and apply for a job?'

'I don't want to be a bank teller, Mama.'

Mother sighs. 'Four years my daughter goes off to college and what does she come home with?' she asks.

'A diploma?'

'A pretty piece of paper,' Mother says.

'I told you. I didn't meet anybody I wanted to marry,' I say.

Mother rises from her chair, comes close so I'll look her in her smooth, pretty face. 'I talked to Fanny's mother and she said Fanny was practically swimming in opportunities once she got that job.'

I'll never be able to tell Mother I want to be a writer. She's gripping the rail, waiting to see if I'll do what fat Fanny Peatrow did to save herself. My own mother is looking at me as if I completely baffle her mind with my looks, my height, my hair. To say I have frizzy hair is an understatement. It is kinky, more pubic than cranial, and whitish blonde, breaking off easily, like hay. My skin is fair and while some call this creamy, it can look deathly when I'm serious, which is all the time. Also, there's a slight bump of cartilage along the top of my nose. But my eyes are cornflower blue, like Mother's. I'm told they're my best feature.

'It's all about putting yourself in a man-meeting situation—'

'Mama,' I say, just wanting to end this conversation, 'would it really be so terrible if I never met a husband?'

Mother clutches her bare arms as if made cold by the thought. 'Don't. Don't say that, Eugenia. Why, every week I see another man in town over six feet and I think, *If Eugenia would just try . . .*' She presses her hand to her stomach, the very thought advancing her ulcers.

I walk down the front porch steps. I shudder with the same left-behind feeling I've had since I graduated from college, three months ago. I've been dropped off in a place I do not belong anymore.

I was not a cute baby. When I was born, my older brother, Carlton Jr, looked at me and declared to the hospital room, 'It's not a baby, it's a skeeter!' and from there the name stuck. I was long and leggy and mosquito-thin. Mother's spent my entire life trying to convince people to call me by my given name, Eugenia.

By sixteen I wasn't just not pretty, I was painfully tall. The kind of tall that puts a girl in the back row of class pictures with the boys. Mother was five foot four and first runner-up as Miss South Carolina.

Mrs Charlotte Boudreau Cantrelle Phelan's Guide to Husband-Hunting, rule number one: a pretty, petite girl should accentuate with make-up and good posture. A tall plain one, with a trust fund.

I was five foot eleven but I had 25,000 cotton dollars in my name and if the beauty in that was not apparent then, by God, he wasn't smart enough to be in the family anyway.

My bedroom is the top floor of my parents' house. It is actually the attic, with long, sloping walls papered in mint-green rosebuds, and I cannot stand straight in many places. It is my sanctuary. The heat swells and gathers like a hot-air balloon up here, not exactly welcoming others, and the stairs are narrow and difficult for parents to climb.

Three days after my conversation with Mother on the porch, I spread out the help-wanted ads from the *Jackson Journal* on my desk. All morning, Mother's been following me around with a new hair-straightening thing while Daddy's been on the front porch growling and goddamning the cotton fields because they're melting like summer snow. Besides boll weevils, rain is just about the worst thing that can happen at harvest time. It's hardly September but the fall drenches have already begun.

I scan the squat, single column under HELP WANTED: FEMALE.

Kennington's Dept. Str. seeks salesgirls w/poise, manners & a smile!

Trim, young secretary wanted. Typing not nec. Call Mr Sanders. Jesus, if he doesn't want her to type, what does he want her to do?

No one could argue that I hadn't worked hard at Ole Miss. While my friends were out drinking rum and colas, I sat and wrote for hours—mostly essays but also short stories, bad poetry, letters of complaint, love letters to boys I'd seen in class, all of which I never mailed. I dreamed of having dates, but my real dream was that one day I would write something that people would actually read.

In my last term I only applied for one job, but it was a good one, being six hundred miles away from Mississippi. I'd seen the ad for an editor position at the Harper & Row publishing house in Manhattan in *The New York Times* down at the library and mailed them my résumé that very day. I never even heard back from them.

'Miss Skeeter, you got a phone call,' I hear Pascagoula holler at the bottom of the stairs.

I go downstairs to the only phone in the house. Pascagoula holds the phone out to me. She is as tiny as a child, not even five feet tall, and black as night. Her hair is curly round her head and her white uniform dress has been tailored to fit her short arms and legs.

'Miss Hilly on the phone for you,' she says.

I sit at the white iron table. The kitchen is large and square and hot.

'He's coming next weekend,' Hilly says. 'On Saturday night. You free?'

'Gee, let me check my calendar,' I say. All traces of our bridge club argument are gone from Hilly's voice. I'm suspicious but relieved.

'I can't believe this is *finally* going to happen,' Hilly says, because she's been trying to set me up for months with her husband's cousin. She's intent on it even though he's much too good-looking for me, not to mention a state senator's son.

'Don't you think we should . . . meet first?' I ask. 'I mean, before we go out on an actual date?'

'There's nothing wrong with him,' Hilly said. 'Ask Elizabeth, she met him last year. Not to mention he dated Patricia van Devender forever.'

'Patricia van Devender?' Most Beautiful at Ole Miss two years in a row.

'Plus he started his own oil business over in Vicksburg. So if it doesn't work out, it's not like you'll be running into him every day.'

I sigh. The date's been cancelled twice already. I can only hope it'll be put off again. And yet I'm flattered that Hilly has so much faith that someone like him would be interested in someone like me.

'Oh, and I need you to come on by and pick up these notes,' Hilly says. 'I want my Initiative in the next newsletter.'

I pause. 'The bathroom thing?' I'd hoped it was forgotten.

'It's the Home Help Sanitation Initiative and I want it in this week.'

I am editor of the League newsletter. But Hilly is president. And she's trying to tell me what to print.

'I'll see. I don't know if there's room,' I lie.

From the sink, Pascagoula sneaks a look at me, as if she can hear what Hilly's saying. I look over at the bathroom off the kitchen. The door's half open and I can see a tiny room with a toilet, a pull string flusher at the top, a bulb with a yellowing plastic shade, a small corner sink. I've never once been inside. When we were kids, Mother told us she'd spank us if we went in Constantine's bathroom. I miss our old maid Constantine more than anything I've ever missed in my life.

'Then make room,' Hilly says, 'because this is pretty darn important.'

Constantine lived about a mile from our house, in a small Negro neighbourhood called Hotstack, named after the tar plant that used to operate back there. If I begged and practised my catechism, Mother would let me go home with Constantine on Friday afternoons.

After twenty minutes of walking slow, we'd pass the coloured store, then a grocer with hens laying in back, and all along the way, dozens of shack-like roadside houses with tin roofs and slanting porches, along with a yellow one that everybody said sold whiskey from the back door. It was a thrill to be in such a different world and I'd feel a prickly awareness of how good my shoes were, how clean my white pinafore dress that Constantine had ironed for me.

There were always dogs, hollow-stomached and mangy, laid out in the road. A little farther on, we'd get to Constantine's house. It had three rooms and no rugs and I'd look at the single photograph she had, of a white girl she told me she looked after for twenty years over in Port Gibson. I used to stare at the toothy smile of that child, a little jealous, wondering why she didn't have a picture of me up too.

After an hour or so, Daddy would pull up, get out, hand Constantine a dollar. Not once did Constantine invite him inside. Even back then, I understood we were on Constantine's turf and she didn't have to be nice to anybody at her own house.

'Don't tell your mama I gave Constantine a little extra, now.'

'OK, Daddy,' I'd say. That's about the only secret my daddy and I have ever shared.

The first time I was ever called ugly, I was thirteen. It was a rich friend of my brother Carlton's, over to shoot guns in the field.

'Why you crying, girl?' Constantine asked me in the kitchen.

I told her what the boy had called me, tears streaming down my face.

'Now you look a here, Eugenia'—because Constantine was the only one who'd occasionally follow Mama's rule. 'Ugly live up on the inside. Ugly be a hurtful, mean person. Is you one a them peoples?'

'I don't know. I don't think so,' I sobbed.

Constantine sat down next to me, at the kitchen table. I heard the cracking of her swollen joints. She pressed her thumb hard in the palm of my hand, something we both knew meant *listen. Listen to me.*

'Ever morning, until you dead in the ground, you gone have to make this decision.' Constantine was so close, I could see the blackness of her gums. 'You gone have to ask yourself, *Am I gone believe what them fools say about me today?'*

She kept her thumb pressed hard in my hand. I nodded that I understood. And even though I still felt miserable, and knew that I was, most likely, ugly, it was the first time she ever talked to me like I was something besides my mother's white child. All my life I'd been told what to believe. But with Constantine's thumb pressed in my hand, I realised I actually had a choice in what I could believe.

Constantine came to work in our house at six in the morning. I came downstairs nearly every day to her standing in the kitchen, Preacher Green playing on the radio that sat on the kitchen table. The minute she saw me, she smiled: 'Good morning, beautiful girl!'

Mother ate her breakfast early in the dining room, then moved to the relaxing room to do needlepoint or write letters to missionaries in Africa. From her green wing chair, she could see everyone going almost anywhere in the house.

'Eugenia, you know there is no chewing gum in this house.'

'Eugenia, go put alcohol on that blemish.'

I learned that socks are stealthier transportation than shoes. I learned to use the back door. But mostly, I learned to just stay in the kitchen.

A summer month could stretch on for years, out on Longleaf. I didn't have friends coming over every day—we lived too far out to have any white neighbours. I took Constantine for granted at times, but I think I knew, for the most part, how lucky I was to have her there.

When I was fourteen, I started smoking cigarettes. I'd sneak them from Carlton's packs of Marlboros. He was almost eighteen and no one minded that he'd been smoking for years anywhere he wanted to in the house or out in the fields with Daddy. Mother told me I wasn't allowed to smoke until I was seventeen.

So I'd slip into the backyard and sit in the tyre swing, with the huge old oak tree concealing me. Mother had eagle-eyes, but almost zero sense of smell. Constantine knew immediately, though. She narrowed her eyes, with a little smile, but said nothing. If Mother headed to the back porch while I was behind the tree, Constantine would rush out and bang her broom handle on the iron stair rail.

'Constantine, what are you doing?' Mother would ask her, but by then I would've stubbed my cigarette out and dropped it in the hole in the tree.

'Just cleaning this here old broom, Miss Charlotte.'

'Well, find a way to do it a little quieter, please. Oh, Eugenia, what, did you grow another inch overnight? What am I going to do? Go . . . put on a dress that fits.'

'Yes, ma'am,' Constantine and I would say at the same time and then pass each other a little smile.

'Just you and me this weekend,' Constantine said, one day.

It was the weekend that Mother and Daddy were driving Carlton to look at Louisiana State University and Tulane. My brother was going to college next year. That morning, Daddy had moved a folding bed into the kitchen, next to Constantine's bathroom. That's where she always slept when she spent the night.

'Go look what I got,' she said, pointing to the broom closet. I went and opened it and saw, tucked in her bag, a five hundred piece puzzle with a picture of Mount Rushmore on it. It was our favourite thing to do when she stayed over.

That night we sat for hours, munching on peanuts, sifting through the pieces spread out on the kitchen table. A storm raged outside, making the room cosy while we picked out the edges. The bulb in the kitchen dimmed then brightened again.

'Which one he?' Constantine asked, studying the puzzle box through her black-rimmed glasses.

'That's Jefferson.'

'Oh, it sure is. What about him?'

'That's—' I leaned over. 'I think that's . . . Roosevelt.'

'Only one I recognise is Lincoln. He look like my daddy.'

I stopped, puzzle piece in hand. 'Because your daddy was so . . . tall?'

She chuckled. 'Cause my daddy was white. I got the tall from Mama.'

I put the piece down. 'Your . . . father was white and your mother was . . . coloured?'

'Yup,' she said and smiled, snapping two pieces together. 'Well, look a there. Got me a match.'

I had so many questions—*Who* was he? *Where* was he? I knew he wasn't married to Constantine's mother, because that was against the law. I picked a cigarette from my stash I'd brought to the table. I was fourteen but, feeling very grown up, I lit it.

'Oh, my daddy looooved me. Always said I was his favourite.' She leaned back in her chair. 'He used to come over to the house ever Saturday afternoon and, one time, he give me a set a ten hair ribbons, ten different colours. I sat in his lap from the minute he got there until he had to leave.'

I listened wide-eyed, stupid.

'One time I was boo-hooing he hugged me to him for the longest time. When I looked up, he was crying too and he . . . did that thing I do to you so you know I mean it. Press his thumb up in my hand and he say . . . he sorry.'

We sat there, staring at the puzzle pieces. Mother wouldn't want me to know this, that Constantine's father was white, that he'd apologised to her for the way things were. It was something I wasn't supposed to know. I felt like Constantine had given me a gift.

'How come you never told me this before,' I said.

She stared at me, and I saw a deep, bleak sadness there, inside of her. After a while, she said, 'Some things I just got to keep for myself.'

When it was my turn to go off to college, Mother cried her eyes out when Daddy and I pulled away in the truck. But I felt free. I was off the farm, out from under the criticism.

I wrote Constantine a letter once a week, telling her about my room, the classes, the sorority. Twice a month, Constantine wrote me back on parchment paper that folded into an envelope. She wrote me every mundane detail of Longleaf: *My back pains are bad but it's my feet that are worse,* or *The mixer broke off from the bowl and flew wild around the kitchen and the cat hollered and ran off. I haven't seen her since.* Our letters were like a year-long conversation, answering questions back and forth, continuing face-to-face in the holidays.

Mother's letters said: *Say your prayers* and *Don't wear heels because they make you too tall* clipped to a cheque for thirty-five dollars.

In April of my last year, a letter came from Constantine that said: *I have a surprise for you, Skeeter. I am so excited I almost can't stand myself.*

And don't you go asking me about it neither. You will see for yourself when you come home.

That was close to final exams, with graduation only a month away. And that was the last letter I ever got from Constantine.

When I got home after graduating, Mother stepped back to get a better look at me. 'Well, your skin looks beautiful,' she said, 'but your hair . . .' She sighed, shook her head.

'Where's Constantine?' I asked. 'In the kitchen?'

And like she was delivering the weather, Mother said, 'Constantine is no longer employed here. Now, let's get all these trunks unpacked.'

I didn't think I'd heard her correctly. 'What did you say?'

Mother stood straighter, smoothing down her dress. 'Constantine's gone, Skeeter. She went to live with her people up in Chicago.'

'But . . . what? She didn't say anything in her letters about Chicago.' I knew that wasn't her surprise. She would've told me such terrible news immediately.

Mother took a deep breath. 'I told Constantine she wasn't to write to you about leaving. Not in the middle of your final exams. What if you'd flunked and had to stay on another year?'

'And she . . . agreed to that?'

Mother looked off, sighed. 'We'll discuss it later, Eugenia.'

By September, not only had I given up hope of ever hearing back from Harper & Row, I gave up on ever finding Constantine. It was like she'd simply disappeared. I had to accept that Constantine, my one true ally, had left me to fend for myself with these people.

On a hot September morning, I wake up in my childhood bed, slip on the huarache shoes Carlton brought me back from Mexico. A man's pair since, evidently, Mexican girls' feet don't grow to size nine-and-a-half. Mother hates them and says they're trashy-looking.

Over my nightgown, I put on one of Daddy's old button-down shirts and slip out the front door. On either side of the drive, the cotton fields are a glaring green, fat with bolls. I head down the steps to see if my mail-order copy of *The Catcher in the Rye* is in the box. I always order the banned books from a black-market dealer in California, figuring if the State of Mississippi banned them, they must be good.

I open the mailbox. There, underneath Mother's *Ladies' Home Journal*, is a letter addressed to Miss Eugenia Phelan. The red raised font in the corner says Harper & Row, Publishers. I tear it open.

September 4, 1962

Dear Miss Phelan,

I am responding personally to your résumé because I found it admirable that a young lady with absolutely no work experience would apply for an editing job at a publisher as prestigious as ours. A minimum of five years in the business is mandatory for such a job.

Having once been an ambitious young lady myself, however, I've decided to offer you some advice: go to your local newspaper and get a job. You included in your letter that you 'immensely enjoy writing.' When you're not making mimeographs or fixing coffee, look around, investigate, and write. Don't waste your time on the obvious things. Write about what disturbs you, particularly if it bothers no one else.

Yours sincerely,

Elaine Stein, Senior Editor, Adult Book Division

Below the type is a handwritten note, in a choppy blue scrawl:

P.S. If you are truly serious, I'd be willing to look over your best ideas and give my opinion. I offer this for no better reason, Miss Phelan, than someone once did it for me.

A truck full of cotton rumbles by on the County Road. The Negro in the passenger side leans out and stares. I've forgotten I am a white girl in a thin nightgown. I have just received correspondence, maybe even encouragement, from New York City and I say the name aloud: 'Elaine Stein.' I've never met a Jewish person.

I race back up the lane, and dash up the stairs with Mother hollering to take off those tacky Mexican man shoes, and I get to work writing down every goddamn thing that bothers me in life, particularly those that do not seem to faze anyone else. Elaine Stein's words are running hot silver through my veins and I type as fast as I can.

By the next day, I am ready to mail my first letter to Elaine Stein, listing the ideas I thought worthy journalism material: the prevalence of illiteracy in Mississippi; the high number of drunk-driving accidents in our county; the limited job opportunities for women.

I take a deep breath and pull open the heavy glass door. A feminine little bell tinkles hello. A not-so-feminine receptionist watches me. She is enormous and looks uncomfortable in the small wooden chair. 'Welcome to the *Jackson Journal*. Can I help you?'

I had made my appointment day before yesterday, hardly an hour after I'd received Elaine Stein's letter. I asked for an interview for any position they might have.

'I'm here to see Mister Golden, please.'

The receptionist waddles to the back then reappears. 'Come on back.' I follow her through the desks of staring men, the haze of smoke, to an interior office.

'Close that thing back,' Mister Golden hollers as soon as I've opened the door and stepped in. 'Don't let all that damn smoke in here.'

Mister Golden stands up behind his desk. He's about six inches shorter than me, trim, younger than my parents. He has long teeth and a sneer, the greased black hair of a mean man. He sits back down, but I keep standing because there are no other chairs in the room.

'All right, let's see what you got.' I hand him my résumé and sample articles I'd written in college. Mister Golden doesn't just look at my papers, he edits them with a red pencil. 'Murrah High editor three years, Chi Omega editor three years, double major English and journalism . . . *Damn*, girl,' he mutters, 'didn't you have *any* fun?'

I clear my throat. 'Is . . . that important?'

He looks up at me. 'You're peculiarly tall but I'd think a pretty girl like you'd be dating the whole goddamn basketball team.'

I stare at him, not sure if he's making fun or paying me a compliment.

'I assume you know how to clean . . .' He looks back to my articles, strikes them with violent red marks.

My face flushes hot and quick. 'I'm not here to clean. I'm here to *write*.'

He sighs heavily, hands me a thick folder of papers. 'I guess you'll do. Miss Myrna's gone shit-house crazy on us, drunk hair spray or something. Read the articles, write the answers like she does, nobody'll know the damn difference.'

I have no idea who this Miss Myrna is. I ask the only safe question I can think of. 'How much . . . did you say it pays?'

He gives me a surprisingly appreciative look, from my flat shoes to my flat hairstyle. Some dormant instinct tells me to smile, run my hand through my hair. I feel ridiculous, but I do it.

'Eight dollars, every Monday.'

I nod, trying to figure out how to ask him what the column is about without giving myself away.

He leans forward. 'You do know who Miss Myrna is, don't you?'

'Of course. We . . . girls read her all the time,' I say, and again we stare at each other long enough for a distant telephone to ring three times.

'What, then? Eight's not enough? Jesus, woman, go clean your husband's toilet for free.'

I bite my lip. But before I can utter anything, he rolls his eyes.

'All right, *ten*. Copy's due on Thursdays. And if I don't like your style, I'm not printing it or paying you squat.'

I thank him more than I probably should. He ignores me and picks up his phone and makes a call before I'm even out the door. When I get to my car, I sink down into the soft Cadillac leather. I sit there smiling, reading the pages in the folder.

I just got a *job*.

I come home standing up straighter than I have since I was twelve, before my growth spurt. Even though every cell in my brain says do not, somehow I cannot resist telling Mother. I rush into the relaxing room and tell her everything about how I've gotten a job writing Miss Myrna, the weekly cleaning advice column.

'Oh, the irony of it. Giving advice on how to keep a home when . . .' Mother lets out a sigh that means life is hardly worth living under such conditions. Pascagoula freshens her iced tea. 'Eugenia, you don't know how to polish silver, much less advise on how to keep a house clean.'

I hug the folder to my chest. She's right, I won't know how to answer any of the questions. Still, I thought she'd at least be proud of me.

'And you will never meet anybody sitting at that typewriter. Eugenia, have some sense.'

Anger works its way up my arms. I stand up straight again. 'You think I *want* to live here? With *you*?' I laugh in a way I'm hoping will hurt her.

I see the quick pain in her eyes. She presses her lips together at the sting. Still, I have no desire to take back my words because finally, *finally*, I have said something she's listening to.

The next day, I stack the Miss Myrna letters in a neat pile. I have thirty-five dollars in my purse, the monthly allowance Mother still gives me. I go downstairs wearing a thick Christian smile. Whenever I want to leave Longleaf, I have to ask Mother if I can borrow her car. Which means she'll ask where I'm going. Which means I have to lie to her on a daily basis. 'I'm going down to the church, see if they need any help getting ready for Sunday school.'

'Oh, darling, that's just wonderful. Take your time with the car.'

I decided, last night, what I need is a professional to help me with the column. My first idea was to ask Pascagoula, but I hardly know her.

Plus I couldn't stand the thought of Mother nosing around, criticising me all over again. Hilly's maid, Yule May, is so shy I doubt she'd want to help me. The only other maid I see often enough is Elizabeth's maid, Aibileen. Aibileen reminds me of Constantine in a way. Plus she's older and seems to have plenty of experience.

On my way to Elizabeth's, I buy a clipboard, a box of number two pencils, a blue-cloth notebook. My first column is due on Mister Golden's desk by two o'clock tomorrow.

'Skeeter, come on in.' Elizabeth opens her own front door and I fear Aibileen might not be working today. Elizabeth has on a blue bathrobe and jumbo-sized rollers, making her head look huge, her body even more waif-like than it is. She generally has rollers in all day, can never get her thin hair full enough.

'Sorry I'm such a mess. Mae Mobley kept me up half the night.'

I step inside the tiny hall. It's a low-ceilinged house with small rooms. Everything has a secondhand look—the faded blue floral curtains, the crooked cover on the couch. I hear Raleigh's new accounting business isn't doing well.

Hilly's Oldsmobile is out front, but she's nowhere to be seen. Elizabeth sits at the sewing machine she has on the dining-room table. 'I'm almost done,' she says. 'Let me just hem this last seam . . .' Elizabeth stands, holds up a green church dress with a round white collar. 'Does it look homemade?'

The hem on one side hangs longer than the other. It's wrinkled and a cuff is already fraying. 'Straight from Maison Blanche's,' I say because that is Elizabeth's dream store. It is five storeys of expensive clothes on Canal Street in New Orleans, clothes that could never be found in Jackson. Elizabeth gives me a grateful smile.

The door to the guest bathroom in the hall opens and Hilly comes out talking, '. . . so much better. Everybody has their own place to go now.'

Elizabeth fiddles with the machine needle, seems worried by it. Then it hits me. Aibileen has her own bathroom in the garage now.

Hilly smiles at me and I realise she's about to bring up the Initiative. 'How's your mama?' I ask, even though I know this is her least favourite subject. 'She get settled in the home all right?'

'I guess.' Hilly pulls her red sweater down over the pudgy roll in her waist. She has on red-and-green tartan trousers that seem to magnify her bottom, making it rounder and more forceful than ever. 'Of course she doesn't appreciate a thing I do. I had to fire that maid for her, caught her trying to steal the damn silver right under my nose.' Hilly narrows her eyes a bit. 'Y'all haven't heard, by the way, if that Minny Jackson is working somewhere, have you?'

We shake our heads no.

I take a deep breath, anxious to tell them my news. 'I just got a job at the *Jackson Journal*,' I say.

There is quiet in the room. Suddenly Elizabeth squeals. Hilly smiles at me with such pride, I blush and shrug, like it's not that big of a deal.

'They'd be fools not to hire you, Skeeter Phelan,' Hilly says and raises her glass of iced tea as a toast.

'So . . . um, have either of y'all actually read Miss Myrna?' I ask.

'Well, no,' Hilly says. 'But I bet the poor white trash girls in South Jackson read it like the King James.'

'Would you mind if I talked to Aibileen?' I ask Elizabeth. 'To help me answer some of the letters?'

'Well . . . I mean, as long as it doesn't interfere with her work.'

I pause, surprised by this attitude. But I remind myself that Elizabeth is paying her, after all.

'And not today with Mae Mobley about to get up or else I'll have to look after her myself.'

'OK. Maybe . . . maybe I'll come by tomorrow morning, then?' If I finish talking to Aibileen by mid morning, I'll have time to rush home to type it up, then get it back to town by two.

Elizabeth frowns down at her spool of green thread. 'And only for a few minutes. Tomorrow's silver-polishing day.'

The next morning at ten, Elizabeth opens her door, nods at me like a schoolteacher. 'All right. Go on in. And not too long now. Mae Mobley'll be waking up any time.'

I walk into the kitchen, my notebook and papers under my arm. Aibileen smiles at me from the sink, her gold tooth shining. She's a little plump in the middle, but it is a friendly softness. And she's much shorter than me, because who isn't? Her skin is dark brown and shiny against her starchy white uniform. Her eyebrows are grey even though her hair is black.

'Hey, Miss Skeeter.'

'Aibileen'—I take a deep breath—'I was wondering if I could get your help on something.' I tell her about the column then, grateful when she nods that she knows who Miss Myrna is.

'So maybe I could read you some of the letters and you could . . . help me with the answers. After a while, maybe I'll catch on and . . .' I stop. There is no way I'll ever be able to answer cleaning questions myself. Honestly, I have no intention of learning how to clean. 'It sounds unfair, doesn't it, me taking your answers and acting like they're mine. Or Myrna's, I mean.' I sigh.

Aibileen shakes her head. 'I don't mind that. I just ain't so sure Miss Leefolt gone approve.'

'She said it was all right.'

'All right, then.'

'Should we sit?' I point to the kitchen table.

Aibileen glances at the swinging door. 'You go head. I'm fine standing.'

I spent last night reading every Miss Myrna article from the previous five years, but I haven't had time to sort through the unanswered letters yet. I straighten my clipboard, pencil in hand. 'Here's a letter from Rankin County.

'*Dear Miss Myrna,*' I read, '*how do I remove the rings from my husband's shirt collar when he is such a pig and . . . and sweats like one too . . .*'

Wonderful. A column on cleaning and relationships. *Two* things I know absolutely nothing about.

'Tell her a vinegar and Pine-Sol soak. Then let it set in the sun.'

I write it quickly on my pad. 'Sit in the sun for how long?'

'Bout an hour. Let it dry.'

I pull out the next letter and, just as quickly, she answers it. After four or five, I exhale, relieved.

'Thank you, Aibileen. You have no idea how much this helps.'

'Ain't no trouble. Long as Miss Leefolt don't need me.'

I gather up my papers. Aibileen picks through a sack of green fiddle-head ferns. The room is quiet except for the radio playing softly, Preacher Green again.

'How did you know Constantine? Were you related?'

'We . . . in the same church circle.' Aibileen shifts her feet.

'She didn't leave an address. I just—I can't believe she quit like that.'

Aibileen keeps her eyes down. She seems to be studying the fiddle-heads very carefully. 'No, I'm right sure she was let go.'

'No, Mama said she quit. Back in April. Went to live up in Chicago with her people.'

Aibileen picks up another fiddlehead, starts washing its long stem, the curly green ends. 'No, ma'am,' she says after a pause.

It takes me a few seconds to realise what we're talking about here.

'Aibileen,' I say, trying to catch her eye. 'You really think Constantine was fired?'

But Aibileen's face has gone blank. 'I must be mis-rememoring,' she says and I can tell she thinks she's said too much to a white woman.

We hear Mae Mobley calling out and Aibileen excuses herself and heads through the swinging door. A few seconds pass before I have the sense to go home.

When I walk in the house ten minutes later, Mother is reading at the dining room table. 'Mother,' I say, clutching my notebook to my chest, 'did you *fire* Constantine?'

'Did I . . . *what*?' Mother asks. But I know she's heard me because she's set the Daughters of the American Revolution newsletter down. It takes a hard question to pull her eyes off that riveting material.

'Eugenia, I told you, her sister was sick so she went up to Chicago to live with her people,' she says. 'Why? Who told you different?'

'I heard it this afternoon. In town.'

'Who would talk about such a thing?' Mother narrows her eyes behind her glasses. 'It must've been one of the other Nigras.'

'What did you *do* to her, Mother?'

Mother licks her lips, gives me a good, long look. 'You wouldn't understand, Eugenia. Not until you've hired help of your own.'

'You . . . *fired* her? For what?'

'It doesn't matter. It's behind me now and I just won't think about it another minute.'

'Mother, she raised me. You tell me what happened!' I'm disgusted by the squeakiness of my voice, the childish sound of my demands.

Mother raises her eyebrows at my tone, takes her glasses off. 'It was nothing but a coloured thing. And that's all I'm saying.' She puts her glasses back on and lifts her DAR sheet to her eyes.

I'm shaking, I'm so mad. I pound my way up the stairs. I sit at my desk, stunned that my mother could cast off someone who'd done her the biggest favour of her life, raise her children, teach me kindness and self-respect. Constantine worked for our family for twenty-nine years.

Twice that week I stop by Elizabeth's to talk to Aibileen. Each time, Elizabeth looks a little warier. The longer I stay in the kitchen, the more chores she comes up with until I leave: the doorknobs need polishing, the top of the refrigerator needs dusting, Mae Mobley's fingernails could use a trim. Aibileen is no more than cordial with me, nervous, stands at the kitchen sink and never stops working. It's not long before I am ahead of copy and Mister Golden seems pleased with the column, the first two of which only took me about twenty minutes to write.

And every week, I ask Aibileen about Constantine. Can't she get her address for me? Can't she tell me anything about why she got fired? Was there a big to-do, because I just can't imagine Constantine saying *Yes, ma'am* and walking out the back door. All Aibileen will do is shrug at me, say she don't know nothing.

One afternoon, when I come home I walk past the relaxing room. The television set is on and I glance at it. Pascagoula's standing about five inches away from the screen. I hear the words *Ole Miss* and on the fuzzy screen I see white men in dark suits crowding the camera, sweat running off their bald heads. I come closer and see a Negro man, about my age, standing in the middle of the white men, with Army men behind him. The picture pans back and there is my old administration building. Governor Ross Barnett stands with his arms crossed, looking the tall Negro in the eye. Next to the governor is our Senator Whitworth, whose son Hilly's been trying to set me up with.

I watch the television, riveted. I am neither thrilled nor disappointed by the news that they might let a coloured man into Ole Miss, just surprised. Pascagoula, though, is breathing so loud I can hear her. She stands stock-still, unaware I am there. The local reporter is nervous, smiling, talking fast. 'President Kennedy has ordered the governor to step aside for James Meredith, I repeat, the President of the United—'

'Eugenia, Pascagoula! Turn that set off right this minute!'

Pascagoula jerks round to see me and Mother. She rushes out of the room, her eyes to the floor.

'Now, I won't have it, Eugenia,' Mother whispers. 'I won't have you encouraging them like that.'

'Encouraging? It's nationwide news, Mama.'

Mother sniffs. 'It is not appropriate for you to watch together.'

On a hot Saturday in late September, the cotton fields chopped and empty, Daddy carries a new RCA colour television set into the house. He moves the black and white one to the kitchen. Smiling and proud, he plugs the new TV into the wall of the relaxing room. The Ole Miss versus LSU football game blares through the house.

Mother, of course, is glued to the colour picture, oohing and aahing at the vibrant reds and blues of the team. I take the Cadillac and head into town. Mother finds it inexplicable that I don't want to watch my alma mater throw a ball around. But Elizabeth and her family are at Hilly's watching the game so Aibileen's working in the house alone. I'm hoping it'll be a little easier on Aibileen if Elizabeth's not there. Truth is, I'm hoping she'll tell me something, anything, about Constantine.

Aibileen seems only the smallest bit more relaxed in Elizabeth's empty house. She eyes the kitchen table, like she wants to sit today. But when I ask her, she answers, 'No, I'm fine. You go head.' She takes a tomato from a bowl in the sink and starts to peel it with a knife.

So I lean against the counter and present the latest conundrum: how to keep the dogs from getting into your trash cans outside.

'Just pour some ammonia in that garbage. Dogs won't so much as wink at them cans.' I jot it down, and pick out the next letter. When I look up, Aibileen's kind of smiling at me.

'I don't mean nothing disrespectful, Miss Skeeter, but . . . ain't it kind a strange you being the new Miss Myrna when you don't know nothing about housekeeping?'

She didn't say it the way Mother did, a month ago. I find myself laughing instead, and I tell her what I've told no one else, about the phone calls and the résumé I'd sent to Harper & Row. That I want to be a writer. It's nice to tell somebody.

Aibileen nods, turns her knife around another soft red tomato. 'My boy Treelore, he like to write.'

'I didn't know you had a son.'

'He dead. Two years now.'

'Oh, I'm so sorry,' I say and for a moment it's just Preacher Green in the room, the soft pat of tomato skins against the sink.

'Made straight As on ever English test he take. Then later, when he grown, he say he gone write himself a book.'

'What kind of book?' I ask. 'I mean, if you don't mind telling . . .'

Aibileen says nothing for a while. Keeps peeling tomatoes round and round. 'He say he gone write down what it was like to be coloured working for a white man in Mississippi.'

I look away, knowing this is where my mother would stop the conversation. This is where she'd smile and change the subject to the price of silver polish or white rice.

Aibileen stops peeling. 'Please don't tell nobody that,' she says, 'him wanting to write about his white boss.' I realise she's still afraid for him.

'It's fine that you told me, Aibileen. I think it was . . . a brave idea.'

Aibileen holds my gaze for a moment. Then she picks up another tomato and sets the knife against the skin. She stops before she cuts, glances at the kitchen door.

'I don't think it's fair, you not knowing what happen to Constantine. I just—I'm sorry, I don't feel right talking to you about it.'

I stay quiet, not sure what's spurred this, not wanting to ruin it.

'I'll tell you though, it was something to do with her daughter. Coming to see your mama.'

'Daughter? Constantine never told me she had a daughter.' I knew Constantine for twenty-three years. Why would she keep this from me?

'It was hard for her. The baby come out real . . . pale.'

I hold still, remembering what Constantine told me, years ago. 'You mean, light? Like . . . white?'

Aibileen nods, keeping at her task in the sink. 'Had to send her away, up north I think.'

'Constantine's father was white,' I say. 'Oh . . . Aibileen . . . you don't think . . .' An ugly thought is running through my head. I am too shocked to finish my sentence.

Aibileen shakes her head. 'No no, no, ma'am. Not . . . that. Constantine's man, Connor, he was coloured. But since Constantine had her daddy's blood in her, her baby come out a high yellow. It . . . happens.'

I feel ashamed for having thought the worst. Still, I don't understand. 'Why didn't Constantine ever tell me?' I ask, not really expecting an answer. 'Why would she send her away?'

At this, Aibileen's face goes blank. The curtain has drawn. She nods towards the Miss Myrna letters, making it clear that's all she's willing to say. At least right now.

That afternoon, I stop by Hilly's football party. The street is lined with station wagons and long Buicks. I force myself through the door, knowing I'll be the only single one there. Inside, the living room is full of couples on the sofas, the chaises, the arms of chairs. I chat my way through until I make it to the kitchen.

'Skeeter, you made it,' Hilly says.

'I can't stay long,' I say, probably too quickly.

'Well, I found out.' Hilly smirks. 'He is definitely coming this time. Three weeks from today.'

I sigh, knowing right away who she means. 'I don't know, Hilly. You've tried so many times. Maybe it's a sign.' Last month, when I'd actually allowed myself a bit of excitement, he'd cancelled the day before the date.

'What? Don't you dare say that.'

'Hilly,' I clench my teeth, because it's time I finally just said it, 'you know I won't be his type.'

'It is *your time*, Skeeter.' She reaches over and squeezes my hand, presses her thumb and fingers down as hard as Constantine ever did. 'It is your turn. And I'm not going to let you miss this just because your mother convinced you you're not good enough for somebody like him.'

I'm stung by her bitter, true words. And yet, I am awed by my friend, by her tenacity for me. Hilly and I've always been uncompromisingly honest with each other, even about the little things. With other people, Hilly hands out lies like the Presbyterians hand out guilt, but it's our own silent agreement, this strict honesty, perhaps the one thing that has kept us friends.

I head back to the country before the game is over. Daddy finished the last harvest weeks ago, but the side of the road is still snowy with cotton stuck in the grass. Whiffs of it blow through the air.

I check the mailbox from the driver's seat. Inside is *The Farmer's Almanac* and a single letter. It is from Harper & Row, hand-written.

Miss Phelan,

You certainly may hone your writing skills on such flat, passionless subjects as drunk driving and illiteracy. I'd hoped, however, you'd choose topics that actually had some punch to them. Keep looking. If you find something original, only then may you write me again.

I slip past Mother in the dining room, invisible Pascagoula dusting pictures in the hall, up my steep, vicious stairs. My face burns. I fight the tears over Missus Stein's letter, tell myself to pull it together. The worst part is, I don't have any better ideas.

I bury myself in the next housekeeping article, then the League newsletter. For the second week in a row, I leave out Hilly's bathroom Initiative. An hour later, I find myself staring out of the window. I turn when I hear Pascagoula's knock on my door. That's when the idea comes to me. *No. I couldn't. That would be . . . crossing the line.*

But the idea won't go away.

AIBILEEN

THE HEAT WAVE finally passes round the middle a October and we get ourselves a cool fifty degrees. In the mornings, that bathroom seat get cold out there, give me a little start when I set down. It's just a little room they built inside the garage. Inside is a toilet and a little sink attached to the wall. Paper have to set on the floor.

On a Tuesday noon, I carry my lunch on out to the back steps, set down on the cool concrete. A big magnolia tree shades most a the yard. I already know that's the tree gone be Mae Mobley's hideout. In about five years, to hide from Miss Leefolt.

After a while, Mae Mobley waddle out on the back step. She got half her hamburger patty in her hand. She smile up at me and say, 'Good.'

'How come you not in there with your mama?' I ask, but I know why. She rather be setting out here with the help than in there watching her mama look anywhere but at her. She like one a them baby chickens that get confused and follow the ducks around instead.

'Mae Mobley? Mae Mobley Leefolt!'

Miss Leefolt just now noticing her child ain't setting in the same room with her. 'She out here with me, Miss Leefolt,' I say.

'I told you to eat in your high chair, Mae Mobley. How I ended up with you when all my friends have angels I just do not know . . .' But then the phone ring and I hear her stomping off to get it.

I look down at Baby Girl, see how her forehead's all wrinkled up between the eyes. She studying hard on something.

I touch her cheek. 'You all right, baby?'

She say, 'Mae Mo bad.'

The way she say it, like it's a fact, make my insides hurt.

'Mae Mobley,' I say cause I got a notion to try something. 'You a smart girl?'

She say, 'Mae Mo smart.'

I say, 'You a kind girl,' and she nod, repeat it back to me. But before I can do another one, she get up and chase round the yard and laugh and that's when I get to wondering, what would happen if I told her she something good, ever day?

She turn from the birdbath and smile and holler, 'Hi, Aibee. I love you, Aibee,' and I feel a tickly feeling, soft like the flap a butterfly

wings, watching her play out there. The way I used to feel watching
Treelore. And that makes me kind a sad, memoring.

After while, Mae Mobley come over and press her cheek up to mine
and just hold it there, like she know I be hurting. I hold her tight,
whisper, 'You a *smart* girl. You a *kind* girl, Mae Mobley. You hear me?'
And I keep saying it till she repeat it back to me.

The next few weeks is real important for Mae Mobley. It's a tricky
thing. You try and get a baby to go in the toilet before its time, it'll make
em crazy. Baby Girl, though, I know she ready. But, Law, if she ain't running my fool legs off. I set her on her wooden baby seat so she don't fall
in and soon as I turn my back, she off that pot.

'You drunk up two glasses a grape juice, I know you got to go.'

'Nooo.'

'I give you a cookie if you go for me.'

We look at each other awhile. She start eyeing the door. I don't hear
nothing happening in the bowl. Usually, I can get them going after
about two weeks. But that's if I got they mamas helping me.

'Go just a little for me, Baby Girl.'

She stick her lip out, shake her head.

'I give you *two* cookies,' I say even though her mama always getting
on me about making her fat.

Mae Mobley, she shake her head and say, 'You go.'

Now, I ain't saying I ain't heard this before, but usually I can get
around it. I say, 'I don't got to go.'

We look at each other. She point again and say, 'You go.'

I just don't know how to go about it. Should I take her out to the
garage to mine or go here in this bathroom? What if Miss Leefolt come
home and I'm setting up on this toilet? She have a fit.

I put her diaper back on and we go out to the garage. 'All right, Baby
Girl, here tis. Aibileen's bathroom.'

I take down my underthings and I tee-tee real fast, use the paper,
and get it all back on before she can really see anything. Then I flush.

'And that's how you go in the toilet,' I say.

Well, don't she look surprise. Got her mouth hanging open like she
done seen a miracle. I step out and fore I know it, she got her diaper off
and that little monkey done climbed on that toilet, holding herself up
so she don't fall in, going tee-tee for herself.

'Mae Mobley! You going! That's real good!' She smile and I catches her fore she dip down in it. We run back inside and she get her two cookies.

That afternoon, Miss Leefolt come home with her hair all teased up.

'Guess what Mae Mobley done today?' I say. 'Went to the bathroom in the toilet bowl.'

'Oh, that's wonderful!' She give her girl a hug, something I don't see enough of. I know she mean it, too, cause Miss Leefolt do *not* like changing diapers.

'Let's see if she do it one more time fore I go home.' We go in the bathroom. I get her diapers off and put her up on that toilet. But Baby Girl, she shaking her head.

'Come on, Mae Mobley, can't you go in the pot for your mama?'

'Noooo.'

Finally I put her back down on her feet. Before I can get her diaper on again, Baby Girl run off fast as she can. Nekkid little white baby running through the house. She in the kitchen. She got the back door open, she in the garage, trying to reach the knob to *my* bathroom.

Baby Girl wagging her head. '*My bafroom!*'

Miss Leefolt snatch her up, give her a pop on the leg. Baby Girl start crying.

'Miss Leefolt, she don't know what she do—'

'Get back in the house, Aibileen!'

I hate it, but I go in the kitchen. I stand in the middle, leave the door open behind me.

'I did not raise you to use the coloured bathroom!' I hear her hiss-whispering, thinking I can't hear, and I think, *Lady, you didn't raise your child at all.*

'This is dirty out here, Mae Mobley. You'll catch diseases! No, no no!' And I hear her pop her again and again on her bare legs.

After a second, Miss Leefolt potato-sack her inside. There ain't nothing I can do but watch it happen. My heart feel like it's squeezing up into my throat-pipe. Miss Leefolt drop Mae Mobley in front a the tee-vee and she march to her bedroom and slam the door. I go give Baby Girl a hug. She still crying and she look awful confused.

'I'm real sorry, Mae Mobley,' I whisper to her. I'm cussing myself for taking her out there in the first place. But I don't know what else to say, so I just hold her. We set there watching *Li' l Rascals* until Miss Leefolt come out, ask ain't it past time for me to go. I give Mae Mobley one more hug, whisper, 'You a *smart* girl. You a *good* girl.'

On the ride home, I don't see the big white houses passing outside the window. I don't talk to my friends. I see Baby Girl getting spanked cause a me. I see her listening to Miss Leefolt call me dirty, diseased.

The bus speeds up along State Street. We pass over the Woodrow Wilson Bridge and my jaw so tight I could break my teeth off. I want to yell so loud that Baby Girl can hear me that dirty ain't a colour, disease ain't the Negro side a town. I want to stop that moment from coming—and it come in ever white child's life—when they start to think that coloured folks ain't as good as whites.

Things is quiet the next few weeks. Mae Mobley's wearing big-girl panties now. After what happen in the garage, Miss Leefolt take a real interest in Mae Mobley's bathroom habits. She even let her watch her on the pot, set the white example. A few times, though, when her mama's gone, I still catch her trying to go in mine.

I hear the doorbell ring and I see Miss Skeeter's car out front. Miss Skeeter been coming over to Miss Leefolt's ever week this month, to ask me the Miss Myrna questions. She ask about hard water stains and I tell her cream of tartar. She ask how you unscrew a lightbulb that done broke off in the socket and I tell her a raw potato. She ask me what happen with her old maid Constantine and her mama, and I go cold. I could tell she don't understand why a coloured woman can't raise no white-skin baby in Mississippi.

Ever time Miss Skeeter finish asking me about how to clean the-this or fix the-that or where Constantine, we get to talking about other things too. That's not something I done a whole lot with my bosses or they friends. I find myself telling her how Treelore never made below a B+ or that the new church deacon get on my nerves cause he lisp. Little bits, but things I ordinarily wouldn't tell a white person.

Today, Miss Skeeter cock her head to the side, wrinkle her forehead. 'Aibileen, remember that . . . idea Treelore had?'

I feel a prickle. I should a never shared that with a white woman.

'I've been thinking about it. I've been wanting to talk to you—'

But fore she can finish, Miss Leefolt come in the kitchen and catch Baby Girl playing with my comb in my pocketbook and say maybe Mae Mobley ought to have her bath early today. I tell Miss Skeeter goodbye, go start the tub.

After I spent a year dreading it, November eighth finally come. Three years ago today, Treelore died. But by Miss Leefolt's book it's still floor-cleaning day. I scrub my way through the morning, through the twelve o'clock news. I miss my soaps cause the ladies is in the dining room having a Benefit meeting and I ain't allowed to turn on the tee-vee when they's company.

About four o'clock, Miss Skeeter come in the kitchen. Before she can even say hello, Miss Leefolt rush in behind her. 'Aibileen, I just found out my mother, Missus Fredericks, is driving down from Greenwood tomorrow and staying through Thanksgiving. I want the silver service polished and all the guest towels washed.'

Miss Leefolt shake her head at Miss Skeeter like ain't she got the hardest life in town and walks out. I go on and get the silver service out the dining room. Law, I'm already tired and I got to be ready to work the Benefit next Saturday night. Minny ain't coming. She too scared she gone run into Miss Hilly.

Miss Skeeter still waiting on me in the kitchen when I come back in. She got a Miss Myrna letter in her hand.

'You got a cleaning question?' I sigh. 'Go head.'

I take a plug a Pine-Ola cream and start rubbing it onto the silver, working the cloth around the rose design. God, please let tomorrow come soon. I ain't gone go to the gravesite. I can't, it'll be too hard—

'Aibileen? Are you feeling all right?'

I stop, look up. Realise Miss Skeeter talking to me. 'I'm sorry I's just . . . thinking about something.'

'You looked so sad.'

'Miss Skeeter.' I feel tears come up in my eyes, cause three years just ain't long enough. A hundred years ain't gone be long enough. 'You mind if I help you with them questions tomorrow?'

Miss Skeeter start to say something, but then she stop herself. 'Of course. I hope you feel better.'

I finish the silver set and the towels and tell Miss Leefolt I got to go home even though it's half a hour early and she gone short my pay. She open her mouth like she want to protest and I whisper my lie, *I vomited*, and she say *go*. Cause there ain't nothing Miss Leefolt scared of more than Negro diseases.

'**A**ll right, then. I'll be back in thirty minutes,' Miss Leefolt say through the passenger car window. Miss Leefolt dropping me off at the Jitney to pick up what else we need for Thanksgiving tomorrow.

'Don't forget the turkey, now,' Miss Leefolt say. 'And two cans of cranberry sauce.'

'Quit squirming, Mae Mobley,' Miss Fredericks snap. She mean old woman.

'Miss Leefolt, lemme take her shopping in the store with me.'

Before I know it, Baby Girl done wormed her way over Miss Fredericks's lap and is climbing out the window in my arms. I pull her up on my hip and we giggle like a couple a schoolgirls. I get a cart and put Mae Mobley up front, stick her legs through the holes. Long as I got my white uniform on, I'm allowed to shop here.

'All righty, Baby Girl. Less see what we need.'

In produce, I pick out six sweet potatoes, three handfuls a string beans. I get a smoked ham hock from the butcher. The store is bright, lined up neat. Nothing like the coloured Piggly Wiggly with sawdust on the floor. It's mostly white ladies, smiling, got they hair already fixed for the Benefit tomorrow. Four or five maids is shopping, all in they uniforms.

In dry goods, I heave the two-pound bag a salt in the cart, to brine the turkey in. I count the hours on my hands, ten, eleven, twelve. If I'm on soak the bird for fourteen hours in the salt water, I'll put it in the bucket around three this afternoon. Then I'll come in to Miss Leefolt's at five tomorrow morning and cook the turkey for the next six hours. I got a apple pie ready to bake, gone do my biscuits in the morning.

'Ready for tomorrow, Aibileen?' I turn and see Franny Coots behind me. She go to my church. Franny bend her head down, say, 'You hear what happen to Louvenia Brown's grandson this morning?'

'Robert?' I say. He a kind, handsome boy, went to high school with Treelore. They was good friends, both on the basketball team.

'Use the white bathroom at Pinchman Lawn and Garden. Say they wasn't a sign up saying so. Two white mens chased him and beat him with a tyre iron.'

Oh, no. Not *Robert*. 'He . . . is he . . . ?'

Franny shake her head. 'They don't know. He up at the hospital. I heard he blind.'

'God, no.' I close my eyes. Louvenia, she is the purest, kindest person they is. She raised Robert after her own daughter died.

That afternoon, I work like a crazy woman, but I don't finish cooking till six o'clock that night, two hours later than usual. I know I ain't gone have the strength to go knock on Louvenia's door. I'll have to do it tomorrow after I'm done cleaning up the turkey. I waddle myself from the bus stop, hardly able to keep my eyes open. I turn the corner on Gessum. A big white Cadillac's parked in front a my house. And there be Miss Skeeter in a red dress and red shoes, setting on my front steps.

I walk real slow through my yard, wondering what it's gone be now. Miss Skeeter stand up, holding her handbag tight like it might get snatched. White peoples don't come round my neighbourhood less they toting the help to and fro, and that is just fine with me.

'I hope you don't mind me coming by,' she say. 'I just . . . I didn't know where else we could talk.'

I set down on the step and ever knob on my spine hurt. The street's full a folks walking to sweet Louvenia's to pray for Robert, kids playing ball in the street. Everbody looking over at us thinking I must be getting fired or something.

'Yes, ma'am,' I sigh. 'What can I do for you?'

'I have an idea. Something I want to write about. But I need your help.'

I let all my breath out. I like Miss Skeeter, but come on. Sure, a phone call would a been nice. She never would a just shown up on some white lady's step without calling. But, no, she done plopped herself down like she got ever right to barge in on me at home.

'I want to interview you. About what it's like to work as a maid.'

'Like the Miss Myrna column?' I say, flat as a pan. 'Bout cleaning?'

'Not like Miss Myrna. I'm talking about a book,' she say and her eyes is big. She excited. 'Stories about what it's like to work for a white family. What it's like to work for, say . . . Elizabeth.'

I look at her. This what she been trying to ask me in Miss Leefolt kitchen. 'You think Miss Leefolt gone agree to that? Me telling stories about her?'

Miss Skeeter's eyes drop down some. 'Well, no. I was thinking we wouldn't tell her. I'll have to make sure the other maids will agree to keep it secret, too.'

I scrunch up my forehead, just starting to get what she's asking. 'Other maids?'

'I was hoping to get four or five. To really show what it's like to be a maid in Jackson.'

We out here in the wide open. Don't she know how dangerous this could be? 'Exactly what kind a stories you think you gone hear?'

'What you get paid, how they treat you, the bathrooms, the babies, all the things you've seen, good and bad.'

'Miss Skeeter,' I whisper, 'do that not sound kind a dangerous to you?'

'Not if we're careful—'

'Shhh, please. Do you know what would happen to me if Miss Leefolt find out I talked behind her back?'

'We won't tell her, or anyone.'

I just stare at her. Is she crazy? 'Did you hear about the coloured boy this morning? One they beat with a tyre iron for *accidentally* using the white bathroom?'

She just look at me, blink a little. 'I know things are unstable but—'

'And my cousin Shinelle? They burn up her car cause she went *down* to the voting station.'

'No one's ever written a book like this,' she say, finally whispering, finally starting to understand, I guess. 'We'd be breaking new ground.'

I spot a flock a maids in they uniforms walking by my house. They look over, see me setting with a white woman on my front step. I grit my teeth, already know my phone gone be ringing tonight.

'Miss Skeeter,' and I say it slow, try to make it count, 'I do this with you, I might as well burn my *own* house down.'

'But I've already . . .' She shut her eyes closed tight. I think about asking her, *Already what,* but I'm kind a scared to hear what she gone say. She write her telephone number on a scrap of paper.

'Please, will you at least think about it?'

I sigh, stare out at the yard. Gentle as I can, I say, 'No, ma'am.'

She set the scrap a paper between us on the step, then she get in her Cadillac. I'm too tired to get up. I just stay there, watch while she roll real slow down the road.

MISS SKEETER

I LOOK INTO MY REARVIEW MIRROR. Aibileen is still on her front steps in her white uniform. She hadn't even looked at me when she said *No, ma'am.*

I guess I thought it would be like visiting Constantine, where friendly coloured people waved and smiled, happy to see the little white girl whose daddy owned the big farm. But here, narrow eyes watch me pass by. I try to think of something more that might convince Aibileen.

A week ago, Pascagoula knocked on my bedroom door.

'There's a long-distance phone call for you, Miss Skeeter. From a Miss . . . Stern, she say?'

I rushed past Pascagoula, down the stairs to the kitchen phone. For some stupid reason, I kept smoothing my frizzy hair down as if it were a meeting and not a phone call.

Three weeks earlier, I'd typed out three pages outlining the idea, the details, and the lie. Which was that a hardworking and respected coloured maid has agreed to let me interview her and describe in specifics what it's like to work for the white women of our town.

I stretched the cord into the pantry, pulled the string on the single bare bulb. The pantry is shelved floor to ceiling with pickles and soup jars, bottled vegetables and preserves. This was my old high school trick to get some privacy.

'Hello? This is Skeet—Eugenia Phelan in Mississippi?'

'I know, Miss Phelan. I called you.' I heard a match strike, a short, sharp inhale. 'I received your letter last week. I have some comments.'

'Yes, ma'am.' I sank down onto a tall tin can of flour.

'What gave you this idea? About interviewing domestic housekeepers. I'm curious.'

I sat paralysed a second. 'I was . . . well, I was raised by a coloured woman. I've seen how simple it can be and—and how complex it can be, between the families and the help.' I cleared my throat. I sounded stiff, like I was talking to a teacher.

'Continue.'

'Well,' I took a deep breath, 'I'd like to write this showing the point of view of the help. The coloured women down here.' I tried to picture Constantine's face, Aibileen's. 'They raise a white child and then twenty years later the child becomes the employer. It's that irony, that we love them and they love us, yet . . .' I swallowed, my voice trembling. 'We don't even allow them to use the toilet in the house.'

There was silence on the other end of the phone.

'And,' I felt compelled to continue, 'everyone knows how we white people feel about the glorified Mammy figure who dedicates her whole life to a white family. Margaret Mitchell covered that. But no one ever asked Mammy how she felt about it.' Sweat dripped down my chest, blotting the front of my cotton blouse.

'So you want to show a side that's never been examined before,' Missus Stein said.

'Yes. Because no one ever talks about it. No one talks about anything down here.'

Elaine Stein laughed like a growl. Her accent was tight, Yankee. 'Miss Phelan, I lived in Atlanta. For six years with my first husband.'

I latched on to this small connection. 'So you know what it's like then.'

'Enough to get me out of there,' she said, and I heard her exhale smoke. 'Look, I read your outline. It's certainly . . . original, but what maid in her right mind would ever tell you the truth?'

I could see Mother's pink slippers pass by the door. I tried to ignore them. I couldn't believe Missus Stein was already calling my bluff. 'The first interviewee is . . . eager to tell her story.'

'Miss Phelan,' Elaine Stein said, and I knew it wasn't a question, 'this Negro actually agreed to talk to you candidly? Because that seems like a hell of a risk in a place like Jackson, Mississippi.'

I sat blinking. I felt the first fingers of worry that Aibileen might not be as easy to convince as I thought.

'I watched them try to integrate your bus station on the news,' Missus Stein continued. 'They put fifty-five Negroes in a jail cell built for four.'

I pursed my lips. 'She has agreed. Yes, she has.'

'Well. That is impressive. But after her, you really think other maids will talk to you? What if the employers find out?'

'The interviews would be conducted secretly. Since, as you know, things are a little dangerous down here right now.' The truth was, I had very little idea how dangerous things were. I'd spent the past four years locked away in college, reading Keats and worrying over essays.

'A little dangerous?' She laughed. 'The marches in Birmingham, Martin Luther King. Dogs attacking coloured children. Darling, it's the hottest topic in the nation. But, I'm sorry, this will never work. Not as an article, because no Southern newspaper would publish it. And certainly not as a book. A book of *interviews* would never sell.'

'Oh,' I heard myself say. I closed my eyes, feeling all the excitement drain out of me. I heard myself say again, 'Oh.'

'I called because, frankly, it's a good idea. But . . . there's no possible way to take it to print.'

'But . . . what if . . .' My eyes started darting round the pantry, looking for something to bring back her interest.

Missus Stein let out a sharp *tsk*. 'I suppose I could read what you get. God knows, the book business could use some rattling. Do the interview and I'll let you know if it's worth pursuing.'

I stuttered a few unintelligible sounds, finally coming out with, '*Thank* you. Missus Stein, I can't tell you how much—'

'Don't thank me yet. Call Ruth, my secretary, if you need to get in touch.' And she hung up.

I lug an old satchel to bridge club at Elizabeth's on Wednesday. It is red. It is ugly. And for today, at least, it is a prop.

It's the only bag I could find large enough to carry the Miss Myrna letters. The leather is cracked and flaking, the thick shoulder strap leaves a brown mark on my blouse where the leather stain is rubbing off. It was my Grandmother Claire's gardening bag. She used to carry her garden tools in it and the bottom is still lined with sunflower seeds.

'Two weeks,' Hilly says to me, holding up two fingers. 'He's coming.' She smiles and I smile back. 'I'll be right back,' I say and I slip into the kitchen, carrying my satchel with me.

Aibileen is standing at the sink. 'Afternoon,' she says quietly. It was a week ago that I visited her at her house.

I stand there a minute, watching her stir the iced tea, feeling the discomfort in her posture, her dread that I might be about to ask for her help on the book again.

As casually as I can, I pull an envelope from my bag. 'I've been meaning to give you this.'

'What you got there?' she says without reaching for it.

'For your help,' I say quietly. 'I've put away five dollars for every article. It's up to thirty-five dollars now.'

Aibileen's eyes move quickly back to her tea. 'No, thank you, ma'am. Miss Leefolt have a fit if she find you giving me cash.'

'She doesn't have to know.'

'I already told you, I'm sorry, I can't help you with that book, Miss Skeeter.'

Hilly's head pops through the door. 'Come on, Skeeter, I'm fixing to deal,' and she disappears.

'I'm begging you,' Aibileen says, 'put that money away so Miss Leefolt don't see it.'

I nod, embarrassed. I tuck the envelope in my bag, knowing we're worse off than ever. It's a bribe, she thinks, to get her to let me interview her. And now I've scared her off for good.

'**D**arling, just try it. It cost eleven dollars. It must be good.'

Mother has me cornered in the kitchen. She pushes me down into a chair and squeezes a noisy, farty tube of goo on my head. She's been chasing me with the Magic Soft & Silky Shinalator for two days now. She rubs the cream in my hair with both hands. I can practically feel the hope in her fingers.

Mother covers my dripping head with a plastic cap. She fastens a hose from the cap into a square grey machine.

'How long does this take, Mother?'

She picks up the booklet with a sticky finger. 'It says here, "Cover with the Miracle Straightening Cap, then turn on the machine and wait for the miraculous—"'

'Ten minutes? Fifteen?'

I hear a click, a rising rumble, then feel a slow, intense warmth on my head. 'The Miracle Cap must remain on the head for two hours without removal or results—'

'Two *hours*?'

'I'll have Pascagoula fix you a glass of tea, dear.' Mother pats me on the shoulder and swishes out through the kitchen door.

For two hours I smoke cigarettes and read *Life* magazine. I finish *To Kill a Mockingbird*. Finally, I pick up the *Jackson Journal*, flick through it. It's Friday, so there won't be a Miss Myrna column. On page four, I read: *Boy blinded over segregated bathroom, suspects questioned*. It sounds . . . familiar. I remember then. This must be Aibileen's neighbour.

At noon, Mother removes the vibrating cap from my head, washes out my hair while I lean back in the kitchen sink. She quickly rolls up a dozen curlers, puts me under her hair dryer hood in her bathroom.

An hour later, I emerge pink and soreheaded and thirsty. Mother stands me in front of the mirror, pulling out curlers. She brushes out the giant circular mounds on my head.

We stare, dumbfounded.

'Ho-ly shit,' I say. All I'm thinking is, *The date. The blind date is next weekend.*

Mother smiles, shocked. She doesn't even scold me for cursing. My hair looks great. The Shinalator actually worked.

On Saturday, the day of my date with Stuart Whitworth, I sit for two hours under the Shinalator (results, it seems, only last until the next wash). When I'm dry, I go to Kennington's and buy the flattest shoes I can find and a slim black crêpe dress. I charge the eighty-five dollars to Mother's account since she's always begging me to go buy new clothes. ('Something flattering for your *size*.') I know Mother would profoundly disapprove of the cleavage the dress enables me to have.

It's past three o'clock by the time I get back home from buying the dress. I'm supposed to be at Hilly's at six to meet Stuart. I check the mirror. The curls are starting to fray on the ends, but the rest of my hair is still smooth. Mother doesn't know about my date tonight and if she somehow finds out, the next three months will be full of excruciating questions like, 'Did he call?' and, 'What did you do wrong?' when it doesn't work out.

Mother's downstairs in the relaxing room with Daddy. My brother, Carlton, is on the sofa with his new girlfriend. They drove up this afternoon from LSU.

When I get Carlton alone in the kitchen, he laughs, yanks my hair like we're kids again. 'So how are you, sister?'

I tell him about the job at the paper, that I'm editor of the League newsletter. I also tell him he better be moving back home after law school. 'You deserve some of Mother's time, too. I'm taking more than my fair share here,' I say through gritted teeth.

He laughs like he understands, but how could he really? He's three years older than me and great-looking, tall with wavy blond hair, finishing LSU law school, protected by 170 miles of badly paved roads.

When he goes back to his girlfriend, I search for Mother's car keys, but I can't find them anywhere. 'Where in the world are your keys, Mama? I'm late for Hilly's. I'm staying there tonight.'

Mother sighs. 'I guess that means you're going to church with them too. And I thought we could all go tomorrow as a family.'

'Mama, please,' I say, rummaging through a basket where she keeps her keys. 'I can't find your keys *anywhere*.'

'You can't take the Cadillac overnight. That's our Sunday church car.'

He's going to be at Hilly's in thirty minutes. I'm supposed to dress and do my make-up there so Mother won't suspect anything. I can't take Daddy's new truck. It's full of fertiliser and I know he'll need it at dawn tomorrow. 'All right, I'll take the old truck, then.'

I huff outside only to find that not only does the old truck have a trailer hitched to it, but a half-ton tractor on top of that trailer.

So I drive into town for my first date in two years in a red 1941 Chevrolet with a John Deere hooked behind me. The engine sputters and churns and I wonder if the truck will make it. It stalls on the main road, sending my dress and bag flying onto the dirty floor.

At three minutes to six, after doing twenty in a fifty with horns honking and teenagers hollering at me, I park down the street from Hilly's house since Hilly's cul-de-sac doesn't provide adequate parking for farm equipment. I grab my bag and run inside, all out of breath and sweaty and windblown and there they are, the three of them, including my date. Having drinks in the front living room.

I freeze in the entrance hall with all of them looking at me. William, Hilly's husband, and Stuart both stand up. God, he's tall, has at least four inches over me. Hilly's eyes are big when she grabs my arm. 'Boys, we'll be right back.'

She whisks me off to her dressing room. 'Skeeter, you don't even have lipstick on! Your hair looks like a rat's nest!'

'I know, look at me!' All traces of the Shinalator's miracle are gone. 'There's no air conditioning in the truck. I had to ride with the damn windows down.'

I scrub my face and Hilly sits me in her dressing room chair. She starts combing my hair out the way my mother used to do, twisting it into these giant rollers, spraying it with Final Net.

'Well? What did you think of him?' she asks.

I sigh and close my unmascaraed eyes. 'He looks handsome.'

I smear the make-up on, something I hardly even know how to do. Hilly looks at me and smudges it off with a tissue, reapplies it. I slip into the black dress with the deep V in the front, the black flats. Hilly quickly brushes out my hair.

I stand up and smooth my dress down. 'All right,' I say, 'give it to me. One to ten.'

Hilly looks me up and down, stops on the dip in the front of the dress. She raises her eyebrows. I've never shown cleavage before in my life; kind of forgot I had it.

'Six,' she says, like she is surprised herself.

We just look at each other a second. Hilly lets out a little squeal and I smile back. Hilly's never given me higher than a four.

When we come back into the front living room, William's pointing his finger at Stuart. 'I'm going to run for that seat and by God, with your daddy's—'

'Stuart Whitworth,' Hilly announces, 'I'd like to introduce Skeeter Phelan.'

He stands up again, and for a minute my head is perfectly quiet inside. I make myself look, like self-inflicted torture, as he takes me in.

'Nice to meet you.' Stuart flips me a brief smile. Then he takes a long slurp of his drink until I hear the ice clink against his teeth. 'So where we off to?' he asks William.

We take Hilly's Oldsmobile to the Robert E Lee Hotel. Stuart opens my door and sits beside me in the back, but then leans over the seat talking to William about deer season the rest of the ride.

At the table, he pulls out my chair for me. 'You want a drink?' he asks me, not looking my way.

'No, thanks. Just water, please.'

He turns to the waiter and says, 'Double Old Kentucky straight with a water back.'

I guess it's some time after his fifth bourbon, I say, 'So Hilly tells me you're in the oil business. That must be interesting.'

'The money's good. If that's what you really want to know.'

'Oh, I didn't . . .' But I stop because he's craning his neck at something. I look up and see he's staring at a woman who's at the door, a busty blonde with red lipstick and a tight green dress.

William turns to see what Stuart's looking at, but he swings back round quickly. He shakes his head no, very slightly, at Stuart and I see, heading out the door, it's Hilly's old boyfriend, Johnny Foote, with his new wife, Celia. They leave and William and I glance at each other, sharing our relief that Hilly didn't see them.

'Lord, that girl's hot,' Stuart says under his breath and I suppose that's when I just stop caring what happens.

At some point, Hilly looks at me to see what's going on. I smile like everything's fine and she smiles back, happy to see it's all working out. 'William! The lieutenant governor just walked in. Let's go speak before he sits down.'

They go off together, leaving us, the two lovebirds sitting on the same side of the table, staring at all the happy couples in the room.

'So,' he says, hardly turning his head. 'What do you do with your time?'

'I write a . . . domestic maintenance column for the *Jackson Journal*.'

He wrinkles his brow, then laughs. 'Domestic maintenance. You mean . . . housekeeping?'

I nod.

'Jesus.' He stirs his drink. 'I can't think of anything worse than reading a column on how to clean house,' he says, and I notice that his front tooth is the slightest bit crooked. I long to point this imperfection out to him, but he finishes his thought with, 'Except maybe writing it.'

I just stare at him.

'Sounds like a ploy to me, to find a husband. Becoming an expert on keeping house.'

'Well, you must be a genius. You've figured out my whole scheme.'

'Isn't that what you women from Ole Miss major in? Professional husband hunting?'

I watch him, dumbfounded. I may not've had a date in umpteen years, but who does he think he is?

'I'm sorry, but were you dropped on your head as an infant?'

He blinks at me, then laughs for the first time all night.

'Not that it's any of your business,' I say, 'but I had to start somewhere if I plan on being a journalist.' I think I've actually impressed him. But then he throws back the drink and the look is gone.

We eat dinner, and from his profile I can see his nose is a little pointy. His eyebrows are too thick, and his light brown hair too coarse. We say little else, to each other at least. Stuart orders yet another drink.

When Hilly and I go to the bathroom, she gives me a hopeful smile. 'What do you think?'

'He's . . . tall,' I say, surprised she hasn't noticed that not only is my date inexplicably rude, but extremely drunk.

The end of the meal finally comes and he and William split the bill. Stuart stands up and helps me with my jacket.

'Jesus, I've never met a woman with such long arms,' he says.

'Well, I've never met anybody with such a drinking problem.'

'Your coat smells like—' He leans down and sniffs it, grimacing. 'Fertiliser.'

The car ride, all three minutes of it, is impossibly silent. And long.

We go back inside Hilly's house. 'Skeeter, why don't you drive Stuart back to his hotel?' William says. 'I'm bushed, aren't you, Hilly?'

'I came in a truck,' I say. 'I'd hate for you to . . .'

'Shoot,' William says, slapping Stuart on the back. 'Stuart doesn't mind riding in a truck, do you, buddy?'

Finally, I just walk out the door. Stuart follows me, doesn't comment that I didn't park in front of Hilly's house or in Hilly's driveway. When we get to my truck, we both stop, stare at the fifteen-foot tractor hooked behind my vehicle.

'You pulled that thing all by yourself?'

I sigh. I guess it's because I'm a big person and have never felt petite or particularly feminine or girly, but that tractor—it just seems to sum up so much.

'That is the funniest damn looking thing I have ever seen,' he says.

I step away from him. 'Hilly can take you,' I say. 'Hilly will drive you.'

He turns and focuses on me for what, I'm pretty sure, is the first time all night. After several long moments of standing there being looked at, my eyes fill with tears. I'm just so tired.

'Ah, shit,' he says and his body loosens. 'Look, I told Hilly I wasn't ready for any damn date.'

'Don't . . .' I say, backing away from him, and head back to the house.

Sunday morning I get up early, before Hilly and William, before the kids and the church traffic. I drive home with the tractor rumbling behind me.

I'd gone back in Hilly's house last night, Stuart trailing behind me. Knocking on Hilly's bedroom door, I asked William, who already had a mouth full of toothpaste, would he mind driving Stuart back. I'd walked upstairs to the guest room before he even answered.

I go into my parents' house. As soon as I see Mother, I give her a hug. I wish I could tell her about my night. I feel guilty for not being nicer to her, for not needing her until my own life turns bad. I feel bad for wishing Constantine was here instead.

At eleven o'clock the next morning, the phone rings. Luckily, I'm in the kitchen and pick it up.

'Miss Skeeter?'

I stand very still, then look out at Mother examining her chequebook at the dining-room table. Pascagoula is pulling a roast out of the oven. I go into the pantry and shut the door.

'Aibileen?' I whisper.

She's quiet a second and then she blurts it out. 'What if—what if you don't like what I got to say? I mean, about white peoples.'

'This isn't about my opinion,' I say. 'It doesn't matter how I feel.'

'But how I know you ain't gone get mad, turn around on me?'

'I don't . . . I guess you'll just have to . . . trust me.' I hold my breath, hoping, waiting. There is a long pause.

'Law have mercy. I reckon I'm on do it. But Miss Skeeter, we gone have to be real careful. And you gone have to change my name. Mine, Miss Leefolt's, everbody's.'

'Of course.' I should've mentioned this. 'When can we meet? *Where* can we meet?'

'Can't do it in the white neighbourhood, that's for sure. I guess . . . we gone have to do it over at my house.'

'Do you know any other maids who might be interested?' I ask.

Aibileen is quiet a moment. 'I guess I could ask Minny. But she ain't real keen on talking to white peoples.'

'Minny? You mean . . . Missus Walter's old maid?' I say, suddenly feeling how incestuous this is turning. I wouldn't just be peering into Elizabeth's life, but Hilly's too.

'Minny got her some stories. Sho nuff.'

'Aibileen,' I say. 'Thank you. Oh, thank you.'

MINNY

MONDAY COMES and I can't stop thinking about Louvenia Brown's grandson, Robert. He got out of the hospital this weekend, went to live with Louvenia. Last night, when I went over there to take them a caramel cake, Robert had a cast on his arm and bandages over his eyes. 'Oh, *Louvenia*,' was all I could say when I saw him.

Robert was laid up on the sofa asleep. They'd shaved half his head to operate. Louvenia, with all her troubles, still wanted to know how each and every person in my family was doing. And when Robert started to stir, she asked if I wouldn't mind going on home because Robert wakes up screaming. Terrified and remembering all over again that he's blind.

'I'm going to the store after while,' I say to Miss Celia. I hold the grocery list out for her to see. Every Monday we do this. She gives me the grocery cash and when I get home I push the receipt in her face. I want her to see that every penny of change matches the paper. Miss Celia just shrugs but I keep those tickets safe in a drawer in case.

Every other day, I hear Miss Celia on the phone in her room, calling and calling the society ladies. The Benefit was three weeks ago and here she is already gunning up for next year. She and Mister Johnny didn't go or I would've heard plenty about it.

'Could you tell her Celia Foote called again? I left her a message a few days back . . .'

Miss Celia's voice is chipper, like she's peddling something on the tee-vee. Every time I hear it, I want to jerk the phone out of her hand, tell her to quit wasting her time. Because never mind she looks like a hussy. There's a bigger reason why Miss Celia doesn't have any friends. Mister Johnny dumped Miss Hilly for Miss Celia back in college, and Miss Hilly never got over him.

I walk in the church on Wednesday night. It's not but half full since it's only a quarter to seven and the choir doesn't start singing until seven thirty. But Aibileen asked me to come early so here I am.

I see Aibileen in our usual pew, left side, fourth from the front, right by the window fan. We're prime members and we deserve a prime spot. The Christmas tree's already up, next to the altar, full of tinsel and a shiny gold star on top. Three windows of the church have stained glass—the birth of Christ, Lazarus raised from the dead, and the teaching of those fool Pharisees. The other seven are filled with regular clear panes. We're still raising money for those.

'So what you want me to come early for?' I ask. 'You miss me or something?'

'Naw, it's no big deal. Just something somebody said.'

'What?'

Aibileen takes a breath, looks around for anybody listening. 'The other day I slipped up and told that Miss Skeeter about Treelore writing coloured things down? Well, she had the gall to ask if me and some a my maid friends might want a put down on paper what it's like to tend for white people. Say she writing a book.'

'Say what?'

Aibileen nods, raises her eyebrows. 'Mm-hmm. I tell her she crazy. I ask her, what if we told the truth? How we too scared to ask for minimum wage. How nobody gets paid they Social Security. How it feel when your own boss be calling you . . .' Aibileen shakes her head. I'm glad she doesn't say it.

'How we love they kids when they little . . .' she says and I see Aibileen's lip tremble. 'And then they turn out just like they mamas.'

'She crazy if she think we do something dangerous as that. For *her*.'

'We don't want a bring all that mess up.' Aibileen wipes her nose with a hankie. 'Tell people the truth.'

'No, we don't,' I say, but I stop. It's something about that word *truth*. I've been trying to tell white women the truth about working for them since I was fourteen years old.

'We don't want a change nothing around here,' Aibileen says and we're both quiet, thinking about all the things we don't want to change. And that's when I see it.

'You thinking about it, ain't you,' I say.

She shrugs and I know I'm right. I can't believe Aibileen wants to tell Miss Skeeter the truth.

Truth.

It feels cool, like water washing over my sticky-hot body. Cooling a heat that's been burning me up all my life.

Truth, I say inside my head again, just for that feeling.

For no reason but to irritate me, we get a heat wave in December. I tote my Fairley Funeral Home fan every place I go. Works good and it was free. Miss Celia actually goes outside and sits by the pool in these tacky white sunglasses and a fuzzy bathrobe. Thank the Lord she's out of the house. At first I thought maybe she was sick in the body, but now I'm wondering if she's sick in the head.

I catch her slipping upstairs to the empty bedrooms almost every day. I hear her sneaky little feet walking down the hall, passing over that little squeak in the floor. I don't think much of it—heck, it's her house. But then one day, she does it again, and then again, and it's the fact that she's so darn *sneaky* about it, waiting until I turn on the vacuum or get busy on a cake, that makes me suspicious.

Today, after she makes her trip upstairs, Miss Celia comes to the kitchen. I wish she'd get on out of here. I'm pulling chicken off the bone. I've got the broth boiling and the dumplings already cut. I don't want her trying to help with this.

But then I look over and see her face has gone flat white, like cheap wall paint. The pricks of sweat on her make-up—that now's gone grey—tell me she's not fine. I help her to bed and bring her the Lady-a-Pinkam to drink. The pink label has a picture of a real proper lady on it with a turban on her head, smiling like she feels better.

Afterward, I wash my hands. Whatever she's got, I hope it ain't catching.

The day after Miss Celia's face goes funny is change-the-damn-sheets day and the day I hate the most. Miss Celia knows about Tuesdays and usually she moves out to the sofa so I can do my work. But at nine, then ten, then eleven the bedroom door's still closed. Finally, I knock.

'Yes?' she says. I open the door.

Not only is Miss Celia still in bed, she's curled up on top of the covers in her nightgown without a drop of her make-up on.

'I got to get them sheets washed and ironed. And then we cooking—'

'No lesson today, Minny.' She isn't smiling either, like she usually does when she sees me.

'You feeling bad?'

'Fetch me some water, will you?'

'Yes'm.' I go in the kitchen and fill up a glass from the sink. She must be feeling bad because she's never asked me to serve her anything before.

When I walk back in the bedroom though, Miss Celia's not in bed and the bathroom door's closed.

'You sick?' I holler outside the bathroom door.

'I'm . . . fine.'

'While you in there, I'm on go head and change these sheets.'

'No, I want you to go on,' she says through the door. 'Go on home for the day, Minny.'

I stand there and tap my foot. I don't want to go on home. It's Tuesday, change-the-damn-sheets day. If I don't do it today, that makes Wednesday change-the-damn-sheets day too.

'What Mister Johnny gone do if he come home and the house's a mess?'

'He's at the deer camp tonight. Minny, I need you to bring me the phone over—' her voice breaks into a trembly wail. 'Drag it on over and fetch my phone book that's setting in the kitchen.'

'You sick, Miss Celia?'

But she doesn't answer so I go get the book and stretch the phone over to the bathroom door and tap on it.

'Just leave it there.' Miss Celia sounds like she's crying now. 'I want you to go on home now.'

'But I just gots—'

'I said go home, Minny!'

I step back from that closed door. Heat rises up my face. And it stings, not because I haven't been yelled at before. I just haven't been yelled at by Miss Celia yet.

Next time I go to her house, she's not in bed when I walk in. She's sitting at the white kitchen table staring out the window.

'Morning, Minny,' she says, not even looking my way.

But I just nod. Miss Celia gets up and comes over to the sink where I'm standing. She grabs hold of my arm. 'I'm sorry I hollered at you like I did. I was sick and I know that's no excuse, but I was feeling real poor and . . .' She starts sobbing then, like the worst thing she's ever done in her life is yell at her maid.

'All right,' I say. 'Ain't nothing to boo-hoo over.'

And then she hugs me tight round the neck until I kind of pat her on the back and peel her off. 'Go on, set down,' I say. 'I'll fix you some coffee.' I guess we all get a little snippy when we're not feeling good.

I try to concentrate on the week. Tomorrow's heavy cooking and I've got the church supper Saturday night and the service on Sunday. When am I going to clean my own house? Wash my own kids' clothes? And Aibileen. She called me again last night, asked if I'd help her and Miss Skeeter with the stories. I love Aibileen, I do. But I think she's making a king-sized mistake trusting a white lady. And I told her, too.

Lord, I better get on with my work.

MISS SKEETER

TONIGHT, I'M GOING to Aibileen's for her first interview. My heart racing, I drive fast on the paved town roads, heading for the coloured part of town. I've never even sat at the same table with a Negro who wasn't paid to do so. The interview has been delayed by over a month. First, the holidays came and Aibileen had to work late almost every night, wrapping presents and cooking for Elizabeth's Christmas party. In January, I started to panic when Aibileen got the flu.

I drive the Cadillac through the darkness, turning into Gessum Avenue. I'd rather have been in the old truck, but Mother would've been too suspicious and Daddy was using it in the fields. I stop in front of an abandoned, haunted-looking house three down from Aibileen's, as we planned. I step into the dark, lock the doors and walk quickly. I keep my head lowered, my heels clicking on the pavement.

A dog barks and my keys jangle to the ground. I glimpse around, pick them up. Two sets of coloured people sit on porches, watching, rocking. There are no streetlights so it's hard to say who else sees me. I keep walking, feeling as obvious as my vehicle: large and white.

I reach number twenty-five, and knock softly. There are footsteps, and something inside slams closed. Aibileen opens the door. 'Come on in,' she whispers and quickly shuts it behind me and locks it.

I've never seen Aibileen in anything but her whites. Tonight she has on a green dress with black piping. I can't help but notice, she stands a little taller in her own house.

'Make yourself comfortable. I be back real quick.'

Even with the single lamp on, the front room is dark, full of browns and shadows. The curtains are pulled and pinned together so there's no gap. I don't know if they're like that all the time, or just for me. I lower myself onto the narrow sofa.

A few minutes later, Aibileen comes back with a tray holding a teapot and two cups that don't match, paper napkins folded into triangles. I smell the cinnamon cookies she's made. As she pours the tea, the top to the pot rattles.

'Sorry,' she says and holds the top down. 'I ain't never had a white person in my house before.'

I smile, even though I know it wasn't meant to be funny. I drink a sip of tea. It is bitter and strong. 'Thank you,' I say. 'The tea is nice.'

She sits and folds her hands in her lap, looks at me expectantly.

'I thought we'd do a little background work and then just jump right in,' I say. I pull out my notebook and scan the questions I've prepared. 'Well, to start, um, when and where were you born?'

She swallows, nods. 'Nineteen o-nine. Piedmont Plantation down in Cherokee County.'

'Did you know when you were a girl, growing up, that one day you'd be a maid?'

'Yes, ma'am. Yes, I did.'

I smile, wait for her to elucidate. There is nothing.

'And you knew that . . . because . . . ?'

'Mama was a maid. My granmama was a house slave.'

'A house slave. Uh-huh,' I say, but she only nods. Her hands stay folded in her lap. She's watching the words I'm writing on the page.

'Did you . . . ever have dreams of being something else?'

'No, ma'am, I didn't.' It's so quiet, I can hear both of us breathing.

'All right. Then . . . what does it feel like, to raise a white child when your own child's at home, being . . .' I swallow, embarrassed by the question, '. . . looked after by someone else?'

'It feel . . .' She's still sitting up so straight it looks painful. 'Um, maybe . . . we could go on to the next one.'

'Oh. All right.' I stare at my questions. 'What do you like best about being a maid and what do you like least?'

She looks up at me, like I've asked her to define a dirty word.

'I—I spec I like looking after the kids best,' she whispers.

'Anything . . . you'd like to add . . . about that?'

'No, ma'am.'

'Aibileen, you don't have to call me "ma'am". Not here.'

'Yes, ma'am. Oh. Sorry.' She covers her mouth.

Loud voices shout in the street and both our eyes dart towards the window. We are quiet, stock-still. What would happen if someone white found out I was here on a Saturday night talking to Aibileen in her regular clothes? Would they call the police to report a suspicious meeting? I'm suddenly sure they would. We'd be arrested because that is what they do. They'd charge us with integration violation—I read about it in the paper all the time—they despise the whites that meet with the coloureds to help with the civil rights movement. This has nothing to do with integration, but why else would we be meeting? I didn't even bring any Miss Myrna letters as back-up.

I see open, honest fear on Aibileen's face. Slowly the voices outside dissipate down the road. I exhale but Aibileen stays tense. She keeps her eyes on the curtains.

I look down at my list of questions, searching for something to draw this nervousness out of her, out of myself.

'And what . . . did you say you disliked about your job?'

Aibileen swallows hard.

'I mean, do you want to talk about the bathroom? Or about Eliz— Miss Leefolt? Anything about the way she pays you? Has she ever yelled at you in front of Mae Mobley?'

Aibileen takes a napkin and dabs it to her forehead. 'I'm sorry, I—' She gets up and walks quickly down the narrow hall. A door closes, rattling the teapot and the cups on the tray.

Five minutes pass. When she comes back, she holds a towel to her front, the way I've seen Mother do when her ulcers make her vomit, and she doesn't make it to her toilet in time.

'I'm sorry. I thought I was . . . ready to talk.'

I nod, not sure what to do.

'I just . . . I know you already told that lady in New York I's gone do this but . . .' She closes her eyes. 'I'm sorry. I don't think I can.' She shakes her head, clutches her towel.

On my drive home, I look over at my notebook on the white leather seat. Besides where she grew up, I've gotten a total of twelve words. And four of them are *Yes, ma'am* and *No, ma'am*.

I park the Cadillac and stare out at Hilly's rambling white house. It's been four days since Aibileen vomited in the middle of our interview and I've heard nothing from her.

I go inside. The bridge table is set up in Hilly's antebellum-style parlour with its deafening grandfather clock and gold swag curtains. Everyone is seated—Hilly, Elizabeth and Lou Anne Templeton, who has replaced Missus Walter. Lou Anne is one of those girls who wears a big eager smile—*all* the time, and it never stops. It makes me want to stick a pin in her. And she agrees with every single little thing Hilly says.

Hilly holds up a *Life* magazine, points to a spread of a house in California. 'A den they're calling it, like wild animals are living there.'

'Oh, isn't that dreadful!' Lou Anne beams.

The picture shows wall-to-wall shag carpet and low, streamlined sofas, egg-shaped chairs and televisions that look like flying saucers.

'Trudy's house looks just like that,' Elizabeth says. I've been so wrapped up in the interview with Aibileen, I'd almost forgotten Elizabeth's trip last week to see her older sister. Trudy married a banker and they moved to Hollywood.

'Well, that's just bad taste, is what it is,' Hilly says. 'No offence to your family, Elizabeth.'

'What was Hollywood like?' Lou Anne asks.

'Oh, it was like a dream. And Trudy's house—TV sets in every room. That same crazy space-age furniture you could hardly even sit in. We went to all these fancy restaurants, where the movie stars eat, and drank martinis and burgundy wine. Not to mention she has live-in help, every day, every *hour.* I hardly had to see Mae Mobley at all.'

I cringe at this comment, but no one else seems to notice. Hilly's watching her maid, Yule May, refill our tea glasses. She's tall, slender, almost regal-looking and has a much better figure than Hilly. Seeing her makes me worry about Aibileen. I've called Aibileen's house twice this week, but there wasn't any answer.

'I was thinking next year we might do a *Gone With the Wind* theme for the Benefit,' Hilly says.

'What a great idea!' Lou Anne says.

'Oh, Skeeter,' Hilly says, 'I know you just hated missing it this year.' I give a pitiful frown. I'd pretended to have the flu to avoid going alone.

Elizabeth taps my arm. She has her handbag in her lap. 'I almost forgot to give this to you. From Aibileen, for the Miss Myrna thing?'

I open the folded piece of paper. The words are in blue ink, in a lovely cursive hand.

I know how to make the teapot stop rattling.

'And who in the world cares about how to make a teapot not rattle?' Elizabeth says. Because of course she read it.

It takes me two seconds and a drink of iced tea to understand. 'You wouldn't believe how hard it is,' I tell her.

Two days later, at eight o'clock at night, I'm stumbling down Aibileen's street as discreetly as one can carrying a fifty-pound Corona typewriter. I knock softly, Aibileen answers and I slip inside. She's wearing the same green dress as last time. I try to smile, like I'm confident it will work this time, despite the idea she explained over the phone.

'Could we . . . sit in the kitchen this time?' I ask. 'Would you mind?'

'All right. Ain't nothing to look at, but come on back.'

The kitchen is about half the size of the living room, and warmer. The black and white linoleum floor has been scrubbed thin.

I set the typewriter on a scratched red table under the window. Aibileen starts to pour the hot water into the teapot.

'Oh, none for me, thanks,' I say and reach in my bag. 'I brought us some Co-Colas if you want one.' I've tried to come up with ways to make Aibileen more comfortable. Number one: don't make her feel like she has to serve me.

'Well, ain't that nice. I usually don't take my tea till later anyway.' She brings over an opener and two glasses. I drink mine straight from the bottle and, seeing this, she pushes the glasses aside, does the same.

I called Aibileen after Elizabeth gave me the note, and listened hopefully as Aibileen told me her idea—for her to write her own words down and then show me what's she's written. I tried to act excited. But I know I'll have to rewrite everything she's written, using up even more time.

Aibileen has a wire-ringed notebook in front of her. 'Want me to . . . just go head and read?'

'Sure,' I say.

She begins reading in a slow, steady voice. 'My first white baby to ever look after was named Alton Carrington Speers. It was nineteen twenty-four and I'd just turned fifteen years old. Alton was a long, skinny baby with hair fine as silk on a corn . . .'

I begin typing as she reads, her words rhythmic, pronounced more clearly than her usual talk. 'Every window in that filthy house was painted shut on the inside, even though the house was big with a wide green lawn. I knew the air was bad, felt sick myself . . .'

'Hang on,' I say. I've typed *wide greem*. I blow on the typing fluid, retype it. 'OK, go ahead.'

'When the mama died, six months later,' she reads, 'of the lung disease, they kept me on to raise Alton until they moved away to Memphis. I loved that baby and he loved me and that's when I knew I was good at making children feel proud of themselves . . .'

I hadn't wanted to insult Aibileen when she told me her idea. I tried to urge her out of it, over the phone. 'Writing isn't that easy. And you wouldn't have time for this anyway, Aibileen, not with a full-time job.'

'Can't be much different than writing my prayers every night.'

'You don't say your prayers, then?'

'I never told nobody that before. Not even Minny. Find I can get my point across a lot better writing em down. I write a hour, sometimes two ever day. Lot a ailing, sick peoples in this town.'

I was impressed. That was more than I wrote on some days. I told her we'd try it just to get the project going again.

Aibileen takes a breath, a swallow of cola, and reads on.

She backtracks to her first job at thirteen, cleaning the silver service at the governor's mansion. She reads how on her first morning, she made a mistake on the chart where you filled in the number of pieces so they'd know you hadn't stolen anything.

'I come home that morning, after I been fired, and stood outside my house with my new work shoes on. The shoes my mama paid a month's worth a light bill for. I guess that's when I understood what shame was and the colour of it too. Shame ain't black, like dirt, like I always thought it was. Shame be the colour of a new white uniform your mother ironed all night to pay for, white without a smudge or a speck a work-dirt on it.'

I hit the return and the typewriter dings. Aibileen and I look each other straight in the eye. I think this might actually work.

Every other night for the next two weeks, I tell Mother I'm off to feed the hungry at the Canton Presbyterian Church, where we, fortunately, know not a soul. Hour after hour, in Aibileen's kitchen, she reads and I type, the details thickening, the babies' faces sliding into focus. Aibileen's writing is clear, honest. I tell her so.

'Well, look who I been writing to.' She chuckles. 'Can't lie to God.'

Before I was born, she actually picked cotton for a week at Longleaf, my own family's farm. Once she lapses into talking about Constantine without my even asking.

'Law, that Constantine could sing. Like a purebred angel standing in the front a the church. Give everbody chills, listening to that silky voice a hers and when she wouldn't sing no more after she had to give her baby to—' She stops. Looks at me.

I wish I could hear everything she knows about Constantine, but I'll wait until we've finished her interviews.

'Any word from Minny?' I ask. 'If Missus Stein likes it,' I say, practically chanting the familiar words, 'I just want to have the next interview set up and ready.'

Aibileen shakes her head. 'I asked Minny three times and she still say she ain't gone do it. I spec it's time I believed her.'

I try not to show my worry. 'Maybe you could ask some others? See if they're interested?'

Aibileen nods. 'I got some more I can ask. But how long you think it's gone take for this lady to tell you if she like it?'

I shrug. 'I can't say for sure.'

Aibileen presses her lips together, looks down at her pages. I see something that I haven't noticed before. Anticipation, a glint of excitement. I've been so wrapped up in my own self, it hasn't occurred to me that Aibileen might be as thrilled as I am that an editor in New York is going to read her story.

On our fifth session, Aibileen reads to me about the day Treelore died. She reads about how his broken body was thrown on the back of a pickup by the white foreman. 'And then they dropped him off at the coloured hospital. That's what the nurse told me, who was standing outside. They rolled him off the truck bed and the white men drove away.' Aibileen doesn't cry, just lets a parcel of time pass while I stare at the typewriter, she at the worn linoleum.

On the sixth session, Aibileen says, 'I went to work for Miss Leefolt in nineteen sixty. When Mae Mobley two weeks old,' and I feel I've passed through a leaden gate of confidence. She describes the building of the garage bathroom, admits she is glad it is there now. It's easier than listening to Hilly complain about sharing a toilet with the maid.

One night she says, 'I was thinking . . .' But then she stops.

I look up from the typewriter, wait. It took Aibileen vomiting on herself for me to learn to let her take her time.

'I's thinking to do some reading. Might help me with my own writing.'

'Go down to the State Street Library. They have a whole room full of Southern writers. Faulkner, Eudora Welty—'

Aibileen gives me a dry cough. 'You know coloured folks ain't allowed in that library.'

I sit there a second. 'I can't believe I forgot that.' The coloured library must be pretty bad. There was a sit-in at the white library a few years ago and it made the papers. When the coloured crowd showed up, the police department simply stepped back and turned the German Shepherds loose. I look at Aibileen and am reminded, once again, the risk she's taking talking to me. 'I'll be glad to pick the books up for you,' I say.

Aibileen hurries to the bedroom and comes back with a long list.

'You want a book by . . . Sigmund Freud?'

'Oh, people crazy.' She nods. 'I love reading about how the head work. You ever dream you fall in a lake? He say you dreaming about your own self being born. Miss Frances, who I work for in nineteen fifty-seven, she had all them books.'

'Aibileen, how long have you been wanting to ask me this? If I'd check these books out for you?'

'A while.' She shrugs. 'I guess I's afraid to mention it.'

'Did you . . . think I'd say no?'

'These is white rules. I don't know which ones you following and which ones you ain't.'

For four days straight, I sit at my typewriter in my bedroom. Twenty of my typed pages, full of slashes and red-circled edits, become thirty-one on thick Strathmore white. I write a short biography of Sarah Ross, the name Aibileen chose, after her teacher. I include her age, what her parents did for a living. I follow this with Aibileen's own stories, just as she wrote them, simple, straightforward.

I read and re-read and then take the pages to Aibileen in the evenings and she does the same. I am surprised by what's in these stories, of separate coloured refrigerators at the governor's mansion, of white women throwing two-year-old fits over wrinkled napkins, white babies calling Aibileen 'Mama.'

I slide the manuscript into a yellow envelope and mail it to New York.

It's a quarter past one and Hilly and Elizabeth and I are sitting at Elizabeth's dining room table waiting on Lou Anne to show up. I've had nothing to eat today and I feel nauseous, jumpy. I've been like this for ten days, ever since I mailed Aibileen's stories to Elaine Stein.

'Is this not just the rudest thing you've ever heard of?' Hilly looks at her watch and scowls. This is Lou Anne's second time to be late. She won't last long in our group with Hilly around.

Hilly deals out a hand of gin rummy. I try to concentrate on the game, but little facts keep jumping in my head every time I look at Elizabeth. About Mae Mobley using the garage bathroom, how Aibileen can't keep her lunch in the Leefolts' refrigerator. Small details I'm privy to now.

'Well, while we wait, I have some news,' Elizabeth says and I recognise the look on her face, the secretive nod, one hand on her stomach.

'I'm pregnant.' She smiles, her mouth trembling a little.

'That's great,' I say. I put down my cards and touch her arm. She truly looks like she might cry. 'When are you due?'

'October.'

'Well, it's about time,' Hilly says, giving her a hug. 'Mae Mobley's practically grown.'

While we play a few practice hands, Hilly and Elizabeth talk about baby names. I try to contribute to the conversation. 'Definitely Raleigh, if it's a boy,' I add. Hilly talks about William's campaign. He's running for state senate next year, even though he has no political experience. I'm grateful when Elizabeth tells Aibileen to go ahead and serve lunch.

By the time Lou Anne Templeton shows up, we've finished our shrimp and grits and are just starting on dessert. Hilly is forgiving. Lou Anne was late, after all, because of a League duty.

Afterwards, I tell Elizabeth congratulations again, walk out to my car. Hilly strides over to me, hands me an envelope.

'For the newsletter next week. You'll be sure and get it in for me?'

When I get home, I work on the newsletter, wishing I was working on the stories instead. I go through the notes from the last League meeting, and open Hilly's envelope.

Hilly Holbrook introduces the Home Help Sanitation Initiative. A disease preventative measure. Low-cost bathroom installation in your garage or shed, for homes without such an important fixture.

  Ladies, did you know that:

- *Ninety-nine per cent of all coloured diseases are carried in the urine*
- *Whites can become permanently disabled by nearly all of these diseases because we lack immunities coloureds carry in their darker pigmentation*
- *Some germs carried by whites can also be harmful to coloureds too. Protect yourself. Protect your children. Protect your help.*

The phone rings in the kitchen and I practically fall over myself racing to it. 'This is Eugenia,' I say quickly.

'Elaine Stein here.'

I breathe deep. 'Yes, ma'am. Did you receive my package?'

'I did,' she says. 'But I still stand by my opinion that a book of interviews . . . ordinarily wouldn't work. It's not fiction, but it's not nonfiction either. Perhaps it's anthropological but that's a ghastly category to be in.'

'But you . . . liked it?'

'Eugenia,' she says, exhaling her cigarette smoke into the phone. 'Have you seen the cover of *Life* magazine this week?'

I haven't seen the cover of my *Life* magazine in a month. 'No, ma'am.'

'Martin Luther King, dear. He just announced a march on Washington DC and invited every Negro in America to join him. Every white person, for that matter. This many Negro and white people haven't worked together since *Gone With the Wind*.'

'Yes, I did hear about the . . . marching . . . event,' I lie. I cover my eyes, wishing I'd read the paper this week. I sound like an idiot.

'My advice to you is, write the book and write it fast. The march is in August. You should have it written by New Year's. And four or five interviews won't be enough for a book. You'll need a dozen, maybe more. You have more interviews set up, I assume?'

I press my lips together. 'Some . . . more.'

'Good. Then get going. Before this civil rights thing blows over.'

That evening, I hand Aibileen three more books from her list. My back hurts from leaning over the typewriter. This afternoon, I wrote down everyone I know who has a maid (which is everyone I know), and their maid's name. But some of the names I can't remember.

'Thank you, oh Law, look at this.' She smiles and flips to the first page of *Walden*, looks like she wants to start reading it right there.

'I spoke to Missus Stein this afternoon,' I say.

Aibileen's hands freeze on the book. 'I knew something was wrong. I seen it on your face.'

I take a deep breath. 'She said she likes your stories. But . . . she won't say if she'll publish it until we've written the whole thing.' I try to look optimistic. 'We have to be finished just after the new year. And she said we have to interview at least twelve maids for her to consider it.'

'But . . . you ain't got any other maids to talk to, Miss Skeeter.'

I clench my hands. I close my eyes. 'I don't have anyone I can ask, Aibileen,' I say, my voice rising. 'I mean, who is there? Pascagoula? If I talk to her, Mother will find out.'

Aibileen's eyes drop from mine so fast I want to cry. *Damn it, Skeeter.* 'I'm sorry,' I say quickly. 'I'm sorry I raised my voice.'

'No, no, it's all right. That was my job, to get the others.'

'What about Hilly's maid, Yule May? You've asked her?'

'She say she too busy trying to get her boys into college next year.'

'Any other maids that go to your church? Have you asked them?'

Aibileen nods. 'They all got excuses. But, really, they just too scared.'

'But how many? How many have you asked?'

'Thirty-one,' Aibileen says. 'I didn't want a tell you,' she says and her forehead wrinkles. 'Until we heard from the lady . . .' She takes off her glasses. I see the deep worry in her face.

'I'm on ask em again,' she says.

A few days later, I sit in the kitchen, bored, smoking a cigarette, something I can't seem to stop doing lately. The kitchen is hot, but I had to get out of my room, where all I do is worry because no other maids have agreed to work with us.

The phone rings like a fire alarm and I answer.

'Minny gone help us,' Aibileen whispers.

I slip into the pantry and sit on my flour can. I can't speak for about five seconds. 'When? When can she start?'

'Next Thursday. But she got some . . . requirements.'

'What are they?'

Aibileen pauses a moment. 'She say she don't want your Cadillac anywhere this side a the Woodrow Wilson bridge. And she say . . . she say you can't set on the same side a the room as her. She want a be able to see you square on at all times.'

'I'll drive our old truck and . . . sit wherever she wants me to.'

Aibileen's voice softens. 'She just don't know you, is all. Plus she ain't got a real good history with white ladies.'

Two days later, Aibileen opens the door and I go in. In the back corner of the living room, Minny stands with her arms crossed over her huge bosom. I've met her the few times Hilly allowed Missus Walter to host bridge club. Minny and Aibileen are both still in their white uniforms.

'Hello,' I say from my side of the room. 'Good to see you again.'

'Miss Skeeter.' Minny nods. She settles in a wooden chair Aibileen has brought out from the kitchen, and the frame creaks. I sit on the far end of the sofa. Aibileen sits on the other end of the sofa, between us.

I clear my throat, produce a nervous smile. Minny doesn't smile back. She is fat and short and strong. Her skin is blacker than Aibileen's by ten shades, and shiny and taut, like a pair of new patent shoes.

'I already told Minny how we doing the stories,' Aibileen says to me. 'You helping me write mine. And hers she gone tell you, while you write it down.'

'And, Minny, everything you say here is in confidence,' I say. 'You'll get to read everything we—'

'What makes you think coloured people need your help?' Minny stands up, chair scraping. 'Why you even care about this? You *white*.'

I look at Aibileen. I've never had a coloured person speak to me this way.

'We all working for the same thing here, Minny,' Aibileen says.

'And what thing is that?' Minny says to me. 'Maybe you just want me to tell you all this stuff so I get in trouble.'

My face is burning red. 'We want to show your perspective . . . so people might understand what it's like from your side. We—we hope it might change some things around here.'

'What you think you gone change with this? What law you want to reform so it say you got to be nice to your maid?'

'Now, hold on,' I say, 'I'm not trying to change any laws here. I'm just talking about attitudes and—'

'You know what'll happen if people catch us? I'd have *guns* pointing at my house.'

There's a still, tight moment in the room.

'You don't have to do this, Minny,' Aibileen says. 'It's all right if you want a change your mind.'

Slowly, warily, Minny settles again in her chair. 'I do it. I just want a make sure she understand, this ain't no *game* we playing here.'

I glance at Aibileen. She nods at me. I take a deep breath. My hands are shaking.

I start with the background questions and somehow we back our way into talking about Minny's work. She looks at Aibileen as she talks, like she's trying to forget I'm even in the room. I record everything she says, my pencil scratching as fast as I can move it. We thought it might be less formal than using the typewriter.

When Minny lapses into news about Miss Celia—'She sneaking upstairs, think I don't see her, but I know that crazy lady up to something'—she always stops herself, the way Aibileen does when she speaks of Constantine. 'That ain't part a my story. You leave Miss Celia out a this.' She watches me until my writing stops.

Besides her furiousness at white people, Minny likes to talk about food. One day, while she's saying, '. . . got a white baby on one arm, green beans in the pot—' she stops. Cocks her jaw at me. Taps her foot.

'Half this stuff don't have nothing to do with coloured rights. Ain't but day-to-day business.' She eyes me up and down. 'Look to me like you just writing *life*.'

I stop my pencil. She's right. I realise that's just what I wanted to do. I tell her, 'I hope so.' She gets up and says she's got more important things to worry about than what I'm hoping for.

The next evening, I'm working upstairs in my room. Suddenly I hear Mother hit the stairs running. In two seconds she's made it in my room. 'Eugenia!' she whispers.

I stand so fast my chair teeters, trying to guard the contents of my typewriter. 'Yes, ma'am?'

'Now don't panic but there is a man—a very *tall* man—downstairs to see you. He says his name is Stuart *Whit*worth.'

'What?'

'He said y'all spent an evening together awhile back but how can that be, I didn't know anything—'

'Christ.'

'Don't take the Lord's name in vain, Eugenia Phelan. Just put some lipstick on.'

I brush my hair because I know it's awful. I even wash the typewriter ink off my hands and elbows. But I won't change clothes, not for him.

Mother gives me a quick up-and-down in my dungarees and Daddy's old button-up white shirt. 'Is he a Greenwood Whitworth or a Natchez?'

'He's the state senator's son.'

Mother's jaw drops so far it hits her string of pearls.

I walk out onto the porch, and there he is. Three months after our date, there is Stuart Whitworth, standing on my front porch in khaki trousers and a blue coat and a red tie, like he's ready for Sunday dinner.

'What brings you here?' I don't smile. I'm not smiling at him.

'I just . . . I wanted to drop by.'

'Well. Can I get you a drink?' I ask. 'Or should I just get you the entire bottle of Old Kentucky?'

He frowns. 'Look, I know it was . . . a long while back, but I came out here to say I'm sorry.'

'Who sent you—Hilly? William?' There are eight empty rocking chairs on the porch. I don't ask him to sit in any of them.

He shoves his hands down in his front pockets like a twelve-year-old boy. 'I know I was . . . rude that night, and I've been thinking about it a lot and . . .'

I laugh then. I'm just so embarrassed that he would come out here and have me relive it.

'Now, look,' he says, 'I told Hilly ten times I wasn't ready to go out on any date. I wasn't even close to being ready . . .'

I grit my teeth. I can't *believe* I feel the heat of tears; it was months ago. But I remember how secondhand I'd felt that night, how ridiculously fixed up I'd gotten for him. 'Then why'd you even show up?'

'I don't know.' He shakes his head. 'You know how Hilly can be.' He runs a hand through his light brown hair. It is almost wiry it's so thick.

I look away because he's cute in an overgrown boy kind of way and it's not something I want to be thinking right now. I hear myself saying, 'What do you mean, not ready?'

'Just not ready. Not after what happened.'

I stare at him. 'You want me to guess?'

'Me and Patricia van Devender. We got engaged last year and then . . . I thought you knew.'

He sinks down in a rocking chair. I don't sit next to him.

'What, she ran off with someone else?'

'Shoot.' He drops his head down into his hands, mumbles, 'That'd be a goddamn Mardi Gras party compared to what happened.'

I don't let myself say to him what I'd like to, that he probably deserved whatever she did, but he's just too pathetic-looking.

'We'd been dating since we were fifteen. You know how it is, when you've been steady with somebody that long.'

And I don't know why I admit this, except that I simply have nothing to lose. 'Actually, I wouldn't know,' I say. 'I've never dated anybody.'

He looks up at me, kind of laughs. 'Well, that must be it, then.'

'Be what?' I steel myself, recalling fertiliser and tractor references.

'You're . . . different. I've never met anybody that said exactly what they were thinking. Not a woman, anyway.'

'Believe me, I had a lot *more* to say.'

He sighs. 'When I saw your face, out there by the truck . . . I'm not that guy. I'm really not such a jerk.'

I look away, embarrassed. It's just starting to hit me what he said, that even though I'm different, maybe it's not in a strange way or an abnormal, tall-girl way. But maybe in a good way.

'I came by to see if you'd like to come downtown with me for supper. We could talk,' he says and stands up. 'We could . . . I don't know, listen to each other this time.'

I stand there, shocked. His eyes are blue and clear and fixed on me like my answer might really mean something to him. I take in a deep breath, about to say yes—I mean, why would I of all people refuse—and he bites his bottom lip, waiting.

And then I think about how he treated me like I was nothing. How he got shit-dog drunk he was so miserable to be stuck with me. I think about how he told me I smelled like fertiliser. It took me three months to stop thinking about that comment.

'No,' I blurt out. 'Thank you. But I really can't imagine anything worse.'

He nods, looks down at his feet. Then he goes down the porch steps.

'I'm sorry,' he says, the door to his car open. 'That's what I came to say and, well, I guess I said it.'

Stuart gets in his car and his door clicks shut. He props his arm up so his elbow pokes through the open window. But he keeps his eyes down.

'Just give me a minute,' I holler out to him. 'Let me get my sweater.'

No one tells us, girls who don't go on dates, that remembering can be almost as good as what actually happens.

We'd driven to the Robert E Lee for dinner last night. I'd thrown on a light blue sweater and a slim white skirt. I'd even let Mother brush out my hair. As she brushed and smoothed and brushed and smoothed, Mother kept asking how I'd met him and what happened on our last date, but I managed to scoot out from under her and dash down the stairs. By the time Stuart and I walked into the hotel and sat down, the waiter said they'd be closing soon. All they'd serve us was dessert.

'What . . . do you want, Skeeter?' Stuart had asked and I'd sort of tensed up then, hoping he wasn't planning on getting drunk again.

'I'll have a Co-Cola. Lots of ice.'

'No.' He smiled. 'I mean . . . in life. What do you want?'

I took a deep breath, knowing what Mother would advise me to say: fine, strong kids, a husband to take care of, shiny new appliances to cook tasty yet healthful meals in. 'I want to be a writer,' I said. 'A journalist. Maybe a novelist. Maybe both.'

He lifted his chin and looked at me then, right in the eye.

'I like that,' he said, and then he just kept staring. 'I've been thinking about you. You're smart, you're pretty, you're'—he smiled—'tall.'

Pretty?

We ate strawberry soufflés and had a glass of Chablis each. He talked about how to tell if there's oil underneath a cotton field and I talked about how the receptionist and I were the only females working for the paper.

'I hope you write something really good. Something you believe in.'

'Thank you. I . . . hope so too.'

The waiter yawned in the corner but we both ignored him and stayed and talked some more. And by the time I was wishing I'd washed my hair this morning and was practically doubled over with gratefulness that I'd at least brushed my teeth, out of the blue, he kissed me. Right in the middle of the Robert E Lee Hotel Restaurant, he kissed me so slowly, with an open mouth, and every single thing in my body filled up with light.

On a Monday afternoon, a few weeks after my date with Stuart, I stop by the library before going to the League meeting. I've come to get more books for Aibileen and check if anything's ever been written about domestic help.

I search through card catalogues and scan the shelves, but find nothing. I spot a single copy of *Frederick Douglass, an American Slave.* I grab it, but when I open it, I see the middle section has been ripped out. Inside, someone has written NIGGER BOOK in purple crayon. I am not as disturbed by the words as by the fact that the handwriting looks like a third grader's. I glance around, push the book in my satchel. It seems better than putting it back on the shelf.

In the Mississippi History room, I search for anything remotely resembling race relations. I find only Civil War books, maps and old phone books. I stand on tiptoe to see what's on the high shelf. That's when I spot a booklet laid sideways across the top of the *Mississippi River Valley Flood Index.* A regular-sized person would never have seen it. The booklet is thin, printed on onionskin paper, curling, bound with staples. 'Compilation of Jim Crow Laws of the South', the cover reads. I open the noisy cover page.

The booklet is simply a list of laws stating what coloured people can and cannot do, in an assortment of Southern states. I skim the first page, puzzled why this is here. The laws are neither threatening nor friendly, just citing the facts:

> No person shall require any white female to nurse in wards or rooms in which negro men are placed.
>
> It shall be unlawful for a white person to marry anyone except a white person. Any marriage in violation of this section shall be void.

No coloured barber shall serve as a barber to white women or girls.
The officer in charge shall not bury any coloured persons upon ground
used for the burial of white persons.
Books shall not be interchangeable between the white and coloured
schools, but shall continue to be used by the race first using them.

I read through four of the twenty-five pages, mesmerised by how many laws exist to separate us. Negroes and whites are not allowed to share water fountains, movie houses, public restrooms, phone booths, circus shows. We all know about these laws, but we don't talk about them. This is the first time I've ever seen them written down.

After several minutes, I make myself stop. I start to put the booklet back, telling myself I'm not writing a book about Southern legislation, But then I realise there's no difference between these government laws and Hilly's bathroom Initiative, except ten minutes' worth of signatures in the state capital.

I scratch my revelation on a piece of paper and tuck it inside the booklet: *Jim Crow or Hilly's bathroom plan—what's the difference?* I slip the booklet in my bag and head for the doors. I have a League meeting in thirty minutes.

Our places of comfort are expectedly different, my friends and I. Elizabeth's is hunched over her sewing machine. Mine is at my typewriter writing pithy things I'll never have the guts to say out loud. And Hilly's is behind a podium telling sixty-five women that three cans apiece isn't enough to feed all those PSCAs. The Poor Starving Children of Africa, that is. Mary Joline Walker, however, thinks three is plenty.

'Isn't it expensive, carting all these tins across the world to Africa?' Mary Joline asks. 'Doesn't it make more sense to send a cheque?'

The meeting has not officially started, but Hilly's already behind her podium. This isn't our normal evening time, but an extra afternoon session Hilly's called. In June, many of the members are going out of town for summer vacations. Then, in July, Hilly leaves for her annual trip down to the coast for three weeks. It's going to be hard for her to trust an entire town to operate properly without her here.

Hilly rolls her eyes. 'You cannot give these tribal people money, Mary Joline. They're likely to go to the local voodoo tent and get a satanic tattoo with our money.'

I make my way across the crowded meeting room, feeling the warmth of attention, as if a beam of light is shining down on my head.

The room is full of cake-eating, cigarette-smoking women all about my age. Some are whispering to each other, glancing my way.

'*Skeeter,*' Liza Presley says before I make it past the coffee urns, 'did I hear you were at the Robert E. Lee a few weeks ago?'

'Are you really seeing Stuart Whitworth?' says Frances Greenbow.

Most of the questions are not unkind. Still, I shrug, try not to notice how when a regular girl gets asked out, it's information, but when Skeeter Phelan gets asked out, it's *news.*

But it's true. I am seeing Stuart Whitworth and have been for three weeks now. Twice at the Robert E Lee if you include the disaster date, and three more times sitting on my front porch for drinks before he drove home to Vicksburg.

The white spotlight of wonder follows me as I make my way back to Hilly. Girls are smiling and nodding at me.

'When will y'all see each other again?' asks Elizabeth.

'Tomorrow night. As soon as he can drive over.'

'Good.' Hilly's smile is a fat child's at the ice-cream kiosk. The button on her red suit coat bulges. 'We'll make it a double date, then.'

I don't answer. I don't want Hilly and William coming along. I just want to sit with Stuart, have him look at me and only me. Twice, when we were alone, he brushed my hair back when it fell in my eyes. He might not brush my hair back if they're around.

'William'll telephone Stuart tonight. Let's go to the picture show.'

'All right,' I sigh.

'I'm just dying to see *It's a Mad, Mad, Mad, Mad World.* Won't this be fun,' Hilly says. 'You and me and William and Stuart.'

She gives the five-minute-till bang with her gavel. I make my way to my chair, lug my satchel onto my lap. I check through the contents, suddenly conscious of the Jim Crow booklet I stole from the library. In fact, my satchel holds all the work we've done—Aibileen and Minny's interviews; the book outline; a list of potential maids; a scathing, unmailed response I wrote to Hilly's bathroom Initiative—everything I can't leave at home for fear Mother will snoop through my things. I keep it all in a side zip-pocket with a flap over it. It bulges unevenly.

At the podium, Hilly looks at her watch, toying with the gavel like she's just dying to bang it. I push my satchel under my chair. Finally, the meeting begins.

I record the PSCA news, who's not brought in their cans. The calendar of events is full of committee meetings and baby showers, and

I shift round in my wooden chair, hoping the meeting will end soon. I have to get Mother's car back to her by three.

It's not until a quarter to, an hour and a half later, that I rush out of the hot room towards the Cadillac. I'll be on the trouble list for leaving early, but what's worse, the wrath of Mother or the wrath of Hilly?

I walk into the house five minutes early, humming 'Love Me Do'.

'Mama, I'm home,' I call down the hallway.

I pull a Co-Cola from the fridge, sigh and smile, feeling good, strong. I head to the front door for my satchel, ready to thread together more of Minny's stories. It's not there. I go outside and look in the car but it's not there either. *Huh,* I think, a slow tingle of panic working its way up my spine. The satchel, it has *everything* in it.

Mother, I think and I look in the relaxing room. But suddenly I realise it's not Mother who has it—the answer has come to me, numbing my entire body. I left my satchel at the League House. And even as the phone is ringing, I already know it is Hilly.

I grab the phone from the wall just as Mother calls goodbye to me from the front door.

'How could you leave this heavy thing behind?' Hilly asks. Hilly never has had a problem with going through other people's things. In fact, she enjoys it.

'Mother, wait a second!' I holler from the kitchen.

'Good Lord, Skeeter, what's in here?' Hilly says. I've got to catch Mother, but Hilly's voice is muffled, like she's bending down, opening it.

'Nothing! Just . . . all those Miss Myrna letters, you know.'

'Well, I've lugged it back to my house so come get it when you can.'

Mother is starting the car outside. 'Just . . . keep it there. I'll be by as soon as I can get there.'

I race outside and jump in the front passenger seat. 'Drive me by Hilly's? I need to pick something up.' I press my hand to my forehead.

'Now look,' Mother says, 'I have some personal errands to run and I just don't think it's a good time to have you tagging along.'

'It'll take you five minutes. Just drive, Mama!'

Mother keeps her white-gloved hands on the steering wheel, her lips pressed together.

'I happen to have something confidential and important to do today.'

I can't imagine my mother has anything more important to do than what I'm staring down the throat of. 'What? A Mexican's trying to join the Daughters of the American Revolution?'

Mother sighs, says, 'Fine,' and moves the gear shift carefully into drive. We roll down the lane at about one-tenth of a mile an hour.

'Mama,' I finally say, 'just let me drive the car.'

She sighs. I'm surprised that she pulls over. I get out and run around the car while she slides over. I put the car in D and press it to seventy, praying, *Please, Hilly, resist the temptation to rummage through my personal business* . . . .

'So what's the big secret, what do you have to do today?' I ask.

'I'm . . . I'm going to see Doctor Neal for some tests. It's just routine, but I don't want your daddy to know.'

'What kind of tests?'

'It's just an iodine test for my ulcers, same as I have every year. Drop me at the Baptist and then you can take yourself to Hilly's.'

I glance at her to see if there's more to this, but she's sitting straight and starched in her light blue dress, her legs crossed at the ankles. I don't remember her having these tests last year. Even with me being up at college, Constantine would've written to me about them. Mother must've kept them secret.

Five minutes later, at the Baptist Hospital, I come around and help her out of the car.

'Eugenia, please. Just because this is a hospital doesn't mean I'm an invalid.'

'Mother, do you . . . want me to come with you?' I ask, knowing I can't—I have to deal with Hilly, but suddenly I don't want to drop her off here, like this.

'It's *routine*. Go on to Hilly's and come back in an hour.'

A minute and a half later, I'm ringing Hilly's bell. If these were regular times, I'd talk to Hilly about Mama. But I can't distract her. It is the first moment that will tell me everything. Hilly is an exceptional liar, except for the moment right before she speaks.

Hilly opens the door. Her mouth is tight and red. I look down at her hands. They are knotted together like ropes. I've arrived too late.

'Well, that was quick,' she says and I follow her inside. My heart is seizing inside my chest. I'm not sure I'm breathing at all.

'There it is, that ugly thing. I hope you don't mind, I had to check something in the minutes from the meeting.'

I stare at her, my best friend, trying to see just what she's read in my things. But her smile is professional, if not sparkling.

'Can I get you something to sip on?'

'No, I'm fine.' Then I add, 'Want to hit balls at the club later? It's so gorgeous out.'

'William's got a campaign meeting and then we're going to see *It's a Mad, Mad, Mad, Mad World.*'

I study her. Didn't she ask me, just two hours ago, to double-date to this movie tomorrow night?

'Yes, um, I heard Spencer Tracy's supposed to be divine,' I say. Casually, I tick through the papers in my satchel. Aibileen and Minny's notes are still tucked deep in the side pocket, the flap closed, the latch snapped. But Hilly's bathroom Initiative is in the open centre section with the paper where I wrote: *Jim Crow or Hilly's bathroom plan—what's the difference?* Besides this is the draft of the newsletter that Hilly has examined already. But the booklet—the laws—they are gone.

Hilly tilts her head, narrows her eyes at me. 'You know, I was just thinking about how Stuart's daddy stood right next to Ross Barnett when they fought that coloured boy walking into Ole Miss. They're awfully close, Senator Whitworth and Governor Barnett.'

I open my mouth to say something, anything, but then two-year-old William Jr totters in.

'There you are.' Hilly picks him up, nuzzles his neck. 'You are perfect, my perfect boy!' she says.

'Well, enjoy the picture show,' I say, going for the front door.

'All right,' she says. I walk down the steps. From her doorway, Hilly waves, flaps William's hand bye-bye. She slams the door before I've even made it to my car.

AIBILEEN

I'VE BEEN IN SOME TENSE situations, but to have Minny on one side a my living room and Miss Skeeter on the other, and the topic at hand be what it feel like being Negro and working for a white woman. Law, it's a wonder they hadn't been a injury.

We had some close calls though. Like when Miss Skeeter showed me Miss Hilly's reasons why coloured folk need they own bathroom.

'Feel like I'm looking at something from the KKK,' I said to Miss Skeeter. We was in my living room and the nights had started to get warm. Minny'd gone in the kitchen to stand in front a the icebox.

'Hilly wants me to print it in the League newsletter,' Miss Skeeter said, shaking her head, disgusted. 'I'm sorry, I probably shouldn't have shown it to you. But there's no one else I can tell.'

A minute later, Minny come back from the kitchen. I gave Miss Skeeter a look, so she slid the list under her notebook. Minny didn't look much cooler. Fact, she looked hotter than ever.

'Minny, do you and Leroy ever talk about civil rights?' Miss Skeeter ask. 'When he comes home from work?'

Minny had that big bruise on her arm cause that's what Leroy do when he come home from work. He push her around.

'Nope,' was all she said. Minny do not like people up in her business.

'Really? He doesn't share the way he feels about the marches and the segregation? Maybe at work, his bo—'

'Move off a Leroy.' Minny crossed her arms.

I gave Miss Skeeter a nudge on the foot. But she had that look she gets when she's all up in something.

'Aibileen, don't you think it would be interesting if we could show a little of the husbands' perspective? Minny, maybe—'

Minny stood so quick the lightshade rattled. 'I ain't doing this no more. You making this too personal. I don't care about telling white people how it feel.'

'Minny, OK, I'm sorry,' Miss Skeeter said. 'We don't have to talk about your family.'

'No. I change my mind. You find somebody else to spill the beans.' We been through this before. But this time, Minny snatched up her pocketbook and said, 'I'm sorry, Aib. But I just can't do this no more.'

So I leaned up, slipped Hilly's piece a paper out from under Miss Skeeter's notebook. My fingers stopped right in front a Minny.

Minny picked it up and started skimming. Pretty soon, I could see all her front teeth. But she wasn't smiling. Then she looked at Miss Skeeter, long and heavy. She said, 'Maybe we keep going then. But you stay out a my personal business, you hear?'

Miss Skeeter nodded. She learning.

After lunch, I take Baby Girl out to the backyard and fill up the green plastic pool. It's already ninety-five degrees outside. Mississippi got the most unorganised weather in the nation. In February, it'll be fifteen degrees and you be wishing spring would come on, and the next day it's ninety degrees for the next nine months.

The sun shining. Mae Mobley's setting in the middle a that pool in bathing bottoms. Miss Leefolt come outside and say, 'That looks like fun! I'm fixing to call Hilly, tell her to bring Heather and Will over here.' And fore I know it, all three kids is playing in there, splashing around, having a good old time.

We grown-ups is setting in the shade a the magnolia tree while the kids play. I put a few feet between me and the ladies so it's proper. They got towels down in them black iron chairs that gets so hot. I like to sit in the plastic green folding chair. Keep my legs cool.

I watch Mae Mobley make Barbie Doll do the skinny dip, jumping off the side a the pool. But I got my eye on the ladies too. Miss Hilly act all sweet and happy when she talk to Heather and William, but ever time she turn to Miss Leefolt, she get a sneer on her face.

'Aibileen, get me a little more iced tea, would you, please?' Hilly ask. I go and get the pitcher from the refrigerator.

'See, that's what I don't understand,' I hear Miss Hilly say when I'm close enough. 'Nobody wants to sit down on a toilet seat they have to share with them.'

'It does make sense,' Miss Leefolt say, but then she hush up when I come over to fill up they glasses.

'Why, thank you,' Miss Hilly say. Then she give me a real perplexed look, say, 'Aibileen, you like having your own toilet, don't you?'

'Yes, ma'am.' She still talking about that pot even though it's been in there six months.

'Separate but equal,' Miss Hilly say back to Miss Leefolt. 'That's what Governor Ross Barnett says, and you can't argue with the *government*.'

Miss Leefolt clap her hand on her thigh like she got the most interesting thing to change the subject to. I'm with her. Let's discuss something else. 'Did I tell you what Raleigh said the other day?'

But Miss Hilly shaking her head. 'Aibileen, you wouldn't want to go to a school full of white people, would you?'

'No, ma'am,' I mumble. I get up and pull the ponytail holder out a Baby Girl's head. Them green plastic balls get all tangly when her hair get wet. But what I really want to do is put my hands up over her ears so she can't hear this talk. And worse, hear me agreeing.

But then I think: why? Why I have to stand here and agree with her? And if Mae Mobley gone hear it, she gone hear some sense. I get my breath. My heart beating hard. And I say polite as I can, 'Not a school full a just white people. But where coloured and white folks is together.'

Hilly and Miss Leefolt both look at me. I look back down at the kids.

'But *Aibileen*'—Miss Hilly smile real cold—'coloured people and white people are just so . . . *different*.' She wrinkle up her nose.

I feel my lip curling. A course we different! Everbody know coloured people and white people ain't the same. But we still just people! I press my lips together.

It don't matter though, cause Miss Hilly already moved on. Ain't nothing to her. She back to her low-down talk with Miss Leefolt.

'. . . government knows best and if Skeeter thinks she's going to get away with this coloured non—'

'Mama! Mama! Look at me!' holler Heather from the pool.

'I see you! I do! What with William running for office next—'

'Mama, give me your comb! I want to do beauty parlour!'

'—cannot have coloured-supporting friends in my closet—'

'Mamaaaaa! Gimme your comb. Get your comb for me!'

'I read it. I found it in her satchel and I intend to take action.'

And then Miss Hilly quiet, hunting for her comb in her pocketbook. Thunder boom over in South Jackson and way off we hear the wail a the tornado bell. I'm trying to make sense a what Miss Hilly just said: *Miss Skeeter. Her satchel. I read it.* I get the kids out the pool, swaddle em up in towels. The thunder come crashing out the sky.

A minute after dark, I'm setting at my kitchen table, twirling my pencil. My white-library copy a *Adventures of Huckleberry Finn's* in front a me, but I can't read it. I got a bad taste in my mouth, bitter, like coffee grounds in the last sip. I take out my notebook, intending to start on my prayers, but I'm just too deep worrying about Miss Hilly. Wondering what she meant when she said, *Read it.*

After while, my mind done drifted to where I wish it wouldn't. I reckon I know pretty well what would happen if the white ladies found out we was writing about them, telling the truth a what they really like.

First thing a white lady gone do is fire you. You upset, but you figure you'll find another job. You got a month a rent saved. People bring you squash casseroles.

But then a week after you lost your job, you get this yellow envelope stuck in your screen door. Paper inside say NOTICE OF EVICTION. Ever landlord in Jackson be white and ever one got a white wife that's friends with somebody. You still ain't got no job prospects. Everwhere you try, the door slams in your face. And now you ain't got a place to live.

Then it starts to come a little faster.

If you got a parking ticket you ain't paid, you going to jail.

If you got a daughter, maybe you go live with her. She tend to a white family a her own. But a few days later she come home, say, 'Mama? I just got fired.' You got to tell her it's cause a you.

Least her husband still working. Least they can feed the baby. Then they fire her husband. They both pointing at you, crying, wondering why you done it. You can't even remember why. Weeks pass and nothing, no jobs, no money, no house. You hope this is the end of it, she ready to forget.

It'll be a knock on the door, late at night. It won't be the white lady at the door. She don't do that kind a thing herself. But while the night-mare's happening, the burning or the cutting or the beating, you realise something you known all your life: the white lady don't *ever* forget.

And she ain't gone stop till you dead.

The next night after supper, Miss Skeeter call me.

'Hey, Aibileen,' Miss Skeeter say and I hear a door shut. 'Sorry to call so late.'

I breathe out. 'I'm glad you did.'

'Aibileen,' Miss Skeeter voice all shaky, 'I have to tell you something.'

'What happen, Miss Skeeter?'

'I . . . left my satchel. At the League. Hilly picked it up.'

I squint my eyes, feel like I ain't hearing too good. 'The red one?'

'The stories were in a flap pocket. On the side, in another folder. I think all she saw were Jim Crow laws, some . . . booklet I'd picked up at the library but . . . I can't say for sure.'

'Oh, Miss *Skeeter*,' I say and shut my eyes. God help me, God help *Minny* . . .

'I know. I *know*,' Miss Skeeter say and start to cry into the phone.

'All right. All right, now.' I try to make myself swallow my anger down. It was a accident, I tell myself. Kicking her ain't gone do us no good. But *still*.

'How long ago this happen?' I ask.

'Three days ago. I wanted to find out what she knew before I told you.'

'You talked to Miss Hilly?'

'Just for a second when I picked it up. But I've talked to Elizabeth and Lou Anne and probably four other girls who know Hilly. Nobody's said anything about it.'

I draw in a breath, hating what I have to tell her. 'Yesterday. Miss Hilly was talking to Miss Leefolt about it.'

Miss Skeeter don't say nothing. I feel like I'm waiting for a brick to come slamming through my window.

'She talking about Mister Holbrook running for office and how you supporting coloured people and she say . . . she read something.' Saying it out loud now, I'm shaking.

'Did she say anything about maids?' Miss Skeeter ask. 'I mean, was she only upset with me or did she mention you or Minny?'

'No, just . . . you.'

'OK.' Miss Skeeter blow air into the phone. She sound upset, but she don't know what could happen to me, to Minny.

'I–I can't say a hundred per cent, but . . .' Miss Skeeter say, 'if Hilly knew anything about the book or you or *especially* Minny, she'd be spreading it all over town.'

I think on this, wanting so hard to believe her. 'It's true, she do not like Minny Jackson.'

'Aibileen,' Miss Skeeter say, and I hear her start to break down again. 'We can stop. I understand if you want to stop working on it.'

If I say I don't want a do it anymore, then everthing I been writing and still have to write ain't gone get to be said. *No,* I think. I *don't* want a stop. I'm surprised by how loud I think it.

'If Miss Hilly know, she know,' I say. 'Stopping ain't gone save us now.'

One evening I have to work real late. I feed Baby Girl supper and put her to bed, cause Mister and Miss Leefolt gone to see a picture at the Lamar. When they get home, they yawning, crickets is cricking. I kind a hang around thinking Mister Leefolt gone offer to drive me home, but he just go right to bed.

Outside, in the dark, I walk all the way up to Riverside. Bus come after while. Ain't but four people on there, two coloured, two white, all mens. I take a window seat behind a thin coloured fella. He got on a brown suit and a brown hat, be about my age.

We cross the bridge, head in the direction a the coloured hospital, where the bus make its turn. I got my prayer book out so I can write some things down.

I look up. The bus done stopped in the middle a the road. A few blocks up they's blue lights flashing in the dark, people standing round, a road block. White driver stare ahead. He turn off the motor and my seat go still, feel strange. He straighten his driver's hat, hop out the seat. 'Y'all stay put. Let me find out what's going on.'

So we all set there in the quiet, waiting. I hear a dog barking, not a house dog, but the kind that sound like he yelling at you. After a full five minutes, driver get back on the bus, start the motor again. He toot his horn, wave his hand out the window, and start backing up real slow.

'Wha happen up there?' coloured man in front a me call to the driver.

Driver don't answer. He keep backing up. The flashing lights is getting smaller, the dog barking fading off. Driver turn the bus around on Farish Street. At the next corner, he stop. 'Coloured people off, last stop for you,' he holler in the rearview. 'White people lemme know where y'all need to get to. I'll get you close as I can.'

The coloured man look back at me. I guess we both ain't got a good feeling. He stand up so I do too. I follow him to the front door. It's eerie quiet, just the sound a our feets.

White man lean up to the driver, say, 'What's going on?'

I follow the coloured man down the steps a the bus. Behind me, I hear the driver say, 'Some nigger got shot. Where you headed?'

Ain't a sound on Farish Street, or a person, cept us two. The man look at me. 'You all right? You close to home?'

'I be all right. I'm close.' My house is seven blocks from here.

'Want me to walk you?'

I kind a do, but I shake my head. 'Naw, thank you. I be fine.'

A news truck whiz by, way down at the intersection the bus turned off of. Big WLBT-TV letters on the side.

'Law, I hope this ain't as bad as it—' but the man gone. They ain't a soul now but me. I get that feeling people talk about, right before they get mugged. Up ahead I see three people walking fast like me. All of em turn off, go into houses, shut the door.

I'm real sure I don't want to be alone another second. I cut between the houses and the back a the auto repair. Finally, up ahead I see Minny's kitchen light, back door open, screen door closed. The door make a whine when I push it. Minny setting at the table with all five kids. I guess Leroy gone to work. They all staring at the big radio in the middle a the table.

'What is it?' I say. Minny frown, fiddle with the dial. The radio man come into tune, hollering, '—almost ten years serving as the Field Secretary for the N-double-A-C-P. Still no word from the hospital but wounds are said to be—'

'*Who?*' I say.

Minny stare at me like I ain't got my head on. 'Medgar Evers. Where you been?'

'Medgar Evers? What happen?' I met Myrlie Evers, his wife, last fall, when she visit our church. I remember how she looked me in the eye, smiled like she was real glad to meet me. Medgar Evers like a celebrity around here, being so high in the NAACP, the National Association for the Advancement of Coloured People.

'Set down,' Minny say. I set in a wooden chair. They all ghost-faced, staring at the radio.

'KKK shot him. Front a his house. A hour ago.'

I feel a prickle creep up my spine. 'Where he live?'

'On Guynes,' Minny say. 'The doctors got him at our hospital.'

'I . . . saw,' I say, thinking a the bus. Guynes ain't but five minutes away from here if you got a car.

'*. . . witnesses say it was a single man, a white male, who jumped from the bushes. Rumours of KKK involvement are . . .*'

Now they's some unorganised talking on the radio, some people yelling, some fumbling round. I tense up like somebody watching us from outside. Somebody white. The KKK was here, five minutes away, to hunt down a coloured man. I want a close that back door.

'*I was just informed,*' the announcer say, '*that Medgar Evers is dead.*'

Minny turn to Leroy Jr. Her voice low, steady. 'Take your brothers and your sisters in the bedroom. Get in bed. And stay back there.' It always sound scarier when a hollerer talk soft.

Minny's hands is in fists. She gritting her teeth. 'Shot him right in front a his *children*, Aibileen.'

'We gone pray for the Everses, we gone pray for Myrlie . . .'

I choke then. The tears roll down. It's all them white peoples that breaks me, standing around the coloured neighbourhood. White peoples with guns, pointed at coloured peoples. Cause who gone protect our peoples? Ain't no coloured policemans.

'What they gone do to us, Aibileen? If they catch us . . .'

I take a deep breath. She talking about the stories. 'We both know. It be bad.'

I turn off the radio, take Minny's hand in mine. We set like that. Minny got the most lonesome look in her eyes. 'I wish Leroy was home,' she whisper.

I doubt if them words ever been said in this house before.

For days and days, Jackson, Mississippi's like a pot a boiling water. On Miss Leefolt's tee-vee, flocks a coloured people march up High Street the day after Mister Evers's funeral. Over three hundred arrested. Coloured paper say thousands a people came to the service, but you could count the whites on one hand. The police know who did it, but they ain't telling nobody his name.

I come to find that the Evers family ain't burying Medgar in Mississippi. His body's going to Washington, to the Arlington Cemetery, and I reckon Myrlie real proud a that. In the newspaper, I read how even the President a the United States telling Mayor Thompson he need to do better. Put a committee together with blacks and whites and work things out down here. But Mayor Thompson, he say—to *President Kennedy*—'I am not going to appoint a bi-racial committee. Let's not kid ourselves. I believe in the separation of the races and that's the way it's going to be.'

For the second time in two months, Jackson, Mississippi's in the *Life* magazine. This time, though, we make the cover.

Ever afternoon, me and Baby Girl set in the rocking chair before her nap. Ever afternoon, I tell her: *you kind, you smart, you important.* But she growing up and I know, soon, them few words ain't gone be enough.

We just rock in the chair awhile. Mae Mobley lean her head against my uniform. We watch the rain dripping on the water left in the green plastic pool. I say a prayer for Myrlie Evers, wishing I'd had work off to go to the funeral. I rock and pray, feeling so sad, I don't know, something just come over me. The words just come out.

'Once upon a time they was two little girls,' I say. 'One girl had black skin, one girl had white.'

Mae Mobley look up at me. She listening.

'Little coloured girl say to the little white girl, "How come your skin be so pale?" White girl say, "I don't know. How come your skin be so black? What you think that mean?"'

'But neither one a them little girls knew. So little white girl say, "Well, let's see. You got hair, I got hair."' I gives Mae Mobley a tousle on her head.

'Little coloured girl say, "I got a nose, you got a nose."' I gives her little snout a tweak. She reach up and do the same to me.

'Little white girl say, "I got toes, you got toes."' And I do the little thing with her toes, but she can't get to mine cause I got my work shoes on.

'"So we's the same. Just a different colour," say that little coloured girl. The little white girl she agreed and they was friends. The end.'

Baby Girl just look at me. Law, that was a sorry story if I ever heard one. Wasn't even no plot to it. But Mae Mobley, she smile and say, 'Tell it again.' So I do. By the fourth time, she asleep.

Miss Hilly call this morning and ask if Miss Leefolt and Baby Girl want to go swimming at the Jackson Country Club and that's a invitation Miss Leefolt ain't had but once or twice.

I put Baby Girl's yellow bikini on. 'You got to keep you top on, now. They don't let no nekkid babies swim at the country club.' Nor Negroes nor Jews. I used to work for the Goldmans. The Jackson Jews got to swim at the Colonial Country Club; the Negroes, in May's Lake.

At the club, Miss Hilly is laid out on a lounge chair, watching her kids swim. I see two maids with other families, but not Yule May.

Miss Leefolt lay down on the lounge chair next to Miss Hilly and I set at the table under a umbrella, few feet behind the ladies. I'm in a pretty good position for hearing what they say.

'Yule May,' Miss Hilly shake her head at Miss Leefolt. 'Another day off. I tell you, that girl is pushing it with me.' Well, that's one mystery solved. Miss Hilly invite Miss Leefolt to the pool cause she know she bring me.

The kids yell they want to get in the big pool now. I pull Mae Mobley's Styrofoam bubble out the bag, fasten it round her tummy. Miss Hilly hand me two more and I put one on William and Heather too. They get in the big pool and float around like a bunch a fishing corks. Miss Hilly look at me, say, 'Aren't they the cutest things?' and I nod.

They talk and I listen, but they ain't no mention a Miss Skeeter or a satchel. After while, Miss Hilly send me to the snack window to get cherry Co-Colas for everone, even myself. And that's when I see Miss Skeeter, back behind the pool, outside the fence. She got on her tennis skirt and her racquet in her hand. She staring at Miss Hilly and Miss Leefolt, tilting her head like she sorting something out. I watch Miss Skeeter come in the gate, walk round the pool.

'Hey y'all,' Miss Skeeter say. She got sweat running down her arms. Her face is pink and swolled up in the sun.

'Hilly,' Miss Skeeter say, 'did Yule May tell you I called?'

Hilly smile kind a tight. 'She's off today.'

'I called you yesterday too.'

'Look, Skeeter, I didn't have time. I have been at the campaign HQ since Wednesday addressing envelopes to practically every white person in Jackson.'

'All right.' Miss Skeeter nod. Then she squint, say, 'Hilly, are we . . . did I . . . do something to upset you?'

'Look, I found that *paraphernalia* of yours.' I swallow hard. Miss Hilly trying to whisper but she really ain't no good at it. 'In your satchel when I was hunting for the minutes? And Skeeter'—she flash her eyes up at the sky and back down—'I don't know. I just do not know anymore.'

'Hilly, what are you talking about? What did you see in my satchel?'

'Those *laws* you were carrying around? About what the—' Miss Hilly look back at me. I keep my eyes trained on the pool. 'What those *other* people can and cannot do and frankly,' she hiss, 'I think it's downright pig-headed of you. To think you know better than our government?' Miss Hilly wag her finger up at Miss Skeeter. 'You are not a politician, Skeeter Phelan.'

'Well, neither are you, Hilly.'

Miss Hilly stand up then. She point her finger to the ground. 'I am about to be a politician's wife, unless you have anything to do with it. How is William ever going to get elected in Washington one day if we have integrational friends in our closet?'

'Washington?' Miss Skeeter roll her eyes. 'William's running for the local senate, Hilly. And he might not win.'

Oh Law. I finally let myself look at Miss Skeeter. Why you doing this? Why you pushing her hot button?

Oh, Miss Hilly mad now. She snap her head straight. 'You know as well as I do, there are good, tax-paying white people in this town who would fight you to the death on this. You want to let them get in our swimming pools? Let them put their hands on everything in our grocery stores?'

Miss Skeeter stare long and hard at Miss Hilly. Then, for one-half a second, Miss Skeeter glance at me, see the pleading in my eyes. Her shoulders ease back some. 'Oh, Hilly, it's just a booklet. I found it at the darn library. I just took it home to *read*.'

Miss Hilly take this in a second. 'But if you're looking at those *laws*, I have to wonder, what *else* are you up to?'

'*Hilly*. You know me better than anybody else in this world. If I was up to something, you'd have me figured out in half a second.'

Miss Hilly just watch her. Then Miss Skeeter grab Miss Hilly's hand and squeeze it. 'I am worried about you. You disappear for an entire week; you're working yourself to death on this campaign.'

And, real slow, I watch Miss Hilly's body slump down, start to give in on itself.

'I'm just so scared,' Miss Hilly whisper through her teeth. I can't hear much. '. . . piled so much money in this campaign, if William doesn't win . . . been working day and . . .'

Miss Skeeter lay a hand on Miss Hilly's shoulder, say something to her. Miss Hilly nod and give her a tired smile.

After while, Miss Skeeter tell them she got to go. I lean back in my chair, and Miss Skeeter look back at me. Everbody around us is sunning and laughing and squinting, not a soul guessing that the coloured woman and the white woman with the tennis racket is wondering the same thing: Is we fools to feel some relief?

About a year after Treelore died, I started going to the Community Concerns Meeting at my church. Lately, the meetings is more about civil rights than keeping the streets clean and who gone work at the clothing exchange. It ain't aggressive, mostly people just talking things out, praying about it. But after Mr Evers got shot a week ago, lot a coloured folks is frustrated in this town. Especially the younger ones.

I walk down the steps to the basement. I look round to see who's here, reckoning I better ask some more maids to help us, now that it look like we squeaked by Miss Hilly. Thirty-five maids done said no and I feel like I'm selling something nobody want to buy.

I wish Minny could help me ask people. Minny know how to put a sell on. But we decided from the start, nobody needs to know Minny's a part a this. It's just too risky for her family.

I settle in. The deacon say we need a quiet prayer meeting tonight. Say we need to heal. We close our eyes and the deacon leads us in a prayer for the Everses, for Myrlie, for the sons. Some folks is whispering, murmuring to God, and a quiet power fill up the room, like bees buzzing on a comb. I say my prayers to myself.

Yule May, Miss Hilly's maid, setting in front a me. Yule May easy to recognise from the back cause she got such good hair, smooth, no nap to it. I hear she educated, went through most a college. Course we got plenty a smart people in our church with they college degrees. Doctors, lawyers, Mr Cross who own *The Southern Times.*

'Deacon Thoroughgood,' a deep voice boom through stillness. I turn—everybody turn—and there's Jessup, Plantain Fidelia's grandson, standing in the doorway. He got his hands in thick fists.

'What I want to know is,' he say slow, angry, 'what we plan to *do* about it?'

Deacon got a stern look on his face like he done talked with Jessup before. 'Tonight, we are going to lift our prayers to God. We will march peacefully down the streets of Jackson next Tuesday. And in August, I will see you in Washington to march with Doctor King.'

'That is not enough!' Jessup say, banging his fist on his hand. 'They shot him in the back like a dog!'

'Jessup.' Deacon raise his hand. 'Tonight is for prayer. For the family. For the lawyers on the case. I understand your anger, but, son—'

'Y'all think *prayer's* going to keep white people from killing us?'

No one answer, not even the deacon. Jessup just turn and leave.

The room is real quiet. Deacon Thoroughgood got his eyes locked a few inches above our heads. Everybody staring at him, everybody wondering what he thinking so that he can't look in our faces. Then I see Yule May shaking her head, real small, but like she mean it and I reckon the deacon and Yule May is thinking the same thing. They thinking about what Jessup ask. And Yule May, she just answering the question.

The meeting ends around eight o'clock. The ones who got kids go on, others get ourselves coffee from the table in the back. They ain't much chatter. I take a breath, go to Yule May standing at the coffee urn.

'I hear the twins gone to Tougaloo College next year. Congratulations.'

'We hope so. We've still got a little more to save. Two at once's a lot.'

'You went to a good bit a college yourself, didn't you?'

She nod, say, 'Jackson College.'

'I loved school. The reading and the writing. Cept the rithmatic. I didn't take to that.'

Yule May smiles. 'The English was my favourite too. The writing.'

'I been . . . writing some myself.'

Yule May look me in the eye and I can tell then she know what I'm about to say. For a second, I can see the shame she swallow ever day, working in that house. The fear. I feel embarrassed to ask her.

But Yule May say it before I have to. 'I know about the stories you're working on. With that friend of Miss Hilly's.'

'It's all right, Yule May. I know you can't do it.'

'It's just . . . a risk I can't afford to take right now. We so close to getting enough money together.'

'I understand,' I say and I smile, let her know she off the hook. But Yule May don't move away.

'The names . . . you're changing them, I heard?'

This the same question everybody ask, cause they curious.

'That's right. And the name a the town, too.'

She look down at the floor. 'So I'd tell my stories about being a maid and she'd write them down? Edit them or . . . something like that?' Yule May lick her lips, look like she imagining it, telling what it's like to work for Miss Hilly. 'Could we . . . talk about this some more? When I have more time?'

'Anytime. Whenever you feel like it.'

She touch my arm and look me straight in the eyes again. It's like she been waiting on me to ask her all this time.

MINNY

NINE MONTHS WITH MISS CELIA and I still don't know if she's sick in the body or fried up her wits with the hair colouring. She does look better than when I started. Her tummy's got a little fat on it, her cheeks aren't so hollow as they were. For a while, Miss Celia was working in the backyard all the time but now she's back to sitting around the bed again.

When I get in for work, Miss Celia comes out of her bedroom. I think she's about to sneak upstairs, but then I hear her on the kitchen telephone asking for Miss Hilly. I get a sick, sick feeling.

'I was just calling again to see about getting a bridge game together!' she says all cheerful and I don't move until I know it's Yule May, Hilly's maid, she's talking to and not Miss Hilly herself.

And half a minute later, she's calling up another name from the back of that stupid paper, like she's gotten into the habit of doing every other day. I know what that thing is, it's the newsletter from the Ladies League, and from the looks of it she found it in a parking lot. She even call Miss Skeeter's house, which I don't like one bit. I told Miss Skeeter myself: *Don't even think about calling her back. Don't tangle up this web any more than it already is.*

So far, not one of those other girls has ever called her back. 'Those ladies ain't worth it, Miss Celia,' I hear myself saying. But she acts like she can't hear me. She goes back to the bedroom and closes the door.

At the end of June, a heat wave of a hundred degrees moves in and doesn't budge. Out in Madison County, the heat officially makes Miss Celia the laziest person in the US of A.

'Minny, would you mind fetching the mail for me?' she asks even though she's sitting here all dressed and I've got butter on my hands and a wash in the machine and a motor blender going.

I clean off my hands and head out to the box, sweat half a gallon on the way. I mean, it's only ninety-nine degrees outside. There's a two-foot package sitting next to the mailbox, in the grass. I've seen her with these big brown boxes before, figure it's some kind of beauty cream she's ordering. But when I pick it up, it's heavy. Makes a tinkling sound like I'm toting Co-Cola bottles.

'You got something, Miss Celia.' I plop the box on the floor of the kitchen.

I've never seen her jump up so fast. 'It's just my . . .' She mumbles something. She heaves the box all the way to her bedroom and I hear the door slam.

An hour later, I go back in the bedroom. Miss Celia's not laying down and she's not in the bathroom. I know she's not in the kitchen or the living room or out at the pool and I just dusted fancy parlour number one and number two. Which means she must be upstairs. In the creepy rooms. I decide it's time I go up there and take a look for myself.

I keep an eye on Miss Celia the next day, waiting for her to sneak upstairs. Around two o'clock, she sticks her head in the kitchen and gives me a funny smile. A minute later, I hear the squeak in the ceiling.

Real easy, I tiptoe for the staircase. At the top, I turn down the long hall. I pass wide-open bedroom doors, one, two, three. Door number four, down on the end, is closed except for an inch. I move in a little closer. And through the crack, I spot her.

She's sitting on the bed by the window and she's not smiling. The package I toted in from the mailbox is open and on the bed are a dozen bottles filled with brown liquid. I know the look of those flat bottles. I nursed a worthless pint drinker for twelve years and when my lazy, life-sucking daddy finally died, I swore to God with tears in my eyes I'd never marry one. And then I did.

And now here I am nursing another goddamn drinker. These aren't even store-bought bottles; these have a red wax top like my Uncle Toad used to cap his moonshine with. Miss Celia picks a bottle up and looks at it like it's Jesus in there and she can't wait to get saved. She uncorks it, sips it, and sighs. Then she drinks three hard swallows and lays back on her fancy pillows.

My body starts to shake, watching that ease cross her face. She was so eager to get to her juice, she didn't even close the damn door. I have to grit my teeth so I don't scream at her.

When Miss Celia comes back downstairs ten minutes later, she sits at the kitchen table, asks me if I'm ready to eat.

'There's pork chops in the icebox and I'm not eating lunch today,' I say and stomp out of the room.

On the first Thursday of July, at twelve noon, Miss Celia gets up from the bed for her cooking lesson. She's dressed in a white sweater so tight it'd make a hooker look holy. I swear her clothes get tighter every week.

We settle in our places, me at the stove, her on her stool. I've hardly spoken one word to her since I found those bottles last week. I'm not mad. I'm irate. But I have sworn every day for the past six days that I would follow Mama's rule number one. To say something would mean I cared about her and I don't. It's not my business or my concern if she's a lazy, drunk fool.

We lay the battered raw chicken on the rack. Then I have to remind the ding-dong for the bobillionth time to wash her hands before she kills us both.

I watch the chicken sizzle, try to forget she's there. Frying chicken always makes me feel a little better about life. I almost forget I'm working for a drunk. When the batch is done, I put most of it in the refrigerator for supper that night. The rest goes on a plate for our lunch. She sits down across from me at the kitchen table, as usual.

'Take the breast,' she says, her blue eyes bugging out at me.

'I eat the leg and the thigh,' I say, taking them from the plate. I thumb through the *Jackson Journal* to the Metro section. I pop up the spine of my newspaper in front of my face so I don't have to look at her.

'Well,' she says, taking the breast, 'I guess that makes us perfect chicken partners then.' And after a minute she says, 'You know, I'm lucky to have you as a friend, Minny.'

I feel thick, hot disgust rise up in my chest. I lower my paper and just look at her. 'No, ma'am. We ain't friends.'

'Well . . . sure we are.' She smiles, like she's doing me a big favour.

'No, Miss Celia. We ain't.'

She blinks at me with her fake eyelashes. *Stop it, Minny,* my insides tell me. But I already know I can't.

'Is it . . .' She looks down at her chicken. 'Because you're coloured? Or because you don't . . . want to be friends with me?'

'So many reasons, you white and me coloured just fall somewhere in between.'

She's not smiling at all now. 'But . . . why?'

'Because you in this house twenty-four hours a day driving me insane. All this time, there I was thinking you were dying a the cancer or sick in the head. Poor Miss Celia, all day long.'

'I know it's been hard . . .'

'I seen you with them bottles upstairs. You act like you want kids but you drinking enough to poison a elephant!'

She's got tears in her eyes. 'If you touch those bottles, I'll fire you right now!'

But the blood's running too hot in my head to stop now. 'Fire me? Who else gone come out here and work while you hang around the house drunk all day?'

'You think I can't fire you? You finish your work today, Minny!' She's boo-hooing and pointing her finger at me. 'You eat your chicken and then you go home!'

She picks up her plate with the white meat and charges through the swinging door. I hear it clatter down on the long fancy dining room table. *I just lost another damn job.*

I wake up Saturday morning at 7 a.m. to a clanging headache and a raw tongue. I must've bitten down on it all night long. I clean my kitchen like it's never been cleaned. Then I walk the two blocks to Aibileen's house.

She's sitting at her table reading one of those books Miss Skeeter got her from the white library. She looks up when she hears the screen door whine. I guess she can tell I'm angry.

'Lord have mercy, who done what to you?'

'Celia Rae Foote, that's who.' I sit down across from her. Aibileen gets up and pours me some coffee.

'What she do?'

I tell her about the bottles I found. I don't know why I hadn't told her a week and a half ago when I found them. Maybe I didn't want her to know something so awful about Miss Celia.

'And then she fired me. Say she gone find another maid. But who gone work for that lady?'

'I tell you, that Celia must be the worst one you *ever* had to tend to.'

'They all bad. But she the worst of all.'

'Miss Celia, though,' Aibileen says. 'Way she treat you? How much she paying you?'

'You know she paying me double.'

'Oh, that's right. Well, anyway, with all her friends coming over, specting you to clean up after em all the time.'

I just look at her.

'And them ten kids she got too.' Aibileen presses her napkin to her lips, hides her smile. 'Must drive you insane the way they screaming all day, messing up that big old house.'

'I think you done made your point, Aibileen.'

Aibileen smiles, pats me on the arm. 'I'm sorry, honey. But you my best friend. And I think you got something pretty good out there. So what if she take a nip or two? Go talk to her Monday.'

I go on home. I don't tell Leroy what's bothering me, but I think about it all day and all weekend long. I've been fired more times than I have fingers. I pray to God I can get my job back.

On Monday morning, I drive to work rehearsing the whole way. *I know I mouthed off* . . . I walk into her kitchen. *And I know I was out of place* . . . I set my bag down in the chair, *and* . . . this is the hard part. *And I'm sorry.*

I brace myself when I hear Miss Celia's feet padding through the house. I don't know what to expect, if she'll be mad or cold or just flat out re-fire me. All I know is, I'm doing the talking *first*.

'Morning,' she says. Miss Celia's still in her nightgown. She hasn't even brushed her hair, much less put the goo on her face. She groans, flattens her hand against her stomach.

'You . . . feel bad?'

'Yeah.'

'Miss Celia, I want you to know—'

But she walks right out while I'm talking and I know I am in some kind of trouble. I go ahead and do my work. Maybe I'm crazy to act like the job's still mine. Maybe she won't even pay me for today. After lunch, I turn on the tee-vee and do the ironing. Usually, Miss Celia comes in and watches with me, but not today.

Finally, I knock at the bedroom and there's no answer. I take a chance and open it. But the bed is empty. Now I've got the shut bathroom door to contend with.

'I'm on do my work in here,' I call out. There's no answer, but I know she's in there. I can feel her behind that door. I'm sweating. I want to get this damn conversation over with.

I go round the room with my laundry sack, stuffing a weekend's worth of clothes inside. I pull the sheets up taut on the bed, smooth the bedspread out.

Finally, I just stop, stare at the door. Am I fired or am I ain't? And if I ain't, then what if she's so drunk, she can't hear me? 'Miss Celia, just say something so I know you still alive in there.'

'I'm fine.'

But she does not sound fine.

The knob turns. Slowly, the door opens. Miss Celia's sitting on the floor. Her knees are drawn up inside her nightgown.

I step a little closer. From the side, I can see her complexion is the colour of fabric softener, a flat milky blue.

I can also see blood in the toilet bowl. A lot of it.

'You got the cramps, Miss Celia?' I whisper. 'You want me to call Mister Johnny?' I try, but I can't stop myself from looking at that red full bowl. Because there's something else deep down in that red liquid. Something . . . solid-looking.

'No.' Miss Celia says. 'Fetch me . . . my phone book.'

I hurry to the kitchen, snatch the book from the table, rush back. But when I try to hand it to Miss Celia, she waves it away.

'Please, you call,' she says. 'Under T, for Doctor Tate.'

I know who Doctor Tate is. He doctors most of the white women I've waited on.

My hands tremble around the rotary dial. A white woman answers.

'Celia Foote, on Highway 22 out Madison County,' I tell her. 'Yes ma'am, lots and lots a blood coming out . . . Do he know how to get here?' She says yes, of course, and hangs up.

'He coming,' I say. 'Maybe we should get you up in the bed, Miss Celia. You think you can stand up?'

Miss Celia leans forward, tries to push herself up. I step in to help her and see that the blood has soaked through the seat of her night-gown. Just as I raise her to her feet, Miss Celia slips in a spot of blood, catches the edge of the toilet bowl to steady herself.

'Let me stay—I want to stay here.'

'All right then.' I back away. 'Doctor Tate be here real soon.'

'Come and set with me, Minny? Please?'

'Come on out of here, Miss Celia. You need some air.'

'I can't get the blood on the . . . rug or Johnny will see it.' Miss Celia's face is getting whiter.

'How long you been bleeding?' I say, settling on the floor beside her.

'Since this morning,' she says and starts crying into the crook of her arm.

'It's all right, you gone be fine,' I say and I sound real soothing, but inside my heart is pounding.

'There's so much blood,' she moans, leaning against me. 'Why's there so much blood this time?'

I look, just a little, in the bowl. But I have to look away quick. 'How far along you think you was?'

'Five months? I don't know.' Miss Celia covers her face with a washrag. 'I was taking a shower and I felt it pulling down, hurting. So I set on the toilet and it slipped out. Like it wanted *out of me*.' She starts sobbing again, her shoulders jerking forward over her body.

'Now you look a here, that's just God's way. Something ain't going right in your innards, nature got to do something about it. Second time, you gone catch.' Then I think about those bottles and feel a ripple of anger.

'This isn't the first time. We got married cause I was pregnant,' Miss Celia says, 'but it . . . it slipped out too.'

I can't hold it in another second. 'Then why in the heck are you drinking? You can't hold no baby with a pint of whiskey in you.'

'Whiskey? Doctor Tate said it's just molasses and water,' she cries down into her towel. 'But I had to try it. I *had* to.'

Well. I'm surprised by how loose my body goes, how relieved I am by this. 'There's nothing wrong with taking your time, Miss Celia. Believe me, I got five kids.'

'But Johnny wants kids now. Oh, Minny.' She shakes her head. 'What's he going to do with me?'

'He gone get over it, that's what. He gone forget these babies cause mens is real good at that. Get to hoping for the next one.'

'He doesn't know about this one. Or the one before.'

'You said that's why he married you?'

'That first time, he knew.' Miss Celia lets out a big sigh. 'This time's really the . . . fourth.'

She stops crying and I don't have anything left to say. For a minute, we're just two people wondering why things are the way they are.

'I kept thinking,' she whispers, 'if I was real still, if I brought some-body in to do the house and the cooking, maybe I could hold on to this one.' She cries down into her towel.

'I'm going to . . . be sick. I'm—'

I grab the garbage can, watch as Miss Celia vomits over it. And then I feel something wet on me and I look down and the blood's coming so fast now, it's leaked over to where I'm sitting. Evertime she heaves, the blood pushes out of her. I know she losing more than a person can handle.

'Sit up, Miss Celia! Get a good breath, now,' I say, but she's slumping against me.

I push her back up but she's gone limp and I feel tears spring up in my eyes because that damn doctor should be here by now. He should've sent an ambulance and in the twenty-five years I've been cleaning houses nobody ever tells you what to do when your white lady keels over dead on top of you.

Many minutes pass before the bell rings. I prop Miss Celia's head on a towel, take off my shoes so I don't track the blood over the house, and run for the door.

'She done passed out!' I tell the doctor, and the nurse pushes past me and heads to the back like she knows her way around. She pulls the smelling salts out and puts them under Miss Celia's nose and Miss Celia jerks her head, lets out a little cry and opens her eyes.

The nurse helps me get Miss Celia out of her bloody nightgown. She's got her eyes open but can hardly stand up. I put old towels down in the bed and we lay her down.

Just before Doctor Tate goes into the bedroom, I touch him on the arm. 'She don't want her husband to know. He ain't gone find out, is he?'

He looks at me like I'm a nigger and says, 'You don't think it's his business?' He shuts the door in my face.

I go to the kitchen and pace the floor. Half an hour passes, then an hour, and I'm worrying so hard that Mister Johnny's going to come home and find out, worrying Doctor Tate will call him, worrying they're going to leave that baby in the bowl for me to deal with, my head's throbbing. Finally, I hear Doctor Tate open the door.

'She all right?'

'She's hysterical. I gave her a pill to calm her down.'

The nurse walks round us and out the back door carrying a white tin box. I breathe out for what feels like the first time in hours.

'You watch her tomorrow,' he says and hands me a white paper bag.

'Give her another pill if she gets too agitated. There'll be more bleeding. But don't call me up unless it's heavy.'

He waltzes out and slams the door behind him.

The kitchen clock reads five o'clock. Mister Johnny's going to be home in half an hour. I grab the Clorox and the rags and a bucket.

MISS SKEETER

IT IS 1963. The Space Age they're calling it. A man has circled the earth in a rocketship. They've invented a pill so married women don't have to get pregnant. Yet my parents' house is still as hot as it was in 1899, the year Great-grandfather built it.

'Mama, please,' I beg, 'when are we going to get air conditioning?'

'We have survived this long without electric cool and I have no intentions of setting one of those tacky contraptions in my window.'

And so, as July wanes, I am forced from my attic bedroom to a folding bed on the screened back porch. When we were kids, Constantine used to sleep out here with Carlton and me in the summer. Next to the bed, now, my typewriter sits on a rusted, white enamel washtable. Underneath is my red satchel.

It's a hundred degrees. I stare at my typewriter with nothing to do, nothing to write. Minny's stories are finished and typed already. Two weeks ago, Aibileen told me that Yule May, Hilly's maid, might help us. But with Medgar Evers's murder and coloured people getting arrested and beat by the police, I'm sure she's scared to death by now.

In a rare breeze, my copy of *Life* magazine flutters. Audrey Hepburn smiles on the cover, no sweat beading on her upper lip. I pick it up and finger the wrinkled pages. A picture of Carl Roberts, a coloured school-teacher from Pelahatchie, forty miles from here. 'In April, Carl Roberts told reporters what it means to be a black man in Mississippi, calling the governor: "a pathetic man with the morals of a streetwalker." Roberts was found cattle-branded and hung from a pecan tree.'

They'd killed Carl Roberts for speaking out, for *talking*. I think about how easy I thought it would be, three months ago, to get a dozen maids to talk to me. Like they'd just been waiting, all this time, to spill their stories to a white woman. How stupid I'd been.

When I can't take the heat another second, I go sit in the only cool place on Longleaf. I turn on the ignition of the Cadillac and roll up the windows, pull my dress up around my underwear and let the bi-level blow on me full blast. As I lean my head back, the world drifts away. I hear a truck pull up into the front drive but I don't open my eyes. A second later, my passenger door opens.

'Damn it feels good in here.'

I push my dress down. 'What are you doing here?'

Stuart shuts the door, kisses me quickly on the lips. 'I only have a minute. I have to head down to the coast for a few days. Wanna come?'

'Right now?'

'Right now,' he says and puts his cool palm on my leg. As always, I jump a little. I look down at his hand, then up to make sure Mother's not spying on us.

'Come on, it's too damn hot here. I'm staying at the Edgewater, right on the beach.'

I laugh and it feels good after all the worrying I've done these past weeks. 'You mean, at the Edgewater . . . together? In the same room?'

He nods. 'Think you can get away?'

Elizabeth would be mortified by the thought of sharing a room with a man before she was married, Hilly would tell me I was stupid to even consider it. They'd held on to their virginity with the fierceness of children refusing to share their toys. And yet, I consider it.

Stuart moves closer to me. He smells like pine trees and fired tobacco, expensive soap the likes of which my family's never known. 'Mama'd have a fit, Stuart, plus I have all this other stuff to do . . .' But God, he smells good. He's looking at me like he wants to eat me up and I shiver under the blast of Cadillac air.

'You sure?' he whispers and he kisses me then, on the mouth, not so politely as before. His hand is still on the upper quarter of my thigh and I find myself wondering again if he was like this with his fiancée, Patricia. I don't even know if they went to bed together.

'I just . . . I can't,' I say. 'You know I couldn't tell Mama the truth . . .'

He lets out a long sorry sigh and I love that look on his face, that disappointment. I understand now why girls resist, just for that sweet look of regret. 'Don't lie to her,' he says. 'You know I hate lies. Oh, and I almost forgot, in three weeks, Saturday night. Mother and Daddy want you and your parents to come have supper.'

'But . . . why all of us?'

'My parents want to meet them. And I want them to meet you.'

'But . . .'

'I'm sorry, baby,' he says and pushes my hair behind my ear, 'I have to go. Call you tomorrow night?'

I'm left alone in the Cadillac to worry. Supper at the state senator's house. With Mother there asking a thousand questions. Looking desperate on my behalf. Bringing up cotton trust funds.

Three excruciatingly long, hot nights later, with still no word from Yule May or any other maids, Stuart comes over, straight from his meeting on the coast. I run down the steps and he hugs me like it's been weeks.

Stuart's sunburnt beneath his white shirt, the back wrinkled from driving, the sleeves rolled up. We both sit straight up on opposite sides of the relaxing room, staring at each other. We're waiting for Mother to go to bed. Daddy went to sleep when the sun went down.

Finally, at half past nine, Mother smoothes her skirt. 'Well, I guess it's time for bed. I'll let you young people alone. Eugenia?' She eyes me. 'Not too late, now?'

I smile sweetly. I am twenty-three goddamn years old. A few seconds pass and we hear the clack-click of her bedroom door shutting. Stuart stands and says, 'Come *here*,' and he's on my side of the room in one stride and he claps my hands to his hips and kisses my mouth like I am the drink he's been dying for all day and I've heard girls say it's like melting, that feeling. But I think it's like rising, growing even taller and seeing sights over a hedge, colours you've never seen before.

I have to make myself pull away. We sit side by side on the sofa. He tries to kiss me again, but I move away. 'Stuart—' I swallow, ready myself for the question. 'When you were engaged, were your parents disappointed? When whatever happened with Patricia . . . happened?'

Immediately a stiffness forms round his mouth. He eyes me. 'Mother was disappointed. They were close.'

'So . . . she'll be comparing me to Patricia?'

Stuart blinks at me a second. 'Probably.'

'Where is Patricia now? Does she still live here or—'

'No. She's gone. Moved to California. Can we talk about something else now?'

I sigh, fall back against the sofa.

'Well, do your parents at least know what happened? I mean, am I allowed to know that?' Because I feel a flash of anger that he won't tell me something as important as this.

'Skeeter, I told you, I hate talking . . .' But then he grits his teeth, lowers his voice. 'Dad only knows part of it. Mother knows the real story, so do Patricia's parents. And of course *her*.'

'Stuart, I only want to know so I don't do the same thing.'

He looks at me and tries to laugh but it comes out more like a growl. 'You would never in a million years do what she did.'

'What? What did she do?'

'Skeeter, I'm tired. I better just go on home.'

I walk into the steamy kitchen the next morning. 'Morning, Pascagoula.'

'Morning, Miss Skeeter. You want your regular breakfast?'

'Yes, please,' I say.

She sets my coffee down in front of me. She doesn't hand it to me. Aibileen told me that's not how it's done, because then your hands might touch. I don't remember how Constantine used to do it.

'Thank you,' I say, 'very much.'

She blinks at me a second, smiles weakly. 'You're . . . welcome.' I realise this is the first time I've ever thanked her sincerely.

I skim the *Jackson Journal* sitting on the table. Down in the national news section, there's an article on a new pill, the 'Valium' they're calling it, 'to help women cope with everyday challenges.' God, I could use about ten of those little pills right now.

I look up and am surprised to see Pascagoula standing next to me.

'Are you . . . do you need something, Pascagoula?' I ask.

'I need to tell you something, Miss Skeeter.' She glances at the door, and comes a little closer. 'Yule May my *cousin*.'

'I . . . didn't know that.'

'We close kin and she come out to my house ever other weekend to check on me. She told me what it is you doing.' She narrows her eyes and I think she's about to tell me to leave her cousin alone.

'She tell me Saturday she gone help you. She try to call Aibileen but couldn't get her. I'd a tole you earlier but . . .' Again she glances at the doorway.

I'm stunned. 'She is? She *will*?' I stand up. Despite my better judgment, I can't help but ask. 'Pascagoula, do you . . . want to help with the stories too? Not Mother,' I say quickly. 'Other jobs, ones you've had before this.'

'This my first job working domestic. I use to work at the old lady home serving lunch. Fore it move out to Flowood.'

'You mean Mother didn't mind this being your first house job?'

Pascagoula looks timid again. 'Nobody else a work for her,' she says. 'Not after what happen with Constantine.'

'What did you think about . . . that?'

Pascagoula's face turns blank. She blinks a few times, clearly out-smarting me. 'I don't know nothing about it. I just wanted to tell you what Yule May say.'

I let out a long, deep breath. One thing at a time.

That night, Aibileen answers on the first ring.

'She'll help us, Aibileen. Yule May said yes!'

'Say what? When you find out?'

'This morning. Pascagoula told me. Yule May couldn't reach you.'

'Law, my phone was disconnected cause I's short this month. You talk to Yule May?'

'No, I thought it would be better if you talked to her first.'

'What's strange is I call over to Miss Hilly house this afternoon from Miss Leefolt's, but she say Yule May don't work there no more and hang up. I been asking around but nobody know a thing.'

'Hilly fired her?'

'I don't know. I's hoping maybe she quit.'

'I'll call Hilly and find out. God, I hope she's all right.' I call four times but the phone just rings. Finally I call Elizabeth's and she tells me Hilly's gone to Port Gibson for the night.

I spend the rest of the night on the back porch, rehearsing questions, nervous about what stories Yule May might tell about Hilly. Despite our disagreements, Hilly is still one of my closest friends. But the book, now that it is going again, is more important than anything.

The next day, I'm sitting in front of the television set watching the twelve o'clock news telling me that sixty American soldiers have been killed in Vietnam. Sixty men, in a place far away from anyone they loved, had to die. I think it's because of Stuart that this bothers me so.

I pick up a cigarette and put it back down. Mother's been nagging me about my smoking and I know I should stop. I'm trying not to smoke, but I'm nervous. I wish I could ask Pascagoula more about what Yule May said, but Pascagoula called this morning and said she had a problem and wouldn't be coming in until this afternoon.

I hear the front door close. A minute passes and Pascagoula comes in the relaxing room. 'Mother's out on the back porch,' I tell her but Pascagoula doesn't smile, doesn't even look up at me. She just hands me a small envelope. 'She was gone mail it but I told her I just carry it to you.' I open the letter. The handwriting is in black pen, written on the straight blue lines of school paper.

Dear Miss Skeeter,

I want you to know how sorry I am that I won't be able to help you with your stories. But now I can't and I want to be the one to tell you why. As you know, I used to wait on a friend of yours. I didn't like working for her and I wanted to quit many times but I was afraid to. I was afraid I might never get another job once she'd had her say.

You probably don't know that after I finished high school, I went on to college. I would've graduated except I decided to get married. It's one of my few regrets in life, not getting my college degree. I have twin boys that make it all worthwhile, though. For ten years, my husband and I have saved our money to send them to Tougaloo College, but as hard as we worked, we still didn't have enough for both. My boys are equally as smart, equally eager for an education. But we only had the money for one and I ask you, how do you choose which of your twin sons should go to college and which should take a job spreading tar? You don't. You find a way to make it happen. Any way at all.

I suppose you could look at this as a confession letter. I stole from that woman. An ugly ruby ring, hoping it would cover the rest of the tuition. Something she never wore and I felt she owed me for everything I'd been through working for her. Of course now, neither of my boys will be going to college. The court fine is nearly as much as we had saved.

Sincerely,

Yule May Crookle

Women's Block 9

Mississippi State Penitentiary

The *penitentiary*. I shudder. I look around for Pascagoula but she's left the room. I want to ask her when this happened, how it happened so goddamn fast? What can be done? I feel sick, nauseous. I switch off the television.

I think about Yule May, sitting in a jail cell writing this letter. I bet I even know what ring Yule May's talking about—Hilly's mother gave it to her for her eighteenth birthday. Hilly had it appraised a few years ago and found out it wasn't even a ruby, just a garnet, hardly worth anything. Hilly never wore it again. My hands turn to fists.

I walk up Aibileen's steps at eight o'clock that night. I kept thinking I would call her to talk about the situation, but I couldn't. Instead, I practically dragged Pascagoula upstairs so Mother wouldn't see us talking and asked her everything.

'Yule May had her a real good lawyer,' Pascagoula said. 'But everybody saying the judge wife be good friends with Miss Holbrook and how a regular sentence be six months for petty stealing, but Miss Holbrook, she get it pushed up to four years. That trial was done fore it even started.'

'I could ask Daddy. He could try and get her a . . . white lawyer.'

Pascagoula shakes her head, says, 'He *was* a white lawyer.'

I knock on Aibileen's door and it is opened by a Negro man, his white clerical collar gleaming. I hear Aibileen say, 'It's OK, Reverend.' He hesitates, but then moves back for me to come in.

I step inside and see at least twenty people packed in the tiny living room and hallway. Aibileen's brought out the kitchen chairs, but most people stand. I spot Minny in the corner and I recognise Lou Anne Templeton's maid, Louvenia, next to her, but everyone else is a stranger.

'Hey, Miss Skeeter,' whispers Aibileen. She's still in her white uniform and white orthopaedic shoes.

'Should I . . .' I point behind me. 'I'll come back later,' I whisper.

Aibileen shakes her head. 'Something awful happen to Yule May.'

'I know,' I say. The room is quiet except for a few coughs. A chair creaks. Hymn books are stacked on the small wooden table.

'I just find out today,' Aibileen says. 'She arrested on Monday, in the State Pen on Tuesday. They say the whole trial took fifteen minutes.'

'She sent me a letter,' I say. 'She told me about her sons.'

'She tell you she only short seventy-five dollars for that tuition? She ask Miss Hilly for a loan, you know. Say she'd pay her back some ever week, but Miss Hilly say no. That a true Christian don't give charity to those who is well and able. Say it's kinder to let them learn to work things out theyselves.'

God, I can just imagine Hilly giving that goddamn speech. I can hardly look Aibileen in the face.

'The churches got together though. They gone send both them boys to college.'

The room is dead quiet, except for Aibileen and me whispering. 'Do you think there's anything I can do? Any way I can help? Money or . . .'

'No. Church already set up a plan to pay the lawyer. To keep him on for when she come up for parole.' Aibileen lets her head hang. 'Court give her four years and a five hundred dollar fine.'

'I'm so sorry, Aibileen,' I say. I glance around at the people in the room, their heads bowed as if looking at me might burn them.

'She evil, that woman!' Minny barks from the other side of the sofa and I flinch, hoping she doesn't mean me. 'Hilly Holbrook been sent up here from the devil to ruin as many lives as she can!' Minny wipes her nose across her sleeve.

The room goes unbearably quiet again. The air is hot and smells like burned coffee. I feel a profound singularity, here, in a place where I've almost grown comfortable. I feel the heat of dislike and guilt.

The bald reverend wipes his eyes with a handkerchief. 'Thank you, Aibileen, for having us in your home for prayer.' People begin to stir, telling each other good night with solemn nods. Handbags are picked up, hats are put on heads. The reverend opens the door, letting in the damp outside air. A woman with curly grey hair and a black coat follows close behind him, but then stops in front of me where I'm standing with my satchel.

Her raincoat falls open a little to reveal a white uniform.

'Miss Skeeter,' she says, without a smile, 'I'm on help you with the stories.'

I turn and look at Aibileen. Her eyebrows go up, her mouth opens. I turn back to the woman but she is already walking out the door.

'I'm on help you, Miss Skeeter.' This is another woman, tall and lean, with the same quiet look as the first.

'Um, thank . . . you,' I say.

I start counting. Five. Six. Seven. I nod back at them, can say nothing but thank you. Thank you. Yes, thank you, to each one.

Eight. Nine. Ten. Eleven. No one is smiling when they tell me they want to help. The room clears out, except for Minny. She stands in the far corner, arms clamped across her chest. When everyone is gone, she looks up and meets my gaze for hardly a second. Minny has made this happen.

With everyone travelling, our group hasn't played bridge in a month. On Wednesday, we meet at Lou Anne Templeton's house, greet with hand-patting and good-to-see-yous.

'Lou Anne, you poor thing, in those long sleeves in this heat. Is it the eczema again?' Elizabeth asks because Lou Anne's wearing a grey wool dress in the heat of summer.

Lou Anne looks at her lap, clearly embarrassed. 'Yes, it's getting worse.'

But I cannot stand to touch Hilly when she reaches out to me. When I back away from her hug, she acts like she doesn't notice. But during the game, she keeps looking at me with narrowed eyes.

'I knew it. I knew that girl was a thief the day she started.' As Hilly tells us the story of Yule May, she makes a big circle with her finger to indicate a huge stone, the unimaginable worth of the 'ruby'.

'I caught her taking the milk after it expired and that's how it starts, you know, first it's washing powder, then they work their way up to towels and coats. Before you know it, they're taking the heirlooms, hocking them for liquor pints. God knows what else she took.'

I fight the urge to snap each of her flapping fingers in half, but I hold my tongue. Let her think everything is fine. It is safer for everyone.

I sit at Aibileen's kitchen table at six o'clock that night. We've arranged for me to come over nearly every night until we're finished. Every two days, a different coloured woman will knock on Aibileen's back door and sit at the table with me, tell me her stories. Eleven maids have agreed to talk to us, not counting Aibileen and Minny. That puts us at thirteen and Missus Stein asked for a dozen. Aibileen stands in the back of the kitchen, listening. The first maid's name is Alice.

I explain that the project is a collection of true stories about maids and their experiences waiting on white families. I hand her an envelope with forty dollars from what I've saved from the Miss Myrna column and my allowance.

'There's a good chance it may never be published,' I tell each individually, 'and even if it is, there will be very little money from it.'

'Aibileen been clear on that,' several say. 'That ain't why I'm doing this.'

I repeat back to them what they've already decided among themselves. That they need to keep their identities secret from anyone outside the group. Their names will be changed on paper; so will the name of the town and the families they've worked for.

'Now, Eula, she gone be like prying a dead clam open.' Aibileen preps me before each interview. She's as afraid as I am that I'll scare them off before it even starts. 'Don't get frustrated if she don't say much.'

Eula, the dead clam, starts talking before she's even sat down in the chair, before I can explain anything, not stopping until ten o'clock that night. Alice, Fanny Amos and Winnie are shy, need coaxing, keep their eyes down to their laps. Flora Lou and Cleontine let the doors fly open and the words tumble out while I type as fast as I can, asking them every five minutes to please, please, slow down. Many of the stories are sad, bitter. I expected this. But there are a surprising number of good stories too. And all of them, at some point, look back at Aibileen as if to ask, *Are you sure? Can I really tell a white woman this?*

'Aibileen? What's gone happen if . . . this thing get printed and people find out who we are?' shy Winnie asks. 'What you think they do to us?'

'We won't know till the time comes, Winnie,' Aibileen says softly. 'Won't be like what you see on the news, though. A white lady do things different than a white man.'

I look at Aibileen. She's never shared with me the specifics of what she thinks would happen. I want to change the subject. It won't do us any good to discuss it.

With Stuart out of town, I concentrate solely on the interviews. The women are tall, short, black like asphalt or caramel brown. If your skin is too white, I'm told, you'll never get hired. The blacker the better. The talk turns mundane at times, with complaints of low pay, hard hours, bratty children.

There is undisguised hate for white women, there is inexplicable love. Faye Belle, palsied and grey-skinned, cannot remember her own age. Her stories unfold like soft linen. She remembers hiding in a steamer trunk with a little white girl while Yankee soldiers stomped through the house. Twenty years ago, she held that same white girl, by then an old woman, in her arms while she died. Each proclaimed their love as best friends. Swore that death could not change this. That colour meant nothing. The white woman's grandson still pays Faye Belle's rent.

Louvenia is my fifth interview. She is Lou Anne Templeton's maid and I recognise her from serving me at bridge club. Louvenia tells me how her grandson, Robert, was blinded earlier this year by a white man, because he used a white bathroom. There is no anger in her voice at all. I learn that Lou Anne, whom I find dull and vapid and have never paid much mind to, gave Louvenia two weeks off with pay so she could help her grandson. She brought casseroles to Louvenia's house seven times during those weeks. She rushed Louvenia to the coloured hospital when the first call came about Robert and waited there six hours with her, until the operation was over. Lou Anne has never mentioned this to any of us. And I understand completely why she wouldn't.

Angry stories come out, of white men who've tried to touch them. Winnie said she was forced over and over. Cleontine said she fought until his face bled and he never tried again.

We cannot talk for several minutes after Gretchen's left. Gretchen is Yule May's first cousin. She attended the prayer meeting for Yule May, but she belongs to a different church.

I'd explained the 'rules' to Gretchen, just like with the others. Gretchen had leaned back in her chair. I thought she was thinking about a story to tell. But she said, 'Look at you. Another white lady trying to make a dollar off of coloured people.'

I glanced back at Aibileen, not sure how to respond to this. Was I not clear on the money part? Aibileen tilted her head like she wasn't sure she'd heard correctly.

'You think anybody's ever going to read this thing?' Gretchen laughed. She was trim in her uniform. She wore lipstick, the same colour pink me and my friends wore. She was young. She spoke evenly and with care, like a white person. I don't know why, but that made it worse.

'All the coloured women you've interviewed, they've been real nice, haven't they?'

'Yes,' I'd said. 'Very nice.'

Gretchen looked me straight in the eye. 'They hate you. You know that, right? Every little thing about you. But you're so dumb, you think you're doing them a favour.'

Aibileen stood up from her stool. 'That's enough, Gretchen. You go on home.'

'And you know what, Aibileen? You are just as dumb as she is,' Gretchen said.

I was shocked when Aibileen pointed to the door and hissed, '*You get out a my house.*'

Gretchen left, but through the screen door, she slapped me with a look so angry it gave me chills.

Two nights later, I sit across from Callie. She has curly hair, mostly grey. She is sixty-seven years old and still in her uniform. She is wide and heavy and parts of her hang over the chair. I'm still nervous from the interview with Gretchen.

Callie begins talking slowly and I start to type, grateful of her slow pace. She stares off as if she can see a movie screen behind me, playing the scenes she's describing.

'I worked for Miss Margaret thirty-eight years. She had her a baby girl with the colic and the only thing that stopped the hurting was to hold her. So I made me a wrap. I tied her up on my waist, toted her round all day with me for a entire year. That baby like to break my back. Put ice packs on it ever night and still do. But I loved that girl. And I loved Miss Margaret.'

She takes a sip of her tea while I type her last words. I look up and she continues. 'Miss Margaret always made me put my hair up in a rag, say she know coloureds don't wash their hair. Counted ever piece a silver after I done the polishing. When Miss Margaret die of the lady problems thirty years later, I go to the funeral. Her husband hug me, cry on my shoulder. When it's over, he give me a envelope. Inside a letter from Miss Margaret reading, "Thank you. For making my baby stop hurting. I never forgot it."'

Callie takes off her black-rimmed glasses, wipes her eyes.

'If any white lady reads my story, that's what I want them to know. Saying thank you, when you really mean it, when you remember what someone done for you'—she shakes her head, stares down at the table—'it's so good.'

Callie looks up at me, but I can't meet her eyes.

'I just need a minute,' I say. I press my hand on my forehead. I can't help but think about Constantine. I never thanked her, not properly. It never occurred to me I wouldn't have the chance.

'You feel OK, Miss Skeeter?' Aibileen asks.

'I'm . . . fine,' I say. 'Let's keep going.'

Callie goes on to her next story. A yellow shoebox is on the counter behind her, still full of envelopes. Except for Gretchen, all ten women have asked that the money go towards Yule May's boys' education.

The Phelan family stands tense, waiting on the brick steps of State Senator Whitworth's house. The house is in the centre of town, on North Street. It is tall and white-columned, appropriately azalea-ed. A gold plaque declares it a historical landmark.

I have on a new light blue skirt and matching jacket. Daddy has on his black funeral suit. Mother is wearing a simple white dress—like a country bride wearing a hand-me-down, I suddenly think, and I feel a rush of panic that we have overdressed, all of us.

'Good evening.' A coloured woman in a white uniform nods to us. 'They expecting y'all.'

We step into the hall and the first thing I see is the chandelier, sparkling, gauzy with light. My eyes rise up the hollow twirl of the staircase and it is as if we are inside a gigantic seashell.

'Why, hello there.' Missus Whitworth is clicking into the hall, hands extended. She has on a suit like mine, thankfully, but in crimson. When she nods, her greying-blonde hair does not move.

'Hello, Missus Whitworth, I am Charlotte Boudreau Cantrelle Phelan. We thank you so much for having us.'

'Delighted,' she says and shakes both my parents' hands. 'I'm Francine Whitworth. Welcome to our home.'

She turns to me. 'And you must be Eugenia. Well. It is so nice to finally meet you.' Missus Whitworth grasps my arms and looks me in the eyes. Hers are blue, beautiful, like cold water. Her face is plain around them. She is almost my height in her heels.

'So nice to meet you,' I say. 'Stuart's told me so much about you and Senator Whitworth.'

'There she is!' Behind Missus Whitworth, a tall, bull-chested man lumbers towards me. He hugs me hard to him, then just as quickly flings me back. 'Now I told Little Stu a month ago to get this gal up to the house. But frankly,' he lowers his voice, 'he's still a little gun-shy after that other one.'

I stand there blinking. 'Very nice to meet you, sir.'

The senator laughs loudly. 'You know I'm just teasing you,' he says, gives me another drastic hug, clapping me on the back.

'Senator,' Daddy says and pumps his hand hard. 'We thank you for all you did on that farm bill. Made a heck of a difference.'

'Y'all come on in,' the senator says. 'I can't talk politics without a drink in my hand.'

The senator pounds his way out of the hall. 'Stuart's still driving over from Shreveport,' he hollers. 'Got a big deal brewing over there.'

We move into a formal living room with ornate moulding and green velvet settees, so full of heavy furniture I can hardly see the floor. 'What can I get y'all to drink?' Mister Whitworth grins. He has a heavy, broad forehead, with thick and wiry eyebrows that wiggle when he talks.

Daddy asks for a cup of coffee, Mother and I for iced tea. The senator's grin deflates and he looks back at the maid to collect these mundane drinks. In the corner, he pours himself and his wife something brown. The velvet sofa groans when he sits.

'Your home is just lovely. I hear it's the centrepiece of the tour,' Mother says. She's been on the dinky Ridgeland County Historic Home

Council forever, but refers to Jackson's home tour as 'high cotton' compared to theirs.

Senator and Missus Whitworth glance at each other. Then Missus Whitworth smiles. 'We took it off the tour this year. It was just . . . too much.'

'Surely you must feel some obligation, for the sake of history . . .' Mother says, and I shoot her a look to let it go.

No one says anything for a second and then the senator laughs loudly. 'There was kind of a mix-up,' he booms. 'Patricia van Devender's mother is head of the council so after all that . . . ruck-a-muck with the kids, we decided we'd just as soon get off the tour.'

I glance at the door, praying Stuart will get here soon. This is the second time *she* has come up. Missus Whitworth gives the senator a deafening look.

'Well, what are we gonna do, Francine? Just never talk about her again? We had the damn gazebo built in the backyard for the wedding.'

Missus Whitworth takes a deep breath. 'Eugenia'—she smiles— 'I understand you aim to be a writer. What kinds of things do you write?'

I put my smile back on. From one good subject to the next. 'I write the Miss Myrna column in the *Jackson Journal*.'

'Stuart said you were trying to get into more serious subjects. Anything particular?'

Now everyone is looking at me, including the maid, as she hands me a glass of tea. I don't look at her face, terrified of what I'll see there. 'I'm working on a . . . a few—'

'Eugenia is writing about the life of Jesus Christ,' Mother pops in and I recall my most recent lie to cover my nights out, calling it 'research'.

'Well,' Missus Whitworth nods, looks impressed by this, 'that's certainly an honourable subject.'

The front door slams, sending all the glass lamps into a furious tinkle.

'Sorry I'm so late.' Stuart strides in, wrinkled from the car, pulling on his navy sports coat. We all stand up and his mother holds out her arms to him but he heads straight for me. He puts his hands on my shoulders and kisses my cheek. 'Sorry,' he whispers and I breathe out, finally relax half an inch. I turn and see his mother smiling like I just snatched her best guest towel and wiped my dirty hands all over it.

'Get yourself a drink, son, sit down,' the senator says. When Stuart has his drink, he settles next to me on the sofa, squeezes my hand and doesn't let go.

Missus Whitworth gives one glance at our hand-holding and says, 'Charlotte, why don't I give you and Eugenia a tour of the house?'

For the next fifteen minutes, I follow Mother and Missus Whitworth from one ostentatious room to the next. There are letters from Confederate soldiers lying on a Federal desk, strategically placed antique spectacles and handkerchiefs. On the second floor, Mother marvels over a canopy bed where Robert E Lee slept. When we finally come down a 'secret' staircase, I linger over family pictures in the hallway. I see Stuart and his two brothers as babies, Stuart holding a red ball. Stuart in a christening gown.

Mother and Missus Whitworth move down the hallway, but I keep looking. His hair was the whitish-yellow of a dandelion. At nine or ten, he stands with a hunting rifle and a duck. At fifteen, next to a slain deer. Already he is good-looking, rugged. I pray to God he never sees my teenage pictures.

I walk a few steps and see high school graduation, Stuart proud in a military school uniform. In the centre of the wall, there is an empty space without a frame, a rectangle of wallpaper just the slightest shade darker. A picture has been removed.

'Dad, that is enough about—' I hear Stuart say, his voice strained. But just as quickly, there is silence.

'Dinner is served,' a maid announces and we trail into the dining room to a long, dark table. The Phelans are seated on one side, the Whitworths on the other. I am diagonal from Stuart, placed as far as possible from him. Waldorf salads are served. Stuart looks over at me and smiles every few minutes. Senator Whitworth leans over to Daddy and says, 'I came from nothing, you know. Jefferson County, Mississippi. My daddy dried peanuts for eleven cents a pound.'

Daddy shakes his head. 'Doesn't get much poorer than Jefferson County.'

'The *young people* so enjoy each other's company.' Mother smiles. 'Why, Stuart comes out to see us at the house nearly twice a week.'

Missus Whitworth has stiffened round the mouth. 'Twice a week? Stuart, I had no idea you came to town that often.'

Stuart's fork stops in mid-air. He casts a sheepish look at his mother.

'Y'all are so young.' Missus Whitworth smiles. 'Enjoy yourselves. There's no need to get serious so quickly.'

The senator leans his elbows on the table. 'From a woman who practically proposed to the other one herself, she was in such a hurry.'

'*Dad*,' Stuart says through gritted teeth.

The maid lays pressed chicken on our plates, tops it with a perky dollop of mayonnaisey dressing, and we all smile, glad for the mood breaker. As we eat, Daddy and the senator talk about cotton prices, boll weevils. I can still see the anger on Stuart's face from when the senator mentioned Patricia. I glance at him every few seconds, but the anger doesn't seem to be fading.

The senator leans back in his chair. 'Did you see that piece they did in *Life* magazine? One before Medgar Evers, about whatsisname— Carl . . . Roberts?'

I look up, surprised to find the senator is aiming this question at me. I blink, confused, hoping it's because of my job at the newspaper. 'It was . . . he was lynched. For saying the governor was . . .' I stop, not because I've forgotten the words, but because I remember them.

'*Pathetic,*' the senator says, now turning to my father, '*with the morals of a streetwalker.*'

I exhale, relieved the attention is off me. I look at Stuart to gauge his reaction to this. I've never asked him his position on civil rights. But I don't think he's even listening to the conversation. The anger round his mouth has turned flat and cold.

My father clears his throat. 'I'll be honest,' he says slowly. 'It makes me sick to hear about that kind of brutality.' Daddy sets his fork down silently. He looks Senator Whitworth in the eye. 'I've got twenty-five Negroes working my fields and if anyone so much as laid a hand on them, or any of their families . . .' Daddy's gaze is steady. Then he drops his eyes. 'I'm ashamed, sometimes, Senator. Ashamed of what goes on in Mississippi.'

Mother's eyes are big, set on Daddy. I am shocked to hear this opinion. Even more shocked that he'd voice it at this table to a politician. I'm suddenly so proud of my daddy, for many reasons. For a second, I swear, I see it in Mother's eyes too, beneath her worry that Father has obliterated my future. I look at Stuart and his face registers concern, but in which way, I do not know.

The senator has his eyes narrowed on Daddy. 'I'll tell you something, Carlton,' the Senator says. 'Those were not wise words to say. But the question I've been asking myself lately is, are they true?'

'*Stooley,*' Missus Whitworth hisses.

'Francine, let me speak my mind. God knows I can't do it from nine to five, so let me speak my mind in my own home.'

Missus Whitworth's smile does not waver, but the slightest bit of pink rises in her cheeks. Stuart stares at his plate with the same cold anger as before. He hasn't looked at me since the chicken course. Everyone is quiet and then someone changes the subject to the weather.

When supper is finally over, we retire to the back porch for after-dinner drinks and coffee. Stuart and I linger in the hallway. I touch his arm, but he pulls away.

'I knew he'd get drunk and start in on everything.'

'Stuart, it's fine,' I say because I think he's talking about his father's politics. 'We're all having a good time.'

But Stuart is feverish-looking. 'It's Patricia this and Patricia that, all night long,' he says. 'How many times can he bring her up?'

'Just forget about it, Stuart. Everything's OK.'

He runs a hand through his hair and looks everywhere but at me. I start to get the feeling that I'm not even here to him. And then I realise what I've known all night. He is looking at me but he is thinking about . . . *her*. She is everywhere.

I tell him I need to go to the bathroom.

Afterwards, I walk by the living room, where the senator is pouring himself another drink. I try to tiptoe past the doorway.

'There you are!' I hear him holler. I back up slowly into the doorway and his face lights up. 'Come here, gal.' He puts his arm round me and the smell of bourbon burns my eyes. 'You having a good time?'

'Yessir. Thank you.'

He sighs, stares off. 'We've had a real hard year with Stuart. I guess he told you what happened.'

I nod, feeling my skin prickle.

'Now, look, everybody says I talk too much when I've had a few but . . .' the senator narrows his eyes at me, like we are old conspirators, 'I want to tell you something. We were worried sick after all that mess last year. With the other one.' He shakes his head, looks down at the glass in his hand. 'Stuart, he just up and left his apartment in Jackson, moved everything out to the camp house in Vicksburg.'

'I know he was very . . . upset,' I say, when truthfully, I know almost nothing at all.

'But ever since the thing with that girl, he's . . . different. He won't tell me anything. I just want to know, is my son all right?'

'I . . . I think he is. But honestly, I don't . . . really know.' I look away. Inside, I'm starting to realise that I don't know Stuart. If this damaged him so much, and he can't even speak to me about it, then what am I to him? Just a diversion?

I escape to the back porch and stand next to Stuart. Lightning bursts in the sky, giving us a flash of the eerily brilliant gardens, then the darkness sucks it all back in. The gazebo, skeleton-like, looms at the end of the garden path.

Stuart puts his hand on my shoulder. He is somehow better, but I am growing worse.

'Stuart, your daddy, he told me . . .' I try to find a way to put it.

He narrows his eyes at me. 'Told you what?'

'How bad it was. How hard it was on you,' I say. 'With Patricia.'

He leans back against the wall and crosses his arms and I see that old anger again, deep and red. He is wrapped in it.

'Stuart. You don't have to tell me now. But, sometime, we're going to have to talk about this.' I'm surprised by how confident I sound, when I certainly don't feel it.

He looks me deep in the eyes, shrugs. 'She slept with someone else.'

'Someone . . . you know?'

'No one knew him. He was one of those leeches, hanging round the school, cornering the teachers to do something about the integration laws. Well, she did something all right.'

'You mean . . . he was an activist? With the civil rights . . . ?'

'That's it. Some Yankee from New York, the kind you see on the TV with the long hair and the peace signs.'

I am searching my head for the right question to ask but I can't think of anything.

'You know the really crazy part, Skeeter? I could've forgiven her. She asked me to, told me how sorry she was. But I knew, if it ever got out who he was, that Senator Whitworth's daughter-in-law got in bed with a Yankee goddamn activist, it would ruin him. Kill his career like that.' He snaps his fingers with a crack.

'So you broke up with her because of your father?'

'No, I broke up with her because she cheated.' He looks down at his hands and I can see the shame eating away at him. 'But I didn't take her back because of . . . my father.'

'Stuart, are you . . . still in love with her?' I ask, and I try to smile as if it's nothing, just a question.

His body slumps some. His voice softens. 'You'd never do that. Lie that way. Not to me, not to anybody.'

He has no idea how many people I'm lying to. But it's not the point. 'Answer me, Stuart. Are you?'

He rubs his temples, stretching his hand across his eyes. Hiding his eyes is what I'm thinking.

'I think we ought to quit for a while,' he whispers.

I reach over to him out of reflex, but he backs away. 'I need some time, Skeeter. Space, I guess. I need to go to work and drill oil and . . . get my head straight awhile.'

I feel my mouth slide open as I hear the soft calls of our parents. It's time to leave.

I walk behind Stuart to the front of the house. The Whitworths stop in the spiralling hall while we three Phelans head out the door. I tell them all goodbye, thank you, my own voice sounding strange to me. Stuart waves from the steps and smiles at me so our parents can't tell that anything has changed.

We stand in the relaxing room, Mother and Daddy and I, staring at the silver box in the window. It is the size of a truck engine, nosed in knobs, shiny with chrome, gleaming with modern-day hope. I flip the knob to '1'. Overhead, the chandelier bulbs dim.

'Oh . . . *my*,' Mother says and closes her eyes. I watch a few tendrils of Mother's hair lift gently into the air. She's been so tired lately and her ulcers are getting worse. Doctor Neal said keeping the house cool would at least make her more comfortable.

'It's not even on full blast,' I say and I turn it up a notch, to '2'. The air blows a little harder, grows colder, and we all three smile, our sweat evaporating from our foreheads.

'Well, heck, let's just go all the way,' Daddy says, and turns it up to '3', which is the highest, coldest, most wonderful setting of all, and Mother giggles. We stand with our mouths open like we could eat it. The lights brighten again, the whirr grows louder, our smiles lift higher, and then it all stops dead. Dark.

'What . . . happened?' Mama says.

Daddy looks up at the ceiling. He walks out into the hall.

'Damn thing blew the current.'

Mother fans her handkerchief on her neck. 'Well, good heavens, Carlton, go fix it.'

For an hour, I hear Daddy throwing switches and clanking tools, boots knocking on the porch. After it's fixed, I sit through a lecture from Daddy to never turn it to '3' again or it will blow the house to pieces. Mother and I watch as an icy mist grows on the windows. Mother dozes in her blue Queen Anne chair, her green blanket pulled to her chest. I wait until she is asleep, listening for the soft snore, the pucker of her forehead. On tiptoe, I turn out all the lamps, the television, every electricity sucker downstairs save the refrigerator. I stand in front of the window and unbutton my blouse. Carefully, I turn the dial to '3'. Because I long to feel nothing. I want to be frozen inside. I want the icy cold to blow directly on my heart.

The power blows out in about three seconds.

For the next two weeks, I submerge myself in the interviews. I keep my typewriter on the back porch and work most of the day long and into the night. Sometimes I catch myself staring off at the fields, but I am not here. I am in the old Jackson kitchens with the maids. I let their coloured memories draw me out of my own miserable life.

'Skeeter, we haven't heard from Stuart in weeks,' Mother says for the eighth time. 'He's not cross with you, now, is he?'

At the moment, I am writing the Miss Myrna column. Once ahead by three months, somehow I've managed to almost miss my deadline. 'He's fine, Mother. He doesn't have to call every minute of the day.' But then I soften my voice. Every day she seems thinner. The sharpness of her collarbone is enough to tamp down my irritation at her comment. 'He's just travelling is all, Mama.'

This seems to placate her for the moment and I tell the same story to Elizabeth, with a few more details to Hilly, pinching my arm to bear her insipid smile. But I do not know what to tell myself. Stuart needs 'space' and 'time', as if this were physics and not a human relationship.

So instead of feeling sorry for myself every minute of the day, I work. I type. I sweat. Who knew heartbreak would be so goddamn hot. When Mother's lying down on her bed, I pull my chair up to the air conditioner and stare into it.

On a rare evening home, I sit with Mother and Daddy at the dinner table. Mother nibbles on her supper. She spent the afternoon trying to keep me from finding out she'd been vomiting. She presses her fingers along the top of her nose to hold back her headache and says, 'I was thinking about the twenty-fifth, do you think that's too soon to have them over?' and I still cannot bring myself to tell her that Stuart and I have broken up.

But I can see it on her face, that Mother feels worse than bad tonight. She is pale and trying to sit up longer than I know she wants to. I take her hand and say, 'Let me check, Mama. I'm sure the twenty-fifth will be fine.' She smiles for the first time all day.

It's nearly August and even though the book's not due until January, we still have five more interviews to sort through. With Aibileen's help, I've moulded and cut and arranged five of the women's chapters including Minny's, but they still need work. There are several dozen made-up names, both white and coloured. 'Niceville, Mississippi' is the name of our town because it doesn't exist. Thankfully, Aibileen's section is done. It is twenty-one pages, beautifully written, simple.

I'm deliberately five minutes late for the Monday night League meeting, our first in a month. Hilly's back from the coast, tanned and ready to lead. She holds her gavel like a weapon. I chew my nails to keep from smoking a cigarette. I haven't smoked in six days.

Besides the cigarette missing from my hand, I'm jittery from the faces around me. I easily spot seven women in the room who are related to someone in the book, if not in it themselves. I want to get out of here and get back to work, but two long, hot hours pass before Hilly finally bangs her gavel. By then, even she looks tired of hearing her own voice.

Before I can escape, Elizabeth catches my eye, waves me over. She is six months pregnant, woozy from the pregnancy tranquillisers.

'How are you feeling?' I ask. Everything on her body is the same except her stomach is huge and swollen. 'Is it any better this time?'

'God, no, it's awful and I still have three months to go.' She takes my hand. 'I heard,' she whispers, 'about you and Stuart. I'm so sorry.'

I look down. I'm not surprised she knows, only that it took this long for anyone to find out. I haven't told anyone, but I guess Stuart has. Just this morning, I had to lie to Mother and tell her the Whitworths would be out of town on the twenty-fifth.

'I'm sorry I didn't tell you,' I say. 'I don't like talking about it.'

I gather my notes quickly, head for the door. Before I make it out, I hear, 'Wait a sec, would you, Skeeter?'

I sigh, turn round and face Hilly. She's wearing a navy-blue sailor number, something you'd dress a five-year-old in. The pleats around her hips are stretched open like accordion bellows.

'I told you *five months ago* to print my Initiative and now another week has passed and you still haven't followed my instructions. I want that Initiative in the newsletter before election time,' she says and points to the ceiling, 'or I'm calling upstairs, missy.'

'If you try to throw me out of the League, I will dial up Genevieve von Hapsburg in New York City myself,' I hiss, because I happen to know Genevieve's Hilly's hero. She's the youngest national League president in history, perhaps the only person in this world Hilly's afraid of.

'And tell her what, Skeeter? Tell her you're not doing your job? Tell her you're carrying around Negro activist materials?'

I'm too angry to let this unnerve me. 'I want them *back*, Hilly. You took them and they don't belong to you.'

'Of course I took them. You have no business carrying around something like that. What if somebody saw those things?'

She licks her lips, takes a deep, noisy sniff. 'You know, it's no wonder Stuart Whitworth dropped you.'

I keep my jaw clenched so that she cannot see the effect these words have on me. 'I want those laws back,' I say, my voice shaking.

'Then print the Initiative.'

I turn and walk out the door. I heave my satchel into the Cadillac and light a cigarette.

Mother's light is off when I get home and I'm grateful. I tiptoe down the hall, onto the back porch, easing the squeaky screen door closed. I sit down at my typewriter.

But I cannot type. I stare at the tiny grey squares of the back porch screen. I stare so hard, I slip through them. I feel something inside me crack open then. I am vaporous. I am crazy. I am deaf to that stupid, silent phone. Deaf to Mother's retching in the house. Her voice through the window, 'I'm fine, Carlton, it's passed.' I hear it all and yet, I hear nothing. Just a high buzzing in my ears.

I pull out the page of Hilly's bathroom Initiative from my satchel. The paper is limp, already damp with humidity. A moth lands on the corner then flutters away, leaving a brown smudge of wing chalk.

With slow, deliberate strokes, I start typing the newsletter: Sarah Shelby to marry Robert Pryor. Please attend a baby-clothes showing by Mary Katherine Simpson. Then I type Hilly's initiative. I place it on the second page, opposite the photo ops. This is where everyone will be sure to see it, after they look at themselves at the Summer Fun Jamboree. All I can think while I'm typing is, *What would Constantine think of me?*

AIBILEEN

'HOW OLD A YOU TODAY, big girl?' Mae Mobley is still in bed. She hold out two sleepy fingers and say, 'Mae Mo two.'

'Nuh-uh, we three today!' I move up one a her fingers.

Her nose wrinkle up cause her whole life she can remember, she been telling people she Mae Mobley *two*. When you little, you only get asked two questions, what's your name and how old you is, so you better get em right.

'I am Mae Mobley three,' she say. She scramble out a bed, her hair in a rat's nest. That bald spot she had as a baby, it's coming back. Usually I can brush over it and hide it for a few minutes, but not for long. It's thin and she's losing them curls. It don't trouble me that she ain't cute, but I try to fix her up nice as I can for her mama.

'Come on to the kitchen,' I say. 'We make you a birthday breakfast.'

Miss Leefolt off getting her hair done. She don't care bout being there on the morning her only child wakes up on the first birthday she remember. But least Miss Leefolt got her what she want. Brung me back to her bedroom and point to a big box on the floor.

'Won't she be happy?' Miss Leefolt say. 'It walks and talks and cries.'

Sho nuff they's a big pink polky-dot box. Got cellophane across the front, and inside they's the doll baby tall as Mae Mobley. Name Allison. She got blonde curly hair and blue eyes. Frilly pink dress on. Evertime the commercial come on the tee-vee Mae Mobley run over to the set and grab the box on both sides, put her face up to the screen and stare so serious. Miss Leefolt look like she gone cry herself. I reckon her mama never got her what she wanted when she little.

In the kitchen, I fix some grits without no seasoning, and put them baby marshmallows on top. I toast the whole thing to make it a little crunchy. Then I garnish it with a cut-up strawberry. That's all a grit is, a vehicle. For whatever it is you rather be eating.

The three little pink candles I done brought from home is in my pocketbook. I bring em out, undo the wax paper I got em in so they don't turn out bent. After I light em, I bring them grits over to her booster chair, at the white linoleum table in the middle a the room.

I say, 'Happy birthday, Mae Mobley two!'

She laugh and say, 'I am Mae Mobley three!'

'You sure is! Now blow out them candles, Baby Girl.'

She blow em clean over. She suck the grits off the candles and start eating. After while, she smile up at me, say, 'How old are you?'

'Aibileen's fifty-three.'

Her eyes get real wide. 'Do you . . . get birthdays?'

'Yeah.' I laugh. 'It's a pity, but I do. My birthday be next week.' I can't believe I'm on be fifty-four years old. Where do it go?

I start washing the dishes. The birthday party tonight just gone be the family and I got to get the cakes made. I clean up the grits plate. Give her some grape juice to drink. She got her old baby doll in the kitchen, the one she call Claudia, with the painted-on hair and the eyes that close. Make a pitiful whining sound when you drop it on the floor.

'There's your baby,' I say and she pats its back like she burping it.

Then she say, 'Aibee, you're my real mama.' She don't even look at me, just say it like she talking about the weather.

I kneel down on the floor where she playing. 'Your mama's off getting her hair fixed. Baby Girl, you know who your mama is.'

But she shake her head, cuddling that doll. 'I'm *your* baby,' she say.

It ain't but eight thirty on Monday morning but Miss Leefolt's phone already ringing its head off.

'Miss Leefolt res—'

'*Put Elizabeth on the phone!*'

I go tell Miss Leefolt. She get out a bed, shuffle in the kitchen in her rollers and nightgown, pick up the receiver. Miss Hilly sound like she using a megaphone not a telephone. I can hear every word.

'*Have you been by my house?*'

'What? What are you talk—?'

'*She put it in the newsletter about the toilets. I specifically said old coats are to be dropped off at my house not—*'

'Let me get my . . . mail, I don't know what you're—'

'*When I find her I will kill her myself.*'

The line crash down in Miss Leefolt's ear. She stand there a second staring at it, then throw a housecoat over her nightgown. 'I've got to *go*,' she says, scrambling round for her keys. 'I'll be back.'

She run all pregnant out the door and tumble in her car and speed off. I look down at Mae Mobley and she look up at me.

'Don't ask me, Baby Girl. I don't know either.'

What I do know is, Hilly and her family drove in this morning from a weekend in Memphis. Whenever Miss Hilly gone, that's all Miss Leefolt talk about is where she is and when she coming back.

'Come on, Baby Girl,' I say after while. 'Let's take a walk, find out what's going on.'

We walk up Devine, turn left, then left again, and up Miss Hilly's street, which is Myrtle. Even though it's August, it's a nice walk, ain't too hot yet. Birds is zipping around, singing. Mae Mobley holding my hand and we swinging our arms having a good ole time. Lots a cars passing us today, which is strange, cause Myrtle a dead end.

We turn the bend to Miss Hilly's big white house. And there they is.

Mae Mobley point and laugh. 'Look. Look, Aibee!'

I have never in my life seen a thing like this. Three dozen of em. Toilets. Right smack on Miss Hilly's lawn. All different colours and shapes and sizes. Some is blue, some is pink, some is white. They's old ones, young ones, chain on top, and flush with the handle.

We get a little closer and now I see they ain't just all over the yard. They's two in the driveway side-by-side, like they a couple. They's one up on the front step, like it's waiting for Miss Hilly to answer the door.

'Ain't that one funny with the—'

But Baby Girl done broke off from my hand. She running in the yard and get to the pink pot in the middle and pull up the lid. Before I know it, she done pulled down her panties and tinkled in it and I'm chasing after her with half a dozen horns honking and a man taking pictures.

Miss Leefolt's car's in the drive behind Miss Hilly's, but they ain't in sight. They must be inside yelling about what they gone do with this mess. Curtains is drawn and I don't see no stirring. I cross my fingers, hope they didn't catch Baby Girl making potty for half a Jackson to see.

When I get back to Miss Leefolt's, the phone rings off the hook the rest a the morning. I don't answer it. I'm waiting for it to stop long enough so I can call Minny. But when Miss Leefolt slam into the kitchen, she get to yapping on the phone a million miles a hour. Don't take me long to get the story pieced together listening to her.

Miss Skeeter done printed Hilly's toilet announcement in the newsletter all right. The list a them reasons why white folk and coloured folk can't be sharing a seat. And then, below that, she follow with the alert about the coat drive too. Stead a coats though, it say something like, 'Drop off your old toilets at 228 Myrtle Street. We'll be out of town, but leave them in front by the door.' She just get one word mixed up, that's all. I spec that's what she gone say, anyway.

Too bad for Miss Hilly there wasn't no other news going on. Nothing on Vietnam or the draft. Next day, Miss Hilly's house with all them pots makes the front page a the *Jackson Journal*. The headline say: COME ON BY, HAVE A SEAT! They ain't no article to go with it. Just the picture and a little caption saying, 'The home of Hilly and William Holbrook, of Jackson, Mississippi, was a sight to see this morning.'

On Thursday morning, I still ain't heard from Miss Skeeter. I set up my ironing in the living room. Miss Leefolt come home with Miss Hilly and they set at the dining room table. I ain't seen Miss Hilly over here since before the pots. I reckon she ain't leaving the house so much. I turn the tee-vee set down low, keep my ear turned up.

'Here it is. Here's what I told you about.' Miss Hilly got a little book-let opened up. She running her finger along the lines. Miss Leefolt shaking her head. 'I can't prove she put those pots in my yard. But this'—she holds up the book and taps it—'this is solid proof she's up to something. And I intend to tell Stuart Whitworth, too.'

'But maybe it really was a mistake, the newsletter. Maybe she—'

'Elizabeth.' Hilly cross her arms up. 'I'm not talking about pots. I am talking about the laws of this great state. Now, I want you to ask your-self, do you want Mae Mobley sitting next to a coloured boy in English class?' Miss Hilly glance back at me doing my ironing. She lower her voice but Miss Hilly never knew how to whisper good. 'Do you want Nigra people living right here in this neighbourhood?

'William had a fit when he saw what she did to our house. I've already asked Jeanie Caldwell to take Skeeter's place in bridge club.'

'You kicked her out of bridge club?'

'I sure did. And I thought about kicking her out of the League, too. But I've decided I want her to sit in that room and see what a fool she's made of herself.'

Miss Hilly nods and, after a while, they get up and drive off together. I am glad I don't have to see they faces for a while.

At noon-time, Mister Leefolt come home for lunch, which is rare. He set down at the little breakfast table. 'Aibileen, make me up some lunch, would you, please.' He lift the newspaper, pop the spine to get it straight. 'I'll have some roast beef.'

'Yessir.' I set a placemat and a napkin and some silverware for him.

'I hear you know Skeeter Phelan. Old friend of Elizabeth's,' he says.

I keep my head down. Real slow, I get to slicing, slicing, slicing the meat off that loin. My heart's pumping triple speed now.

'She ask me for cleaning tips sometimes. For the article.'

'That right?' Mister Leefolt say.

'Yessir. She just ask me for tips.'

'I don't want you talking to that woman anymore, not for cleaning tips, not to say hello, you hear?'

'Yessir.'

'I hear about you two talking and you'll be in a heap of trouble. You understand?'

'Yessir,' I whisper, wondering what this man know.

Mister Leefolt pick up his newspaper again. 'I'll have that meat in a sandwich. Put a little mayonnaise on it. And not too toasted, I don't want it dry now.'

That night, me and Minny's setting at my kitchen table. My hands started shaking this afternoon and ain't quit since.

'That ugly white fool,' Minny say.

'I just wish I knew what he thinking.'

They's a knock on the back door and Minny and me both look at each other. Only one person knock on my door like that, everybody else just come on in. I open it and there Miss Skeeter. 'Hello, Minny,' she say when she step inside.

Minny look over at the window. 'Hello, Miss Skeeter.'

Fore I can get a word in, Miss Skeeter set down and start right in.

'I've had some ideas. Aibileen, I think we should lead with your chapter first.' She pull some papers out a that tacky red satchel. 'And, Minny, I think your section should definitely come last.'

'Miss Skeeter . . . I got some things to tell you,' I say.

Minny and me look at each other. 'I'm on go,' Minny say, frowning like her chair got too hard to sit in. She head for the door, but on her way out, she give Miss Skeeter a touch on the shoulder, real quick, keep her eyes straight like she ain't done it. Then she gone.

I rub the back a my neck. Then I tell her that Miss Hilly pulled that booklet out and showed it to Miss Leefolt. And Law knows who else.

Miss Skeeter nod, say, 'I can handle Hilly. This doesn't implicate you, or the other maids, or the book at all.'

And then I tell her what Mister Leefolt say, how I ain't to talk to her no more about the cleaning article. I don't want a tell her these things, but she gone hear em and I want her to hear em from me first.

She listen careful, ask a few questions. When I'm done, she say, 'He's full of hot air, Raleigh. I'll have to be extra careful, though, when I go over to Elizabeth's,' and I can tell, this ain't really hitting her, what's happening. The trouble she in with her friends. How scared we need to be. I tell her what Miss Hilly say about letting her suffer through the League. I tell her she been kicked out a bridge club. I tell her that Miss Hilly gone tell Mister Stuart all about it, just in case he get any 'inclination' to mend things with her.

Skeeter look away from me, try to smile. 'I don't care about any of that ole stuff, anyway.' She kind a laugh and it hurts my heart. Cause everbody care. Black, white, deep down we all do.

'I just . . . I rather you hear it from me than in town,' I say. 'So you know what's coming. So you can be real careful.'

She bite her lip, nod. 'Thank you, Aibileen.'

The summer rolls behind us like a hot tar spreader. Ever coloured person in Jackson gets in front a whatever tee-vee set they can find, watches Martin Luther King stand in our nation's capital and tell us he's got a dream. I'm in the church basement watching. Our own Reverend Johnson went up there to march and I find myself scanning the crowd for his face. I can't believe so many peoples is there—250,000. And the ringer is 60,000 a them is *white*.

'Mississippi and the world is two very different places,' the deacon say and we all nod cause ain't it the truth.

We get through August and September and ever time I see Miss Skeeter, she look thinner, a little more skittish in the eyes. She try to smile like it ain't that hard on her that she ain't got no friends left.

In October, Miss Hilly sets at Miss Leefolt's dining-room table. She stick her pinky out from her tea glass and say, 'Skeeter thought she was so clever, dumping all those toilets in my front yard. Well, they're working out just fine. We've already installed three of them in people's garages and sheds. Even William said it was a blessing in disguise.'

I ain't gone tell Miss Skeeter this. That she ended up supporting the cause she fighting against.

It's already the third Wednesday a October, so it's Miss Leefolt's turn to host bridge club. It's all changed up now that Miss Skeeter been thrown out. It's Miss Jeanie Caldwell, the one who call everybody honey, and Miss Lou Anne who replaced Miss Walter, and everybody's real polite and stiff. They ain't much fun listening to anymore.

I'm pouring the last ice tea when the doorbell go *ding-dong*. When

I open it, the first word that pop in my head is *pink*. I never seen her before but I've had enough conversations with Minny to know. Who else round here gone fit extra-large bosoms in a extra-small sweater?

'Hello, there,' she say, licking her lipsticky lips. She raise her hand out to me and I think she giving me something. I reach out to take whatever it is and she give me a funny little handshake.

'My name is Celia Foote and I am here to see Miss Elizabeth Leefolt, please.'

I'm so mesmerised by all that pink, it takes a few seconds to hit me how bad this could turn out for me. And Minny. It was a long time ago, but that lie stuck.

I look back and all four a them ladies is staring at the door with they mouths open like they catching flies. Miss Caldwell whisper something to Miss Hilly. Miss Leefolt stagger up, slap on a smile.

'Hello, Celia,' Miss Leefolt say. 'It's certainly been a long time.'

Miss Celia clears her throat and says kind a too loud, 'Hello, Elizabeth.' Her eyes flicker back to the table where the other ladies is setting. 'I'm here to offer my help for the Children's Benefit.'

Miss Leefolt smile, say, 'Oh. Well, I . . .'

'I got a real knack for arranging flowers, I mean, everybody back in Sugar Ditch said so. Even my maid said so, right after she said I'm the worst cook she's ever laid eyes on.' She giggle at this a second and I suck in my breath at the word *maid*.

Miss Hilly get up from the table. She lean in, say, 'We really don't need any more help, but we'd be delighted if you and Johnny would attend the Benefit, Celia. It's on Friday night, November the fifteenth at the—'

'—the Robert E Lee Hotel,' Miss Celia finish. 'I know all about it.'

'We'd love to sell you some tickets. Johnny'll be coming with you, won't he? Go get her some tickets, Elizabeth.'

Miss Leefolt come back with the envelope. Miss Hilly take out two tickets and hand the envelope back to Miss Leefolt, who goes in the back to put it away.

'Lemme just get my cheque writ out. I'm lucky I have this big ole bag with me today. I told my maid Minny I'd pick up a ham bone for her in town.'

I stay still as I can, hoping to God Miss Hilly didn't hear what she just said. She hand the cheque over but Miss Hilly all wrinkled up, thinking.

'Who? Who'd you say your maid was?'

'Minny Jackson. Aw! Shoot.' Miss Celia pop her hand over her mouth. 'Elizabeth made me swear I'd never tell she recommended her and here I am blabbing my mouth off.'

'Elizabeth . . . recommended Minny Jackson?'

Miss Leefolt come back in from the bedroom. 'Aibileen, Mae Mobley's up. Go on and get her now. I can't lift a nail file with my back.'

I go real quick to Mae Mobley's room but soon as I peek in, Mae Mobley's done fallen asleep again. I rush back to the dining room. Miss Hilly's shutting the front door closed, looking like she just swallowed the cat that ate the canary.

'Aibileen,' Miss Leefolt say, 'go on and get the salads ready now, we're all waiting.'

I go in the kitchen. When I come back out, the salad plates is rattling like teeth on the serving tray.

'. . . mean the one who stole all your mama's silver and . . .'

'. . . thought everybody in town knew that Nigra was a thief . . .'

'. . . I'd never in a million years recommend . . .'

'. . . you see what she had on? Who does she . . .'

'I'm going to figure this out if it kills me,' Miss Hilly say.

MINNY

I'M AT THE KITCHEN SINK waiting for Miss Celia to come home. That crazy woman woke up this morning, squoze into the tightest pink sweater she has, which is saying something, and hollered, 'I'm going to Elizabeth Leefolt's. Right now, while I got the nerve, Minny.' Then she drove off in her Bel Aire convertible with her skirt hanging out the door.

I was just jittery until the phone rang. Aibileen was hiccupping she was so upset. Not only did Miss Celia tell the ladies that Minny Jackson is working for her, she informed them that Miss Leefolt was the one who 'recommended' me.

So, now I have to wait. Wait to find out if, number one, my best friend in the entire world gets fired for getting me a job. And number two, if Miss Hilly told Miss Celia those lies that I'm a thief. And number two and a half, if Miss Hilly told Miss Celia how I got back at her for telling those lies that I'm a thief. I'm not sorry for the Terrible Awful Thing I done to her. But now that Miss Hilly put her own maid in jail to rot, I wonder what that lady's going to do with me.

It's not until ten after four, an hour past my time to leave, that I see Miss Celia's car pull in. She jiggles up the walk like she's got something to say. I hitch up my hose.

'Go, please! We'll talk tomorrow,' she says, but for once, I don't want to go home, I want to hear what Miss Hilly said about me. But Miss Celia won't tell me anything.

The next morning before work, Aibileen calls my house.

'I call poor Fanny early this morning cause I know you been stewing about it all night.' Poor Fanny's Miss Hilly's new maid. Ought to call her Fool Fanny for working there. 'She heard Miss Leefolt and Miss Hilly done decided you made the whole recommendation thing up so Miss Celia would give you the job.'

Whew. I let out a long breath. 'Glad you ain't gone get in trouble,' I say. Still, now Miss Hilly calling me a liar *and* a thief.

'Don't you worry bout me,' Aibileen says. 'You just keep Miss Hilly from talking to your boss lady.'

When I get to work, Miss Celia's rushing out to go buy a dress for the Benefit next month. She says she wants to be the first person in the store. It's not like the old days when she was pregnant. Now she can't wait to get out the door.

The phone rings. 'Miss Celia residence.'

'This is Hilly Holbrook speaking. Who is this?'

My blood whooshes down from my hair to my feet.

I lower my voice, make it deep like a stranger. 'This Doreena. Miss Celia's help.' *Doreena? Why I use my sister's name!*

'Doreena. I thought Minny Jackson was Miss Foote's maid.'

'She . . . quit.'

'Is that right? Let me speak to Missus Foote.'

'She . . . out a town. Down at the coast.'

'Well, when she gets back, you tell her I called. Hilly Holbrook, Emerson three sixty-eight forty?'

'Yes, ma'am. I tell her.' In about a hundred years.

Four hours later, Miss Celia walks in with five big boxes stacked on top of each other. I help her tote them back to her bedroom and then I stand very still outside her door to hear if she'll call up the society ladies like she does every day. Sure enough, I hear her pick up the phone. But she just hangs it back up again. The fool's listening for the dial tone again, in case someone tries to call.

Three days after Miss Hilly called, I walk into work half an hour early. The coffee grinds go in the fancy percolator, the water goes in the pot. I lean my bottom against the counter. Quiet. It's what I've been waiting for all night long.

'You're awful early, Minny.'

I open the refrigerator and bury my head inside. 'Morning,' I say from the crisper. All I can think is, *Not yet*.

'*Minny*, what happened?' Miss Celia has made her way around the refrigerator door without me even realising it. My face bunches up. The cut on my eyebrow breaks open again, the hot blood stinging like a razor. Usually my bruises don't show.

'I'm fine,' I say, trying to turn so she can't see me. But Miss Celia's moving with me, bug-eyeing the cut like she's never seen anything so awful. I take a wad of cotton from my pocket, hold it to my face.

'It's nothing,' I say. 'I banged it in the bathtub.'

'Minny, that thing's bleeding. I think you need you some stitches,' she says, picking the phone up.

'Them doctors ain't gone work on no coloured person, Miss Celia.'

I turn and face the sink. I keep thinking, *This ain't nobody's business, just do your work,* but I haven't had a minute's sleep. Leroy screamed at me all night, threw the sugar bowl upside my head, threw my clothes out on the porch. I mean, when he's drinking the Thunderbird, it's one thing, but . . . *oh*. The shame is so heavy I think it might pull me to the floor. Leroy, he wasn't on the Thunderbird this time. This time he beat me stone-cold sober.

'Go on out a here, Miss Celia, let me get some work done,' I say because I just need some time alone. At first, I thought Leroy had found out about my working with Miss Skeeter. It was the only reason I could come up with while he was beating me with his hand. But he didn't say a thing about it. He was just beating me for the pure pleasure of it.

That afternoon, I do a terrible thing. I drive past Aibileen walking home from the bus stop. Aibileen waves and I pretend I don't even see my own best friend on the side of the road in her bright white uniform.

When I get to my house, I fix an icepack for my eye. The kids aren't home yet and Leroy's asleep in the back. I don't know what to do about anything, not Leroy, not Miss Hilly. I just sit and stare at my walls.

'Minny *Jackson*. You too good to give old Aibileen a ride?'

I sigh and turn my sore head so she can see.

'Oh,' she says. 'Come on over. I make you some coffee.'

Before I walk out, I peel that glaring bandage off, slip it in my pocket with my icepack. On some folks around here, a cut-up eye wouldn't even get a comment. But I've got good kids, a car with tyres, and a refrigerator freezer. I'm proud of my family and the shame of the eye is worse than the pain.

In her little kitchen, Aibileen puts the coffeepot on for me, the tea kettle for herself.

'So what you gone do about it?' Aibileen asks and I know she means the eye. We don't talk about me leaving Leroy. Plenty of black men leave their families behind like trash in a dump, but it's just not something the coloured woman do. We've got the kids to think about.

'Thought about driving up to my sister's. But I can't take the kids, they got school.'

'Ain't nothing wrong with the kids missing school a few days. Not if you protecting yourself.'

I fasten the bandage back, hold the icepack to it so the swelling won't be so bad when my kids see me tonight.

'How come Miss Celia chase after Miss Hilly like she just begging for abuse?' I say this even though Miss Celia getting her feelings hurt is the least of my worries right now. It just feels kind of good to talk about someone else's screwed-up life.

'Almost sounds like you care,' Aibileen says, smiling.

'She just don't see em. The *lines*. Not between her and me, not between her and Miss Hilly.'

Aibileen takes a long sip of her tea. 'You talking about something that don't exist.'

I shake my head at my friend. 'Not only is they lines, but you know good as I do where them lines be drawn.'

Aibileen shakes her head. 'I used to believe in em. I don't anymore. They in our heads. People like Miss Hilly is always trying to make us believe they there. But they ain't.'

'I know they there cause you get punished for crossing em,' I say. 'Least I do.'

'Lot a folks think if you talk back to you husband, you crossed the line. And that justifies punishment. You believe in that line?'

I scowl down at the table. 'You know I ain't studying no line like that.'

'Cause that line ain't there. Except in Leroy's head. Lines between black and white ain't there neither. Some folks just made those up, long time ago. And that go for the white trash and the society ladies too.'

'So I ain't crossing no line if I tell Miss Celia the truth, that she ain't good enough for Miss Hilly?' I pick my cup up. I'm trying hard to get this, but my cut's thumping against my brain.

Aibileen laughs. She pats my hand. 'All I'm saying is, kindness don't have no boundaries.'

'Hmph.' I move the icepack round my head. 'Well, maybe I'll try to tell her. Before she goes to the Benefit and makes a big pink fool a herself.'

'You working there this year?' Aibileen asks.

'If Miss Hilly gone be in the same room as Miss Celia telling her lies about me, I want a be there.'

'I be there too,' says Aibileen. 'I feel bad for Miss Skeeter. I know she don't want a go, but Miss Hilly tell her if she don't, she lose her officer job.'

I drink down the rest of Aibileen's good coffee, watch the sun sink. The air turns cooler through the window.

'I guess I got to go,' I say, even though I'd rather spend the rest of my life right here in Aibileen's cosy little kitchen, having her explain the world to me.

It took me a few days, but I finally came up with a plan. It's not a good one, but at least it's something. I know that every minute I wait is a chance for Miss Celia to call up Miss Hilly. I wait too long and she'll see her at the Benefit next week. This morning, I saw the list by Miss Celia's bed. Get fingernails done. Go to pantyhose store. Get tuxedo pressed. Call Miss Hilly.

'Minny, does this new hair colour look cheap?'

I just look at her.

'Tomorrow I am marching down to Fanny Mae's and getting it recoloured.' She's sitting at the kitchen table and holds up a handful of sample strips. 'What do you think? Butterbatch or Marilyn Monroe?'

'Why you don't like you own natural colour?' Not that I have any idea what that might be.

'I think this Butterbatch is a little more festive, for the holidays and all. Don't you?'

'If you want your head to look like a Butterball turkey.'

Miss Celia giggles. She thinks I'm kidding. 'Oh, and I have to show you this new fingernail polish.' She scrambles in her bag, finds a bottle of something so pink it looks like you could eat it.

'Look, isn't it the thing? And I've found two dresses to match it!'

She scoots off and comes back holding two hot-pink gowns, smiling all over them. They're long to the floor, covered in sparkles and sequins, slits up the leg. Both hang by straps thin as chicken wire. They are going to tear her up at that party.

'Which one do you like better?' asks Miss Celia.

I point to the one without the low-cut neckline.

'Oh, see now, I would've chosen this other one. Listen to the little rattle it makes when I walk.' She swishes the dress from side to side.

I think about her rattling round the party in that thing. Whatever the white version of a juke joint hussy is, that's what they'll be calling her. She won't even know what's happening. She'll just hear the hissing.

'You know, Miss Celia'—I speak kind of slow like it's just now coming to me—'instead a calling them other ladies, maybe you should call up Miss Skeeter Phelan. I heard she real nice.'

I asked Miss Skeeter this favour a few days ago, to try to be nice to Miss Celia, steer her away from those ladies. Up to now, I've been telling Miss Skeeter not to dare call Miss Celia back. But now, it's the only option I have.

'I think you and Miss Skeeter would get along just fine,' I say and I crank out a big smile.

'Oh, no.' Miss Celia looks at me all wide-eyed, holding up those saloon-looking gowns. 'Don't you know? The League members can't *stand* Skeeter Phelan anymore. I heard all about it at Fanny Mae's. They said she's the biggest embarrassment this town's ever seen. Said she was the one who put all those toilets on Hilly Holbrook's front yard.'

I grind my teeth together to keep my real words in. 'Have you ever met her?'

'Well, no. But if all those girls don't like her, then she must be . . . well she . . .' Her words trail off like it's just hitting her what she's saying.

Sickness, disgust, disbelief—it all wraps together in me like a ham roll. To keep myself from finishing that sentence for her, I turn to the sink. I knew she was stupid, but I never knew she was a hypocrite.

'Minny?' Miss Celia says behind me.

'Ma'am.'

She keeps her voice quiet. But I hear the shame in it. 'They didn't even ask me in the house. They made me stand out on the steps like a vacuum salesman.'

I turn round and her eyes are down to the floor.

'Why, Minny?' she whispers.

What can I say? Your clothes, your hair, your boobies in the size-nothing sweaters. I remember what Aibileen said about the lines and the kindness. I remember what Aibileen heard at Miss Leefolt's, of why the League ladies don't like her.

'Because they know about you getting pregnant that first time. And it makes them mad you getting knocked up and marrying one a their mens.'

'They *know* about that?'

'And especially since Miss Hilly and Mister Johnny went steady for so long,' I say. 'I reckon they broke up right around the time he met you.'

I'm waiting for it to hit her, that her social life is doomed. That there's no sense in calling the League ladies anymore. Then her face starts to clear like she's figured something out.

'Well, no wonder she can't stand me!' she says, grinning with all she's got. 'I'm just going to have to explain it to Hilly, let her know I am not a boyfriend stealer. In fact, I'll tell Hilly when I see her at the Benefit.'

She's smiling like she just discovered the cure for polio, the way she's worked out a plan to win Miss Hilly over.

At this point, I am too tired to fight it.

On Benefit Friday, I work late cleaning that house top to bottom. At four thirty I wipe the counters one last time, then head to the back where Miss Celia's been getting ready for the past four hours.

'Now what is going on in here?' I mean, she's got stockings dangling from chairs, pocketbooks on the floor, enough costume jewellery for a whole family of hookers, forty-five pairs of high-heel shoes, under-things, overcoats, panties, brassieres, and a half-empty bottle of white wine on the dressing table with no coaster under it.

'What time is it, Minny?' Miss Celia says from the bathroom.

'Ain't even five yet,' I say, 'but I got to go soon.'

'Oh, Minny, I'm so excited.' I hear Miss Celia's dress swishing behind me. 'What do you think?'

I turn round. 'Oh my Lord.' I might as well be Little Stevie Wonder I am so blinded by that dress. Hot-pink and silver sequins glitter from her extra-large boobies all the way to her hot-pink toes.

'Miss Celia,' I whisper. 'Tuck yourself in fore you lose something.'

Miss Celia bats her fake-lashed eyes. She is rouged, painted and plastered with make-up. The Butterbatch hairdo is pouffed up around her head like an Easter bonnet. One leg peeks out in a high, thigh-baring slit and I turn away, too embarrassed to look. Everything about her oozes sex, sex, and more sex.

'Oh, Minny, I'm so nervous, I've got butterflies.' She takes a heavy swig from her wineglass, kind of teeters a little in her high heels.

'Miss Celia,' I say, and I close my eyes, praying for the right words. 'Tonight, when you see Miss Hilly . . .'

She smiles into the mirror. 'I got it all planned. When Johnny goes to the bathroom, I'm just going to tell her. That they were over with by the time me and Johnny started getting together.'

I sigh. 'That ain't what I mean. It's . . . she might say some things about . . . me.'

'You want me to tell Hilly you said "hi"?'

'No, ma'am. Don't tell her nothing.' I sigh.

Just stay home, fool, is what I want to say to her, but I don't. It's too late. With Miss Hilly at the helm, it is too late for Miss Celia and, Lord knows, it is too late for me.

THE BENEFIT

THE JACKSON JUNIOR LEAGUE Annual Ball and Benefit is known simply as 'the Benefit' to anyone who lives within a ten-mile radius of town. At seven o'clock on a cool November night, guests will arrive at the Robert E Lee Hotel bar for the cocktail hour. At eight o'clock, the doors from the lounge will open to the ballroom. Swags of green velvet have been hung around the windows, adorned with bouquets of real holly berries.

Along the windows stand tables with auction lists and the prizes. The goods have been donated by members and local shops, and the auction is expected to generate more than six thousand dollars this year, five hundred more dollars than last year. The proceeds will go to the Poor Starving Children of Africa.

In the centre of the room, beneath a gigantic chandelier, twenty-eight tables are dressed and ready for the dinner to be served at nine. A dance floor and bandstand are off to the side, opposite the podium where Hilly Holbrook will give her speech. After the dinner, there will be dancing.

At seven on the dot, couples begin drifting through the front doors, handing their furs and overcoats to the coloured men in grey morning suits. Hilly, who's been there since six o'clock sharp, wears a long taffeta maroon-coloured dress. Ruffles clutch at her throat, swathes of material hide her body. Tight-fitted sleeves run all the way down her arms. The only genuine parts of Hilly you can see are her fingers and her face.

Some women wear slightly saucier evening gowns, with bare shoulders here and there, but long kid-leather gloves ensure they don't have more than a few inches of epidermis exposed.

Celia Foote and Johnny arrive later than they'd planned, at seven twenty-five. When Johnny came home from work, he stopped in the doorway of the bedroom, squinted at his wife, briefcase still in his hand. 'Celia, you think that dress might be a little bit too . . . um . . . open at the top?'

Celia had pushed him towards the bathroom. 'Oh, Johnny, you men don't know the first thing about fashion. Now, hurry up and get ready.'

Johnny gave up before he even tried to change Celia's mind. They were already late as it was.

They walk in behind Doctor and Missus Ball. The Balls step left, Johnny steps right and, for a moment, it is just Celia, standing under the holly berries in her sparkling hot-pink gown.

The air seems to still. Husbands drinking their whiskies stop in mid-sip, spotting this pink thing at the door. It takes a second for the image to register. They stare, but don't see, not yet. But as it turns real—real skin, real cleavage, perhaps not-so-real blonde hair—their faces slowly light up. They all seem to be thinking the same thing—*Finally* . . . But then, feeling the fingernails of their wives, also staring, digging into their arms, their foreheads wrinkle. Their eyes hint remorse, as marriages are scorned (she never lets me do anything fun), youth is remembered (why didn't I go to California that summer?), first loves are recalled (Roxanne . . .). All of this happens in a span of about five seconds and then it is over and they are left just staring.

William Holbrook tips half his gin martini onto a pair of patent-leather shoes. The shoes are attached to the feet of his biggest campaign contributor. 'Oh, Claiborne, forgive my clumsy husband,' says Hilly. 'William, get him a handkerchief!' But neither man moves.

Hilly's eyes follow the trail of gazes and finally land on Celia. The inch of skin showing on Hilly's neck grows taut.

Celia grabs for Johnny's arm as they make their way into the room. She teeters a bit as she walks, but it's not clear if it's from alcohol or the high heels. They drift around, talking to other couples. Or at least Johnny talks; Celia just smiles. A few times she blushes, looks down at herself. 'Johnny, do you think I might've overdressed a little for this thing?'

Johnny gives her a sympathetic smile. He'd never tell her, 'I told you so,' and instead whispers, 'You look gorgeous.' He squeezes her hand, gets her another drink from the bar, her fifth, although he doesn't know this. 'Try to make some friends. I'll be right back.' He heads for the men's room.

Celia is left standing alone, tapping her foot, looking round the room for somebody she recognises. She stands on tiptoe and waves over the crowd. 'Hey, Hilly, yoo-hoo.'

Hilly looks up from her conversation a few couples away. She smiles, but as Celia comes towards her, Hilly heads off into the crowd.

Celia stops where she is, takes another sip of her drink.

'Oh, hey there, Julia,' Celia calls. They'd met at one of the few parties Celia and Johnny attended when they first got married.

Julia Fenway smiles, glances around.

'It's Celia. Celia Foote. How are you? Oh, I just love that dress. Where'd you get that? Over at the Jewel Taylor Shoppe?'

'No, Warren and I were in New Orleans a few months ago . . .' Julia looks around, but there is no one near enough to save her. 'And you look very . . . glamorous tonight.'

Celia leans closer. 'Well, I asked Johnny, but you know how men are. Do you think I'm a tad overdressed?'

Julia laughs, but not once does she look Celia in the eye. 'Oh, no. You're just *perfect*.'

A fellow Leaguer squeezes Julia on the forearm. 'Julia, we need you over here a second, excuse us.' They walk away, heads leaned close together, and Celia is alone again.

Five minutes later, the doors to the dining room slide open. The crowd moves forward. Guests find their tables using the tiny cards in their hands as oohs and aahs come from the bidding tables along the walls. They are full of silver pieces and hand-sewn daygowns for infants, monogrammed hand towels, a child's tea set from Germany.

Minny is at a table in the back polishing glasses. 'Aibileen,' she whispers. 'There she is.'

Aibileen looks up, spots the woman who knocked on Miss Leefolt's door a month ago. 'Ladies better hold on to they husbands,' she says.

Minny jerks the cloth round the rim of a glass. 'Let me know if you see her talking to Miss Hilly.'

'I will. I been doing a super power prayer for you all day.'

'Look, there Miss Walter. Old bat. And there Miss Skeeter.'

Skeeter has on a long-sleeved black velvet dress, scooped at the neck, setting off her blonde hair, her red lipstick. She has come alone and stands in a pocket of emptiness. She scans the room, looking bored, then spots Aibileen and Minny. They all look away at once.

Skeeter jots a note for the newsletter article about the Benefit. She looks around the room, taking in the swags of green, the holly berries, red roses and dried magnolia leaves set as centrepieces on all the tables. Then her eyes land on Elizabeth, a few feet away. She looks exhausted, having had her baby only a month ago. Skeeter watches as Celia Foote approaches Elizabeth. When Elizabeth looks up and sees who she's been surrounded by, she coughs, draws her hand up to her throat as if she's shielding herself from some kind of attack.

'Not sure which way to turn, Elizabeth?' asks Skeeter.

'What? Oh, Skeeter, how are you?' Elizabeth offers a quick, wide smile. 'I was . . . feeling so warm in here. I think I need some fresh air.'

Skeeter watches Elizabeth rush away, at Celia Foote rattling after Elizabeth in her awful dress. That's the real story, Skeeter thinks. Not the flower arrangements or how many pleats are around the rear end of Hilly's dress. This year, it's all about The Celia Foote Fashion Catastrophe.

Moments later, dinner is announced and everyone settles into their assigned seats. The room is full of chatter, praise for the party, praise for the Chateaubriand. After the main course, Hilly stands behind the podium. There is a round of applause and she smiles at the crowd.

'Good evening. I sure do thank y'all for coming tonight. Before we start the announcements, I'd like to go ahead and thank the people who are making tonight such a success.' Without turning her head from the audience, Hilly gestures to her left, where two dozen coloured women have lined up, dressed in their white uniforms. A dozen coloured men are behind them, in grey and white tuxedos.

'Let's give a special round of applause to the help, for all the wonderful food they cooked and served, and for the desserts they made for the auction.' Here, Hilly picks up a card and reads, 'In their own way, they are helping the League reach its goal to feed the Poor Starving Children of Africa, a cause, I'm sure, dear to their own hearts as well.'

The white people at the tables clap for the maids and servers. Some of the servers smile back. Many, though, stare at the empty air just above the heads of the crowd.

Hilly goes on, thanking and recognising in a musical, patriotic voice. Coffee is served and the husbands drink theirs, but most of the women keep rapt attention on Hilly. She concludes the list with, 'And of course we thank our anonymous contributor of, ahem, *supplies*, for the Home Help Sanitation Initiative.'

A few people laugh nervously, but most turn their heads to see if Skeeter has had the gall to show up.

'I just wish you'd step up and accept our gratitude. We honestly couldn't have accomplished so many installations without you.'

Skeeter keeps her eyes on the podium, her face stoic and unyielding. Hilly gives a quick, brilliant smile. 'And, finally, a special thanks to my husband, William Holbrook, for donating a weekend at his deer camp.' She smiles down at her husband, adds in a lower tone, 'And don't forget, voters. Holbrook for State Senate.'

The guests offer an amicable laugh at Hilly's plug.

Once the dinner and the speech have ended, people get up to dance, husbands head for the bar. There is a scurry to the auction tables for last-minute bids. Two grandmothers are in a bidding war over the child's tea set. The price shoots up from fifteen dollars to eighty-five in no time.

In the corner by the bar, Johnny yawns. Celia spots Hilly. For the moment, Hilly has only a few people around her.

'Johnny, I'll be right back,' Celia says.

'And then let's get the hell out of here. I'm sick of this monkey suit.'

Richard Cross, a member of Johnny's deer camp, slaps Johnny's back. They say something, then laugh. Their gazes sweep across the crowd.

Celia almost makes it to Hilly this time, only to have Hilly slip behind the podium table. Celia backs away.

As soon as Celia disappears into the ladies room, Hilly heads for the corner. 'Why, Johnny Foote,' she says. 'I'm surprised to see you here. Everybody knows you can't stand big parties like this.' She squeezes the crook of his arm.

Johnny sighs. 'You are aware that the doe season opens tomorrow?'

'You can miss a day of hunting season, Johnny. You used to for me.'

Johnny rolls his eyes. 'Celia wouldn't have missed this for anything.'

'Where *is* that wife of yours?' Hilly asks. She's still got her hand tucked in the crook of Johnny's arm and she gives it another pull. 'Not at the LSU game serving hot dogs, is she?'

Johnny frowns down at her, even though it's true, that's how they met.

'Oh, now you know I'm just teasing you. We dated long enough to get to where I can do that, can't I?'

Before Johnny can answer, Hilly's shoulder is tapped and she glides over to the next couple, laughing. Johnny sighs when he sees Celia headed towards him. 'Good,' he says to Richard, 'we can go home. I'm getting up in'—he looks at his watch—'five hours.'

Richard keeps his eyes locked on Celia as she strides towards them. She stops and bends down to retrieve her dropped napkin, offering a generous view of her bosoms. 'Going from Hilly to Celia must've been quite the change, Johnny.'

Johnny shakes his head. 'Like living in Antarctica all my life and one day moving to Hawaii.'

Celia walks up, sighs with a disappointed smile.

'Hey, Celia, how are you?' Richard says. 'You sure are looking nice tonight.'

'Thanks, Richard.' Celia lets out a loud hiccup and she frowns, covers her mouth with a tissue.

'You getting tipsy?' asks Johnny.

'She's just having fun, aren't you, Celia?' Richard says. 'In fact, I'm fixing to get you a drink you're gonna love. It's called an Alabama Slammer.'

Johnny rolls his eyes at his friend. 'And then we're going home.'

Three Alabama Slammers later, the winners of the silent auction are announced. As names are read, items are received with the excitement of someone winning a real contest, as if the booty were free and not paid for at three, four, or five times the store value. Then there are the desserts: cakes, slabs of pralines, divinity fudge and pies.

'. . . and the winner of Minny Jackson's world-famous chocolate custard pie is . . . Hilly Holbrook!'

There is more applause for this one, not just because Minny's known for her treats, but because the name *Hilly* elicits applause on any occasion.

Hilly turns from her conversation. 'What? Was that my name? I didn't bid on anything.'

'Hilly, you just won Minny Jackson's pie! Congratulations,' says the woman to her left.

Hilly scans the room, eyes narrowed.

Minny, having heard her name called in the same sentence as Hilly's, is suddenly very alert. She is holding a dirty coffee cup in one hand, a heavy silver tray in the other. But she stands stock-still.

Hilly spots her, but doesn't move either, just smiles very slightly. 'Well. Wasn't that sweet? Someone must've signed me up for that pie.'

She doesn't take her eyes off Minny and Minny can feel it. She stacks more cups on the tray and heads for the kitchen as fast as she can.

'Why, congratulations, Hilly. I didn't know you were such a fan of Minny's pies!' Celia's voice is shrill. She's come up from behind without Hilly noticing. As she trots towards Hilly, Celia stumbles over a chair leg. There are sideline giggles.

Hilly stands very still, watching her approach. 'Celia, is this some kind of joke?'

'Hilly,' Celia says, grasping Hilly's arm, 'I've been trying to talk to you all night. I think there's been some kind of miscommunication between us and I just think if I *explained* . . .'

'What have you done? Let me go—' Hilly says between gritted teeth. She shakes her head, tries to walk off.

But Celia clutches Hilly's sleeve. 'No, wait! You got to listen—'

Hilly pulls away, but still Celia doesn't let go. A ripping sound cuts through the air. Celia stares at the red material in her fingers. She's torn the maroon cuff clear off Hilly's arm.

Hilly looks down, touches her exposed wrist. 'What are you trying to do to me?' she says in a low growl. 'Did that Nigra maid put you up to this? Because whatever she told you and whatever you've blabbed—'

Several more people have gathered around them, listening, all looking at Hilly with frowns of concern.

'Blabbed? I don't know what you—'

Hilly grabs Celia's arm. '*Who* did you tell?' she snarls.

'Minny told me. I know why you don't want to be friends with me.'

Susie Pernell's voice over the microphone announcing the winners grows louder, forcing Celia to raise her own voice. 'I know you think me and Johnny went behind your back,' she yells, and there is laughter from the front of the room over some comment, and more applause. Just as Susie Pernell pauses over the microphone to look at her notes, Celia yells, '—but I got pregnant *after* you broke up.' The room echoes with the words. All is silent for a few long seconds.

The women around them wrinkle their noses, some start to laugh. 'Johnny's wife is *d-r-u-n-k*,' someone says.

Celia looks around her. She wipes at the sweat that's beading on her make-uped forehead. 'I don't blame you for not liking me, not if you thought Johnny cheated on you with me.'

'Johnny never would've—'

'—and I'm sorry I said that, I thought you'd be tickled you won the pie.'

Hilly leans closer to Celia so no one else can hear. 'You tell your Nigra maid if she tells anybody about that pie, I will make her suffer. You think you're real cute signing me up for that auction, don't you? You think you can blackmail your way into the League?'

'What?'

'You tell me right this *minute* who else you've told ab—'

'I didn't tell nobody nothing about a pie, I—'

'You *liar*,' Hilly says, but she straightens quickly and smiles. 'There's Johnny. Johnny, I think your wife needs your *attention*.' Hilly flashes her eyes at the girls around them, as if they're all in on a joke.

'Celia, what's wrong?' Johnny says.

Celia scowls at Hilly. 'She's not making sense, she called me a—a liar, and now she's accusing me of signing her name on that pie and . . .' Celia stops, looks round like she recognises no one around her. She has tears in her eyes. Then she groans and convulses. Vomit splatters onto the carpet.

'Oh shit!' Johnny says, pulling her back. Celia pushes Johnny's arm off her. She runs for the bathroom and he follows her.

Hilly's hands are in fists. Her face is crimson, nearly the colour of her dress. She marches over and grabs a waiter's arm. 'Get that cleaned up before it starts to smell.'

And then Hilly is surrounded by women, faces upturned, asking questions, arms out like they are trying to protect her.

'I heard Celia's been battling with drinking, but this problem with lying now?' Hilly sows the rumour she'd intended to spread about Minny, in case the pie story ever got out. 'What do they call that?'

'A compulsive liar?'

'That's it, a compulsive liar.' Hilly walks off with the women. 'Celia trapped him into that marriage, telling him she was pregnant. I guess she was a compulsive liar even back then.'

After Celia and Johnny leave, the party winds down quickly. Member wives look exhausted and tired of smiling. There is talk of the auction, of babysitters to get home to, but mostly of Celia Foote retching.

When the room is nearly empty, at midnight, Hilly stands at the podium. She flips through the sheets of silent bids. Her lips move as she calculates. But she keeps looking off, shaking her head. Then she looks back down and curses because she has to start all over again.

'Hilly, I'm headed on back to your house.'

Hilly looks up from tallying. It is her mother, Missus Walter, looking even frailer than usual in her formal wear. She wears a floor-length gown, sky blue and beaded, from 1943. A white orchid wilts at her clavicle. A coloured woman in a white uniform is attached to her side.

'Now, Mama, don't you get in that refrigerator tonight. I won't have you keeping me up all night with your indigestion. You go right to bed, you hear?'

'I can't even have some of Minny's pie?'

Hilly narrows her eyes at her mother. 'That *pie* is in the garbage.'

'Well, why'd you throw it out? I won it just for you.'

Hilly is still a moment, letting this sink in. '*You?* You signed me up?'

'I may not remember my name or what country I live in, but you and that pie is something I will never forget.'

'You—you old, useless . . .' Hilly throws down the papers she's holding, scattering them everywhere.

Missus Walter turns and hobbles towards the door, the coloured nurse in tow. 'Call the papers, Bessie,' she says. 'My daughter's mad at me again.'

MINNY

On Saturday morning, I get up tired and sore. The phone rings and it's Mister Foote.

'I'm up at deer camp but I just want you to know, Celia's real upset. She had a rough time at the party last night.'

'Yessir, I know.'

'You heard, then, huh?' He sighs. 'Well, keep an eye on her next week, will you, Minny? I'll be gone and—I don't know. I'll come home early if I need to.'

I didn't see myself what happened at the party, but I heard about it while I was doing dishes in the kitchen.

When I get to work on Monday, Miss Celia's still laid up in bed with her face buried under the sheets.

'Morning, Miss Celia.'

But she just rolls over and won't look at me.

On Tuesday morning, Miss Celia's still in the bed. Yesterday's lunch tray's on the floor without a single bite missing.

'Come on, lemme get to them sheets.'

But she just lays there.

Later on, I bring her a tray of chicken pot pie. 'Now, Miss Celia, I know it was terrible what happened at the Benefit. But you can't set in here forever, feeling sorry for yourself.'

Miss Celia gets up and locks herself in the bathroom.

I start stripping the bed. When I'm done, I pick up all the wet tissues and glasses off the nightstand. I see a stack of mail; at least the woman's gotten up to go to the mailbox. I see the letters H W H across the top of a card. Before I know it, I've read the whole note:

> Dear Celia,
>
> In lieu of reimbursing me for my dress you tore, we at the League would gladly receive a donation of no less than two hundred dollars.
>
> Furthermore, please withhold from volunteering for any non-member activities in the future, as your name has been placed on a probationary list. Your cooperation in this matter is appreciated.
>
> Do kindly make the cheque out to the Jackson League Chapter.
>
> Sincerely,
>
> Hilly Holbrook
>
> President and Chairman of Appropriations

On Wednesday morning, Miss Celia's *still* under the covers. I do my work in the kitchen, try to appreciate the fact that she's not hanging round with me in here. But I can't enjoy it because the phone's been ringing all morning, and for the first time since I started, Miss Celia won't pick it up.

By the next afternoon, I can't stand it another minute. Miss Celia's still in the same spot she's been all week. Her face is thin and that Butterbatch is greasy-looking. The room is starting to smell too, like dirty people. I bet she hasn't bathed since Friday.

'Miss Celia,' I say.

I hear Miss Celia sniffle, then hiccup, then start to cry full-on. 'None of this would've happened if I'd just stayed where I belonged. He should've married proper. He should've married . . . *Hilly*.'

'Come on, Miss Celia. It ain't—'

'The way Hilly looked at me . . . like I was *nothing*. Like I was trash on the side of the road. Why does she hate me so much? She doesn't even know me,' Miss Celia cries. 'And it's not just Johnny, she called me a liar, accused me of getting her that . . . *pie*.' She bangs her fists against her knees. 'I *never* would a thrown up if it wasn't for that.'

'What pie?'

'H-H-Hilly won your pie. And she accused me of signing her up for it. Playing some . . . trick on her.' She wails and sobs. 'Why would I do that? Write her name down on a list?'

It comes to me real slow what's going on here. I don't know who signed up Hilly for that pie, but I sure *know* why she'd eat alive anybody she thought did it.

'Miss Celia . . .' I say, 'I know why Miss Hilly got so mad,' I say. 'About the pie, I mean.'

'What?' she sniffs. 'What happened, Minny?'

'Miss Hilly, she call me up at home last year, when I's still working for Miss Walter. To tell me she sending Miss Walter to the old lady home. I got scared, I got five kids to feed. Leroy already working two shifts.'

Miss Celia sits up in bed, wipes her nose. She looks like she's paying attention now.

'For three weeks, I be looking for work. Ever day after I get off from Miss Walter's, I went looking. I go over to Miss Child's house. She pass me up. I go on to the Rawleys' place, they don't want me neither. The Riches, the Patrick Smiths, the Walkers, not even those Catholic Thibodeaux with them seven kids. Nobody do.'

'Oh, Minnie . . .' says Miss Celia. 'That's awful.'

I clench my jaw. 'When they was two days left at Miss Walter's and I still didn't have no new job, I start getting real scared. And that's when Miss Hilly, she come over to Miss Walter's to talk to me.'

'She say, "Come work for me, Minny. I pay you twenty-five more cent a day than Mama did." I tell her, "No, thank you, Miss Hilly." And so she say she pay me fifty cent more and I say, "No, ma'am. No, thank you." Then she tell me she know bout the Childs and the Rawleys and all them others that turn me down. Said it was cause she'd made sure everbody knew I was a thief. I've never stole a thing in my life but she told everbody I did and wasn't nobody in town gone hire a sass-mouthing thieving Nigra for a maid.

'And that's how come I did it.'

Miss Celia blinks at me. 'What, Minny?'

'I tell her to eat my shit.'

Miss Celia sits there, still looking dazed.

'Then I go home. I mix up that chocolate custard pie. I puts sugar in it and Baker's chocolate and the real vanilla my cousin bring me from Mexico. I tote it over to Miss Walter's house, where I know Miss Hilly be setting round, waiting for the home to come and get her mama, so she can sell that house. Go through her silver.

'Soon as I put that pie down on the counter top, Miss Hilly smiles, thinking it's a peace offering. And then I watch her eat it. Two big pieces. She stuff it in her mouth like she ain't ever eaten nothing so good. Then she say, "I knew you'd change your mind, Minny. I knew I'd get my way in the end." And she laugh.

'That's when Miss Walter, she ask for a piece a that pie. I tell her, "No, ma'am. That one's special for Miss Hilly."

'Miss Hilly say, "Mama can have some if she wants. Just a little piece, though. What do you put in here, Minny, that makes it taste so good?"

'I say, "That good vanilla from Mexico," and then I go head. I tell her what else I put in that pie for her.'

Miss Celia's still as a stone staring at me, but I can't meet her eyes.

'Miss Walter, her mouth fall open. Nobody in that kitchen said anything for so long, I could a made it out the door fore they knew I's gone. But then Miss Walter start laughing. Laugh so hard she almost fall out the chair. Say, "Well, Hilly, that's what you get, I guess. And I wouldn't go tattling on Minny either, or you'll be known all over town as the lady who ate *two* slices of Minny's shit."'

I sneak a look up at Miss Celia. She's staring wide-eyed, disgusted. I start to panic that I told her this. She'll never trust me again. I walk over to a chair and sit myself down.

'Miss Hilly thought you knew the story. That you were making fun a her. She never would a pounced on you if I hadn't done what I did.'

Miss Celia just stares at me.

'But I want you to know, if you leave Mister Johnny, then Miss Hilly done won the whole ball game. Then she done beat me, she beat you . . .' I shake my head, thinking about Yule May in jail, and Miss Skeeter without any friends left. 'There ain't many people left in this town that she ain't beat.'

Miss Celia's quiet awhile. Then she looks over at me and starts to say something, but she shuts her mouth back.

Finally, she just says, 'Thank you. For . . . telling me that.'

She lays back down. But before I close the door, I can see her eyes are wide smack open.

The next morning, I find Miss Celia's finally managed to get herself out of bed, wash her hair, and put all that make-up on again. It's cold outside so she's back in one of her tight sweaters.

But Miss Celia doesn't say much. There's a tiredness in her eyes. She's not so quick to smile at every little thing. She points her finger out the kitchen window. 'I think I'll plant a row of rosebushes. Along the back of the property.' I take this as a good sign.

The next morning I come in and find Miss Celia at the kitchen table. She's got the newspaper out, but she's staring out at that mimosa tree. It's chilly outside.

'Morning, Miss Celia.'

'Hey, Minny.' Miss Celia just sits, looking out at that tree, fiddling with a pen in her hand. It's started to rain.

'What you want for lunch today? We got a roast beef or some a this chicken pie left over . . .' I lean in the refrigerator. I've got to make a decision about Leroy, tell him how it is. *Either you quit beating on me, or I'm gone. And I'm not taking the kids either.* Which ain't true, about the kids, but that ought to scare him more than anything.

'I don't want anything.' Miss Celia stands up, slips off one red high heel, then the other. She stretches her back, still staring out the window, then she walks out the back door. I shake my head and look down at the newspaper.

That's when I see Miss Hilly's note tucked underneath it and Miss Celia's cheque for two hundred dollars. I look a little closer. Along the bottom of the cheque, in the little space for the notes, Miss Celia's written the words in pretty cursive handwriting: *For Two-Slice Hilly.*

MISS SKEETER

I STARE AT THE PHONE in the kitchen. No one's called here in so long, it's like a dead thing mounted to the wall. There's a terrible quiet looming everywhere—at the library, at the drugstore where I pick up Mother's medicine, in our own house. President Kennedy's assassination, less than two weeks ago, has struck the world dumb.

On the rare occasion that the phone does ring lately, it's Doctor Neal, calling with more bad test results, or a relative checking on Mother. And yet, I still think *Stuart* sometimes, even though it's been five months since he's called. Even though I finally broke down and told Mother we'd broken up.

I take a deep breath, dial zero, and close myself up in the pantry. I tell the operator the long-distance number and wait to be connected.

'Elaine Stein.'

I blink, surprised it's not her secretary. 'Missus Stein, I'm sorry, this is—Eugenia Phelan. In Jackson, Mississippi.'

'Yes . . . Eugenia.' She sighs, evidently irritated that she took the chance to answer her own phone.

'I was calling to let you know that the manuscript will be ready right after the new year.'

There is silence, except for an exhale of cigarette smoke. 'Oh, no, January is not acceptable. The last editor's meeting of the year is on December twenty-first,' Missus Stein continues. 'If you want a chance at getting this read, I've got to have it in my hands by then.'

'But . . . you told me January!' Today is December second. That gives me nineteen days to finish the entire thing. I swallow, 'I don't know if . . .'

'It's just occurred to me, you'll need a section about your own maid.'

'Yes, ma'am,' I say, even though I have no idea how I'll finish two maids in time, much less write stories about Constantine.

I get off the phone, stunned. I know I need to get to work immediately, but I check on Mother in her bedroom. In the past three months, her ulcers have got much worse. She's lost more weight and can't get through two days without vomiting.

Mother eyes me up and down from her bed. 'Don't you have bridge club today?'

'It's cancelled. Elizabeth's baby is colicky,' I lie. Mother still doesn't know that I've been kicked out of bridge club or that Patsy Joiner got a new tennis partner. I don't get invited to cocktail parties or baby showers anymore, or any functions where Hilly will be there. Except the League. At meetings, girls are short and to the point with me when discussing newsletter business. I tell myself, that's what you get when you put thirty-one toilets on the most popular girl's front yard.

It's not as if I hadn't expected consequences. I just hadn't thought they'd last so long.

Hilly's voice over the phone that morning was gravelly sounding, low, like she'd been yelling all morning. 'You are sick,' she hissed at me. 'Do not speak to me, do not look at me. Do not say hello to my children.'

'Technically it was a typo, Hilly,' was all I could think to say.

'You turned my yard into some kind of a sideshow,' Hilly'd said. 'Just how long have you been planning to humiliate my family?'

What Hilly didn't understand was, I hadn't planned it at all. When I started typing out her bathroom initiative for the newsletter, typing words like *disease* and *protect yourself*, it was like something cracked open inside of me, not unlike a watermelon, cool and soothing and sweet. I always thought insanity would be a dark, bitter feeling, but it is drenching and delicious if you really roll around in it. I'd paid Pascagoula's brothers twenty-five dollars each to put those junkyard toilets onto Hilly's lawn.

'And you call yourself a *Christian*,' were Hilly's final words to me and I thought: God. When did I ever do that?

This November, Stooley Whitworth won the senator's race for Washington, but William Holbrook lost the local election, to take his state seat. I'm quite sure Hilly blames me for this too.

A few hours after talking to Missus Stein over the phone, I tiptoe back to check on Mother one last time. Daddy's already asleep beside her. Mother has a glass of milk on the table. She's propped up on her pillows but her eyes are closed. She opens them as I'm peeking in. 'Can I get you anything, Mama?'

'I'm only resting because Doctor Neal told me to. Where are you going, Eugenia? It's nearly seven o'clock.'

'I'll be back in a little while. I'm just going for a drive.' I give her a kiss, hoping she doesn't ask any more questions. When I close the door, she's already fallen asleep.

I drive fast through town. My conversation this afternoon with Missus Stein is still racing through my head. I've been trying to prioritise everything left to do. But the hardest part is, I have to ask Aibileen, again, about what happened to Constantine.

I hurry into Aibileen's kitchen. The look on my face must tell her something's wrong.

'What is it? Somebody see you?'

'No,' I say, pulling papers from my satchel. 'I talked to Missus Stein this morning.' I tell her about the deadline. 'And . . . she wants me to write about Constantine.'

Aibileen sets her cup of tea down.

'I can't write it if I don't know what happened, Aibileen. So if you can't tell me . . . I was wondering if there's someone else who will.'

Aibileen shakes her head. 'I reckon they is,' she says, 'but I don't want nobody else telling you that story.'

'Then . . . will you?'

'I'll write it down. Give me a few days. I'll tell you everthing.'

On Thursday night, I go to the League meeting. It's pathetic, but I'm glad to still have the newsletter. Once a week, I actually feel like I'm a part of things.

But the minute I walk in, backs turn. My exclusion is tangible, as if concrete walls have formed around me. Hilly gives me a smirk, whips her head round to speak to someone else.

Instead of my usual seat up front, I slip in the back row. Hilly steps up to the podium and announces the upcoming gimme-drives (coat drive, can drive, book drive and a plain old money drive). 'Now, we have something very exciting to discuss. The committee has decided that our newsletter could use a little updating.'

I sit up straighter. Shouldn't I decide on changes to the newsletter?

'First, we're changing the newsletter from a weekly to a monthly. And we're adding a fashion column, highlighting some of the best outfits worn by our members, and a make-up column with all the latest trends.

'OK, then. It is time to choose an editor for our new, modern monthly. Any nominations?'

Several hands pop up. I sit very still.

'Jeanie Price, what say ye?'

'I say Hilly. I nominate Hilly Holbrook.'

'Aren't you the sweetest thing. All right, any seconds to . . .' Hilly looks down at the podium, like she can't quite remember who's been nominated. 'To Hilly Holbrook as editor?'

'I second.'

'I third.'

Bang-bang goes the gavel and I've lost my post as editor.

I head straight for the doors when the meeting is over. No one speaks to me, no one looks me in the eye. I keep my head high.

I don't go straight home after the League meeting. I know I need to work on the stories, but I turn onto the wide lanes and just drive. I've never felt so empty in my life. I can't help but think of all that's piling on top of me. *I will never make this deadline, my friends despise me, Stuart is gone, Mother is . . .*

I don't know what Mother is, but we all know it's more than just stomach ulcers.

'I wish I could just leave here,' I say and my voice sounds eerie, with no one to hear it.

A couple of hours later, I pull up in front of our house and see Stuart sitting on the top porch step. Daddy's in a rocking chair. They both stand when I turn off the engine.

'Hey, Daddy,' I say. I don't look at Stuart. 'Where's Mama?'

'She's asleep, I just checked on her. Turn the lights out when you're done.' Daddy goes inside and Stuart and I are left alone.

I sit on the front step and put my head down on my arms. He moves closer to me, but not so close that we are touching. I wish we were touching.

'I came to tell you something. I came to say that I saw her.'

I lift my head up. The first word in my head is *selfish*. You selfish son of a bitch, coming here to talk about Patricia.

'I went out there, to San Francisco. I told her I thought that was the ugliest thing you could do to a person. Lie that way. She looked so different. Had on this prairie-looking dress and a peace sign and her hair was long and she didn't have any lipstick on.

'And then she called me a whore.' He rubs his eyes hard with his knuckles. 'She, the one who took her clothes off for that guy—said I was a whore to my daddy, a whore to Mississippi.'

'Why are you telling me this?' My fists are clenched.

'Because of you. After we broke up, I knew I had to get her out of my head. I drove two thousand miles there and back and I'm here to tell you. It's dead. It's gone.'

'Well, good, Stuart,' I say. 'Good for you.'

He moves closer and leans down so I will look at him. And I feel sick, literally nauseated by the smell of bourbon on his breath. And yet I still want to fold myself up and put my entire body in his arms. I am loving him and hating him at the same time.

'Go home,' I say, hardly believing myself. 'There's no place left inside me for you.'

'Can I come by on Saturday? To talk some more?'

I shrug, my eyes full of tears. I won't let him throw me away again. It's already happened too many times, with him, with my friends. I'd be stupid to let it happen again.

'I don't really care what you do.'

I wake up at 5 a.m. and start working on the stories. I realise I do not have seventeen more days. How *dumb* of me. I have ten days, because of the time it will take to mail it to New York.

That night, I tell Aibileen about the new deadline, and she looks like she might cry. 'Also, we need to decide on the title,' I say. 'I've been working on a few. I think we should call it *Coloured Domestics and the Southern Families for Which They Work*.'

'Say what?' Minny is at the kitchen table, drinking a cola, looking out the window.

Aibileen says 'What you think about just calling it . . . *Help*?'

'*Help*,' Minny repeats, like she's never heard of the word.

'I like . . . *Help*,' I say, because I really do.

With just six days left, Aibileen gives me a letter when I arrive for our session. 'Fore I give this to you . . . I think I ought to tell you some things. So you can really understand.

'Remember, I told you Constantine had a daughter. Well, Lulabelle was her name. Law, she come out pale as snow. Grew hair the colour a hay. Not curly like yours. Straight it was.'

'She was that white?' I ask. I've wondered this ever since Aibileen told me about Constantine's child.

She nods. 'When Lulabelle was four years old, Constantine . . .' Aibileen shifts in her chair. 'She take her to a . . . orphanage in Chicago.'

'An orphanage? You mean . . . she gave her baby away?'

Aibileen looks me straight in the eye. I see something there I rarely see—frustration, antipathy. 'A lot a coloured womens got to give they children up, Miss Skeeter. Send they kids off cause they have to tend to a white family. But most send em off to family. A orphanage is . . . different altogether.'

'Why didn't she send the baby to her sister's?'

'Her sister . . . she just couldn't handle it. Being Negro with white skin . . . in Mississippi, it's like you don't belong to nobody.'

'Was she already working for my mother then?'

'She'd been with your mama a few years. That's where she met the father, Connor. He worked on your farm, lived back there in Hotstack.'

'Was it a coloured orphanage or a white one?' Because I am thinking, I am hoping, maybe Constantine just wanted a better life for her child. Maybe she thought she'd be adopted by a white family and not feel so different.

'Coloured. White ones wouldn't take her, I heard. A few years later, Constantine wrote the orphanage, told em she made a mistake, she wanted her girl back. But Lula been adopted already. She was gone.' Aibileen leans back in her chair. 'Constantine said if she ever got Lulabelle back, she'd never let her go.'

I sit quietly, my heart aching for Constantine. I am starting to dread what this has to do with my mother.

'Bout two years ago, Constantine get a letter from Lulabelle. I reckon she was twenty-five by then, and it said her adoptive parents give her the address. They start writing to each other and Lulabelle say she want a come down and stay with her awhile.'

Two years ago. I was up at school then. Why didn't Constantine tell me in her letters what was going on?

'She took all her savings and bought new clothes for Lulabelle. She told us at prayer meeting, "What if she hate me for what I done?"'

I remember my last letter from Constantine, that she had a surprise for me. I realise now, she'd wanted to introduce me to her daughter. I swallow back tears coming up in my throat. 'What happened when Lulabelle came down to see her?'

Aibileen slides the envelope across the table. 'I reckon you ought a read that part at home.'

At Longleaf I go upstairs. Without even stopping to sit down, I open Aibileen's letter. Afterwards, I put my hands on the typewriter keys.

I write that Constantine had a daughter and had to give her up so she could work for our family—the Millers I call us. I don't put in that Constantine's daughter was high yellow; I just want to show that Constantine's love for me began with missing her own child. Perhaps that's what made it so unique, so deep. While she was wanting her own daughter back, I was longing for Mother not to be disappointed in me.

For two days, I write all the way through my childhood, my college years, where we sent letters to each other every week. But then I stop and listen to Mother coughing downstairs. I hear Daddy's footsteps, going to her. I light a cigarette and stub it out, thinking, *Don't start up again.* I light another cigarette and smoke it down to my fingers. I can't write about what's in Aibileen's letter.

That afternoon, I call Aibileen at home. 'I can't put it in the book,' I tell her. 'About Mother and Constantine. I'll end it when I go to college. I just . . .'

'Miss Skeeter—'

'I know I should. I know I should be sacrificing as much as you and Minny and all of you. But I can't do that to my mother.'

'No one expects you to, Miss Skeeter. Truth is, I wouldn't think real high of you if you did.'

The next evening, I go to the kitchen for some tea.

'Eugenia? Are you downstairs?'

I tread back to Mother's room. Daddy's not in bed yet. I hear the television on out in the relaxing room. 'I'm here, Mama.'

I sit in the straight cane chair beside her bed. I think about how I should begin. 'I want to talk about Constantine,' I say.

'Oh, Eugenia,' Mother chides and pats my hand. 'That was almost two years ago.'

'Mama,' I say and make myself look into her eyes. 'What happened? What happened with her daughter?'

Mother's jaw tightens and I can tell she's surprised that I know about her. 'Now, you look, I was good to Constantine. Oh, she talked back plenty of times and I put up with it. But, Skeeter, she didn't give me a choice this time.

'That girl—' She shakes her finger at me. 'She showed up here. I had the entire DAR chapter at the house. They were all in the living room having cake, ninety-five *people* in the house, and she's drinking coffee. She's walking round the house like a guest and then she's filling out the form to become a *member*.'

Again I nod. Maybe I didn't know those details, but they don't change what happened.

'She looked white as anybody, and she knew it too. She knew exactly what she was doing and so I say, "How do you do?" and she laughs and says, "Fine," so I say, "And what is your name?" and she says, "You mean you don't know? I'm Lulabelle Bates. I'm grown now and I've moved back in with Mama. I got here yesterday morning." And then she goes over to help herself to another piece of cake.

'Thank God nobody heard her. I pulled her into the kitchen and I said, "Lulabelle, you can't stay here," and, oh, she looked at me haughty. She said, "What, you don't allow coloured Negroes in your living room if we're not cleaning up?" That's when Constantine walks in the kitchen and she looks as shocked as I am. I say, "You get your daughter out of my house right now."'

Mother's eyes seem more deep-set than ever. Her nostrils are flaring.

'So Constantine, she tells Lulabelle to go on back to their house, and Lulabelle says, "Fine, I was leaving anyway," and heads for the dining room and of course I stop her. "Oh no," I say, "you go out the back door, not the front with the white guests." And do you know what she did?'

Yes, but I keep my face blank. I am still searching for the redemption.

'Spit. In my face. A Negro in my home. Trying to act white.'

I shudder. Who would ever have the nerve to spit at my mother?

'I told Constantine that girl better not show her face here again. Nor would I tolerate her keeping terms with Lulabelle, not as long as your daddy was paying Constantine's rent on that house back there.'

'But it was Lulabelle acting that way. Not Constantine.'

'What if she stayed? I couldn't have that girl going round Jackson, acting white when she was coloured.'

'She hadn't seen her daughter in twenty years. You can't . . . tell a person they can't see their child.'

But Mother is caught up in her own story. 'And Constantine, she thought she could get me to change my mind. "Miss Phelan, please, just let her stay at the house, she won't come on this side again, I haven't seen her in so long."'

'And that Lulabelle, with her hand up on her hip, saying, "Yeah, my daddy died and my mama was too sick to take care of me when I was a baby. She had to give me away. You can't keep us apart."'

Mother narrows her eyes. 'It's time you learned, Eugenia, how things really are. You idolise Constantine too much. You always have.' She points her finger at me again. 'They are not like regular *people*.'

I can't look at her. I close my eyes. 'And then what happened, Mother?'

'I asked Constantine, just as plain as day, "Is that what you told her? Is that how you cover your mistakes?"'

This is the part I was hoping wasn't true. This is what I'd hoped Aibileen had been wrong about.

'I told Lulabelle the truth. I said, "Your daddy didn't *die*. He left the day after you were born. And your mama hadn't been sick in her life. She gave you up because you were too high yellow. She didn't want you."'

I let my head sink into my hands. There is no redeeming piece of the story. A child should never know this about her own mother.

'I never thought Constantine would go to Illinois with her, Eugenia. Honestly, I was . . . sorry to see her go.'

'You weren't,' I say. I think about Constantine, after living fifty years in the country, sitting in a tiny apartment in Chicago. How lonely she must've felt. How bad her knees must've felt in that cold.

'I was. And even though I told her not to write you, she probably would've, if there'd been more time.'

'More time?'

'Constantine died, Skeeter. I sent her a cheque, for her birthday. But Lulabelle . . . sent it back. With a copy of the obituary.'

'*Constantine*,' I cry. I wish I'd known. 'Why didn't you tell me, Mama?'

Mother sniffs, keeping her eyes straight ahead. She quickly wipes her eyes. 'Because I knew you'd blame me when it—it wasn't my fault.'

'When did she die? How long was she living in Chicago?' I ask.

'Three weeks.'

Aibileen opens her back door and lets me in. Minny is sitting at the table, stirring her coffee. I put the finished manuscript down on the table with a thump.

'What if they find out?' Aibileen says. 'What if folks find out Niceville is Jackson, or figure out who who.'

'They ain't gone know,' Minny says. 'Jackson ain't no special place. They's ten thousand towns just like it.'

My skin prickles. I'm not so afraid for myself, but for what I've done to Aibileen, to Minny. To Louvenia and Faye Belle and eight other women. The book is sitting there on the table. I want to put it in my satchel and hide it.

Instead, I look to Minny because, for some reason, I think she's the only one among us who really understands what could happen. She doesn't look back at me though. She's lost in thought.

'Minny? What do you think?' I ask.

Minny keeps her eyes on the window, nods at her own thoughts. 'I think what we need is some *insurance*.'

'Ain't no such thing,' Aibileen says. 'Not for us.'

'What if we put the Terrible Awful in the book,' Minny asks, 'then Miss Hilly *can't* let anybody find out the book is about Jackson. She don't want *anybody* to know that story's about her. And if they start getting close to figuring it out, she gone steer em the other way. Nobody know that story but Miss Hilly and her own mama,' Minny says. 'And Miss Celia, but she ain't got no friends to tell anyway.'

'What happened?' I ask. 'Is it really *that* terrible?'

Aibileen looks at me. My eyebrows go up.

'If we put the Terrible Awful in the book and people *do* find out that was you and Miss Hilly, then you in so much trouble'—Aibileen shudders—'there ain't even a name for it.'

'That's a risk I'm just gone have to take. I already made up my mind.'

Aibileen sighs. 'I reckon you better tell her then.'

I write all night, grimacing over the details of Minny's story, and all the next day. At four in the afternoon, I speed to the post office.

When I get home, Doctor Neal's car is here. Down the hall, through the open front door, I can see that Mother's bedroom door is closed. A little while later, Doctor Neal comes out.

'I gave her something to help the pain,' he says.

'The . . . pain? Was Mama vomiting this morning?'

Old Doctor Neal stares at me through his cloudy blue eyes. 'Your mother has cancer, Eugenia. In the lining of the stomach. She didn't want to tell you.' He shakes his head. 'But since she refuses to stay in the hospital, you need to know. These next few months are going to be . . . pretty hard.' He raises his eyebrows at me. 'On her and you too.'

'Few months? Is that . . . all?' I cover my mouth with my hand, hear myself groan.

'Maybe longer, maybe sooner, honey.' He shakes his head.

I walk back to Mother's room. Daddy is on the settee by the bed, staring at nothing. Mother is sitting straight up. She rolls her eyes when she sees me.

'Well, I guess he told you,' she says.

Tears drip off my chin. I hold her hands. 'How long have you known?'

'About two months.'

'Oh, *Mama*.'

'Now stop that, Eugenia. It can't be helped.'

I sink down on the settee and Daddy puts his arm round me. I lean against him and cry.

Christmas Eve is depressing and rainy and warm. Every half hour, Daddy comes out of Mother's room and looks out the front window and asks, 'Is he here?' even if no one's listening. Carlton Jr is driving home tonight from LSU law school and we'll both be relieved to see him. All day, Mother has been vomiting and retching.

'Charlotte, you need to be in the hospital,' Doctor Neal said that afternoon. I don't know how many times he's said that in the past week.

'At least let me get the nurse out here to stay with you.'

'Charles Neal,' Mother said, not even raising her head from the mattress, 'I am not spending my final days in a hospital, nor will I turn my own house into one.'

At six o'clock that night, Carlton finally pulls up, comes in the house.

'Hey there, Skeeter.' He hugs me to him. He is rumpled from the car drive, handsome in his college cable-knit sweater.

Mother sits up when she sees him, holds her thin arms out. 'Oh, Carlton, you're home,' she says.

Carlton stops still. Then he bends down and hugs her, very gently. He glances back at me and I can see the shock on his face. I turn away. I cover my mouth so I don't cry, because I won't be able to quit. Carlton's look tells me more than I want to know.

When Stuart drops by on Christmas Day, I don't stop him when he tries to kiss me. But I tell him, 'I'm only letting you because my mother is dying.'

I've heard nothing from Miss Stein. When the club reopens the first week of January, I put my tennis skirt on and grab my racket. I walk through the snack bar, ignoring Patsy Joiner, my old tennis partner who dumped me, and three other girls, all smoking at the black iron tables. I'll be skipping the League meeting tonight, and for ever, for that matter. I gave in and sent a letter three days ago with my resignation.

I slam the tennis ball into the backboard, trying my best not to think about anything. Lately I've found myself praying, when I've never been a very religious person. I find myself whispering long, never-ending sentences to God, begging for Mother to feel some relief, pleading for good news about the book, sometimes even asking for some hint of what to do about Stuart.

When I get home from the club, Doctor Neal pulls up behind me in his car. I take him back to Mother's room, where Daddy's waiting, and they close the door behind them. Mother's gone four days now without vomiting. She's eating her oatmeal every day, even asked for more.

'I've seen this before, Eugenia,' Doctor Neal tells me. 'Sometimes people get a burst of strength. It's a gift from God, I guess. So they can go on and finish their business. But that's all it is, honey. Don't expect anything more.'

On the first Friday of 1964, I can't wait any longer. I stretch the phone into the pantry.

'Elaine Stein's office.'

'Hello, it's Eugenia Phelan, calling long-distance. Is she available?'

The phone goes silent, and a minute or so later she comes back.

'I can confirm that we did receive your package during the holidays. Someone from our office will notify you after Missus Stein has made her decision. Thank you for calling.'

Stuart and I have been seeing each other once a week now. We went to a movie after Christmas and once to dinner in town, but usually he comes out to the house because I don't want to leave Mother. He is hesitant around me, kind of respectfully shy.

'Listen,' Stuart says on one visit. 'I didn't want to bring this up before but . . . I know what people are saying in town. About you. And I don't care. I just want you to know that.'

My first thought is *the book*. He's heard something. My entire body goes tense. 'What did you hear?'

'You know. About that trick you played on Hilly.'

I relax some, but not completely. I've never talked to anyone about this except Hilly herself.

'And I could see how people would take it, think you're some kind of crazy liberal, involved in all that mess.'

I study my hands, still wary of what he might have heard, and a little irritated too. 'How do you know,' I ask, 'what I'm involved in?'

'Because I know you, Skeeter,' he says softly. 'You're too smart to get mixed up in anything like that. And I told them, too.'

On Saturday evening, Stuart takes me to the Robert E Lee for dinner. 'Here's to new beginnings,' he says and raises his bourbon.

I nod, sort of wanting to tell him that all beginnings are new. Instead, I smile and toast with my second glass of wine. I've never really liked alcohol, until today.

By the time we make it back to Longleaf, it's eleven o'clock. The lights in my parents' bedroom are off, so we sit on the sofa.

I rub my eyes and yawn. When I open them, he's holding a ring between his fingers.

'Oh . . . Jesus.'

'I was going to do it at the restaurant but . . .' He grins. 'Here is better.'

I touch the ring. It is cold and gorgeous. Three rubies are set on each side of the diamond. I am smiling and about to cry at the same time.

'I have to tell you something, Stuart,' I blurt out. 'Do you promise you won't tell anyone?'

He stares at me and laughs. 'Hang on, did you say yes?'

'Yes, but . . .' I have to know something first. 'Can I just have your word?'

He sighs, looks disappointed that I'm ruining his moment. 'Sure, you have my word.'

I do my best to explain. Looking into his eyes, I spread out the facts and what details I can safely share about the book and what I've been doing over the past year. I leave out everyone's name and I pause at the implication of this, knowing it's not good. Even though he is asking to be my husband, I don't know him enough to trust him completely.

Then I tell him that the manuscript has been sent to New York. That if they decide to publish it, it would come out in, my guess is, eight months, maybe sooner. Right around the time, I think to myself, an engagement would turn into a wedding.

'It's been written anonymously,' I say, 'but with Hilly around, there's still a good chance people will know it was me.'

But he's not nodding his head or pushing my hair behind my ear, and his grandmother's ring is sitting on Mother's velvet sofa like some ridiculous metaphor. We are both silent. His eyes don't even meet mine. They stay a steady two inches to the right of my face.

'Why would you want to go stirring up trouble?'

'I'm not making trouble, Stuart. The trouble is already here.'

But clearly, this isn't the answer he is looking for. 'I don't know you.'

I look down, remembering that I'd thought this same thing.

'I don't . . . think I can marry somebody I don't know,' Stuart says.

'I had to tell you,' I say, more to myself than to him. 'You needed to know.'

He studies me for a few moments. 'You have my word. I won't tell anyone,' he says, and I believe him. He stands and gives me one last, lost look. And then he picks up the ring and walks out.

That night I wander from room to room, dry-mouthed, cold. At midnight, I hear Mother's voice calling from her bedroom.

'Eugenia? Is that you?'

I walk down the hall. The door is half open and Mother is sitting up in her starchy white nightgown. Her hair is down round her shoulders. I am struck by how beautiful she looks.

'I have something to tell you,' I say.

'Oh? Well, go on then.'

'Stuart proposed,' I say, faking a smile. Then I panic, knowing she'll ask to see the ring.

'I know,' she says. 'He came by here two weeks ago and asked Carlton and me for your hand.'

Two weeks ago? Of course Mother was the first to know something so important. I'm happy she's had so long to enjoy the news.

The date is Friday, January 18, 1964. 'Harper and Row,' I announce, 'wants to publish it.'

'You kidding me,' says Minny.

Aibileen lets out a whoop like I've never heard come out of her before. 'Law, I can't believe it!' she hollers, and then we are hugging, Aibileen and me, then Minny and Aibileen. Minny looks in my general direction.

'Listen,' I tell them, 'she said not to get too excited. That the number of copies they're going to put out is going to be very, *very* small. And she said it's one of the smallest advances she's ever seen . . . Eight hundred dollars,' I say. 'Divided thirteen ways.'

Aibileen splits open in laughter. I can't help but laugh with her. But it makes no sense. A few thousand copies and $61.50 a person?

Tears run down Aibileen's face and finally she just lays her head on the table. 'I don't know why I'm laughing. It just seem so funny all a sudden.'

Minny rolls her eyes at us. 'I *knew* y'all crazy. Both a you.'

'She said it'll be at least six months until it comes out. Sometime in August.'

'So six months from now, we'll finally know what's gone happen,' Minny says, 'good, bad, or nothing.'

AIBILEEN

THE HEAT DONE SEEPED into everything. For a week now it's been a hundred degrees and ninety-nine per cent humidity. Get any wetter, we be swimming.

We been living in anticipation. Me, Minny, Miss Skeeter, all the maids with stories in the book. Feel like we been waiting for some invisible pot a water to boil for the past seven months.

'You want you a snack, Baby Girl?' I ask when she get home from school on Thursday. Oh, she a big girl! Already four years old. She tall for her age—most folks think she five or six. Skinny as her mama is, Mae Mobley still chubby. And her hair ain't looking too good. She decide to give herself a haircut with her construction scissors and you know how that turn out.

I fix her a little something low-calorie to eat cause that's all Miss Leefolt let me give her. Crackers and tuna fish or jelly with no cream.

'What you learn today?' I ask even though she ain't in real school, just the pretend kind. Today when I ask what she learn, Mae Mobley just say, 'Nothing,' and stick her lip out.

'How you like your teacher?' I ask her.

'She's pretty,' she say.

'Good,' I say. 'You pretty too.'

'How come you're coloured, Aibileen?'

Now I've gotten this question a few times from my other white kids. I used to just laugh, but I want to get this right with her. ''Cause God made me coloured,' I say. 'And there ain't another reason in the world.'

'Miss Taylor says kids that are coloured can't go to my school cause they're not smart enough.'

I come round the counter then. Lift her chin up and smooth back her funny-looking hair. 'You think I'm dumb?'

'No,' she whispers hard, like she means it so much. She look sorry she said it.

'What that tell you about Miss Taylor, then?'

She blink, like she listening good.

'Means Miss Taylor ain't right all the time,' I say.

She hug me round my neck, say, 'You're righter than Miss Taylor.' I tear up then. My cup is spilling over. Those is new words to me.

At four o'clock that afternoon, I walk as fast as I can from the bus stop to the Church of the Lamb. I wait inside, watch out the window. After ten minutes a trying to breathe and drumming my fingers on the sill, I see the car pull up. Miss Skeeter pull a big brown box out the back seat, then carries it up to the church door, like she dropping off old clothes. She stop a second and look at the door, but then she get in her car and drive away.

Soon as she gone, I run out and tote the box inside and grab out a copy and I just stare. I don't even try not to cry. Be the prettiest book I ever seen. The cover is a pale blue, colour a the sky. And a big white bird—a peace dove—spreads its wings from end to end. The title *Help* is written across the front in black letters, in a bold fashion.

Tomorrow, I'm on take early copies to all the women whose stories we put in. Miss Skeeter gone carry a copy up to the State Pen to Yule May. In a way, she's the reason the other maids even agreed to help. I carry that big box home and take out one copy and put the box under my bed. Then I run over to Minny's house.

'Copies gone show up in the bookstores and the libraries tomorrow. Twenty-five hundred in Mississippi, other half all over the United States.' That's a lot more than what Miss Stein told us before, but since the freedom rides started and them civil rights workers disappeared in that station wagon here in Mississippi, she say folks is paying more attention to our state.

'How many gone to the white Jackson library?' Minny ask. 'Zero?'

I shake my head with a smile. 'Three copies. Miss Skeeter told me on the phone this morning.'

Even Minny look stunned. Just two months ago the white library started letting coloured people in. I been in twice myself.

Minny open the book and she start reading it right there. I set there awhile. Time to time she grin. Few times she laugh. And more an once she growl. I don't ask what for. I leave her to it and head home. After I write all my prayers, I go to bed with that book setting on the pillow next to me.

By Wednesday, they still ain't even a ripple in the water. Not one person's bought a copy in the white bookstore. The Farish Street store say they done sold about a dozen, which is good. Might a just been the other maids, though, buying for they friends.

On Thursday, day seven, before I even left for work, my phone ring.

'I've got news,' Miss Skeeter whisper. I reckon she must be locked up in the pantry again.

'What happen?'

'Missus Stein called and said we're going to be on the Dennis James show.'

'*People Will Talk*? The tee-vee show?'

'She said it'll be on Channel Three next Thursday at one o'clock.'

On Friday night, a week after the book come out, I get ready to go to the church. Deacon Thomas call me this morning and ask would I come to a special meeting they having, but when I ask what about, he get all in a hurry and say he got to go.

Soon as Minny and me step in the church entrance, one a the Brown brothers slip behind us and he lock the door. I'm about to ask why, would a got scared if I had the time, but then the thirty-odd peoples in the room start clapping. Minny and me start clapping with em. Figure somebody got into college or something.

'Who we clapping for?' I ask Rachel Johnson. She the Reverend wife. She laugh and it get quiet. Rachel lean in to me.

'Honey, we clapping for you.' Then she reach down and pull a copy a the book out a her bag. I look around and now everbody got a copy in they hands. All the important officers and church deacons are there.

Reverend Johnson come up to me then. 'Aibileen, this is an important time for you and our church. We want you to know, for your safety, this will be the only time the church recognises you for your achievement. I know a lot of folks helped with this book, but I heard it couldn't have been done without you.'

I look over and Minny's smiling, and I know she in on it too.

He hand me the book. 'We know you couldn't put your name in it, so we all signed for you.' I open up the front cover and there they is, not thirty or forty names, but hundreds, maybe five hundred, in the front pages, the back pages, along the rim a the inside pages. All the peoples in my church and folks from other churches too. Oh, I just break down then. All that doing and trying and hoping all come out at once.

'There may be some hard times ahead,' Reverend Johnson say to me. 'If it comes to that, the church will help you in every way.'

Then the reverend hands me a box, wrapped in white paper, tied with light blue ribbon, same colours as the book. He lays his hand on it as a blessing. 'This one, this is for the white lady. You tell her we love her, like she's our own family.'

On Thursday, I wake up with the sun and go to work early. Today's a big day. I get my kitchen work done fast. One a clock come and I make sure I got my ironing all set up in front a Miss Leefolt's tee-vee, tuned to Channel Three.

In the box pops Dennis James. He start telling us what we gone discuss today. His black hair is sprayed down so heavy, it don't even move. He is the fastest-talking Southern man I ever heard. Then, at 1.22 p.m., a woman come set next to him by the name a Joline French. She say she the local book reviewer.

That very second, Miss Leefolt walk in the house. She all dressed up in her League outfit and her noisy high heels and she head straight for the living room.

'I am so glad that heat wave is over I could jump for joy,' she say.

Mister Dennis chatting bout some book called *Little Big Man*. I try to agree with her but I feel real stiff in the face all of a sudden. 'I'll—I'll just turn this thing off.'

'No, keep it on!' say Miss Leefolt. 'That's Joline French on the television set! I better call Hilly and tell her.'

She clomp to the kitchen and get on the phone with Miss Hilly's third maid in a month. Ernestine ain't got but one arm. Miss Hilly's pickings getting slim.

'Ernestine, this is Miss Elizabeth . . . Oh, she's not? Well, you tell her the minute she walks in that our sorority sister is on the television set.'

Miss Leefolt rush back in the living room and set on the sofa, but it's a commercial on. I get to breathing hard. What is she doing? We ain't never watched the tee-vee together before.

All a sudden there be Mister Dennis with my book in his hand! He holding it up and poking his finger at the word *Anonymous*. For two seconds I'm more proud than I is scared. I want to yell—*That's my book on the tee-vee!* '. . . called *Help* with testimonies from some of Mississippi's very own housekeepers—'

'Oh, I wish Hilly was home! Who can I call? Look at those cute shoes she's got on, I bet she got those at The Papagallo Shoppe.'

Please shut up! I reach down and turn it up a little, but then I wish I hadn't. What if they talk about her? Would Miss Leefolt even recognise her own life?

'. . . read it last night and now my wife is reading it . . .' Mister Dennis talking like a auction man, eyebrows going up and down, pointing at our book. '. . . and it is truly touching. Enlightening, I'd say, and they used the made-up town of Niceville, Mississippi, but who knows?' He whisper real loud, 'It could be Jackson!'

I freeze, feel a tingle on my neck. Mister Dennis be laughing and talking, but that sorority sister, Miss Joline, got a face on red as a stop sign.

'—a disgrace to the South! A disgrace to the good Southern women who've spent their lives taking care of their help. '

'Why is she frowning like that on tee-vee?' Miss Leefolt whine at the box. 'Joline!' She lean forward and *tap-tap-tap* her finger on Miss Joline's forehead. 'Don't frown! You don't look cute that way!'

'Joline, did you read that ending? About the pie? If my maid, Bessie

Mae, is out there listening, Bessie Mae, I have a new respect for what you do every day. And I'll pass on the chocolate pie from now on!'

But Miss Joline holding up the book like she want to burn it. 'Do not buy this book! Ladies of Jackson, do not support this slander with your husbands' hard-earned—'

'Huh?' Miss Leefolt ask Mister Dennis. And then poof—we on to a Tide commercial.

'What were they talking about?' Miss Leefolt ask me.

I don't answer. My heart's pounding.

'My friend Joline had a book in her hand.'

'Yes, ma'am.'

'What was it called? *Help* or something like that?'

I press the iron point down in the collar a Mister Raleigh's shirt. I got to call Minny, Miss Skeeter, find out if they heard this. But Miss Leefolt standing there waiting for my answer and I know she ain't gone let up.

'Did I hear them say it was about Jackson?' she say.

I keep right on staring at my iron.

'I think they said Jackson. But why don't they want us to buy it?'

A second later there's Dennis James again holding up the book and Miss Joline's still all red in the face. 'That's all for today,' he say, 'but y'all be sure and pick up your copy of *Little Big Man* and *Help* from our sponsor, the State Street Bookstore. And see for yourself, is it or is it not about Jackson?' And then the music come on and he holler, 'Good day, Mississippi!'

Miss Leefolt look at me and say, 'See that? I told you they said it was about Jackson!' and five minutes later, she off to the bookstore to buy herself a copy a what I done wrote about her.

MINNY

I'VE A MIND TO CALL THAT Dennis James on the phone and say, *Who do you think you are, spreading lies like that?* You can't tell the whole metro area our book is about Jackson!

I rush to the kitchen and call Aibileen, but after two tries the line's still busy. I hang up. I wonder for the millionth time what's going to happen when Miss Hilly reads the last chapter. She better get to work soon, telling people it's not our town.

The phone rings and I snatch it up.

'Oh, Minny,' Aibileen says. 'They figure out the town, ain't no time fore they figure out the *people.'*

'He a fool is what he is.'

'I just talk to Louvenia,' Aibileen whisper. 'Miss Lou Anne just come home with a copy for herself and a copy for her best friend, Hilly Holbrook.'

Here we go.

Next morning, I pull up to the house. The first thing I see is Mister Johnny's truck's still home. I wait in my car. He's never once been here when I come in.

I step into the kitchen. I stand in the middle and look. Somebody already made coffee. I hear a man's voice in the dining room. Something's going on here.

I lean close to the door and hear Mister Johnny, home on a weekday at 8.30 in the morning, and a voice in my head says run right back out the door. Miss Hilly called and told him I was a thief. He found out about the pie. He knows about the book. 'Minny?' I hear Miss Celia call.

Real careful, I push the swinging door, peek out. There's Miss Celia setting at the head of the table with Mister Johnny setting next to her. They both look up at me.

'I told him about the baby,' Miss Celia whispers. 'All the babies.'

'Minny, I would've lost her if it hadn't of been for you,' he says, grabbing hold of my hands. 'Thank God you were here.'

I look over at Miss Celia and she looks dead in the eyes. I already know that doctor told her that there won't ever be any babies born alive. Mister Johnny squeezes my hands, then he goes to her. He gets down on his kneecaps and lays his head down in her lap. She smoothes his hair over and over.

'Don't leave. Don't ever leave me, Celia,' he cries.

'Tell her, Johnny. Tell Minny what you said to me.'

Mister Johnny lifts his head. His hair's all mussed and he looks up at me. 'You'll always have a job here with us, Minny. For the rest of your life, if you want.'

'Thank you, sir,' I say and I mean it. Those are the best words I could hear today.

I reach for the door, but Miss Celia says, real soft, 'Stay in here awhile. Will you, Minny?'

So I lean my hand on the sideboard and I wonder how it is that I have so much when she doesn't have any. He's crying. She's crying. We are three fools in the dining room crying.

I keep dropping things, broke my last measuring cup tonight and Leroy's eyeing me like he knows. Right now he's drinking coffee at the table and the kids are all over the kitchen doing their homework.

I jump when I see Aibileen standing at the screen door. She puts her finger to her lips and nods to me. I disappear out the screen door. Aibileen's standing on the side of the house in her white uniform.

'What happen?' I ask.

'Ernestine call and say Miss Hilly's talking all over town about who's in the book. She telling white ladies to fire they maids and she ain't even guessing the right ones!' Aibileen looks so upset, she's shaking.

'Miss Hilly told Miss Lou Anne, "Your Louvenia's in here. I know she is and you need to fire her. You ought to send that Nigra to jail."'

'But Louvenia didn't say a single bad thing about Miss Lou Anne!' I say. 'And she got Robert to take care of! What Miss Lou Anne say?'

Aibileen bites her lip. She shakes her head and the tears come down her face. 'She say . . . she gone think about it.'

'Which one? The firing or the jail?'

Aibileen shrug. 'Both, I reckon.'

'Jesus Christ,' I say, wanting to kick something. Some*body*.

Aibileen's eyes jerk up to the door and there's Leroy, watching us from behind the screen. He stands there, quiet, until I tell Aibileen goodbye and come back inside.

'What's the big secret, Minny?'

I can feel him watching me, feel his liquor breath on my shoulder. I don't move.

'You know I'll find out,' he hisses. 'I always do.'

People probably assume I don't care if he finds out—oh, I know what people think. They think big strong Minny, she sure can stand up for herself. But they don't know what a pathetic mess I turn into when Leroy's beating on me. I'm afraid to hit back. I'm afraid he'll leave me if I do. How can I love a man who beats me raw? One time I asked him, 'Why? Why are you hitting me?' He leaned down and looked me right in the face.

'If I didn't hit you, Minny, who *knows* what you become.'

Who *knows* what I could become, if Leroy would stop hitting me.

MISS SKEETER

MY EYES POP OPEN. My chest is pumping. I'm sweating. What woke me? I get out of bed and listen. It didn't sound like Mother. It was too high-pitched. It was a scream, like material ripping into two shredded pieces.

I press my hand to my heart. It's still pounding. Nothing is going as planned. People know the book is about Jackson. A maid named Annabelle was fired, white women are whispering about Aibileen and Louvenia and who knows who else.

What if the book was a horrible mistake?

I take a deep, painful breath. I try to think of the future, not the present. A month ago, I mailed out fifteen résumés to Dallas, Memphis, Birmingham, and five other cities, and once again, New York. Now, even if I did get a job offer in a big city, I can't abandon Aibileen in the middle of this mess.

I lie down and watch the first rays of sun coming through the window. I shiver. That ripping scream, I realise, was *me*.

I'm standing in Brent's Drug Store while Mr Roberts works on a prescription. Mother says she doesn't need the medicine anymore. I'm just grateful she's better. If my fifteen-second engagement to Stuart is what spurred Mother's will to live, the fact that I'm single again fuelled her strength even more. She was clearly disappointed by our breakup, but then bounced back superbly.

The front bell tinkles. I look over and in walk Elizabeth and Lou Anne Templeton. I slip back into beauty creams, hoping they don't see me. But then I peek over the shelves to look. They're heading for the lunch counter, huddled together like schoolgirls. Lou Anne's wearing her usual long sleeves in the summer heat and her constant smile. I wonder if she knows she's in the book.

Elizabeth's got her hair pouffed up in front and she's covered the back in a scarf, the yellow scarf I gave her for her twenty-third birthday. I stand there a minute, letting myself feel how strange this all is, watching them, knowing what I know. She has read up to chapter ten, Aibileen told me last night, and still doesn't have the faintest idea that she's reading about herself and her friends.

'Skeeter?' Mr Roberts calls out. 'Your mama's medicine's ready.'

I walk to the front of the store, and have to pass Elizabeth and Lou Anne. They keep their backs to me, but I can see their eyes in the mirror, following me. I pay for the medicine and work my way back through the aisles. As I try to escape along the far side of the store, Lou Anne Templeton steps from behind the hairbrush rack.

'Skeeter,' she says. 'You have a minute?'

I stand there blinking, surprised. 'Um, sure,' I say, wary.

Lou Anne glances out of the window and I see Elizabeth heading for her car. Lou Anne motions me closer.

'I know we haven't talked in a while but,' she lowers her voice, 'I just thought you should know what Hilly's saying. She's saying you wrote that book . . . about the maids.'

'I heard that book was written anonymously,' is my quick answer, not sure I even want to act like I've read it. Even though everyone in town's reading it. All three bookstores are sold out and the library has a two-month waiting list.

She holds up her palm, like a stop sign. 'I don't want to know if it's true. But Hilly . . .' She steps closer to me. 'Hilly Holbrook called me the other day and told me to fire my maid Louvenia.' Her jaw tightens and she shakes her head.

Please. I hold my breath. *Please don't say you fired her.*

'Skeeter, Louvenia . . .' Lou Anne looks me in the eye, says, 'she's the only reason I can get out of bed sometimes.'

I don't say anything. Maybe this is a trap Hilly's set.

'And I'm sure you think I'm just some dumb girl . . . that I agree with everything Hilly says.' Tears come up in her eyes. Her lips are trembling. 'The doctors want me to go up to Memphis for . . . *shock treatment . . .*' She covers her face but a tear slips through her fingers. 'For the depression and the . . . the tries,' she whispers.

I look down at her long sleeves and I wonder if that's what she's been hiding. I hope I'm not right, but I shudder.

'Skeeter, Louvenia is the bravest person I know. Even with all her own troubles, she sits down and talks to me. She helps me get through my days. When I read what she wrote about me, about helping her with her grandson, I've never been so grateful in my life.

'I just want you to know, I will never fire Louvenia. If Hilly Holbrook ever says that to me again, I will tell her to her face she deserved that pie and more.'

'How do—what makes you think that was Hilly?' *Our protection—our insurance, it's gone if the pie secret is out.*

'Maybe it was and maybe it wasn't. But that's the talk.' Lou Anne shakes her head. 'Then this morning I heard Hilly's telling everybody the book's not even about Jackson. Who knows why.'

I suck in a breath, whisper, 'Thank God.'

She turns for the door, but looks back at me as she opens it. 'And I'll tell you one more thing. Hilly Holbrook's not getting my vote for League president in January. Or ever again, for that matter.'

On that, she walks out, the bell tinkling behind her.

I linger at the window and watch Lou Anne slip away, thinking, There is so much you don't know about a person. I wonder if I could've made her days a little bit easier, if I'd tried. If I'd treated her a little nicer. Wasn't that the point of the book? For women to realise: *We are just two people. Not that much separates us. Not nearly as much as I'd thought.*

But Lou Anne, she understood the point of the book before she ever read it. The one who was missing the point this time was me.

It's Wednesday. Tomorrow I turn in my Miss Myrna column that I wrote six weeks ago. I've stockpiled two dozen of them, because I have nothing else to do. After that, there's nothing left to think about.

I slip on my huaraches and walk out into the warm night. The moon is full and there's just enough light. I forgot to check the mailbox this afternoon and I'm the only one who ever does it. I open it and there's one single letter. It's from Harper & Row, so it must be from Missus Stein. I'm surprised she would send something here since I have all the book contracts sent to a box at the post office, just in case. It's too dark to read, so I tuck it in the back pocket of my blue jeans.

Instead of walking up the lane, I cut through the orchard, feeling the soft grass under my feet, stepping round the early pears that have fallen. It is September again and I'm still here. Even Stuart has moved on. He has moved his oil company down to New Orleans.

I hear the rumble of gravel. I can't see the car driving up the lane, though, because for some reason, the headlights aren't on.

I watch Hilly park the Oldsmobile in front of the house and turn off the engine, but she stays inside. She's leaning over her steering wheel, like she's trying to see who's home. What the hell does she want?

I approach the car quietly. She lights a cigarette, throws the match out the open window into our drive.

'Waiting for someone?' I say.

Hilly jumps and drops her cigarette into the gravel. She scrambles out of the car and slams the door closed, backing away from me.

'Don't you get an inch closer,' she says.

So I stop where I am and just look at her. Who *wouldn't* look at her? Her black hair is a mess. Half her blouse is untucked, her fat stretching the buttons, and I can see she's gained more weight. And there's a sore in the corner of her mouth, scabby and hot red. I haven't seen Hilly with one of those since Johnny broke up with her in college.

'Hilly, why are you here?'

'To tell you I've contacted my lawyer, who happens to be the number one expert on the libel laws in Mississippi, and you are in big trouble, missy. You're going to jail, you know that?'

'You can't prove anything, Hilly.' I've had this discussion with the legal department of Harper & Row.

'Well, I one hundred per cent know you wrote it because there isn't anybody else in town as tacky as you. Taking up with Nigras like that.'

It is truly baffling that we were ever friends. I think about going inside and locking the door. But there's an envelope in her hand, and that makes me nervous.

'I know there's been a lot of talk, Hilly, and a lot of rumours—'

'Oh, that talk doesn't hurt me. Everyone in town knows it's not Jackson. It's some town you made up in that sick little head of yours.'

Hilly waves the envelope at me and it crackles. 'I am here to inform your mother of what you've *done*.'

'You're going to tell my *mother* on me?' I laugh, but the truth is, Mother doesn't know anything about it. And I want to keep it that way. What if it makes her sick again?

'I most certainly am.' Hilly walks up the front steps, head held high.

I follow quickly behind Hilly to the front door. She opens it and walks in like it's her own house.

But then Mother appears. 'Why, *Hilly*,' she says. She is in her bathrobe and her cane wobbles as she walks. 'It's been such a long time, dear.'

Hilly blinks at her several times. I do not know if Hilly is more shocked at how my mother looks, or the other way round. Mother's once thick brown hair is now snow white and thin. The trembling hand on her cane probably looks skeleton-like to someone who hasn't seen her. But worst of all, Mother doesn't have all of her teeth in, only her front ones. The hollows in her cheeks are deep, deathly.

'Missus Phelan, I'm—I'm here to—'

'Hilly, are you ill? You look horrendous,' Mother says.

Hilly licks her lips. 'Well, I—I didn't have time to get fixed up before—'

Mother is shaking her head. 'Hilly, *darling*. No young husband wants to come home and see this. Look at your hair. And that . . .' Mother frowns, peering closer at the cold sore. 'That is not attractive, dear.'

I keep my eye on the letter. Mother points her finger at me. 'I'm calling Fanny Mae's tomorrow and I'm going to make an appointment for the both of you.'

'Missus Phelan, that's not—'

'No need to thank me,' Mother says. 'Now, I'm off to bed,' and Mother hobbles towards her bedroom. 'Not too late, girls.'

Hilly stands there a second, her mouth hanging open. Finally, she goes to the door and flings it open and walks out. The letter is still in her hand.

'You are in a lifetime of trouble, Skeeter,' she hisses at me, her mouth like a fist. 'And those Nigras of yours.'

'Exactly who are you talking about, Hilly?' I say. 'You don't know anything.'

'I don't, do I? That Louvenia? Oh, I've taken care of her. Lou Anne's all set to go on that one. And you tell that Aibileen, the next time she wants to write about my dear friend Elizabeth, uh-huh,' she says, flashing a crude smile.

My nostrils flare. I want to hit her, at the sound of Aibileen's name.

'Let's just say Aibileen ought to've been a little bit smarter and not put in the bit about the L-shaped crack in poor Elizabeth's dining table.'

The goddamn crack. How stupid could I be to let that slip?

'And don't think I've forgotten Minny Jackson. I have some *big* plans for that Nigra.'

'Careful, Hilly,' I say through my teeth. 'Don't give yourself away now.'

Her eyes fly open. 'That was not me WHO ATE THAT PIE!'

She turns and marches to her car. She jerks the door open. 'You tell those Nigras they better watch out for what's coming to them.'

My hand shakes as I dial Aibileen's number. I take the receiver in the pantry and shut the door. The opened letter from Harper & Row is in my other hand. It feels like midnight, but it's only eight thirty.

I blurt it out. 'Hilly came here tonight and she *knows*.'

Then I hear Minny's voice in the background. 'Hilly? What about Miss Hilly?'

'Minny's . . . here with me,' Aibileen says.

'Well, I guess she needs to hear this too,' I say, even though I wish Aibileen could tell her later, without me. As I describe how Hilly showed up here, stormed into the house, I wait while she repeats everything back to Minny. It is worse hearing it in Aibileen's voice.

'It was the crack in Elizabeth's dining-room table . . . that's how Hilly knew for sure.'

'Law, that *crack*. I can't believe I put that in.'

'No, *I* should've caught it. I'm so sorry, Aibileen.'

'You think Miss Hilly gone tell Miss Leefolt I wrote about her?'

'She can't tell her,' Minny hollers. 'Then she admitting it's Jackson.'

I realise how good Minny's plan was. 'I agree,' I say. 'I think Hilly's terrified, Aibileen. She doesn't know *what* to do. She said she was going to tell my *mother* on me.'

Now that the shock of Hilly's words has passed, I almost laugh at this thought. That's the least of our worries.

'I reckon they's nothing we can do but wait, then,' Aibileen says, but she sounds nervous. It's probably not the best time to tell her my other news, but I don't think I can keep myself from it.

'I got a . . . letter today. From Harper and Row,' I say. 'I thought it was from Missus Stein, but it wasn't.'

'What then?'

'It's a job offer at *Harper's Magazine* in New York. As a . . . copy editor's assistant. I'm pretty sure Missus Stein got it for me.'

'That's so good!' Aibileen says, and then, 'Minny, Miss Skeeter got a job offer in New York City!'

'Aibileen, I can't take it. I just wanted to share it with you. I . . .' I'm grateful to at least have Aibileen to tell.

'What you mean, you can't take it? This what you been dreaming of.'

'I can't leave now, right when things are getting bad. I'm not going to leave you in this mess.'

I hear her whisper to Minny, 'She say she ain't gone take it.'

'Miss Skeeter,' Aibileen says back on the phone, 'I don't mean to be rubbing no salt on your wound but—'

I hear muffled words and handling of the receiver and suddenly it's Minny on the phone. 'You listen to me, Miss Skeeter. I'm on take care a Aibileen and she gone take care a me. But you got nothing left here but enemies in the Junior League and a mama that's gone drive you to drink. You done burned ever bridge there is. And you ain't *never* gone get another boyfriend in this town and everbody know it. So don't walk your white butt to New York, *run* it.'

Minny hangs up, and I sit staring at the dead receiver in one hand and the letter in the other. *Really*? I think, actually considering it for the first time. *Can I really do this?*

Minny is right. I have nothing left here except Mother and Daddy and staying here for my parents will surely ruin the relationship we have, but . . .

I lean against the shelves, close my eyes. I'm going. I am going to New York.

AIBILEEN

MISS LEEFOLT'S SILVER SERVICE got funny spots on it today. Must be cause the humidity's so high. I go around the bridge club table, polishing each piece again, making sure they all still there. Mae Mobley's brother, Li'l Man, he's started swiping things, spoons and nickels and hair pins. He stick em in his diaper to hide. Sometimes, changing diapers can be like opening treasure.

The phone ring so I go in the kitchen and answer it.

'Got a little bit a news today,' Minny say on the phone. 'Miss Renfroe say she *know* it was Miss Hilly who ate that pie.' Minny cackle but my heart go ten times faster.

'Law, Miss Hilly gone be here in five minutes. She better put that fire out fast.' It feel crazy that we rooting for her. It's confusing in my mind.

'And Miss Clara, she know about Fanny Amos.'

'She fire her?' Miss Clara put Fanny Amos's boy through college, one a the good stories.

'Nuh-uh. Just sat there with her mouth open and the book in her hand.'

'Thank the Lord. Call me if you hear more,' I say.

A few minutes after we hang up, the doorbell ring and I pretend I don't even hear. I'm so nervous to see Miss Hilly's face after what she said to Miss Skeeter. I can't believe I put in that L-shaped crack. I go out to my bathroom and just set.

When I come back in, I hear all the ladies at the table talking. Miss Hilly's voice is loud. I hold my ear to the kitchen door, dreading going out there.

'—is *not* Jackson. This book is garbage, is what it is. I'll bet the whole thing was made up by some Nigra—'

I hear a chair scrape and I know Miss Leefolt about to come hunting for me. I can't put it off no more.

I open the door with the ice tea pitcher in my hand. Round the table I go, keeping my eyes to my shoes.

'I heard that Betty character might be Charlene,' Miss Jeanie say with big eyes. Next to her, Miss Lou Anne's staring off like she don't care one way or the other. And I can't tell nothing on Miss Leefolt cause she just frowning like usual. But Miss Hilly's face, it's purple as a plum.

'And the maid in chapter four?' Miss Jeanie going on. 'I heard Sissy Tucker saying—'

'The book is *not about Jackson!*' Miss Hilly kind a scream.

I have to sit late that night for Miss Leefolt. While Mae Mobley sleeping, I pull out my prayer book, get started on my list. I'm so glad for Miss Skeeter. She call me this morning and say she took the job. She moving to New York in a week! But Law, I can't stop jumping ever time I hear a noise, thinking maybe Miss Leefolt gone walk in the door and say she know the truth.

By the time I get home, I'm too jumpy to go to bed. I walk through the pitch-black dark to Minny's back door. She setting at her table reading the paper.

I pull out a chair and set down. 'I just want a know what's gone happen,' I say. 'I know I ought a be thankful it ain't all blowed up in my face yet, but this waiting's driving me crazy.'

'It's gone happen. Soon enough,' Minny say, like we talking about the kind a coffee we drink.

'Minny, how can you be so calm?'

She looks at me. 'You know Miss Chotard, who Willie Mae wait on? She ask Willie Mae yesterday if she treats her bad as that awful lady in the book.' Minny kind a snort. 'Willie Mae tell her she got some room to grow but she ain't too bad.'

'She really ask her that?'

'Then Willie Mae tell her what all the other white ladies done to her, the good and the bad, and that white lady listen to her. Willie May say she been there thirty-seven years and it's the first time they ever sat at the same table together.'

Besides Louvenia, this the first good thing we heard. I try to enjoy it. But I snap back to now. 'What about Miss Hilly?'

Minny put her newspaper down. 'Look, Aibileen, I ain't gone lie. I'm scared Leroy gone kill me if he find out. I'm scared Miss Hilly gone set my house on fire. But,' she shake her head, 'I can't explain it. I got this feeling. That maybe things is happening just how they should.'

'Really?'

Minny kind a laugh. 'Lord, I'm starting to sound like you, ain't I? Must be getting old.'

Minny looks back down at her paper, but after a little while I can tell she ain't reading. She just staring at the words, thinking about something else. Somebody's car door slam next door and she jump. And I see it then, the worry she's trying to hide. But why? I wonder. Why she hiding that from me?

The more I look, the more I start to understand what's going on here, what Minny's done. I don't know why I'm just now getting this. Minny made us put the pie story in to protect us. Not to protect herself, but to protect me and the other maids. She knew it would only make it worse for herself with Hilly. But she did it anyway, for everbody else. She don't want anybody to see how scared she is.

I reach over and squeeze her hand. 'You a beautiful person, Minny.'

She roll her eyes and stick her tongue out like I handed her a plate a dog biscuits. 'I knew you was getting senile,' she say.

On Monday morning, I get to work on Miss Hilly's eight-place silver setting that Miss Leefolt borrowed for some big luncheon for her church yesterday. I wash it and spend the next hour polishing it.

When Miss Leefolt come in, she put her bag on the table and tisk. 'Oh, I meant to return that silver this morning but I'm late for my hair appointment. When you're finished polishing, go ahead and walk that silver on over to Hilly's for me. I'll be back after lunch.'

When I'm done, I wrap all a Miss Hilly's silver up in the blue cloth. I go get Li'l Man out a bed. He just woke up from his nap and he blink at me and smile.

'Come on, Li'l Man, let's get you a new diaper.' I put him up on the changing table and take off the wet one and Lord almighty if there ain't three tinker toys and one a Miss Leefolt's bobby pins in there.

'Boy,' I laugh, 'you like Fort Knox.' He grin and laugh. He point at the crib and I go over and poke through the blanket and sho nuff, there's a hair roller, a measuring spoon and a dinner napkin. Law, we gone have to do something about this. But not now. I got to get over to Miss Hilly's.

I lock Li'l Man in the pushchair and we go over to Miss Hilly's house. It's hot and sunny and quiet. We stroll up her drive and Ernestine open the door. She got a skinny little brown nub that poke out the left sleeve. I don't know her well. She go to the Methodist church.

'Hey, Aibileen,' she say.

'Hey, Ernestine, you must a seen me coming,' I say, and I hand her the heavy cloth full a silver. She reaches out with her good hand to take it.

That night, there's a terrible storm. The thunder's booming and I'm at my kitchen table sweating. I'm shaking, trying to write my prayers. It's just too much not knowing and worrying and—

Thunk thunk thunk. Somebody knocking on my front door.

'Who—who is it?' I say. I check that the lock is on.

'It's *me.*'

Law. I let out a breath and open the front door. There's Miss Skeeter, wet and shivering. Her red satchel's under her raincoat.

'I couldn't make it to the back door. The yard's so thick with mud I couldn't get through.'

She barefoot and holding her muddy shoes in her hand. I close the door quick behind her. 'Nobody see you, did they?'

'You can't see a thing out there. I would've called but the phone's out with the storm.'

I know something must a happened, but I'm just so glad to see her face before she leaves for New York. We ain't seen each other in person in six months. I give her a good hug.

'The stores are asking for more books, Aibileen. Missus Stein called this afternoon.' She take my hands. 'They're going to do another print run. Five *thousand* more copies. There'll be more money coming. At least one hundred dollars to each of you.'

I put my hand on my heart. I ain't spent a cent a the first sixty-one dollars and now she telling me they's more?

'And there's something else.' Miss Skeeter look down at the satchel. 'I went to the paper on Friday and quit the Miss Myrna job.' She takes a deep breath. 'And I told Mr Golden, I think the next Miss Myrna should be you.'

'Me?'

'I told him you've been giving me the answers all along. He said he'd think about it and today he called me and said yes, as long as you don't tell anybody and you write the answers like Miss Myrna did.'

She pull a blue-cloth notebook out a her satchel, hand it to me. 'He said he'll pay you the same as me, ten dollars a week.'

Me? Working for the white newspaper? I go to the sofa and open the notebook, see all them letters and articles from past times. Miss Skeeter set beside me.

'Thank you, Miss Skeeter. For this, for *everthing*.'

She smile, take a deep breath like she fighting back tears.

'I can't believe you gone be a New Yorker tomorrow,' I say.

'Actually, I'm going to go to Chicago first. Only for one night. I want to see Constantine, her grave. It's right outside of town. Then I'll go to New York the next morning.'

'You tell Constantine Aibileen say hello.'

We set there a second, listening to the storm. I think about the first time Miss Skeeter came over to my house, how awkward we was. Now I feel like we family.

'Are you scared, Aibileen?' she asks. 'Of what might happen?'

I turn so she can't see my eyes. 'I'm all right.'

'If something happens to you . . . how am I going to live with that, knowing it was because of me?' She presses her hand over her eyes, like she don't want to see what's gone happen.

I go to my bedroom and bring out the package from Reverend Johnson. She take off the paper and stare at the book, all the names signed in it. 'I was gone send it to you in New York, but I think you need to have it now.'

'I don't . . . understand,' she say. 'This is for me?'

'Yes ma'am.' Then I pass on the reverend's message, that she is part of our family. 'You need to remember, ever one a these signatures means it was worth it.' She read the thank-yous, the little things they wrote, run her fingers over the ink. Tears fill up her eyes.

'I reckon Constantine would a been real proud a you.'

Miss Skeeter smile and I see how *young* she is. After all we written and the hours we spent tired and worried, I ain't seen the girl she still is in a long, long time.

'Are you sure it's all right? If I leave you, with everything so . . .'

'Go to New York, Miss Skeeter. Go find your life.'

That night I lay in bed thinking. I am so happy for Miss Skeeter. Part a me wishes I could have a new start too. The cleaning article, that's new. But I'm not young. My life's about done.

I get a few hours' sleep before dawn. I put on my clean uniform I washed in the tub last night. In the kitchen, I drink a long, cool glass a water, turn off the light and head for the door. My phone ring.

I pick up and I hear *wailing*. 'Minny? That you? What—'

'They fired Leroy last night! And when Leroy ask why, his boss say Mister William *Holbrook* told him to do it. Holbrook told him it's Leroy's nigger *wife* the reason and Leroy come home and try to kill me with his bare hands!' Minny panting and heaving. 'He throw the kids in the yard and lock me in the bathroom and say he gone light the house on fire with me locked inside!'

Law, it's *happening*. I cover my mouth, feel myself falling down that black hole we dug for ourselves. All these weeks a hearing Minny sound so confident and now . . .

'Where you now, Minny, where the kids?'

'The gas station, I run here in my bare feet! The kids run next door . . .' She panting and hiccupping and growling. 'My sister Octavia coming to get us. Say she gone drive fast as she can. Just stay on the phone with me till she get here.'

'Is you OK? You hurt?'

'I can't take this no more, Aibileen. I can't do this—' She break down crying into the phone.

It's the first time I ever heard Minny say that. I take a deep breath, knowing what I need to do. The words is so clear in my head and *right now* is my only chance for her to really hear me, standing barefoot and rock bottom on the gas station phone. 'Minny, listen to me. You never gone lose your job with Miss Celia. Mister Johnny told you hisself. And they's more money coming from the book. Minny, hear me when I say, *You don't have to get hit by Leroy no more.*'

She take a deep, shaky breath. She say, 'I hear what you saying, Aibileen. We gone go stay with Octavia till we find a place a our own.'

I let out a breath.

'She here,' she say. 'I'll call you tonight.'

When I get to Miss Leefolt's, the house is real quiet. I reckon Li'l Man still sleeping. Mae Mobley already gone to school. I put the coffee on and say a prayer for Minny.

I fix a bottle a milk for Li'l Man and take a deep breath. I feel like my day's already done and it's only eight o'clock in the morning. But I still ain't tired. I don't know why. I push open the swinging door into the dining room. And there be Miss Leefolt and Miss Hilly setting down at the dining-room table on the same side, looking at me.

For a second, I stand there, gripping the bottle a milk. 'G'morning,' I say and start to walk to the back.

'Ross is still sleeping,' Miss Hilly say. 'No need to go back there.'

I stop where I am and look at Miss Leefolt, but she staring at the funny L-shaped crack in her dining-room table.

'Aibileen,' Miss Hilly says and she lick her lips. 'When you returned my silver yesterday, there were three pieces missing. One silver fork and two silver spoons.'

I suck in a breath. 'Lemme—lemme go look in the kitchen, maybe I left some behind.' I look at Miss Leefolt to see if that's what she want me to do, but she keep her eyes on the crack.

'You know as well as I do that silver's not in the kitchen, Aibileen,' Miss Hilly say.

'Miss Leefolt, you checked in Ross's bed? He been sneaking things and sticking em—'

Miss Hilly scoff real loud. 'Do you hear her, Elizabeth? She's trying to blame it on a toddler.'

My mind's racing, I'm trying to remember if I counted the silver before I put it back in the felt. I think I did. I always do. Law, tell me she ain't saying what I think she saying—

'Miss Leefolt, did you already check the kitchen? Or the silver closet? Miss Leefolt?'

But she still won't look at me and I don't know what to do. I don't know, yet, how bad this is. Maybe this ain't about silver, maybe this is really about Miss Leefolt and *chapter two* . . .

'Aibileen,' Miss Hilly say, 'you can return those pieces to me by today, or else Elizabeth is going to press charges.'

Miss Leefolt look at Miss Hilly and suck in a breath, like she surprised. And I wonder whose idea this whole thing is, both of em or just Miss Hilly's?

'I ain't stole no silver service, Miss Leefolt,' I say and just the words make me want a run.

Miss Leefolt whisper, 'She says she doesn't have them, Hilly.'

Miss Hilly don't even act like she heard. She raise her eyebrows at me and say, 'Then it behooves me to inform you that you are fired, Aibileen.' Miss Hilly sniff. 'I'll be calling the police.'

'*Maa-maaaa!*' Li'l Man holler from his crib in the back. Miss Leefolt look behind her, then at Hilly, like she ain't sure what to do. '*Aaai-beee,*' Li'l Man call, starting to cry.

'Aai-bee,' call another small voice and I realise *Mae Mobley's home.* She must not've gone to school today. I press on my chest. *Lord, please don't let her hear what Miss Hilly saying about me.* Down the hall, the door opens and Mae Mobley walks out. She blinks at us and coughs.

'Aibee, my froat hurts.'

'I—I be right there, baby.'

Mae Mobley coughs again and it sounds bad, like a dog barking, and I start for the hall, but Miss Hilly say, 'Aibileen, you stay where you are, Elizabeth can take care of her kids.'

Miss Leefolt look at Hilly like, *Do I have to?* But then she get up and trudge down the hall. She take Mae Mobley into the bedroom and shut the door. It's just two of us left now, me and Miss Hilly.

Miss Hilly lean back in her chair, say, 'I won't tolerate liars.'

My head swimming. 'I didn't steal no silver, Miss Hilly.'

'I'm not talking about silver,' she say, leaning forward. She hissing in a whisper so Miss Leefolt don't hear her. 'I'm talking about those things you wrote about Elizabeth. She has no idea chapter two is about her and I am too good a friend to tell her.

'And your friend, Minny? She's got a nice surprise coming to her. I'm calling Johnny Foote and telling him he needs to fire her right now.'

The room getting blurry. I'm shaking my head and my fists is clenching tighter.

'Miss *Hilly*.' I say it loud and clear. 'I know something about you and don't you forget that.'

She narrow her eyes at me. But she don't say nothing. She fish her tongue out and touch that sore with it. Then she drop her eyes.

Before she can say anything else, the door flies open down the hall. Mae Mobley runs out in her nightie and she stop in front a me. She hiccupping and crying and her little nose is red as a rose. Her mama must a told her I'm leaving.

Baby Girl grab the skirt a my uniform and don't let go. I touch my hand to her forehead and she burning with fever.

'Baby, you need to get back in the bed.'

'*Noooo!*' she bawls. '*Don't gooo, Aibee!*'

Miss Leefolt come out a the bedroom, frowning, holding Li'l Man.

'Aibee!' he call out, grinning.

'Hey . . . Li'l Man,' I whisper. I'm so glad he don't understand what's going on. 'Miss Leefolt, lemme take her in the kitchen and give her some medicine. Her fever is real high.'

Miss Leefolt glance at Miss Hilly, but she just setting there with her arms crossed. 'All right, go on,' Miss Leefolt say.

I take Baby Girl's hot little hand and lead her into the kitchen. She bark out that scary cough again and I get the baby aspirin and the cough syrup. Just being in here with me, she calmed down some, but tears is still running down her face.

I put her up on the counter and crush up a little pink pill, mix it with some applesauce and feed her the spoonful. She swallow it down and I know it hurts her. I smooth her hair back. That clump a bangs she cut off with her construction scissors is growing back sticking straight out. Miss Leefolt can't hardly look at her lately.

'Please don't leave, Aibee,' she say, starting to cry again.

'I got to, baby. I am so sorry.' And that's when I start to cry. I don't want to, it's just gone make it worse for her, but I can't stop.

'Why? Why don't you want to see me anymore? Are you going to take care of another little girl?' Her forehead is all wrinkled up, just like when her mama fuss at her.

I take her face in my hands, feeling the scary heat coming off her cheeks. 'No, baby, that's not the reason. I don't want a leave you, but . . .' How do I put this? I can't tell her I'm fired, I don't want her to blame her mama and make it worse between em. 'It's time for me to retire. You my last little girl,' I say, because this is the truth, it just ain't my choosing.

'Baby Girl,' I say. 'I need you to remember everthing I told you. Do you remember what I told you?'

I look deep into her rich brown eyes and she look into mine.

And then she say it, just like I need her to. 'You is kind,' she say, 'you is smart. You is important.'

'Oh *Law*.' I hug her hot little body to me. I feel like she done just given me a gift. 'Thank you, Baby Girl.'

'You're welcome,' she say, like I taught her to. But then she lay her head on my shoulder and we cry like that awhile, until Miss Leefolt come into the kitchen.

'Aibileen,' Miss Leefolt say real quiet.

'Miss Leefolt, are you . . . sure this what you . . .' Miss Hilly walk in behind her and glare at me. Miss Leefolt nods, looking real guilty.

'I'm sorry, Aibileen. Hilly, if you want to . . . press charges, that's up to you.'

Miss Hilly sniff at me and say, 'It's not worth my time.'

Miss Leefolt sigh like she relieved. For a second, our eyes meet and I can see that Miss Hilly was right. Miss Leefolt ain't got no idea chapter two is her.

I push back on Mae Mobley real gentle and she looks at me, then over at her mama through her sleepy, fever eyes. She look like she's dreading the next fifteen years a her life, but she sighs, like she is just too tired to think about it. I put her down on her feet, give her a kiss on the forehead, but then she reaches out to me again. I have to back away.

I go in the laundry room, get my coat and my pocketbook.

I walk out the back door, to the terrible sound a Mae Mobley crying again. But at the same time feeling, in a way, that I'm free, like Minny. I head down the hot pavement at eight thirty in the morning wondering what I'm on do with the rest a my day. The rest a my life.

The paper gone pay me ten dollars a week, and there's the book money plus a little more coming. Still, it ain't enough for me to live the rest a my life on. I ain't gone be able to get no other job as a maid, not with Miss Leefolt and Miss Hilly calling me a thief. Mae Mobley was my last white baby.

The sun is bright but my eyes is wide open. I stand at the bus stop like I been doing for forty-odd years. In thirty minutes, my whole life's . . . done. Maybe I ought to keep writing, not just for the paper, but something else, about all the people I know and the things I seen and done. Maybe I ain't too old to start over, I think and I laugh and cry at the same time at this. Cause I thought I was finished with everthing new.

Kathryn Stockett

What was the starting point for this novel?

Growing up in Mississippi, almost every family I knew had a black woman working in their house—cooking, cleaning, and taking care of the white children. That was life in Mississippi. I was young and assumed that was how most of America lived. When I moved to New York, though, I realised my 'normal' wasn't quite the same as the rest of America's. I knew a lot of Southerners in the city, and every now and then we'd talk about what we missed from the South. Inevitably, somebody would start talking about the maid they grew up with, some little thing that made us all remember—Alice's good hamburgers or riding in the back seat to take Willy May home. Everybody had a story to tell. It was probably on one of those late nights, homesick, when I realised I wanted to write about those relationships from my childhood.

Tell us about your own family maid and your family's relationship with her.

My grandmother's maid was named Demetrie. She started working for my grandparents in 1955, when my father and uncle were still boys and she was twenty-eight. When they were grown, she looked after us, the grandchildren. I loved Demetrie dearly, and I felt so loved too. We got the best part of her. She wasn't our mother, so it wasn't her job to discipline us or make us sit up straight.

She just played with us and fed us, and she liked to make us laugh. I think another reason my siblings and I had such a close connection with Demetrie is that she never had children of her own. She'd grown up poor and lived with an abusive husband. When a person has that much sadness and kindness wrapped up inside, sometimes it just pours out as gentleness. She was a gentle soul. There haven't been enough people like her in this world.

You interviewed both African-Americans and whites from this time period. Was there anything surprising in what they told you?

It is hard to approach someone and say, 'Excuse me, but what was it like to work for a white family in the South during the 1960s?' I guess I felt a lot like Skeeter did in *The Help*. But I did hear plenty of interesting stories. One black woman from Birmingham told me she and her friends used to hide down in a ditch, waiting for the bus to take them to work. They were that afraid to stand on a street corner because white men would harass them. Still, all of the black women I spoke to were very proud of the jobs they'd had. They wanted to tell me where their white children live today and what they do for a living. I heard it over and over: 'They still come to see me' and 'They call me every Christmas'. The surprises actually came with the white women I interviewed. I realise there's a tendency to idealise the past, but some of the women I spoke to, especially the middle-aged generation, just fell apart before they even started talking. They remembered so many details: she taught me to tell time; she taught me to iron a man's shirt before I got married; she taught me how to wait for the green light. They'd remember and sigh. After a while, I started to better understand what they were feeling. I felt it, too. It wasn't just that they missed these women so deeply. I think they wished that they could tell them, one last time, 'Thank you for everything.' There was a sense that they hadn't thanked them enough.

Were you nervous that some people might take affront that you, a white woman in 2008—and a Southern white woman at that—were writing in the voice of two African-American maids?

At first, I wasn't nervous writing in the voice of Aibileen and Minny because I didn't think anybody would ever read the story except me. I wrote it because I wanted to go back to that place with Demetrie. I wanted to hear her voice again. But when other people started reading it, I was very worried about what I'd written and the line I'd crossed. And the truth is, I'm still nervous. I'll never know what it really felt like to be in the shoes of those black women who worked in the white homes of the South during the 1960s and I hope that no one thinks I presume to know that. But I had to try. I wanted the story to be told. I hope I got some of it right.

Condensed from www.kathrynstockett.com

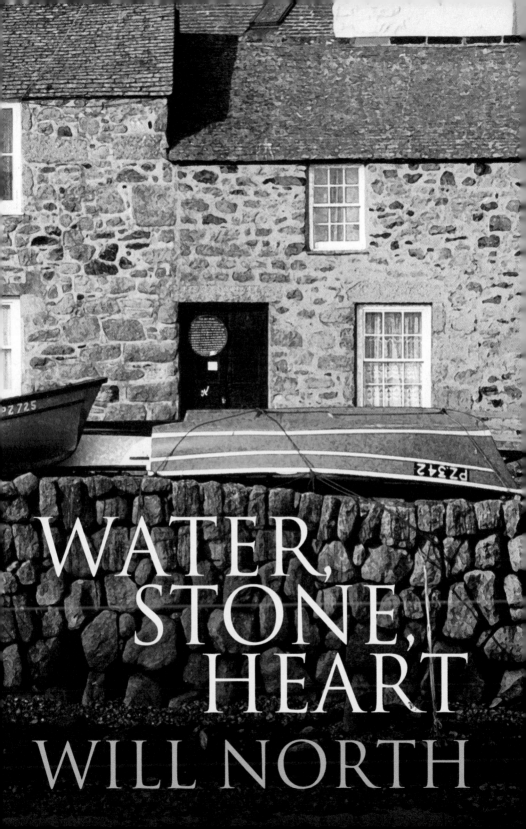

WATER,
STONE,
HEART

WILL NORTH

A reader once asked me, 'Why do you write love stories about mature people?' I was so stunned I laughed. Are we not still alive? Do we not still long for companionship and love? *Water, Stone, Heart*, like my debut novel *The Long Walk Home*, is about people who have been knocked around a bit by time and experience, people who yearn for connection and yet fear it, people burdened by histories but who sense a second chance and must find the courage to seize it. In short, real people with real lives struggling with real challenges . . . and the opportunity for joy. People like us.

ONE

'YOU ALL RIGHT down there?'

Andrew Stratton looked up towards the cliff top, ten feet above his head, but the afternoon sun was in his eyes and all he could make out was the silhouette of a woman's head and shoulders, etched against a Wedgwood-blue sky. Stratton was standing on a narrow grassy ledge above the sea, which he shared with a loudly bleating, black-faced sheep. The shape of a dog appeared beside the woman. The shape barked.

'Um, yes,' he called back. 'I was just walking along and saw this sheep stranded down here.'

'And you decided to join it?'

'Yes . . . Well, no . . . I mean, I thought I'd try to help it back up to the top. But whenever I get near it, it looks as if it's going to jump.'

'Do you always have that effect?'

'What?'

'Oh, nothing.'

From the slender shelf that he and the sheep occupied, it was, he guessed, at least 200 feet straight down to the Atlantic breakers crashing far below. He'd been walking along the cliff path just north of the Cornish village of Boscastle, and had paused to watch the waves roll in and dash themselves to foam and mist on the jagged rocks below, when he'd heard the sheep. There was a scar of loose rock and torn vegetation where the sheep had descended to the ledge, in the theory, Andrew imagined, that the grass there was greener.

'That's Darwin's sheep, that is,' said the voice above.

'You know the farmer?' Andrew was suddenly more hopeful.

He heard the woman laugh. 'No, I mean that what you have there is the dimmest sheep in the flock, the one that has to die to protect the gene pool and assure the survival of the species.'

'Oh.' There was something in her tone that implied she thought he and the sheep had more in common than just the thin sill of grass they shared. 'Any suggestions?' he called.

'Not a one. The general idea is to let nature take its course.'

He let this sink in.

'Right, then,' she said. 'As long as you're OK, I'll leave you to it.' The head pulled back from the cliff edge and disappeared. He could hear her whistling as she crunched off along the path.

Andrew Stratton—professor, from Philadelphia—did not know a great deal about sheep. He hadn't a clue, now that he was down here, how he would get the sheep back up. Come to think of it, he wasn't at all sure how he'd get himself back up, either. He approached the skittish animal once more, and it backed away again, until it was perched at the very lip of the precipice.

He gave up. He turned towards the cliff face and started climbing, only to slip back almost immediately when a chunk of rock came off in his hand. He could almost hear his wife Katerina's voice—ex-wife, to be accurate: 'Never climb shale or slate if you can help it. It flakes off and you fall.' She had taken up rock climbing more than a year earlier—taken up with a rock climber, too, and left Andrew for him shortly after. Now he remembered some of her safety rules: plan your ascent several moves in advance; maintain three reliable points of contact with the rock before you reach for the next hold; test each hold before you use it to bear weight. He'd often wished, in the weeks following her departure, that there had been similar rules for protecting oneself in the case of domestic landslides.

In a few moments of more careful climbing, he regained the rim and hoisted himself up to the footpath. In the far distance, he could see a figure, a woman, striding along the cliffs, a large brown and white dog running circles around her. He looked down. The sheep had returned to munching, utterly oblivious to the fact that it would soon be out of grass and luck. The woman had been right: this was a very dim sheep—although in his experience, limited though it was to the few days since his arrival in Cornwall, in the stupidity sweepstakes all sheep seemed equally qualified. He resolved to tell the manager at the Visitor Centre in the village about the stranded sheep and let someone who knew what they were doing rescue it.

The day had begun pleasantly enough. He'd taken a guided tour of the Valency river valley. His tour guide was an expert who knew every twist and turn of the tumbling stream, every nook and cranny in the valley. Her name was Lilly Trelissick, and the valley was her favourite place in the whole world. Lilly was nine. She hated her name and preferred to be called 'Lee'. Naturally, she called Andrew 'Drew'.

Lilly—or rather, Lee—was the only child of Roger and Anne Trelissick, who lived at Bottreaux Farm on a hill above Boscastle, a small village in a steep-sided, V-shaped valley on Cornwall's stormy Atlantic coast. On the lush pastures above the valley, Roger raised Devon Ruby Red cattle, a breed much prized for its flavourful meat, and Anne worked part-time as a freelance illustrator of children's books. Andrew was renting a seventeenth-century stone cottage off in one corner of the farm, which the couple had renovated. Roger and Anne's house was newer—Georgian, Andrew thought, given its tall windows and pleasing proportions.

Lee Trelissick charged a small fee for her tours, payable in the form of an ice cream—specifically a 'Chunky Choc Ice'—readily purchased from the newsagent's shop just up the main road from the harbour and conveniently situated near the beginning of the footpath up the Valency valley. A few steps downhill from the shop, just above the narrow stone bridge that carried the only road through the village, the Valency met the Jordan, a smaller river that tumbled down the lesser arm of the valley towards the sea. In truth, both were little more than streams. Normally, at this time of year—it was high summer—water levels in both streams would be low. But August had begun with unusually muggy, sunny days punctuated by sudden, short rain squalls, so the ground was saturated and both streams were flowing picturesquely fast and full.

Below the bridge, the conjoined streams followed an arrow-straight channel neatly bounded by ancient, hand-laid stone embankments. The little river clattered over rock shelves, ducked under another, even smaller stone bridge, and then lost itself in the harbour. Tiny and tidal, protected by two massive stone jetties, Boscastle harbour was the only sheltered cove along twenty miles of wild, shipwrecking Atlantic coast.

The harbour had once been a bustling cargo-shipping port. These days, Boscastle's economic survival depended on the tourist trade. The tortured sedimentary cliffs, the crashing sea spray and the scenic harbour netted the quaint old fishing village great shoals of visitors every summer. August was high season, the make-or-break month for the gift shops and cafés that lined the narrow street.

Lee, however, was having none of it. 'I can't wait till all these people leave!' she hissed between licks along the exposed vanilla core of her chocolate-coated ice cream. She and Andrew were standing outside the newsagent's, just uphill from the big car park that had been built along the north bank of the Valency to accommodate the tourists. 'And anyway, just look at 'em,' she sputtered, as a tour bus stopped to disgorge a stream of travellers who then waddled off downhill like so many overnourished ducks. 'Bet you none of 'em makes it to the top of Penally. They're all too fat!'

'I don't know, Lee. Keep eating those ice creams and you could end up the same way,' Andrew said calmly.

The girl lifted an eyebrow. 'You want the tour or not, Drew?'

Andrew laughed. 'OK, OK. You're the boss. Lead on.'

Stratton had only been in Boscastle for a few days, but he'd already developed a fondness for the wiry little girl. There was nothing fussy about this kid. She seemed to live every day in the same worn khaki shorts, a T-shirt from someplace called the 'Eden Project', and olive-green rubber boots—the better to wander through the woods below the farm and along the river's soggy upper reaches. Her arms and legs were bony and browned by the sun, and her sandy hair was cropped close to her skull, with a ragged fringe at the forehead. When she looked up at him, and especially when she smiled, her eyes narrowed to slits so thin he marvelled she could see out of them at all. He never saw her with any other children; she seemed perfectly happy in her own company. And whenever he saw her crossing the fields beyond his cottage, her strides were strong and determined. Lee always seemed to be on a mission.

It worried him a bit that she wandered the countryside all alone. It was a city-dweller's worry, he knew, and, anyway, Anne had told him she'd long since stopped trying to keep track of her daughter. 'She's a bit of an old soul, is our Lilly. She goes her own way,' Anne had said. 'Mind you, she's a good girl, smart and trustworthy, but stubborn as a goat. And she either likes you or she doesn't.'

Apparently, she liked Andrew. At least, he guessed she did, since most mornings he found her sitting on the stone wall by the gate to his cottage, facing the front door, as if impatient for him to get a move on. She'd been there the first day after he arrived from the States. Jet lag had kept him asleep until midmorning. Yawning, a cup of tea in his hand, he'd opened the top half of the split door at the front of his cottage and been greeted with, 'Who are you?'

He'd had no idea who she was.

'I'm Andrew. Who are you?' he'd replied.

'Lee. I live here.'

'No you don't, I do.'

'On this farm, I do.'

'I see. So Anne's your mother?'

'Yup.'

'But Anne told me her daughter's name was Lilly.'

The girl screwed up her face in disgust. 'I hate that name.'

'I see.'

'What are you doing here?'

'I'm renting this cottage.'

'Are you on holiday?'

'Not really. I'm taking a course, starting Monday. It's like being at school.'

'School? In the summer? That's daft. What are you going to school for?'

'Stone-wall-building. I'm learning how to make walls . . . like the one you're sitting on.'

'Why? We've already got plenty of them.'

Andrew could see the door opening to a very long discussion, one he wasn't really prepared to enter, especially with an inquisitive little girl. Why, he realised, was a very complex question. So he dodged it. 'Would you like a cup of tea?'

'Had some already.'

'Like some more?'

'Nope. Got to get going. Busy day.' And with that, her curiosity apparently satisfied at least for the moment, the girl hopped down and dashed off across the meadow beyond the wall.

And ever since Wednesday, that's how their days had begun. He'd throw open the top half of the door and shout, 'Good morning, madam!' She liked that.

'Guess what, Drew?' she'd begin, hopping off the wall and skipping

to the door. Lee seemed to think every new thought needed to be introduced this way: 'Guess what? The cat's had kittens.' Or: 'Guess what?
S'goin' to rain later.'

Andrew had taken to answering, 'I don't know, what?' just to tease
her, but she ignored him and launched right into the latest bit of local
news. It was better than any morning newspaper. The news was always
varied, interesting and unexpected. It was a delightful way to start the
day—a cup of hot, sweet, milky tea and Miss 'Guess What?'

That's how today, Saturday, had started.

'Guess what, Drew?'

'I don't know, what?'

'It's a good day for you to have my famous and exclusive guided
walking tour of the river valley. Complete with sacred wells and witches!'

'Famous, is it?'

'It is. Far and wide.'

'How often have you conducted this tour?'

'Loads of times.'

'Hmm. Doesn't sound very exclusive.'

She hesitated.

'A few times, then?' he ventured.

'Nearly once!' she said, giggling behind her hand.

'Ah, now that's what I call exclusive. When do we leave?'

'Soon's you finish that tea, because—guess what?—Mum's taking me
to Wadebridge this afternoon to get new wellies; my feet've got too big
for these ones.' She hopped round on one foot and shook the other by
way of emphasis.

'Well then, I guess I'd better get a move on. I'll just get my boots.'

When he emerged again, a day pack slung over one shoulder, she
was waiting by the gate. 'Where shall we begin?' he asked.

'At the bottom, of course. In the village.'

Given that he knew there was a back route from the farm directly
into the valley, this seemed odd, but he didn't argue. 'Right, then. Down
to the village it is!'

It was a luminous morning. A bit of ground fog drifted up in wisps
from the cooler fingers of the valley, evaporating quickly in the warming
air. They followed a narrow lane that dipped into the side valley cut by
the little River Jordan, passed a whitewashed old mill perched above
the stream, briefly joined the main road from Camelford, then turned
into steep, one-way Fore Street and followed it as it twisted downhill.

Over the centuries, Boscastle had evolved two centres: 'Top Town', high above the valley, where they were now, and 'Quay Town', down round the harbour. Fore Street—which somewhat confusingly changed its name to Dunn Street halfway down the hill—linked the two. Andrew loved the almost medieval character of the narrow street, lined as it was on both sides with squat stone cottages leaning one against the other. They passed the village hall, the old Methodist chapel, the primary school Lee attended, and the post office. Beyond the post office, the street turned sharply right and plunged downhill, paralleling the course of the Jordan, which clattered through the valley far below. Although it was barely ten o'clock when they reached the bottom of the road, tourists already packed Quay Town as tightly as salted sardines in a barrel.

It was here that Andrew was informed matter-of-factly by his guide that there was a small fee for the tour. Ice cream seemed to Andrew a fine breakfast, so he bought Chunky Choc Ices for them both. Soon they'd left behind the crowded car park and were heading upstream through the trees bordering the Valency, where they had the leafy riverside footpath to themselves.

Here, just above the port area, the valley's wooded slopes climbed steeply up from the banks of the stream, leaving just enough room for the riverbed and the narrow footpath. But a little farther on, the floor of the valley opened, and the path meandered through a grassy meadow.

'You've missed most of the flowers,' Lee said, as if Andrew hadn't been paying attention.

'What do you mean?'

'There are masses and masses of primroses, and daffodils, and blue-bells, and things here in the spring. You should see Minster churchyard then. There's so many daffodils then you can barely see the gravestones. But they're all gone now. You came too late.'

Andrew felt as if he should apologise. 'Still lots of flowers here, though,' he countered, somewhat defensively. 'Like this, for instance.' He pointed to a bush flecked with pale pink blossoms maturing to ivory.

Lee snorted. 'That's just dog rose. It's a weed, like these nasty, prickly blackberry brambles. They get everywhere. I hate them.'

'Your mother told me she makes blackberry wine.'

'Lot of good that does me.'

Andrew couldn't argue with this line of reasoning.

A gentle bend revealed a pool created by a low stone dam that slowed the stream's flow. They stopped and sat on a rock, where Lee said, 'That's a weir, that is.' She pointed towards an outlet just upstream of the dam. 'It used to shunt water to the leat.'

'Leat?'

'You know, leat . . . what carries the water to the mill. I thought you Americans spoke English.'

'I used to think so,' Andrew said, 'but now I'm not so sure.'

'OK, you know that big red wooden water wheel, down near the car park? Used to be a mill there. Water that ran it came from here.'

'What kind of mill?'

'A mill that grinds stuff, silly.'

'What kind of stuff?'

'You do have a lot of questions for a grown-up.'

'You sure know a lot for a kid.'

'Is that a compliment?'

'I never compliment before lunch.'

Lee smiled. 'You remind me of my friend Nicki. She says things like that. You'd like her. She's funny.'

'Am I funny?'

'Not before lunch.'

Lee hopped off the rock and spun off up the path again, sometimes walking, sometimes skipping. Andrew was amazed at how much Lee already knew about the natural world. 'Where did you learn all this?' he asked when he caught up with her.

'Mostly from Elizabeth. Mum says I'm to call her "Mrs Davis", but she says I can call her Elizabeth. She runs the Visitor Centre and knows loads of stuff.'

'But you're not a visitor.'

Lee looked at him a moment, as if trying to decide whether he was teasing or just stupid. 'That's silly,' she said, and off she skipped again.

Andrew followed happily, his eyes sweeping the hillsides. The trees climbing the slopes included ash, beech and hazel, but mostly they were gnarled sessile oaks, which looked to him like something from a fairy tale, their mossy branches twisted and dense. It was the kind of woodland that should have fairies and elves, and he said so.

'I never saw none, but Nicki says there are piskies down here.'

'Piskies?'

'You know—little folk.'

'Has she seen them?'

'Never asked. If Nicki says something, that's good enough for me.'

Andrew was admiring the elaborate structure of one particular oak, a very old one that overhung the river, when Lee piped up.

'Guess what, Drew?'

'I don't know. What, Lee?'

'That's my secret tree.'

'Is it, indeed?'

'Yup. I climb way high up in it sometimes with a book and read there.'

'I bet it's peaceful up among the leaves.'

Lee's secret tree was made for climbing. Its branches began low and continued, ladder-like, far up its thick, knobby trunk. Andrew swung up onto the lowest branch and said, 'Come on. Show me where you sit!'

Lee scrambled up past him with the sureness of a monkey, until the two of them were deep in a cylinder of green leaves, virtually invisible from the ground. She settled into the crotch of one of the branches and leaned against the trunk. Andrew balanced on a branch beside her. 'Sometimes I sit here and spy on people walking along the footpath,' she confided.

'No kidding! See anyone interesting?'

'Yeah. Saw the vicar once.'

'What was he doing?'

'Not "he", silly, "she". Don't you go to St Symphorian's?'

'I've only been here a few days, Lee. Gimme a break.'

Her eyes narrowed to slits. 'You're not one of those Methodists, are you?' She asked this as if Methodists had horns.

'No, I'm not. Wait a minute. How can St—what was it?'

'Symphorian's.'

'Right, Symphorian's. How can they have a priest who's a woman? I didn't think Catholics allowed that.'

'It's not Catholic. It's C of E.'

'Huh?'

'Church of England. You don't know much, do you?'

'I guess not.'

'Me and Mum, we're C of E. Dad is, too, I think, but he's too busy with the farm most Sundays to go to church.'

'And the C of E has lady priests?'

The girl shot him a look. 'D'you have a problem with that?'

'No!'

' 'Cause some people do. My friend Nicki calls them "Nanderthals".'

'Ne-anderthals. Boy, your friend sure uses big words.' He wondered if all the kids in Boscastle were as precocious as these two.

'Yeah, Neanderthals. That's it. It means backward, sort of. You're not one of them, are you?'

Andrew placed his hand over his heart. 'Neither a Methodist nor a Neanderthal, to the best of my knowledge. Promise.'

This seemed to satisfy Lee. Back on the ground, the two of them continued along the riverbank until they reached a narrow wooden footbridge that crossed the stream to a path that led up the thickly wooded hillside opposite. 'End of tour,' Lee announced.

'That's it? What about the wells and witches?'

'Have to wait till next time. Got to meet my mum so's we can go to Wadebridge. For the boots.'

She dashed across the footbridge.

'Thanks for the ice cream,' she called over her shoulder.

'I'm going to complain about this to the Visitor Centre,' Andrew called after her. He thought he heard a distant giggle.

He slipped off his day pack and pulled out an Ordnance Survey Explorer Map. He checked it for a moment, shouldered his pack, and continued upstream. At a tiny cluster of cottages the map identified as Newmills, he climbed out of the valley and turned seawards. He was heading for the coast path and, unbeknown to him, an encounter with a stranded sheep.

TWO

NICOLA RHYS-JONES was berating herself. And not quietly. She was shouting into the wind.

'Idiot! Bloody idiot! Meet a nice-looking guy with a conscience, toss off a few wisecracks, walk away. Brilliant!'

Randi, her seven-year-old Siberian husky, rocketed round her, barking, as she tramped along the coast path. Nicola stopped and looked back along the cliffs to the north. High above Pentargon, near the stream of the same name, she saw the tiny figure of a man. The handsome man who'd tried to help the idiot sheep. The handsome man with the thick, curly, pepper-and-salt hair and gentle, caring face. She would not wait for him to catch up. She wanted to, sort of, but mostly she didn't. Too obvious. She trudged down the steep path towards Boscastle harbour and her tiny stone cottage-cum-studio near the jetty.

Nicola Rhys-Jones, single—divorced, if you wanted to be technical about it—was rapidly approaching 'woman of a certain age' status and pretending it didn't matter to her in the least, though it did. Anyone—any man, at least—passing her on the coast path would have observed a woman beautiful by any definition but her own: long, softly wavy dark brown hair; big brown eyes beneath thick, expressive brows; a handsome nose admittedly a bit too big for her face; high, angular cheekbones; skin slightly olive and remarkably unlined; and full lips that curved up at the corners with the perpetual hint of a smile, as if she was keeping a secret. She was nearly forty, but didn't look it. Yet. She stood three inches shy of six feet (a little too tall, she thought), and had broad shoulders (a little too broad, she worried), generously proportioned breasts (too generous—her Italian heritage) and slender legs attached to shapely hips she worked hard to keep from spreading (thus, the dog-walking, not that she didn't enjoy it).

Nicola unlocked the low wooden door to her tiny stone cottage, went into the kitchen, filled a bowl with water for Randi, then mixed herself a gin and tonic and climbed the steep stone steps to her studio. She loved the house, especially the light-filled studio with its view of the harbour. She lay back on the chaise opposite her easel and put her glass on the floor. The upper storey of the cottage had once been a loft for drying fishing nets. The ground floor had been an office and a storage room for crab pots. The place suited her, at this stage of her life, though it was a far cry from the gracious home she had shared with Jeremy.

Jeremy. What a disaster. Ten years of marriage to a rich, well-educated, hopelessly narcissistic Englishman who also happened to have an abusive streak. As if she hadn't had enough of that as a girl.

Nicola DeLucca, graduate student at the Art Institute of Boston, had met Jeremy Rhys-Jones, son of an English peer, while she was on a fellowship in Florence, Italy. His family had a modest estate on Cornwall's rocky, wind-wracked Penwith peninsula, near the artists' colony of St Ives. She was the sole daughter of a working-class immigrant family from the claustrophobic Italian enclave that was Boston's

North End. She had had two brothers: one younger, James, the older one, John—named after saints, though only James warranted that honour. Her father, Anthony, had abandoned his family when she was only six, and her mother, Angela, had been forced to go to work cleaning offices in the State House at night—a source of shame in the neighbourhood.

After high school, Nicola had won an art scholarship to Boston College. Four years later, she graduated and landed a part-time job as a book-jacket designer for a publisher. In her free time she took advanced painting courses at the Art Institute. Winning the fellowship freed her from the need to work and forced her to take seriously her talent as a painter.

In Florence, she floated in a nearly perpetual state of sensory overload. Her breakfast was cappuccino and biscotti amid the continuous hiss of the espresso machine behind the long marble counter of the steamy corner café near her student rooms. Then she wandered out into the city. She quickly realised that the elaborate palaces left her cold. The places that stirred her were far more pedestrian: tiny shops lining the narrow stone-paved alleys and arched arcades; the agricultural abundance of the public markets; the black and red capes the Florentine police wore as they sat astride horses so white and muscular they seemed carved from the same dazzling Carrara marble as Michelangelo's *David*. She spent hours sketching in the piazzas for oil studies she would later complete in class.

Jeremy was not in Florence studying art; Jeremy was in Florence studying Italian women. It was just her luck that he preferred his Italian women to be English-speaking. Though a year younger than she, he was mature, cultured and charming. And tall. And dishy. And unlike anyone she'd ever met.

Nicola fell hard. Many afternoons, she and Jeremy climbed the hill opposite the city to watch the setting sun gild the stone and stucco walls and red-tiled roofs stretching towards the distant, mauve hills. When Jeremy returned to England while she continued studying in Florence, he wrote ardent letters to her almost daily. No one had ever done that for her before. He flew down every few weekends. Then, as winter approached, he invited her to spend Christmas with his family in Cornwall.

She flew to London, then took the long train ride down nearly to the tip of Britain's southwest peninsula. Jeremy met her at the station in St Ives in a draughty, beaten-up Land Rover. He was wearing an oily-smelling, waxed-canvas waterproof jacket, a flat tweed cap and green rubber boots she learned were called 'Wellingtons'.

Jeremy had described his family's home as a 'country house', and Nicola had in mind something small, sweet and ivy-clad. So, when they passed through pillared gates, she was completely unprepared for either the scale or the grandeur of the granite mansion to which the long, tree-lined drive led. Compared to the cramped row houses of the North End—or, for that matter, to the houses in Florence—the house seemed to her palatial.

Trevega House, as it was called, lay in a sheltered valley cut by a stream that raced west from the high moor tops before emptying into the sea. The estate ranged for several hundred acres and included a clustered hamlet of former tenants' cottages, a farm complex, even a disused water mill. Over the generations, the Rhys-Joneses had created lush landscape gardens and broad lawns around the manor house, as well as a massive walled vegetable garden.

Inside the house, the rooms were high ceilinged and spacious. Its furnishings, which were informal, comfortable and decidedly English, were a hotchpotch of patterns, colours and textures that somehow worked as a whole. For the holiday, evergreen boughs, red-berried holly branches and ropes of ivy were arranged on windowsills and tabletops. There were candles everywhere.

The coastal landscape beyond the valley, however, was a far cry from the 'green and pleasant land' Nicola envisioned when she thought about England. The hills round the estate were rugged and wind-whipped. Miles of ancient stone walls crawled across bare, rocky slopes, which rose to massive granite outcrops. What trees there were, and they were few, were twisted and salt-stunted, their trunks and limbs bent away from the wind screaming in from the Atlantic.

Someone else might have found this midwinter world impossibly bleak, but Nicola felt strangely at home. It took her a few days of wandering to understand why: the rocky crags and the windswept cliffs, she realised, were simply colder, windier, wetter versions of pictures she'd seen, as a child, of the sparsely clad hills her father and mother had come from in Sicily.

For all the estate's ruggedness, the grazing meadows nestled within its snaking stone walls were green, even at Christmastime. The climate here was gentle, even if the wind wasn't, and the rainfall plentiful. The coastal land was prime grazing land, and Jeremy's father's farm manager,

Nigel Lawrence, ran a large herd of Black Angus cattle on this land.

Jeremy's small family—his father, Sir Michael, and his younger sister, Nina—received her warmly. Nicola knew that his mother, Jemma, had died years earlier not far from their London town house when she flipped her antique MG convertible while driving too fast—'As usual,' Jeremy had said with disgust.

And, after a few days (and a few large whiskies), Sir Michael, a large man in his mid-seventies with an unruly mane of white hair and a sparkle in his clear, blue eyes, told Nicola that she reminded him of his wife. 'Strong-minded and high-spirited, she was,' he had rumbled, his gentle, jowly face creasing in fond remembrance. 'Just like you, my dear, just like you; fine thoroughbred stock, both of you.' Nicola had simply smiled, not knowing how to respond.

Jeremy had described his father as intimidating, but Nicola and Sir Michael got along famously right from the start. He was courtly and kind and made her feel at home. She simply adored him—as the father, perhaps, she'd always dreamed of but had been denied. Nicola and Sir Michael shared a language of aesthetics that Jeremy did not comprehend. Sir Michael's artistic passions were on display on walls throughout the great house. He was a lifelong collector of the works of the English artists who had painted in the Cornish coastal art colonies at the beginning of the twentieth century: Stanhope Forbes, Frank Bramley, Laura Knight and Alfred Wallis, among others. But it was Laura Knight's talent for capturing the intensity and purity of the light unique to the far southwest of Cornwall that affected Nicola most—and later influenced her own painting.

On Christmas Day, Jeremy gave her a complete set of Winsor & Newton oil paints and a portable easel. Sir Michael gave her a charcoal sketch of a woman with a small boy in her lap. It was some days later that she learned, from Jeremy, that it was a portrait of his grandmother and his father as a boy, by Stanhope Forbes.

Then, on New Year's Eve, Jeremy surprised her by asking her to marry him, and Nicola surprised herself by accepting.

At the beginning, everything seemed perfect. The wedding was in late May, just after Nicola's fellowship ended. The ceremony was performed at the eleventh-century church in Zennor, the hamlet closest to the Rhys-Jones estate. The Anglican rector graciously allowed Nicola's brother James, who'd recently been ordained a Catholic priest, to participate in the ceremony. Sir Michael had flown both her brother and her mother 'over the pond' for the event. The stone sanctuary had been bedecked with white roses and chrysanthemums. Her mother had cried.

After a damp honeymoon of island-hopping in Scotland's Outer Hebrides, she and Jeremy moved into Trevega House. It wasn't her husband's first choice. Jeremy had taken an economics degree at Cambridge and planned to work at the London headquarters of his father's financial-management firm, tending to the arcane investment problems of his father's many wealthy clients by day and enjoying the city's social scene by night. But Sir Michael had other ideas. He sent Jeremy off to apprentice at the firm's Penzance office and gave them Trevega House in which to live. Sir Michael tended to stay in London, close to the House of Lords and his club.

Jeremy was furious with this arrangement, but Nicola was thrilled. She loved the rambling old house, the gardens, the peaceful evenings by the fire, the long walks along the coast and the horseback rides deep into the prehistoric granite hills. And then there was Sir Michael's wedding present to her—a little painting studio of her own overlooking the harbour in nearby St Ives, where the light was diamond bright and the aquamarine water in the little port looked positively Mediterranean. The truth, of course—the white sand beach notwithstanding—was that the water sweeping in from the Atlantic was so cold, even in midsummer, that only children could tolerate it for more than a few minutes.

Children. They'd had none, though not for want of trying. Nicola's secret was that her own sexuality was complicated and fraught—she could be frisky and flirtatious one moment, remote and disengaged the next. It troubled her, but she kept it to herself, and the fact was that her husband was too involved in his own needs to even notice the shifts. A few years into the marriage, years in which her husband increasingly lurched from solicitous to abusive, Jeremy decided it was time they started a family. When months had passed with no pregnancy, he had turned brutally primal.

And as she had once before, she stopped eating, as if to purify herself, as if the pain of hunger could expunge whatever it was that she had done, whatever sin she had committed, to bring this abuse upon herself. When Jeremy began to take ever-longer business trips to London, she found herself relieved. She suspected that he had a lover in the city, and she realised she didn't care. It should have felt like loss, but instead it felt like relief.

Nicola's only confidante in those days was Annabelle Lawrence, the farm manager's wife. A leggy, tomboyish blonde, she and Nigel had a child, Jesse, who, at two, seemed to be permanently and happily grafted to Annabelle's left hip. Annabelle was one of those relentlessly upbeat women who take everything easily in their stride.

Annabelle liked Nicola and was worried about her. In recent months, Nicola had lost weight and seemed to have gone pale. One dreary autumn morning, Annabelle paid her a visit with a plate of freshly baked scones. She let herself in through the back door, called out, and found Nicola sitting alone at the scrubbed-pine trestle table in Trevega House's cavernous kitchen, staring out of a window towards the ocean as a cold mist crept in from the Atlantic.

'Foul day is what it is out there,' Annabelle announced gaily as she stripped off her wet jacket and set Jesse down in his carrier chair. 'What say we girls have tea and get fat on these scones?'

Nicola looked up and gave her a wan smile.

'You all right, then, love? You're lookin' a bit peaky lately.'

'I'm fine, Annabelle, really; just tired.'

'You're spendin' too much time in that studio of yours. Wearin' yourself out getting ready for that exhibition.'

Nicola had been working hard preparing canvases for an opening at the Great Atlantic Gallery in nearby St Just, but that wasn't it. 'I'll put the kettle on,' Nicola said, rising and heading for the counter where it sat.

She never made it. She had only gone a few steps before the room began to swim round her. She shot an arm out for support, found nothing, and collapsed. She had blacked out.

Having had some training as a nurse before she'd married Nigel, Annabelle checked Nicola's breathing and pulse, then raced to the sitting room, grabbed cushions from the couch, and returned, using one to support Nicola's head and the rest to prop her legs above her heart.

It was when she unzipped Nicola's hooded sweatshirt that Annabelle saw the bruises on her neck. Someone had throttled her. There was only one likely candidate. A fury built inside her. She was holding a cool, damp cloth over her friend's forehead when Nicola came to.

'Well, that was stupid, wasn't it?' Nicola said, blinking and struggling to sit up.

'No, sweetie,' Annabelle whispered, pulling Nicola close. 'Stupid is lettin' him do this to you and not tellin' anyone.'

It had taken months, Annabelle's persistence and several visits to a social services adviser in Penzance for Nicola to leave her husband. When she did, in the middle of a freakishly cold March, she did it quietly one day when he was away. She took only her car, her clothes and her art supplies.

She drove north along the coast, following narrow, rural lanes, intuitively unwilling to stray far from the sea that gave her so much pleasure and that informed so much of her art. On the third day of her meandering journey, she turned down a steep hill and found herself at the harbour in Boscastle at low tide. Something about it was right—the way the colourful local boats leaned this way and that on the mud flats, waiting for the tide to turn; the river twisting through the village; the protective folds of the valley.

Tucked beneath the cliff on the south side of the little harbour was a small, honest, stone building with a WELL-APPOINTED COTTAGE TO LET sign in the window. She agreed to rent the place for a week. A few days later, she extended her stay another week. Eventually, she came to an understanding with the owner for a year-to-year lease.

About a month later, Nicola was working in her upstairs studio when she heard a knock at the door. When she got downstairs and opened it, she found Sir Michael there, leaning on his cane in the rain, with a large parcel under his arm.

'Good afternoon, my dear,' he said, his great head tilting downwards. 'Do you suppose I might come in out of the elements?'

Nicola felt a surge of fear. 'Jeremy?'

'I come alone, Nicola. I should like a word with you, if you'll permit me.'

Nicola stepped back from the door and the big man entered. He set down the parcel, leaning it against the wall, straightened, and shrugged off his wet coat. Finally, he turned to her and smiled, his sagging, bloodhound face transformed with warmth.

'Hello, dear Nicola,' he said softly. 'I have missed you.'

Tears slipped down Nicola's cheeks, and Sir Michael took her into his arms. 'Oh, Dad,' she said into his shoulder, 'I'm so sorry. It's just that I couldn't . . .'

'I know, dear one. You couldn't tell me. But I found out. Nigel told me, in the end. He didn't want to, of course; managing the farm is his life, and he didn't want to jeopardise that. Annabelle made him. Disgusting. My own son.' Sir Michael looked around the tiny sitting room and dropped into a chair by the coal fire. 'I don't suppose you have a whisky?'

Nicola shook herself out of her shock. 'Um, no. Brandy? I have a nice cognac . . .'

'Splendid.' He inched the chair closer to the fire.

When she returned with the drink, Nicola sat on the floor and wrapped her arms round her father-in-law's knees. 'How did you find me?'

The old man shrugged. 'Not so difficult, really, for a man in my position. Put in a word at the Yard. They traced your car.'

'But why?'

Sir Michael looked at her, placed a wrinkled, age-spotted hand upon her shoulder, and chuckled. 'Thoroughbred stock, my dear, thoroughbred stock. Knew it from the moment you walked through the door. Told him that Christmas—someone like you came along once in a lifetime, and it was time he settled down. But I had no way of knowing my only son was a brute, I promise you. How could I? What do we ever really know about our children, except what they allow us to know? Feel like a fool, and worse. Lost someone very dear to me when you left. Love my daughter, of course, but you . . . well, you were—*are*—something else entirely.'

Nicola saw the watery shimmer in Sir Michael's eyes and hugged his knees closer. 'I can't come back, Dad. I won't.'

'I know that, my dear, and I have no intention of asking you to.'

'Then why are you here? Why did you track me down?'

'My son, I am sorry to say, is not a gentleman. But I am. It is my responsibility—and my great joy—to ensure you are provided for.'

'I don't want anything from—'

'Hush, Nicola. I know you don't. Don't you see that's partly why I am here? You conducted yourself throughout this horror like a perfect lady. In some respects, I rather wish you hadn't. I would have understood what was happening sooner. I've come to tell you that I have arranged for the divorce and made Jeremy sign the papers. That is what you desire, is it not?'

Nicola nodded.

'Good. That's sorted, then. In addition, I aim to make sure you experience no further hardship. You've had quite enough.'

'But—'

He put up a hand to quiet her. 'There will be a small stipend—nothing embarrassing, I assure you—but you will not be uncomfortable. It will be deposited in an account in your name every month. I have also kept your studio in St Ives, and am leasing it out. Of course, should you ever wish to have it again . . .'

'Dad, you know how I love St Ives and that studio. But so long as Jeremy is at Trevega House, I couldn't possibly . . .'

'I know. I haven't yet decided what to do about him. But in the meantime, I'm doing quite well on the rental, if I do say so myself!' His old eyes sparkled like those of a thief with a diamond. He took another sip of the brandy. 'Oh, and there is one more thing.'

He hoisted himself from his chair and moved slowly towards the door, where the parcel leaned against the wall.

'Nicola, I want you to have this. I know you love it, and it would please me immensely to know it was with you.'

He lifted the parcel, which was wrapped carefully in heavy brown paper, and set it before her. Nicola unwrapped it slowly, but thought she knew what it was. It was the painting she admired most in Sir Michael's collection: Laura Knight's exquisite *Ella, Nude in Chair*. When she lifted it from its wrapping she stared at her father-in-law, shaking her head. 'No. I couldn't—'

'I'm afraid you must, my dear. It's already written into my will.'

Laura Knight had produced a number of studio paintings, including this nude of her best friend, Ella Naper, whom she'd posed in a gilded armchair draped with a black and red silk robe. The painting had a slightly unfinished look, though the figure in the chair was perfect.

'Pleasure to give it to someone with your talent,' Sir Michael said. 'Maybe she'll be your muse—eh, my girl?'

Nicola rose from the chaise and descended to her kitchen. Outside, the sun had set and the harbour was in shadow. She fed Randi, refilled his water bowl, and made herself another gin and tonic. Then she went into her sitting room, lay down on the sofa, sipped her drink, and stared at the painting of Ella Naper that now hung above the rough granite mantel. She thought of Ella as her spiritual companion— a free spirit, confident in her world. It was who she wanted to be. It was, in fact, who she'd become in the nearly four years she'd lived in Boscastle.

Moments later, she was asleep. After a while, Randi came in from the kitchen, nuzzled his mistress's hand, got no response, and curled up in his usual place, on the rug in front of the hearth.

THREE

'GUESS WHAT, DREW?'

Andrew had just opened the door of his cottage to a soft August Sunday morning. Lee was in her usual place. She had on her new wellies. 'You're going to finish the tour today and take me to see the sacred wells and the witches?'

'No, silly. It's nearly time to go to church! You'd better hurry.'

'Well, thank you for that reminder, but I'm afraid I have other plans. I'm going walking this morning, since somebody I know cut short yesterday's outing . . .'

Lee squinted at him from the wall. 'You sure you're not one of those Methodists?'

'Positive.'

'Well, suit yourself, then. I'm off.' She hopped off the stone wall and dashed across the meadow towards home.

Lee Trelissick made Andrew's heart ache, the way it does when you long for something you know you will never have. Lee was exactly the kind of child he'd dreamed of having with Katerina—and was glad they hadn't. Andrew was a professor of architecture at the University of Pennsylvania when he and Katerina Vogel met, at an awards dinner for the school's most promising graduate students. She'd worked in real estate but had discovered that her strength was in finance. When she completed her MBA, Mellon Bank snapped her up and put her on their executive fast track.

Katerina—'Kat' to her friends—was all sharp angles and hard edges. Even her shiny, jet-black hair was asymmetrically cut. Almost painfully thin and taller than average, Kat stood apart from her classmates and, Andrew noticed, spent most of her time talking with the professors. That evening, when she noticed him in the crowd, she simply lifted an eyebrow. He was mesmerised.

When they married a year later, she was far too busy with her career to consider children. That made perfect sense to him at the time and, though he was a full ten years older than she, Katerina, at thirty, had plenty of time left on her biological clock. But he also sensed that she was ambivalent about children, as if she feared she wasn't mother material. When she passed her thirty-fifth birthday, Andrew began to resign himself to childlessness.

Then she had left him. Now, he'd learned, she was pregnant. It was hard to know which had been more of a surprise. Or more painful.

He finished his tea, laced up his boots, grabbed his day pack, and headed north along a single-track lane above the farm. After a half-mile or so, he turned left onto the path that led down through Minster Wood to the footbridge over the Valency where Lee had left him the day before. He was headed for St Juliot's, an isolated parish church the young architect Thomas Hardy had restored before he became a novelist and poet.

Andrew hadn't seen the end coming. When Kat had announced she was leaving, one Saturday just before the end of spring term, he had been so stunned, so utterly blind-sided, he'd simply stared at her.

'When?' he'd finally said.

'Today. Now. I've already packed my car. My lawyer will contact you. Don't worry. I don't want anything that's yours.'

But Andrew was still back at the leaving. 'Why?'

She looked at him with a mixture of pity and disgust. 'You really don't have a clue, do you?'

His forehead furrowed, as if he was puzzling out a design problem. 'I'm sorry. No, I don't.' And he didn't.

'I can't believe I have to spell this out for you. I want to spend my life with a man who wants to make a mark on the world. You call yourself an architect. But what do you actually do? You sit in your tidy, minimalist university studio and develop abstract notions about shape and form and space. You lecture to your doting students. I used to think it was great to be "Mrs Professor Stratton", until I realised how dull your life is. *Our* life is. Tell me something, Mr Architect: where are your clients? Where are your buildings? Not to mention that you could be making ten times as much as they pay you at that damned university.'

'I guess I'm just not that interested in money,' he'd said. 'And I don't see what this has to do with money, anyway.'

'Everything has to do with money, but that's not even the point.

The point is, you have no passion. It's like you have ice in your veins instead of blood.'

'That's not true. I love working with my students—'

'And here's the saddest thing.' She was on a roll now. 'You don't even know this is a lousy way to live! You don't even know you're only half alive. You know what being half alive means? That you're also half *dead*! And I'm dying being here with you. *That's* why I'm leaving!'

Andrew had heard some of this before, but never delivered with such fury. 'Have you arranged someplace to stay?' he asked when Katerina finally flared out.

She stared at him in disbelief. 'I am so out of here,' she said.

And then she was.

Andrew and Kat lived in an early nineteenth-century brick row house on Delancey Street. Andrew had spent years renovating the old house, turning its stacked warren of dark, cramped rooms into a flowing, light-filled, contemporary space. An inventive cook, he'd built himself a sleek commercial-grade kitchen on the ground floor that opened to a dining room overlooking an urban garden. An hour after Katerina left—an hour spent staring blankly out at the garden and replaying the scene on a continuous loop in his head—Andrew left the house and walked across Rittenhouse Square, picked up a couple of bottles of Australian Shiraz at the liquor store, then went on to the Italian delicatessen on South 19th Street, where he bought a selection of cured meats and some black olives. He felt scorched. Blistered. Charred.

On the walk back across the square, he paused at the play area. The day was warm and fragrant from the flowers in the formal plantings at the square's four corners. All around him, children dashed about in spring outfits. Their young mothers lounged on the dark green benches lining the walkway. At the corner, while he waited for the light, a hand touched his elbow and a silky voice purred, 'Hey, handsome.'

The voice belonged to a rather Rubenesque beauty called Phyllis Lieberman, a colleague in the art and architecture school, who lived a few blocks away. Single, roughly the same age as he, Phyllis never missed an opportunity to flirt with him. Phyllis was a walking embodiment of eroticism, squeezed into a small but lush package.

The light changed, but he didn't cross. He thought briefly of giving Phyllis a jaunty, deflecting response. Instead, he turned towards his friend and said, 'Kat's left me.'

The woman hesitated a moment, then slid her arms round him and gave him a warm, full-body hug. Then she stood back and said, 'How about we two go for a walk?'

'Sure,' Andrew replied, but without much enthusiasm.

Phyllis slipped her arm through his and steered him towards the river. They walked slowly, Phyllis, in her customary three-inch heels, gracefully picking her way along the uneven brick sidewalk. They'd reached Washington Square and were taking a turn round Independence Hall when she said, 'You might as well hear this from me, ducks: not many people are going to be surprised by your news.'

'No, apparently I haven't been a particularly satisfactory husband. That's what Katerina says, anyway.'

'That's nonsense, for starters. Stratton, you're a first-class gent. And anyway, the affair's been going on for months. She hasn't exactly been discreet about it.'

Andrew stopped dead and stared at her. 'Affair?'

Phyllis blanched and clapped a hand over her mouth. 'Oh my God! You don't know, do you?' She sounded like someone being strangled. In a moment, she recovered and tugged him to a bench.

'Look, it's a guy she met at the climbing gym,' she whispered, 'a fat-cat lawyer. That's what I hear, anyway.' She took one of his hands in both of hers. 'Oh, ducks, I'm so sorry.'

He looked around the square. He'd always loved the old colonial part of Philadelphia—the brick, the stone, the history. But none of it gave him comfort on this day.

He felt like his life had just ended.

Andrew climbed high up the west slope of the Valency valley. A side stream cut across the footpath he'd been following as it raced downhill. He picked his way across steppingstones and then stopped to take in the view. Over the aeons, the almost infinitesimal friction of water slipping over stone had cut a winding channel deep into the surrounding plateau. At the outer edge of the sharpest curves, he could see where seasonal floods had chewed away at the friable slate bedrock, creating bluffs. Away to the east, the hills were patterned with neat, green fields. And for as far as he could see, the fields were defined by ancient stone walls.

Andrew had had no idea, not the faintest inkling, how to respond to Katerina's attack the day she left. So, he got on with things. Except that things didn't go well. It wasn't just that Andrew felt shell-shocked by the breakup, but his work seemed to have hit a brick wall as well. He had been researching what he believed would be an important contribution to his field: a book he was calling *The Anatomy of Livable Places*. One summer when he was in grad school, he'd hitchhiked across Europe and been captivated by the way hill towns in Italy or Spain, or fishing communities in Greece, or villages in rural England, seemed to possess a kind of wholeness, a certain harmony of form and material, the result of which was that they made you feel 'at home', even if you didn't live there. These places settled into him, into his bones and, years later, while wrestling with the problem of the increasing soullessness of American communities, the comforting livability of those places came back to him. And an idea grew.

Andrew was convinced that if you could deconstruct that feeling of livability, of 'home-ness', if you could identify its component parts and understand how they worked together, you could design new communities with the same comforting character. There were certain components of livability he thought were obvious. Most places that felt livable seldom had a building more than three or four storeys high. Also, the buildings tended to be clustered together companionably, with breathing space provided by small plazas. They also tended to have what Andrew called 'public living rooms'—coffee shops, outdoor cafés or pubs, for example, where people gathered to chat or simply watch the world go by. He noticed that such places were constructed of local materials. As a result, they looked as if they had grown organically from the ground, rather than having been imposed upon it.

But his editor at the University of Pennsylvania Press didn't get it. 'If you're trying to define what "home" means, why are you looking in Europe? You're an American!' To Andrew, the answer was personal and visceral: he'd never felt at home in America. Growing up in the suburbs of Boston, he'd known few of his family's neighbours. And to do anything—shop, go out to eat, see a movie—you had to get into a car. The result, for Andrew at least, was a sense of alienation, of not belonging to the place he was from.

But there was another problem with his project, too. His department chairman didn't think the subject of his research was sufficiently 'professional', which meant it flirted with the real concerns of everyday people. In academia, that was the kiss of death. The more he argued with his editor and his chairman, the more he felt like he was banging his head against a wall.

Still, he had his champions, and steadfast, candid Phyllis was one of them. When Andrew hit rock bottom, both emotionally and intellectually, on the first anniversary of Katerina's departure, it was she who suggested he get away. 'Go someplace where the landscape speaks to you, and just become a part of it, if only for a few weeks. Don't think. Just find out how the place *feels*. Figure out why later.'

The idea both intrigued and unsettled him. It had always been his nature to study the world from a distance. It was easier, and safer, to be an observer than a participant. After the summer break had begun, he'd been taking a walk through the colonial part of Philadelphia. Not far from Independence Hall, two men were restoring the pavement of a plaza. The new pavement was being made with large rectangular blocks of blue-grey granite—Belgian blocks, he knew they were called— roughly four inches wide, ten inches long and six inches deep. The two men had laid down a bed of gravel and levelled sand and now were setting the granite blocks in a handsome herringbone pattern.

Andrew sat on a bench and watched the men work. Every so often, one of the men would pause, lean back on his haunches, look at the pattern developing, and smile. The result of their work—nothing more than stone and sand—was breathtaking in its artistry and simplicity.

So it was that Andrew Stratton decided it was time he got his hands dirty. And in that strange way events sometimes transpire, the opportunity presented itself. As part of his research, Andrew had contacted several organisations in Europe devoted to historic preservation and sustainable building techniques, and they regularly emailed him their newsletters. The day after he'd sat watching the workmen, he heard from the Southwest Council for Sustainable Building in England. Among other bits of news, he noticed that a course on mortarless stone-wall-building was being offered by the Guild of Cornish Hedgers in partnership with the National Trust, a land-protection organisation. The week-long course would be held in August in Boscastle, on Cornwall's wild Atlantic coast. Boscastle was not far from the town from which Andrew's father never tired of telling him his ancestors had come: Stratton, in north Cornwall.

On impulse—in itself a breakthrough for him—he emailed to register for the course. A few hours of Internet-searching later, he'd also found Shepherd's Cottage, and emailed the owners. Anne Trelissick had written back, and he reserved the seventeenth-century stone cottage for two weeks.

As Philadelphia slouched into the dog days of August, he escaped, arriving in Boscastle on a clear, warm afternoon just after a brief summer shower that left the air freshly laundered and the narrow, wet streets shimmering. He was immediately entranced. He felt as if he'd come home.

At the top of the Valency valley, Andrew climbed over a stile in a stone wall, walked through the cemetery of St Juliot's church, with its lichen-encrusted headstones leaning this way and that, and ducked under its fifteenth-century porch. He'd been looking forward to this moment. He wanted to see what Hardy had done during the restoration of the church in the late 1800s. But when he pushed open the church's heavy oak door, he found a small clutch of parishioners, Lee and Anne included. A female priest—the one Lee had been telling him about, he guessed—stood at a raised pulpit.

He mumbled an apology and took a seat in a pew at the rear.

Heads turned to regard the stranger who had joined them. Lee grinned at him and waved. The priest looked across the tiny congregation and smiled. 'Welcome,' she said. 'I was just about to tell one of my favourite stories.'

The priest's informality won him over immediately. Andrew smiled back and nodded. She began.

'I'm sure you've all heard variations of this joke: a mountain climber loses his footing and begins to fall from a cliff—perhaps a cliff like those along the coast path here in Boscastle. He grabs the branch of a shrub growing from the cliff face and it arrests his fall. But the branch is slender and brittle, and he knows it will not hold him long.

'"Help!" he cries. "Is anyone up there? Help!"

'And a deep voice answers, "I am the Lord, your God. I can save you if you believe in me. Do you believe?"

'"Oh, yes, Lord, I do—with all my heart, especially right now!"

'"Good," says the Lord. "Let go of the branch."

'The climber hesitates. "Is there anyone *else* up there?" he asks.'

There was a faint titter of laughter in the congregation.

'The Bible tells a similar story,' the priest continued. 'In this case, Jesus has just performed the miracle of feeding the multitudes. Five thousand people gather to hear him preach and, afterwards, he tells his disciples to feed them. They reply that they have only two fish and five loaves of bread, and it is impossible.

'But Jesus takes this meagre larder and somehow manages not only to extend it to the entire crowd, but to have leftovers as well! Now, I don't know about you, but I think that would have made me a believer for life. But apparently some of the disciples were slow learners. When the crowd disperses, Jesus tells his disciples to get into their boat and set out across the sea. He stays behind to pray and reflect, and tells them he will join them soon.

'That night a storm rakes the sea and the disciples' boat is tossed for hours. Finally, as Matthew tells us, on the fourth watch, early in the morning, they see Jesus walking towards them on the surface of the water. They cry out in fear, "It is a ghost!" But Jesus says, "Take heart. It is I. Be not afraid." Then Peter jumps up and says, "Lord, if it is you, command me to come to you over the water."

'And here's where I think Jesus shows us his sense of humour—in a way not all that different from the joke we began with. What does he do? He says, simply, "Come." And so, Peter clambers out of the boat. He lets go with one hand. He lets go with the other. And he walks across the water towards his Lord.

'So here is Peter, striding across the surface of the sea, when he sort of wakes up and looks around. He sees that the sea is rough and the sky is stormy. And suddenly he is afraid. He has, to put it simply, a crisis of faith. He fears that the branch of salvation, like the branch our climber was clutching, is slender and brittle.

'What happens next? Well, it's useful to remember that the name "Peter" means *rock*, which is exactly what he begins sinking like. "Lord, save me!" Peter cries.

'And Jesus reaches out, pulls him up, and returns him to the safety of the boat. "O ye of little faith, why did you doubt?" Jesus asks. And the rest of the disciples, in awe, declare, "Truly, you are the son of God." '

The priest paused and rested her eyes on the villagers before her.

'We are only human,' she said. 'Our day-to-day lives test our faith repeatedly—in ourselves, in those we love and in God. And sometimes we sink. What does Matthew's account of this episode in the life of Jesus and his disciples tell us? That faith can buoy us up. That faith can calm the storm. That faith can produce miracles—big ones, little ones, it hardly matters. Faith can enable each and every one of us to "walk upon the water" of our lives. Faith can be our salvation.

'Now, let us pray . . .'

The service continued, but Andrew was still thinking about the vicar's sermon. Though he had gone to church dutifully every Sunday with his parents as he was growing up, Andrew had never had much faith in faith. He had even less in organised religion.

As he matured, Andrew found a new faith—a faith in the power of rational thought. He believed that the universe was explainable. He believed that the mysteries of religious faith were nothing more than natural phenomena awaiting logical explanation. Andrew had faith in science. But he had faith, too, in the essential goodness of human beings. He had also had faith in himself, in the importance of his work and in the security and fullness of his love for his wife. But now his marriage was shattered and the value of his work was in question. In the year since Kat dropped her bomb, Andrew had felt his belief in himself seeping away. It was as if his soul had sprung a leak. 'O ye of little faith,' Jesus had said. Yes, precisely.

Lee yanked him out of his bleak meditation at the end of the service.

'Come on,' she said, tugging at his pocket. 'You have to meet Janet!'

'This is Drew,' Lee announced, dragging him over to the priest. 'He's living with us.' Andrew felt like the farm's new dog.

The vicar smiled and offered Andrew her hand. 'Janet Stevenson. It was nice you could join us this morning,' she said.

'Yes, well, I apologise for barging in like that. Look, I'm sorry to be so ignorant, but what does one call an Anglican priest?'

She chuckled. 'Technically it's "The Reverend Janet Stevenson of Davidstow, Forrabury, St Juliot, Lesnewth, Minster, Otterham and Trevalga parishes". But most people just call me Janet.'

'Thank goodness,' Andrew said. The Reverend Janet was a tall, angular woman with shoulder-length, rather severely cut brown hair shot through here and there with strands of grey. But her eyes were gentle, and her smile was warm and genuine. 'Your sermon's given me something to think about,' Andrew confessed.

'Yes, I noticed you seemed to have drifted away afterwards.' The priest leaned a bit closer and spoke quietly: 'If there's something you'd like to discuss, the rectory's next to St Symphorian's, at the top of the village, by Forrabury Common.'

Andrew wondered whether clairvoyance was an essential skill among priests. 'Thank you,' he replied.

Lee was tugging at his pocket again. 'Come *on*, Drew, or you'll be late at the Cobweb, too!'

'The Cobweb?'

'The pub,' Janet explained. 'Nearly everyone goes there for Sunday lunch, there or the Wellington—you know, roast lamb and the works.'

'And if you don't get moving,' Lee chided, 'there'll be none left!'

'You seem to have a friend,' the priest said.

Andrew laughed. 'It feels more like I've been adopted. Or maybe kidnapped. Will I see you there?'

'I usually put in an appearance; have a pint at least. Professional responsibility, you see.'

Andrew smiled and gave her a wave as Lee tugged him across the churchyard towards Anne's car. He never did get to look around at Thomas Hardy's handiwork.

The Cobweb occupied the first two floors of a massive, four-storey, eighteenth-century stone warehouse built deep into the black slate hillside across the road from the Visitor Centre. A formal dining room and function room occupied the upper floor, but the heart of the pub was two large, low-beamed, stone-walled, virtually windowless adjoining rooms on the ground floor. There were big stone fireplaces in each room, along with an eclectic collection of tables, chairs, high-backed settles and miscellaneous artwork and wall ornaments. From the thick beams overhead in the room nearest the door hung hundreds of antique beer bottles. Andrew, who was just over six feet tall, felt as if he needed to duck to move through the place.

On this Sunday, the room was packed with tourists and locals alike. Andrew had finally reached the long bar that spanned the two rooms and was about to order a pint of St Austell's Doom Bar ale when a woman's voice rang out. 'Well, if it isn't the sheep whisperer. Flora! It's that bloke I was telling you about!'

Andrew turned to his right and saw a darkly beautiful woman perched on a high stool at the end of the bar. She had on a black, paint-splattered, ribbed cotton sleeveless tank top, and a pair of faded cut-off jeans. One very long, very tanned leg crossed the other at the knee. From the suspended foot dangled a hot-pink flip-flop. Her dark brown hair was long and gathered to one side in a ponytail held by a rolled and knotted kerchief. She smiled.

'Um . . . I'm sorry,' Andrew stuttered. 'I don't think we've . . . Wait—you must be that woman on the cliff. With the dog.'

'And you're the saviour of stranded sheep, the Ovine Ranger.'

Another older, plump, rosy-cheeked woman—Flora presumably—

bustled up behind the bar and gave him a broad smile. 'Pay no attention to her. She's just havin' you on a bit. What'll it be, me 'an'sum?'

'A pint of Doom Bar, please.'

'On me, Flora,' the woman on the stool said, and the barmaid lifted an eyebrow as she pulled down the long-handled vacuum pump to draw the fresh ale up from the cellar casks. She slid the pint over to Andrew with a wink.

'How's that sheep, then?' the woman in the cut-offs teased, bouncing her crossed leg rhythmically. Andrew watched the pink flip-flop dance.

'No idea.' He took a long slug of his pint. He loved British ales: amber, creamy, almost no fizz. 'Thanks for the drink.' He moved down the bar to join her.

'I was a little worried, frankly, about whether you'd get yourself up from that ledge.'

'But not worried enough to stick around to help.'

'Oh, no. I know too well how fragile is the male ego.' She tilted her head to one side and gave him a crooked, amused smile.

Suddenly, Andrew remembered the sermon. 'I could have fallen,' he said.

'That would have been Darwin at work again. But you didn't, did you?'

'Actually, I did. Fell nearly a hundred feet towards the knife-edged rocks and boiling surf, but arrested the fall by grabbing the branch of a shrub growing from the cliff face. Unfortunately it was gorse, so my hand was impaled by thorns. Still, it held long enough for me to find a route back to the top, no thanks to you.'

She grabbed his hand, flipped it over to see his palm, which was unscarred, wiped her own palm over his, then let it go. 'Liar.'

Andrew was trying to recover from the galvanic jolt of her touch. His blood sizzled. 'I used the other hand,' he said.

'Liar twice,' she said. 'You're right-handed. That's the hand you use to lift your glass.'

'How's your dog?' Andrew asked, trying to buy time, trying to recover.

'Randi!' the woman called—then a big, furry dog that looked for all the world like a wolf appeared from the crowd, trailing several small children, including Lee.

'So *there* you are!' Lee called out amid the din of voices in the pub. 'Guess what, Drew? This is Randi, and he's the bestest dog in the world.' The dog sat on his haunches beside the woman on the stool and regarded her with helpless adoration, tongue lolling.

'And Nicki!' Lee cried, noticing the woman on the stool. 'Drew! Drew!' She was hopping with delight. 'This is my best friend, Nicki!'

Andrew looked at the woman across from him, then back to Lee. 'Wait . . . I thought Nicki was one of your girlfriends. I mean a girl like you . . . not a . . . a grown-up!'

'Not an old crone, you mean,' the woman said, with something less than her former feistiness. Andrew glanced at her and wondered how old she actually was. Mid-thirties; forty, tops. Pretty young as crones go. Pretty, period. Something lush, slightly exotic about her. He was still buzzing inside from her touch.

Lee bailed him out. 'Nicki's not like other grown-ups. She's like me. A "free spirit". That's what Mum says, anyway.'

Nicola slid off her stool and swept the girl into a bear hug, thinking just how wrong Lee was, but loving her for believing it. Lee giggled and squirmed away into the crowd, her introductions apparently now completed.

The woman stood facing Andrew, squinting, thoughtful.

'So you're Drew . . . I should have guessed.'

Andrew smiled. 'Why? Is my fame so widespread?'

'It is when Lee's your publicity agent, and yes, thank you, I'd love another drink.'

Andrew laughed and signalled Flora. 'My treat this time,' he said to the barmaid when she arrived.

Flora fairly leered at him. 'Aren't *we* becomin' chummy! Same again, Nicki?'

'Sure, but as long as he's buying, make it a double.'

'So what do you do when you're not cadging free drinks at the Cobweb?' Andrew asked.

'Oh, that's so American: *What do you do?* As if that defined you! You're in Europe, my friend. Here we enquire about your family, about life, about truth, about beauty . . .'

'OK, then, tell me about your family.'

'Don't have any. At least not here.'

'Your life, then?'

'Chequered.'

'Is that the truth?'

'Truth enough.'

'OK, then, beauty? Besides your own, which is perfectly obvious to anyone with at least one functioning eye.'

This seemed genuinely to take Nicola aback. She turned to the tall gin and tonic Flora had left her and downed a third of it in one go. She stared at the glass for a moment, then turned towards him. 'Thank you,' she muttered. Then she smiled. 'Liar.'

'You're right, I'm lying. I spend my days photographing gorgeous, scantily clad models for fashion magazines, and I've just gotten used to telling women they're beautiful. Apart from you, most of them seem willing to accept the compliment.'

'You're a fashion photographer?'

'No. That's the "liar" part.'

She smacked his arm playfully and laughed, then raised her glass and clinked his. 'You win this round.'

'I didn't know it was a competition.' This, too, was a lie. He felt as if he'd been fencing ever since he arrived.

'It's always a competition.'

'What is?'

'Flirting.'

'Is that what we're doing?'

'Isn't it?'

'Wait. This is making my head hurt. I asked first.'

'And I dodged the question.'

'You certainly did.'

Andrew felt weirdly off-balance with this lovely but curious woman. And he realised this whole business of interacting with someone new was a little scary. It had been years. How do you behave? What do you say?

Andrew did a verbal feint. 'Look, I'm told the reason to be here on Sunday afternoon is the roast dinners. Are you eating?'

'Heavens, no; far too much food for midday.'

'So why are you here?'

She scanned the packed pub. 'For the company, I guess.' She waved at the Reverend Janet, who was working the crowd. 'My work is pretty solitary.'

'Ah,' he said, 'we're back to what you do.'

'Clever how you did that.'

'You brought it up, actually. Let me guess. You're either an exceptionally messy interior decorator or an artist.'

'Aren't you observant!'

'You're an artist?'

'No. I'm an exceptionally messy decorator, and I'd better get back to my paint cans.' She drained her glass and slung a canvas bag over her shoulder. 'Nice meeting you, Drew. Thanks for the drink. Lee was right about what she said about you.'

'Which was?'

Nicki smiled a conspirator's smile. 'Oh, that's just between us girls.'

'Do you have a name, besides Nicki?' Andrew felt as if he was trying to lasso Nicola and pull her back.

'Nicola Rhys-Jones, formerly DeLucca.'

'Married, then?'

'Not any more.'

Andrew smiled. She didn't.

'And you're called?' she asked.

'Stratton, like the village up the coast. Andrew Stratton.'

'Married?'

'Not any more.'

This time Nicki did smile.

Then she was gone.

FOUR

IT WAS STILL TOO EARLY for the sun to have crested the steep hills to the east as Andrew made his way down through Minster Wood to the footpath along the river on Monday morning. The street through Quay Town was nearly deserted.

The coastal fog was beginning to break up; it promised to be another fair day. He stood at the edge of the car park where he was to meet his instructor, watched the river race past, and thought about Nicola. She intrigued him. And there was that seismic shock when she touched his hand. It amazed him. It confused him. It nagged at him. What was that about?

A little knot of men was gathering by the slate-stone Visitor Centre. Andrew wandered over to join them.

' 'Morning! We all waiting for the teacher?' he asked.

He received two curt nods and one, 'I reckon.' Men of few words.

'Where're you from?' asked the talkative one, a wiry, balding fellow of perhaps thirty-five with a sharp, ferret-like face. Andrew's accent had given him away.

'Philadelphia,' he answered.

Three pairs of eyes widened. Finally, another of the men, a tall, heavily built fellow in manure-splattered green wellies and blue coveralls looked him over. 'Better fit you stayed 'ome, lad. No 'oliday, this. This be 'ard lowster.'

Andrew stared at the man for a moment, smiling what he was sure was an idiot's smile, while he waited for his brain to translate. He thought he got the gist. 'Yeah, reckon it will be,' he answered.

Now the third gent spoke up. 'There's a lot of fine stonework around Philadelphia. It was the Pennsylvania Dutch, was it not?'

Andrew looked at this fellow in frank amazement. How would he know that? The man seemed overdressed for the task ahead—neatly pressed denim shirt with button-down collar, sharply creased khaki trousers and what appeared to be brand-new work boots. He looked like a Bostonian, sounded like a Londoner, and was certainly no Cornishman. He extended his hand to Andrew.

'Ralph Newsome. I studied engineering at Drexel for a year.'

'Andrew Stratton. I teach architecture at Penn.'

'Small world,' Newsome said.

The ferret didn't want to be left out. 'Jacob Casehill,' he said, taking Andrew's hand. 'Stonemason. Everyone calls me Case.'

The three of them turned to the big fellow, who suddenly seemed as shy as a child. 'Burt Pencarrow. Farmin' out Holsworthy way.' He kept his hands in the pockets of his coveralls.

It was at this point that a beaten-up white van lurched into the car park. On the side of the van was written THE STONE ACADEMY.

The teacher's name was Jamie Boden, and Andrew had expected, given the diminutive first name, a young spark of a fellow. But the man who climbed out of the van was, Andrew guessed, at least sixty, his face weathered, freckled and deeply creased, his head crowned with a tangle of ginger hair going white. He wore stiff canvas trousers and a collarless blue shirt, both of which seemed impregnated with fine, grey dust.

'Coffee!' he said by way of greeting.

Case jerked his head to the left. 'Bakery's open. Few doors down from the village shop.'

'Excellent,' the man responded, and took his leave. 'One more coming,' he said over his shoulder. 'Gel, thank the good Lord.'

Burt lumbered after the instructor, big and slow as a draught horse. Andrew mumbled, 'Gel?'

'A woman,' Newsome explained. 'And, like all women, late.'

As if to prove him wrong, a dark green Land Rover with NATIONAL TRUST stencilled on its doors roared into the car park and whipped smartly into a space. The driver's door snapped open, and a young woman who looked to be in her mid-twenties fairly exploded from the car and strode towards them. She was stocky and sported a deep tan, dramatically set off by a helmet of close-cropped platinum-blonde hair. She was wearing olive-drab hiking shorts, and her calves looked carved from stone.

'This it? Just the three of you?' she said without introduction.

'Lovely to meet you, too,' Newsome answered with a grin.

Her manners caught up with her, and she thrust out her hand. 'Sorry. Becky Coombs. Got stuck behind a bloody bus full of tourists.' She shook hands all round. 'Where's Jamie?'

'You know him, then?' Andrew asked.

'Oh, yes, Jamie's by way of being a god around here. Reckoned it was time I took one of his classes, especially since the project's on my patch. Volunteers will join us next week.'

'You're at the National Trust office here in Boscastle?' Andrew ventured.

'Yes, when I'm not out in the field, that is.'

'Must be great to have a job that takes you out into countryside this beautiful,' Andrew said.

'It is that . . . except maybe in the winter. Rains constantly, and the wind never lets up. Storms take a toll, especially along the coast path. We've a lot of stonework needs doing.'

Case had been quiet. Now he gave the girl a sly look and said, 'Reckon you can hoist all the stone we'll be shiftin'?'

Becky smiled at Case. 'No, not all of it. Just my share.'

Andrew glanced at the sturdily built 'gel' and chuckled.

Jamie Boden was back, big Burt close behind, both of them clutching Styrofoam coffee cups. They gathered in a circle, and Boden looked each of them over as if they were rocks he was sizing up. 'Right, then, what're you chaps driving?'

'Thought we was workin' right here, by the car park,' Case said.

'Will be,' Boden said. 'That's our remit: build a barrier between the verge and the river. But not this morning. Today we learn things. And to do that we go to my place, up on the moor. But it's rough going. Becky's got her Land Rover, so that's good. The rest of you?'

Burt rumbled that he had a Toyota pick-up. Case was driving a Ford Fiesta. Newsome had a BMW 3 Series.

'Well, that's out,' Boden said. 'Fiesta too, most likely. You?' he said to Andrew.

'I walked here.'

'You'll be the American, then. You ride with me in the van. Becky, you take Mr BMW here. Burt, can you take Mr Casehill? Right, then, stick close, or you'll never find it.'

A little after eight thirty, Randi dragged Nicola out for his morning walk. It was a splendid day, and she wasn't scheduled to start her shift at the Museum of Witchcraft until ten. She smiled at the thought of her 'job'. She'd been volunteering at the museum—'the world's largest collection of witchcraft-related artefacts'—for more than two years now. It was all Randi's fault. He had belonged to an elderly woman in a nearby village—a practising witch known only as Joan—and Colin Grant, the museum's owner, had taken the dog in after she died. Nicola met Colin while out walking along the cliffs just after sunrise one morning. He was sitting atop a ledge on Penally Point, meditating, and Nicola hadn't noticed him. When he wished her a soft-spoken good morning, she'd nearly jumped out of her skin. She recognised the fellow—the museum was next to the lower bridge over the Valency, directly opposite her own cottage. She'd often thought him rather sweetly gnomish—small in stature, shy in speech, with a slightly too-large head aswirl with grey curls. He had climbed down from his perch and joined her on the coast path. 'You're up early,' he'd observed.

'As are you,' she'd noted.

'Oh, I'm here most mornings, communing,' he'd said.

He'd asked if she took walks every day and, when she said she did, he mentioned he'd inherited a lovely dog that needed walking and that, given the press of work at the museum during the tourist season, he didn't have enough time to do it himself. Somehow she'd agreed to walk the animal, and she and Colin arranged a time later that day to meet. The dog's name was Randi. Colin explained that Joan had claimed the dog had extraordinary powers, most notably knowing instantly whether anyone who came to their door was friend or foe.

Looking back, her first meeting with Randi still seemed like something of a miracle. The dog, who was three at the time, took one look at her and immediately began running joyous circles around her, long tail wagging furiously, bouncing on all fours like a lamb. He didn't let out a single bark. Colin stood there with his mouth agape.

'That's exactly what he used to do with Joan,' he said finally. 'He connects the two of you. You're not a witch, perchance?'

Nicola laughed. 'Not to the best of my knowledge!'

'Well, he seems to think you are. Perhaps you should consider whether you have the gift.'

'The only gift I have is being a sucker for a sweet dog, and you'd already sussed that out, hadn't you?'

'Actually,' Colin said with a mischievous smile, 'yes.'

'You're not a witch, too, are you?'

'Um . . . yes. I thought you knew that.'

'Look, I didn't even know men could *be* witches, but it doesn't mean a thing to me. I'll take the dog.'

'I only wanted you to walk him.'

'The hell you did . . .'

'Are you sure you're not a witch? Because you're a dab hand at reading minds.'

And so, Randi came home with Nicola, and the two of them had been inseparable ever since. He was a handsome animal. His lush coat was tan and black on his back, but snow-white on his belly. His legs and paws, too, were white. His most distinctive feature was a dark charcoal widow's peak on his forehead with a lightning slash of white in its centre. Best of all, as fearsome as he sometimes looked, the dog had a sweet, gentle soul.

Randi usually chose the route for their morning walks, and on this occasion he turned right out of their front door, trotted up to the main road, crossed the road bridge, and headed uphill past the Visitor Centre and the Cobweb, finally turning right onto the footpath leading up the Valency valley.

They'd passed the wide part of the stream behind the weir, when Randi stopped and looked up into one of the trees. He looked at

Nicola, looked up at the tree, and looked at Nicola again. Lost in a reverie vaguely to do with the American, she kept walking. But Randi didn't follow, and eventually he barked once.

'What?' Nicola said, exasperated.

The dog barked again, but kept looking up.

That was when she heard the giggling. She recognised it immediately. 'Lilly Trelissick! What are you up to?'

'I'm up to about half the tree,' Lee said, giggling louder now.

'Well, you're driving Randi round the twist, so come on down and walk with us.'

There was a scuffle of boots on bark, a shaking of leafy branches, and then a pair of skinny, tanned legs emerged from the canopy. Nicola caught Lee as she dropped the last few feet to the ground and gave her a hug.

'Listen here, you ragamuffin. You'll break your neck one of these days.'

'Will not, 'cause that's my special tree, and we have an agreement. If I climb it carefully, it won't let me fall.'

Nicola looked at the girl and realised there was no rebuttal to such an argument. So she changed the subject. 'So tell me about this Andrew Stratton.'

'I told you. He's a nice man. We're mates. That's all. Why? *Wait!* You like him, don't you!'

'That's ridiculous.'

'You do. You *do!* Nicki and Drew, Nicki and Drew!'

'Stop that! What's he doing here? That's what I want to know.'

'Goin' to school is what. Stone-wall school. Told him we already had plenty, but he wouldn't listen.'

They set off up the valley. A little way upstream of the footbridge, at a point where a tributary stream plunged over a rock shelf and joined the river, they stopped to chuck stones. Randi was off rummaging around in the undergrowth on one of the slopes.

'Why's an American going to stone-wall-building school?' Nicola muttered, as much to herself as to Lee.

'I think it's to do with his work,' Lee ventured. 'He's an *art*-something . . . art-*tech*.'

'An *architect?*'

'Yeah, ar-chi-tec. Means he builds stuff, he said. Like walls, I guess. Is that a good thing?'

'Well, let's just say it makes him interesting. Maybe he understands something about beauty.'

'He thinks *you're* beautiful. Said so yesterday, coming back from the Cobweb. I told him you were a witch.'

'You *what?*'

'Well, you are, right? You work at the museum.'

Nicola hung her head in her hands. 'I don't believe this . . .'

The fact was that Nicola had indeed become intrigued by witchcraft, at least the gentle form of it that had been a part of Cornish culture for centuries. Nicola wasn't sure when it was, exactly, that she'd fallen away from the Catholicism she'd been raised with. Maybe it was when the vows she'd spoken during her marriage ceremony turned to bitter blood the first time her husband had hit her. Maybe the rot had set in long before any of that when, despite going to Mass every Sunday, bad things kept happening to her when she was a girl scarcely older than Lee. Modern witchcraft, she'd learned, was merely a religion that reveres nature. It didn't promise salvation or threaten damnation; it simply offered a way of fitting oneself into the complex web of the universe. And here, in a landscape littered with prehistoric stone circles, enigmatic standing stones, hilltop burial quoits, sacred wells and remote hermits' cells, witchcraft just seemed, well, natural.

'So what did he say when you told him I was a witch?'

'He said you had a funny way of casting spells, but I didn't understand.'

But Nicola did. She'd done what she always did: flirted and fled, leaving behind little but the sting of her barbed tongue.

They had driven through Camelford and were climbing out of the valley of the River Camel when Jamie Boden said to Andrew, 'Notice anything different?'

'It's getting steeper?'

'True enough, and that's part of the answer. Let me ask you this: when you look at buildings in Boscastle, what do you see?'

'A lot of black slate, at least where it hasn't been painted over.'

'Right. Now look around again.'

'Granite! I hadn't even noticed the change.'

'That's the thing about this country. The underlying geology is so complex that it seems like it changes every dozen miles or so. That's why neighbouring villages can look so different sometimes. They're built of whatever material was close at hand. Mind you, the granite's fairly new, geologically speaking. It's the result of volcanic activity only three hundred million years ago. Slate's much older.'

'*Only* three hundred million years. I like that.'

'Round here, you get used to thinking about time differently. Show you what I mean in a moment.'

They turned from a narrow, winding road hemmed by hedgerows to a rutted dirt track. Ahead on the horizon, the moorland was barren, virtually treeless, almost otherworldly. The slopes were littered with scree broken off by frost. Jamie's van lurched to a stop beside a rocky field. The other two cars pulled up behind them, and everyone got out and followed Jamie across the springy turf.

'The fields hereabout are all part of my land, but I feel more like a museum curator than a landowner,' Jamie commented. They stood on the edge of what Andrew now realised was a wide, circular stone wall, the remnants of a rampart of some sort. And within the circumference of the circle, which had a diameter of perhaps fifty yards, there were eight or ten smaller circles.

'This was a settlement,' Newsome said quietly.

'Right. Round about four, maybe five thousand years ago.'

Andrew tried to get his mind wrapped around such antiquity. 'And it's still here,' was all he could say.

'That's the thing I want you lot to understand,' Jamie said as they returned to their vehicles. 'Building with stone is the nearest we get to immortality. When you build a stone hedge, you're building for all time.'

'Stone *hedge*?' Andrew asked.

'Aye, lad. You're in Cornwall now, and we call 'em hedges. Doesn't matter if it's all stone, or all earth and turf, they're all hedges here, not walls. Right, then. To the classroom!' Jamie hoisted himself into the van, Andrew followed, and they roared off, the others following.

Another hundred yards or so later, they pulled up in a cleared parking area and walked through a gate in an old stone hedge that led to Jamie's house, an ancient, gable-ended, two-storey, slate-roof granite cottage. A sturdy stone barn stood some distance from the house. 'Thirteenth century, some of it,' Jamie replied to their unspoken question. 'With various later bits.'

The yard was rimmed with stone hedges. Andrew glanced around and realised the hedges varied in style every few yards. It was a display area for the craft of hedge-building.

'There's something like thirty thousand miles of hedges here in Cornwall,' Jamie said. 'Some of them are even older than that settlement I showed you. Since then, as you can see with these demonstration hedges here, different styles have evolved, driven mostly by what rock was available and, later, what tools could be used to shape the stone.'

Andrew looked around. There were hedges built of raw fieldstone; hedges with alternating courses of regular, shaped granite; hedges with horizontal layers of slate and shale.

'I've got a hedge half built from a previous class,' Jamie said. The group walked round the back of the big stone barn to a sort of outdoor workroom. Jamie took them to the unfinished end of a new stone hedge. 'So, what do you notice?'

'It curves inwards from the base,' Becky commented.

'Right. That centralises the weight and pushes the hedge into the ground.'

'It's hollow in between the two sides,' Andrew noted. 'Well, not hollow, but filled with dirt.'

'That's part of the traditional Cornish hedge design. But that's not dirt. Dirt is part organic and, over time, it breaks down and sinks, creating weakness. Soon enough, the stone faces will collapse inwards. Around here, there's a lot of rotted granite that breaks down to something like sand. We call it "growan". When I'm building a granite hedge, I look for a deposit of that stuff to fill the centre—which is called the "heart", by the way. Down Boscastle way there's usually a layer of shillet—broken-up bits of slate—just below the turf. We'll be using that. Speaking of which, we'd best be getting back down there. Time to get to work.'

When their little caravan got back to the Visitor Centre car park, they drove to the far end. The county council had hauled in several loads of stone, all slate, but in an earthy array of colours, from sandy brown to blue-black. They'd left a small 'Bobcat' front loader as well. Jamie gave them the bad news. 'First job's the nastiest. We need to excavate a bed for the grounders.'

'Grounders?' Newsome asked.

'The stones that make up the footing. They need to be set into the ground, which means digging a trench. Come on, then. Tools are in the van.'

Jamie had an impressive array of shovels, spades and picks, and something that looked like a combination pick and spade, called a mattock.

He passed them out and then ran two twenty-foot parallel lines of twine between stakes at the edge of the macadam, each about five feet apart.

'Why so wide?' Newsome asked. 'We're not trying to stop tanks!'

Jamie laughed. 'The gentleman wishes to know why I'm having you dig such a wide trench. There are rules of proportion in hedge-laying. The first is that the base must be as wide as the hedge is to be tall; the standard height of a hedge is five feet. Also, the width of the top should be roughly half the width of the base. We're trying to stop gravity from pulling the hedge down once it's laid.'

The five students set to work. Case took his shovel and began to cut a line in the turf. Becky watched him for a few moments, then grabbed a mattock and asked him to step aside.

'That'll take for ever,' she said. She swung the mattock above her head, then, her strong shoulders arching, brought the broad blade down and, in one smooth stroke, peeled back an inch-thick strip of sod as wide as the mattock blade. She moved her feet slightly to one side and repeated the movement. Working like a machine, she'd stripped the five-foot-wide trench surface to a length of ten feet in a matter of a few minutes. She stopped, drenched with sweat, stepped aside, smiled, and said, 'All yours now, gents.'

Andrew shook his head. 'Wow, Becky.'

'We do a lot of footpath maintenance at the Trust; I'm well acquainted with this fellow,' she said, hefting the heavy mattock.

Even silent Burt was moved to observe, 'Lass does a fitty job, she does.'

They continued like this, Becky peeling sod and the rest of them clearing subsoil, while Jamie, working alone, manoeuvred the biggest stones into the bucket of the Bobcat and dumped them along the edge of the car park, a couple of yards from the new trench. By mid-afternoon, they'd begun laying the big footing stones that were the grounders.

At about four thirty, Jamie killed the Bobcat's engine and yelled, 'All right, you lot, we'll leave it there till tomorrow. First round at the Cobweb's on me!'

Andrew was thankful the pub was just on the other side of the car park. As they dragged themselves across the shimmering macadam, Jamie chattered on about the next day's lesson, but Andrew guessed the students weren't retaining much of it. They were all sweat-drenched, filthy and weary.

Jamie, Burt and Case, who had the farthest to drive, left after their first pint, Newsome and Becky after their second. 'Reck'n ah'll be orf t'me 'oosbund,' Becky said, mimicking Burt's thick Cornish accent. She clapped Andrew on the back and strode out of the door.

Flora had just come on duty and she made a beeline for Andrew. 'Don't you be flirtin' with yon Becky, me 'an'sum,' she whispered with a wink. 'That husband of hers is a right terror.'

'I should think "yon Becky" would be terror enough, but we're only working together.'

'On the new hedge, I heard.'

'How'd you hear about that?'

'From Nicki. Saw her on the way to work.'

'How'd *she* find out?'

'A little bird, I expect,' Flora said, smiling.

'Lee.'

'Thick as thieves, those two,' Flora said. 'Another pint of Doom Bar, Drew? It is Drew, isn't it?'

Andrew smiled and nodded. 'Sure, but I need to eat, Flora. What do you recommend?'

'What you need is a big plate of sausage and mash, smothered with caramelised onions. Just the ticket for a workin' man.'

'Done. Bring it on, m'dear.'

The meal was perfect. Later, walking along the footpath in the waning midsummer evening light, Andrew was visited by several small epiphanies. In a matter of days, he had already made friends in this village, friends who meant something important, something he couldn't quite identify but knew he had not felt before. It had to do with honesty, the absence of pretence, something that did not exist in the competitive university community he'd lived in for so long. What's more, he felt enfolded and comforted by the thick cloak of history that seemed draped over the entire landscape. And the landscape itself—lush in the valley, bleak on the hilltops, wild and wind-blown on the coast—centred him in a way he'd never experienced before. His ancestors were from nearby; maybe there was something to heritage after all. And then there was this Nicola—Nicola with the electric touch.

Andrew took the footbridge over the river, climbed up through Minster Wood, passed the tiny Minster church huddled in a remote notch in the valley, crossed the fields, let himself into Shepherd's Cottage, and was asleep in seconds.

FIVE

Diffuse light flooded through the seven-foot-tall, multi-paned window on the north wall of the studio. It had once been the door through which fishing nets were winched up from the quayside below. The thick oak winch arm still hung out high over the pavement. The ceiling of the upper floor of Nicola's cottage was open to the roof peak, and on the south side two skylights had been fitted in between the rafters.

Nicola stood at her easel, working quickly, adding confident bursts of a dusky yellow the colour of Dijon mustard to a canvas already awash in pigment. She was working on one of her 'tranquillity panels', part of a series of large, abstract paintings commissioned by a private hospital in London. The idea was that they helped people heal.

Randi, in pride of place on a throw blanket on the Victorian 'fainting couch' she'd rescued from a jumble sale, looked up, barked once, and dashed downstairs. One sharp, happy bark meant a friend. A low growl meant uncertainty. Repeated angry barks meant trouble. It was magical how he seemed to know. There was a light knock, a short pause, the creak of the front door opening, then a thin voice.

'Nicki?' the voice called.

It was Lee. Nicola decided to pretend she wasn't there, and tiptoed behind the sailcloth scrim that served as the wall of her bedroom area. Lee closed the door, mumbled something to Randi, and climbed the stairs to the studio.

'Nicki?' the girl repeated.

Before she could call her name again, Nicola swept out of her hiding place and snatched the girl up in her arms.

'Oof! You're getting too big for me to ambush you any more!' she cried.

'Why didn't you answer the door?'

'The truth? Because, sweetie, sometimes when I'm working I don't want to be interrupted, and . . .'

'Sometimes you do?'

'By you? Anytime.'

Lee looked at the canvas on the easel. 'What's this?'

Nicola laughed. 'You tell me.'

The painting was large, and taller than it was wide, almost as tall as Lee. Its principal colours were an almost Mediterranean blue, a rosy pink and a pale green the colour of spring leaves. But there were also dozens of shades in between, punctuated by slashes of mauve, lavender, violet and yellow, with occasional flashes of orange and red.

After a while, Lee heaved a sigh and said, 'It feels peaceful.'

'What's that supposed to mean?' Nicola asked, probing.

'It's like being in my tree. I get all calm, and I feel like I could be in that place, in that feeling, for ever.'

'That's what the painting's about,' Nicola said. 'It's going to a hospital in London, where it's supposed to make sick people feel more comfortable.'

Lee was quiet for a moment. 'I think it will,' she said finally, sagely nodding her head.

'Meanwhile,' Nicola said, 'what are you doing down here at this hour? Isn't it time for your supper?'

Lee grinned. 'I was watching Drew and those other people building the new hedge up by the car park. They've all gone to the Cobweb again. They looked knackered.'

'I'll bet they are. How's the wall coming along?'

'Well, it's only the second day. They're laying grounders. They're the big bottom stones. I think it'll be a good hedge. You should see.'

'Perhaps I will.'

'Drew would like it if you did.'

'What?'

'You know. If you took an interest. He's a really nice man, Nicki.'

'That's as may be. But you're not my matchmaker.'

'Well, someone should be!'

Nicola could not believe she was getting advice from a nine-year-old. 'Listen,' she said gently, 'I love you, and I appreciate that you care about me, but being Cupid's not your job.'

Lee looked at the painting for a while.

'Whose job is it, then?' she asked.

'Nobody I know,' Nicola answered. 'Now, I think it's time you headed up to the farm. Do you want me to call ahead and let your mum know you're OK?'

Lee gave Randi a hug, answering, 'Yeah, maybe. Don't want to give Mum fits.'

Nicola stood outside her door, in the lane between her house and the river, and watched Lee cross the bridge and head towards the path up the Valency. She called Lee's mother, cleaned the paint off her fingers, changed quickly, and walked over to the Cobweb. This time, she left Randi behind.

Andrew was standing at the bar, nursing his pint and chatting to Flora.

'First it's hoisting sheep, then it's hoisting rocks,' Nicola said as she stepped up beside him. 'I can't say that's much of an improvement!' She winked at Flora.

'You're telling me,' Andrew said wearily.

Nicola eyed his dirty clothes. 'Love your ensemble.'

'Love your perfume,' he countered. 'What is that, eau de turpentine?'

'Touché,' she said, laughing.

'Can I get you somethin', Nicki?' said Flora. 'Or are you just goin' to talk dirty to each other in French?'

'A G and T, please, Flora,' she answered. This time, she paid for her own. Then she said to Andrew, 'So how are your grounders?'

'Grinding. Did you know there's a ton of stone in every three cubic feet of hedge? I'm sure I lifted that much already today.'

'You mean wall?'

'No, I mean hedge. That's what they're called in Cornwall. I thought you were local.'

'Me? Hardly.'

'Yeah, I guess your accent's a little soft for this area. What part of the country are you from?'

'The Boston part.'

'Up in Lincolnshire?'

'No, up in Massachusetts.'

'You're joking.'

'Can't be. You're not laughing.'

'I'm just surprised. That's where I'm from. Originally, at least.'

'You're from Boston? What neighbourhood?'

'Well, outside of Boston, actually: Lexington.'

'Ooh, the ritzy side of the tracks. No wonder.'

'No wonder what?'

'No wonder no accent.'

'And you?'

'The North End.'

'Hmm. You've lost your accent, too—and adopted a faux-British one, I see.'

'Fee, fi, faux, fum, I smell marriage to an English-mun,' Nicola sang. 'Thankfully, the only thing that survived that debacle was the accent.'

'Sore subject, I gather.'

'Dead subject.'

'Your husband?'

'Ha! I wish! No, just the marriage.'

'I'm sorry.'

'I'm not. Couldn't be happier.'

Andrew glanced at Nicola for a moment, then turned away. 'I'm not sure I believe that.'

'I was referring to the divorce.'

'Want to talk about it?'

'No more than you'd like to talk about yours, I suspect.'

'Oh, I talked about mine constantly, incessantly, to any- and everyone. Then I stopped.'

'Stopped, or just ran out of listeners?'

Andrew laughed. 'Just got bored with the subject, I guess.' He clinked the lip of his glass to hers and said, 'To hell with the past!'

'I'll drink to that,' Nicola replied.

The two of them stood looking at each other for a moment. Then Andrew turned back to the bar and searched for a menu. 'I've got to eat something. I'm going to pass out from hunger.'

'Please don't. Flora so hates scenes.'

Andrew took a breath and said, 'Would you care to join me?'

Her eyes widened, but she shook her head. 'On my income, I can afford to eat here or drink here, but not both. It's a lovely offer, though.'

'Play your cards right and I might treat,' Andrew teased.

'Only if I get to see the cards first.'

'Where's your sense of adventure?'

'Can't afford that, either.' Then Nicola surprised herself. 'Look, I've probably got enough wilted lettuce and mouldy vegetables at home to put together a passable salad for two. Interested?'

'With that mouth-watering description, how could one fail to be? But I'm filthy.'

'I know things seem a little primitive here, but believe it or not my cottage has hot water. Even soap. But the wine's on you and, if you hurry, you can get something lovely and expensive before the Rock Shop across the street closes.'

'I don't even know if I can move, much less hurry.'

'You run the risk of having me pick it out, then.' She swung her bag onto her shoulder. 'See you there.'

Andrew stood looking at the door, dumbfounded. He was having a date.

Flora was back. 'Orderin' supper, Andy-boy?'

'I guess not. I have a dinner invitation, sort of,' he answered.

'What, with Nicki?' Flora's forehead furrowed. 'Careful how you go, then, me 'an'sum.'

The comment took him by surprise. 'What do you mean?'

'Don't get me wrong, now. Nicki's a good soul. But she blows hot and cold when it comes to men—stormy, like. Bit of a loner is our Nicki. Lot of artists like that, I reckon.'

'Thanks, Flora. Careful is how I'll go.'

The Rock Shop, it transpired, did not sell rocks. It took its name from the rock candy it had sold to visitors for years—along with boxes of handmade chocolates, a selection of local beers and hard ciders, and wine. 'You should call this place "Guilty Pleasures",' Andrew said to the middle-aged woman at the till.

'You'd be Andrew. Nicki said you'd be along.' She pushed a bottle of wine across the counter. 'She chose this,' she said.

Andrew studied the bottle, an inexpensive Beaujolais-Villages.

'Hmm,' he said, looking at the shelves of wine bottles. 'Let's see if we can't choose something a little better than this, something with a bit more backbone. Ah!' He pulled down a bottle of Moulin-à-Vent. Then another.

'Good choice,' the woman said. 'It's one of Nicki's favourites, actually.'

'Then why'd she choose the Villages, I wonder?'

'Maybe because the Beaujolais-Villages is simpler, a bit safer?'

'I don't think of Nicola as the simple, safe type,' Andrew commented. 'Do you?'

The woman behind the counter had a giggle the sound of a silver bell. She blushed. 'I'm sure I couldn't say,' she said.

Andrew paid for the wine, thanked her, stepped out of the door, then turned and re-entered. 'Um, this is sort of embarrassing, but I've just realised I have no idea where she lives.'

The silver bell again, then: 'Over the bridge, right into the lane down the south bank of the river, carry on to the bottom, where the quay begins. Hers is "The Loft". Can't miss it. Enjoy the wine!'

Andrew thanked her again and backed out of the door. He felt like an idiot. He stopped in at the Cornish Stores, a little convenience shop, and rescued the last bunch of carnations, which were languishing, like huddled orphans, in a nearly dry bucket outside the door.

'**W**hat the hell have I got myself into, Randi?'

The dog barked, then resumed panting happily.

Nicola was shredding romaine with a vengeance. An egg was boiling in a pot on the stove, along with four small new potatoes. She had some limp green beans 'refreshing' in a bowl of ice water.

She had no idea why she'd invited this man to dinner. She'd never had a man in her cottage, much less one she'd known for only a couple of days. What was he *really* doing in Boscastle? Nobody came to Cornwall from America to build stone hedges—nobody sane, anyway. Maybe he was on the run from someplace or something or someone. Good Lord, the man's sole character reference was a nine-year-old girl! Oh, and a sheep!

OK, he was pretty good-looking, and neither too young nor too old. Tall enough, too; in heels she could probably look him straight in the eye. Cute, curly, dark brown hair with a little grey scattered about. Eyes—she didn't even know what colour they were. They'd spent all their time together in the dimness of the Cobweb.

Plus, in a week he'd be gone.

This last thought nagged at her—not that she might never see him again, but because that was part of the attraction. He was safe. Not much chance of getting 'involved'. Not much chance to mess up, either. But mostly, not much chance of risking her heart. She'd done that once, with Jeremy, and he'd brutalised it. In the few years she'd lived in Boscastle, she'd seen two or three men socially. But these dates had never got much beyond dinner at the pub, and the truth was, that had suited her just fine. The best men—men like Anne's Roger—were all taken. Besides, no one she met seemed able or willing to keep up with her. She used her sharp wit as a sort of entrance exam, and most men failed.

But this Stratton chap gave as good as he got. That took courage. She liked that.

There was a small slate sign with the name of the cottage attached to the whitewashed wall, beside the door. Just before Andrew knocked, he heard the dog bark, just once.

'Door's open!' he heard Nicola yell.

He stepped directly into a low-beamed room that ran the full width of the house. The floor was made of massive slabs of slate, rounded and worn by centuries of heavy use. There was a small dining table at one end of the room and a shallow fireplace surrounded by comfortable-looking furniture at the other. The overall colour scheme was white and nautical blue, with accents of lemon yellow. There was an expensively framed oil painting over the mantel, but the rest of the artwork was posters and prints suitable for a seaside cottage. He wondered if the house belonged to Nicola or was a rental.

Randi sat in a bright doorway at the back and barked a second time. A summons. Andrew went through to a long, narrow kitchen that ran across the back of the house. It was brightly lit, but the only window, over the deep porcelain sink, looked out on to the cliff face not two feet away. Nicola was squeezing lemon juice into a small bowl with olive oil in it. The tiny room was tangy with citrus.

He held out the carnations. 'Wilted flowers to go with the wilted lettuce,' he said.

She laughed. 'Did you get the wine?'

'Got something better. You have lousy taste in wine. I may look like a mere labourer, madam, but in fact I am a connoisseur of fine wines.'

She looked at one of the bottles and beamed. 'OK, Mr Common-sewer of Wine, are you equally expert at operating a can opener?'

'I think I could cope.'

'Good. There's a tin of very expensive Italian tuna just there, and the opener is in that top drawer. We're having *salade niçoise*.'

'Ah, I understand now,' he said as he cranked the can opener. 'Romaine lasts for ever without wilting, and most of the other ingredients are tinned, preserved in salt or brine, or, like the hard-boiled egg, in a protective shell. So it doesn't matter how old they are. It's like the wine: a vintage salad.'

'Hey! Beggars can't be choosers and you, my friend, look every inch the beggar.'

Andrew looked down at his clothes. 'Good point. Where can I wash?'

'The bathroom's upstairs, beyond the bedroom. But first open the wine!'

Andrew found a corkscrew, opened the first bottle, poured her a glass, delivered it with a flourish, and departed, picking his way up the narrow stairs, with Randi leading the way.

The painting on the easel at the top of the stairs stopped him in his tracks. He'd never seen anything like it. Outside, the light was fading, and yet the canvas seemed to glow from within, the colours radiant. There was nothing representational about the piece, but it reminded him of water at sunrise. Nicola was a fine painter.

He looked around. The upper storey was a big, airy space. The walls and cathedral ceiling were painted white, and the exposed crossbeams were bare, lime-washed timbers. The studio had a wonderfully earthy smell of linseed oil.

He stepped behind the billowy canvas curtain and into Nicola's bedroom, which was simply a section of the loft. It was sparsely furnished: a wrought-iron double bed that stood on a multicoloured rag rug, a dresser, a tall Victorian wardrobe. A few books were stacked on a side table with a lamp and some framed photographs. That was it—no television, no other decoration. Almost a hermit's cell. Suddenly feeling like a voyeur, he went through to the bathroom and washed up.

The salad was nearly gone, and they were well into the second bottle of wine when Nicola asked Andrew how long he planned to stay in Boscastle. They'd got past the basics: family, school, career—at least, the parts each was willing to share.

'Just a couple of weeks. I signed on to the hedge project for a week and came a few days early to beat the jet lag. Then I thought I'd spend a few more days poking around Cornwall before I leave.'

'Why are you really here?' Nicola asked.

He smiled. 'For the salad, which was pretty terrific, by the way.'

She made a face. 'You know what I mean. Why are you here, in Boscastle, three thousand miles from home . . . building a stone wall, for God's sake?'

'Hedge,' he corrected.

'You're hedging, all right.' In the light of the curious collection of candles she'd set on the simple pine dining table—some short and squat, some slender and tall, all of them white—her eyes shone like freshly mined anthracite. The coppery highlights in her long, wavy brown hair flashed in the changing light of the candle flames.

'It seemed like a good idea at the time. Still does, actually.'

'Is that supposed to be an answer?'

'It's all I have. You ask as if you suspect I'm an escaped felon.'

'Are you?'

He laughed. 'No. Though it feels that way sometimes.'

'Because you left your wife?'

He looked up at her sharply. 'I didn't. She . . . we . . . separated.'

'How many years ago?'

He took a breath. 'One.'

Nicola blanched. 'I'm so sorry. I had no idea it was that recent. It's just you seem so, I don't know . . . calm. Under the circumstances.'

'Do I?'

'On the outside, anyway.'

'Yes, well, I suppose I do.'

'And are you?'

A surge of emotion took him by surprise, a kind of panic. The truth was, he didn't know. He looked around the room, as if the answer were hidden there. 'Probably not,' he answered finally.

She reached across the table and touched his hand. 'Good,' she said, smiling. 'You'd be a freak if you were.'

'Thank you . . . I think.'

'She left you, didn't she?'

Andrew sighed. 'Is my inadequacy that obvious? Yes, she left me. We didn't separate. I lied about that.'

'She was a fool, whoever she was.'

'I don't know . . .'

'Andrew, please.' Nicola made a face. 'I've only known you for a few days, but it doesn't take a clairvoyant to see that you are a good man. For heaven's sake, you try to save sheep!'

'But I couldn't save the marriage.'

'None of us can do that single-handedly.' Then a thought occurred to her. 'Did you beat her?'

'What? Of course not!'

'My husband beat me.'

Andrew looked at the woman across the table, speechless. 'Your husband *beat* you? I . . . I can't imagine . . .'

'You know what? I believe you. I believe you can't imagine doing harm to anyone, much less a woman. I suspect you're cursed.'

'Cursed?'

'With being a gentleman.'

'I never thought of it as a handicap.'

Nicola seemed to study him for a moment, then said, 'She left you for someone else, didn't she?'

Andrew looked away. 'Maybe Lee's right. Maybe you are a witch. Or a mind-reader.'

'I'm so sorry. I shouldn't have—'

'Yes. She left me. For a lawyer, someone who earns a lot more than a university professor.' He stared at his empty plate, then looked up again. 'And now, Nicola, I think it's time I trundled home to bed.'

Nicola suddenly felt like a vampire who had sucked the life out of this lovely man. 'Andrew, please don't. I didn't mean—'

'I know, Nicola. I'm still a little raw is all, like some reptile that's shed its skin and is waiting for the layer underneath to toughen up.'

'I remember how that feels,' she said.

Andrew stood. 'Look,' he said, 'dinner was wonderful—almost as wonderful as your company, but not quite. I've got a big day tomorrow. We start building the rest of the hedge, now that the foundation is laid.'

She rose. 'Thank you for the flowers, Andrew.'

'Sorry they weren't a bit more, um . . . lush. You deserve better.' Andrew stood at the door for a moment, waiting for Nicola to open it. She seemed riveted to the floor. He lifted the latch, stepped out into the warm evening, then turned and smiled.

'Good night, Nicola,' he said quietly, 'and thank you.'

Nicola managed to smile. 'Good night, Andrew.'

She watched him walk up the lane, then closed the door.

'Damn!' she said.

SIX

'HOW MANY of those stones you reckon you'll pick up and put down before you find one you fancy?' Jamie had walked up behind Andrew and was smiling.

They were working on the 'filler' level, laying stone on top of the uneven grounders to create a level base on which to build the rest of the hedge. Earlier that morning, Jamie and Becky had gone through the rock pile and sorted the stones in rows, placing the largest closest to the wall. Jamie explained that you always lay the biggest stones first, so you don't have to lift them very high.

Andrew studied the rock he'd just lifted. 'I'm searching for one that fits.'

'Makes sense, but for one thing: you're doubling your work every time you lift one and put it back. You'll soon be exhausted and have little to show for your sweat.'

'So what's your solution?'

'You don't search for the right stone, lad, you discover it.'

'Huh?'

Jamie laughed and patted him on the shoulder. 'I'm being a bit unfair to you. It takes years. Lads! Becky! Over here for a moment.'

The crew gathered round the area where Andrew was working.

'You've all got the physics down pretty well,' Jamie said to his crew. He'd taught them how to lift big stones safely and how to find the right side for the face of the hedge. 'Now it's time for the metaphysics,' he said.

They all looked at him like pilgrims at the oracle.

'There's a trick to make this easier. When you look at the hedge face you're working on, I want you to remember this: you can find a stone to fit the space in front of you, or you can find a space to fit the stone. You have two choices, not one. Hedge-building's like doing a jigsaw puzzle. You have pieces and spaces, and you just match them up. The difference here is that the pieces are bloody heavy. So never pick up a stone twice. As you make your rows, try to keep several of its spaces in your mind's eye, then pick up a stone that fits one of those spaces. In a sense, it's simple: you just put the stone where it goes. So spend more time looking at your stones, but leave them on the ground. You'll soon learn to discover what fills the spaces, just by looking and rotating the stone in your head. Get the picture?'

They all nodded, though tentatively.

'Plus, there's the practical problem: if you keep picking up stones and putting them down again, we'll never get to the pub.'

They laughed, then went back to work, each of them doing a lot more staring than lifting, moving more slowly but, increasingly, with more confidence. Soon there were more 'ahs!' of satisfaction than 'uhhs' of effort as they discovered the stones they were looking for.

'**I** think you're round the twist,' Nicola said.

Anne Trelissick looked up from her drawing board, where she'd been putting the final touches on a pen-and-ink illustration.

'No, you don't,' Anne said. 'You know I'm telling you the truth, and it scares you.'

'Look,' Nicola exploded. 'Don't be daft; his wife left him!'

'And you left your husband.'

'And how do I know Andrew isn't violent, too?'

'May I remind you that this is a guy who tried to save a bloody sheep? OK, that makes him rather stupid, but nothing more. Besides, Lee really likes him, and one thing I've learned about my daughter, bless her quirky heart, is that she's a good judge of character. The evidence stands before me: you're her best friend.'

Nicola looked at her friend for several long moments. 'Thank you, Anne,' she said finally. 'But there's the other point, the obvious one . . .'

'Which is?'

'He'll be gone in—what—a week? I'm not about to fall in love with him.'

'Well, you're right there. You're not about to, you already have. You're not immune, you know, just because you got stung once.'

Nicola stood and gave Anne a hug. 'Thanks, love,' she said.

Anne shrugged. 'Damned if I know what for.'

Lee Trelissick was lying in wait. She'd seen the hedgers go into the Cobweb and sat on the wall opposite, waiting for Andrew to emerge. After only one pint, he did. He stood outside the door, blinking in the bright light, and considered which way to go home. He chose the road, over the valley path, and had taken only a few steps before he heard the familiar greeting: 'Guess what, Drew?'

He swivelled his head and there she was. It lifted his spirits immediately. 'I don't know. What, Lee?'

'Today's Wednesday!'

'So I gathered. Thankfully, it's nearly over.'

'No, it isn't.' She was skipping along at his side now.

'Listen, kid. By my reckoning it's coming up on five thirty. I've been here since eight this morning. Wednesday's over.'

'You're wro-ong!' she sang.

He stopped on the bridge over the river. 'OK, what?'

'Wednesday's Welly night.'

'Huh?'

'The singing! Don't you know?'

Andrew started laughing. He couldn't help it. Lee was facing him with her hands on her hips, like a schoolmarm lecturing to the class dunce . . . which was him. She positively vibrated with impatience. 'Why don't you tell me about it as we walk home, Lee?'

They passed the Wellington, Boscastle's oldest hotel, on their way up Dunn Street. It was a compact, handsome construction, several storeys high and vaguely Victorian-looking. It had the unusual distinction of having been built directly over the little River Jordan. Andrew stopped to admire the threshold of the hotel's entrance, where there was a steel grating beneath which he could hear the stream rushing through its ancient stone culvert.

Lee pulled at his hand, reclaiming his attention. 'Every Wednesday night, there's singing at the Welly.'

'What, *karaoke*?'

'No, silly! Old-timey songs. Some people bring instruments, too. There's been singin' at the Welly for ages and ages,' Lee continued. 'People turn up and, after a while, they just start singing, though Jack's the one who gets it going.'

'Jack?'

'Jack! The Boscastle Busker! You know . . . the guy with the big hat who walks around town singing?'

Andrew, focused as he was on the hedge-building, had missed this bit of local colour.

'He has loads of songs in him. But absolutely *everyone* goes and sings along!'

'And that includes you?'

'Yup. Mum and Dad take me, but I can't sit in the bar. I sit in a corner and no one complains. So you'll be there, right?'

Andrew sighed. He'd planned a bath, a bowl of spaghetti Bolognese, and bed, but there was no denying Miss 'Guess What?'

'**W**hat'll it be, friend?'

Andrew was standing at the Wellington's famous Long Bar. Before him was an array of hand pumps, each with a name more bewildering than the next: Cornish Knocker, Betty Stogs, Keel Over (that one sounded lethal), Figgy's Brew. He looked at the barman and shook his head. 'A pint of something, but I've no idea what.'

The nattily dressed fellow behind the bar laughed. 'Common problem here at the Welly. What do you like?'

'Amber ale. Smooth, not too hoppy.'

'That'll be Figgy's Brew. Here, have a taste.' The barman pulled a short measure into a small tumbler and handed it to him.

Andrew tasted and nodded. 'Perfect.'

The pub was packed. Andrew felt a hand on his shoulder. 'Come for the singing, lad?'

'Jamie! I thought you'd gone back up to Bodmin Moor.'

'Not on a Wednesday, not when Jack's in town.'

'What are you drinking, Jamie? My treat.'

'Well, thank you, son. Same as yours—a pint of Figgy.'

His drink came and Andrew clinked Jamie's glass with his. 'To the fine art and craft of Cornish hedging,' Andrew said.

'I'll always drink to that. And to you as well. Been watching you. You've a head for it, hedging, now you've got the spaces notion down. Expect that's partly from your training.'

'We didn't have hedge-building courses in architecture school.'

'Not what I mean. You've a good spatial sense. I think you see the hedge as a whole, in your mind, not just the stones and the spaces between them. One thing I don't get, though, lad. What you're doing here—building hedges when you could be making buildings. Odd sort of holiday, if you take my meaning.'

Andrew smiled at his stone master. 'I've never made a building, Jamie.' He could hear his ex-wife's tirade and shook it out of his head. 'I teach architectural theory. That's different.'

'Not much theory in hedging.'

'That's not true, Jamie, and you know it. You don't teach hedge-building, anyway. What you really teach is a reverence for the stone. You want us to listen to the stone, the story it wants to tell—how it was formed, what it's been through since, what it can do and can't do, what it wants to be.'

'Seems like somebody's been paying attention.'

'I have, Jamie, and it's partly because I've been trying to puzzle out something that's vaguely related.' And Andrew told Jamie about his ideas about livable places, about the almost organic integrity of such places, about the honesty of simple vernacular buildings, the beauty of working with local materials and building to human scale, and about how this art, this way of being in the world, was disappearing in America.

Jamie said, 'Seems to me you're living in the wrong country, lad. Around here, that stuff still matters. But what are you going to do, build Cornish hedges in Philadelphia?'

Andrew laughed. They both did.

'I don't know, Jamie,' Andrew said. 'I didn't even really know I was searching for something until I got here. It's like you told us this morning: you can find a stone to fit the space, or you can find a space to fit the stone. I used to think I was the stone. Now I think maybe I'm the space that needs filling.'

Jamie's face crinkled like a piece of brown paper. 'That's a step towards enlightenment, lad.'

'Drew!'

Andrew turned to find Lee at his side. Anne and Roger were weaving through the crowd. The barman, whose name was Brian, came round the end of the bar and bent down. 'Now, missy, I'll need you to be movin' towards the family area,' he said gently.

'It's not *missy*, it's Lee, as you well know, Brian Shaheen!' Lee said, her chin stuck out like the prow of a ship.

'An apple and mango for the lady, please, Brian,' Andrew said.

Lee got her drink and vanished. Then, apropos of nothing, an unaccompanied baritone voice rang out from the rear of the room:

> 'Come all jolly fellows, that love to be mellow,
> Attend unto me and set easy;
> A pint when it's quiet, come lads let us try it,
> For thinking can drive a man crazy.'

Andrew was amazed as voices around the room picked up the tune. By the time the leader got to the chorus, it seemed to Andrew half the crowd had chimed in.

Jack Vaughan was a slender, handsome man of about sixty, with a shiny, balding pate, a neatly trimmed greying beard and brilliant blue eyes. His voice was splendid. Beside him, singing alto harmony, was an apple-cheeked woman Andrew took to be Jack's wife. Opposite them at their table was a stockier fellow who occasionally played guitar with a deft touch and filled in the tenor harmonies. The crowd was some thirty strong.

Andrew was singing the chorus of 'John Barleycorn', when a voice in an upper register joined him. He knew the voice even though it had never sung for him before. The song ended.

'Hello, sailor,' Nicola said. She was wearing a simple but flattering raw linen wrap dress tied at the hip, and heels.

'Not me. I get seasick,' Andrew said with a grin.

'When you're sailing, or when you're drinking?'

'Yes.'

She punched his shoulder. 'You could be a regular here, with that voice.'

Andrew feigned shock. 'I believe that was a compliment!'

'I think you're right. I must be slipping.'

'Careful. You have a reputation to protect.'

'A reputation?'

'You know: prickly, pugnacious.'

'I prefer to think of it as proactive.'

'Get 'em before they get you?'

'Something like that.'

'Is it so unsafe out there?'

'You have no idea.'

'No. I suppose I don't. Then again, I'm not a woman.'

'Yes, I noticed that.'

'How about another drink?'

Nicola smiled. 'I wouldn't say no.'

It was nearly eleven o'clock when Jack's voice rang out on another song and the crowd picked right up:

> 'In South Australia I was born.
> Heave away! Haul away!
> South Australia, round Cape Horn.
> We're bound for South Australia.'

Thunderous applause and much hooting followed this song, and Andrew realised it was their traditional closing number. The crowd began milling about and drifting towards the entrance.

Lee found him and said, 'See? See? I *told* you!'

Andrew laughed. Roger scooped up his daughter and Anne whispered something to Nicola. Slowly, the rowdy energy in the room dwindled to a happy sigh, like air from a leaky balloon.

Nicola asked Andrew to walk her to her door, but all the ale he'd consumed suddenly demanded attention. 'Sure, Nicola,' he said, 'but I need to make a quick stop at the gents first.'

'You do that, Mr Stratton,' she said with a slightly woozy slur that made his name come out 'Sshtratton'. 'You can catch up with me. Think you can remember the way?' Then she winked and headed for the door, hips swinging.

When Andrew got back from the gents, most of the crowd was gone. He crossed the hotel's car park, walked a few steps down to the end of Dunn Street, then turned left before the bridge and walked beside the river towards the harbour. He felt like an imbecile. He didn't understand Nicola's invitation. Or maybe it was the beer making him stupid. No, he felt perfectly clear-headed. What, then? A woman with whom most of his previous interactions were best described as jousting matches had invited him back to her place—for what? A nightcap? It was completely bewildering. It was also exciting, a feeling he hadn't felt since . . . well, he couldn't remember when.

He knocked lightly at Nicola's door.

'Come upstairs. I've something I want to show you. The door's open.' The voice was above him, and he looked up. She was leaning out of the studio window. The cream-coloured linen dress glowed in the light of the moon.

He entered Nicola's cottage. Randi greeted him with his standard single bark, then raced up the stairs. Andrew followed. Nicola was waiting for him beside her easel.

'Hi,' he said, feeling suddenly awkward. 'You look so lovely.'

She made a teasing, and slightly unsteady, curtsy and said, 'Thank you, sir. But I'm not what I wanted you to see.'

'Nicola, I think you may be the only thing I want to see, ever again,' he said, amazed to hear himself say the words.

She smiled, a wide, bright-eyed grin, but then said, 'Stop that, you silly man, and pay attention.'

Andrew realised then that her watery painting was no longer on the easel. Something else was in its place, covered with a sheet.

'Close your eyes,' she ordered.

He obeyed and heard her sweep the sheet off the easel.

'Right. Open them.'

Before him was a painting of a girl dancing across a flower-strewn meadow by a stream. But not just any girl. He recognised Lee instantly. And it was not just any painting. Nicola had captured not only the image but also the spirit of the girl and the world she inhabited, a world of trees and grasses and wild flowers and water that shimmered with light.

He sat on the edge of the chaise. 'My God, it's . . . it's perfect.'

Nicola sat beside him. The two of them looked at the painting for a long while and said nothing. Andrew could feel the warmth of Nicola's skin radiating through the thin linen.

'You're the first person I've shown it to,' she said, finally.

'Then I am deeply honoured.' Hesitantly, Andrew put his right arm round Nicola's shoulder and drew her gently towards him. She leaned her head on his shoulder.

'I love that little girl,' she whispered.

'Me too,' Andrew said. 'I always wanted a kid just like her.'

'But your wife didn't?'

'Right. Except now she's having a baby with my replacement. What about you and your ex?'

'We tried. It didn't work. Thank God.'

'I think you'd have made a pretty terrific mother,' he said. They were both still staring at the new painting. Andrew turned his head and placed a light kiss on Nicola's left temple.

She leaned into him a little closer. 'Thanks.'

'For the compliment or the kiss?' he asked.

'Yes.'

Nicola turned and looked at the man beside her. His eyes were green-grey, she now knew. It was a good and gentle face. A caring face. She straightened and kissed his lips lightly, tentatively.

'I think you are a good man, Andrew Stratton,' she said, her voice barely a whisper.

She watched his face fall. 'I used to think I was, but since Kat—'

'Shh,' she said, and kissed him again. But then he drew back.

'Wait. I need to tell you that I lied to you last night,' he said. 'She didn't just leave me for someone richer. I was too embarrassed to tell you the truth, partly because I think she was right. She said she was divorcing me because I was passionless. Because I have "ice in my veins", she said.'

Nicola looked at him, her head tilted to one side. 'She was wrong, you know,' she said.

'Why?'

'Because your lips are warm. Very warm. And sweet.'

Andrew smiled at Nicola and said, 'I think one of us is drunk.'

'Um-hmm. You shouldn't drink so much.'

She kissed him again, harder this time. He responded in kind, his hands cupping her chin. She swivelled to her left and straddled Andrew's lap, facing him, eyes closed, pressing her lips to his, running her hands beneath his shirt.

Andrew could barely credit what was happening, and was struggling to keep his head clear. A wonderful, talented and undeniably lovely woman was kissing him, clutching him, her breath ragged, her desire undisguised. He wasn't at all sure how it had come about. The two of them had been so busy trading snappy remarks, he hadn't noticed that he'd been falling in love for days. And Andrew suddenly also understood—the way someone struck by lightning comprehends the fragility of life in a way no one else can—that he'd never loved this way before. He'd never felt the way he did now: amazed, entranced, transported.

He took her by the shoulders and laid her down on the chaise, stroking her face, then her neck, moving his hands gently. Slowly her dress fell open and his fingertips slid down the curve of her breast, exploring the landscape of her body.

Suddenly Nicola went rigid. Her eyes flew open.

'No! Johnny, don't! *Please!*'

Andrew tried to hold her, but again she screamed, '*No!*'

Her feet found purchase on the chaise, and she struggled backwards, pushing herself up the sloped arm of the chair till she teetered on its edge, flailing her arms in defence, yanking at her dress.

Andrew had shot to his feet and now stood beside the chaise, transfixed with shock. Nicola was staring straight ahead, eyes wild with fear, but also glazed. He suddenly understood that she was somewhere else—not with him in her studio, but off in some distant, private hell. He grasped her shoulders, as much to keep her from tumbling off the chair as anything else.

'Nicola!' he said, trying to get her to focus on his face. 'It's OK.'

'No! It's *not*! I'll *tell!*'

She was crying now, her arms clutched round her stomach, her body convulsing. Andrew eased her back down the chaise, and she curled into a ball on her side. He knelt on the floor and held her close, whispering her name, telling her she was safe. Her sobs shook them both. After a while, they lessened and then ceased altogether. He realised she was asleep.

He looked around the room and saw Randi watching from the shadows of a far corner of the studio. He was amazed that the dog had not barked. Perhaps the dog had been through this before.

Andrew stood and tried to come to terms with what had just happened. Had Nicola fallen asleep as he caressed her and then woken from a nightmare? Was she drunk and hallucinating? Had he frightened her?

What Andrew understood was that he needed to get her to bed. He slipped behind the sailcloth room divider and turned back the covers of Nicola's bed. Then he went back to the chaise, gathered her in his arms, and lifted her. As he settled her in bed, she mumbled something anxiously, but he couldn't make it out. He pulled the covers round her, kissed her forehead, and turned out the light on the side table. He sat beside her for a long time, wondering what the hell had just happened.

After a while, he rose and went back into the studio, where he found Randi sitting patiently in the middle of the room.

'Well, my friend,' he said, 'what do you suggest we do now?' Andrew was troubled by the idea of spending the night in Nicola's cottage, but was also afraid of leaving her alone.

Randi got up and walked to the chaise, made a single quiet woofing sound, yawned, and lay down on the floor.

'Good suggestion,' Andrew said, chuckling. He gathered a couple of dust sheets to use as blankets and lay down on the chaise. The whole experience had shaken him. Nicola had seemed in a trance, as if she were possessed. She'd been terrified.

Andrew looked around the room for something tangible to ground him in reality and found the painting of Lee, in the meadow by the stream. He wondered if Lee didn't represent Nicola's own childhood spirit—innocent, alive to the world, for ever at play.

But who was 'Johnny'?

Andrew was moving stone like a machine. He'd reached a nearly Zen-like state with the hedging, a zone of quiet concentration in which he had very little sense of the world around him.

They'd completed the first section, mounded turf at the top, and moved on. Becky and Ralph had stripped the second twenty-foot segment of topsoil and started on the third, while Jamie and Case moved stone with the Bobcat and laid grounders. Andrew worked with Burt in companionable silence and, in that silence, Andrew thought about Nicola.

He'd left her cottage quietly, just after dawn. The streets were deserted, the shops shuttered. As he wandered up the valley, he kept replaying the stages of the evening before: the by-now expected early verbal skirmishes at the Welly; the growing harmony between them; the unexpected invitation; the magical intimacy . . . and then her blind fear.

He thought about the tranquillity panels she painted—how peaceful they were, and how apparently at odds with her soul. He wondered how, or even if, he should approach the subject of her terror.

It took until afternoon, but he thought of something. And it calmed him. When the crew knocked off for the day, Andrew took a pass on their usual pint at the Cobweb.

Janet Stevenson answered his knock wearing blue jeans and a University of Michigan sweatshirt.

'Reverend Janet?' Andrew said, thinking, absurdly, that the priest would be in her vestments.

'It's Andrew, isn't it?' she said, smiling.

'That's some memory you have, ma'am,' he replied.

'It helps in this trade,' she said. 'Would you like to come in?'

Andrew looked down at his dirty clothes, then smiled. 'Perhaps not, given the state I'm in.'

'I'm not exactly overdressed myself,' she said. 'It's my son's sweat-shirt. I was cleaning. I'm the help as well as the vicar.'

'Look, I've just barged in without an appointment, so let me begin with an apology. Do you have a moment? Maybe we could take a short walk?'

'Yes, and yes. My husband's doing dinner tonight. Let me just tell him where I'm going. Where am I going, by the way?' she said, smiling again.

Andrew looked around. The church sat on high ground, looking out to sea. 'The churchyard?'

'I've been before,' she said. 'But it has its charms. I'll just be a tick.'

A few minutes later, they were strolling among the ancient, lichen-encrusted headstones that surrounded the church. They stopped at a gate that looked west, towards the sea. Andrew leaned on the top of the gate and began: 'Reverend Janet—'

'Just "Janet" is fine.'

'Janet . . . Let's say you knew someone to whom something terrible seems to have happened. Maybe a long time ago. But it's clear it haunts the person still.'

'How can I help?'

He took a deep breath. 'I don't know. That's what I came to ask *you*.'

The priest folded her hands together before her, as she might in church. 'I have to confess, Andrew, that the Church isn't very good at this sort of thing. We're charged with looking after the faith of our "flock", of trying to be of comfort in crises. But it sounds as if your friend is beyond that, and we're ill equipped to serve as either social workers or psychologists.'

She looked at him steadily for a moment and he saw a deep sadness.

'My tools are so limited,' she said. 'I could counsel this person about the everlasting love of God, about the redemption inherent in faith in His love. But she—may I guess it is a "she"?—would have to embrace that love. And I suspect, given her trauma, that may be a lot to ask.'

Andrew was amazed. In his experience, ministers always claimed to have all the answers. And suddenly he felt embarrassed. What had he really expected? What did he hope to achieve?

'Janet,' he said finally, 'I'm sorry. I should have thought about this more, I guess. I'm just trying to help someone I care about.'

'I know you are,' she said softly, 'and she is lucky to have you—*if* she will have you. I sense you are a good soul, Andrew. I believe you can reach her.'

'I don't know that. How can you?'

'Think about Peter, Andrew. Think about the lesson of his faith. If you believe you can help, if that belief comes from a good heart—which I believe it does—then you can walk on that water, and perhaps carry her with you.'

Andrew nodded to the priest, and said, 'Thank you. I'm sorry to have interrupted your evening.'

'You did nothing of the sort.'

'Good evening, Reverend Janet.'

'Good evening, Andrew. And good luck.'

He'd nodded and had walked just a few steps when she said, 'Have you thought of talking to Colin Grant?'

'The witch? I wouldn't have thought you had much in common with Mr Grant.'

'More than you might guess. Besides, I'll take someone who believes in something over someone who believes in nothing any day.'

'But witchcraft?'

' "There are more things in heaven and earth, Horatio . . . ," ' she said, quoting Shakespeare.

And Andrew thought, This is not your average priest.

He did not go to see Colin Grant next. It was late, and he needed to think that suggestion through. He was preparing a salad in the tiny kitchen at Shepherd's Cottage when he saw Nicola walking across the meadow from Roger and Anne's house. He met her at the door.

'Some hot date you are,' she said, flashing a grin. 'You're so exciting you put me right to sleep!'

Andrew was so startled by the absurdity of this greeting, he just stared. Then he regained his composure. 'Would you like to come in?'

'No, I just walked all the way up here to give you a hard time.'

Andrew stood aside, and Nicola danced in and plopped herself down in the overstuffed easy chair by the stone hearth.

So,' she said, 'I have two questions.'

'First?'

'Do you have a decent wine in this house?'

'Yes, a chilled Pinot Grigio. Will that be adequate, madam?'

'We'll see.'

'And the second question?'

Nicola tilted her head and smirked. 'Was it good for you? Because I certainly don't remember,' she added, rolling her eyes.

'I'll just get that wine, shall I?' Andrew answered, shaking his head as he disappeared into the kitchen. He was glad to have the excuse to leave the room, because he hadn't the first inkling what he should say next, if anything.

'Would you like to stay for dinner?' he called from the kitchen. 'I was just making a sort of Italian salad—mixed baby greens, tomato, prosciutto, mozzarella, onion and black olives.'

'Wait!' Nicola called back. 'You mean you have no fresh basil?'

Andrew walked to the door of the kitchen and leaned against the jamb. Nicola was sitting sideways in the big chair, her back against one arm, her tanned legs over the other. She was wearing a simple, sleeveless printed cotton sundress with a deeply scooped neckline. She looked delicious. 'Of course I have fresh basil,' he said. 'I just thought it would be wasted on you.'

'Ooh, that was below the belt.'

Andrew went back to the kitchen, opened the Pinot Grigio, and returned with it and two simple tumblers. He poured, and they clinked glasses. 'To the ever-unpredictable Ms Nicola Rhys-Jones, née DeLucca.'

'To the phantom date,' she countered, with some bemusement. 'There one moment, gone . . . well, at some point.'

He smiled, but sadly. 'You don't remember, do you?'

Nicola closed her eyes for a moment and when she opened them, the bemused look was gone, replaced with what Andrew could only describe as self-disgust. 'I'm sorry, Andrew, truly. I don't usually drink that much—well, actually, I do—but I don't usually pass out. I'm utterly embarrassed. I have no memory of last night, apart from your kissing me and my loving it.'

Andrew's voice was gentle. 'It's OK, Nicola. You have nothing to apologise for.'

'Oh, but I do. Because I have a confession to make. I've never invited a man to my cottage since I moved here from St Ives. In fact, I haven't been involved with another man since Jeremy.'

'It sounds to me like Jeremy would put any woman off men for a very long time.'

'Thank you. Yes. That's it, you see. I'm terrified of men.'

'I understand.'

'With one possible exception: you. Want to know why?' she asked.

Andrew nodded.

'Because you *do* understand. You're not like other men.'

'You can't know that,' Andrew said.

'Actually, I can. Want to know how? First, I'm a witch. I know these things.'

'How come you didn't know about Jeremy?'

'I wasn't a witch then, and don't interrupt. Second, Lee adores you. And third . . .' Nicola paused and looked at him with affection. 'A chap who risks his neck for a sheep is not abusive.'

'Oh, thank you.'

Nicola grinned. 'So there you have it: my indisputable, three-point, Jesuitical proof of your goodness.'

'My head is spinning, but that could be hunger. Dinner?'

She sank further into her chair. 'Dinner would be splendid. Thank you.'

OK, he thought as he finished assembling the salad, one of two things is going on here. Either she has no idea what happened last night or she does and doesn't want to broach it. Either way, it's not a topic for discussion.

He whisked together a Dijon vinaigrette, dressed the salad, added torn basil, and brought the bowl out to the tiny dining table by the window looking out towards the sea.

'You will, I'm afraid, have to bestir yourself if you wish to eat.'

Nicola had simply been watching him, like someone at a pavement café. Now she swung her legs off the chair arm and rose in one fluid motion, and he was struck again by how lovely this odd woman was. He held her chair and she slipped into it.

'Hello,' he said. 'My name is Andrew, and I'll be your waiter tonight. May I top up your glass?'

'You may.'

After dinner, as Andrew was walking her back, Nicola slipped her arm through his. 'Do you mind if I ask you something serious?'

'Of course not. What?'

She squeezed his arm gently. 'Did we make love last night? We didn't, did we?'

'If you mean did we have intercourse, then no.'

'But we were intimate.'

'Yes, rather magically so, I thought.'

'But I passed out.'

'Yes . . . Well, no, not exactly.'

She laughed lightly. 'What is that supposed to mean?'

'I don't know, really. Maybe you could tell me.'

'Tell you what? You're talking in riddles.'

He took a deep breath, looked down the empty lane, then turned to her. 'Nicola, I just need to ask you this . . . who's Johnny?'

Nicola stiffened, halted, and slid her arm out of Andrew's. 'How do you know about Johnny?' she said, stepping away from him as if he was radioactive.

'I don't know anything about Johnny. You screamed, "No, Johnny, don't!" last night. It was like you were in a trance. Then you passed out. That's all I know.'

It was as if Nicola had been turned to stone. She stood still, her eyes wide and wary. Finally, frostily, she said, 'Johnny does not exist.'

'Nicola, look . . . I saw you go rigid; I saw you struggling to get away. You were terrified.'

'It's none of your business,' she said through clenched teeth. Then she turned on her heel and walked quickly down the street towards the harbour. Andrew jogged to catch up with her.

'Nicola, I'm just trying to help.'

'Then leave me *alone!*' she snapped.

Andrew stopped. Nicola continued.

'Don't you understand how I feel about you?' he cried.

Now she stopped and spun round. Her mouth opened but no sound escaped. She turned again and ran headlong down the hill.

He did not follow. And as he stood there in the lane, watching her fleeing form dissolve into the gathering darkness, he realised he had never been in love before. Not with Kat. Not with anyone. But he was now.

Nicola woke in darkness, her body taut, her sheet pulled to her throat in two clenched fists. She had been dreaming again about Johnny, something she hadn't done for years.

Johnny. Her elder brother. The handsome one, with their father's broad shoulders and sleek, black hair. The brilliant one, with the effortless straight As right into high school. The ambitious one, who started his drug dealing small in the ninth grade—a few ounces of marijuana here and there, mostly for friends—but who later developed a talent for dealing cocaine. Johnny, the cocky one, who thought he could outsmart everyone, including his mother (at which he succeeded) and his drug-selling competitors, whose territory he took, incrementally, street corner by street corner, but who were not, in the end, either outsmarted or amused.

Johnny, who began sneaking into her room at night, when their mother was cleaning offices in the State House. Johnny, who raped her. Johnny, who got himself killed before she'd ever had a chance to confront him as an adult, and demand acknowledgment, and extract apology, and confer forgiveness.

Damned Johnny.

SEVEN

LEE WAS HALFWAY UP her favourite tree, but the climbing was slow, what with having to hook the umbrella over a branch each time she climbed higher. After having been drenched more than once by summer showers while reading in her tree, she'd had the brilliant idea of keeping her old red umbrella with the white polka dots there permanently, hooked over a limb to be used when necessary. She thought this arrangement exceptionally clever.

Today, however, she wasn't reading. She'd come up to have a think. The tree was a good place to think, what with the water bubbling along below and the birds and the privacy and all. Today's think was about Nicki—well, Nicki and Drew, really. Nicki had rung while she and Mum were having breakfast and, after listening a bit and glancing at Lee, her mum had taken the phone out into the hall, where she talked in urgent whispers. Naturally, Lee went to the door to listen—Nicki was *her* best friend, after all. She couldn't hear what Nicki was saying, of course, and all she could catch were snatches of what her mum was saying in response: 'Andrew said *what*?' and, 'Why'd you run away, you silly cow?' and, 'Sweetie, you need to let go of Johnny.'

Obviously, Nicki liked Drew but was seeing somebody named Johnny whom she needed to 'let go of'. In her perch high above the river, now, Lee realised she felt rather hurt that Nicki had a boyfriend she didn't know about. After all, she told Nicki absolutely *everything*. Why had Nicki kept this a secret? She scrunched her eyes and made her mind sail above the village, on a reconnaissance mission, but she couldn't think of anybody named Johnny in Boscastle.

Lee decided she needed to talk to Drew about this situation. She felt she'd sort of pushed him and Nicki together, and now she worried he might be sad about whatever had happened between them yesterday. Plus, there was the whole problem of Drew returning to America next week. If Nicki liked him, that would make her sad, too, probably. She left the umbrella hanging from a branch, returned to the ground, and headed down the valley towards the harbour.

'**R**eckon yon child wants to ask you somethin', Andrew,' Burt said, nodding towards the end of the wall. The hedge-laying crew was sitting by the river, finishing lunch.

Andrew followed his gaze and saw Lee, who was standing, stork-like, with one knee bent, foot resting against the opposite knee. He had no idea how long she'd been there. When she saw he'd noticed her, she grinned and waved.

'Don't go getting snared by these local lasses, now, Andrew,' Jamie teased. 'We've work to do yet.'

Andrew got to his feet and walked stiffly to where Lee waited. 'Hiya, toots. Whatcha doing down here?' Andrew asked.

'Came to see you,' she answered, dropping her foot to the ground. 'We need to talk.' Her pale eyebrows knitted together to signal serious business.

'We do?'

'Yup. Can you?'

'Sure, for a bit anyway.'

Lee turned and started walking towards the entrance to the car park. Andrew followed. When they were out of earshot from the others, she said, 'You like Nicki, right?'

Andrew kept walking. 'Well, yes, Nicola is a lovely woman, plus she's your best friend, too, and any friend of yours . . .'

Lee levelled a look at him. 'Don't treat me like a kid.'

Andrew was about to protest, but he caught himself. 'All right, yes. I like her. I think she's pretty terrific, although a lot of the time we seem to be at daggers drawn.'

'What's that supposed to mean?'

'Oh, you know, sort of teasing each other all the time.'

Lee nodded, and said nothing for a few moments.

'Lee, what's troubling you? Something is, or you wouldn't have come down here when you could be in your tree.'

'Nicki called Mum this morning, all upset. About something that happened between you two, I guess.'

'Yes, well. We . . . um . . . had a bit of a disagreement.'

Lee reached the bridge and stopped. 'I think Nicki's got another boyfriend. His name is Johnny. Mum told her she should let him go. I don't think Mum likes him. Mum likes you, though,' she added.

Andrew leaned on the parapet beside the gangly girl. He sighed. 'It must have been hard for you to come down here to tell me that,' he said.

'A little,' she confessed.

Andrew turned and scooped up the bony child in his arms in a giant hug. 'I love you to pieces, Lee Trelissick, and if I had a daughter I'd want her to be just like you.'

She wriggled away, giggling, and he let her go. He was a little surprised by his own impetuousness. Something inside him was softening, uncurling, anxiety calving off him like a glacier melting. This new gentleness was, he knew, partly a legacy of the hedge-building. He didn't need to anticipate or prepare for anything; he could let things take their natural course. He could just 'be'. He could even admit to himself the pure joy and wonder he felt whenever he was with this solemn little girl.

They were walking back to the worksite.

'What are you going to do about this Johnny?' Lee asked.

Andrew stopped and knelt in front of her. 'Look, I'm a visitor here, Lee. I'm just passing through. I have no business being involved in the troubles and cares of those who live here.'

Lee nodded. 'But you love Nicki. That makes it different.'

Andrew just stared at her. 'You're right. I do. And I'm going to take care of this Johnny guy. Thank you for telling me. But now I have to get back to work. It's our last day. That OK with you?'

Lee nodded, and Andrew set off for the hedge site.

'You won't hurt him, will you?' Lee called after him.

He looked back at the girl. 'I don't think that will be necessary.'

But, of course, he had no idea what would be necessary.

Jamie had seen the rain coming.

'All right, you lot,' he'd called out as the first drops splattered the dusty ground, 'get the tools in the van and your sorry selves to the pub. You've been reprieved!' Though there was still another twenty yards of hedge to be laid, what they'd built looked clean and solid. And he'd turned his crew from a group of clumsy amateurs into skilled craftspeople—proper hedge-layers he'd be proud to work beside. It was always like this at the end. He hated to let them go. Ever since his wife of forty years died—what, five years ago now—his students had been his family.

Now here they were, this latest lot, shambling in from the street, sweaty, dirty, smiling, their shirts pockmarked with raindrops.

'Flora, my dear, sweet lass,' he called to the barmaid after they'd muscled their way through the crowd of tourists who were also sheltering from the shower, 'drinks for my crew, on me.'

When their glasses were delivered, he lifted his in a toast.

'You're ugly as sin, every last man of you—the lovely Becky, of course, excepted—but you're Cornish hedgers now, and damned fine ones!'

Nicola sat on a stool in the bar on the other side of the double fireplace wall. Only the back of the bar communicated with the two rooms. She was wolfing down a delightfully sinful and messy hamburger smothered in caramelised onions and melted Cheddar, along with a plateful of chips, and washing it all down with her usual gin and tonic. Flora had told her that Andrew was in the adjoining bar with Jamie's crew, but she stayed put. She didn't want to see him. Well, actually she did, but she had no idea what to say if she did, how to begin and, having begun, where to stop. And then there was the repeated refrain, the leitmotif: he was as good as gone anyway.

The shower passed, the tourists drifted outside again, and Flora plonked herself down next to Nicola on her break, a half pint of lager in front of her. She leaned close to Nicola's ear.

'Tell you what, love. That there Jamie, if he weren't always so bloody filthy, I could get to likin' him. Hard body, soft eyes. What's not to like, eh?'

'Flora, you trollop, you shock me!' Nicola said, giggling.

'What, you think 'cause I'm old enough to be your mother I can't hanker after a good man?'

'No! It's just . . . I don't know . . . I thought you were sweet on Brian, over at the Welly.'

'What, *him*? Oh, Brian's OK as far as that goes, good for a laugh and a bit of a flirt, but I don't see him ever makin' much of hisself. Men who bartend, well, most of them are a bit short of ambition, y'know? Like they're just markin' time. Unless they own the place, which Brian don't.'

'But is Jamie Boden that much better a prospect? I mean, the chap's a hedge-builder.'

Flora laughed. '*Hedge-craftsman*, to you, m'dear. But he wasn't always, is what I hear. Been at that less than ten years, for all his skill. Before that he was in finance, up in London. Made a pile in hedge funds, got fed up, and moved back here to live in his wife Lydia's family's place up there on the moor. Then lost her to cancer, poor soul.' She went quiet for a moment and then started laughing, her ample body rippling with mirth. 'Old Jamie went from hedge funds to hedge-building! Just thought of that, I did. Pretty good, eh?'

After several more rounds than usual, Jamie's students began to take their leave—Burt and Ralph first, with a salute from Ralph and a standing invitation from Burt to come up to the farm for a visit anytime. A nod from Casehill, and a handshake. Becky hugged Jamie and said, 'See you Monday,' and was gone.

'Monday?' Andrew asked his teacher.

'Got a crew of National Trust volunteers coming to continue work on the hedge. What're your plans next week, lad?'

Andrew sighed. 'Leaving. Probably Wednesday or Thursday.'

'A shame is what that is, now I got you nearly useful.'

Andrew laughed. 'I can't spend the rest of my life building Cornish hedges, Jamie.'

'Why not? Market demand's growing, and I can't begin to keep up with it. Pay's good, too, plus no one's your boss.'

'I'm an architect, Jamie.'

'You like being an architect?'

This stopped Andrew cold. It wasn't a question he'd ever consciously entertained. He'd known he wanted to be an architect almost from childhood. He'd never even considered anything else. It was what he did. It was who he was. But were you an architect if you never built anything?

'How old d'you reckon I am?' he heard Jamie ask.

'Sixty-something?' Andrew answered.

'Pushing seventy. And feeling every year of it. Been looking for someone to pass the Stone Academy on to for a while now, and I'm thinking you're a natural for it.'

Andrew looked at his friend. 'Well, sir, that's as fine a compliment as I've been paid in a very long time.'

'It isn't a compliment, you bloody numskull. It's the offer of a lifetime!'

'Jamie, look, I've got a house in Philadelphia and a new semester of classes to teach in less than a month. I'm sorry. I can't.'

'Can't or won't? I'm not offering you a job. I'm offering you a life. The only question is whether you have the courage to live it.'

Andrew stared at him for a moment, finally saying, 'It's not that simple.'

'Isn't it? Remember what you were telling me at the Welly last Wednesday? About honest architecture, livable communities and local materials? That's not a scholarly pursuit, lad, that's your passion, even if you're too blind to see it. And while I'm at it, let me tell you something else. You were born to work with stone. Never seen anyone take to it so naturally.'

Andrew felt honoured. 'Look, I hear you. I just think it's . . . I don't know . . . crazy. Not to mention that if I didn't show up at school next month, that would probably be the end of my career.'

Jamie nodded. 'Right, then,' he said, 'here's my fall-back position. What are you doing on Monday?'

Andrew laughed hard. He'd planned on seeing a bit of the county before he left, but the truth was, he really would prefer to work some more on the hedge. He hated unfinished business. And he could hardly turn Jamie down, now.

'See you in the car park at eight,' Andrew said.

'Good lad,' Jamie said.

Andrew clapped an arm round his friend, thanked him for the lessons and the drinks, and took his leave.

Flora had been watching this exchange while serving customers at the two bars, and now she sidled over to Jamie.

'What are you up to, you old rascal?' she asked.

Jamie smiled, but it was a tired smile. 'Looking for a successor, Flora; looking for a successor.'

'You retirin'?'

'No, love, just thinking ahead. Plus, I like that chap.'

Jamie paid the bar bill and turned to leave.

'See you again Monday, Jamie?'

Jamie looked at her for several moments, as if something was dawning on him, then grinned. 'If not sooner,' he said.

When all the crew had left, Flora mixed an unrequested gin and tonic and slapped it down in front of Nicola.

'My shout,' she said about the drink, 'but only if you tell me what the hell's going on between you and the American.'

Nicola slumped. 'Is my private life such public knowledge?'

'No, just to me and those who care about you, which includes, oh, I don't know . . . maybe half the village?'

'Bloody hell.'

Nicola knew Wednesday night had gone all wrong. She woke up in bed the next morning, fully dressed and alone. Andrew had asked her about Johnny. What did he know? She sighed.

'I'm just wrestling with some old ghosts, is all,' she said.

'Nicki, let me tell you something from my long years of romantic experience. The calendar is a bum way to measure the passage of time. Time's more like the Valency out there,' she said nodding towards the door. 'It just rushes by. And it don't give much of a damn about your history . . . or your ghosts. I'm not sayin' this because I'm so wise, love. I'm sayin' it because I haven't been, and an awful lot of time has passed under my bridge, and I've been standin' on it alone. That Andrew of yours is not the kind of man who's goin' to hurt you. Ain't got it in him, for one thing. And cares for you a lot, for another. Like Jamie does me. I know he does—he just hasn't tumbled to it yet, poor sod. You been solitary so long I don't think you even remember what it's like to have a warm body beside you. We aren't meant to live solitary, especially us women.'

'But—' Nicola interjected.

'I know, I know; he's leavin'. But is that any reason why you shouldn't have a few moments of togetherness? Of happiness?'

Early on Saturday morning, Andrew stood at the kitchen window and waited for the kettle to boil. Roger and Anne's house was invisible, drowned in a miasma of milky white. In the meadow across the road, one of Roger's cows materialised from the fog and, just as suddenly, vanished. Andrew welcomed the mist. He had a walk planned that would take him up along the high ridge east of the Valency River, then west to the coast and High Cliff. The fog would keep the air cool for what he could tell from his Ordnance Survey map would be several steep climbs.

After a breakfast of fresh eggs from the farm and crusty bread, he tossed a water bottle, a rain jacket and the map into his day pack, laced up his boots, and stepped out of his door. Lee was not waiting for him on her wall, which came as a disappointment. Apparently she drew the line at sitting on cold, damp rocks.

He struck off along a narrow, single-track road that skirted a wood in which huddled Minster church. The lane carried on high above the Valency valley. After a mile or so, the lane dipped steeply into a rocky ravine, climbed up again, and zigzagged through a tiny hamlet of cottages and barns called Treworld, then stretched out across the shoulder of the valley again.

Just outside Lesnewth, a signpost pointed to a footpath that cut across a meadow to another lane that led to the village of Tresparrett, where there was a pub Andrew thought he might try for lunch. He was halfway across the field when a voice called out to him. He peered down-slope and there was Roger, sitting on top of an open all-terrain vehicle, a knitted cap pulled down against the mist, surrounded by cattle. Andrew walked down the hill towards him, just as the sun began to burn through the fog.

'Running away from home?' Roger called, climbing down from his perch.

'It's my day off,' Andrew said. 'No hedge-building on Saturdays. It's a rule in Cornwall, I understand.'

'Not on my farm, it isn't. When are you starting?'

'Starting?'

'On my hedges, man! They need attending to!'

Andrew laughed, and then realised they were surrounded by large, quietly chewing cattle. Roger caught his momentary flash of concern.

'Needn't worry about these fellows. Sweetest breed in the country. These are Devon Rubies.' Roger walked among his cattle, stroking their backs. 'Where're you off to?' he asked.

'The Horseshoe in Tresparrett, for lunch.'

'Want a lift?'

'Sure! Buy you a pint?'

'Sure!'

'Then I believe we have a deal, my friend,' Andrew said, climbing onto the back of the ATV. Roger started the engine and they were off, bumping across fields so rugged that Andrew thought he'd lose his teeth before he had a chance to use them on lunch.

At the top of the hill, they whipped a quick left turn and promptly entered the little hamlet of Tresparrett. The Horseshoe Inn was a low, whitewashed stone cottage set back from the main road. It was just opening.

'Good day to you, Derek!' Roger shouted to the bearded fellow behind the bar as they entered. 'Derek, Andrew; Andrew, Derek,' Roger said by way of introduction. 'Him and me go back a ways.'

'And it never gets any better,' Derek said, smiling.

'Derek's never got over losing Anne to me, you see. Sweet on her, he was, weren't you, lad?'

'And who wouldn't have been, I ask you! How is your fine lady, then?'

'Oh, tolerable, Derek. Tolerable,' said Roger.

Derek shook his head and, addressing Andrew, said, 'Haven't a clue why she chose him. Nor why she's stuck it out with him this long. Horrible fate for a nice girl. Horrible.'

Roger had a packed lunch, so Andrew ordered two pints and a bacon and brie sandwich for himself. They took their pints to a table and, after delivering the sandwich, Derek drifted off to tend to new arrivals.

'That's nice work you lot have been doing down there by the harbour,' Roger said, as Andrew ate.

'The hedge? Thanks, but it's all due to Jamie.'

'Not what he tells me. Word is, you're gifted.'

Andrew laughed. 'Oh? And what else does the Boscastle grapevine have to say about me?'

The other man's face became serious. 'I also hear there's some trouble between you and Anne's friend Nicki.'

Andrew felt suddenly defensive. 'Look, Roger, I don't know what you think of me, but I've done nothing that—'

The farmer interrupted, waving his free hand. 'Nay, friend; not what I meant, not at all. I'm not supposed to know anything, if you follow, but it's not about you.'

'Yeah. Lee says Nicola's got some guy named Johnny in her life.'

'Not any more, she don't,' Roger replied. 'He's dead.'

'Her boyfriend died?'

'Not her boyfriend, Andrew. Her elder brother. And a nasty piece of work, is what I hear. A drug dealer. Happens he also, um, fiddled with her, as a kid.'

Andrew looked blank.

'You know, incest and all. Then got himself killed.'

'Oh God.'

'Look, the missus tells me Nicola's sweet on you, but scared. This dead brother, it's like he's sleeping under her bed. Way I look at it, Nicola's hiding here in Boscastle. But not from that upper-class ass of an ex-husband of hers. I reckon she's hiding from the dead brother—and the rest of the world as well. You're the first thing she's really taken notice of, besides that dog of hers, since she got here. And it's been years.'

Andrew struggled to take it in. He felt swept by waves of compassion for Nicola and fury about this dead, but not dead, brother.

Roger was still talking. 'But you didn't hear it from me, right? Anne will kill me if she knows I've told you.'

Andrew looked at the man for a moment. 'Thank you,' he said finally. He put out his hand and Roger took it.

Andrew stood at a window in the upstairs library of the Museum of Witchcraft, gazing at the little river below and waiting for Colin Grant to finish a phone conversation. He'd been immensely relieved to find someone other than Nicola at the ticket desk when he asked after Colin. Nicola had had the morning shift.

'My good fellow, please accept my apologies,' Colin said, putting down the receiver. 'One of my board members, a somewhat trying chap, but well intentioned. What can I do for you? A book, perhaps?' he added, gesturing to the shelves that lined the walls.

'A question, really,' Andrew said. 'Something the vicar suggested you might be able to help with.'

'Ah, yes, the Reverend Janet. It wouldn't be the first time. You have a matter she can't address?'

There was an uncomfortable pause, then Andrew nodded and dived in. 'Let's say someone, a woman, was sexually abused as a child, by an elder brother. And let's say that brother died soon thereafter, but the memory of his abuse still haunts the woman in adulthood, so much so that it makes forming normal relationships with men extremely difficult.'

'An all-too-common phenomenon, I'm afraid,' Colin said, shaking his head in dismay.

'Are there practices or . . . "cures" in witchcraft that might apply?'

'Oh, yes, certainly, though perhaps nothing quite so specific.' Colin went to one of the shelf units. 'You're really talking about two broad categories of concerns: visitations—you used the word "haunts", and it is apt—by an evil spirit, in this case the dead brother, but also issues associated with love in general. There is a long history of witches applying what we might call "white magic" to address such problems. On this shelf,' he said, sweeping a hand along a row of book bindings, 'we have volumes to do with matters of the heart. And over there,' he added, pointing across the room, 'is a section on dealing with banishing evil spirits. I'd be happy to lend you however many books you'd like to examine.'

'Mr Grant—'

'Colin.'

'Colin. I was thinking more along the lines of direct intervention. I gather there is a community of believers in and around Boscastle, though I know that they don't exactly advertise themselves.'

'This is true. People have peculiar and rather lurid ideas about witchcraft and witches, almost all of which are wrong.'

'Let's say you knew a witch who could act on this person's behalf. What might they do to intervene in such a matter?'

Colin was quiet for a moment. 'We're speaking in purely theoretical terms, you understand.'

Andrew nodded.

'Right. Well, for a start, the witch might scry in a dark mirror.'

'I'm sorry, scry?'

'Oh. Sorry. An old word derived from the verb *descry*, which means, "to catch sight of". Witches sometimes use dark mirrors to see into the world of the spirits. She would ask the spirits, or "old ones", to give her advice, and might see visions in the mirror and use those visions to find a solution. She would wait for a waning moon, because that's believed to be the best time for banishing terrors. Then the witch might advise the woman to tear off a bit of a photograph of her brother each night of the waning moon, then burn the pieces on the night of the dark of the moon.'

'So the woman would have to be an active participant?'

'That's best, but the witch might perform this herself on behalf of the woman, with or without her knowledge. Of course, she'd have to have the picture, or something once owned by the brother.'

Andrew thought about this for a moment and remembered a photograph in Nicola's bedroom, a picture of three children at a beach. 'Would a photocopy of a picture work?'

'Oh, yes, certainly. And if there is a new relationship involved'—here Colin looked briefly at Andrew—'she would use a waxing moon to bring about a good relationship. The witch might secretly bind two sticks together, one gathered from the garden of the woman and one from the garden of the man. This would encourage the relationship.'

Andrew listened to Colin with respect, as he might have any colleague at the university, and yet Andrew's faith in reasoning left little breathing space for such arcane notions. Scepticism rose in him like a spiritual seasickness, but he fought it down. What choice was there, really? It did not seem there was anything in the world as he knew it that could banish the ghost that plagued the woman he now, to his utter surprise, thought of as his beloved.

'The next question, I suppose, is whether you can think of anyone who might perform such a ceremony?'

The museum owner surprised Andrew with an almost childlike grin. 'You already know such a person, my dear fellow, and I would recommend her whole-heartedly, although I cannot promise she would do it. Flora Penwellan.'

'Flora at the Cobweb?'

'The very same. A gifted and gentle witch. Runs in her family. I knew her mother.'

'Colin, I think she might just help after all. This person's her friend.'

'Well, then, I leave it to you. And welcome to our particular bit of old Cornish culture.' Colin extended his hand, and Andrew took it. The two nodded, and Andrew left.

From her studio, across the narrow river from the museum, Nicola saw Andrew emerge and turn upriver. At first she thought she would call out to him, but she decided against it. What would she say?

Then an idea bubbled up out of her confusion, and she picked up the phone.

EIGHT

ON SUNDAY MORNING, Andrew was woken by a peculiar, episodic rattle. He opened his eyes, got his bearings, and saw the morning was already well advanced.

The rattle ceased, then began again, like hail against a roof. No, like gravel against a window. His kitchen window. He pulled on a pair of jeans, stumbled to the kitchen, and peered out. Sure enough, there was Lee, sitting on the stone wall. Also Nicola. Both of them grinning and chucking gravel at the cottage. He sighed, put water in the kettle, turned it on, and opened the door.

'Ladies!' he barked. 'It is barely daylight!'

'Uh-uh!' said Lee.

'Uh-uh!' said Nicola.

They seemed immensely pleased with themselves. He wandered back inside, desperate for tea. The girl and the woman skipped in behind him as if they belonged there.

'We thought you were goin' to sleep *for ever,*' Lee chided as she hopped up to sit on the counter by the sink.

'Why aren't you getting ready for church?' Andrew asked her.

'Nicki and me are going to a different church, a *really* old one!'

'Older than St Symphorian's?'

'Yup,' Lee said.

'What's your mother think of this arrangement?' he asked. The kettle clicked off, and he poured the steaming water into a teapot.

'Mum's poorly,' Lee said. 'Says she has a summer cold or something. She said it was fine.'

'And you two needed to inform me of your devotional plans'—he glanced at the clock—'at this ungodly hour, because . . .?'

' 'Cause you're meant to come with us! Right, Nicki?'

'If you'd like,' Nicola said, looking at him, her eyes soft, her voice signalling a kind of apology.

'I need some breakfast,' Andrew groused, now playing up the role of the put-upon victim.

Nicola came over to the counter, used her hip to push him gently aside, cut a thick hunk of crusty bread from the loaf Andrew kept under a kitchen towel, slathered it with butter, and then drizzled it with honey from the crock on the windowsill. '*Petit déjeuner, monsieur,*' she said, handing it to him on a paper napkin. 'Come on, you'll like it,' she added.

Andrew slumped his shoulders in resignation and shuffled off to the bedroom to look for a shirt. Then he came back out and asked, 'What's the appropriate dress for this church?'

'Oh, it's quite casual,' Nicola said lightly, flashing a quick wink at Lee. 'And it's a bit of a hike to get there.'

Lee was wearing her usual faded khaki shorts, T-shirt and wellies. Nicola had on hiking sandals with lugged soles, a flatteringly snug pair of black capri trousers, a tailored white cotton broadcloth shirt with the collar turned up at the back, and a black-and-white-striped silk scarf tied to hold back her hair. Andrew marvelled at how lovely she was with so little artifice. He retreated to his room and put on a faded blue chambray shirt, socks and his boots. In the kitchen, he grabbed his honeyed bread, filled a lidded traveller's mug with milky tea, and followed the ladies out to Nicola's car, which turned out to be a rugged old olive-green Land Rover. Lee climbed in the back, joining a delighted Randi. Andrew took the passenger seat, and the moment he clicked his seat belt, Nicola rocketed up the farm track and turned right onto the main road south towards Tintagel.

At a hairpin curve in a narrow, lushly forested valley about three miles from Boscastle, Nicola pulled the car onto the left shoulder of the road and brought it to a stop. Andrew slugged back the last of his tea and followed his guides to a trail along a stream.

The girls chattered away and Randi raced ahead, coming back every few minutes like a child checking in with his mother. The trail passed a handsome old stone gristmill, crossed the stream, and then edged round a series of ever-higher rock outcrops.

'What's this place called?' Andrew asked.

His question met with an incredulous look from Lee and a forgiving smile from Nicola. 'Rocky Valley,' she said.

'Duh,' Andrew said, grinning.

A little farther down the valley, they arrived at the ruins of two stone structures. Another mill, Andrew realised when he discovered the grindstones half buried in the rubble. He was about to ask Nicola about the place when he realised she and Lee had disappeared.

He found them bent over and staring at the face of an exposed wall of shale behind one of the ruined buildings. As he approached, he realised that, with their forefingers, they were tracing the circuitous outlines of a labyrinth design cut into the rock face. The carving was delicately incised and a little over a foot in diameter. As he watched, they moved on to a second, nearly identical labyrinth a few feet away. Again, they traced it with their fingers, as if performing some silent ritual. Andrew found a brass plaque attached to the rock face that said that the stone-carved labyrinths dated from the Bronze Age and were believed to have religious significance.

Tucked into every nook and cranny of the cliff face, wedged into every crack and seam, as high as a human being could reach, there were tiny, fetish-like objects: a miniature baby shoe, a toy dog, a tiny model boat, and simpler items—a button, a key, a pyramid of small shells. Nicola herself was pushing a polished cowrie shell into a cleft in the rock. Lee stood off to one side, her hands clasped loosely below her waist, and was preternaturally quiet, as if in a trance.

Nicola turned to Andrew and smiled peacefully and with unabashed affection. 'Welcome to church.'

Andrew blinked.

'Here in Cornwall, the practice of witchcraft survives and thrives. It's very gentle and mostly about acknowledging the power and the blessings provided by each of the turning seasons, revering the flow of the natural world.'

'So you really are a witch?'

Nicola laughed. 'No, I'm just learning about witchcraft, from working at the museum.'

Andrew looked again at the artefacts strewn about the area. 'And all this?'

'Offerings—prayers, if you will. This place has been holy for millennia. Believers in this area are simply carrying on a very long tradition of

communing with the spirits and with nature in this special place.'
Nicola took his hand. 'Come on, there's more to see.'

The three of them followed the dog across another footbridge and
continued downstream. Randi raced ahead and disappeared round a
bend. Lee dashed after him. When Andrew turned the corner, too, he
came to an abrupt stop and said, simply, 'Wow.'

Nicola smiled. 'I thought you might like this,' she said.

Invisible until you rounded the bend, what lay before them was
Bossiney Cove, a wedge-shaped pocket of deep, boiling ocean into
which the stream they'd been following flung itself. Charcoal-black
slate cliffs rose almost vertically on both sides, creating a sharp contrast
to the brilliant-white surf foaming on the rocks below with each
incoming surge. Out over the ocean, vast tracts of milky-blue sky were
broken by towering cumulus cloud masses and, closer to the water,
fast-moving squall bands ruffled the water. The colours dancing on the
surface of the water put him in mind of one of Nicola's paintings.

On their way back up the narrow valley towards the car, Andrew
stopped by the ruined mill to look again at the labyrinths. Something
about them bothered him and, after a few moments of studying, he
grasped what it was.

'Lovely, aren't they?' Nicola said.

'Yes, and that's the problem. They're *too* lovely.'

'I don't follow you.'

'You see how clean and delicate these incisions are? There's no way
they could be Bronze Age. The tools they had then were too primitive.
To do something this precise, you'd need hardened steel. But materials
like that didn't exist then.'

'I thought you were an architect. Since when did you become an
archaeologist?' There was an edge in her voice, and instinctively Lee
moved off with the dog.

'OK, let's forget the matter of tools. This rock is shale. Shale is
sedimentary and relatively soft. It erodes when exposed to water.
Anything carved in this rock three thousand five hundred years ago
would have disappeared altogether in just a few centuries of rain.'

'Listen, Mr Know-it-all,' Nicola said, her voice rising, 'this has been a
holy place for centuries. Just ask anyone round here! Who the hell are
you to say it's not? A week of stone-wall-building and now you're a rock
expert, too? Give me a break!'

Andrew could hear the shrill edge to her voice. He softened his. 'Look,

Nicola. I'm not trying to insult you. It's just that, well, I don't think these labyrinths are any older than that tumbled-down mill behind you. I think they both date back about a hundred and fifty years. Tops.'

'Nicki? Drew?' It was Lee. 'The wind's changed, and look at the sky back that way.'

She pointed towards the ocean, and the two adults followed her finger. The girl had sensed what neither of them had. The sky over the cove was black, and the wind had picked up. At that moment, there was a crack of lightning; then drops of rain the size of marbles began hammering the ground. The argument instantly forgotten, the three of them ran up the path. Randi led the way.

By the time they climbed into the Land Rover, the squall had passed, but they were soaked. Apart from the damp panting of the dog in the back, no one spoke, and the atmosphere in the car was electric as they drove back to Bottreaux Farm.

At Shepherd's Cottage, Andrew got out. He stood with the door open, leaned in, and said quietly, 'I'm sorry I spoiled things.'

Without turning away from the windscreen, Nicola said, 'Not everything in creation is amenable to rational analysis.'

Andrew nodded and closed the door. The vehicle sped away down the track towards the farm.

'I don't think Nicki was very happy with you yesterday.'

'Thank you, Harry. What a wise wizard you are.'

Lee shot Andrew a look. She had been sitting on the wall outside his door again, reading a Harry Potter book, when Andrew emerged from his cottage on Monday morning. Now she had the book buried in her little forest-green knapsack. The two of them were walking through the Valency valley towards the port. Andrew had promised to help with the new hedging volunteers. He wasn't entirely sure what Lee's agenda was, other than to point out that he'd blown it the day before.

'I'm just saying,' Lee continued, 'that maybe it's not so bad to believe Rocky Valley is magical. A lot of people do. Just because maybe the labyrinths aren't so old doesn't mean there isn't magic there anyway.'

This was a reasonable position, Andrew mused, so long as you believed in magic in the first place. Certainly, Rocky Valley was an enchanting place. Was there a sort of continuum from 'enchanting' to 'enchanted'? From 'magical' to 'magic'?

It was an odd morning, the air close, almost sticky on the skin.

There was almost no birdsong, as if there were insufficient oxygen from which to create trills and chirps.

'S'goin' to rain this afternoon,' Lee announced. 'A lot.'

Andrew looked up at the blue sky. 'What makes you so sure?'

'I just know. Dad was goin' to cut hay today, but I told him not to. He always listens to me about stuff like that.'

This sort of thing no longer surprised him. More magic, perhaps. Or just the magic of childhood.

They stopped by the weir. 'This is as far as I go,' Lee said.

'Got plans, have you?'

'Yup. You know, exploring.'

'OK, kiddo. Thanks for the company this morning. And the advice.'

Lee smiled, turned, and skipped back the way they'd come. He watched her until she rounded a bend and disappeared. The girl was enough to make you believe magic was an everyday occurrence. Then he turned downstream to meet Jamie and Becky.

The new hedging crew had been at it for nearly four hours when the rain started. A cloud, like a massive black-and-blue bruise, had appeared in the otherwise blue sky to seaward. The valley was so narrow, they hadn't seen it coming.

Jamie squinted at it for only a moment and shouted, 'Right, lads, time for lunch. Indoors, I should think. The Cobweb!'

The rain began as a mist as they put their tools away in Jamie's van. But by the time they'd hurried across the road to the inn and ordered drinks, the clattering hiss of raindrops on the steaming pavement outside could be heard even within the pub.

High up in the Valency valley, near the village of Lesnewth, where Andrew had walked to two days earlier, the rain gauge recorded that it was raining at the rate of nearly two inches per hour.

Jamie was sitting on a stool at the bar of the Cobweb, chatting up Flora, who was wearing a plunging, décolletage-revealing blouse.

'You mark my words,' Flora said, as she leaned on her elbows opposite Jamie, 'in fifteen minutes, this place'll be cheek-by-jowl. Here we are, a seaside village, and everyone comes to walk the cliffs and see the harbour, but when the rain comes, everyone wants to be in the pub. You watch.'

'I don't know, Flo,' Jamie said. 'Might be the scenery in here that draws 'em.'

'Go on, you dirty old man,' Flora protested, with a grin. She slipped off to attend to another customer, but not without giving the stone craftsman a lascivious wink.

And, sure enough, in they came, tourists who'd been nosing about the harbour and the gift shops and had dashed up the street to shelter, ramblers in dripping anoraks who'd been out hiking the coast path, and passers-through who decided a shower was a good excuse to stop for a pint. In no time at all, the pub was jammed.

The rain stopped entirely at about 12.45, and the sun came out a few minutes later.

All morning, Lee had been hunting newts in the boggy spots higher up in the Valency valley. But it wasn't until she was returning downstream again, to the shadier parts of the valley, that she began to find the creatures. Apart from the on-again, off-again bursts of rain, she'd had a lovely time. The showers were more an annoyance than anything else; they came and went so quickly it was hardly worth one's while to look for shelter.

She'd been poking around just below the Newmills cottages when she heard the dull rumble of thunder. She looked at her watch and was surprised that it was already coming up to three o'clock, and she still had a long way to go to get back down the valley towards home. A bolt of lightning flashed directly above her, and then the air sizzled and erupted into the loudest, closest, scariest crack of thunder she'd ever heard. Almost immediately, the rain hit. She grabbed her backpack and raced downstream to a spot where the curving river had cut overhanging ledges out of a cliff of night-black slate. She ducked beneath one of them and was amazed that she could barely see the other bank of the stream; the rain was falling so hard it was like being behind a waterfall.

Jamie's gang had returned to their labours. Though it was at that moment sunny in Boscastle, Andrew heard the thunder and looked up at Jamie. Jamie, in turn, was looking up at the sliver of sky above the narrow valley. There was a flash of lightning.

'Lads and lasses, you're in luck,' Jamie announced. 'It's an early day we'll be having today. But I'll expect you all bright and early tomorrow, raring to go!'

The novice crew cheered and began the process of cleaning up the worksite and putting away tools. A few headed for their cars, but several returned to the Cobweb. Jamie locked the van, looked at Andrew, and they, too, repaired to the pub.

A little after three o'clock, beneath the darkest of the clouds, the Lesnewth rain gauge registered rainfall at the rate of nearly six inches per hour.

The Cobweb was even more crowded than at lunchtime. The two men eased their way through the throng and, when Flora saw them coming, she had two pints of Doom Bar ready for them. Jamie executed an awkward bow in her direction. Andrew took a quick slug from his glass but found himself feeling oddly restless.

'Back in a bit,' he shouted into Jamie's ear above the din.

Out on the street, Andrew was struck by how loud the rain was. He pulled the drawstring on the hood of his anorak tight and wandered down the street. As he rounded the corner of the Riverside Hotel, the sun came out, and he realised the roar was not the rain, but the river. He peered over the parapet and was stunned by what he saw. A stream that was normally clear as tap water was now black as graphite and flowing at a terrific speed, its normally comforting burble an angry, fraught rumble, as stones carried by the flood tumbled along the bedrock. He realised it was only a matter of time before the muddy flood reached the cottages downstream, including Nicola's. He ran off the bridge and down the lane to her house and pounded on the door. No answer. He opened the door and called out. Again, no response. He then looked across the tumbling river and saw the Museum of Witchcraft. Of course. She was at work. He dashed across the foot-bridge and saw the river just upstream slip over its banks and spread, slowly, like an ugly tide.

Lee knew it was time to do something. She had been huddling beneath the ledge for nearly half an hour and there had been no letup in the rain. For most of that time, she'd been excited by the scene before her. She loved lightning and thunder. But that part of the storm seemed to have passed now, and there was only the relentless rain.

She didn't notice until it was too late that while she was safe in her niche in the cliff, the footpath up and downstream from her had been flooded. And the slightly elevated platform beneath the slate overhang where she'd been sheltering was getting smaller by the moment as the water rose.

A high-pitched screech pulled Lee's attention to the river upstream. This was followed by a strange whooshing sound, and then a thud. And suddenly she knew it was a tree that had crashed into the river. Almost as suddenly, she realised the footpath was re-emerging: the river was dropping. She picked up her backpack and ran pell-mell towards home.

It took a while, but eventually Jamie realised Andrew hadn't yet returned to finish his pint. So he set off through the bar to the front door to see what had become of his friend.

He knew almost the moment he stepped into the street that something was wrong. He understood instantly what the deep, thundering noise was, and he took off at a dead run to the car park. It was filled with cars, and dozens of people stood beside the stone hedge his crews had been building, watching the roiling river, which even here was close to bursting its banks.

'People,' he said calmly as he reached them, 'I think it might be wise for you to stand back from the river and, if you have cars in the car park, to move them to higher ground. You are in some danger here.'

Two men nodded and moved away towards their cars, but the rest seemed hypnotised by the scene before them: the churning black water had now topped the channel edge and was inching towards the base of the new hedge. Jamie climbed into his van, reversed out of the car park, and drove up the steep road to the north, pulling onto the verge just above the newsagent's shop. He locked the doors and jogged back downhill to the pub.

Inside, no one seemed to have the slightest idea what was happening outside. He wrestled his way to the bar and got Flora's attention. 'Listen, love, this is important. The river's burst its banks, and I reckon there's more to come. So we need to get these folks out to their cars and heading up the hill. And I want you to promise me you'll stay upstairs, in the dining room, out of harm's way. You'll be safe here.'

There wasn't the slightest indication of a problem in the confines of the Cobweb, and Flora lifted an eyebrow and gave him a look.

Jamie caught it. 'Flora, I'm going to tell you right here and now: I love you, lass. But you're in danger. We all are.'

Flora stood stock-still for a moment, then grabbed Jamie's shirt front, pulled him across the bar, and gave him the longest kiss of his life. Then she released him, and while he tried to catch his breath, she bellowed, 'All right, you lot, here's the latest news: the river's risin' fast, and the car park's about to be flooded! If you value them fancy BMWs and Land Rovers out there, you'd all better look to your vehicles. No rushin' about, mind you; nice and easy out the door, please.'

No one moved.

She slammed her beefy hands on the bar. Glasses danced. 'Oi!' she shouted. 'Is there somethin' about *out* you don't understand? Bar's closed, got it? Out you go, then, everyone.'

Lee reached the footbridge for the path up to Minster Wood and the farm just in time to see the river lift the delicate wooden structure off its footing on the north bank. Slowly, even gracefully, it pirouetted some ninety degrees until it angled downstream, dangling from the footing on the south side. Then it toppled sideways into the flood and was gone.

As Lee continued running along the sodden path downstream, from upstream she heard a groan, a crash and then a low rumble. She quickly looked back, even though she'd already intuited what had happened. The fallen tree that had dammed the river and lowered its level downstream had given way. Squeezed between the slate outcroppings on the north bank and the steep, forested slopes on the south, a ten-foot wall of water was twisting its way down the valley with the speed of a train, tearing at everything in its path.

Lee did the only thing she knew to do, the only thing she had time to do. She sloshed as fast as she could through the rising water by what had once been the riverbank and threw her arms round 'her tree', the one steadfast, familiar thing left in the landscape. The wall of water and debris hit when she'd climbed halfway up to her accustomed perch. The gnarled sessile oak lurched, but its deep roots held. Lee clung to her tree with the passion of a child clutching a parent; the oak was her protector. After the first surge passed, she climbed higher. She expected the flood would lessen after the wall of water passed, but it did not. It kept rising, inching up the twisted trunk of the ancient oak.

At 3.35 p.m., though the sun was shining in Boscastle, the rain gauge at Lesnewth recorded another surge in rainfall, to the astonishing rate of nearly a foot an hour.

Colin Grant was descending the exterior stone stairs from his library and office at the Museum of Witchcraft just as Andrew arrived. Colin had been working upstairs and had only just noticed the river out of his window. He'd come down more out of curiosity than worry. Andrew changed that instantly.

'River's over its bank upstream, Colin,' he yelled above the din of the rapids behind him. 'Where's Nicola?'

'Ticket window.' Colin went to peer round the corner of the building and immediately returned. He yanked open a door beneath the stairs and pulled out a uniform jacket for the coastguard. 'Tell Nicola and the others to shift what exhibits they can to the upper floor. I'm the town's coastguard. I've got to get to the bridge and warn people away.'

Andrew went into the museum. The light was dim and there was soft New Age music playing. The river's roar barely penetrated the museum's ancient, thick stone walls. Nicola looked up and smiled. Then she saw the tension in Andrew's face.

'The river's flooding. Colin says get your visitors out and take what you can upstairs. He's gone to warn people on the bridge. The water's already risen to within a few feet of your cottage.'

Nicola came to the door and looked across the river to her house. Randi stood beside her.

Andrew looked at them, then said, 'I'm going to go help Colin. The river is full to overflowing. That means it's raining hard somewhere up in the hills. And the way this valley's shaped, there's no place for that water to go but straight through this village. The tourists are strolling round the flooding banks gawking like this is some kind of a spectacle. That's how people get killed.'

'You're right,' she said. 'Go. I'll look after things here.'

A moment after he left, she ran out of the building and called after him, 'Take care of yourself, OK?'

But the noise of the furious river drowned her out.

By the time Andrew reached Colin on the upper bridge it was raining torrents again. Colin had the coastguard vehicle parked there with its emergency lights flashing. They were joined by a team from the fire brigade from the nearby village of Delabole, who were shepherding people towards higher ground.

'It's still rising!' Colin shouted. 'I just phoned an incident report to headquarters in Falmouth. You can hardly credit it, but people keep trying to get on the bridge to watch. Bloody idiots! Help me string emergency tape across the road.'

Andrew nodded. They stretched the blue and white tape between two poles on one side of the bridge and were just crossing to the other side when, upriver, they saw a small red Ford shooting down the river's channel like a kayak. Colin looked at it in disbelief as it swept beneath the bridge towards the sea.

'Definitely speeding,' he deadpanned.

'Nobody in it, thank God,' Andrew noted. Seconds later, it slammed into the smaller, lower bridge downstream.

As they were cordoning off the bridge, Andrew looked up Dunn Street, the road that ran from the upper village to the harbour. The narrow street had become a river itself, channelling water nearly a foot deep downhill at frightening speed.

'Oh, bloody hell!' he heard Colin cry. Andrew thought Colin was looking up Dunn Street, too, but when he turned he realised the man was facing upriver, his mouth open. Andrew followed his gaze and froze. Far up the Valency, at the curve just above the car park, a wall of water at least a building-storey high was bearing down on the village. And not just water. Tons of debris and entire uprooted trees were borne along by it, bouncing and twisting on the foaming crest of the wall.

NINE

ELIZABETH DAVIS, manager of the Visitor Centre, at the south end of the main car park, was at a distinct disadvantage as the flood waters rose. The centre was designed to face the car park, not the river behind it, so it was a surprise when she realised there was water flowing through the entry hall. The storm had been an annoyance all afternoon, and the power in the building had failed several times, but she'd been too busy rebooting the centre's computer to pay much attention to what was happening outside. When she understood that a safe exit was no longer possible, she closed the entrance's double doors and called the fire brigade.

She also turned off the power. There were two families of five in the Visitor Centre at the time, along with Elizabeth's assistant.

Despite the closed doors, water rose in the centre. First, the group moved to a raised children's play area. Then, when Elizabeth realised that this area, too, would soon be under water, she shepherded parents, children and her assistant up a ladder into the storage loft. They had just reached safety when the wall of water smashed into the building. The whole structure shuddered. The front doors could not withstand the attack. The ground floor was immediately inundated.

Andrew and Colin, still on the south side of the main bridge, had been astonished when the wall of water Colin had spied failed to follow the course of the river and instead had disappeared behind the Visitor Centre and Bridge Walk. Moments later, they watched helplessly as, one after another, waterborne vehicles careened down the road, past the turning to the bridge, and carried on downhill.

Something had been nagging Andrew's subconscious, and now it came to him. As he and Colin had been left no task other than to watch what felt like the whole village being washed into the sea, he yelled to Colin, 'Back in a few minutes. Need to check something!'

Colin nodded but did not turn his gaze from the flood before him.

Andrew plodded uphill along Dunn Street until he reached the Welly. He wasn't surprised to find its owner, Peter Williams, staring worriedly at the water rushing through the culvert beneath the building. Williams looked up, recognised Andrew, and said, 'It'll never hold. It's just not meant to carry so much water.'

'We need to get everyone out,' Andrew said.

'My wife's already going from room to room,' Peter said, 'but half the village is in the bar.'

'Then you'll just have to evict them,' Andrew said.

'And the sooner the better,' replied Peter, 'though I don't imagine they'll much appreciate being driven out into this.'

Peter was right, they didn't. There was a murmur of dissent, but the crowd dissipated. Andrew followed them and headed down the street to rejoin Colin. Peter and his wife were the last people to leave the hotel.

Moments later, the Jordan River smashed through the upstairs wall of the hotel, broke into the floor below, and cascaded through the Welly's Long Bar, shattering its beams, flooding it with thirteen feet of debris-choked flood water and filling it with 120 tons of mud.

Elizabeth, her assistant and her two-family brood in the loft of the Visitor Centre had been able to keep their spirits up by means of the stories, games and songs she improvised to distract the children. This strategy had been largely successful . . . until, at about 5p.m., another massive wall of water and debris smashed into the building. When Elizabeth saw that the water was now up to the top rung of the ladder they'd used, she pushed the Velux skylight open as far as it would go and she and her assistant helped the parents and children up to the apex of the roof.

Exposed to the downpour, straddling the roof peak of the Visitor Centre, Elizabeth felt that if they didn't drown from the flood, they would surely drown from the rain itself. Visibility was nil. So when a new sound found its way through the thunder of the river and the scream and thud of collapsing buildings, Elizabeth struggled to place it: a rhythmic *whomp-whomp-whomp* that throbbed in her bones, not just in her ears.

'And then I realised what it was,' she would later tell a reporter. 'I felt like Radar O'Reilly on *M*A*S*H*. Incoming helicopters!'

Earlier, in far northern Scotland, the rescue coordination centre at the Royal Air Force base at Kinloss had responded to initial police and coastguard reports of a flood at Boscastle by scrambling rescue helicopters based at RAF Chivenor, fifty miles north of Boscastle, and the Royal Navy Air Squadron base at Culdrose, forty-five miles to the southwest. Rescue 169, a big yellow RAF Sea King, was first on the scene. Moments later, another Sea King, the red and grey RNAS 193, approached from the south along the coast. Marine captain Pete McLelland, peering down from his copilot's seat, watched as a swollen fan of coffee-coloured water surged out of the harbour into the bright green sea.

Responding to a police report, the yellow RAF helicopter went off to deal with a reported heart attack. RNAS 193 then dipped into the mouth of the valley; what they saw below horrified them. The valley, from hillside to hillside and in both directions—indeed, the entire lower village—was one vast, raging river. McLelland radioed the rescue centre at Kinloss: 'Pass to all emergency services. This is a major incident, repeat major incident. We require all standby aircraft and all available land-based emergency crews, as we are in danger of losing Boscastle and all the people in it.'

Hovering only fifty feet above the rooftops, RNAS 193 first winched to safety a family of four from a rental property near the bridge. They had barely cleared the helicopter doors when McLelland saw something that clenched his heart: two little girls in pink blouses sitting on top of the spindly remains of a structure he would later learn had been the Visitor Centre, a now-ruined building that was the first line of defence against the tons of water that tore through the valley.

Anne Trelissick was in her flagstone-floored farmhouse kitchen, drinking tea and trying to shake off the last vestiges of the cold she'd been fighting. She was listening to the afternoon programme on BBC Radio Cornwall when she heard the breaking news that roads around Boscastle were being closed due to flooding. Though the rain had been heavy up on the hills above town, there hadn't been the slightest indication that something terrible was happening down in the valley. Anne's first reaction was scepticism. Her second sent her flying out into the rain to the barn, where Roger was mucking out manure.

'Roger! Where's Lilly?'

Her husband looked up, smiling. 'In a world of her own, I expect.' Then he saw the fear in his wife's eyes. 'Annie. What is it?'

'The radio says Boscastle's flooding. Lilly told me she was going hunting for newts in the valley today. She's not back.'

'Lilly's a smart, resourceful girl, Anne.'

'Roger! The valley's flooding; she could be anywhere!'

He put down his pitchfork. 'I'll attend to it.'

Roger Trelissick was by nature unflappable and, while his wife worried about their daughter all the time, he did not. He climbed up onto his all-terrain vehicle and raced up the farm track. For the first time in his life, he was terrified about his girl.

Just beyond Minster church, where the footpath down to the river began, he skidded to a stop and ran as fast as he could down through the woods, calling out his daughter's name. But before he'd descended even two-thirds of the way into the valley, his ears told him what his heart had been trying not to admit: the valley was inundated. The sleepy Valency River had become evil, a destroyer.

When Andrew returned from the Welly, he was elated by the sight of the two helicopters sweeping in from the harbour. But Colin was nowhere to be seen. He glanced round in the murky light and caught a glimpse of the coastguard jacket to the south of him, in the direction of

Nicola's cottage. Colin was clawing his way back upstream. Andrew waded down to help the man.

'Had to check the cottages,' Colin gasped as they reached higher ground. 'All empty, I think.'

'You think?' Andrew said.

'I hope,' he said between breaths. 'Nicola.'

Andrew's head turned as if jerked by a wire. 'What about her?'

'I tried to get her out, but she was adamant about having to save someone called Ella,' Colin shouted over the noise of one of the now-hovering copters. 'Don't know who she was talking about. I couldn't get her to come with me. She said she'd be fine. Nothing more I could do. Now look,' he said, jerking his head downstream.

Andrew looked and was stunned.

Far downstream, he could just make out Nicola's cottage—or what was left of it. The river had gnawed its way through the front wall on the ground floor. The door and two small, multi-paned windows were gone, leaving only a gaping hole with the upper storey suspended above it.

'I have to find her,' Andrew said. He set off into the water, but Colin grabbed him.

'Don't be an idiot!' he shouted. 'She's either safe or gone, and you can't do anything to change that. God only knows how many we've lost already!'

Much as he struggled, Andrew knew Colin was right. The river, if that was even the right word for the roaring beast before them, was destroying everything it encountered in its headlong rush to the sea. He wouldn't have stood a chance. He felt something now that he hadn't felt throughout the entire afternoon: a crushing personal terror. Nicola might be gone.

'Andrew!'

He looked uphill towards the voice. Just above the cordon, Roger Trelissick was climbing down from his ATV.

'Have you seen Lilly?' her father yelled.

Andrew glanced downstream again to the ruins of Nicola's cottage and then trudged up to meet Roger. 'Not since this morning. We walked together for a bit. Said she was going up-valley.'

'Lord help her. She's missing!'

'Did you check below Minster Wood?'

'Tried, but the bridge is gone. The whole bottom of the valley up there is under water! I was hoping she was with you. Or Nicola.'

'Nicola was alone when Colin saw her a while ago.'

The man's face went from hopeful to desperate. Only this morning, Andrew and Lee had been strolling happily through the meadows along the quiet riverbank in the sun . . . And suddenly, Andrew knew.

'Roger!' he shouted.

The farmer was climbing back onto the ATV.

'I might know where she is!' Andrew raced up the hill. 'Can we get to the river below your farm?' he asked, as he climbed up and straddled the seat behind his friend.

'The Jordan's overtopped the road. Police have everything closed off. We'd have to go overland. Where is she?'

'I want you to understand it's only a hunch, Roger, OK? She has a favourite tree. A big twisted oak by the river near the weir. She likes to climb into it and read. It's like she thinks she and the tree are friends.'

Roger gunned the ATV. 'Hang on!'

Andrew gripped the handles at his hips, and they raced up the switchback main road south out of the lower village. Soon, they were plummeting downhill through fields Andrew knew were Roger's. 'Do you have any rope at the farm?' Andrew bellowed into Roger's ear.

Roger simply nodded, and they barrelled across fields and farm lanes. They lurched to a stop by one of the barns. It was still raining, but not with the intensity that it had been. In moments, Roger was back with a thick loop of rope tossed over his shoulder.

'Where's this tree?' he yelled as they rocketed off again.

'Below the footbridge and just above the weir.'

Roger finally stopped at the edge of a thicket of brush and trees and tore off into the woods. Andrew followed. The two men crashed through the undergrowth and clambered down the steep slope of the valley. When they reached the racing river, Andrew could recognise nothing.

'Where's the weir?' he called.

'Under there!' Roger called back, pointing to the swirling maelstrom of water and debris below them.

Andrew headed upstream, gripping branches to give him stability in the slimy morass of mud and leaves on the hillside. Roger was right behind him. A few minutes later, Andrew stopped. Below him, still stubbornly clutching the ground with its roots, was Lee's tree. Around it swirled a torrent of brown, whitecapped water. The noise was incredible. There was no way Lee could have heard him if he called, so he peered through the rain looking for a sign of her in the tree's canopy. He searched to no avail until the wind picked up and shuddered the leaves, and there, in the crotch of two branches, was a little girl in khaki shorts and a T-shirt. She was clutching a battered red and white umbrella.

Nicola had been standing on a dining chair in front of the fireplace, lifting Laura Knight's exquisite *Ella, Nude in Chair* from the wall when the river tore her front door off its hinges and flung it across the room. She leaped from the flimsy wooden chair to the floor as a three-foot wall of inky water surged through the room. Moments later, when she reached the stairs to the studio, the portrait under one arm, both front windows imploded.

With the water rising quickly, she clawed her way up to her studio. Upstairs, she pulled a dustsheet from the floor and wrapped the painting in it, clutching it to her breast because it was her one tangible connection to Sir Michael.

She stood at the long window. Outside, the stone footbridge was buried beneath the flood. Cars, vans, recycling bins, even the venerable red public telephone box that had stood across the street from the Welly, sped by below her on the waves. Suddenly, she felt very alone; she had left Randi with the museum staff when she ushered them out to the terrace above the building. A power failure had thrown the windowless museum into pitch darkness and halted their work rescuing artefacts. Now, beneath her, furniture thudded against the walls as water whirlpooled through the sitting room. But despite the chaos downstairs, she felt safe in her sturdy fishermen's loft.

This illusion lasted for perhaps two minutes. Nicola gasped as she saw, speeding through the gloom on the surface of the rushing river, an entire tree, as big as a bus, hurtling directly towards her house. She grabbed *Ella* and fled to the back of the loft, praying the tree would slide by.

But her prayers went unanswered.

Andrew grabbed Roger's shoulder and pointed towards the oak in the middle of the flood. Roger's face flashed from desperation to almost heartbreaking relief when he, too, saw the umbrella. While Roger tried vainly to call out to his daughter, Andrew studied the current. It was an architectural problem, he realised: a matter of angles and forces. After a few minutes of silent calculation, he started crawling upstream, pulling the rope behind him. Roger understood immediately and followed. The idea was to fix the rope to a tree on land and have one of them go downstream with it to Lee's tree. If they could get to it, and get Lee down, they might be able to get her back to the hillside to safety.

There was a brief shouting match about who would stay ashore and who would go with the rope. But Roger was much bigger and stronger than Andrew, and they agreed he needed to be at the pulling end. They clove-hitched one end of the rope to a young alder. Andrew wrapped the other end round his waist, cinching it with a quick-release knot. And then he entered the river.

His plan was to ease himself into the flood, slip downstream, and use his feet to stop whenever he got swept away. This strategy worked well for perhaps twenty seconds, at which point subsurface debris knocked his legs out from under him and he spun on the end of the rope, above and below the water, until his feet found purchase again and he sputtered to the surface. The principal advantage of this unintentional manoeuvre was that Lee saw him.

'Drew!' she screamed.

'It's OK! Come down!'

'No way!'

Andrew concentrated on his footing, inching closer to the tree. The boulders in the streambed were constantly on the move. He'd steady his feet on one and, almost immediately, it would be swept out from under him.

After perhaps ten minutes of this battering, Andrew was closing in on the tree. Lee's father let out one last length of rope and timed it perfectly. Andrew slammed into the trunk of the tree, caught his breath, and began climbing towards Lee.

The massive tree trunk tore through the front of Nicola's cottage. The entire building shuddered. Nicola clung to the banister at the top of the stairs as the house lurched. There was no way to know how long the structure would last, and she knew she needed to flee. But there was only one way out: down the stairs. And the lower floor was flooded to the ceiling.

When she heard the rescue helicopters thumping up the valley, her head instinctively jerked upwards and she saw, at last, her escape. She placed the wrapped portrait on her paint stand and, with her eyes clenched tight, smashed a wooden chair through the glass of the old skylight in the loft's sloping rear roof. Then she tied the dustsheet holding *Ella* round her neck and, grateful at long last for her height, pulled herself out onto the wet slate roof.

Andrew had just managed to coax Lee down through the tree limbs towards the rushing water and the rope when he heard a shout.

'Andrew!'

He peered through the branches and saw Roger scrambling furiously upslope and, a moment later, saw why. Yet another wall of water was funnelling down the narrow valley. Effortlessly, the tidal wave ripped the young tree that held their rope from the ground like so much brush. Andrew tore open the quick-release knot at his waist and watched the rope whip away through the branches like a line on a harpooned whale.

'See?' Lee yelled, and just for a fraction of a second, he wanted to throttle the wise little kid. Instead, they climbed higher into the old oak.

And there they sat. Roger had disappeared.

'Where's Daddy?' Lee cried, clinging to Andrew's soaked shirt. And Andrew prayed that he hadn't been sucked into the flood.

What Andrew didn't know was that Roger had heard the helicopters farther down the valley. He'd scrambled back up the hillside to his ATV. At the edge of the woods, he threw downed limbs, leaves and a bale of just-mown hay into a pile. Then he poured half the contents of his spare fuel can on the pile and lit it. There was a towering explosion of flame, and then a thick, white cloud of smoke as the wet leaves and hay burned.

Then he waited. He looked at his watch. It was nearly 6 p.m. The rain had stopped. He willed a helicopter up-valley.

It was the copilot of a helicopter from RAF St Mawgan who noticed the pillar of smoke in the valley. The chopper was on its way to respond to a report of stranded motorists in a shallow valley near Otterham when Tim Llewellyn, who, like the crew men in RNAS 193, had also seen service in the Gulf War, tapped his pilot's shoulder and pointed down. A hundred feet below, beside the smoky fire, a man was pointing frantically west, towards the centre of the flooded Valency valley. They circled once but, seeing nothing obvious, continued to Otterham.

It was thirty minutes later, as the helicopter returned to Boscastle after having lifted and dropped the motorists to safety, that the copilot saw the smoke again and, almost immediately thereafter, a flash of orange flame. Roger had thrown the rest of his petrol onto the smouldering pile.

This time, the helicopter dropped and pivoted round the signal fire. Again, the fellow below was waving them towards the centre of the valley.

Llewellyn peered into the canopy of trees as the pilot banked sharply and brought the aircraft low into the valley and hovered. And then, amid the mass of green and brown that was the valley floor, a flash of red appeared. Bizarrely, a man in a tree was waving an opened red and white umbrella. Llewellyn radioed his winchman in the back to prepare to descend.

In moments, Robbie Campbell, the winchman, was down. He balanced on a limb and cinched the girl to his chest, then signalled to be lifted. And up they went, spinning slowly in the backdraught, until another crewman pulled them both in through the side door. Then Campbell descended again for the man, and Andrew, too, was carried up to the hovering craft.

In the field beside the smoky bonfire, Roger Trelissick waved with both arms like a madman. Then he sat down in the wet grass and wept.

Lee clung to Andrew's soggy shirt like a limpet to a rock once the helicopter dropped them at the soccer field above town, like everyone else who'd been airlifted. Volunteers guided them down to the rectory, where Janet Stevenson, the vicar, enveloped them in care, served hot tea, and found them dry clothes. Suddenly, Andrew realised that he was utterly spent. He slouched in an easy chair and Lee, dry now, curled into his chest. He held her there for all he was worth, as if she were life itself.

But his love for Lee, and his joy at having found her, could not ease the dread he felt about Nicola. The woman he knew now with absolute clarity to be the love of his life, the matching half of his splintered heart, had not been seen or heard from for hours. And he knew she was nowhere near as tough as she pretended to be.

Colin, still in his coastguard jacket, appeared out of nowhere with a van, and began shuttling survivors from the rectory to the village hall, where arrangements were being made to take those who needed medical attention to the clinic in Camelford, and those who needed shelter to the big leisure centre there.

Roger and Anne arrived at the village hall, having had to drive miles out of their way to avoid the roads the police had blocked. Lee was asleep in Andrew's arms. Both parents knelt on the floor on either side of the mat on which Andrew sat holding her, and, very gently, stroked her hair and bony legs until she woke.

'Mum! Daddy! It was so cool! You should have been there, up in my tree!'

Andrew smiled. Anne stood and gathered her daughter in her arms. 'Come home, Drew. We're dry up there.'

'I need to find Nicola,' he replied, and Anne nodded.

'Do it for all of us,' Roger said. 'Lilly needs her.'

And then they left, and Andrew ached at the completeness of them: mother, father, daughter . . . family.

Andrew had just left the hall and turned down towards the ruins of the lower village when Nicola arrived in the van from the rectory. She stepped down to the road hugging a rag-covered package and looked round, blinking, as if she'd been left on another planet. Andrew would remember this moment for the rest of his life. She was shattered, lost, a waif in borrowed clothes. He didn't call out, for fear he'd frighten her. He reached her just as she entered the village hall.

'Nicola . . .'

She turned towards the sound of her name. She stared, hollow-eyed, for a moment, and then a light came on. A smile rose from somewhere deep, and she held it for a moment. Then she began to sag. Andrew slipped his arms under hers and lifted her towards him.

'Nicola,' he said again.

'I saved her,' she said into his shoulder.

'Of course you did,' he said quietly. He had no idea what she was talking about.

After they'd been fed by volunteers and had their dried clothes returned, they spent the night, side by side, wrapped in blankets on gym mats at the leisure centre in Camelford, along with dozens of others. Though she was dry and warm, Nicola trembled uncontrollably. Andrew wrapped his arms round her and held her close until the trembling passed and she was asleep. Then he unwrapped the package and understood whom she'd saved.

TEN

TUESDAY, AUGUST 17 was cruel. The heavy weather having passed, the morning dawned sunny, warm and preternaturally clear. A perfect day for tourists, but the only people moving in the lower village were emergency workers.

Nicola and Andrew were standing on the edge of the main road, halfway up the hill above the harbour. Though they were told the police had cordoned off the area, they'd hitchhiked back to Boscastle from Camelford anyway. Nicola had been adamant about returning. Now the two of them, along with a small crowd of others, tried to take in the scene before them. No one said a word. The only sound was the muted roar of the river, still flowing filthy and fast through the ravaged town, but no longer at full flood stage. The main road through the lower village had survived, but the bridge that carried it over the normally sparkling river had been stripped of most of its stone railing walls. At the Riverside Hotel and, for that matter, at all of the buildings as far as they could see, the ground-floor doors and windows had been ripped out, and tree branches hung out of them like claws. The lower bridge was invisible, buried beneath a tangle of trees and cars.

'It's still there,' Andrew heard Nicola say.

'What is?'

'My house.' At the bottom of the hill, they could see that the police were refusing to let anyone across the bridge. Nicola grabbed Andrew's arm. 'Come on,' she ordered, directing him to a footpath along the hill-side that led to the coast. 'We'll go in the back way.'

'What for? There's nothing left down there.'

'I need to get Lee.'

'Lee's at home, Nicola,' he said gently, wondering if Nicola was still in shock.

She stopped and turned to face him, a hand on one cocked hip, one eyebrow raised. 'The *painting* of her!'

'Oh. Right.'

'How did you ever get to be a professor? Affirmative action for the hopelessly dim?'

'Nicola?'

'What?'

Andrew grinned. 'Nice to have you back again, love.'

To his utter surprise, she stepped forward, held his face in her hands, and kissed him.

'Thank you,' she said. 'Now get a move on!'

When they reached the cliffs, they picked up another footpath that dropped down to the harbour entrance. With Nicola leading, they ducked behind buildings so the police wouldn't see them. It was slow going, plodding through stinking mud. They were both wearing what they'd worn the day before—Andrew his hedging work clothes and boots, Nicola black slacks, sandals and a museum T-shirt. They were both filthy in minutes.

When they finally came out of the shadows and turned the corner, Nicola gasped. Where only yesterday there had been a postcard-worthy cottage there now was nothing but a raw, gaping hole, much of it filled with a huge, mud-caked tree trunk.

'My God, what's keeping it from collapsing?' Nicola said.

'Post-and-beam construction,' Andrew replied. 'The stone walls really just function as filler; it's the posts and beams that hold it up. If they're intact, the structure will survive. Problem is, there's no way of knowing the condition of the posts without going inside.'

He was peering into the dim interior when he heard shouts from upstream. Men in yellow hard hats were waving at them. Nicola bolted inside, clambering over the tree towards the back.

'Nicola! I don't know whether—'

'Neither do I, but I'm getting Lee! Hold off the goons!'

Daylight cascaded down the worn stone steps from the skylights in the roof as she crawled upstairs. Her heart leaped when she reached the top and saw Lee's portrait, clean and dry, leaning against the wall. She grabbed the spread from her bed, wrapped it round the canvas, then started back down the stairs. But the treads were greased with mud, and she hadn't descended halfway when her feet shot out from under her. Desperate to protect the painting, she twisted and fell heavily on her side, landing on the sharp edge of the stone treads and slithering to the bottom, into the mud. Pain shot through her. She lay still for a moment, breathing shallowly.

Andrew was beside her in seconds. 'Are you OK?'

She shook her head. 'No, but Lee is. I think I cracked a rib.'

'Take a deep breath, but slowly,' Andrew ordered.

She took a deep breath and let it out again.

'No change?' Andrew said.

'No.'

'Good. Sharp pain would mean you'd broken a rib, which could puncture a lung if you moved. Now, let's get out of here.'

They'd just stumbled out through the ragged arch of the front wall when one of the policemen arrived in his reflective yellow emergency jacket. 'Oi! What d'you think you're doing, then?'

'Visiting my house. What does it look like?' Nicola barked.

'She lives here,' Andrew said, as if that explained everything.

The policeman looked at the ruin behind them and then said, almost tenderly, 'Not any more she doesn't. Look, we can't have people trying to enter buildings that may be on the verge of collapse. I'm afraid everyone's got to be evacuated.'

Nicola softened, and the three of them made their way up the lane to the main road. Andrew carried the draped canvas.

'Which way are you heading?' the officer asked when they reached the bridge.

In pain, emotionally spent, Nicola looked first one way and then the other, and said, 'I don't know. I have nowhere to go.' Tears zigzagged down her cheeks through the dirt.

'Yes, you do,' Andrew said, taking her hand. And he led her towards the road to the upper village.

They'd just reached the switchback above the harbour when Roger found them. 'You two are even more trouble to find than that vagabond daughter of mine. Been to Camelford and back trying to locate you. Somebody back at the farm wants to see you. Truck's at the top of the hill.'

It was nearly four o'clock before they finally jounced into the yard at Bottreaux Farm. There were animated voices in the kitchen, and they could smell the heavenly aroma of a beef-rib roast as they came through the side door of the house.

'Drew! Nicki!' Lee threw herself at Andrew and scaled him as if she was climbing her oak tree. Nicki showered her with kisses.

'And aren't you two an attractive pair,' a voice cracked. 'Look like a couple of mud wrestlers.' It was Flora. She and Jamie were sitting at the end of the big scrubbed pine table in the middle of the kitchen, drinking red wine from thick tumblers. Anne was bent over the stove, checking the roast. When she straightened up, she screeched, 'Out! Out of my kitchen, you two. Look at you!'

It was the first time Andrew and Nicola realised just how filthy they were. Their trousers were encased with dirt to the knees, and the rest of their clothes were plastered with caked silt.

The ever-gentle Roger said, 'Perhaps you'd like a bath . . .'

'Not till I get a drink!' Nicola protested.

Jamie took charge, and poured three more glasses. Then he held his own up and suddenly his ageing, weather-browned face lost its levity.

'You gave us a hell of a fright, lass,' he said to Nicola. 'Thank God you're with us again. Thank God we're all here and safe.'

'Amen, brother,' Flora intoned.

Andrew nudged Nicola. He still had the covered painting under his arm. She looked at him and understood, then took the package, unwrapped it, and laid the painting of Lee on the table before Anne and Roger. 'This was meant to be for your anniversary, but maybe now's the right time,' she whispered.

Anne's hand flew to her mouth. Roger slipped his arms round his wife and tears inched down his weathered face.

'*Way* cool!' Lee cried.

'**A**nnie! I don't have any clothes!' Nicola was standing at the top of the stairs wrapped in a big white Turkish towel.

'Music to a man's ears!' she heard Jamie shout from the kitchen. And then, 'Ow!'

Anne called from her bedroom, 'In here, Nicki!' She'd laid out several pieces of clothing and was shaking her head. Anne was petite; Nicola was not. 'These are the biggest things I have, love,' she said as Nicola entered. 'The only thing we share is shoe size. Good luck!'

There was an ankle-length black challis skirt and a hand-knitted, V-necked yellow jumper in a fluffy angora-blend yarn. With Nicola's lush figure, it left little to the imagination. She slipped into a pair of flats Anne had left and descended to the kitchen again. Andrew was there in his own clean clothes; Roger had fetched them from his cottage.

'Woo-hoo,' Jamie crowed when she entered. This got him another cuffing from Flora.

'Go on, you randy old man,' Flora said, smiling.

Nicola was stricken. 'Oh my God! Randi!'

'Not to worry, love,' Anne said. 'Colin's got him, and he's safe.'

Andrew slipped his hand round Nicola's waist, and she leaned into him, feeling safe, too, for the first time in what seemed for ever.

Dinner was the sort of event that often follows a disaster, a mix of giddy exultation at having survived and recognition of just how close some of them had been to perishing. They ate in the kitchen, round the big table, the radio tuned into BBC Radio Cornwall the whole time. Gradually, the news reports from Boscastle turned brighter. The number of people thought to be missing had dropped sharply. No bodies had been found in either the ruined cars or in the buildings that had been searched. The reporters had already begun calling it the 'Boscastle Miracle'.

Jamie and Flora had spent the night on the floor of the dining room above the Cobweb, along with others. 'Gettin' too old for that sort of nonsense,' Flora complained. Jamie allowed that it was the most romantic night he could remember.

Flora snorted. 'Either your memory is rubbish or you need a better life!'

'I'm hoping for the latter,' Jamie said with a grin. Under the table, Flora squeezed his hand.

The police had cleared them out of the pub in the morning. Jamie had bundled Flora into his van, and they were bouncing along single-track lanes around the fields above town when they ran into Roger on his ATV. Roger had told Jamie his chances of making it home were slim, and invited the two of them to stay at the farm.

They lit candles as the August light waned but, between the rich food, the wine and the nearly continuous stress of the last two days, the celebrants were flagging by nine o'clock. It was Flora who called a halt to the proceedings. 'Right, then. I don't know about the rest of you lot, but I'm knackered. Where're we kippin'?'

Andrew felt a tug at his sleeve.

'Let's go home,' Nicola whispered.

'Are you sure?' he asked.

'Oh, yes,' she said, smiling.

'Me, too!' Lee cried, leaping from her chair.

'No, you don't, you little ragamuffin!' Roger said, sweeping his daughter into his arms. 'It's early to bed for you, too. For all of us, I should think.'

'The sheets aren't clean,' Andrew apologised as he pulled back the coverlet on the antique double bed in his cottage.

'Good,' Nicola said, pulling the fuzzy yellow jumper over her head and stepping out of Anne's skirt. She had nothing else on underneath. She slipped into bed, pulled up the sheets, and patted the mattress beside her. He sat. 'Andrew?'

'Yes?'

'Do you love me?'

'Yes. I do.'

'That's what you were trying to tell me that night I ran away, isn't it?'

'Yes . . . although, honestly, I'm not sure I really knew it then.' He leaned down and kissed her.

'I know I love you, too, Andrew. But it scares me to death.'

'I know it does. We can take this slowly. I don't want you ever to be afraid again.'

Nicola sat up. 'When are you going back to the States?'

'Never.'

'What?'

'Never. I'm staying here. I'm resigning from the university.'

Nicola stared at him for a moment. 'Andrew?' she asked again. 'Would it be OK if I just curled up with you? Could you do that? Just hold me?'

And he did, drawing her into his arms, her back curled against his chest. She pressed herself into him and he felt her tension ease. They were both asleep in moments.

Andrew was frying eggs and bacon when Lee burst through the cottage door on Wednesday morning. 'Mum says to tell you that the radio says folks will be allowed into the lower village to collect valuables later this morning! Where's Nicki?'

'Here, sweetie,' Nicola said, emerging from the bedroom wearing one of Andrew's shirts and the skirt from the night before.

'Mum also says, your clothes will be out of the dryer in a few minutes.'

'Have you ever considered a career as a newscaster?' Andrew grumped. He hadn't had his tea yet.

Lee shot him a look. 'Is that supposed to be funny?'

'I'm never funny before lunch.'

'You got that right,' she said.

Andrew chuckled. He was deeply happy. Awakening earlier with

Nicola beside him had felt like a miracle; he'd lain motionless for a long time, watching the slow rise and fall of her chest, the tumble of dark hair across her face, the relaxed curve of her full lips in slumber. When the morning sun had reached her face, she'd opened her eyes, seen him watching her, and smiled.

'Good morning, darling,' she'd said, grinning.

'"Darling"?'

'Yes, because you are. I'm just a slow learner, is all.'

'I'll say.'

She'd punched him playfully. 'For that, you get to make me breakfast!'

'You call that punishment? I'd gladly do that for the rest of my life!'

She'd grinned again. 'You may have to.'

It was past noon when Andrew and Nicola reached the bridge. A crowd of shell-shocked residents milled about behind an emergency cordon, waiting for a policeman to let them through, but there was a holdup of some sort. There were television satellite trucks in the road and reporters everywhere.

Then the walkie-talkie of the police officer manning the tape squawked. He mumbled 'Roger' into the device and then unhooked the tape, gently herding everyone away from the bridge.

'Please,' he said, his arms spread wide to move people back, 'it's only for a few minutes. The prince is arriving, you see.'

A cavalcade of funereally black vehicles rounded the switchback, descended the hill, and swept past the cordon and across the bridge. A few moments later, Prince Charles emerged from a large black Range Rover. He was deeply tanned and wearing a dove-grey double-breasted suit in a faint glen plaid. The prince waved to the clutch of residents on the other side of the bridge and was immediately escorted by officials round the corner of the ruined Riverside Hotel and uphill towards the Cobweb.

Nicola said, 'Let's hope he's come to offer assistance. In addition to being Prince of Wales, he's also the Duke of Cornwall. They say he cares a lot about rural England. Here's his chance.'

They stood there for a moment, taking in the spectacle, and then Nicola gave Andrew a nudge. The officer was letting people in.

'Come on, we've work to do.' And they headed down towards Nicola's cottage. They saw Colin beside his coastguard vehicle and called to him.

'Hang on a bit,' the museum director yelled back.

He pulled open the rear door of the car and Randi leaped out. The dog danced across the debris pile that once had been the lower bridge, and tried to launch himself into Nicola's arms.

'Bloody ungrateful, I call it!' Colin called, smiling broadly.

'Thank you, dear man!' Nicola called back as she struggled to calm her dog, who now was leaping at Andrew with equal enthusiasm.

Then they entered the wreck that had once been Nicola's home.

Nicola had finished packing her paintbox and was stuffing clothing into a suitcase when Randi barked, just once. She looked wearily at Andrew. 'Would you see what that's about?'

'I'm on it.' He picked his way down the muddy steps and, a few moments later, called back, 'Nicola? A gentleman to see you.'

She cursed and descended. Then she saw him. 'Dad!'

Sir Michael stood in the shelter of the hole that had been her front wall. Andrew was at his side. Randi panted happily.

Muddy from climbing over the tree lodged in what remained of her sitting room, she hesitated. Then the elegantly dressed old man stepped forward, and she threw herself into his arms.

'Nicola, thank God. Oh, thank God.' That was all he could say. There were tears in his eyes. The two of them, the old man and the woman, clung to each other as if they'd drown if they let go.

Andrew had no idea what was happening.

Nicola saw his bewilderment, and laughed. 'Andrew Stratton, allow me to introduce Sir Michael Rhys-Jones, my father-in-law. Well, former, actually. Dad, this is Andrew, an American architect, a formidable Cornish hedge-builder and the man I love.'

Now it was Sir Michael's turn to be flummoxed, but he recovered quickly and said, 'Nicola, I am very pleased, indeed.'

Andrew bowed slightly, took the old man's extended hand, and said simply, 'Sir Michael, my pleasure.'

'What the hell are you doing here?' Nicola erupted.

Sir Michael laughed. 'That's my girl—right to the point! All right, I'm here with Charles.'

'You know the prince?'

'My dear, yes, I know the prince. I've been one of his financial advisers for most of his adult life, and I'm on the board of the Prince's Trust. There are certain other connections I have that made it possible for me to prevail upon him to let me come along on this visit. I was desperate to know how you were, and the local authorities hadn't a clue. Now, I will have to leave in a few minutes, my dear. You will need a place to live . . .'

'I have one, Dad,' she said quietly, nodding towards Andrew.

'Yes,' he said, scrutinising Andrew. 'Yes. Good. That's for the best. But I shall be in touch. And please, Nicola, stay out of this place in future.' He gestured around the ruined room. 'It is dangerous.'

Nicola nodded. The old man turned and began walking back upstream towards the bridge and the prince's entourage. Andrew had never seen Nicola so happy.

'**D**rew!'

It was Nicola. It was September now, and she had adopted Lee's nickname for him. She dashed across the lower bridge to where he and Jamie were working to repair the witchcraft museum. She waved a letter she had clutched in her hand. 'It's from Dad!'

It had taken Andrew a while to get used to Nicola calling her former father-in-law 'Dad', but now he smiled and sat down on a nearby rock. 'Listen!' she demanded.

'*My dear Nicola,*

'*For various boring tax reasons, I have arranged to donate Trevega House and its lands to the National Trust. But I have done so with the proviso that it remain in a lifetime tenancy so long as my family is in residence. I have named you as the family tenant. I have also named you and my daughter as my beneficiaries. Jeremy is no longer employed in my firm and I no longer acknowledge him as my son. I have settled an amount upon him with his promise that he will relinquish any claim on Trevega or my estate. He has accepted these terms. No one since my dear wife has loved Trevega House as you have, Nicola, and it should be yours. My daughter agrees.*

'*I have also—I hope you will forgive me—examined the background of Andrew Stratton. You have chosen well. I should like to request that Andrew begin at once a survey of the properties appurtenant to Trevega House—the cottages, the mill—and advise me as to their restoration and potential as rental properties, all income therefrom to go to you.*

'*Please advise if this is acceptable . . . and please say yes.*

'*With love abiding,*

'*Michael.*'

Andrew smiled. 'Tell me about Trevega House, Nicola.'

And she did, sitting on a pile of rocks beside him, the joy pouring out of her like sunshine.

When she was finished, Andrew said, 'Do you think I could finish what I'm doing here first? It seems as though Sir Michael's work will be long-term, and I'd like to invite Jamie to be my partner.'

'And Flora and Jamie could have one of the cottages!' she enthused. 'What will we tell Lee?'

Nicola winked.' 'She and I already have something planned. She'll spend summers with us. She wants to learn how to paint.'

'I see. So, you just assumed I'd agree to all this?'

'No, I didn't. That's why I threw Lee in as the clincher,' she said with a mischievous smile. 'I know you're a sucker for her, and I didn't want to take any chances.'

Andrew grabbed Nicola and pulled her onto his lap.

'Come here, you. I'll show you the clincher!'

EPILOGUE

THE TWO WOMEN sat on the ground beside a primitive well, framed in rough stone, from which a spring seeped. They were just a few hundred yards downhill from Minster church, in the woods above the River Valency. It was the last night of the waning moon, and pitch-dark, but for the candle flickering between them.

They had been here for some nights, now, quietly going through the same ancient rite. The older woman reached her hand into the water and then flicked it over the head of the younger woman.

'Amen, hetem,' intoned the older woman.

'Amen, hetem,' the younger one repeated.

'Mighty ones and old ones,' the older one continued. 'Witness Flora and Nicola anointing themselves, that we might be great like you. Thout! A thout! Throughout and about!'

The women sat quietly, taking in the sounds and spirits of the place—listening for owls, badgers, deer and foxes. After a while, Flora held up the remains of a photograph—the one from Nicola's bedroom that depicted her and her two brothers at the beach—and began a chant: 'Johnny DeLucca, be dead and past. Nicola DeLucca, be whole at last.'

The younger woman joined in the chant, and gradually it built in volume and power. After perhaps ten minutes, Flora held up her hands, and they stopped. Then she took what remained of the photo—just the head of Nicola's dead brother—tore it, and set it afire in the flame of the candle.

Both women let out a *whoop!* and then Flora shouted into the night, 'The work is done. So mote it be!'

Nicola shuddered involuntarily and fell to one side.

Not far away in the darkness, Andrew Stratton struggled to get to his feet, but the girl beside him dragged him down again.

'Drew!' Lee hissed. 'It's all right. It's what has to be.'

Jamie put his arm round his friend. 'Let it happen, lad. Let the magic work. Flora knows what she's about.'

Farther up the hill and just beyond the parish boundary, Colin Grant, unbeknown to any of them, tied together two small sticks—one from Andrew's garden, the other from Nicola's former cottage—with red string, and left them as an offering beside the secret grave of a witch who had been known to have success with love spells.

Then he slipped into the darkness.

Will North

Can you tell us a little about your life and why you decided to become a writer?

Ever since my eighth grade teacher, Mrs D'Ascoli, gave me three As for an essay on Longfellow's epic poem, *Evangeline*, writing has been my 'meal ticket'. It was my ticket to scholarships for an undergraduate degree in English, and then a graduate degree in journalism. It carried me through a series of jobs and ultimately, at the age of thirty, to a position in the Jimmy Carter Administration. Much as I loved that job, one of the best things that ever happened to me was the election of Ronald Reagan, who promptly fired me and forced me to choose between holding a job and becoming an author. I chose the latter.

When did you first come to Britain and what is it about this island that makes you feel so at home?

I first came to England in 1968 and the moment my foot hit the tarmac at Heathrow I felt an overwhelming sense of having come home at last. I'm not a believer in past lives, and I have only a small bit of English ancestry (my heritage is mostly German), but at that moment I knew I'd found the place where I belonged. I returned often. Indeed I'm the author of a three-book series called *The Best of Britain's Countryside*, now out of print. The books—guidebooks that follow a two-week itinerary and read like travel narrative—aimed to get visitors away from London and the tourist traps and into those off-the-beaten track places that I'd discovered over the years; places that seemed to me to capture Britain's essence. Still, the question of why I felt so deeply at home in Britain dogged me for decades. Finally, in 2004, I hit upon an idea. I would strap on a backpack and walk for three and a half months, focusing on southern England. The idea was simple: slow down to walking speed, pay very close attention, and sort out the individual bits and pieces of experience that held such meaning for me. I walked roughly 1,200–1,400 miles and one of the villages I passed through was Boscastle.

That was two days before the flood. How did you feel, knowing that you had come so close to being caught up in the disaster?

Because I was walking the coastal path, I didn't hear about it for a couple of days. I was somewhere south of Padstow, I think. It seemed surreal. I remember August 16th being a strange day: sunny, muggy, with occasional very short, furious squalls racing in off the ocean. The rain was horizontal; I'd shelter against a hawthorne hedge or a wall and it would blow right past me. Never did get wet. What happened, I later learned, was that all those little storm cells gathered and simply sat above the hills east of Boscastle. And the only place the water could go was down that narrow valley. There's an oft-photographed sway-backed building near the harbour that housed a gift shop. All you need to know to understand the ferocity of the flood is that the building had been there for three hundred years, and it simply vanished. It's astonishing no one was killed.

You have an interest in architecture, which seems to be reflected in the character of Andrew. How did that come about?

My son is an architect and, had I known there was such a thing when I was growing up, I might have been one, too. Instead, I've renovated a half-dozen houses over the years, including two originally built in the 1700s. I've also studied dry-stone wall building, which features in *Water, Stone, Heart*. But there is a larger subject that has fascinated me for years: 'What do we mean when we say we feel at home somewhere? What are the bits and pieces of experience that, added up, make us feel a sense of belonging to a particular place?' I never felt at home where I grew up (for the record, New York). The only place I ever felt utterly at home has been England and, only recently, the island I now live on in the Pacific Northwest. I have already researched much of a nonfiction book that I'm calling *The Anatomy of Home*, but right now I'm having too much fun writing fiction.

How did you come to the story of Andrew and Nicola?

In each of my novels, there is an underlying theme or issue that matters to me deeply. In *Water, Stone, Heart*, it is this question: 'How does a woman who was abused as a child ever form a normal, healthy, loving, and trusting relationship with a man?' It is a terrible tragedy and most women never fully recover. Perhaps it takes an equally destructive calamity to break through the barriers. Like a flood . . .